LOVE STRADDLE

by

M.P. KNOX

Book Title: LOVE STRADDLE

Author: © M.P. KNOX

National Library of Australia Cataloguing-in-Publication entry

Author:	Knox, M.P., author.
Title:	Love Straddle / M.P. Knox.
ISBN:	9780992462307 (paperback)
Subjects:	Interpersonal relationships–Fiction.
Dewey Number:	A823.4

Published by Love of Books, Brisbane, Australia, 2014
www.loveofbooks.com.au

Cover designed by Donna Munro

Website:lovestraddleanovel.wordpress.com
mpknox46@aapt.net.au

Paperback available from all Amazon websites and www.loveofbooksclub.com

eBook available from Amazon Kindle and all major eBook sites.

To the real Vicki

with many thanks

M.P. Knox

Contents

PROLOGUE

It is July 2006.

As we climb away from Calgary, the seat belt indicator gongs. I loosen the strap and recline in my business class seat. I have this mental skill of being comfortable and enjoying air flights. I imagine that I am a pupating insect, like a silkworm caterpillar. I have woven a cocoon around me, taking up all the space I am allowed. I am in suspended animation. I have found out all the controls and resources at my disposal and how to use them. Fully reclining seats, footrests, air blowers, lights, video, audio, attendant summonsing: I know them all and make myself comfortable. I am a glass half-full person. Rather than being confined in a space that limits me and denies comfort, my capsule is a perfect size for comfort, with controls that empower me to metamorphose and emerge ready for different conditions.

The flight to London will take long enough for me to reflect on past events that have caused this journey and the natural laws of behaviour that I have recently discovered. If I had known them before, this journey would not be necessary, or I would have made it many years ago.

Now I will tell you my story – at least, my part in events – including my own and other people's emotions, that engineers like me normally ignore. But emotions are important, as I have lately discovered.

PART 1: LOVE EXPOSED (1966)

In which Vicki tricks me into revealing my affections.

CHAPTER 1   ASK NO QUESTIONS

Things had started going wrong at Boston, USA in the Summer of '66. The only way seemed up for Vicki and me, as I waited to see her during the summer vacation, at the end of our second year at Liverpool uni, forty-one years ago, when I was an engineering student.

I sit on the edge of a chair and pretend to look at a brochure about this Department of Applied Psychology at New England University, Boston, USA. Maybe the girls' vacation jobs here fell through, although Vicki had written saying they are expecting us at this time.

Tom looks archly down his hooked nose, as he thrusts and retracts his jaw to the reggae rhythm from his portable LP player. The rest of his face is Nordic, with white skin, high cheekbones and a blonde forelock spilling over his forehead. He wears a colourful tropical beach shirt with a cravat at his throat. Below his long body, his legs are short and his jeans are turned up at the bottoms. He gyrates jerkily around the reception room. When the vinyl record finishes, he sits down.

"Where is your woman, man?" he asks me in his high voice and singsong Jamaican accent.

"Vicki wrote that she would be here, " I looked at my watch again. "They are six minutes late."

People expect me to have a Saxon or Teutonic face, rectangular in shape with a square hairline, because of my unemotional nature and preoccupation with independence and efficiency. But my face has the heart shape, widow's peak hairline, high overhanging brow and shaven dark beard of the Celts. These distant ancestors retreated to mountainous areas of Wales or Cornwall or Scotland, out of reach of successive waves of Roman, Saxon, Viking, Dane and Norman conquerors. Nevertheless, I look okay and girls don't usually keep me waiting. By now, even my idol, Dr Spock, would be growing impatient.

Just then the two girls breeze in, wearing white lab coats, smiling broadly.

"Selwyn!" Vicki says. "It's great to see you."

"Hello, Vicki," I say. "It's terrific to see you. I didn't know you are selling ice creams."

We hug. Her clean smell and the firmness of her body are reassuring. Tom hugs petite Angela, only slightly smaller than him. Like Vicki and me, the two are seeing each other, but are not yet an item. We hoist our packs and Vicki leads us along a corridor.

We pass through a reception area with "Pediatric Psychology" on a sign above the desk.

"My feet have a mind of their own," Tom says, doing a couple of reggae steps.

"Pediatrics is not feet, it is children," I tell Tom.

"Same thing," he says. "Children always get under your feet."

We come to a door labelled "Adolescent and School Psychology".

"Is the problem with adolescents that they won't submit to the discrimination that their school has to do?" I ask.

"You are cynical," says Vicki turning to look at me. "We can't allow them to be themselves, can we?"

"Definitely not," I say. "They have to learn to work and pay taxes. Look, Vicki and Angela, I hope we are not interrupting what you are doing?"

"No, not at all," Vicki says. "Actually, I think you may be able to help us," she says in her plummy Oxford voice. "We would appreciate your participation in some tests."

"Okay. Sounds interesting," I agree automatically. "What kind of tests?"

"Changing behaviour."

"They use the cane to change behaviour in schools, "says Tom. "They force people to—"

"No, not any more. That used to be the way. Social scientists used to explain the way people behave as conditioning by the environment. Did you hear on the news about unethical experiments being conducted by 'behaviourists'?"

"Yeah, I heard about Skinner," I say. "He starves pigeons down to 60% of their bodyweight. Then he puts each pigeon into a small box, just big enough to turn around in."

We arrive at a lift. There are seven floors and it is at the top. Vicki calls it and it starts coming slowly.

I continue, "Skinner had these letters, 'F.O.O.D.', written on buttons inside the box. When the bird pecked the buttons in the correct order, a food pellet was released. Skinner went home for the weekend leaving the pellet machine to reward progress. When he came in on Monday, some pigeons had learned to peck the sequence, FOOD."

"The others were probably feet up," Tom says. "That is cruel, man."

"It is cruel, I agree," Vicki says. "Um, do we want a world ruled by behaviourism?"

As always, Vicki's serious talk is jerky, punctuated with ums and ohs. Her hesitancy is neither lack of ideas nor lack of vocabulary. It signals something like "Pay attention. My message may not be what you expect."

"Behaviourism is what most of us do now, " I reply. "We change people by Skinner-ing them, or by making others do it for us."

"Alas, I agree. We do, Selwyn."

"Is there a problem with that, Vicki?"

"It treats individuals like blocks of wood. An, um, authority controls groups of people and pushes them into any position it wants. It does not allow for individual differences or allow them any say."

The lift arrives. We all get in, with several others, and the lift starts upwards.

"Is a behaviourist a fascist, then?" Tom asks.

Everyone looks at him. He is an extrovert.

"They could be," Vicki says. "Fascism conditions the masses to want nationalism."

"Rule Britannia, marmalade and jam—" Tom sings, gyrating his shoulders with a reggae rhythm and clicking his fingers in time.

We stop at the first floor, where there is a sign, "Industrial and Organisational Psychology". Two people in white lab coats get out. They have been silent in the corners of the lift. Then we continue upwards.

"Were they observing us?" I ask, putting on a furtive face. The girls laugh.

"Possibly," says Vicki. "A study at Chicago has found that when workers are observed by anonymous strangers, they work harder."

"Are you working harder Angela?" asks Tom kindly.

"Absolutely. My brain is flat out."

"Doing what?"

"Trying to figure out whether those creepy guys were observing us."

"Observation is a different way of controlling people and is individualised. So it isn't fascist."

"What if there is no control?" asks Tom.

"Voluntary behaviour can be self-controlled," I say. "for example when people change their minds it —"

"— is called cognition."

"That's what I was going to say, cognition."

"Like starting a car when it is in gear," says Tom. "You get a jerk."

We all grin broadly and look at him, but no one says anything.

"Hmm, a little," says Vicki, encouraging him. "When you have a sudden insight."

Tom is pleased with himself. "How do you know when someone has an insight," he says. "You can't look inside their head."

"We infer it from their behaviour," Vicki replies.

"When they start in neutral," says Tom.

"When people change their behaviour by cognition, we say they have learnt," I add, recalling Vicki's textbook. "This may be by imitation, insight, problem-solving, intelligence or conscious thought. When these occur, it is inferred that there has been a change in the mind. They can—"

"Yes, Selwyn," Vicki says. "You are correct again. There are any many learning methods we use to change minds – for example, an aim of justice is to correct criminals' minds and behaviour."

We get off at "Forensic and Legal Psychology". We walk along a corridor and pass doors inscribed "Witness Memory Research" and another labelled "Trial Consulting".

I pause in front of the doors.

"I guess witnesses forgetting to turn up at trials is a big problem."

I keep a straight face, as usual.

"Yes, but here we are looking into what meanings people, um, take from certain words. When humans see the letters, F.O.O.D., for example, some may think of hunger and others of dieting, depending on their cognition. People make up their own minds. The problem is how to ask witnesses to recall their experience without bias. We are looking into cognitive persuasion that recognises that."

"Perjury sends them to prison."

"Persuasion is more humane and accurate than conditioning people with fear."

"Out with behaviourism and in with cognition?"

"Correct."

Vicky walked on, with us following.

"Before questioning a witness we need a method for finding out their true background attitudes and preferences."

We come to a door labelled "Interrogation and Confessions Research Unit".

"Let's ask here, " says Tom. "Though we might have to slap them around a bit."

"This is us," says Vicki.

We go in, take off our packs and sit in a small reception area. We can see a passage leading away with rooms on both sides. Tom rubs his back against his chair. He has acne from his waist to his neck and it causes itching.

"I hope the methods you use are not questionable," I say. I don't often make jokes, so I give a small laugh, so the others will know it is a joke.

The three burst out laughing. It isn't that funny and they seem to be laughing at me. I like to be the centre of attention.

"Coffee? Tea?" Angela asks.

"Or me?" Tom prompts.

"Me not available. Sorry, Tom."

"Me want Vicki," I say with a goofy laugh.

"Me not stupid. Me know what Selwyn want Vicki for," Vicki says.

"That's not fair," I say. "I imagine you are alluding to coitus. I had verbal intercourse in mind."

"That's what I was worried about," Vicki says quickly and we all laugh.

They are used to my bluntness now. With me, they always know where they stand and this time they like it. Sometimes I upset them without meaning to.

When I first met Vicki, I had thought the hesitations in her speech marked indecision, giving her time to think. I realize now that Vicki's ideas are carefully tended and self-confident, so that her response to any incident is razor sharp. Her hesitations seek attention to profundities. She is as neat, stylish and understated on the inside as she is on the outside. When I am with her I am self-conscious and clumsy. My understanding seems shallow, my opinions facile and my humour juvenile.

We order our drinks and Angela goes to get them.

"So you are investigating interrogation," I say.

"Yes. We are trying to find out how people respond when questioned," says Vicki.

"Questioned about what?" Tom asks.

"Criminal activities," Vicki says.

"How do you know that they have been doing criminal activities?" I ask.

"We infer it from their behaviour."

"Hmm. I'm going to be on my best behaviour," Tom says.

"We measure involuntary behaviour," says Vicki. "For example, if you were involved in a crime, when asked about it, your feelings may cause you to sweat."

"Why?" I asked.

"Anxiety may stimulate your metabolism, generating heat that you try to lose by perspiring."

"What if it was a murder in cold blood."

"Even if your circulation is unaffected, you could be anxious, causing sweating and your skin's electrical conductivity may increase."

"Are you going to use electricity on me?" asks Tom, showing anxiety.

"Only to measure your behaviour, not to cause it. We use a low voltage across electrodes on your skin. Suppose we asked you What is your favourite food?"

"My favourite food is ackee with saltfish," says Tom." Just thinking of it makes me feel hungry, man."

"A remarkable result," I say.

I look around to see if they like my sarcasm, as I have been practising.

"Yes, Selwyn, his feelings are remarkable," says Vicki. "If his mother in Jamaica makes his ackee with saltfish, he might feel anxious and sweat, because he misses her."

"Isn't that the same as saying that he is anxious because he misses his mother's ackee with saltfish?" I ask.

"No. They are two different feelings. He might miss his mother and feel anxious, while not being hungry at all."

"Tom is always hungry," I say.

"Tom, do you miss your mother?" asks Vicki.

"No. Only when I'm hungry," he answers. He gives me a tiny wink. "Then I feel anxious. But I only sweat if it is a hot day."

"There," says Vicki in exasperation. "You see, he is only capable of one feeling: hunger. It is the foundation for all his behaviour, just as Pavlov's dogs salivated when a bell was rung, whether they were hungry or not."

"The way to an engineer's heart—"

"That'd be right!" Vicki says. "Pavlov could have used engineering students instead of dogs!"

"Hmm. He would have rung a bell when he fed them and observed how they drooled even if there was no food."

"They would also salivate if the observer was a girl," Tom adds.

Angela brings our hot drinks. We sip them.

"Thanks, Angela," I say. "I was fresh out of saliva."

"Engineers have one-track minds," laughs Vicki.

"Not our fault," I say. "It is endemic to our profession. Engineering has traditionally been a masculine pursuit, having iconic technologies that mimic sexual intercourse, such as trains and tunnels and reciprocating motion. Some technologies have been granted female status, such as ships, which are always referred to affectionately by the feminine pronouns, "she" and "her". Consequently, sex is never far from engineer's minds, as indicated by the frequency of sexual innuendo in engineering communication. For example, uncertain situations are—" .

"Thank you, Selwyn. You do not need to remind us how sexist engineers are," Vicki interrupts.

I do not feel good about being labelled as sexist. All engineering students at LUT are males, whereas Vicki and Angela are in Biological Science, which has a handful of females.

"Anyway, "Vicki continues, "if Tom has strong feelings and anxiety triggered by thinking about his favourite food, he may perspire more and we can see the change in electricity flow between two points on his skin. Let's go and test some other associations," she says, getting up.

She leads the way to a laboratory, where she introduces us to her supervisor, a large man, Tony, with a shock of unruly hair. He shows us into a soundproof room with a chair like a dentist's. To one side there is a control room.

"Welcome to the Lie Detection Laboratory," Tony says. "Today Vicki and Angela have asked me to demonstrate a simple test."

"Did you say 'lie detection'?" I ask, puzzled. He nods.

I turn to Vicki. "Do you think I tell lies?"

She shakes her head. "No, Selwyn. We all tell small ones from time to time."

I do not think I do. I regard lying as a very low behaviour. Lying is incompatible with science, which requires scrupulous honesty. In my home, honesty is the greatest virtue, rated higher even than Ayn Rand's other six: rationality, productiveness, pride, independence, integrity and justice. I have them on a list beside my bed.

We listen as Tony explains the test. I see a side of Vicki that I have not seen before: the serious student. She is listening to Tony intently, with an occasional nod or shadow of a frown. She senses me watching her and turns, giving me a big smile. My heart melts. What we have between us is unique. I want her, with every fibre of my being.

The psychologist continues, "The test you will do today is informal, for research purposes only and there is no stigma attached.

"We are only going to look for changes in your behaviour shown by what you say in response to a stimulus or question. Our lie detector measures physiological changes from which psychological causes can be inferred.

"For example, we will measure your responses by word association. A suspect in a crime may hesitate and become anxious before they reply to a word, for example, 'gun', that could connect them with the crime. Their anxiety or fear triggers adrenalin release, their heart beats faster and they sweat more, which the electrocardiogram can measure. The sweat moistens the skin and the current flow between two electrodes touching the skin increases. A pen writing on a rotating chart is given a jiggle by the current flow. It is alongside other measurements, such as pulse rate, blood pressure, respiration rate and muscular reflexes, which also jiggle. The chart with all these traces is called a polygraph. The bigger the lie, the bigger the jiggles.

"Today we will only have a brief informal test to show how a lie detector works," he says. "Vicki and Angela are investigating techniques for accessing subjects' true beliefs, rather than when their response is merely to get them off the hook."

"It sounds like you are developing a method to interrogate Soviet spies!" Tom says.

"No comment," the psychologist is curt.

I turn to Vicki. "I don't get it. I never lie to you!"

She laughs. "No, I know that, Selwyn. We are comparing people's true feelings with what they actually say."

"What if I say I want one thing but choose something else? Would that be lying?"

Vicki looks at me and smiles, as if she knows something that I do not.

"It depends on the situation. It's just a bit of fun," she says. "No big deal. It could help you to understand any difficulties you may be having."

"Am I having difficulties, Vicki?" I say.

I think she is my major difficulty. She has been eluding a steady relationship with me all term, despite a promising start.

"I don't know," she shrugs, smiling. "You seem to me to be doing all right for yourself," she pauses. "I hear you did well in second year exams. Congratulations."

"Thanks. It was not unexpected. I usually top the class. However, I didn't get everything I wanted last semester," I look at her meaningfully.

"Could you have wanted too much?" she replies seriously.

She could mean I had been too impatient to have sex with her. I wonder how much she knows about me and Barbara. I haven't tried to hide our relationship from her. Neither have I mentioned it to her.

Suddenly I realize I had agreed to go on a real lie detector. This is no joke. Should I feel threatened? No. I have no secrets from Vicki.

"Are you willing to be tested?" Tony asks. "Perhaps you have some questions?" I have plenty of questions but I do not ask them because Vicky is there. His explanation has made me uneasy. I have a bad taste in my mouth, as though they regard me as a suspect who refuses to confess. It is an insult. I expect to be treated with the respect due to me as a truthful person. The premise of the test is that either I am a congenital liar or that I am concealing something of import. It is a shameful suggestion. What am I being accused of? What do they want to find out? Is my honesty in doubt?

"Vicki and Angela have made up the questions, " says Tony. "You don't have anything to worry about. Will you do it?"

I have always dealt with Vicki openly. Now I want to show her I have nothing to hide and trust her. But Tom is not so easily persuaded. For once he looks defensive.

"My life is private. I think I'll give it a miss."

The psychologist is disappointed. "I'm sorry to hear that, Tom. What about you, Selwyn?"

I ask myself, "What is Tom up to, that he won't answer a few questions? Surely it is not merely his routine caution? It's not like him to hold back like this."

I cannot refuse to take the test, as this would admit to Vicki that I have something to hide. Putting me on a lie detector is a fussy way of asking questions that she could ask me politely. I do not have any secrets I am ashamed of. Vicki said it is just a bit of fun, and I trust her.

"I'll give it a go," I say. "My life is an open book."

"What kind of book?" asks Tom. "Engineering?"

"Truths," I say.

"We'll soon see," says Vicki smiling.

I end each chapter with a Rule that I have learnt by reflecting on my experiences. I hope it will help the reader avoid some of the difficulties I have encountered in my life.

Rule 1: *Men limit lying to the speaking of untruths, whereas women include men's insincerity and withholding of truths.*

CHAPTER 2   LIE DETECTOR

"Okay, Selwyn, let's begin," says Tony, the psychologist.

A technician sits me in the dentist's chair and adjusts it for a relaxed posture. They tape electrodes smeared with gel against my skin on my face, head and arms. They attach wires to each electrode, gather these into bundles, and connect them to a heavy cable into the control room.

"What are these straps for?" I ask, as the technician fastens my arms and waist to the chair.

"Some people forget that they are wired up. If they move, the electrodes get dislodged."

They all go out, closing the soundproof door behind them. I can still see them through a glass panel. The two girls are sitting beside Tony beside the polygraph recorder. We are all wearing headsets.

There is a camera pointing at my face. I make sure my expressions hide my feelings, as usual. I habitually put my face in one of two standard looks: an expressionless public mask that reveals neither positive nor negative emotions, conveying alert interest. This gives me the most time to work out a smart response. People wanting to know my feelings about something go away empty handed. Alternatively, I put on a face with mouth and eyes turned down, reflecting. People who don't know me think I am sad, until I tell them to look at the relaxed face of a higher primate.

"Hello, Selwyn."

"Hello."

"Do you own a car?"

"Yes."

"Do you have a girlfriend?"

There is Vicki, sometimes. Barbara regularly.

"Yes," I answer

"What is she called?"

"Vicki."

"Do you have another girlfriend?"

"Yes."

"What is her name?"

"Barbara."

I think, "Why are they putting me through this?" Vicki knows I will have these answers. But I have never discussed Barbara with her.

"Do you have a driving licence?"

"Yes."

"Have you ever had an erection?"

"Yes."

"Have you ever masturbated?"

I blush. I have never admitted this to anyone and I feel foolish. My skin conductance probably goes off-scale.

"Yes," I admit. "But not into the family liver," I add with more bravado than I feel, recalling an incident in the novel, "Portnoy's Complaint".

No-one laughs.

"Who do you think of when you masturbate, Barbara or Vicki?"

It is a loaded question and not fair. I am not used to telling girls who I think of when I masturbate. This isn't fun.

"I don't want to do this."

I try to get out of the chair but I am strapped in and can't move. "Let me out, please."

"Answer the question, please. Do you think of Barbara or Vicki?"

I think sometimes it is Barbara, but more often Vicki.

"Vicki."

"Have you ever engaged in sexual activity with another family member?"

I think of the forbidden looking and touching with my siblings when I was small, that I had never admitted to anyone before.

"Yes."

"Have you ever had sexual intercourse with a girl?"

"Yes," I answer. Two weeks ago I would have said no, truthfully. I can see the girls' faces in the control room and they are frowning.

"How many times have you been to the United States?"

"Twice," I answer, counting a day excursion over the border from Canada.

"How many times altogether have you had sexual intercourse with girls?"

"Twice."

"How many times have you had sexual intercourse with a girlfriend?"

This is pretty damned intrusive, I think. There is no longer any doubt in my mind that Vicki has thought up these questions to find out about my relationship with Barbara. I am not sure why. I try again to get out of the chair, by breaking the straps on my arms, but they are too strong.

"Let me out," I demand, panting. "Restraining the liberty of an individual against their will is a felony, and those responsible may be charged with an offence."

"Don't worry; this information will be kept confidential."

That isn't the point. It is Vicki who I don't want to know everything. But I am too nonplussed to articulate this.

"I don't want to answer. Let me out."

"We will let you out very soon, after a few more questions. Now again; how many times have you had sexual intercourse with your girlfriend? Never, once, twice, more than twice?"

He is now asking about my "girlfriend". I wonder if I should nominate Vicki or Barbara. If Vicki was my girlfriend, I would answer "never".

"Twice," I answer. "But it's none of your damn business."

"Do you like this girlfriend?"

"Yes," I answer.

"Is there any other girl you like more than her?"

I hesitate. He, of course, means Vicki. Is this the way for Vicki to find out where she stands with me? I don't like it but I can't put my finger on exactly why not. There doesn't seem to be any harm. Vicki will find out that I am crazy about her, which I have been concealing from everyone. I always try and conceal my emotions from people. That way I don't give anything away that I might want to keep to myself, at least until I have thought things through.

"Yes," I answer. I just want this grilling to be over.

"Is this other girl Vicki?"

"Yes," I reply.

"Who is more attractive to you, your girlfriend or Vicki?"

"Vicki."

"Who do you feel more possessive about, your girlfriend or Vicki?"

"Vicki."

"Who would you rather be with, in the future?

"Vicki."

"Would it be hard for you to get along without your girlfriend?"

"No."

"Have you promised to stay with your girlfriend?"

"No."

"Have you made a plan to finish with your girlfriend?"

"Yes," I say, and it isn't a lie.

"When will you finish with your girlfriend?"

"When I get back to Liverpool."

"Would it be easy for you to get along without Vicki?"

"No," I say truthfully. Hopefully Vicki will recognize that I want her very badly.

"Do you love Vicki?"

"Yes."

"How much on a scale from 1 to a maximum of 10 do you love her?"

"Ten."

"Has there ever been a time when you have wanted to have two girlfriends at the same time?"

Until that moment I have not had to face my ambivalence. Men who lead women on are anathema. Since meeting Vicki I have had flings with several other girls. Although I am rapt over Vicki, I am not going to become monogamous until she gives me more attention.

I hesitate but not for long.

"No," I lie.

I would love to have two females, the more the merrier. The girls in the control room frown. It is my first lie in the interview, a little white one. I know that the lurch my heart has taken has been registered.

The psychologist ends the test. I feel gutted. There should be no doubt that I am besotted with Vicki. My only duplicity has been to minimize the importance to me of my ongoing relationship with Barbara. Having a bit on the side is okay, but it has become more than that, now we are sleeping together. Vicki knows that now.

As the technician undoes the straps, takes off the wires and lets me out of the chair, the psychologist speaks to me.

'Thank you for your cooperation."

I glare at him. "Did you find what you were looking for?"

18

"Vicki and Angela wanted to practise using a lie detector in a situation where a couple doubts each other. They made up the main questions, and I demonstrated how to follow up on questions where there are issues.

"We have plenty of cases where the machine has discovered that a 'neglected wife' and her roving husband still have some affection left for each other. On the other hand, we have also tested a young man who truly loved a wealthy girl but subconsciously was seeking her money. Others have shown that a young couple are in love, even though they are engaged to other people.

"You confessed to a crush on Vicki and at the same time having a sexual relationship with another girl. You did not try to conceal that, and therefore there is not necessarily a problem in your relationship with Vicki. It depends what you want.

"You have been an unusually honest subject, Selwyn. Goodbye and the best of luck."

He turns away and continues writing notes beside the peaks on the polygraph.

I am indignant when I speak to Vicki. "Why didn't you ask me directly?"

I am angry at the way they have treated me. They didn't give me much respect.

"I'm sorry if we have upset you."

"I would have answered honestly, and you would know I truly do love you, very much more than Barbara," I say. "What were you trying to find out?"

Vicki takes us into a meeting room where the four of us discuss the meaning of lie detector tests. Afterwards, the girls show us around the campus and then take us back to the family home where they are staying. We spend the afternoon and evening with them and are guests of honour at a barbecue.

Vicki is friendly but distant. She seems unimpressed by the strength of my feelings for her on the lie detector and does not mention it.

We sleep in our sleeping bags on the floor of the games room. The girls go to bed early, leaving us there. I had been hoping for more time with Vicki, but she does not seem to want to get involved with me. I do not understand why. I assume that I am not good enough for her.

I lie awake, sadly reviewing my behaviour with her, but am unable to reach any conclusion. Fortunately, I am tired and go to sleep.

The next day, the girls come with us to the bus station. I kiss Vicki goodbye.

"I'm going to miss you and I am not lying," I say, holding her.

"I believe you will," she says, "and I will miss you, too. It won't be long until we are back in Liverpool."

"I love you."

She seems embarrassed and draws away from me, to arms' length. "And I like you very much," she says, smiling perfunctorily, worried. "I am sorry about the lie detector test, that it upset you."

"It's okay now," I say, although I still smart.

I think her acknowledgement shows respect and I am pleased.

"See you soon."

"Bye."

I give her a hug and follow Tom onto the Greyhound, to take us to Miami. From there we will fly to stay with his family in Jamaica and then back to Liverpool for our Finals year at university.

As we bowl down the freeway, I am smarting from her cool response to my crush on her, verified by the lie detector. I cannot get her out of my mind. The driver plays The Beatles' "You've Got to Hide Your Love Away". I talk with Tom about her.

"I thought she would be all over me, after the test," I complain to Tom.

"You have been found out," he laughs. "She doesn't like you fucking Barbara! It serves you right for being greedy," he smirks.

"She knows I would give up Barbara if we had something going."

He thinks it is funny. "Some of us survive with only one female at a time."

I now wish I had done as he did and refused to be tested.

I wonder how Vicki will respond to what she has found out. At least she knows now that I truly love her. What hurts is that she does not seem to love me back. Perhaps it was not smart to go to Barbara when I could not get sex from Vicki. Now Vicki is unwilling to compete but not because she is uncompetitive. From the very start, Vicki has had it in spades with me.

Rule 2: *A woman requires that she alone has the man's attention*

CHAPTER 3 VICKI

Vicki and I first met ten months earlier, at the beginning of second year.

Trying to be social, I scan the crowded coffee lounge for a familiar face. I had studied hard as a fresher and I seldom came here. Socialising is not my scene but I need a new girlfriend. I had finished with my girlfriend, Bridget, at the end of the year. Now at the beginning of second year, I feel geeky and awkward.

At the far end of the room sprawls a group so casual, fashionable and confident, that they must be third year students from wealthy families. An exceptionally good-looking girl ornaments the group. I focus on her as I sip my coffee. She is like the glittering central stone in a diadem. She seems to be holding court with her group, at once absorbed and yet aloof, possibly a little bored. Her head moves, swinging her ponytail. Sincerity and good humour alternate with scepticism and ridicule. I want to hear her talk and have to get closer. Trying to look inconspicuous, I push through the crowd towards her, apologising repeatedly.

I work my way to the back of the room. Groups lounge chatting in arm chairs or sit cross-legged on the floor around coffee tables. The groups grow with circles of onlookers. I do not see anyone I know. While I was hard at work studying in first year, they were forging friendships. I regret not having made any friends and will try harder this year.

Ceiling speakers pump out "Help" by The Beatles, but it is drowned out by the hubbub of talk and laughter. I bump into students with coffee mugs cruising looking for girls, looking for friends or just looking for a space to stand and gaze at the action. I keep pushing on through towards my target.

As I get closer, I can see she is a magnet holding her group together. She sits back in a maroon silk blouse, her breasts bulging under a pattern of bunches of shiny red cherries with dark green leaves. Tight blue jeans encase her long slim legs and maroon knee-length leather boots. She is smoking a cigarette delicately, with straight fingers, blowing it upwards in a narrow jet. Other students, male and female, are smoking, too. There is a pall of smoke over the room.

From time to time, she uncrosses her legs and leans forward to tap ash into an ashtray on the table. She is talking, discussing something with her group. Her posture is self-conscious, and I can see it is costing her effort to speak loudly enough to be heard amid the uproar. She seems to have a personal interest in the topic. She shows a curious mixture of strength and vulnerability. Other quieter conversations are going on between twos and threes around her. I hear her say "Smith" and "Wilson" in a melodic BBC voice. I guess she went to a posh private school and is studying law. She seems to be talking about Rhodesia's Unilateral Declaration of Independence threat, ridiculing Wilson's weak stand against white racism.

I stand to one side, where I can study her face. She looks up at me and I return her gaze, putting on my happy face. She smiles back with brilliant green eyes and looks away. She is breathtakingly beautiful and used to admiring stares. Her long thick hair, the colour of old copper, is tied high at the back of her head and swings as she talks. She has slender hands, wrists and arms. On one hand, she wears an old classic gold Cartier watch, presumably an heirloom. On the other is a plain gold bracelet, a solid ring from the absence of any join mark. She is wearing jewellery more valuable than most students' total possessions. Her ear is white and fragile like a seashell, with a light gold circle swinging by a chain from a stud in the lobe.

When she turns, her face is almond-shaped and fair, with a light sprinkling of freckles across the centre. Her nose is narrow, straight, and finely chiselled, with the end upturned away from a sensual mouth. A smile habitually plays on her full lips. It is the face of an aesthete, someone with a passion for refined experiences. Her eyes are also playful, up for adventure. I get an impression of kindness, intelligence and fun.

"What do you think Smith will do when, um, Harold arrives in Rhodesia?" she asks, looking at the students around her for an answer, ignoring me. She seems accustomed to speaking in public on issues. She is a knight errant who rides a high horse of ideals and fights passionately for what she believes in.

"Smith will show him how he is in charge there. He won't listen to Wilson at all, Vicki," says someone. "The situation will escalate."

A pretty name, I think. She shakes her head, ponytail jiggling. "No. Smith will make some piddling concession, so that Wilson can save face, like promising to have an election, away in the future. Wilson will claim it is, ah, a back-down."

I know some Rhodesian students and I have been following these issues with interest. I am blown away by Vicki's handle on the situation. I decide to express my admiration – and get her attention. Although I am excluded, I know that groups will accept a stranger who brings support for the leaders.

"Vicki's right," I interrupt loudly, over the top of a student who is replying to her. He is surprised and falls silent. Vicki turns her head and looks me up and down. I continue, "Harold is most interested in getting re-elected. Justice for black Rhodesians won't get many votes." Everyone looks at me. The group falls silent as they strain to listen. "If he sends the troops in against Smith, British settlers in Africa will be rooted. There will be a rout. They will be out of Africa. Voters with relatives in Africa will hate Wilson. He will have made powerful enemies in the corporate world, too, miners who want to continue sending minerals here. As Vicki told you, Wilson will desert the blacks, pulling out and leaving Ian Smith to crush the very same movement that Labour has encouraged up to now. It's a double-cross."

I finish there. Vicki nods thoughtfully and looks at me again. I kneel down and sit cross-legged on the carpet beside her. As always when I speak to a group, the silence afterwards hurts, and I feel rejected. Even so, I always do it as a test of my intelligence. Presently, the buzz of conversation resumes. Vicki turns to speak to the student seated on her other side from where I am standing. As I watch she asks him a question, but I can only see the side of her head.

I try to lip-read his answer and recognise some words: engineer, second year, studious, first year girlfriend, Chemistry, finished. They are talking about me and Bridget, who I was going with during most of last year. She studies Chemistry.

Then another in the group starts rebutting my argument, stating that because Rhodesia depends on our mineral markets, economic sanctions would be successful and that is the way Wilson will go. It makes good sense and I learn from it. I have already achieved what I want. I have made a favourable impression on Vicki and the group. I have guessed correctly that they are not Labour stalwarts, and my attack on Wilson is acceptable.

I watch Vicki's eyes and I try to imagine being her, aware of her deep beauty and unique features. Dark green irises nestle quietly but alert in her pure white sclera beneath long copper eyelashes. Her eyes retract as brow and cheeks come together in deep smiles that crinkle at her temples. She is totally alive to her surroundings, feeling others' emotions and moods, giving her mind to understanding, rather than pronouncing judgements, her awareness composed rather than fearful. She is her own person in every way. Her friends return her smiles.

She is aware I am watching her by her lingering small smile, her feigned interest in others' conversations and the way she combs her hair through her fingers. I feel myself falling under her spell. She has infected me with joy, lifting me up. Again, I wonder what subject she studies. She is too alive to her surroundings to be a lawyer. She could be an art student or maybe in Education.

After half an hour, everyone gets up and goes off to lectures. Vicki passes me politely, with an encouraging smile, as if she wants to meet me, but I am too shy. She leaves an odour of wild flowers. Where her bare arm brushes against mine, my hairs spring erect and my skin tingles. I can feel my heart pounding jubilantly in my chest as I hurry to my lecture. Suddenly, my whole world has changed. As I stride along, I puff a tune, whistling through my teeth, "Help me get my feet back on the ground".

I have a goal and my studies can take second place for a while.

I want Vicki.

In the days following, Vicki is often with her group, older male students, law students. Group members affect tiredness or perhaps boredom and make cynical remarks or laconic jokes. They laugh at each other and call each other by nicknames, lolling on the furniture, putting up their feet and striking poses, having a great time. I can't get close to her. I think of going boldly up to her but dismiss the idea because she seems so sophisticated, while I am so naïve.

For the first time in my life I feel out of my class. I have never before thought about a girl's social class, at least not consciously. Vicki and her group seem to be sophisticated and middle class, but it could be superficial. I can imagine myself as one of them next year. I feel the equal of Vicki on the inside, where it counts.

I endeavour to meet Vicki socially. The Students' Union holds dances on Saturday nights, called 'hops', with music by popular bands. The Beatles were to come but they broke their contract when they became famous. Spencer Davies and Georgie Fame are coming this weekend. Perhaps I will meet her there. I do not dance but the dance floor is too crowded anyway.

On Saturday evening I look for her at the hop in vain. There are plenty of girls who live and work in the town. They teeter around in groups on high-heeled platform-soled shoes, enjoying the music and dancing, hoping to meet the boy of their dreams. Students call these girls "totty". I learn to call the hops "cattle markets". I learn that Vicki wouldn't come to a hop. She would probably be at a middle-class private party, out on a date, or at home.

On the following Monday, in the Union coffee lounge, when one of her companions vacates a chair, I sit down next to her.

"Hi," I say. I am self-conscious, trying to hide my Yorkshire accent, saying as little as possible. "I'm Selwyn."

"Hi." She gives me a perfunctory smile and looks away, quickly enough to be disinterested.

I am tall and fair with the straight nose of an aristocrat, school principal or inspector of police, and high cheekbones. I am upright with a distinguished bearing. I have broad shoulders tapering to a slim waist with strong arms, thighs and legs. My movements are deliberate and powerful. I am adept at swimming, skiing and simple dances but awkward at soccer. I am unable to follow even simple routines such aerobics and yoga.

I am dressed in a brightly coloured shirt and jeans. I have large feet wearing desert boots.

I offer her a cigarette. She accepts and I light it.

"Paula, isn't it?"

"No," she replies, drawing on her cigarette and looking away. "Vicki."

"Sorry, Vicki. I'm terrible at names. Where are you from?"

"Salisbury."

"Wiltshire?"

"Yes. Not Rhodesia."

She continues to look away. I suppose male students pester her all the time.

"Are you going to the protest?" I ask in my broad Yorkshire accent. The Students' Union is organising a rally in support of increased government grants to students.

"Maybe."

"I will be going," I tell her, "though it won't make any difference to me. I'm on the minimum grant."

She looks interested. Her face is soft and mobile but sets in a few expressions that hide what she is thinking.

"You must be rich?"

She sounds middle-middle class. I want to speak like her, hiding my accent. However, I am proud of where I come from. I have never exchanged more than a few words with a middle class girl from down south before.

"No," I tell her. "My parents have a bit of brass and they pay my bills, but every time I save up a C or two I lose it speculating."

"What on?"

"Share puts or calls or commodities, usually. I will eventually win, in a big way."

"I'm on the minimum, too," she mimics my accent. I acknowledge with a smile.

"I like your gold things." I speak carefully with an Oxford accent, as spoken by BBC newsreaders.

'Thanks. I have them on to cheer me up."

"Is something wrong?"

"My father is ill."

"What do your parents do?"

She speaks hesitantly, as if the situation is tentative.

"My mother has, um, chemists' shops. My father has, um, dementia."

I deduce she is middle-middle.

"I'm sorry to hear about your father. Is he bad then?"

"Pretty bad. He doesn't know who I am any more. Look, I have a lecture. I'll see you around."

She is not a snob. She has come out of her shell and is talking to me as an equal. There is nothing more that I could want. She is the girl I have dreamed of.

"See you around. I'm Selwyn, by the way."

"You said. I'll remember."

"Bye, Paula – I mean Vicki."

She smiles and is gone.

I am besotted.

In aiming to win this girl, I know I am an outsider, at odds that are long.

Rule 3: *A woman who gets male group attention is attractive to individual males.*

PART 2: FRESHER LOVE (1946 –1965)

In which I relate experiences growing up on our farm to pursuit of girls in my first year at university.

CHAPTER 4   ANIMAL LOVE

Going back even further to the start of first year, I was a naïve farm boy setting off from home to Liverpool University of Technology.

I feel special as I drive my old Volkswagen beetle up Nidderdale from our farm in the West Yorkshire Dales. It is September 29th, Michaelmas Day traditionally the last day of the harvest season, the end of the annual farming cycle and the beginning of autumn. It is the start of a new phase in my life and it heightens my appreciation of the world I am leaving, where I have no place but have been given the opportunity to enter another distant one.

From an early age, my treatment had been different from other boys. I am the second son, and my mother tried to turn me into the girl she wanted, with kisses, cuddles and ribbons in my curly blonde hair. When my sister was born, she discarded me. I must have been horrible, because I cried so much she shook me and hurt me. I was afraid of her. As the second son I was destined to leave the farm. She may have wanted to avoid affection that could make ejection painful. Fear of desertion became my constant companion. Then she had twins, a boy and a girl, who became the centre of her interest.

I seemed to get the least care and attention of all five of us. To be the centre of delicious attention, my ruse was to dive off the garden wall and land on my head, repeatedly. My mother ignored this behaviour, except to put iodine on my cuts. She said she could not take me out with her, because I looked like a victim of child abuse. It may have been vindictiveness, or possibly to stop masturbation, that made her decide to have me circumcised, the only one of her three boys to be thus mutilated. I coped with the worry I felt around her by transferring my affections unconditionally to my father. He accepted me the way I was, a little different.

I attended the village school. The work was too easy for me and as I did not have any friends in that class I was put up a year level.

These children were bigger than I was and when I surpassed them I was ostracised and excluded from games in the playground, and became unhappy. When I did not make any friends I realised I was different. My worrying increased. I was taken away then and sent to a private school.

From age nine my schooling prepared me for the 11-plus. My abilities were not unlike the others. Our classroom was a jungle of hierarchies and territories that I knew about from the outside, as friendships eluded me. The only companionship I knew was with my younger sister, Heather. My mother was a highly-strung, strange and volatile woman, bitter from a life that had been impoverished socially by recession and war. In her own view, she was a farmer's wife trapped by male dominance on a farm, without independent financial security, excluded from the farm office, required to bring up five thankless children. She would skulk in her bedroom for days at a time. In those days depression was hidden and ignored.

When farming talk drifted towards a sexual subject, my mother abruptly changed the topic. She may have been in denial. My father had never admitted any sexual propensities, as if we children had germinated like seeds without his involvement. Consequently, I was left to construct my own understanding of my sexuality from observing the way domestic and farm livestock animals behaved.

The sex I saw as I watched our bull serving the dairy cows was consistent with Thomas Hobbes' view of the human condition as 'solitary, poor, nasty, brutish and short'. He was a huge and fearsome animal, imprisoned in a pen behind high walls, with a barred and padlocked door. About once a week, a cow was brought to an outside pen. When his unlocked door swung open, he trotted out with a long pink erection and without hesitation jumped straight on to her and into her. Two thrusts later, it was all over and he would eye off any other cows around. Sometimes a heifer's legs would buckle under his massive weight, and he would be more circumspect in a second attempt. When he had done his job, he would show no interest in his amour and stand gazing over the gate to the freedom of the field beyond. Then the men would drive him with sticks back into his cell and padlock him in again. It was the only sexual intercourse I saw until I was twenty.

I came away from these trysts in the bull's pen with a troublesome erection. It was painful. Touching it seemed natural but was forbidden. It was shameful and not to be talked about. It was never to be imagined in action.

The sexual stimulus I experienced from horse riding could not be talked about, either. The rhythm of the hip thrusts I used to control the pony's gait was answered by pressure in my groin from the pommel of my saddle. It induced a state of priapia that only ended when I dismounted. However, if the pony suddenly jumped or shied, the pain from my squashed testes could be excruciating. It surprises me that western saddles, with pommels high enough to hang a lariat from, were accepted before cowboys wore jock straps or jockey shorts. Perhaps testicles that receive a drubbing benefit by increased sperm production.

This was not a matter for discussion. Even when my father plastered red ochre paint between the rams' front legs, the explanation was simply that it was to "mark" the ewes. The rams were fat from summering in the long grass of the orchard, where they had taken turns to mount the one infertile ewe, put in to stop them practising on each other. They were released into flocks with hundreds of females. A month later, we retrieved them exhausted, having lost twenty percent of their body weight. Nearly every ewe's rump had been painted red. Curiously, a few ewes had paint all over them, as if there had been unconventional indulgence.

On a farm, with procreation all around, it was impossible to be unaware of my own sexuality. I started a meat rabbit enterprise with one buck and one doe. Within a year, I had hundreds of white rabbits. A truck from the rabbit abattoir called weekly.

The fecundity of rabbits is amazing. A doe can be almost continually pregnant. The same day as she gave birth to a litter of ten to twelve kits, I put her with the buck again. When I reached into the buck's cage, if I was not careful, he bit the skin on my forearm to hold on, mounted my hand and thrust away vigorously, feeling for an aperture.

Young calves were kept in pens and bucket fed with milk. They sucked on fingers held under the surface, drawing in the milk, until after several weeks, they learned to drink. While this was going on, the other hungry calves engaged in a frenzy of sucking, on any protuberance available. They sucked the bolt on the pen door, they sucked each other's ears and they sucked each other's scrotums. The objects they liked to suck most were in warm body corners, and they sucked on my pocketknife through my clothes. When no milk was forthcoming the hungry calf put all its weight behind a muzzle thump to the supposed udder, to release milk. I have been knocked off my feet and winded by hungry calves.

On weekends I sometimes milked our herd of about thirty cows with a milking machine. It was an old-fashioned dairy where the cows stood in stalls, with the milk being sucked out by a pulsating cluster of rubber teat cups. The teats of young cows were mere buttons, but those of older cows were like carrots. The teat cups could accommodate the various shapes.

One day, when I was washing the milking equipment, being troubled by an erection, I wondered if the milking machine would ease my discomfort. I put my erect penis in a teat cup and turned on the vacuum. I felt an immediate huge pain. The rubber linings contract in a wave that undulates down the teat to eject the milk. A cow's teat is spongy and compressible. However, the spongy tissue in an erect penis is engorged with blood and has valves that stop its egress even under the full force of atmospheric pressure. I managed to quickly turn off the machine and I was released, bruised, but without sufficient tissue damage to require medical treatment. Such equipment should have a warning notice affixed.

RULE 4: *Livestock and pet behaviours that have been artificially selected for reproduction effectiveness can distort human understanding of animals' sexual behaviour.*

CHAPTER 5   GREAT EXPECTATIONS

As a teenager in a boys school without friends, I was delighted to make friends with girl students on the local bus to and from school. When the bus was crowded, my intrepid organ made its presence felt when girl students sat on my lap. If I stood up to let adults sit down, I had to bend double, with my hand in my pocket to affect a casual pose, to disguise the tent in my trousers. But I did not conceal it when I danced pelvis to pelvis with buxom Sharon Wright at parties in the village hall. She did not seem to mind it pressing against her, and her seraphic smiles encouraged me to hold her close as we danced to Adam Faith's "Poor Me". When we went outside, I discovered kissing. If I delved in her mouth with my tongue, she would suck it invitingly.

I had no idea that sex is normally part of a relationship. The topic of sexual relations was entirely taboo at home and rigorously excluded from the school curriculum. When I was a final year student, a conclave of Church of England parsons tried to have us discuss, with students from the girls' school, moral issues in boy-girl relationships. The topic seemed rather abrupt for our first cross-gender discussion, and we were shy and tongue-tied. When we were asked our views of how emotions should affect sexual relations, we had no idea.

I didn't get it at all. The clergy's advice was oblique, but my intuition was that I could be missing out on something worth knowing. I complained to my mother, who upbraided my school principal for exposing me to such experiences without parental permission. In her opinion, the whole topic should be left to the family.

"You have no right to put these ideas in his head. He is more interested in chemistry," she complained.

When this was broadcast in the staff room, I was nicknamed "Chemistry" Archer by the teachers, to my acute embarrassment.

33

My mother had received no sex education herself and regarded sexual relations as largely unnecessary and offensive to decent living. My parents had little understanding of their sexuality, having met and married during the war, when coitus would have been too hurried between bombing raids for any pleasure. My mother did not acknowledge that a boy needed to meet girls of the same age, and when I did, she tried to stop it, in the same way that my father chained up our dog when the Collie bitch up the road was on heat.

A tenant farmer lives at his workplace and is always on duty caring for animals twenty-four seven. Days off are rare and holidays not to be counted on. In the tenant farming fraternity, a few parents still selected partners for their sons and arranged marriages. To be a farmer's wife, a girl has to have discipline, be capable of unremitting toil and able to withstand social isolation. Parents arranging relationships look for these qualities in a girl's descent, virginity and social conformity.

Young blades thus betrothed sometimes stray to a more adventuresome local girl for sex, causing problems. Parents therefore encourage young males to go abroad to sow their wild oats, to attain manhood there before returning and settling down. Farmers' sons from England backpack on working holidays in the USA, Canada or Australia. They have casual sexual liaisons and acquire the maturity needed to take over from their retiring fathers.

As second son, born between my brothers, Howard and Matthew, my destiny is to leave Priory Farm.

"You can't go farming," I am told at an early age. "Matthew has to have a farm and we can't afford to start him and you as well. You have to go away. If you do well at school you will be able to get a good job."

I grow up in the farming community, never to be a farmer, as a spectator. I feel rejected until I decide my life's mission. One night, standing under the stars, I vow to better the lives of the poor, the helpless and those living under bigotry.

I become a frequent visitor to the town library. I read The Saint, James Bond, Hemingway, Conrad and "Lady Chatterley's Lover". This last book is banned but I borrow it from a classmate. The sexually explicit pages are sweat stained and dog-eared.

These adventurers' dalliances are romantic. I want romance, adventure and excitement. I have clandestine dates with several local girls, including passionately embracing my sister's French pen friend in a dangerously rocking dinghy on our farm pond. There is another episode with secret kissing in the mossy glades of a local wood. There is the blackness of Christmas Eve in the back of a Landrover bumping along farm roads, carrying drunken carol singers from farm to farm, with furtive groping under duffle coats. I find that girls have a small appetite for secretive sex and want relationships to be out in the open with moral respectability. This my mother will not allow, frustrating my ambition to have sexual intercourse.

I badly want to experience sexual intercourse, partly from peer pressure but mostly because of the troubling hard-ons that plague my life. I had heard of masturbation and orgasms but my rubbing just made matters worse. The problem with masturbation is that until I have sex for the first time, I don't know what to expect. It is rather like being given a yoyo, never having seen one being used. When it reaches the end of its string and stops, it seems rather pointless. I am as horny as hell but cannot do anything about it. The topic is taboo among my school and university friends, probably because our churches regard it as sinful.

"Masturbation is unnatural," they preach.

The evidence conflicts. Every few weeks, quite unpredictably, I wake up lying in a cold puddle. It is highly embarrassing, and cleaning up the sticky mess cannot hide what has taken place. I suspect that the processes that produce a wet dream occur in default of sexual intercourse. It is evident that my gun is loaded but neglected and discharging involuntarily. I become more and more desperate to experience coitus.

Because of my mother's hubris, no girl in our district is good enough for me. She can find no good in anyone. She particularly looks down on any girl with any hint of family gossip or scandal, who is illegitimate, working class, or from a family without property, wealth, prospects or civility. Most unsuitable is a girl from a family with a disability, a health issue, mental or inherited illness, tuberculosis, alcoholism or unemployment. Imprisonment and poverty are prohibitive, as are Jews, Communists, Roman Catholics, Irish, gypsies, dark-skinned people and foreigners. She has a litany of prejudices that keep her friendless in self-imposed misery. Her redeeming feature is that she does a great job of providing nourishment for my physiological needs, such as growth, sporting contests and the thuggery called rugby.

In my final year at school, I take the advice of my chemistry teacher and apply to study engineering at university. It is required in the UK that students go away to study, and I visit several universities for interview. I am most attracted by Liverpool University of Technologies' option of petroleum engineering in the second and third years, because I want to become an oil tycoon.

My A level results are good enough to secure a place at LUT.

I drive noisily in my wreck of a car around the market square of my local town, Wortam, in the West Riding of Yorkshire. The fighting men used to gather here with their weapons under the direction of the Lord of the Manor, to defend against marauders from the north and east. The square is now used for markets and an annual sheep fair. The houses have a pleasing rectangular uniformity and are regimented shoulder to shoulder around the square for mutual shelter and warmth. It is an environment that affords few luxuries. I realise I am going to miss my community of humorous, hardy Dales people.

I cross a narrow-walled bridge and farewell the quilted sheep pastures, a patchwork of emerald meadows, stitched around by dry stonewalls of flat rocks, gathered and stacked long ago, in sunken, grassed erosion channels. The swell of each patch seems held down by its walls. The whole quilt is draped across the bottom of a broad glaciated valley, the dale rising a short way up the sides to where the moor starts above.

In the lowest part, the road intertwines with the river as it ripples cleanly between banks where tall oak, birch, sycamore, horse chestnut and ash trees grow like sentinels. Occasionally, there are rectangular patches of woodland with Douglas firs and other trees. How well I know these covers from the inside, from walking through them beating out game birds for parties of shooters. Crows' nests are built cleverly on the leafless furthermost branches that are too slender to hold the weight of the boy that was me who climbed up to steal their eggs.

Heavy box-like farmhouses alternate at intervals on each side of the road, set back behind lush sheep "in" pastures. Each farmhouse has outlying field barns filled to the rafters with hay from "out" meadows, with flyways left above the bales for ghostly barn owls to bring in mice for their young. Below the hay are floorboards, under which barrow ducks creep to their nests, as they have done for hundreds of years.

The "in" pastures hold few sheep now, in autumn. As I climb up the dale, the moors encroach from misty heights where clouds and rain prevail, and I gallop my pony along sheep tracks with the wind in my hair. The trees and bushes become black shapes as the light fades to the hilltops.

Sunlight breaks through, here and there, adding distant patches of pale purple from heather and the soft brown and light greens of cotton grass, bilberry heath and mosses. The sheep with their lambs are up there grazing. Before winter, shepherds will bring them down to the grass, hay and root crops in the lowland dales.

Finally, I am above the fields and trees and into the pass where mist is descending in wisps from the high peaks, oozing down the hillsides. The road goes through a railway arch, like the keyboard of a giant, made with ten million bricks. I emerge from the arch, and there ahead is a greener land where, in the distance, I am to start a new life.

I turn my portable transistor to Radio Luxembourg. The Beatles' song, "Ticket to Ride", is playing. I turn the volume up loud. "She ought to think right. She ought to do right by me. I am going away and I don't care." I can't think of anything that can stop me now, and I yell out the words as I wind down towards my new home.

RULE 5: *In close-knit communities, there are familiarity, trust and promiscuity.*

CHAPTER 6   PRUDISH ONSET

I arrive at LUT with an immense desire for sex with a girl, without knowing how to begin a relationship with one. After age nine, all my education was with only males. Apart from younger sisters, I have had little association with females. I have much to learn.

On Orientation Day, I browse along the avenue of extra-curricular stalls in the Great Court. I sign up for the Film Production Unit, wanting to try out as a cameraman. A few days later, there is a message in my pigeonhole about a meeting today at the Refectory coffee shop. Two students are already there, sitting at a small table, deep in conversation.

Jade, the convenor, is a second year Arts student. He is unkempt, nonchalant and a chain smoker. He matches the stereotype of a film director interested in art for art's sake.

Deborah is an attractive, compact and self-assured actress. She has an unusually mobile face, and I feel admiration and dislike for her in sequential moments. Her prominent Roman nose is the weather vane of an intense attention, simultaneously superior and condescending. She has the tiny arched feet of a ballerina, or Chinese concubine. She glides from place to place with tiny steps. This rare flower of femininity fascinates me. I am used to people who project their feelings, whereas this actress's real feelings are nowhere in sight on her whitened and painted face, like a clown at a circus.

After I introduce myself, I sit down with them, and Jade continues his conversation with Deborah. I wonder what she is going to do next.

"Will that be okay?" Jade asks her laconically.

"Yes, I'll do it," she agrees. "It will be fun."

Jade turns to me.

"What would you like to do, Selwyn?"

"Camera work?"

"Maybe, later. What about some acting?"

I hesitate. I am a hopeless actor. I find it difficult just being myself.

"What is the part?" I ask. "Can I see a script?"

"You and Deborah will be together. No script. We will work it out as we go. Experimental film. Anything can happen."

"Who else is in it?"

"No-one else. You two are enough. We can begin shooting on Saturday morning at my flat. Any problems?"

"What do I have to prepare?"

"Get together with Deborah before then. Get to know each other better."

I look at Deborah. She smiles reassuringly. This could be fun.

"How about going into town together and having a look around the shops. I need to buy a couple of things."

I hate shopping. On the other hand, Deborah is a striking looking girl.

"Okay."

"Good," says Jade. "One more thing, Selwyn. Will you be okay with taking off your clothes for the camera?"

It suddenly seems to go very quiet as they both look at me.

I gulp.

"By, by myself?" I ask, my voice hoarse.

Jade shakes his head emphatically. "No. With Deborah."

"Oh."

I try to imagine what we will be doing.

"Will there be rehearsals?"

"Yes, of course. What do you say, Selwyn?"

Deborah is looking as though she is about to eat me.

"Okay," I say, with a shrug, as if I do this all the time and am indifferent, but want to show my willingness.

'Right," says Jade. "Then that's settled. Here's my address. We'll meet at eleven on Saturday morning."

Deborah and I go into the city centre on a bus. She is chatty and intense, demanding my attention all the time. After a while she starts holding my hand. I go back with her to her digs but she doesn't ask me in. We have a long kiss on the doorstep. She is an expert and clinical kisser. She explores my mouth thoroughly. We arrange to meet the next day, Friday evening at the Students' Union.

When we arrive, students are thronging in for a dance with the Merseybeats, a local band. Deborah and I start dancing to The Beatles' "A Hard Day's Night". Our dancing is apart. She is stylish and I get a good look at her.

Deborah's appearance affects me with a strange illusion that she has a horse's head. I keep thinking of the joke about the horse that goes into a bar.

"Why the long face?" the barman asks.

Deborah gives whiffling snorts of contentment. The more I imagine her without any clothes, the less attractive she becomes. I have been repelled by girls before. I imagined one girl as a witch and another as a Pekingese. I make an excuse to Deborah of not feeling well and go home. My intuition rejects cavorting naked with Deborah for Jade and his camera.

The next day, I don't go to Jade's flat as I had promised. I don't run into either of them subsequently. So I don't know if they ever made a film. That was the end of my brief career as a movie actor.

Deborah could have been an ideal opportunity to have sex, without making any commitment. However, I am unusually old-fashioned. Privacy and affection are more important. Although I have a strong desire to have sex with attractive girls, I feel inadequate to negotiate the conventions that I imagine are involved. I want to learn these, as I have been unable to make close enough friends to find out. I cannot get Tom to disclose his experience. I suspect that he, too, has not gone all the way. The alternative is to learn sexual behaviour by trial and error, which could be inefficient, or from a female with sexual experience, which could be humiliating.

I am intrigued how the uni students pair off. The girls seem to compete informally for male attention to get as high as possible on a ladder, like a squash ladder, which is the agreed competition hierarchy. The most attractive single girls are those rated highest by all the male students, whereas those with least man-pulling ability are left down near the bottom. Unattached male students are rated according to female attention, with those getting most attention from girls at the top. Fresher males like me are near the bottom.

The most desirable female is expected to pair off with the most desirable male, with a little flexibility for personal preferences. The second most desirable female would gladly accept the most desirable male but when he is already taken she settles for the second most desirable, again with a little flexibility. The process continues until, because there is a surplus of males, the least desirable males remain untaken and have to chase skirt off-campus or spend their time in the bar playing darts and suchlike.

Fresher men like me are not rated high enough up the ladder to pair off with a university girl but they get their chance in second year. Few first year relationships last into second year.

This traditional matching process is not always followed. Women's liberation enables a minority of women to highly rate bizarre low-rated men. Weird pairings disrupt but do not destroy the hierarchies. Availability of The Pill has meant that men are no longer expected to take responsibility for offspring from sexual relations. Consequently, the coupling process is more for instant gratification and ratings awarded more for fashionable qualities, such as socialism, social connections and sports cars, than for traditional values such as heredity, virginity and family support. I am looking forward to going into second year and getting a pairing.

By my reckoning, the best way to get a classy chick is to get a First Class degree. Instead of spending my time at extra-curricular activities with high kudos, such as debating, I plan to hit the academic straps. I see plenty of other male students who are after the same chicks as me, decide the other way and pursue fame in the Students' Union. Which of us will score best in the end is going to be tested.

Rule 6: *In a closed social community, pairings are between males and females in order of position determined by relative attractiveness judged in interaction with the other gender.*

CHAPTER 7   MARATHON MAN

The lecture theatre is bursting at the seams, with students sitting in the aisles right down to the front. There are eighty-two students, all males, at our orientation lecture for the three-year engineering course. We are Victory in Europe babies, the first batch of Baby Boomers. The classes I am in are the largest there have ever been. Crowding and shortages of teachers, or of rooms, have occurred throughout my education.

"At the end of the year," announces the course coordinator, "ten percent of you, those lowest in exams, will have your enrolment in Engineering cancelled. We simply won't have room for you in second year."

We are in a competition for survival.

I like competition. Peer pressure doesn't affect me. My most outstanding feature is my ability to concentrate, to shut out the World and give my full attention to one thing at a time. Conversely, once I have started something it is hard to stop me until I have finished it. I am able to analyse situations, focus on key problems and create solutions. I do not allow emotions and feelings to affect me. Not even criticism throws me off my stride.

I feel like I have come home. Engineering is what I like doing best of all, when time stops for me. I have spent my school holidays on the farm building racing carts, tree houses, rafts, dams and waterwheels, generating hydroelectricity, building siege catapults, flying foxes, modifying farm machinery and using calcium carbide, from our rook scarer gun, to blow things up. I have a thirst for engineering and use every opportunity to learn as much as I can. Although we have not yet been assessed, I have a feeling from observing my classmates that I am going to be very good, maybe the best.

I want to get First Class honours. The esteem from a top degree will get a good job, a high salary and classy women. I want to become a tycoon in the international petroleum industry, earning enough to fly, ski, sail and drive a fast car. Six days per week, oil engineering is my escape. When I cannot get a girl, also on the seventh. While my classmates are at parties or in a bar, I study engineering textbooks and conference papers.

Whether working very hard will result in coming first, is less clear. It might be true in top-level sports, where training effort relates closely to performance in the competition. But in engineering, our training in practical problem-solving by open-book tutorials has little resemblance to the closed-book Finals exams at the end of the third year. These will test, under conditions of arduous endurance, our recall and understanding of theories from three years of study. It is not obvious to me how best to prepare.

That night, lying in bed thinking about how to do well, I have an epiphany. I am at the starting line of a three-year marathon. To win, I will have to be ahead and win the Finals sprint. I know a little about the psychology and strategies used in endurance events from travelling to school and talking with a distance runner in my class who competed in the national titles.

The first principle is to establish superiority from the start. None of us has a previous degree, or has studied engineering before. So we are all equal. Some have done better than others at A levels, and quite a few have straight As. With my A, B and C in chemistry physics and maths I am fairly ordinary, but I figure this reflects my unhappy adolescence and I can be as good as anyone on the course if I put in enough work. I will start out at a blistering pace. When others go to the Students' Union bar I will study. When the others go to parties all weekend I will study. I will allow myself only one night off per week. I accept that I am going to miss a lot of fun but I'll catch up on that after the finish.

Getting away at the start, we are tightly bunched. It is difficult to pick the frontrunners, as everyone is inscrutable. I keep notes on opponents' traits that may indicate ability, such as questioning of lecturers outside class. It takes a cluster of signs, such as library borrowing and assiduous note-making, to confirm very high achievement potential. I try to establish mutuality with the better opponents, by conversation and sharing of answers. However, the high flyers are suspicious of me and only share within a group of friends. People who do share with me return little of use. Nevertheless, I persevere, and people start coming to me for help.

The competition is like playing pinball, trying to make things go the way I want until the ball drops.

After a while, I am regarded as a pace-setter and I ease off a little for comfort. I love being a university student, living away from home like the others. At last, I have freedom from my mother's control even though I have not yet used much of it. When my radio plays The Beatles' "Run For Your Life" I hum along, but I am chasing a race leader in my imaginary marathon rather than a girl.

I thrive in a strict routine. I study fourteen hours a day for six days of the week and see other students, lacking motivation or strength, decline and give up. Some students try to exert peer pressure and slow me down. I share a room in digs with a student who soon recognises that he is out of his depth.

"I thought engineering was designing things, not doing fucking maths," he grumbles. For a term he struggles. Then for some reason he starts taking down lecture notes on toilet paper. Towards the end of the year, he is trying to revise from tall piles of notes on the floor leaning against the bedroom wall. When a pile falls over, he tries to put the sheets back in order, but he has not numbered the sheets. I try to help but it is impossible.

"Fuck it!" he explodes. He throws all the sheets of notes into the air, where they drift down like large snowflakes into a valueless heap. The next week he goes home to stay.

"I'll get a job," he says. "I'm not cut out for studying."

It suits me fine. I feel that I am in the leading group and look for ways to improve my efficiency for the long haul ahead. Most important of these is to have a steady girlfriend to avoid the distraction of unfulfilled sex.

I figure that to be successful with university girls, I have to have lost my virginity previously, no matter where. It is a precondition that I embrace with alacrity.

Rule 7: *If a person is in a competition, they can try to win by accepting loss of competitiveness in another dimension.*

CHAPTER 8   ROMANTIC INTENT

I have not found any attractive university girls to get off with, apart from the equine Deborah. I accept defeat and turn my attention to women students from teaching and nursing colleges who I meet at hops.

One Saturday night I meet Margaret, a girl who has come with a group from a teachers' college two hours drive away in the Midlands. She is a buxom brunette and a wonderful kisser, with a body that fits nicely against mine. Before going home, she jokes that I can visit her at her college, if I bring a tent. As I am up to date with my work, I reckon I deserve a few days off. I accept on the spot, saying I will hitchhike down and arrive on Monday afternoon. She gives me the address, and I tell her I will be waiting for her outside the college gates after her last class.

I look for company on this expedition but the other mate in my digs and my friend, Tom, already have dates. On Sunday I finish off an assignment, pack my tent and sleeping bag, catch a bus out to the motorway and start thumbing a ride south.

My second ride drops me at the wrought iron gates of a magnificent redbrick building with Doric pilasters, hexagonal corner rooms, and a copper-clad cupola. I sit on the grass outside reading a book until Margaret comes out through a side gate and beckons me to follow her. We walk hand in hand down a lane, through a broken-down wooden gate into a hayfield with rolling swards of long grass. We are concealed from the upper storey of the college by a high and thick bramble hedge. We kiss, and Margaret says I should put up my tent behind the hedge and she will be back later. I had not realised my visit would be so clandestine but I am happy that Margaret is reliable in meeting me and that this location has promise.

I set up my tent on a patch of grass eaten short by rabbits. When she returns, she brings some food and three giggling friends. They inspect me, as if I am a peculiar wild animal Margaret has caught. I am pleased when they leave and I am alone with her.

We eat together and alternately talk and kiss through the long evening. The evening air is scented with the sweet smell of cowslips, hanging their yellow heads in clumps. I want to walk back to the college with her but she bids me stay where I cannot be seen. I have picked a bunch of blue forget-me-nots and bluebells for her and give them to her when we have kissed goodnight.

As twilight settles, there are scuffling noises in the dark hedge, which has white flowers of blackberry brambles studding it like diamonds. I find a run where a fox passes through the hedge as it patrols its territory and hunts mice.

I spend the next day playing Margaret's radio and trying to read. The Beatles' "Norwegian Wood'" sets me to doubting that my seduction will be successful unless I can get Margaret to loosen up. I am starving. I walk the elm and hawthorn hedgerows and find a clump of hazel but the nuts are green, milky and sour. I come to an oak wood and at one end find a stand of chestnut trees. In the leaf litter beneath are delicious nuts inside spiky shells. I peel off the brown skins and eat so many I get a stomach ache.

In the afternoon, Margaret comes with food and water. After I have eaten we lie in the tent, fully clothed. We kiss and touch each other in the secret places whose sensations are new to me, but I can't get her to go any further. Nevertheless, it is enjoyable and difficult to part at sundown.

The next day I read and in the evening we fondle each other again. It becomes plain to me that this is as far as Margaret will go until I make a major commitment. Although I like her, I can't see myself in a permanent relationship with her because we can find little to talk about. I leave the following morning, promising to phone, but I forget to, and never see or hear from her again. I learn that females have a large capacity to absorb romantic gestures, but these are insufficient for the trust needed in sexual intercourse.

Frustrated, I realize that females are homogeneous in denying fresher men sexual experience without strings despite demanding romantic gestures. I return to the university determined to pursue coitus, accepting strings that I can break with an easy conscience.

Rule 8: *When love has trust, from commitments, sacrifices and romantic gestures, then intimacy and passion can follow.*

CHAPTER 9   BREAKING FREE

Bridget and I are a devoted couple in first year, studying together, working side by side. Her only faults are her appearance and frequent blushes, which remind me of my mother. It is my mother's oppression at home that has made it a novelty for me to have a regular girlfriend now, for the first time, at age eighteen. We live far apart in lodgings and there is nowhere obvious where we can have sex. However, if we had really wanted sex together, we would have found somewhere.

We enjoy longer and longer kisses in a lounge of the Students' Union, because we have nowhere better where we can go. We hug and I tease her with my tongue and she tries to catch it and suck it. She bit my lip until it bled. I realise she is suffering an agony of frustration like mine. Her soft sweet mouth is intoxicating and when we pull apart the pupils of her eyes are wide like a child's but dulled as though emerging from a private world of emotion, into the bright world of vision and reason.

I run my hands up her sides, across her back and around to hold her firm breasts. She seems overcome with tenderness for a few seconds, pulling in her breath sharply and hugging me tightly. While she holds me thus my anxiety recedes and is replaced first by unbounded joy and then by gratefulness for Bridget.

I share most of the remainder of the year studying at the uni with Bridget for long hours. She is the first intelligent female of my own age I have conversed with. Towards the end of the year it seems likely that we will move in together somewhere for second year. But I am uneasy. Although Bridget is idealistic and a passionate activist against racial discrimination in South Africa, she lacks a spirit of adventure.

One day she shows me photos taken at the German concentration camps when the war ended. I had been unaware of the horror and am profoundly shocked.

"I don't think I will ever be the same again," I say to her.

"I know what you mean."

"It has made me sad to be human."

Even if she continues her human rights campaigning, life with Bridget would be too sedate for me. She wants to get a good degree and do PhD research into ethical drugs for treatment of mental conditions, such as the manic depression her brother suffers from. She wants a sensible job, sensible home life, sensible holidays, sensible mortgages, sensible superannuation and sensible babies. They are not what I want, yet.

The amygdala in my brain, where my emotions are processed, is urging me to do the opposite, to take risks that will generate adrenalin. I want sleeping around. I am still a virgin, and commitment to Bridget would mean staying sober, leaving parties early, ugly pregnancy, noisy babies, whinging children, going shopping together, family gatherings, being conforming and predictable, and getting onto a career treadmill. My life would be over before it had started.

I think of the combined weight of these and other disadvantages of committing to Bridget. She would be a good partner to have, but there are not nearly enough advantages to tip the balance and settle me down. The biggest advantages would be sex and companionship. Later, children. They are not enough to tip the balance. I have a lot of living to do, like James Bond, before I will tip over. It will probably be in ten years from now, when I will be thirty.

I am very fond of her but I know I am out of my depth. I can choose to get sex with her and be unhappily dependent, or enjoy independence and lose my virginity when opportunity affords. The philosopher Buradan posed the dilemma of a hungry donkey that comes upon two equal piles of hay. It cannot decide which to eat from first. Unable to resolve the dilemma, it eventually starves to death.

The dilemma is resolved when she tells me she irons her hair, to remove her natural curls. I like them. I am amazed that an intelligent woman is so influenced by arbitrary fashion. I am fond of her but I am not ready to settle down to a life of hair ironing. I am unable to make the commitment she deserves.

"Goodbye, Bridget," I say. "You are a wonderful person but I met you ten years too early."

"How can you be so unfeeling?" she says.

She takes it hard. I want to take away her hurt but the best way is to be decisive and abrupt so that her healing is unhindered. For weeks, her unhappy face pops up around the university. I am pleased when she takes up with Wyatt, an engineering student who is my best friend. He often made up a threesome to eat, study or go to a movie. A woman takes up with a man's best friend for three reasons. First, he is safe. Second, the absconder may become jealous and return. Third, the two of them can share opinions of him, good and bad. I wish them well together.

Free from Bridget, I immerse myself in our group of engineering students as a single man. I enjoy returning to life as a single man with our engineering group. Whereas my behaviour has been limited by Bridget, now I discover that a social group exercises subtle controls on its members.

Rule 9: *Relationships are unlikely to survive when the proponents' wants are divergent.*

CHAPTER 10   PEER CONTROL

One fine morning at the end of the academic year, our group of engineers is hanging around the Union coffee lounge when Larry suggests we hitchhike up to the Lake District for a few days. We can sleep rough in our sleeping bags. He is an enthusiastic leader, and this excursion has potential for heaps of fun. It is the first time I have done anything with a group of friends. It will be an all-male outing. My virginity is a secret, a source of shame. I hope that there may be an opportunity on this adventure to relinquish my innocence.

"Right," says Larry, "we'll hitchhike in pairs and meet in the pub at Ambleside. Any questions? Okay, starting – now." He and Ken leave by bus to go out to the main road to hitchhike north.

Thomas and I get our sleeping bags and hitch up the A6 to Kendal. We get plenty of lifts, but they are short ones, and it is seven o'clock before we are drinking beer in the pub in Ambleside. Larry and Ken and some of the others are there well before us.

A group of girl students from a college in Ambleside comes in for an end-of-week drink. We introduce ourselves and join them at their table. The girls drink a mixture of mild beer with cider they call moonshine. Our socialising proceeds at a rapid pace.

There are twelve of us. We have seen a farmer's barn by the road, and leaving the girls at the pub we all walk up there. I go up to the farmhouse and ask permission to sleep there. The farmer is reluctant, but I explain exactly who we are and acknowledge his concerns, especially that we will not smoke. In the end, he agrees.

We put our bags inside the hay barn and go back to the pub. At chucking-out time, we each take a girl back to the barn in the dark. Larry, our leader, pairs off with Louise, their leader. Anne-Marie, Louise's best friend, is with me.

Someone has a radio and it plays The Beatles' "Michelle". We lie in the hay, listen to the plaintive music, kiss and grope. People call out comments.

A male voice says, "Is that your hand, Thomas?"

Tom replies, "No. What do you want it for?"

Anne-Marie stays with me until midnight.

Next day the girls have college, and we guys swim in the lake and walk six kilometres to Windermere and back. There are patches of oak woodland rich with bryophytes and lichens, due to very high rainfall. Moss tussocks and ferns are common. In the sodden ground near the water, I find wild plants I know from Priory Farm: bog asphodel, bog orchid and bladderwort. Jozef, an architecture student who lives with us at Sidmouth Hall, has a hobby of growing insectivorous plants. Resplendent in his lucky deerstalker hat, he shows us butterwort, a mauve insectivorous plant, and sundew. The mixed woodland is drier, and there are primrose, wood anemone, snowdrop and bluebell, many still in flower. There are rosebay, knapweed, angelica, wild parsnip and harebells coming into flower. I have a lasting image of him standing leaning forwards, inspecting these plants, with his hands clasped behind his back.

The girls continue to visit us in the barn for the next four nights at chucking-out time, until we leave to return home. Anne-Marie continues to resist sexual intercourse. I suspect that the girls, led by Louise, have decided how far they will go with us. They are lovely girls and we respect their limits on sex. This is the happiest time of my life so far, when I am accepted as one of a group. I am not sure whether it is because I have changed; or that these guys are more tolerant; or that I am valued for my engineering talents. I don't care which; I enjoy myself.

The unthinkable has happened. first year is ended and I am still a virgin. I am desperate.

It seems to me I have wheel-spin and I need a different approach. So I decide to stop doing the things to get girls that have not worked and adopt a fresh approach.

Rule 10: *Guys and gals pair off, and their sex behaviours are controlled by their gender hierarchies.*

PART 3: SECOND YEAR SPREAD (1965-1966)

In which I find I can attract college girls and university girl students, but my offers of sexual intercourse are not taken up. I become infatuated with Vicki. The girls seem to require me to have more experience at sex, which I cannot get until I have sex. Frustrated, I hedge my investment of precious time across a spread of females.

CHAPTER 11   LOVE PAIR

In the exams at the end of first year, I come top of the main subject, Engineering.

"You are lucky to be so intelligent," says one of my classmates.

"No. I worked very hard; that's all," I reply.

Intelligence is not a useful concept. Every situation requires different abilities. For our course, much hard work is essential. When I have a steady girl, as I did with Bridget, I can work harder than most.

"Get yourself a steady girlfriend," I advise him.

I have established my superiority after the first leg of our three-year marathon. As the administration had warned, they send down half a dozen in the class who failed to hand in work or whose work was of too low a quality. For the survivors, the pressure is off and we can loaf and follow our whims. My second principle is to establish control and conserve energy. I want to hold down the pace as much as possible in second year, enjoy myself and still finish ahead. The class is happy when I set a slow pace. I work in with a group intent on having a good time. I get myself elected secretary of the Engineering Society and get to meet everyone through helping organise events.

When I go home to Priory Farm, I am seedy and studious. My mother ridicules me.

"Here's the professor," my mother chides. "I don't suppose you even know what day of the week it is!"

When I go up for second year, I am determined to redefine myself as a can-do person, getting rid of my first year nerdiness. I desert the provincials and start hanging around with Larry, Roger and Thomas, who are happening types. We have had enough of living in digs and we want to live in a place where we can screw.

I am able to persuade my parents of the social advantages of living in a student residence. After the vacation, I move into Sidmouth Hall, still being constructed. Adjoining it is a new women's residence, Exmouth Hall. It seems like I have entered a philanderer's paradise.

We soon develop a camaraderie with the girls amid the plasterboard and bits of two-by-four. Although the girls' rooms are in a different building, we can meet in a shared dining room for meals. We plan activities together, such as going to movies. We share transport into the university and to parties. There are only a couple of us who have cars. Mine is an old VW beetle, but I usually have passengers wherever I go. We also meet in each other's rooms.

I am delighted to find that Vicki, the girl of my dreams from the Students' Union coffee lounge, is living in Exmouth Hall. I see her in the dining room but I don't have enough nerve to ask her out on a date.

The best place to score crumpet is at Saturday night parties. When I don't have a party to go to, I gate-crash. There are usually a couple of bouncers hanging out near the door limiting who can get in. If I don't recognize anyone, I say that I am a friend of Dave. There are so many Daves around, it usually works.

One Saturday night, I am gate-crashing with our gang when I come across Vicki. She is dancing with her female friends. She stands out as an independent fun-loving girl with a wonderful body. I am only a little drunk and she seems pleased to see me.

"Hello, Selwyn."

"Hi, Paula. Dance?"

"It's Vicki."

"Sorry. Vicki. Dance?"

"Okay."

We show each other our routines with feet, arms and body. She dances mechanically with a bored look on her face, as is the fashion. I try not to look awkward. When The Beatles' "Girl" is playing, we dance close together. Her body fits perfectly against mine, and I soon become aroused. I close my eyes and imagine we are spinning endlessly in a Viennese waltz, in a magnificent ballroom. She is in a white spreading gown, with me in black tie and tails.

When the music finishes, I lead her out into the garden and we hold each other and talk for a while about ourselves. She is shy and I have to prise out her personal information. As I thought, she went to an exclusive girls' school. I doubt that her classmates would go with a boy from a plebeian public grammar school like mine.

She asks why she hasn't seen me around in first year. I tell her about Bridget and finishing with her recently. She wants to know why we finished. I say that I didn't like her enough to make a commitment and settle down. I had cut free before it got too serious. It sounds reprehensible but Vicki makes no comment.

I ask her whether she had a boyfriend in first year but she won't tell me. I take this to mean she did. We talk about our dreams and plans, for travel and jobs. I want to be an oil tycoon. Her dreams are travel and scholarly research. I find myself revising my plans, trying to fit in with hers. Born within a few days of each other, we are two of a kind, both dreamers. Like me, she is introverted and a little nervous in company, putting on forced joviality and a supercilious grin, fiddling with her hair as a come-on. I want to help her overcome her lack of confidence, her little-girl word clutters under the group conversation spotlight. Most of all, I like the way she seems to understand me, listening to me uncritically.

We hug and her hair smells clean and her skin of flowers. Then we kiss. Her mouth is soft and tastes of sweet apricots. I try to French kiss her but when I delve with my tongue, she twists her head away.

"No," she gasps.

We kiss some more and I grind my erection into her pelvis. I feel at a disadvantage about what to do next, as I am a virgin. I can't make up my mind whether she is, too. In an earlier age she could have been called demure. I manage to get rid of my rides and take Vicki back to Exmouth. As she doesn't ask me in, I kiss her outside. They forbid visitors at night. She seems friendly; that is all.

"See you tomorrow, Vicki," I say carefully.

"I expect so, Selwyn," she says. "Goodnight."

"G'night."

She has me on my back foot; so I don't try for a date. I don't want to have her turn me down. For several weeks after our first kiss, we spend time together and have a lot of fun. I soon take up with long kisses and hugs where I had left off with Bridget, with the difference that we now had the privacy of "pashing" in my room in hall. We lie on my bed while my hands caress and massage her back under her top. I write messages on her silky smooth back with my finger, for her to sense and interpret as letters and words.

"What does this say?" I ask her.

"T.O.U.C.H," she says.

Her body is wonderful, with firm curves and soft recesses. She lets me go so far and then stops me.

We kiss as we hang out the windows and jeer in unison at pranksters, as officials try to maintain order, for example, when the police come to find out who put the warden's car in the lake. We kiss during food fights in the kitchen. We kiss when our gang creates a disease hoax and quarantines everyone. We kiss as we watch a beer-vomiting race. And we kiss at the formal ball.

She is lovely, a positive spirit. She looks at flowers, speaks to birds, strokes cats and pats dogs. She smiles wryly at strangers, with a suggestion of naughtiness. But when you meet her, she is trusting and open, looks levelly, shakes hands firmly, holds eye contact. She is gentle and graceful, with fine-boned legs, long skirts and hips with some width that swing alluringly; she wears soft materials and pastel colours. On some matters such as cruelty to children and animals, she displays a campaigner's zeal and will not brook compromise.

I am delighted to find she is neither vain nor precious. She is beautiful without make-up and wears it invisibly. She is intelligent and insightful and can read the emotions I try to hide like a book, albeit a short one.

After kissing to get to know her, there is kissing to build up trust, and then kissing to undress her. Kissing and a painful bulge in the front of my jeans is all I get. We don't shag because I am too inexperienced. I don't take the lead because I don't have her support. I have always found myself unable to make love to a passive woman, for then it is just sex. Love has to be a shared experience, equal and lasting.

We see each other every day. Counter to my intuition, she wants to spend more and more time socialising with the others. I blame myself for lack of sexual experience to keep her interested. It is the same with my conversation but I learn to tease out her deep thoughts. They are critical and incisive. I have never known anyone as intelligent and I learn so much from her about people, their motives and their deceptions. We go to the movies together with our group and she holds my hand. When I ask, she explains who is who because in a complex plot, I forget which character has done what.

When she takes on too much, which is often, she tends to neglect those closest to her. Her inertia, her tendency to keep doing what she is already doing, is large. Her days are filled with activities and routines she has engaged in for many years and has scheduled forward in her mind. She lacks flexibility to vary her schedule to deal with new and emerging needs. She fits me in but it costs her a big effort to be flexible.

Unlike me, she is gregarious and hangs out in groups. Whereas some girls speak to draw attention to themselves, Vicki speaks for effect, quietly in measured tones, occasionally with explicit reflection. She is disorganised and untidy but makes an effort occasionally to create an ambitious event, such as a theme party, with others' support.

I am very happy. I am doing well in the course, and I have Vicki who is wonderful. I have surprised myself that I have as my girlfriend the best-looking girl in our year. Since I first saw her in the Students' Union coffee lounge, she has been at the centre of my life. I find myself tipping over from my wants for independence when I was with Bridget, to waiting for Vicki to settle down with me.

Our relationship doesn't settle down and it doesn't seem to be going anywhere. Vicki stops coming to my room. Empathy is not my forté, but I have the idea that Vicki won't have sex with me because I am a virgin. It is a Catch-22 situation. Vicki will not put out until I make a commitment, but I will not make a commitment until Vicki has put out. It is a standoff.

Rule 11: *A woman gives short shrift to a man who shows no sign of being ready to make a commitment.*

CHAPTER 12   BULLY BOY

I followed the Principal up the stairs and we stopped outside a door. Inside we could hear a woman's voice issuing instructions. She knocked and a middle-aged woman came out.

"Yes, Mrs Lacey?"

"Miss Fettler, this is a new student, Selwyn Archer."

"Is he—"

"Yes, Howard Archer's brother. I'll leave him with you. Goodbye, Selwyn. Come and see me at any time if you have any problems."

It was my first day at the private school where I would be crammed to pass the Eleven Plus scholarship exam in three years' time.

Miss Fettler introduced me to her class.

"Class, this is Selwyn, brother of Howard Archer, the knife thrower." I was ashamed. My heart sank as she warned me sternly, "Selwyn, we won't have that sort of behaviour in this school. What do you say?" "No, Miss Fettler."

My brother had recently been suspended for sticking a knife in another student's leg.

"I was throwing it to stick it into the stair riser when he walked in the way," he told my parents, who believed him.

At morning break my new classmates clustered around me and recounted story after story of my brother's torturing and beating up of any student who told on him. He made them give him their pocket money and lunches. He threatened clever students, getting them to copy their homework into his book. They threatened that if my brother tried anything on them again, they would 'do me in'.

My worrying increased. I hoped he would be expelled. He was dark, broad and fat, whereas I was fair, medium wide and skinny. He used his greater strength and weight to bully me mercilessly. He was careful to assault me behind closed doors, in dark corners, and when our parents were out. I felt helpless to stop his neck and arm locks, punching, pinching and hair pulling. Or he would throw me over his hip to the ground, drop on top of me and press my shoulders to the ground.

"Give in?" he asked.

I was no wimp. He had weight and strength advantages. I struggled to get free, unsuccessfully.

"Yer beaten," he says, with a slap, because a hit would leave tell-tale bruising.

Meanwhile, our father was increasing Howard's responsibility and authority for farm work. As his deputy, Howard got management experience with our workforce of half a dozen workers. I got none.

The custody of livestock, even those soon to be killed, was undertaken by most farmers with tolerance and kindness. Howard treated the farm animals with disrespect. He was like Goebbels who experimented on prisoners of war, revelling in cruel surgical and medical operations. Howard considered we had bred them for death and seemed to enjoy dehorning, ear tattooing, nose ringing, castration, tail cutting, assisted births, stabbing bloated stomachs, slaughtering and autopsies. He investigated what organs did by finding out what would happen without them. He used no anaesthetic. His activities would not have been unusual, but he had a sadistic interest in causing pain to animals in his care, and if the animal resisted he increased it.

He seemed to resent the animals for their dumb dependence on him, tying him down to look after them, when he would rather have been away at university like me. When driving them, he used stick and dog without mercy. He would not tolerate disobedience and vented his anger, exacting punishment by threshing or slaughtering an animal at the least sign of defiance. His surgery was radical and ruthless. When butchering a dead animal, he would play with its organs. I protested when he pushed a still-warm liver down my trousers.

"What did you do that for?"

"Ha ha!" he replied.

I believe he fancied himself as a Hemingwayesque man of violence. He cultivated a beard and swarthy appearance, with a reputation as an unprincipled brute.

One evening fairly late, when he was going to bed to get the rest he needed for heavy physical work next day, I was bent over my textbook making notes, with a mug of hot cocoa beside me.

"What have we got herr, then?" he asked. "It's a funny looking thingg. Having a party all by itself, is it?"

I sipped from the mug and waited for him to go.

"Bring your own drink, is it?"

I ignored him. He gave my arm a poke and splashed cocoa across my notes.

"Leave me alone," I say.

"Hark! It speaks. What sayest thou?" he asked, trying to spill more cocoa.

"Pull your horns in, calf shagger!"

The teasing went out of his voice. "Shut up. I'll get you for that."

He grabbed the hot drink and poured it across my notes and textbook.

"I'll kill you," I yelled as I chased him like a banshee with my sheath knife, down the stairs and into the dining room, where he took refuge on the opposite side of the table, while I tried to wrong foot him and run around the end. I had no intention of catching him or injuring him.

"Help! You're crazy," he shouted, cowering.

In his tiny mind I am mad to oppose him.

"You're the one who's bent – calf shagger," I jeered.

"Shut up."

My mother came in. "Selwyn, put down that knife. Get on with your study."

"It was him. He—"

"I am not interested," she says. "If you don't pass these exams you'll have to leave school and get a job."

"But—"

"That's enough. You heard me." She walked out.

"Crazy bastard," Howard jeered.

There was no justice, as he could do no wrong in my mother's eyes, and my father automatically backed her up. They condoned his bullying. When I defended myself, the fighting was always my fault. I worried that I was alone against the World. Nevertheless, it was empowering to see him cringe, and for the first time I realized that I could overcome him

About a month later, I was climbing up the narrow stairs carrying a full mug of coffee when I met Howard coming down. To let him pass, I stood aside on the landing. He paused opposite me.

"Well, look, it's crazy boy!"

He poked my arm holding the hot drink and a little spilled on to my hand, burning it.

I threw the scalding contents of the mug into his face. He screamed.

"You just wait," he says wiping coffee from his eyes with the backs of his hands.

I went to push past him and he tried to punch me. I had grown taller than he had, with a longer reach. I punched him hard, one fist in each eye, and he was temporarily blinded. He sat down on the landing.

"I'll get you," he sobbed.

"Howard, the coward," I intoned.

I went back to my books. Radio Luxembourg was playing Dylan's "The Times They Are A-changing."

After that, Howard gave me a wide berth. He stopped taking me with him in his car to parties and on social outings. I had no social life and few distractions from study.

When Howard shot my dog, there was nothing I could do about it immediately. He was a young dog, a mongrel bred from our best working dog. I had taken him to help me beat for a pheasant shoot in the woods and copses on local farms. When he got excited and ran too far ahead of the advancing line of guns, Howard shot him dead. I was outraged, but his drastic solution was applauded by the other shooters. It strengthened my determination to go far away when I left home.

Howard's jealous bullying was intended to prevent my success and discourage me from getting to university, but it had the opposite effect. I felt trapped at home but could escape by doing well at school. I was desperate to leave, not only home, but the district, to get away from him and the closed society that tolerated him.

After I leave home, my father stands aside from most day-to-day operation of Priory Farm. Howard takes over. As boss man, he no longer has to get his hands dirty. He aspires to a higher social class, for which he has neither the education nor the ethics. He tries to learn these by befriending middle class people. He starts riding in the local foxhunt, a middle class pursuit.

The hunt is opposed by local farmers and idealists. The hunt members make Howard Master of Foxhounds, an office with scope for his brutality. On a tall horse, in a crimson jacket and top hat, with leather boots and carrying a whip, he is an intimidating figure. His manners, invective and use of the whip are no less imposing. However, rather than acquiring the manners of a middleclass gentleman, he has become a boorish, pigheaded tyrant.

"Get out of my way or I'll ride over you," he tells protestors against hunting when they block the road at the hunt meet. "You touch this horse and you'll feel this whip!"

He goes to local pubs night after night and gets drunk. When he is drunk he likes to impose himself on the local girls, as if he has a right to no-strings-attached sex with them.

Howard is hated by the workers for being lazy, imperious and cruel. The more a worker kowtows to his demands, the more Howard imposes on him. He believes that the poorer a worker is, the more compliant he will be, and therefore he should be paid minimum wages. The minimum wage barely meets the basic needs of a small family. Fortunately, my father has not yet retired and retains control over wages and pays above the minimum. He is fair and our workers do their best for him but not for Howard. Under Howard, Priory Farm becomes unprofitable.

When I go away to university, my troubles with Howard seem to be over. Then my mother informs me that he is coming to visit me.

Rule 12: *A bully dominates others in every context where he is not stopped.*

CHAPTER 13   SIBLING VISIT

I had longed to get away from my bullying brother, Howard. Unfortunately, he intrudes into my life when he is least wanted, like a spammed pop-up that you can't get rid of.

I look out the window again, and then sit on the bed with Vicki as we wait in my room at Sidmouth Hall for my visitors from home to arrive. She looks at her watch.

"They're late. Are you sure you told them how to get here?"

"Yes. I sent them a map with the route marked right into the car park."

I had asked her if she would like to meet my visitors and, to my surprise, she had agreed, willingly giving up time when she could otherwise study. We are friends and I hope we will soon be lovers. This is a step in the right direction.

"Who did you say are coming?" she asks again.

"My elder brother Howard, younger sister Heather and Robert, a friend."

I am not looking forward to seeing Howard. The weekend visit is my mother's idea. I can hardly refuse, as my parents are paying for my hall of residence and have recently given me a decent car.

I asked Vicki if she would be my girlfriend during their visit and she agreed even though both of us have been going out with others. I want an exclusive relationship with her and want her to get a good impression of my family.

Just then an open-top sports car pulls up outside in the No Stopping area.

We go down the stairs.

"Hey, you!" I call through a window. "You can't park there!"

The three have climbed out and are stretching. My brother looks like a slob, with his beer gut hanging over his belt and showing bum crack behind.

Startled, they look around and see us.

"Oh, look what we have here," says my brother, "a useless student!"

Robert stutters with gusto, "U–uni students have got to be s-smartasses."

We walk over and I introduce Vicki as "my friend".

"Hello, Vicki my friend," says Howard.

"Pleased to m–m—" says Robert.

"That's enough of that," says Howard. "We haven't got all day."

"Don't be rude," I admonish Howard. Turning to the others, I gesture towards Howard and shake my head, saying, "He's getting worse."

My brother punches me hard on the upper arm. I wince. The pain makes me angry. He is showing off in front of Vicki.

"Keep your fists to yourself, fat bastard," I say. I turn to Vicki. "Howard is a bully."

It is not an impressive start. I expect Vicki to leave at any moment. We exchange pleasantries with Heather and Robert about their journey. Howard interrupts, scratching his behind.

"Let's have a drink. Is there a bar in this dump?"

We drive to the Ball and Powder, a public house just off campus. There he and Robert down about six pints apiece of Cain's best bitter, the local brew. I have two pints, and Vicki and Heather have Babycham. It is late Saturday afternoon and the pub is in an uproar, with sports teams letting off steam.

As night falls, Howard is amused to see drunken louts lobbing glass mugs into the passing heavy traffic. He and Robert go to join in. There is the smash of a windscreen, squeal of breaks and a succession of impacts from a serial crash. I am appalled. Vicki, Heather and I leave immediately. I hope never to see Howard or Robert again.

We make our way to the Students' Union where an engineering society dance, called "Public Hanging", has started. Howard and Robert catch up with us as we enter. I buy tickets for the girls but Howard and Robert disappear around the side of the building. As we climb the stairs to the concert hall, they appear at the top looking pleased with themselves.

"Climbed up a drainpipe," Howard says. "They shouldn't leave the windows open."

"It was a toilet window," stutters Robert. "He fell in."

We look at Howard's wet foot. Vicki looks at me and rolls her eyes. We are drawn into the concert hall where the Spencer Davies Trio is belting out "Keep on Running". The students are packed in trying to dance shoulder to shoulder with local girls imported to balance out the excess of male engineering students. The audience far exceeds the loading limit of the wooden floor and it bounces like a massive trampoline. The Administration manager stops the band because the floor has become unsafe.

I see Howard trying to chat up girls, yelling at the top of his voice. I don't know what his line is but they usually shake their heads, look gobsmacked and back away, as if from a dangerous animal. He is a rugby forward and pushes through to us, knocking people off their feet. He starts chatting up Vicki. I suggest we go in another room where a new group called The Who are playing songs from their album, "My Generation".

Vicki dances the same way that she talks – quietly, with elegance and reserve. She is an understated person and perhaps that is why I love her to distraction. All the females I have known before seem to be cut-outs trying to be someone else, but she is the real thing. Beside her, I feel vulgar, provincial and Philistine.

Larry is president of the Engineering Society. He loves nothing better than to have a loud hailer or public address system to control people. Dressed in black, tall and elegant, he interrupts the dancers and announces a public hanging. Spotlighted on stage is the noose of a full-size gallows we have built. The concert hall is jammed full of people and they slowly hush.

"Ladies and Gentlemen, we are sorry to disappoint you but Professor Shapner, the Head of Engineering, has forbidden the public hanging tonight of any student, whatever his or her crimes. They will be dealt with by the disciplinary committee.

"However, is there anyone here among you, who is not a student of engineering, who has committed crimes punishable by public hanging? If so, nominate them now."

I call out, "Howard Archer."

Howard goes pale, turns and looks at me, shaking his head.

"Shut up!"

I nod to Larry, smiling. Larry, dressed all in black, responds gleefully.

"Ladies and gentlemen, one Howard Archer is guilty of the crime of —", he cups his ear towards me.

"Bestiality," I yell.

"Bestiality," Larry announces.

The audience howls as Howard tries desperately to get away. It takes several students to seize him and frog-march him up on to the stage. Roger and Tom bind him, gag him and blindfold him as he struggles. They stand him on the trap door and put his head in the noose.

Larry talks quietly to him, as if giving him absolution.

"Drum roll!" Roger calls and he begins the countdown, his gravelly voice reaching the furthest corners of the crowded hall. It is taken up loudly by the audience.

"Ten. Nine. Eight. Seven. Six. Five. Four. Three. Two. One—"

There is a loud bang as the trap door swings downward and Howard drops. The rope jerks taut and he hangs with his head at knee height, with blood squirting from his mouth and trickling down his chin.

Several girls near the front faint. There is a deathly hush. It is no longer a joke.

Howard climbs out and back on to the stage. He has landed on his feet on a table under the stage, bending his knees for the rope to tighten a little. He swaggers to the front, takes the empty tomato ketchup sachet from his mouth and bows. The laughter lasts for several minutes, ending with applause.

Larry announces, "A big hand for Howard Archer!"

He comes back to us, inflated even more than usual.

He thumps me on the arm. "I'll get you for that."

I draw Vicki outside on the veranda, where we look over the city lights. She shivers and I wrap my arms around her bare shoulders. When she turns to say something, I kiss her gently then passionately. I want her badly but I do not know how to go about achieving what I want. I am a virgin, and the arts of seduction are unknown to me. I am gentle with her and I try to be courteous, but I am at a loss as to what to do next.

As I drive back to hall, a horn blares and a car draws alongside. Four ugly male faces glare at us, shouting abuse.

"You cut him up," says Howard. "Nice."

He shakes his fist at them, "Mother fuckers."

They pull past me and block my way. Howard gets out. Robert gets out, too, and gives them a middle finger salute, stuttering "F-fight, you f-fuckers!"

Within seconds, all the males except me are fighting in the middle of the road. Because Vicki is there, I get out as slowly as I think will be respectable and square up to one of them. My brother and Robert punch the other three. I trade a few taps and obscenities until the others have had enough. I try to calm their driver. I probably lose face with Vicki for not punching but I never have been able to fight unless it seems necessary. After a short while, they are losing. So they get back in their car and drive off as if nothing has happened.

"That s-showed them!" says Robert.

I think Vicki must be as revolted by Howard and Robert as I am. Heather is a schoolgirl and in awe of Vicki. Vicki asks me about them.

"You say he works with your father on the farm. Did he go to university?"

"No. I am the only farm boy in the Wortham area who stayed on into the sixth form. Farmers' sons do not go to university or even stay on into the sixth form. Oldest sons of tenant farmers are always kept at home to take over the tenancy when their fathers retire."

"Is Howard jealous of you?"

"Of course. He lives with my parents who are narrow-minded about relationships with girls. His every move is scrutinized. He is jealous of the freedom I have."

"What about your sister?"

"She is in the final senior year at school and is thinking about going to university. She has come up to see if she would like it."

"What about Robert?"

"He lives on a nearby farm, also a tenant of Lord St Tanby. He is in the same boat as Howard."

"Is he Heather's boyfriend?"

"No, she's not allowed to have a boyfriend."

During that weekend, Vicki helps me show them a good time. Uni life is a novel experience for them, and I am grateful to Vicki for putting herself out.

When they are gone, I take a box of chocolates up to her room. She is on her bed holding court to two male students who I have not met. I am jealous. They are listening to The Beatles' "Nowhere Man". They smirk at me as if my gallantry is ridiculous.

"Thank you, Selwyn," she says. That's really sweet of you."

"You were wonderful, Vicki."

"It was a pleasure."

I leave, wondering whether she will continue in the role of my girlfriend. Howard had been openly envious of my access to quality skirt like Vicki. I am incensed a few weeks later when Vicki tells me Howard has written to her. It is typical of him to try and steal my girlfriend. It is so disrespectful to me. I assume she does not reply.

I like being with Vicki because I have learnt to read some of her postures and am beginning to understand her. She has much more social experience than I am and is able to talk about how she feels, which is beyond me. My communication is always reticent because I have difficulty empathizing and need time to think. What I particularly like about her is how she offers her experience honestly and humbly, without dressing it up to mislead people.

When Vicki talks, she is not a cool weigher of words or a purveyor of stock monologues. She offers intelligent observations spontaneously, her words coming naturally in streams of consciousness with rushes and hesitations that convey her strong emotions and idealism. This contrasts with me and my engineer's robotic talk and my predilection for empirical theories, detached from emotion. Our viewpoints are so different that when we try to persuade each other, it is more a process of enlightenment than one of negotiation or compromise.

Vicki is a fabulous listener. She knows the lyrics of all The Beatles' songs, whereas I don't even know the titles. When I talk, she can pick up nuances and emphases that reveal my emotions and explain my behaviour. She is able to delve into my subconscious. Since the lie detector test, I have no secrets from her.

I have never before encountered a girl with such good taste in fine things, fine sentiments and feminine gentility. She comes from a world of privilege, foreign holidays, restaurant eating, sailing and wealth. I want to learn about these from her, to understand the experiences that have made her the cultured person she is.

Vicki has brought me to a tipping point where I would be happy to settle down with her although we are both only nineteen. Until I met her, I didn't want to settle down until age thirty. She would be my best friend with whom I could share my dreams and worries. We would help each other succeed in our careers, have a wonderful family and be loyal partners throughout our lives.

There would be unlimited sex, evolving to unite us in passion. We would be good for each other. She would help me socialize and I would help her to be well-organized. It seems unlikely that I will meet another woman as attractive and accomplished who I love as much as Vicki. We could have children in a few years' time and we would be young enough to be part of their lives.

I am convinced. Now all I need to do is convince her.

Although I am attentive in the following weeks, she doesn't seem to want us to become a couple. She seems to be looking for someone better, and that hurts. It never occurs to me to tell her that I love her or why I do, even when she declines dates with me. I can't work out what is wrong and it seems too demanding to ask her. She gives me just enough encouragement to keep me on a piece of string. I suspect that she has lost interest in me because of my lack of sexual experience and I set out to remedy that with other girls from her hall.

Rule 13: *A woman does not take love for granted.*

CHAPTER 14   CINDERELLA'S RENEGE

"I am getting a friend at Cambridge to buy Angela and me tickets to their college's May Ball. Do you want a pair of tickets to come with us?"

"What sort of a do is it?" I ask him.

"Black tie, the apex of their social season."

I am curious to see what separation from plebeians like us has done for Cambridge University students, who are reputed to regard us redbrick students as second rate. I want to lend the lie to that. Most of all, I am looking forward to having Vicki as my partner.

"I'll let you know," I reply.

"Do you want to go?" I ask Vicki.

"Oh, yes, please! Groovy," she replies.

A few days before the ball, Vicki puts her hands on my shoulders and looks me straight in the eyes.

"Thanks for asking me, Selwyn. I would like to drive down with you and Tom and share the cost. I like you but I want to, um, go with Angela. I'll give you the money for my ticket. Um, don't take it the wrong way. Okay?"

Her hesitancy marks the care with which she speaks. She seems to want me to understand something important, but I don't get it. There is only one way to take it, and that is as a put-down. Even so, I trust her and hope time will reveal to me a better way to take it.

"Okay," I mumble.

But it isn't. I no longer want to go. I have little interest in going to a black tie affair on my own. The prospects for scoring crumpet are dismal. I am locked in. Angela does the same with Tom and he is as upset as I am. We assume they want to pick up Cambridge guys. Their renege is bloody rude after we have bought our tickets.

When the day of the Ball comes, the two girls look stunning with their hair tied back. Their beauty makes their rejection all the more painful. Tom drives down with me in the front and the girls in the back. There is little conversation.

We arrive and hand in our coats. Vicki is wearing a long glittery figure-hugging sheath, with bare shoulders. We thread our way past the ebullient St John's students assembling in groups at the entrance, extravagantly dressed in formal attire. The girls say they will meet us there in six hours' time at 4.00am.

"See you later," Vicki says.

She and Angela disappear into the throng.

The forecourts and banquet halls of old Cambridge are a romantic setting. The Ball is spread through the ancient college buildings and spills over into a handful of marquees on the quadrangle lawns. The cloisters are lit by the soft light of candles and lanterns. We wander around looking for girls without partners but there aren't any.

There are half a dozen different dance floors, with trad, jazz, folk, steel band, pop and swing music. The dance venues are adjacent to cosy bars with cascades of bottled drinks. The dining hall is resplendent with a luxurious cold buffet of venison, pheasant, caviar, oysters, lobster and smoked salmon. After that there are gateaux, crème brulée, tiramisu and cheesecakes.

Tom and I get stuck into the food. I know him well from travelling together and we live in neighbouring flats. He has gone home with me to the farm a couple of times and we sometimes study together. I always have difficulty with small talk but his commentary on the people there is amusing. By about 1.00am we are ready to go. The three-hour wait until we will meet the girls is the longest of my life. It seems such a wasted opportunity to be there without a girl.

"I wonder why the girls are snubbing us?" I ask Tom, wanting to hear him deny this.

"Bitches," he replies. "No taste."

"What did Vicki mean about 'not taking it the wrong way'?"

"I don't know," he says. "The wrong way would be that they don't want to be with us."

"Well, the right way could be that they want to be with us but can't for some reason."

"What reason?" Tom asks. "Aren't they under pressure to get long-term boyfriends?"

"Well, they don't seem to have other guys," I muse.

Tom thinks for a few minutes.

"We have gone with some other girls in hall – a few times. That could be the problem."

I am seeing Linda, a lithe first year doll studying drama and dance. Before that I was with Annette, an elegant bird from American Samoa. Both live in Vicki's hall. We spend some joyous times on my bed without coitus. Vicki probably knows about these affairs, as I have made no effort to keep them a secret. If Vicki wants me to pursue her monogamously, she should be more responsive to me.

Tom has been playing the field, too.

"We took a chance," says Tom. "Girls talk to each other."

"I only date other girls when Vicki turns me down. Surely she can't expect me to sit in my room waiting for her?"

"She probably does."

"No way," I say. "This is the age of Free Love."

"Do you think so? The difference is that girls want to call the shots now."

Our ideas of who should make the first move may be different. I wonder, not for the first time, what the rules are for dating girls. I always have trouble with social situations because the rules are not written down and people expect you to know. I don't have any close friends to ask, except for Tom, who is from Jamaica and unfamiliar with English ways.

"Girls are expecting to be able to call the plays," I say. "There is an Australian woman doing a PhD at Cambridge about the ethics of love and marriage, who wants women to play around, keep men waiting."

"You mean Germaine Greer. She is bringing consumerism into how women choose men. Women are becoming choosey. Don't you think Vicki is worth waiting for?" asks Tom. "She's pretty special. You are lucky she likes you."

"Yeah, I know, but she's also a prick teaser," I say. "I need a regular screw without complications, so I can get on with my work."

"There is no such woman, Selwyn."

"So what about Vicki?"

"You have to wait around for her until she wants you."

"I can't afford the time. She is driving me crazy!"

"You are too wrapped up in your work, Selwyn. It will be your downfall."

"I'm not looking to settle down until I'm thirty."

"There won't be any females of our age left; maybe a young chick will have you."

"That's okay. What about you and Angela?"

"We were getting to know each other – until tonight." Tom sounds very down. "I'm not impressed with these flaky uni girls. Girls with jobs know what they want. Larry is doing okay with Lisa. I'll ask her if she has a girlfriend."

Lisa works as a business secretary in the town and lives with her parents. She is intense, insightful and pretty. Larry spends a lot of time with her. I am envious of his steady relationship, as the university girls are erratic.

Vicki and Angela arrive back punctually for our return trip to Liverpool. It is not long before dawn and the Ball is still in full swing. They are both alone. They don't say what they have been doing or whether they have met any men. We haven't seen them at all during the Ball. There is a certain iciness between us, as if we are together from necessity rather than choice.

Like most of our gang, we are not able to talk about our feelings. If we could, then I would ask the girls why the hell they had deserted us tonight. I stop seeing Vicki. She has snubbed me and even though she apologised in advance she has not explained why she stood me up. I can only conclude that she is looking for a stranger with a better academic pedigree. Like most redbrick students, I resent it that access to the Cambridge and Oxford Universities is privileged. Vicki's endorsement is very unwelcome. Consequently, I cease asking Vicki for dates.

A few weeks later, she comes up to my room when I am alone.

"Selwyn, are you doing anything this evening?".

"I'm seeing Linda. Why?"

'Never mind. It was just an idea."

"Sorry. I thought you didn't want to do anything. Another time?"

"I'll let you know."

It seems that Vicki is going to invite me to something. That is a breakthrough and I should accept. But I never break dates. "First come, first served" is my rule for dealing with people and it is Linda's turn next. Too bad; I would sooner be with Vicki than Linda, but rules are rules.

I seem to be outside the maze again with Vicki, without knowing why. I wish I knew how to ask her what is happening. I begin to think there may be a deep-seated difference between us that we are unable to discuss: social class.

Rule 14: *A woman usually plays to the gallery, and her motives may be invisible to the man on whom her effect is greatest.*

CHAPTER 15   CLASS DIFFERENCE

Vicki continues to snub me back at Liverpool. I think she is rejecting me as a serious boyfriend because of our difference in social class. At school, we did not study the British Class System, nor did we discuss it at home. At university, people pretend it does not exist. I try to find out my own class and Vicki's using books from the library.

The classes are social groups with greater similarities within than without. Hatred between the classes gives each a boundary and coherence within. The lower classes defer to the higher classes as leaders, uniting the British against foreign enemies. The fabric of society and the economy are woven on a warp of social classes with historical antecedents.

When I try to identify my own social class, it is defined in relation to others by historical relationships. At Priory farm, my family are tenants on Wortham Estate, owned by Lord St Tanby. He is a patrilineal descendant of a French knight, Tresize, who William the Conqueror rewarded after the invasion of 1066 with a chunk of West Yorkshire. William subjected rural England to a brutal feudal system under a rigid hierarchy from within his inviolable fortress, the Tower of London. The hierarchy he imposed survives to this day in the distant Yorkshire Dales.

Tresize gave Priory Farm to John Fordham, a villein, or serf, who is an ancestor of my father. He belonged to the Frenchman, and he and his family were unable to leave. They paid rent in tithes, or tenths of their produce, when the knight demanded them. When marauding invaders laid waste to the surrounding lands, Tresize provided free shelter and food to locals who defended under siege his home, Barton Castle.

Wortham Estate is a large slice of Yorkshire county, with fifty-three large farms under tenancy and four villages with churches. While Barton Castle has fallen into disuse, Tresize's descendants, currently Lord St Tanby, occupy Wortham House, a prestigious

Elizabethan country house, built in an E-shape with four round towers. It has thirty-eight bedrooms and two bathrooms, a three-acre maze, and a one-hundred-acre park with a landing strip for guests' planes. There are extensive gardens and conservatories maintained by a handful of full-time gardeners, a dovecote, a carp pond, bee hives, a weather station, an astronomical observatory, lime-burning kilns, a wind mill, stables, kennels for a pack of hounds and a private carriageway to the local waterfalls, a popular beauty spot.

I was aware I was from a lowly class. Once a year Lord St Tanby, in his old Morris Minor, draws up outside, in his muddy Priory Farm yard, setting the dogs barking. My mother rushes out of sight any signs of bourgeois living, such as processed foods or new appliances. She believes possession of these could cause an increase in the annual farm rental. She welcomes Lord St Tanby effusively and humbly, with tea and cupcakes, preferably stale ones, in our "best" room, reserved exclusively for his visits. The five of us small children are primed to stand by silently and hungrily watching him eat.

"They are a fine lot of children," he would say. "I'll get Smithers to come and see you about an indoor toilet. It's going to be a cold winter."

His hobby is measuring the weather.

"I have been corresponding with a friend in Russia," he says. "We think that a cold winter over there is followed by a cold winter here."

His Lordship's rental income has been diminished by inheritance and wealth taxes and his lifestyle is quite modest. His forebears passed on the property to him in stewardship, under perpetual tenancies. The estate income is only sufficient to repair the worst of decay. The great house has a hole in the roof, and he and his two elderly sisters live in a few rooms with one servant and a cook. He is under pressure not to renew expired tenancies and sell off land to pay for the maintenance of the remainder.

Lord St Tanby has exclusive rights to come on to our land at any time with his guests, usually aristocrats, who come to hunt deer and foxes from horseback. His guests also shoot grouse, pheasants, partridges, duck, woodcock and snipe. They may join the local middle class who hunt otters and hares with hounds. He has gamekeepers to protect game animals from hungry poachers and vermin such as hawks, stoats, weasels, pole cats, feral cats, squirrels and zoo escapees such as minks.

Tenant farmers have rights and cannot be evicted unreasonably. This gives us more security than our farm workers. Remaining unaltered since feudal times, our farm includes narrow strips of land for making hay on a shared moorland common. In most places the Enclosures Acts of around 1800 reallocated the strips more rationally, enabling more efficient use of machinery. Priory Farm has rights to graze cattle as part of a large herd run on the common after hay-making. There are other rights that are merely curiosities now. We have a right of pannage, which is to keep pigs in the woods to feed on fallen acorns, beechmast, chestnuts and other nuts. We have rights to flotsam, the collecting of material floated in along our river bank. We can coppice trees, pruning them back to yield saplings for fodder, thatch and fuel.

Our farm workers have rights, too, that we have granted by tradition, such as shooting of pigeons and hares, supply of free firewood and free use of the farm machinery for cultivating cottage gardens. Rights to rabbiting, at warrens in our banks and hedges, are eagerly sought. When rabbit disease struck, farm workers' families went hungry because they could ill-afford butchers' meat.

My parents regard our workers with respect for their loyalty but deride their wanton lifestyles. As a child I was forbidden from playing with the children of workers, because I could acquire incorrect grammar, bad manners, swearing, disease and lice. My mother regarded working class adults as bad role models, because they drank, smoked, fought, fornicated, were promiscuous, spent unwisely, gambled, borrowed money and were too stupid to save for a rainy day.

"They live as if there is no tomorrow," she complains.

Howard and his cronies drive sports cars, take days off for hunting and shooting and manage their farm workers authoritatively. Howard spends many evenings at pubs around the district, in the lounge bar with other farmers' sons, farm suppliers and professionals who service farm businesses. If he spots a worker in the public bar, he sends through a pint of ale with the barman, when he needs a favour.

Farm succession is a major priority. Tenancies traditionally pass down the male line, and eldest sons destined to take over rich farms go to private boarding schools where the emphasis is on sport rather than university entrance.

Second sons of lower middle class tenant farmers are seldom afforded funding to follow a military career or to enter the church or academia. With state grants available, many go to teacher training colleges; very few gain entrance to university.

When I pass the entrance exam to the boys' grammar school in the nearby town, I am confronted by a more complex assessment of class. I am in a school with a cross-section of the classes. As the only farm boy in my grade, I am regarded with curiosity, as if from a foreign world. My school is a pressure cooker, and after age fourteen, I study only science and maths.

A few days before I go away to university, Lord St Tanby, asks me up to Wortham House for tea. I am nervous as I cycle past the gamekeepers' cottages, up the long drive through the Great Park with its deer and past the laurel maze, and walk up the balustraded steps to the vast mansion to pull the doorbell handle. I am received by the sole remaining servant, a decrepit woman, and led into a sumptuous drawing room where the elderly bachelor, lord of the manor, dressed as usual in a threadbare Harris Tweed suit, is taking tea with his two elderly spinster sisters beside a large log fire.

The upper class is sometimes regarded as a separate species, unable to breed with lower classes and produce fertile offspring. Consequently, inbreeding has led to a decline in their gene pool, resulting in incoherent speech, impediments and various other disabilities. An alternative interpretation is that they are so wealthy they can never trust that a lover is not a gold digger. Consequently, none of them has married.

Lord St Tanby is a bumbling, kindly man, well-liked within the world he owns.

"Ah, Selwyn! So glad you could come," he says genially.

He introduces me to his sisters who question me about my schooling. They want to know about the university application process I followed and what I will be studying. Their curiosity seems to be in "meritocracy", a catch cry of the political Left that threatens the aristocratic tradition.

The Right Honourable Lord St Tanby, formerly Chief Whip for the Conservatives in the House of Lords and near the apex of England's social hierarchy, eyes me with suspicion.

"Hmm. Engineering. I suppose we do need engineers. Liverpool is just the sort of place that needs them. I went to Cambridge myself. Not much engineering around there, by Jove. Mostly hot air, what?" he laughs hollowly. "Your parents must be proud of you. Now, what do you think about the election? Are you a supporter of MacMillan's lot? I mean, what do you think about this new, er, chap, Harold, er, Wilson?"

"I like Mr Wilson," I admit bravely, knowing this would be heresy. In those days I expected honesty to be more valued than tact. His lordship starts, slopping tea into his saucer, while his sisters shake their heads sadly.

"Really? And why do you like him?" Lord St Tanby looked over his glasses at me, genuinely puzzled, as if I am treasonous.

I mumble a few words about social reform, and the visit is over. He shakes hands, wishes me well and rings for the servant to show me out.

RULE 15: *Social class affiliations enable people with intractable differences to co-exist with respect and dignity.*

CHAPTER 16   CHANGING CLASS

Although I have inherited a social class that runs very deep, I want to be more like Vicki and to do this I must shed my provincial, rural, farm tenant, lower-middle class identity. School rugby friendships haven't lasted at uni, and I am losing my Dales accent.

Brits tend to classify a person by the way he or she speaks. George Bernhard Shaw, in his play, "Pygmalion", tested having a lower class girl pass as upper class after education in speech. Education is a great leveller. Education may be a better indicator than breeding. A Labour politician says:

"At university, an aristocrat and the son of a coal miner can rub shoulders."

This is the thesis in DH Lawrence's "Lady Chatterley's Lover", with an unbridgeable chasm between a well-born but educationally and socially deprived gamekeeper, Mellors, stuck in the working class, and an upper class and well-educated lover. They both have birth, brains and intimacy, but he lacks education. It is a tryst between nature and nurture.

For a marriage match, both nature and nurture used to be considered. Jane Austen put love above both in "Pride and Prejudice". Although education, skills and social connections are ascendant under American influence, heredity nevertheless persists in the UK. Class in Britain cannot be bought. "Old money" is required for entry to the upper class and is often frozen in hereditary assets. Because "new" money is more available for luxury cars and yachts, such items are sour grapes and bourgeois, middle class or vulgar to the impoverished upper class.

Each class has distinct occupations, habitats, ownership, possessions, education, behaviours, languages, customs, recreations and entertainments. The subspecies, "Farmer", can vary from lower class at a subsistence farm with a cottage plot and a few animals, to middle class where the owner is the partner operating a food production conglomerate with large-scale mechanical monocultures, intensive meat-growing factories and robotic dairying. Somewhere along this spectrum, tenant farmers like the Archers lie.

"We are working class," my mother says, exuding hubris as she waits to be corrected that my father is an employer of workers and therefore cannot be working class.

Tenant farmers are somewhere between working and middle class. They do not have the independent income of the professional, military and clergy, or the investment income of land and property owners. They work for themselves in a secure occupation, and this puts them a cut above the wage-earning labouring classes.

Vicki seems to be middle-middle. She speaks plummy BBC English, is demure and good- humoured and went to a private school for girls. It must be a school for middle class girls, because she has a much wider understanding of cultured life than I do. She drives a new car and holidays on the Continent off the beaten track. She shops at Selfridges, Debenhams and Waitrose, but not with aristocrats and the nouveau riches at Harrods. Vicki used to sail on her father's yacht. She no longer goes to church, but takes an interest in politics and goes to the theatre regularly.I haven't asked Vicki about her ancestry. If it were high class, she probably wouldn't be at a redbrick uni and would be in a job where she would meet high-class males, such as arts, fashion or publishing.

Social groups of engineering students often have similar social class and come from places related geographically. Middle class students often can afford to live in residential halls, whereas working class students live in digs. One social group of working class students is from northeast England. Other groups include the Iraqis, the Europeans and the Colonials. These overseas groups are considered to have no assessable class. A counterculture group hangs out in the Union playing snooker instead of going to lectures.

I try to join a middle-middle class group, dominated by ex-public schoolboys, involved in rugby and cricket-playing, from "county" professional homes in the southeast. They drive sports cars in rallies at weekends. I quickly find out they don't want me.

"Selwyn, as you don't have a sports car, you can stay and keep time when we cross the finish line."

I am left stranded there when they forget to tell me which pub they are gathering at.

Next I fall in with several provincial lower middle class grammar school types like myself, led by an impoverished middle-middle class ex-public schoolboy. Our provincial dialects distinguish his BBC English. My Yorkshire identity amuses them as much as it embarrasses me. They make me say, "Eee lad, tha'll zoon be olt'nuff t'go down't pit" (meaning "Well, boy, you will soon be old enough to go underground mining").

By the end of the first year, my provincial identity is preventing me from mixing with some students I am planning to move into hall with. At the start of second year, I decide to redefine myself as middle-middle class. This is a bold plan because one's social class normally cannot change. However, becoming more like Vicki is highly desirable. Although opposites are sometimes said to attract, it is also said the effect does not last. There is little evidence that couples from different social classes complement each other. Matches of like with like are said to be most resilient. Accordingly, I desert my former friends and fall in with a middle-middle group of expatriates and Jews. Some of them have vestiges of colonial accents that they are losing and I begin, like them, to speak BBC English. Vicki and several of her girlfriends start to hang around with us. As a rural provincial, I am something of a curiosity but I am not lampooned as I was in first year.

I try to morph my social class into Vicki's, using my new identity. After her Cambridge snub, there seem to be three tactics I can use to become more acceptable. First, I distance myself from my family and former class peers by absenting myself from their company. Second, I climb to Vicki's class by acquiring her speech, conversation, colloquialisms, slang, swearing, values, attitudes, materials, locales, experiences and media interests. Third, I learn to mimic a range of regional accents and postures, within which I can lose my own. I soon have a repertoire of comic dialects that I use to showcase the neutral speech I am developing.

I admire Vicki so much, I would happily end my search for love and sex in a relationship with her. However, I realize that it will take some time to develop a relationship and that early sex with her is unlikely, whatever commitment I make. The major obstacle between Vicki and me could be our different customs for exclusive relationships, which I don't understand. If I pursue another girl, I do so openly. Yorkshire people take pride in straight dealing and straight talking, at the risk of bluntness and terseness. A Wortham girl would never have deserted me at the May Ball in Cambridge the way Vicki did.

By contrast, we find southerners insincere, devious and reticent to call a spade a spade. I fear that Vicki may be a "prick teaser" who enjoys keeping me, as well other guys, on a piece of string, to haul us in when she wants us. I don't have time for that and will sniff around for a girl who is more accommodating. I assume Vicki will understand that I want to get sexual experience to take our relationship further.

Bright, adventurous and beautiful, Vicki stands very high in the female hierarchy. I am making it my business to claw my way up the male ladder as high as hard work can get me. She seems to me to be my ideal match, and class no longer is a barrier between us.

I learn too late that the customs of her class lead her to expect that a guy should pursue her exclusively, whereas at home we do not expect a guy and a girl to become exclusive until they are engaged.

Rule 16: *Differences of breeding are manifest in physical appearance and learning capacity, which underpin attraction. The rest of social class can be learnt. Therefore, an attracted couple can overcome a social class difference through learning.*

CHAPTER 17 VIRTUOUS PHILANDERER

My dedication to course work is opposed by my classmates. In first year, they found me excessively conscientious and scrupulous, prepared to spend all day cranking equations and splitting intellectual straws. I am top in the first year exams, and my self-confidence is boosted. I distinguish myself again in the Easter exams. Now, classmates display a Tall Poppy Syndrome, common in Baby Boomer groups, and try to diminish my stature by nicknaming me Prat. It is slang for an incompetent or ineffectual person. It is obviously untrue and I am not offended. However, it is hurtful as an undeserved abuse.

I realize that my success is affronting to those who are floundering. It is made worse because I have little interest in male company and am never around to help my fellow students understand the concepts we must learn. I am resented and rejected as a perfectionist. My response is to increase my effort level.

The guys I live with want me to behave less competitively and let work take second place to women.

"Come on, Selwyn," says Richard. "Leave the books for once. We're going out in the country for the afternoon."

"No, thanks. I'd rather study."

"You study too much," he wags his finger. "What are you doing? Trying to make us look lazy?"

"No. I find the work interesting and I enjoy doing it."

"Well, it is not appreciated. You have become a nerd. You are an embarrassment," he says angrily as he storms off.

It is hard to hurt my feelings. Anyway, because I am in front of the field, my strategy this year is to do as little as possible. So I slack off and spend my spare time dating.

I date girls living in Exmouth Hall. I meet them at social functions and take them to my room for talking, kissing and fondling. Always I crave that initial rush I had with Vicki. With these second-year university girls, I have to invest a lot of time and make a commitment, which I am not prepared to do, as I prefer Vicki. I am impatient with them, and our relationships do not last for long. When they talk about homes, babies and bank accounts, I finish with them.

The Exmouth Hall girls' defection from the Free Love movement has me puzzled. Mick Jagger's gyrations suggest a sex bonanza, but the girls next door seem oblivious. Feminine sexuality is getting a radical make-over, but the uni girls seem content to demand the traditional virtues of loyalty and prospects. When I declare my engineering genius, it gets scant regard.

All the girls seem to be swapping boyfriends. In an epiphany, I realise that young women are exploring their sexuality with various partners before making a commitment, in the same way that men do. There is a revolution in women's rights, allowing them rights men have assumed are theirs alone.

Women are demanding rights to careers within marriage, equal to men's. I am alarmed that Vicki may not be prepared to sacrifice her own career prospects to achieve my career goals. I am nineteen and I don't want children until I'm thirty. I want to explore alternative lifestyles for living together as a couple, for example, in a commune. My goals are my career and   expensive recreation, paid from my high earnings. I want to be president of an oil exploration company and I intend to achieve that, starting with a top degree.

 Women are questioning men's behaviour towards them and asserting equal rights. I fear I am in pursuit of goals that are reducing in value and being replaced by ones for which I am uncompetitive. The prevailing male mood is that women are stroppy, refusing to be discriminated against any longer for being female. Radios and record players pump out Nancy Sinatra's "These Boots Are Made for Walkin", sending a chill through men. In the plaintive song, "Michelle", males pretend female angst is a communication problem. Eventually, the paradigm of heterosexual encounter changes to one of "If it feels good, do it." This doesn't help me because I don't know what it feels like.

At Liverpool uni, my social group are a new generation, the first of the post-war baby boom. We value achievement. Our women are suddenly ambitious. Our pre-drug environment is transfixed by a liberation movement rooted in California. In our all-male engineering department, hippiedom is slowly being absorbed from San Francisco.

University women are attracted to the Beach Boys, the flower children, the cannabis-induced explorations of The Beatles in "Paperback Writer" and the Rolling Stones in "Get off of My Cloud". Love relationships such as mine with Vicki are being re-evaluated and found wanting. I worry that Vicki will forget me and seek a different kind of heterosexual love from within one of the emerging cells of hippy counter-culture.

I have a stream of girls visit me in my room, with plenty of kissing and fondling. My relationships with these girls don't last long. I try to have several girls on the go so as not to be left high and dry. I prefer to make a clean break and finish with one before becoming embroiled with another, but there isn't time for all the necessary courtesies. Instead, I have one relationship losing interest, while two or three others are progressing and another is kindling. It is harmless fun, but I am becoming increasingly frustrated. I do not understand what is happening to me and why I am dating so many girls. I am getting muddled about what I have told and to whom.

I have an appointments schedule for the half dozen or so females I am involved with and it is posted on the inside of my door with their room numbers or telephone numbers. It shows the activity planned in my dates a week ahead, with a code for sexual progress, from 0 to 10. Every day I meet a girl for lunch and another in the evening. I am constantly refining my techniques. There are also mistakes to be avoided. I have found that forgetting the girl's name or using the wrong name sets things back significantly. On the other hand, mention of a desire to settle down in domestic bliss is a leg-opener. Mention of babies or children is counter-productive, presumably because guys of my age with this interest are weird.

I am becoming frantic trying to lose my virginity to an attractive girl. There is a sex revolution going on all around me and I keep missing out. As every day passes, I gain in experience of girls. The outcome is always the same. They are in no hurry to have sex with me and won't be rushed by me. If I make a sexual advance and the girl stops me, I always comply and then try the same move again on our next date. It normally requires several dates before I can take them to my room, lie on the bed with them, hold them, hug them, hold their breasts and get my hand into their pants.

The closest I can get to intercourse is a "dry fuck", with me lying on top in my clothes. By this, I hope to ease my pain. My thrusts and banging of my thighs seldom produce the sticky ejaculation in my pants I want, even though the mess is unpleasant when it goes cold. My banging usually draws complaints from the girl who fears injury. It is frustrating and painful for me when I have to stop, as I suffer terribly afterwards from "blue rocks", excruciating pains in the testicles. It is all very embarrassing. I can get no relief from masturbation, as my mind is filled with Christian guilt and ignorance of what I am trying to simulate. It is like learning to swim without getting into the water.

It has become difficult to make credible commitments to girls who live in Exmouth Hall, as the girls are prone to exchange information. Consequently, I have to go further and further afield in my quest to obtain sexual intercourse. There are plenty of women's halls of residence nearby.

I am entertaining a girl in my room when there is a knock on the door. When I open it, I am surprised to see Vicki. She seems very embarrassed that there is a girl she knows on my bed. Flushing deeply, she turns to go.

"Oh, sorry, Selwyn. I'll see you later."

"Vicki, I—" She is gone.

I bump into her in the dining room and ask her on a date, but she shakes her head.

"Selwyn, all you care about is sex."

She is not wrong. I wonder how else it could be with her. Perhaps I could show more emotions, even if I don't understand what they should be. I resolve to become aware of females' feelings when I am with them. During these halcyon days I discover that girls' intelligences are different from mine and superior in certain areas, contradicting what I had learnt at school. Each girl has her own special magic, and all are kind, sincere and distrustful of men. They are tolerant of my ingénue attempts at gallantry but are on a different timetable with sex. I can attract women easily, but I am a hopeless suitor.

One day when Vicki turns me down for a date, I ask Linda up to my room for tea. I am very fond of Linda. As I wait in my room, I hear footsteps getting closer. Her quiet knock sounds loud.

"Come!" I call.

Linda comes in and goes to the window with its view across a lake, where white Peking ducks in families sail on the rippled surface, with ducklings bobbing in lines behind.

I am sitting cross-legged on the bed, watching her three-quarter profile through the viewfinder of my Nikon SLR camera. Her face is an inverted triangle with a broad forehead, high cheekbones and cheeks scalloped to a pert nose with a finely chiselled chin. I find her face of irresistible classical beauty.

Click. I record reality for my fantasy.

"Nice view," she says, primping her hair and sucking her cheeks in for the camera.

Click.

I am shooting black and white film, which brings out the textures in her hair and skin. Her body is an athlete's, firm, with muscular legs in shorts, her T-shirt riding up to reveal a washboard taut tummy. She is a sprinter and prowls my room as if there may be blocks.

Click. I grab her. She feels like a cat, one of those half-Siamese felines whose sleek bodies vibrate with pleasure when you stroke them, sinuous and slinky like a cheetah.

"Is female portraiture your thing?" she asks. She puts on a top hat from an ornate black wooden hatstand with a boater, sombrero, umbrella, tennis racquet and camera tripod. She takes a silver-ferruled cane and shows me a music hall pose.

Click.

"Not exactly portraiture," I murmur.

"Then what is it?" she asks, trying other looks. She walks like a gymnast or ballet dancer with pointed toes.

Across the room inside the window, a king-size bed reposes from wall to wall. Its area takes up one-third of the room. The bedposts and bedhead are blackened wood ornately carved with cupids and intertwining ivy. The bed sheets are white cotton with black Japanese kanji symbols and maroon flourishes, with a bedspread of maroon and gold patches. At the bedside, there is the end of a Queen Anne wooden side-table with chair under, in white and gold, serving as a desk. By the bed is an art deco table light, of a green female figure in amber, up-stretched and holding a lamp bulb. At the ends stand a pair of Chinese ceramic urns, with glazed concubines in maroon and gold, filled with artificial sunflowers and white ostrich feathers. In front of the desk, fastened to the wall, is a cork notice board with several cards and invitations to weddings and coming-of-age parties.

"My thing," I say, adjusting my camera, "is love."

I mean sex. To me, sex and love are the same thing.

"Love?" Linda's laugh is nervous. She sits down on the other end of the bed with her legs crossed. She is impish, with naughtiness barely controlled. She has several parts of her body that are double-jointed, that she can bend or flex in an unnatural manner. She is wearing tight-fitting blue jeans and a shiny red vinyl jacket.

She gazes at the titles on the spines of my books.

"Do you read love stories?" she asks.

"Sometimes. But I prefer the real thing." I wink at her mock-lecherously. "Have you ever been in love?" I ask curiously.

She reflects for a moment. "I don't think so. Not totally," she says.

"Me too, hardly at all," I admit. "But I'm trying. What sort of music do you like?"

I put on reggae music.

"Tea?"

There is a coffee table, with a fine china tea set, set for two, including a teapot and a box with assorted teabags. I switch on an electric kettle. On the table are an open box of chocolates and a box of Turkish Delight in icing sugar.

"Sweet?" I say, proffering them.

She takes a piece of Turkish Delight and sits back, relaxed.

"You have a great face – and body," I say. "Everything. I could fall in love with you."

"I'll bet you say that to all the girls," she replies, chewing. "Well, forget it. I'm not interested,"

"Why aren't you interested in love? Are you seeing someone already?"

She shrugs. "That's for me to know and you to find out."

I kiss her and we lie on the bed. I try to take her jeans off. When she protests, I assume it is a game and try briefly to access through strength where I have not succeeded with stealth. It is an error for, without saying a word, she gets up and leaves. When I see her the following evening, she is off-hand with me, and we never get together again. I regret it, as I like her, but I soon forget her. I never am rough with a girl again.

My education at a boys' grammar school has denied me female company, and now I am catching up, becoming aware that my lack of emotion in relationships is worthy of Attila the Hun. I want urgently to get sexual experience and satisfy Vicki. At home, farming men believe women want to be forced to have sex; their reluctance is said to be a sham, which they use to avoid responsibility. I learn with Linda that when uni women try to push me away, it is time to quit. I never use force with women and respect these girls' wishes at all times.

I see Vicki almost every day, and although we sometimes speak, it is only briefly. I ask her out regularly but although I don't see her out with other guys, she always turns me down. I think my sexual inexperience is the problem.

"Vicki, can I go to bed with you?" I plead jokingly.

"No. Why should you do that?" she plays the game.

"I wouldn't take up much room. You would hardly know I was there."

"Ha ha."

My love for Vicki is so intense that my failure to have a continuing relationship with her is worrying. I am stirred up and high on adrenalin. I could challenge Vicki to tell me what is wrong, or abandon her, but I am soothing my concerns in sex fantasies with other girls in Exmouth Hall.

Because I lack experience, sexual intercourse is a subject of never-ending interest to me. As secretary of the Engineering Society, I organise an excursion to an oil refinery at Rotterdam, and afterwards we all go to Amsterdam's Red Light District. There we observe the open traffic in sex with a mixture of awe, disgust and scientific interest. I timed one customer, from reception to departure, at 20 minutes. Such brevity is consistent with the intercourse of cattle and sheep on the farm. Pigs, however, stay on the job for hours, and dogs sometimes lock together overnight. I hear that a lion may keep his wick dipped for days. The theory is that they are establishing paternity by preventing interlopers.

This was not a concern with red light women. Their fecundity was controlled by the government.

Obviously, loving and fucking are separate matters. Sexual intercourse is understood to be a service or favour that females render to males. The solution, I imagine, is to have two women, one to pursue for love and another for sex. One girl, Vicki, is for courting, and the other for fucking. If I limit myself to a meaningless sexual dalliance with another woman (preferably a woman of a lower social class who I would be unlikely to marry) this would be far less threatening to Vicki's reputation than if she has sex with me. I begin looking for a girl for casual sex.

I go jogging regularly to prepare for the exigencies of an indulgent sex life.

"Why are you training?" a class mate asks me.

"For sex," I reply.

Fortunately, he doesn't call my bluff and ask who I am having sex with. I would lie rather than admit I am still a virgin. My peers seem to be scoring, and my deficiency is hard to countenance. The worst aspect is public perception of a new age of promiscuity. Males assume that females must be enjoying a new age of plenteous sex with The Pill, Free Love and Women's Liberation. When I fail to share in the booty, it can only be that I am not trying hard enough to get my share.

Sexual and academic endeavours are so serious and proscribed that students are encouraged to vent their creativity in pranks and stunts. When an opportunity arises to participate in one and Vicki is going to be in it, too, I gladly join in.

Rule 17: *The possibility of safe sex does not mean that sex is devalued. Rather, a woman is able to engage in it more discriminately.*

CHAPTER 18   LOGICAL DESIGN

We are in the Union coffee lounge lolling around, with Vicki trying to preside over a disorderly meeting. In group situations, I take the role of progress evaluator.

"Okay, Vicki," I say. "Let's get a decision."

"I'll try," Vicki tells me.

I am too introverted to stay in the spotlight for long but I delight in solving problems and like to have the leader's ear. Vicki is a skilled group facilitator, and we have asked her as an outsider to facilitate an Engineering stunt for Rag Week, when students traditionally go off-campus with schemes to raise money for charities. There are Larry, Tom, Roger, Jozef, Richard, half a dozen others and me.

She claps her hands. "Okay, everyone. The most popular proposal so far is take a car across the Channel on floats using sails," Vicki summarises. "Do you want to stay with that, or go into other alternatives?"

"Would we need a mast and a keel?" asks Roger, who has done little sailing but is the most practical of us. We know he would take the lead with construction.

"Even with them, I think sails would be too slow," Vicki says. She is an experienced offshore sailor. "Are there any other ideas?" She thrives on male attention like a flower under a sprinkler.

"What about paddles?" suggests Jozef.

"What? Row all the way?" asks Vicki, her tired tone dismissing the idea. "It's twenty-one miles."

"No, paddle wheels, extending from the back axle. It would not be very fast, but quick enough to get there," says Jozef.

"How about a boat on floats," Tom suggests. Everyone laughs. We talk a bit about what would have to be done to build a paddle car.

"We need to get a car from somewhere," Larry says. "I'll see to that."

Larry has a knack for getting things done. We are confident that he will get the local newspaper to run our story and that a reader will donate a suitable car.

"Who would help construct it?" he asks, taking over from Vicki. Several of us raise our arms.

"All in favour then, say aye!" Vicki wraps up the meeting.

There is a chorus of "Aye."

"Those against?"

No-one. Engineers have a credo about meetings: "Put up, shut up and pitch in."

"Carried," says Larry. "Now, we have one month to do it, before exams. Let's meet here again tomorrow."

Although we will soon be professional engineers, none of us has had responsibility in a project of this size before. It requires teamwork and we have to work out our roles. Larry assumes leadership. I consider contesting this but Larry always listens to me. His plan for our Lake District jaunt worked. I have confidence in him and prefer to back him up with my skills.

The local paper runs an article with a photo of us on the front page.We are offered several cars and choose an old Vauxhall.

Larry asks me to design floats and paddlewheels.

"Dead easy," I say. "As good as done."

My experience on the farm making rafts and waterwheels is relevant. I know exactly what calculations are needed and how to present them. Engineers present designs in rigorously logical order. It is a method begun at school that has continued at university, with deductive reasoning that has required increasing concentration as we have matured. Now, after seven years, boredom is taking over and we are ready to rebel.

A couple of others and I are holding the field together in the marathon of course work. Our pace has slackened off while we are off chasing women and people have had some time for fun and shenanigans.

Recently there was chaos in our main lecture theatre. Dr Bishop, our well-liked thermodynamics lecturer, had stopped writing equations on the chalkboard and turned to face us. He is bewildered behind his pebble glasses and dishevelled, with a paper plane stuck under his collar. His seedy-suited appearance, with underarm salt rings and suit rot, belie the brilliantly logical mind of a very persuasive lecturer.

"Next, we calculate the entropy gained by the system."

He turns back to the chalkboard but another fleet of paper airplanes descends around him, one becoming stuck in his mop of unkempt grey hair, another bouncing off his shoulder and thudding into the blackboard. We do not understand the significance of entropy, nor do we care to find out today.

"Gentlemen, would you, er, desist?" he turns around and pleads.

A further wave of planes is launched towards him.

Without another word, Dr Bishop closes his notebook and walks to the exit from the lecture theatre. The door on the right is into the senior common room. We watch as he opens the door on the left, goes in and shuts it behind him.

Someone calls out, "He's in the broom cupboard!"

There is a gale of laughter. He is too frightened to come out. We leave boisterously to go to the Union coffee lounge, rapping on the cupboard door with our knuckles as we pass.

"We know where you are," we chant as we pass.

As I drink my coffee, my epiphany is to realize that Dr Bishop has set us free to be autonomous learners. We no longer have to be taught. We can choose the path of independent learning.

"We are no longer children," Larry says. "Only 2.5% of people of our age go to uni, and we behave like idiots." We decide there and then to stop throwing paper planes.

Now I step up my intensity and it gets serious again. The fourth principle of the marathon is to hide pain, and my aim is to demoralize the others. Several have quit recently and there will be more.

The next day Dr Bishop is back as if nothing has happened. He begins as usual with an unequivocal proposition, such as $1 + 1 = 2$ and introduces assumptions and axioms one at a time until he finally induces and deduces the theory of entropy in all its profound glory.

My world never seems the same again. It is an engineers' world, with the infinite possibilities for logical changes. I copy down every line of Dr Bishop's theorem and I write the Greek algebra equations of the proof, later practising the examples until they are familiar friends. I know I can trust the equations in a world where almost everything else is changing.

I love engineering. When I start solving a problem, such as designing a chemical plant to manufacture a product, I feel every part of me engaging with the task. I go with the flow and time stands still.

I am self-confident and wonder if I am an engineering savant. I read about savants and their skills and get a feeling of empathy I don't have with ordinary people. When I visit industrial plants, I am rocked by a delightful stream of epiphanies as I realize how everything works and fits together into a whole. I ask the tour guide question after question until I understand. I feel blessed to have these experiences. Too bad that I monopolise the tour guide.

I become a professional engineer at this time, taking on a new persona, twenty-four hours per day, every day. Through it is channelled my interest in the World. I no longer care about the psychology, sociology, anthropology or history of situations. I concern myself only with bringing change to meet demand efficiently. Engineers make things happen.

My engineer's view is a narrow one, but I am proud of it. Society is bogged down in the past and the present. Change and a new future will bring benefits, and when there are enough, old systems will give way. Expecting different results when you do the same old thing over and over again is insane (adapted from Rita Mae Brown).

Designing a paddle-car is fun. To calculate the length and diameter of each pontoon, I calculate the diameter and length of a cylinder, whose volume when half-submerged displaces water that is equal in weight to half the weight of the car and six passengers. I make the pontoons long to increase hull speed but not so small in diameter as to be too flexible. I submit my drawings and working to the others, who give their approval.

I write to a handful of local engineering companies and beg them to make our floats and paddle wheels in a good cause. Two weeks later a mobile crane and a low-loader, carrying the floats and bent metal rings for the paddles, pulls up in front of the Engineering Department. They unload the pontoons, like two fat pencils, in a construction bay.

Tom and I learn to weld by trial and error. We complete the construction. A crane and truck, again generously donated, carry the paddle-car to a nearby canal for testing. It floats when we lower it into the water, but when the six of us go aboard, the back-end submerges. The others look at me. I am crimson.

"Selwyn, the floats are too small."

Shit. Shit. Shit. I check my working and discover the equation I have used was $V=2\varpi rL$, which is the curved surface area, rather than $V=\varpi^2 L$ which is the volume. It is a primary-school error. I am so embarrassed. We are able to reduce weight by cutting off the rear half of the car body. Then it floats high enough for the paddle system to work well. From then on I look up equations when I can, rather than relying solely on my memory.

This error is traumatic for me. It seems to contradict my earlier claim that I have a savant ability at engineering. At mathematics I am only average. At many life skills, particularly relationships, I am below average. I tend to be a dreamer and absent-minded. I am often nicknamed Professor. Sometimes I put my hot coffee in the fridge and leave the milk out.

We cram into a handful of cars. With much fanfare, we set off for Dover on the English Channel, whooping and yelling at puzzled people who watch us go by. When we get to the harbour, we lower the paddle-car into the water and tie up at the quay. That night we crash on someone's floor, too exhausted even to go out for food.

Next morning, after a hearty breakfast, we shinny down the harbour wall, clamber aboard and, with the motor rumbling, set off for France. Once clear of the harbour, we throttle-up to a snarl and plough across an empty sea, our flag streaming out behind us in a light headwind. Ahead, giant oil tankers loom up from the mist and slide silently away.

As the tide floods up the English Channel, we watch the French coast ahead swing right to over our shoulder. Somewhere off Belgium, the ebbing tide begins to carry us back. When Calais harbour mouth comes into view ahead, with its two protruding jetties, it seems like we are going to be swept across sideways into oblivion. We gun up to full power. With the paddles tossing back an avalanche of green sea water, we claw our way between the jetty pylons and into the still waters of Calais harbour.

Our nose bumps into the harbour wall where a man is fishing. He is puzzled by the sudden appearance of a family car with paddlewheels and winds in his fishing line. Vicki shinnies up a ladder and kisses him on both cheeks.

"Que fait?" he asks Vicki (What are you doing?)

"Nous venons d' Angleterre!" (We have come from England.)

"Ah, les Anglais! Sont fous" (Oh, the English! They are mad), he says, as if craziness explains this further episode in his lifetime of encounters with these bizarre foreigners. He scratches his head and goes further along the quay to continue fishing.

We send Larry to the only food shop open during the siesta, but he comes back empty-handed and outraged. "The bastards speak French," he tells us.

Vicki goes and returns with French sticks and bottles of red wine. She likes to play bounteous universal provider.

On the way back to Dover, aboard the fishing smack that accompanies us with the car in tow, I sit with Vicki. We are too tired to talk. She goes to sleep with her head on my shoulder.

I have spent several days with Vicki on this stunt. We have not talked much, but it is an experience that will hold us together.

Despite our camaraderie, I am not dating Vickie and am increasingly frustrated through lack of success in playing the field with the hall girls. I need to establish a stable sexual relationship within the next two months to compete outstandingly in Finals year. When an opportunity arises unexpectedly, I grab it without considering all possible consequences.

Rule 18: *Responsibility for one's actions is chosen, not imposed.*

CHAPTER 19 TOWN GIRL

The Liverpudlian dialect, Scouse, is a barrier between the townspeople and uni students. Although we live in Liverpool, few of us understand or speak the dialect. There are other cultural differences. Few students have jobs because our government grants enable us to maintain a modest standard of living without doing paid work. We enjoy a lifestyle that workers envy. Town and gown relations are often a matter of resentment on the one hand and arrogance on the other.

"Students!" a townie complains in broad Scouse. "I reckon they're having a lovely time doing nothing, at the expense of taxpayers like us!"

An engineering student replies in a southern accent. "We'll be designing things for you to make and keep you in a job, mate."

But the townie is not satisfied. "We have to slave away at the boring stuff while you enjoy yourself designing things. It is not fair, man!"

Lisa tells me about a former school friend who also works in the town. She is a dental assistant. She could be a better prospect for sex than the university girls. So I accept Lisa's offer to meet her. I hope Barbara can provide sex. I need a mistress while I am waiting for Vicki to make up her mind. There is no question of making a long-term commitment to Lisa. I am keeping myself for Vicki.

Lisa arranges for Tom to meet another of her school friends, Margot.

Engineering is learnt mostly in solo study, in a library or at home. When I am not getting regular female attention, I waste my time chatting up female students, getting nowhere with the girls from the halls, or daydreaming. In contrast, if my appetite for attention has been sated, I am placid and pliable and take on new ideas readily. I can stay in a work routine day after day and plough through the assignments, producing high-quality output. I need a steady sexual relationship to succeed.

"Do you think you'll ever want to settle down, Selwyn?" asks Lisa, looking at me intently and warily, as if I might be a strange species. I suppose Larry has told her of my gallivanting around with girls from Exmouth Hall, and she wants to protect Barbara.

"Getting hitched is not on my agenda," I tell Lisa, "not until I'm thirty."

"Are sure of that, Selwyn?" she asks. "A girl could come along who changes your mind."

"She would have to be pretty special to do that!"

"Barbara is pretty special, Selwyn."

I don't expect to have much to talk about with a non-university girl, but I am not a snob and want to please Lisa, whom I like. She gives me a phone number, and I call and make a date.

Later that week I pull up in my wreck of a car in front of a tidy detached house, in a better part of a suburb near the university. I knock at the front door and Barbara comes out. She is a slim, rather angular girl with a shy face that comes alive when she smiles. Her small fine hand is firm as I lead her to my battered car

"Car, meet Barbara. Barbara, meet car."

"Do engineers always believe machines are alive?"

"More or less. They like them and take good care of them."

"Like in 'Zen and the Art of Motorcycle Maintenance'?"

"Got it."

"So your car could be a competitor of mine?"

"Oh, no. It's too slow. Sorry."

I catch Barbara grinning, and we both laugh. She is tastefully understated, and I immediately like her. We go to a pub several suburbs away and talk over drinks. She is a receptionist at a dental practice. She is intelligent but under-confident and often blushes. She tells me how she failed to achieve university entrance grades. I am the other side of a rift from her, due to the education system, and I feel embarrassed.

When I pull up outside her house to drop her off, we kiss hungrily

"Do you think I'm dumb because I don't go to university?" she asks.

"Being a good dental receptionist requires as much skill as pulling teeth. One day, when there's justice, a receptionist will drive a Porsche like a dentist."

I run my hands over her body. She has a skinny Twiggy appearance that includes some delightful curves. I meet with no resistance, not even the "no that means yes" that I am used to. Eventually I reach her hidden place. Feeling its moistness, I conclude she has sexual experience. We arrange a date for a few days' time.

I am surprised when she asks me into her home to meet her parents. They do not have a place in my plan. They are respectable people; he is a solicitor. I am embarrassed and tongue-tied. They ask me about my studies, and her father pours me a malt whisky. He is interested in my studies. I like him and I know that I will treat Barbara as well as I can.

"Do you like engineering?" he asks in a friendly manner.

"Most of the time. I'm not keen on complex numbers or sewage treatment plants, though."

Her mother usually talks about what I will do when I finish my course, insinuating that I have an obligation to stay with Barbara. I become aware that my intentions with their daughter do not honour her parents' concerns. I try to avoid her parents when I pick her up.

Barbara is gracious, thoughtful and lives to please others. She submits to my ideas without thinking of her own needs. She doesn't talk much and only about straightforward matters.

It is an old-fashioned idea but I think of Barbara as a mistress. It used to be the custom for a buck to have a bit on the side while he is in the process of publicly committing himself to the partner chosen by his family. The mistress provides for his physical needs while he is kept from enjoying his intended's favours by chaperoned meetings. A mistress could be rewarded by gift, paid-for accommodation, or employment. It lifts the relationship to a respectable level, avoiding the context of common prostitution that payment in cash could imply.

"'Are you seeing Vicki?" Barbara asks, only mildly interested.

"No, not in the last week," I reply.

It is a relief to have Barbara and a simple relationship. When I am with Barbara, I do most of the talking. I tell her about difficulties with my work and my ambition to be an oil tycoon. She seems to listen but does not offer comment or insights, and eventually I stop telling her my concerns.

She does not share with me her concerns, except the dental practice gossip. She enjoys her work and takes her responsibilities seriously. She does not seem to mind my taking her out for a token drink at a pub and then back to my room for foreplay. With this girl, unconditional sex seems likely to follow soon.

I wonder if Vicki knows I am seeing someone else regularly. Vicki has been seeing me with other Exmouth girls, but these relationships last for only a week or two. I play my cards close to my chest. Vicki is a frequent visitor at Larry's flat.

"You won't tell Vicki about Barbara, will you?" I tell Larry.

"No. Of course not. If you want to double-time Vicki, that's up to you. She's only a good friend."

The way he said this puzzled me. I worry that Lisa will hear about us from Barbara and tell Vicki. A few days later, as I am escorting Barbara to my room, I run into Vicki in the dining room. I give a friendly smile but she looks through me as if I'm not there. My relations with Vicki reach an all-time low.

"Hi, Vicki. What are you doing these days?"

"Busy."

"Can we do something together?"

"No, thanks, Selwyn. Maybe later."

Unfortunately, Vicki does not let me know when she is free. She is either forgetful or complicated or both. Although I still have a crush on Vicki, she seems to have little interest in me. I am not used to being thwarted and intend to win her over, even if it takes me all third year to do it. I predict she will be more interested in me in third year, as I near graduation. I can wait.

RULE 19: *A woman will want her role with a man to exclude any other women from competing with any part of the role she wants for herself.*

CHAPTER 20 SHE WON'T SEE ME

I see Vicki in casual encounters almost every day, setting my heart racing and my blood tingling. More than ever I am in love with her. In the dining room at halls, I take my dinner over to join Vicki, who is eating with a couple of girlfriends. They smile politely and continue their talk for a while. Then the two depart, leaving Vicki and me alone together, for the first time since before the May Ball.

"How is your revision for exams going?" I ask.

"I haven't started yet," she sighed. "I can't get motivated."

I am sarcastic. "Is that because it is psychology? Perhaps you lack self-control; in the same way a cobbler's shoes always need mending?"

"Ha ha," comes her riposte. "You mean, the way you are doing engineering but your car needs fixing?"

'Ow!" I grimace. "Touché. Anyway, what have you been doing?"

"Stop it," Vicki snaps at me.

"What."

"You are making me account for my time. Get off my back," she says angrily. "I am stressed enough already."

"Sorry."

She finishes her meal, gets up and goes to fetch a cup of coffee. She lights a cigarette. I light one, too.

I change to a different topic. "I have been playing The Beatles."

"Which one?"

"'Rubber Soul'. What do you think of 'You Won't See Me'?" I ask.

"I love it. Why?"

"It could be me." I try to sound hurt.

"Can't you get together with your girl?"

"That's you, Vicki!"

"I'm not your girl."

"That is the problem!" I protest. "It is not for want of trying."

"There's trying and there's trying, Selwyn," she calms down and is condescending. "Paul McCartney doesn't go about it in the right way, either. Did you see the story in *The Guardian* about him and Jane Asher?"

"No," I say, bored. "Are they fighting again?"

"Yes, and she is standing up to him." Vicki is pleased. She taps ash into the ashtray.

"I call it being uncooperative."

She rolls her eyes up as if I am stupid. "Jane won't do what McCartney wants, because they are fighting for control," she says approvingly. "She won't wait around for him the way Cynthia waits for Lennon. She has a terrible time. The four go off recording all day and leave her. They are very close, with their own language and jokes. It's hard for her to get a look in."

"Jane is a different class," I reply, blowing smoke up. I have raised the class thing to suss out Vicki's views, as we are from different classes. "He's working class Liverpool and Jane's upper middle Willesden."

"Willesden phooey," replies Vicki. "Paul has been living for the last three years at the Asher's other place at Wimpole St in central London. It's a pretty fancy address, close to the West End. Jane's father is a hospital consultant and her mother is a Professor of Music and Drama. Her family has, um, culture in spades. Paul is new to all that and relishing it."

Having reinvented my own class identity, I can understand Paul. But not Jane. Millions of females seem to want to be like her.

"What does Jane want from Paul, then?" I am genuinely puzzled.

"Middle class women have career expectations these days," says Vicki stubbing out her cigarette. "It is a principle."

"Do you mean she doesn't need him?"

"She needs more control. Jane doesn't have time to see him when he wants. He expects her to drop everything for him. She expects to have an independent career, like her mother. They are from different worlds."

"Like you and me, Vicki. You come from a different world from me."

She tries to downplay her class superiority. "Oh, but coming from a farm in the Dales is so much more romantic than coming from Salisbury!"

"There's not much romance at Priory Farm. I told you the bull's style, didn't I?"

"How could I forget?" she rolls her eyes. "Tell me, do you think Paul is smart, Selwyn?"

I wonder what she is getting at.

"Yes, Paul is intelligent, very," I inform her. "He was one of three out of ninety students to pass the 11 plus to the best school in Liverpool. He learned the value of hard work and preparation. He's always first into the studio. Do you think he is intelligent?"

"Not when it comes to understanding Jane."

Now I get it. It was a rhetorical question. She already had an answer. Fair enough. Understanding women requires a different type of intelligence, as I am learning the hard way.

"Art and marriage are seldom compatible."

Vicki loves art.

"Are you suggesting that creative people should have casual relationships"

"Paul and Jane are hardly casual."

"I get it. You are you thinking that what artists do today, an engineer can do tomorrow?" she says.

"Take Leonardo. He was an artist first, then an engineer."

"I hear Paul doesn't often sleep alone," says Vicki.

"Artists have traditionally been single," I say. "Being separated gives both Paul and Jane better conditions to innovate."

"Cheating won't help their relationship." Vicki is emphatic.

Shit. Vicki is a great listener and she has worked out what I am driving at. She isn't going to accept Barbara, unless I can persuade her.

"Isn't it within his rights, seeing as how they aren't married?" I rebut her.

"I'll bet Jane doesn't see it like that. It could be why she has taken herself off to Bristol. You can't blame her if he is having one-night stands."

"That chicken and egg stuff won't wash, Vicki. It takes two to make a downwards spiral, and they both have to compromise.

Obviously, her inertia is the lesser of the two, and she has to sacrifice more."

"She could stay with him, at least some of the time," Vicki agrees.

"It may not be enough. Jane is really hurting him," I tell her. "He is writing from the heart. 'I'm Looking through You and You're Not There' is a bitter song. The words show Paul is disappointed and pessimistic. He wants her desperately and sings: 'And I will lose my mind if you won't see me.' He is badly hurt, feels sorry for himself and threatens to withdraw his affections "

"That would be sad," Vicki says. "They go together well."

I am persuasive. "Earlier there had been talk about them getting engaged. If she will not, why should he sleep alone? For him, having girls is like – brushing his teeth."

Vicki is pensive. "The thing is, Jane has to take a stand for her career. She represents the hopes and ambitions of all English women who have seen their skills atrophy under the thumb of their husband's careers. She wants independence within marriage, but not cheating. The package has monogamous sex. That is a principle, too."

"Well, she is seeking it from the one man who most wants her to give up her career," I reply.

"I think I can tell you are on Paul's side. It is classical power struggle, and the lines are drawn," Vicki declares hostilely.

"No," I say patiently. " I am logical and on the side of the one who should compromise least."

"You mean Paul."

"In this case, yes. The evidence is, he needs her more than she needs him. Paul yells out 'I'm looking through you, and you're not there!' He is indignant about her going off: Jane is deserting him when he needs her. His job is not easy. Every day at the top is an ordeal for him."

"He is trying to blame her, as if she is letting him down," Vicki shakes her head. "There are millions of women out there, telling her to resist him and do what she wants."

"Is she their champion?"

"Yes," says Vicki. "If Jane is strong enough to say no to McCartney, then they are strong enough to defy their lesser men."

"The lie is that she is not like them."

"Stronger."

"Yes."

"Are you on Jane's side, then?"asks Vicki.

"Yes and no," I say. "How can he go to her when he's in a band with three other people? It has to be a publicity stunt, a mock contest of words. The real contest for control is how they change each other's behaviour. They both have too much inertia for compromise to be easy. He is more committed to his career than she is to hers. Traditionally, a man's woman has gone to support him when he is on a crusade. It's as if Jane wants The Beatles to fail."

"I feel sorry for him," I continue. "What is amazing is that McCartney, who has never had a woman turn him down in his whole life, now has Jane telling him to get lost. Why can't she put her acting on hold for a few years?"

"So you think Jane should give in to him?" Vicki seems surprised.

"No," I am thoughtful. "I think that 'Rubber Soul' is about flexibility wrung out of the tension in their relationship. I suppose I am on the side of art. I don't want them to stop each other creating—"

"And you believe Paul can continue? Honestly? What if she doesn't make it in theatre and comes crawling back to him after The Beatles have gone down? Would he ever forgive her?"

"Possibly," I say.

I think how kind and caring Vicki is. Whereas I seldom bother to think about other people, relationships are almost everything to Vicki. Whereas I judge situations from my selfish interest, she believes every situation has a best solution for the people involved. She reaches judgements with reluctance.

"So you think his need for her is dire?" asks Vicki.

"Absolutely, but not terminal." I am cynical. "The songs in 'Rubber Soul' are more passionate than precipitate. He has inertia to keep him going, whatever she does."

"I'm not so sure. You know what I'm thinking?" she asks, changing the subject.

"No idea."

"The words of a song keep going through my head. Guess which one."

"Hmmm. 'I Can't Get No Satisfaction'? "

"Selwyn! I mean a Beatles song! Come on, try!"

I concentrate.

"My favourite song is 'I'll Get You in the End. Yes, I Will, Oh Yeah!'"

"No," she shakes her head. "I am thinking of 'Nowhere Man'. Isn't he a bit like you and me?"

"But I do have a point of view – and I am going places."

"But I'm nowhere," she says sadly. "Maybe you just want me to help you with your job, like Paul wants Jane?" says Vicki. "How long would that last?"

"Maybe if you were with me I wouldn't work so hard."

"You know that's not true."

I reflect. She is right. "Let me take you out, to a restaurant or a movie?"

"Not just now, Selwyn. I have to start studying."

We hug as we part. I don't know what to do with Vicki. But I have a date with Barbara to look forward to.

Rule 20: *When a matter of principle separates a man and a woman, it may be possible to compromise in the dimension of separation, unless the principle is too precious for compromise.*

CHAPTER 21   PROTOSEX

Whereas virginity in a girl is attractive, in me, a male engineering student of over twenty years, it is a rite of passage into adulthood that distorts my every interaction with a female. I do not care about being different but I am worried about my sexuality. I feel alone in my predicament. There is no-one to discuss it with as no-one I know talks about losing their virginity, even as a joke. For the initiated, it is no big deal. It is like car drivers, who readily recount experiences behind the wheel, but forget about their first driving lesson.

When I encounter a female, a voice inside me asks: Is this the one who will have sex with me? It depends not on love but whether she will provide no-strings sex soon, before I have to make any commitment requiring me to end the relationship. These half-relationships are all that I have ever known.

I listen to The Who sing "Substitute" and hope that sex with Barbara will further my relationship with Vicki, even though she no longer seems interested in me. Unfortunately, Barbara starts talking about the possibility of a permanent relationship, but I assert I am looking no further ahead than the end of my course, in just over a year's time. Although I am desperate for sex, I do not pressure Barbara, for then I would have a commitment to honour. There is a sexual revolution in progress and the media have guys and gals jumping into bed together in droves. If I can get Barbara to jump in with me willingly, we will be free agents.

Second year exams will soon be upon us, and I start swotting. I have taken it easy most of the year, like most of the guys. Now is the time to distinguish myself. I study all week and see Barbara one day at weekends.

"If we don't do it soon, I am going to explode," I tell Barbara.

"Me, too. I don't care about the consequences," she says.

"We will have to be careful," I warn her.

The consequence I am most worried about is pregnancy.

"Mmmm," she kisses me.

I plan to finish with her at the end of the year in the unlikely event that Vicki and I revive our relationship. I know, intuitively, that I need to be in a steady relationship to perform at my best academically from the start of the coming final year. Before the end of second year, in a few weeks' time, I have to lose my virginity and establish a satisfying sexual relationship with a reliable girl so that I can get away to a flying start in Finals year.

Vicki has never been reliable for long and she has not been interested in dating since I started with Barbara. My affection for Barbara has increased, as she has been reliable at foreplay and I may be able to have sex with her, without committing to anything. There are no other candidates; there is insufficient time to do the groundwork with another girl, and there seems no point in delaying doing the deed that has bothered me for so long.

I investigate how to get no-strings sex with Barbara. The French psychoanalyst, Jacques Lacan, proposed that one can make the absence of sexual relations seem most refined by pretending that the obstacle is of one's own making. If I set up an obstacle and she overcomes it, I can enjoy sex without strings.

I try the gambit out in discussion with Barbara, as we take a break during some foreplay. I am focussed on going all the way with her, like a golfer about to play a green. My words are carefully planned.

"It's not fair to you if we have sex," I tell her. "I might take a job overseas and then where would we be?"

"I could come, too."

"It might not be possible. I could be away at an all-male drilling camp for months on end. You could be stuck somewhere waiting for me, all by yourself."

"I wouldn't mind."

"So you can get along without me?"

"If I have to, yes. But it may be better if I stay here where I have a job, family and friends."

It is exactly what I want her to say. I plan on going to a job overseas when I finish. I am using her no more than she is using me. When I leave at the end of the course, she will have the fortitude to stay behind. With Barbara available for third year, I can concentrate on competing strongly in second year exams.

When exams are over, our group begins moving into three flats vacated by third years. The engineers have a party to celebrate finishing uni. It is in a flat, and after some smoochy dancing, I borrow a bedroom. Barbara is magnificent naked, and I have the opportunity I have sought for so long.

"Are you on The Pill?" I ask.

"No."

"Why aren't you?" I ask her.

"I haven't needed to be."

I have a condom in my wallet. I have been carrying it since the lower sixth and it has embossed a circle in the soft leather. The mark embarrasses me because it shows a very long period of denial. I dread being questioned about this mark, and so I always keep my wallet well-hidden. The imprinted ring symbolises the many years of frustration I suffered.

It takes some time to get going. Fortunately, I find some Vaseline in a drawer and take a chance that it will not weaken the rubber.

I begin to enjoy myself. But nothing could prepare me for what happens next. Without warning, I am teetering on the brink of ecstasy before plunging into the delight of an orgasmic snowdrift. I give my body and mind over to instinct, for an interval somewhere between a few precious seconds and an eternity, during which time I am sure I am immortal. No words can express the joy I feel from this first sex act.

Barbara is passive and quiet.

"Do you want some more?" I ask her.

"No. It was lovely."

"Did you have an orgasm?"

"I don't think so."

"Have you ever had one?"

"No."

"Do you mind?"

"No. It was okay."

Without accolades, I feel grateful to Barbara. I wish I had the experience to bring her to orgasm, for her to have an experience as amazing as mine.

I take her home around midnight and then go back to bed. I awake in the early morning with a new glorious world before me and another painful hard-on, as if my member had discovered its vocation at last. For the first time I masturbate to orgasm. Now that I have experienced the real thing, simulation is possible. Until now, substitution has not been possible, because I didn't know how.

When I go into uni, Richard and Bruce can sense a change in me and corner me in the coffee lounge.

"Did you have sex with Barbara last night?" Richard asks.

"Maybe." I am smug.

"Was it good?" Bruce asks.

"Compared to what, do you mean?" I answer, drawing out their envy.

"Compared to say 0 and 10."

"Umm. Maybe 9," I smile.

Richard is impressed. "Nine! Hey, Selwyn. Congratulations!"

Bruce asks, "Did you have 10 previously, or is that your ideal for the future?"

"Future."

"Who with?" says Richard. "Vicki?"

"Fuck off, nosey bastard."

I have enacted the final rite of passage into adulthood. Sex is supposed to be the ultimate human experience. I have sublime enjoyment from dispelling deeply felt fears that I might somehow be sexually inadequate, doomed to a partial existence and dying unfulfilled. Even if I die tomorrow, I will have lived fully. At last, I know I am okay. I will be able to renew my pursuit of Vicki with confidence. Nothing can stop me now.

Although for Barbara this first time lacks much fulfilment, there is a new intimacy between us and a physical passion that dominates our relationship. She is content to meet each Saturday for an evening out followed by sex. This keeps my uppity organ satisfied.

When we are kept apart, I find relief by masturbation. The warnings of church, parents and teachers try to intrude, but I push them aside and obtain release with a free conscience. I feel strongly empowered and am able to apply myself to my studies with new-found concentration.

"You are putting in some long hours," says Richard. "Barbara seems to have settled you down."

"Regular sex is so good," I say, full of hubris.

"You are playing with matches," he says. "Be careful you don't get burnt."

"No chance."

Sex with Barbara does not increase my commitment to her. I think of our intercourse as existential Free Love, between close friends and without strings. Barbara's is a casual love. However, she never does go on The Pill and does not explain why. I am always careful to use a condom.

"I hate putting on these things," I tell her.

"Well, I appreciate it."

"They might not always work. They can overfill."

"Really? How impressive," she laughs. "Perhaps you can get a high-capacity type."

But the other types I try have the same problem. I conclude that our weekly sex is infrequent enough for an excessive volume to accumulate. So we get together on Wednesdays as well, and the problem is solved.

On the other evenings, Barbara tells me she stays home or goes out with friends, but she never shares her social life with me. I do not meet any of her friends. She has married friends living in the apartment above ours but she never introduces us. She could be reticent due to the 'town and gown' divide. Would I, a student, get on with her townie friends? Probably not. I am not a social person. The explanation I prefer is that ours is a casual relationship, for sex rather than sociality. When Barbara hints that she possibly has another relationship, I feel sure she has another guy. But she could possibly want to make me jealous, to get some commitment from me.

At the end of term, in the hiatus of waiting for exam results, our group alleviates the boredom with pranks to amuse students in our halls. When we visit Richard, who has several times complained of constipation, we come across a sign "To the Exhibitionà". We wonder what is being exhibited. The signs are going our way, towards his room. They lead to the door of the toilet along the corridor from his room. On the door is a sign "Exhibition: The Great Turd." The title is not exaggerated, and we regard Richard with new respect.

As second year draws to a close, I say goodbye to Barbara for the summer, because I am going overseas with Tom to vacation work in Montreal.

My crush on Vicki remains, and I wish I could get together with her over the holidays to revive our relationship for final year, through Finals and hopefully permanently. Now that I have experienced sex, I hope Vicki and I will become closer.

"How did you get on in the exams, Selwyn?" she asks.

"Quite well. I think I might have come top in the engineering subjects."

"Well done. You worked for it."

"Thanks. How did you go?"

"Not well. I failed the main subjects."

"'I'm sorry. You didn't seem to study much."

"I'm going to switch over to counselling."

"Well, if you have found out what you are good at, you have used your time well."

"I hope I'm good at it."

"You seem like a counsellor."

"Oh?"

"I always want to open up to you and tell you my problems. You like helping people and you really care about them. You're a natural."

'Thanks, Selwyn."

"You are welcome."

I spend quite a bit of time with Vicki, usually with the rest of our group. We hang out in the Union coffee lounge together, eating fish and chips in the refectory or curry at hall, or go to the movies.

"Tom and I are going to Montreal," I tell Vicki. "His father has arranged jobs for us."

"Good ol' dad," says Vicki to Tom. "Does he work there?"

"He used to be manager of the oil refinery in Montreal," says Tom, "but he now manages a sugar company in Jamaica. He is friends with the current manager in Montreal. He buys tankers of oil products from him and was able to get us vacation jobs."

"A sugar daddy, hey? Then you'll have to be on your best behaviour," Vicki replies.

"I always am, Vicki," I say.

"Your problem is that you believe it," Vicki says wryly. "You will get caught out one of these days."

"With you I am clean-bowled," I reply.

"You have had a knock, but have failed to score?"

That's what you think, I tell myself. Sooner or later you will find out that I am fucking Barbara. What will happen to us then, I wonder.

"So I'm not out?" I say.

"No, I haven't given up on you – yet."

Vicki's feistiness is very attractive. I am pretty sure she likes me a little. All the experience in the World won't fix "bad chemistry" with a girl. I wonder how I can revive our relationship.

Then, on the last day of the academic year, Vicki and Angela tell us they have vacation work at New England University, at Boston. They ask us to drop in and see them, after our jobs finish.

Vicki's invitation surprises me, being her first intimacy with me in a while. Had she made this approach the previous week, I would still be a virgin, because I would have delayed doing it with Barbara. On the other hand, I think she could be responding to my more manly bearing.

"What are you going to be doing, Vicki?" I ask.

"Our vacation work is in the psychology department."

"What project?"

"Don't know. They'll tell us when we get there."

"Could you study the psychology of a Boston Tea Party?" I suggest. "It is a fascinating piece of history. The US tea shippers threw their tea into the harbour rather than pay taxes under the British Tea Act. This led to the American Revolution. The War of Ind— "

"Yes, yes. Thank you, Selwyn," says Vicki. "It was simply the overthrow of British power by revolting Americans." Everyone laughs.

"When we have a tea party in Jamaica, the most powerful person has the pot," says Tom. "He is usually a Rastafarian."

Again, we all laugh. Recreational drug use has taken off in the USA. Returning English bands are being searched and miscreants jailed. Drug use has not yet become common at uni.

Maybe I will be able to get off with Vicki in Boston. I will be happy just to revive our relationship; sex with her would be the icing on the cake.

I wish my first time had been with Vicki. I love her for the way she smells, because she is gentle, because she makes me laugh – many reasons. My sexual involvement with Barbara could be an obstacle to renewing my relationship with Vicki, if she knows about it. I may finish with Barbara while I am away, depending on how I get on with Vicki in Boston.

Rule 21: *Unconditional sex is seldom possible.*

PART 4: THIRD YEAR STRADDLE (1966)

In which love becomes a commodity, relationships are investments, and I adopt the portfolio strategy of a spread between two relationships.

CHAPTER 22   DAMNED LIES

I am feeling mentally bruised as Tom and I leave behind Vicki's lie detector test in Boston and travel south on a Greyhound bus. The lie detector test may have been a whim for Vicki, but for me it was an invasion of privacy. It was underhand of her. While she has found out my feelings, her own have remained hidden. Vicki is one up on me and I feel vulnerable. I regret having taken part.

"I reckon I am innocent, and the results should not be used against me," I tell Tom.

Tom nods and I see he is half-asleep. He is looking forward to going home to Jamaica. The bus driver is playing country and western. My favourite is Johnny Cash's gravelly voice crooning "Folsom Prison Blues".

I relax and go over in my mind how Tom and I met with Vicki and Angela at the research centre after I was tested. We had coffee and discussed the lie detector and its history.

"Deception is a part of life," I begin. "The old warning is 'Caveat emptor', meaning 'Let the buyer beware'. Without deception, most businesses would go bankrupt. Some deception is discouraged, for example, by trade practices regulations, such as lies about used cars. Some deception is criminalized, for example, fraud.

"It is difficult to legislate against some crimes, for example, witchcraft. A law is only as good as its enforcement and that may be difficult. They did not bring in a law against witchcraft until the practice had virtually ceased.

"In mediaeval times in Europe, women suspected of witchcraft were bound and thrown into a river. If they floated, it signified guilt and they were burned at the stake. If they sank, they were innocent."

"It was enough to be suspected," says Angela. "The trial was a farce."

"A lie detector is most useful where truthful behaviour is the norm."

119

"Religion but not adultery," says Tom.

"Correct. The aim of most lie detection is to get a confession," I say. "Torture was used to obtain confessions but more humane methods are now preferred."

"Humane lie detection is an oxymoron," says Vicki. "It is never pleasant."

"There are three levels or degrees of investigation. First-degree interrogation is by interview. Second-degree is scientific interrogation, such as voice analysis. Third-degree is by harassing, browbeating, deprivation of sleep, food and light, use of sweat boxes and various tortures that do not endanger life or health, or leave visible marks. It is covert torture and not at all humane."

Vicki nods. "How do you know all this, Selwyn?" she asks me.

"I used to play a game called Detective. Lie detection can now sway a court trial. Previously, barristers and physical or psychological tests assessed guilt. In Africa in the 1930s, the suspect had to plunge his or her arm into boiling water to retrieve an object from the bottom of the boiler. If their arm blistered, they were guilty. Recent experiments have validated this method. Guilty people expect to blister and thereby cause blistering to occur.

"Trial by ordeal, such as walking over hot coals or hot metal, invokes the same principle.

"Truth drugs were administered openly or covertly. Sodium amytal was thought to cause the suspect to boast of his crime. Unfortunately, he also admitted to crimes he did not commit.

"Scopolamine is an anaesthetic and makes the suspect too drowsy to devise lies. He will confess to anything suggested."

Vicki interjects. "Is that the preferred police method?"

I smile at her. "It probably is somewhere, such as for prisoners in the Vietnam war. But observing behaviour has long been a favoured method."

"That was what we did," says Vicki. "We observed your skin moisturising."

"Involuntary behaviour. The Bible reports that when Joseph suspected Mary of adultery, he applied the standard test of having her circle the altar, when any guilt would show in her face. The cause was mystical and psychological."

"It could have been dizziness and morning sickness he saw," Angela jokes.

I smiled briefly. "Personal demeanour, diction and body language have sometimes been used to detect deceit while preserving the suspect's rights. When a speaker averts his or her eyes, blushes, hesitates, scratches their nose or pulls on their collar, a cluster of these behaviours can indicate they are lying."

"A person's gaze is predicted to be steady when lying, and unsteady when telling the truth. This can be measured mechan—"

Vicki interrupts, "Don't you mean when telling the truth the gaze is steady?"

"No," I repy. "Surprisingly, most liars have an unwavering gaze. But you are right: it is difficult to test and the method has been abandoned.

"Tests show that clever liars can control their breathing and heart rate. Then other behaviours that change with anxiety have to be used.

"Lie detectors use several measures. During the McCarthy era in the 1950s, fear of communism led to rapid growth in their use. At the National Security Agency, 4000 to 8000 employees and all new employees had a lie detector test with six questions: Are you an alcoholic? Are you a homosexual? Have you ever associated with communists? Have you ever done anything you are ashamed of? Are you now or have you ever been in sympathy with leftist ideas? If you are an unmarried female, have you ever slept with a man?"

"Maybe I'm a communist," Angela says and we all laugh.

I continue. "McCarthy had the test repeated every six months and used the positive answers to purge the agency of people regarded as security risks.

"But lie detectors have also been used to get innocent people off the hook. Criminals on death row have been reprieved. Prominent citizens charged with crimes, such as rape, by an irresponsible or neurotic person, or by a child, have been protected by lie detector tests.

"From July 1965, polygraphs were limited to investigations where the crime was punishable by death or by a year or more of confinement. It was difficult for an accused person to escape taking the test: to refuse was a fairly clear admission of guilt."

"That was very interesting, Selwyn," says Vicki. "I will bear all of it in mind when I am analysing your polygraph."

"We are only here for another three weeks," says Angela. I wonder if that is sarcasm.

"We will have to leave out the historical part," says Vicki. "But thank you for taking part in the test, Selwyn. Yours is one of the more unusual minds that has been tested here."

I am flattered. "Oh? In what way?"

"You only apply literal meanings to the questions. You show great intelligence, based on logic and reason, rather than emotions, and do not seem to care how your responses come across to others."

It seems correct, and I am pleased to have Vicki praising me.

"Is that good?" I ask as she stands up to finish the meeting.

"Analysis should be easy. As for whether you will get a reprieve, it will depend on your follow-through."

"What do you mean?"

"Think about it."

Reprieve? Follow-through? I wonder what she is getting at.

After the meeting, we went on a tour of the campus and then back to where the girls were staying. At a party in the evening, we didn't talk about the test. This morning they were bleary-eyed when they came with us to the bus station, and we simply kissed and got on the bus.

At this very moment, the girls are probably at work analysing the polygraph results from the test. Whereas the test cannot be sure that I am lying, it can support that I am telling the truth.

If Vicki can read in the test what is in my heart, she will want to be with me when we get back, unless my behaviour with Barbara repels her. I have to decide whether to finish with Barbara.

Rule 22: *A lie detector can reveal questions that the subject is fearful of answering.*

CHAPTER 23   CHEAT'S COME-UPPENCE

The bus stops at Tampa and we go in for coffee. I have a nagging worry that I have over-exposed myself during the lie detector test and bared my soul.

I am still smarting from the embarrassment of our stupid behaviour at the Montreal oil refinery during our vacation work. Tom had led me astray but that was no excuse, because I had allowed myself to be led.

Tom is my best friend. His talk is slightly out of control, ahead of his thoughts. When he says anything, he flushes and looks around at people's faces to see if he has provoked any ridicule before continuing. For example, whenever his safety is threatened by road traffic, he is indignant.

"If they hit me, they'll have to pay my insurance," he says. He then flushes as if this may be ridiculous, which it is.

Tom's shyness may originate in his diminutive stature. He isn't much over five feet tall, with a body that seems too long for his stumpy legs. When others are striding it out, he has to trot to keep up. He is a terrific field hockey player, with acceleration that leaves other players for dead.

Tom is always a good starter but doesn't follow through and is a poor finisher. He often jumps to the wrong conclusion.

Through Tom's father, we had employment in the laboratory at Montreal oil refinery, to gain engineering experience. Our job was to collect samples from various places in the refinery, take them to the laboratory and test them with a gas chromatography analyzer for presence of volatile components needed to start cars in cold weather.

We put the samples in a machine that slowly heated them, collecting, condensing and measuring the distillate volumes. The percentages distilled at 70, 100, 180, and 220°C were recorded automatically. If percentages were below 20, 50, 90 and 98, respectively, the gasoline was below specification.

"If you measure a sub-spec sample, call this number immediately. It is the control room," said the Laboratory Manager, Francois Dumas.

Collecting the samples from around the plant was unpleasantly hot. Each sample involved climbing steep stairs, and the job was tiring. We had to go around every two hours. In between, we had to analyse the samples. We were constantly under pressure to get the work done.

No-one commented on the table of results we printed out daily. After several weeks, during which every sample was within specification, the work seemed inactionable and pointless.

"Cold starts aren't a problem in summer," I said. "There's no lack of volatiles."

"I think what we are doing is meaningless," Tom said. "No-one gives a tinker's cuss about our findings. Let's save ourselves the sweat of collecting samples. We could just take one and fiddle the sensitivity to vary the results to what we have been getting."

"No, it is wrong to do that. I believe we should do what we agreed to."

"C'mon, Selwyn. Wouldn't you rather read a book than waste your time with this shit?"

Reluctantly, I agreed. From thereon we concocted samples with credible variations. This saved going out to collect them, and we now had time to lie back in armchairs in the general manager's office, reading and snoozing.

One night, when we arrived for work, we were surprised to find the manager, Francois Dumas, there.

We followed him into his office. He kept us standing.

"What happened last night?" he asked in an unfriendly manner.

"Nothing unusual," I shrugged. "Why?"

"There was an outage of one of the heating elements in the main fractionating column at some time after midnight," Dumas told us. "The product was sub-spec. You should have picked that up. It should have been recycled and rectified. Instead, a large slug of gasoline has been piped to Chicago, another loaded into a lake tanker, some was sent west by rail and the remainder trucked out to service stations all over Ontario. The fault was not recognised until 9.15 am when the switchboard was jammed with complaints that cars would not start. We are currently recalling that entire batch. As we speak, there are hundreds, even thousands, of service station mechanics draining and refilling petrol tanks. Some customers will never trust this company again and will switch over to our competitors' brands.

"Now tell me exactly where the samples came from that you tested."

We told him everything. We said we were sorry and that we had not realised that our results mattered.

Dumas' voice had an edge that could cut glass. "I told you when and where to get the samples and you cheated. I told you the control room wanted any off-spec results, but you thought you knew better and that there couldn't be any. You didn't do your work. Normally, I would fire you both. However, Thomas's father is a mate of mine. I feel sorry for him that he has a son like you. So I'm giving you another chance. Remember this: I trusted you and you let me down. I am very unpopular around here now and it is your fault. Get out of my sight, you lazy cheating smart-asses."

As we sip our coffees on the way to Miami, I tell Tom, "We are fortunate Dumas knows your old man."

"Do you think so? He is sure to tell him and he will go mad at me."

"Would you have confessed to substituting concocted samples if it was a crime and we could go to jail?"

"Maybe not."

"Is that why you wouldn't go on the lie detector? You had something to hide from Angela?"

"Dead right. Margot and I. Too much to lose."

"So would you have lied on the lie detector?"

"Probably not. They can tell. Did you tell some porkies?"

"What do you think? Of course not. I told the truth, the whole truth, so help me. Jesus, I've stuffed it!"

The truths I told were the problem: a confession of guilt. Anguish floods through me. I had failed at being honest with Vicki all along.

"You certainly admitted to more than you had told me," says Tom. "I hadn't realised you were such a sex fiend. If I were Vicki, I would have been quite shocked yesterday by how cold-blooded you are. I think she is a deeply caring and loving person. Your shenanigans with Barbara would probably have upset her."

"Why would she be upset?"

"That you show no remorse in using Barbara for sex. It violates a principle that she probably adheres to: sex should be for love."

"She may not give me the chance now," I say mournfully.

"I don't think you realized that Vicki has certain rules about how a guy should behave. Did you not realize that you could lose her by agreeing to take part?"

"I do not know the rules. I just do what comes naturally. The lie detector held no threats for me. I thought I could use it to show her how much I loved her. I could hardly refuse. I trusted she would understand why I had Barbara, that the end justifies the means."

"People like Vicki do not accept Machiavelli's assertion that morally wrong actions are sometimes necessary to achieve morally right outcomes. You were wrong to use Barbara for sex experience so that you could apply it to Vicki. She might even worry that some would see her as partly to blame for not keeping you satisfied."

"It was not as clear-cut as that. I have feelings for Barbara."

"Well, Vicki is not a bit impressed."

"I thought I had nothing to lose." My words are heavy with regret.

"She may be pissed off if she thinks you have been cheating on her. For example, if a girl finds out you are double-timing her, you can lose her."

"Thanks for telling me," I say bitterly.

We get back on the bus.

"Do girls cheat when they wear make-up and falsies to deceive a guy?" Tom asks, trying to cheer me up.

"Not if the guy accepts it."

"Girls are experts at deception. They snow guys with it," Tom says.

"So why is it that a girl is so down on a guy who double-times her?" I ask.

"You know how we talked about monogamy being a principle with Paul McCartney's girlfriend?" says Tom, drinking from his Coca Cola can.

"Yes, of course."

"The churches vehemently oppose free love without marriage, promiscuity, the gospel of feminists and hippies, because they contradict monogamy."

"It is not as if promiscuity isn't natural," I answer. "It is common in nature and has a positive role in diversifying the gene pool. Bonobo monkeys have frequent sexual intercourse with various members of their group to maintain cohesion and reduce social tension. That's cool."

"No, human females in western countries always want monogamy. I daresay you would prefer polygamy, with several wives. Would you have a double standard, wanting each to be a 'captive' mate to be sure any offspring are yours? Monogamy prevents competition and stops disease spreading. In these days of feminine equality, you are a dinosaur."

I am indignant, and Tom shuts up.

"Tom, Vicki has seen into my heart and how it beats for her but she does not care. Her indifference pierces me to the core."

"If that is true, you should finish with her," says Tom. "Anyway, how do you know she doesn't care for you?"

"Her behaviour towards me is indifferent. She has given me no sign that I occupy more than a superficial place in her affections. She always seems calm and pleasant, as if her life is going just the way she would like it. Her feelings for me at most have been lukewarm. Last term, she did not seem to care that I suffered torments of extreme love. They threatened my ability to work, until I took up with Barbara. In short, my interaction with her is with a sphinx whose purpose is a mystery to me." I try to get Tom on my side. "Vicki would have been better off to question me," I tell Tom. "The lie detector was a ruse to get Tony to ask the questions, turning over stones to see if incest, infidelity, homosexuality and anything else would crawl out. She didn't have the nerve to do it herself. She knows I am not a congenital liar or cheat. I am an honourable person who has a different perception of where we are at in the mating game."

"I doubt Vicki is playing games with you," says Tom. "She seems to be a sincere person who would try to cooperate with the people she cares for. What stage is she at, then?"

"I am just any bloke, a stranger, to her," I reply, "one of many who want to be her boyfriend. I am not likely to give up my existing girlfriend without more encouragement."

"Perhaps she does expect that."

"Well, she should tell me."

"It's a rule of the mating game. Everyone knows that you don't play two girls against each other."

"Well, I didn't know that," I protested. "Vicki does not live by a set of rules; she treats people as individuals. She knows from the lie detector that she is not in competition with Barbara."

"She would know that, but what about everyone else?" Tom reminded me. "She is not the kind of smooth socialite who could brush Barbara under the carpet. She hasn't much confidence and she would imagine herself in difficulty explaining to her friends how you also have a girl from off-campus."

"I suppose she may revert to the traditional rules as a lifeline," I admitted. "I thought that true love was enough, but evidently it isn't. I wish I knew why people treat me with so much suspicion."

"It's because you are different."

"Different is bad, hey."

"Sometimes. That's enough for caution."

Tom got out a book as if he didn't want to talk about it anymore.

I am now feeling angry with Vicki about the lie detector. She has done something to me with the lie detector, but I don't know what it is. I feel as though I have been mentally raped. I conclude that by exposing all my secrets, she has the evidence. I feel vulnerable to her derision or rejection and I am awaiting her verdict. It is not about whether I am honest but about whether I am a cheat. I wish I knew the rules.

Vicki does not have the personality of an inquisitor. She is too introverted and shy to question me directly. The lie detector extends her senses to be able to perceive cheating from my responses. She will interpret the answers with her feelings rather than by rational thought. Will she fix on duplicity in my starting a relationship with Barbara? I do not know what new information was exposed by the test. Will she overlook my basic honesty? I feel doomed.

The Greyhound Bus driver plays "Eleanor Rigby", a mournful song about a spinster that catches my mood. One line is "Ah, look at all the lonely people". When I look at the window all I can see is my reflection in the glass. I feel stupid for having thought the lie detector could show Vicki my feelings for her.

RULE 23: *Lie detectors can create environments in which confessions are made.*

CHAPTER 24   CONDITIONAL TRUST

When we arrive in Miami, it is late afternoon and getting dark. We get off the bus at a backpackers' hotel, leave our packs in our room and walk along the beach to a jetty where there is a crowd waiting to watch wild dolphins being fed. People are filling the benches of a small grandstand overlooking the shallows, where wavelets are breaking and surging up the beach. We buy tickets and wait with them. People are speaking softly and there is an atmosphere of anticipation.

"This is going to be good," Tom says.

"Yup. Dolphins are the most intelligent of animals."

"More intelligent than me?" asks Tom.

"Definitely," I reply.

The golden orb of the Sun plunges below the horizon. The floodlights come on, and the tinny address system plays the Beach Boys' "Good Vibrations".

"There's one," someone yells, pointing.

The water is torn apart by a high-speed fin trailing spray. Beneath it, a long dark shape torpedoes in towards the beach, closely following a glint of fish. The racing shadow turns white and curls around, extinguishing the fish. It rolls over to blackness again and glides away.

"Wow!" Tom says. "Did you see that? It corralled the fish up against the surface. Dolphin eyes can't see upwards, and so it rolls belly up to see and grab the fish."

The music stops.

"Good evening ladies and gentlemen," says the announcer. "Now that the Sun has set, we can expect the rest of the dolphins any minute."

She recounts the history of dolphin feeding there, going back twenty years, recalling the names of four generations of dolphins from one family pod.

Without warning, the flat water is sliced open by dolphins torpedoing in, chasing fish. Their silvery quarry leap into the air but there is no escape. The predators breach in flurries of foam.

A dozen young marine park rangers in uniform spread out along the waterline. They walk out into the surf together, as far as waist deep. Dolphins slowly dock with them, one on one, like submarines. We disinfect our hands, take small dead fish from a bucket by the tail and wade out to a ranger facing a long dark body lying underwater, its menace suspended.

"This is Dione," says the ranger. "Do not touch her. We know it's her by the notch in her dorsal fin," he points. "She is twenty-two years old, the daughter of Saturn, who was our first dolphin."

Farther out, we can see a small dolphin threshing about exuberantly.

"That's Ceres, Dione's two-year-old baby. He is still nursing but soon he will stop taking milk. Already he is catching lots of fish."

Tom reaches down, puts his fish under the water by her bottlenose. She snatches it with her serrated mouth.

"She is so trusting," I say.

The ranger hands us fish from his pouch and we feed them to the dolphin. When we stop, she gently moves back, turns around and goes out to her baby.

"Is it unconditional trust?" I ask.

"No, it's fragile but we're getting there. Unconditional trust cannot happen overnight. It does not lie waiting at the end of a path, but all along it. It is not a smooth path, either. You only realise what trust you have gained when you have almost lost it. Dolphins learn to trust us by trial and error. With these animals, it's two steps forward and one back."

"You mean their trust is conditional?"

"Of course. Our intentions, feelings and talk mean nothing to them. It is what we do that counts."

"Dolphins have cooperated with humans before," he continued. "There is a long history of indigenous fishers in a mutually beneficial relationship with dolphins. When a fisher gives a signal, dolphins form a line and muster a school of fish. They bail them up, driving them into cast nets. The dolphins' pay-off is to take turns in cutting through the churning fish, swallowing several in one pass. Indigenous people would never harm a dolphin. They regard each dolphin as personal property and have sued people for using their dolphin without permission."

Dione comes back and we feed her some more fish.

"It's a wonder that their trust has been preserved."

"It hasn't. It is being regained. When whales became scarce, whaling stations killed dolphins. The flensing decks ran red with dolphins' blood. Ignorant European colonists hunted them almost to extinction. Then, about fifty years ago, killing of dolphins was banned. It has taken until now to re-establish trust. It is being regained slowly, year by year."

We finish our feeding and wade back with the ranger to the beach.

"One bad incident with a dolphin could ruin the relationship," he tells us. "Our nightmare is that some psychopath attacks a dolphin while it is feeding. A few years ago some drunk rammed a bottle into a dolphin's blowhole and killed it."

"What happened?" I ask.

"The dolphins stopped coming to daily sessions for a while. They can live without us. They only get twenty percent of their food from us."

"Trust develops the same as when humans make commitments to each other and keep them. Breaking promises, or cheating, obviously destroys trust."

"The imbalance may be more subtle," says Tom. "If one side gives too much, the other side may waste it. If the other is taking too much without giving back anything, the giver may quit. Unless the relationship is balanced, it will not last."

"That was the problem at the oil refinery: we didn't think we were getting enough attention."

"What about dependants? A relationship between a parent and a child is not balanced."

"I suppose the parent receives something, too, and it is enough – a feeling of being wanted, respected and responsible."

"So we are talking emotional exchange as well as material give and take."

"Yes. For example, monogamy is usually reciprocated." Tom pouts and looks at me with raised eyebrows, as if I have surprised him.

I thought about Vicki and her other boyfriends. I had no evidence she was having sex with anyone. I had cheated without meaning to. Now our relationship lacked trust and might not last. Oh, Hell!

The ranger had to go, so we thanked him and left.

"Let's get some lunch, Tom," I propose. "You can pay if you want."

Rule 24: *Trust is conditional within an arena bounded by fulfilled commitments.*

CHAPTER 25   BOWER BIRD

After feeding the wild dolphins, we walk along the beach front looking for somewhere to have dinner. We come to a diner, order spaghetti and sit at the bar side by side. The server keeps us supplied with coffee. Tom plays reggae on the juke box.

His passion is reggae music and dance. He wins every limbo competition he enters, being able to bend so far back his shoulders almost touch the floor as he sashays forward with the music.

"Let's limbo some more.

Limbo lower now."

Reggae resonates in his body, even for hours after the music has stopped. If he is happy, which is most of the time, he mouths the lyrics.

"I was walkin' along de road

'Concentratin' on truckin' right."

When the music is played by a live steel band, he is in heaven. He is friends with a university group that plays for student dances. Their mellow warbling tremolos alternate with heavy metal chimes like church bells. These sounds are produced from the ends of metal oil drums beaten into hemispheres, the swellings carefully tuned with metal punches and mallets.

Tom went to a public school in England and has impeccable manners, but his speech has retained the lilt and dropped consonants of the West Indies. He has an engaging personality, and his good humour ensures he makes friends wherever he goes.

I value Tom for his sound common sense about females, whose behaviour I seldom understand. His experience of girls is from the expatriate party scene in Jamaica, where teenagers are liberated from the stuffy class-consciousness that stifles relationships in England.

"When a guy and a girl fall in love, does trust happen automatically, do you think?" I ask Tom.

"Are you kidding me?" he looks over his sunglasses at me. "Girls give their trust slowly and carefully. It is the sine qua non of the relationship."

"What do you mean?"

"In your terms, Spock, trust is the leg-opener. Of course, trust isn't automatic. Where did you find out about girls, Selwyn? A James Bond novel? Do you know what a love relationship is?"

"Maybe not. We do not have love relationships in my family; at least, none to speak of."

The drinks server brings us water and pours us a glass each disdainfully, as if he thinks we are cheapskates.

"That's sad," says Thomas. "A couple's life together revolves around trust. Imagine you are Vicki. As she gains trust of a guy, she can set in train a series of linked traditional events that will carry her through family life. After a respectable interval of monogamous courting, they can become engaged to be married. After that, if they are still young enough, they can expect to have children and the joys of caring for them, christening them, confirming them and supporting them materially and morally, as they repeat the cycle, for the rest of her life. That's what females want initially and what males want, too, eventually. She superimposes this structure over other preoccupations, such as homemaking, her career and her social life. Her skills will go to children and grandchildren; her travails manifest in their lifestyles, security and happiness. They provide her life with purpose."

"I know all that. But it just happens, doesn't it?"

"As long as there is trust in a loving relationship with a male. If she chooses well and is fortunate, their relationship will have the locomotive power to pull her through to the end of her life. There is no room for mistakes as there is no turning back or much prospect of finding a substitute engine, or another good man, if the first one fails. Consequently, your dalliance with Barbara is stopping your relationship with Vicki in its tracks. Until there is trust between you, you are not going anywhere together."

I realise then that my stock of trust with Vicki is rather low. Tom asks the server where our food has got to. We are hungry.

"So what are you going to do about Vicki and Barbara?" he asks.

"I said on the lie detector I would finish with Barbara when I get back. Maybe I won't."

"Do you know that in the UK bigamy is illegal?" says Tom. "So why do you want more than one girlfriend?"

"I'm not up to marriage yet. No girlfriend has everything. I need to find out what is as much as I can get from one girl."

The server tells us our food is coming.

"Vicki may think, because you have Barbara, that you will be a cheat in the mating game," says Tom.

"But I am not playing the mating game. I am into self-actualization. My sex with Barbara is not sneaky. Vicki can easily find out when I am with Barbara."

"She may be more concerned than if you were to try and hide the affair. Your openness shows no remorse. Where does that leave her?"

The spaghetti is good. As I eat I mull over my dilemma. Why should I finish with Barbara for Vicki on spec? Vicki has given me no undertaking that she will accept me as a suitor or, indeed, that her attention will be on me exclusively. I had offered to partner her at the Cambridge May Ball and declared my love for her on the lie detector in Boston. She has declined to reciprocate both times. My gallantry on both occasions appeared not to be recognized. Her neglect is hurtful and distracts me from study. I suspect that she is toying with me and doubt that she will accept me. Therefore, I decline to make myself exclusively available to her until she has shown more commitment. It seems like my strong feelings are being wasted on a shrew.

A server takes our orders for banana splits and coffee.

"Building trust from her whims is what courting is all about," Tom says. "When an animal is courting, each exposes itself to the other, building up trust for when it has to surrender its defences during mating. The more harm the animals can do to each other, the longer and more elaborate is the courting ritual; like praying mantis who do a slow mating dance for six hours, with the possibility of the female biting the male's head off."

The server brings our banana splits and coffee.

"Our farm bull is dangerous," I say, "but there's no mating ritual. He goes straight in."

"Your farm is an artificial environment. In the wild, courting establishes bonding and parental care by the male."

"How do animals start their courting?"

"One enters the other's territory or space and is accepted there," says Tom. "The male bower bird adorns his nest, the female is attracted, and they mate."

"I haven't got that far with Vicki."

"You already have a bird in your bower, mate. Vicki must wonder what you are up to."

"A bird in the hand—"

We go to the till and pay half each.

For the rest of my vacation in the USA and Jamaica, my feet barely touch the ground. I am extremely in love with Vicki. I am hoping she will reciprocate the commitment I will make when we see each other back at university. The lie detector should have shown her I have no secrets from her and want a trusting relationship. Will we be able to communicate well enough to find a way out of our impasse?

Rule 25: *The more a couple can hurt each other, the more elaborate and prolonged will be the courting ritual.*

CHAPTER 26   KNOCKBACK

I recall promising Vicki in Boston I will stop seeing Barbara, not that I will finish with her. I have kept my word and have not contacted Barbara since I got back.

I can scarcely wait to see Vicki and I go looking for her at her flat. Angela tells me she is out for the evening. She does not know when she will be back. I wonder who Vicki is with, and jealousy wells up inside me. I ask Angela to tell her I called.

When I get back, I find Richard and Bruce have each taken a bedroom in our flat, leaving me with the lounge. They think this arrangement gives them the right to lounge in my bedroom whenever they please, which misapprehension I am quick to dispel. I buy an enormous old carved wooden bed. Now all I need is a steady girl to go in it and I will be all set for a year of hard study.

By the time I find Vicki the next day in the Union coffee lounge, I am frantic with worry. Does she want me? I hope she will be able to see that my involvement with Barbara is in the past, that it is her that I want. I forgive her for her intrusive lie detector test. Our eyes lock briefly and then she looks down, as if remembering what she has to say. I walk towards her, my heart thumping in my ears. Only a month ago, I had left her in Boston poring over my polygraph, presumably looking for my lies. When I did the test, I had thought she would be impressed by how very much I honestly do want her. But she had not been pleased then and she is not now. Once again, I have failed to understand a female.

She greets me in a friendly enough manner, but I sense she is waiting for me to tell her something.

"Selwyn! Good to see you."

"How are you, Vicki?"

"Dreading starting work."

"Me, too," I agree, although I am looking forward to it. "This is the big one." I am starting Finals year.

"Not for me," says Vicki. "I am starting again, doing counselling; another three years."

"Why are you leaving Biological Science?"

"I'm not interested, except in Psychology. It is only a small part of Biological Science," she replies. "I want to do counselling."

She hadn't seemed to settle into study during the previous year. She had never had a steady boyfriend since I met her near the beginning of the year, although for a few weeks we had been close enough that some people inferred we were a couple.

I wonder if Vicki has outside troubles affecting her studies. Her father has become seriously ill, leaving her without his support. At the same time, she may be called on to support her younger brother and her mother in the trauma of her father's illness. It is characteristic of Vicki not to readily share her worries with others. I lack the ability to draw them out of her.

"You'll be a great counsellor," I say. "You have fabulous listening skills."

"Thank you, Selwyn."

She must realize that my affection for her is extraordinary; at least it is for me. Nevertheless, she is treating me like a stranger in a lift. I could have been anyone, temporarily sharing some space. We chat about the rest of our holidays after leaving Boston.

Then she turns away and starts talking to someone walking by. I soon feel dismissed. My disappointment is so acute I feel like vomiting. I refuse to wait around to speak with her like a servant and I leave. I only manage to exchange a few words with her that week.

"How did the lie detector test turn out?" I ask her.

She shrugs. "How do you mean?"

Her innocent eyes do not fool me. That lie detector test was reprehensible.

I want to say, "Aren't you thrilled at how much I love you?" but I do not have the words.

I merely say, "Did you get what you wanted?"

"Yes, sort of," she says, vaguely, keeping her intentions hidden, as always. "Now I have a lecture. Will you excuse me?" She gets up and leaves.

For me, the lie detector test has changed things between us; it is her move now, to reciprocate the feelings I have shown. I am not in the business of boosting women's vanity for nothing. She doesn't seem to realize that she has brought me down from the apogee of self-confidence to feel like a useless sycophant. Stung and fighting anger, I turn away and return to the flat to do some calming study.

"What's happening with you and Vicki?" asks Tom when he comes over for a visit.

"Nothing," I reply, "unfortunately."

"I thought that lie detector test would have brought you closer together."

"The opposite. Why is Vicki acting so unfriendly towards me?" I ask Tom.

"Yes, I noticed that. She's avoiding you. Maybe she's expecting you to make the next move."

"I made the last move!" I protest. "I answered all her fucking lie detector questions. It's up to her to make the next move. I laid bare my soul on that lie detector test. It should be enough that she knows I'm crazy about her. Why doesn't she respond to that?"

"She could be waiting for you to finish with Barbara. You told her you would finish with Barbara, didn't you?"

"When I say I am going to do something, I do it. I haven't contacted Barbara once since I made that promise. It is a tacit relationship termination. If Vicki would show me some affection and interest in dating, then of course I'll formally finish with Barbara. She is expecting too much if she thinks I will dismiss Barbara on the off chance that she will have me. Why does she have to have a clear field? Guys and girls have one night stands all the time these days. She can't be a total prude."

"But you used to have something going with her. Why not again? All you have to do is give her some face. She would not like competing with Barbara."

"Why not?"

Tom is impatient with me.

"Because Barbara's a 'town' girl, you Eric."

"I'm not going to pander to her snobbery!" I say.

"Vicki doesn't talk like a snob, Selwyn."

"Then why shouldn't she want to compete?"

"No-one wants to, because there will be a loser," Tom says. "Vicki may figure she shouldn't have to compete."

"Why not?"

"Vanity. She may feel she has it in spades and it's a lay-down Grand Slam."

"Vulnerable?"

"She is vulnerable. You have Vicki to fall back on."

"Her vanity is keeping us apart, not me."

"But a girl's vanity is what gives her confidence and makes her feel attractive."

"Do you think so? Men don't have vanity. It seems girly and silly."

"Men not have vanity? You're joking! What about their hair, their car and their job. It's one-upmanship, competitiveness."

"It's ridiculous."

"If Vicki was seeing a truck driver, would you bother?"

"I would let his tyres down."

"Ha! Ignore vanity at your peril. Let Vicki feel like she's special to you."

"I have done that, on the lie detector test."

"That was there and then. Show her here and now. I have to go," says Tom. "You and Vicki seem to be stymied by mutual distrust. I hope you can work it out to trust each other."

My radio plays the plaintive Beatles song, "Michelle", endlessly rearranging the same few sounds just as I sadly try to work out what to do to fulfil my love for Vicki without giving in to her.

When my anxiety about Vicki gets too much, I turn to studying not only my course notes but also books I bring back from the library in other disciplines, such as psychology.

Our neighbours, Tom, Larry and Roger, come into my room for a lounge visit. Richard and Bruce also join in. Bruce puts his hand on my typewriter as he comes in, and says, "Giddaymate," as he always does with every machine, car, or electrical device, as if it is an animate being. He says it is Zen and peacemaking. Their noise, as they sit around talking, annoys me. I am trying to study. It gets so loud I have to say something.

"Hey, guys! Keep it down, would you please? "

"What's up, Spock?" asks Bruce.

We watched Star Trek on TV yesterday.

Peer normative pressure doesn't bother me at all; I like being noticed for being different.

"I'm trying to concentrate. This stuff is hard."

"Why bother?"

"It is sure to be in the exam."

"Exams are not everything," says Richard. "University isn't about getting a ticket to a good job. It's where you get an education to last you all your life. Leave your books for once. We're going out for a curry."

"Not me," I say. "I would get bad guts."

"You would get bad guts anyway," says Richard. He turns to the others. "How about you guys?"

"We were thinking of going to the Chinese," says Larry as if it was decided. He is usually the leader in such discussions. "We went for a curry the other night."

"I need a curry so badly, I can practically taste it," says Richard, rolling his eyes and licking his lips. "We always have a curry on Fridays. Isn't that right, Bruce?"

Richard is often stubborn, especially when dealing with Larry, whose leadership he envies.

"Yeah, Friday night is curry night," says Bruce in his precise way. "But it would be good to catch up with these guys. The last time we got together was in the first week of term." Bruce can be relied on for new perspectives.

While this discussion drags on, I am revising for the exam. It is a ritual negotiation and a waste of time. They should go back to somewhere they have liked before.

"Maybe the Chinese has curries, too," says Tom, pleased with his idea. "Or maybe the Balti house has some Chinese dishes?" Everyone looks at him and he laughs nervously. He always tries to create harmony.

"No, they don't," says Richard, as if the idea is ridiculous.

"I don't mind, either way," says Roger. "It's just food."

Roger is always unpretentious, ready for anything.

"What about you, Spock?" asks Larry. "Would Chinese stuff up your guts, too?"

"Hmm. It's not worth the risk. Leave me out."

"We have two for a curry and three for Chinese," says Larry. "Richard and Bruce, you are overruled."

"Bullshit," says Richard. "Roger is okay with either. So it's two against two."

"I'll toss a coin. You call," says Tom to Richard.

"Excuse me," I say. "Why is it necessary to use chance to resolve it?"

"Because chance is not biased," says Tom.

"You wish. There is no such thing as chance. A coin tosses the number of spins you give it. It is the same with everything. As soon as you describe how to generate a random outcome, it is no longer random .It would be better to decide in terms of nutrition and cost, including transport."

"We can walk to the Chinese," says Larry.

"True enough," says Bruce, "but you pass the Balti on the way."

"The Chinese is cheaper," says Roger.

"Shut up, Roger. Whose side are you on?" says Bruce.

"Chinese food is better for you," says Larry. "That's why there are so many people in China."

I cough and clear my throat. "If I might interrupt. The question is which is more nutritious, Chinese or Indian; say, chicken tandoori or stir-fried chicken. The tandoori has higher temperature cooking, with more dairy products and more saturated fats."

"That decides it, Chinese is better," says Larry.

"Wait," I say. "The stir fry would have lightly cooked but oily vegetables. Hot spicy tandoori could be easier to digest because hot cooking breaks down animal tissues. Stir fry would have more cellulose and unsaturated oils to break down."

"I told you Indian is healthier," Richard says. "Thank you, Spock."

"I go for taste," says Tom. "Indian food is more hot and spicy; Chinese is more sweet and saucy. This evening I am feeling like sweet and saucy."

"You are always sweet and saucy, Tom," says Bruce, simpering. "I prefer duck, tandoori duck."

"Never heard of it," says Larry. "Has anyone heard of it?"

"Then I will have to go Chinese," says Bruce. "Sorry, Richard."

"Fuck your duck," Richard says. "I was so looking forward to a curry."

"We can go for a curry next time, Richard," says Tom, harmonizing as usual.

"Well, that's decided," says Larry. "Selwyn, are you going to change your mind and come with us?"

"I never change my mind," I say, "unless I get new information that changes the weight of evidence."

"You have heard our opinions," says Bruce, "weighty ones, except for Roger's."

"I don't take any notice of opinions," I say. "Your so-called discussion was merely a ritual that confirmed the pecking order in your group. Each of you has been able to assert your pre-established position."

"Isn't that what groups usually do?" says Richard. "What's your position, Selwyn?"

"I choose not to be a part of your hierarchy."

"Why not?" asks Larry. "You wouldn't have to start at the bottom. We would value you. Being part of a group is good fun."

"No, thank you. Being independent is more important to me. I can do what I like, without having to think about keeping in with the group."

"You spend too much time studying," Larry says. "Just because you are intelligent doesn't mean you can ignore the rest of us."

"Because I prefer to work does not mean I am preventing you from succeeding. Whether you achieve your goals is up to you. I am not stopping you."

"What Larry means is that you will need to socialize with other engineers, in your job," says Richard.

"Who says? Some engineers do need to do that, I agree, but I aim to be a one-man band."

They all look at me in silence.

"You are one weird fucker," says Bruce.

"Isambard Kingdom Brunel was a one-man band," I say. "He accomplished a lot by himself. He designed the *SS Britain*, the first ocean-going steamship and the largest ship built up to that time. I'll bet he didn't dream it up with his friends at the local Chinky."

"Maybe his friends would have talked him out of it. But new designs come from teams nowadays," says Richard. "Do you think you will be able to get a job as a one-man band, Selwyn?"

"The fashion is for a design to be claimed by the team who develops it. However, a new design often originates with an independent individual working alone who can see that a design makes sense within economic, social and psychosocial contexts."

"If you think you can master all those contexts as well as engineering, good luck to you. You have a lot of studying to do," says Larry. "I do as little studying as possible. Enjoy your band practice. Let's go, guys."

"See ya, guys. Have a good time."

"Go fuck yourself, Spock," says Roger good-naturedly as he goes out. I suspect he is finding being in the group too limiting. He, too, wants a First Class degree and could be envious of my freedom from social obligations, without the courage to go solo.

They leave. I can imagine them talking about me.

"Selwyn is focussed, isn't he?"

"He is nuts," Richard would answer.

Let them think what they like. It is good not to have to take part in social activities I despise. When I am not studying, I feel anxious. I worry about Vicki. Why is she ignoring me? Will I finish with Barbara and take a chance on her?

Rule 26:*A woman will not acknowledge another woman as a competitor for a man, if this may be construed as an unwanted parity or as a weakness in her own position.*

CHAPTER 27 COMPROMISE

I have not contacted Barbara since my return. Presumably, Vicky would hear of it from Lisa, Barbara's friend, or from her boyfriend Larry, who knows my movements. Vicki would also know that I have not told Barbara we are finished.

Womens' Liberation at this time is encouraging women to be uncompromising in their dealing with men. Although I talk with Vicki about this and that, I do not hear her making any demands, perhaps because our talk is so stilted. We talk about the psychology she is studying, as I am interested in why people behave the way they do. It has always puzzled me.

When I see Angela and Vicki in the coffee lounge, I go over to them.

"Hi."

"Hi."

"What's today's psych topic, Vicki?"

"Motivation."

"That's important to me. What do you think my motives are?"

"Abraham Maslow, who we are studying, would probably answer that they differ from one context to another."

"How about the context of me trying to get off with you?"

"That would be a low level physical need to have sex, wouldn't it?" Vicki and Angela laugh unpleasantly.

"Vicki, you know that's not true. I also want to share my life with you."

"Hmm. That sounds like you also want esteem from me. Why should I esteem you?"

"Because with me you will have a wonderful life."

"No, that's not esteem; that's self-esteem. You think you're great, don't you? According to Maslow, once a person gets esteem, they are able to advance up the hierarchy to self-esteem at the next level above, and then higher to achievement and higher again to self-fulfilment."

"I think I like this Maslow's theory. I am quite high up already."

"No, not in our relationship you are not, Selwyn. You are very low still. You are stuck at getting esteem."

"But people do esteem me already!"

"Not in our relationship they don't. Go on: who esteems you?"

"The guys think I am okay."

"The guys," echoes Vicki, laughing nastily. "The guys don't esteem you. They think you're a woman crazy socio-phobe. Who else?"

No-one; she is right. My guts twist in pain. It would not help my case to tell her Barbara does. It occurs to me that because I haven't been in touch with her for three months she probably doesn't any longer.

I shrug my shoulders.

"Okay, you win. You can continue to treat me like a piece of shit, if you must."

"Aw, Selwyn. Now you are fishing for compliments."

"Just because you are a psych student, you figure you can outsmart everyone. You don't even know what you want yourself. Now if you will excuse me, I am going to get myself a piece of 1st Class honours degree."

I walk off. It doesn't seem likely Vicki will come across soon. We have been back in Liverpool for two weeks and Vicki is pointedly ignoring me. She does not acknowledge the crush on her that must have shown on the lie detector test, leaving me up in the air. I see little of her. Sometimes she studies at the other guys' flat. She never comes to our flat; at least, not while I am there.

It was only much later that I realised that women at this time were caught in a maelstrom of re-evaluation of their careers, their sexuality, their relationships – everything. It was possible that when Vicki looked at me she saw a male to be spurned, rather than someone whose intention was to benefit her in any and all the ways she might want during all of her life.

Tom came over to our flat, and we had a cup of coffee.

'What's happening with Vicki?" he asked.

"Nothing," I answered.

We talked about how I still thought it would be courteous if she acknowledged how I had exposed my infatuation for her on the lie detector. Tom told me that it was a stand-off.

"You are waiting for some sign of interest from Vicki, and she is waiting for you to finish with Barbara. It's a classic."

"Okay. Thanks. I didn't think it was that obvious that she was waiting for me. I am not good at understanding women's behaviour."

I have to find out how long I have until Vicki will give up on me. Tom thinks I may not have long.

"She must think you are being a stick-in-the-mud about Barbara," he says. "No wonder she is unfriendly."

"I have an analogy for our behaviour in our relationship, based on physics. I have imagined Vicki's and my unwillingness to change as amounts of 'inertia' determining how much we would have to sacrifice to get a fair compromise."

Tom is not impressed. The last time I tried him on something like this he told me I was crazy. Theory is not something he embraces.

"Why inertia?" he asks patiently, humouring me.

"It is the tendency of a person to continue doing behaviours that they been doing unless there is a stopping force."

"What sort of behaviours?"

"Being single or in a relationship, or living in a certain place, or wearing certain clothes or living a certain lifestyle. Inertia increases with time as we adapt to our habitat, acquire possessions, developing habits and relationships that become more intense and enduring. The more set we become in our ways, the larger is the inertia. It takes a larger and larger force to deflect us from our course."

"What sort of stopping force?"

"A change in motivation, pathway, opposition or friction."

"Interesting. But does knowing about inertia help?"

"If you estimate a person's inertia relative to yours, you can balance your relationship with them."

"What's so good about having a balance?"

"It is rational and comfortable, with no-one dominating. Here, let me show you."

My bookshelf is a plank resting on two piles of house bricks. I take off the books and pick up the plank.

"Oh goody goody, a see-saw," says Tom.

"Correct. Suppose Vicki and I are at opposite ends trying to decide for how long to go on a camping holiday. I want to go for 10weeks but Vicki wants to go for only 4 weeks? How will we resolve it?"

"You will capitulate and you will go for 4 weeks."

"Will I be happy about that?"

"No, but next time there is a conflict, it will be your turn to get your own way."

"Okay, but taking turns to be unhappy is not very satisfactory. Is there a better way?

"You could split the difference and go for 7 weeks. ?"

"Probably," I reply. "We would each be put out 3 weeks. Is that better?"

"Yes, it is an equal sacrifice." says Tom.

"Because we have equal rights to have your own way?" I ask.

"I guess so."

"Is that realistic?" I query. " What if I have twice as much inertia as Vicki? Suppose I have arranged to meet with my friends at our 10 week destination and I have been planning this with them for ages. I might prefer to go by myself. On the other hand, Vicki would not be much put out by going for longer. She has never been camping with me before, or for 10 weeks with anyone, but she is adventurous and her inertia for going longer than 4 weeks is quite low. She plumped for 4 weeks quite arbitrarily . So her inertia is to be considered, but is lower than mine, say half as much. Do you agree that compromise is possible?"

"Not if you would go by yourself."

"That would suggest my inertia is impossibly high, whereas we decided that Vicki's is a half as much as mine. Suppose we can change our plans and still meet with my friends, so we both can compromise."

"She should compromise twice as much as you." says Tom. He looks pleased with himself.

"Brilliant! But what is fair about that?"

"It balances. Look."

He put the plank, about one metre long, on my study table, resting liking a see-saw across my engineer's triangular ruler. He picked up two books, one twice as heavy as the other.

"Now, this book, which is twice as heavy, will represent your inertia acting at this end. The other book is Vicki at the other end."

Tom put the two books at the ends of the plank. He adjusts the position of the pivot to a shorter distance from the heavy book, until the two sides balance.

"Okay, done," he said, standing back admiring his work.

"Tell me what fraction of the length is the distance to the balance point?"

"From your end, about one third."

"Correct. In fact, exactly one third," I say. "Why is that?" "Two inertias times one third of the distance equals one inertia times two thirds."

"Correct," I say. "Each side has an equal "moment" of two thirds, by the Law of Momentum."

"It is just common sense," says Tom, who has an aversion to theories. "Inertia is the same as mass."

"By Newton's Second Law."

"Of course. Well then, what is the compromise for your camping trip?" asks Tom.

"One third of ten minus four, equals two. I have to compromise 2 weeks, less than the 10 I want, making 8 weeks. Vicki would make twice the concession I do, increasing by 4 weeks to 8 weeks. Does that make sense?"

"Hmm. It is logical," Tom admits.

"This method is a way of keeping the peace. It can be used to balance all the difficult compromises that couples have to make."

"You are trying to work out how long you should expect to wait for Vicki, to begin a relationship with you after you finish with Barbara," Tom reminded me.

"Wouldn't that be immediate?" I say. "It is already 2 weeks since I got back and I haven't seen Barbara since before the holiday."

"No. Vicki would expect you to wait from when you finish."

"I cannot afford much time for settling into a new relationship. Two weeks is enough."

"Are you kidding?' says Tom. "Vicki would want much more."

"Four weeks?"

"More. Say eight weeks."

"Jesus. Okay, suppose Vicki wants 8 weeks and I want 2 weeks," I say. "Assume your inertia is higher from having a previous relationship, at 2 to 1. Then the compromise is 4 weeks, with you conceding 2 weeks and Vicki 4 weeks."

"Holy cow! I will have to wait a month even if I give Barbara the flick today. I should have worked this out before. I must finish with Barbara immediately and start with Vicki as soon as possible or I'm going to be all alone when I am revising for the end of term exams."

"Well, I think your calculations point to one thing: you need to talk to Vicki. If you keep going like this your brain is going to overheat."

I have to make up my mind immediately: can I afford the distraction of changing girlfriends now?

RULE 27: *For a balanced compromise, concede a proportion equal to their share of total inertia.*

CHAPTER 28   BURADAN'S ASS

It is probably already too late to take up with Vicki, even if I were to finish with Barbara. I don't want the uncertainty and disruption of changing girlfriends at this time. Then I think another week won't hurt while I wait for Vicki to register that I have stopped seeing Barbara. It is three months since I contacted Barbara.

"What's happened with you and Barbara since you have been back?" Tom asks me on one of my daily visits to his place, the extent of my social life on days when there are no uni classes.

"Nothing. I haven't contacted Barbara yet," I tell him.

"So what are you waiting for?" Tom asks me.

"I'm thinking of continuing with her."

"In a permanent relationship?

"No. Casual."

"What about Vicki?"

"I have been waiting ever since we got back for a sign that Vicki wants a relationship with me. But I haven't seen one. Have you?"

"No, but that doesn't mean anything," says Tom, lighting a cigarette. "Vicki always plays her cards close to her chest. She wants to save the World but is still figuring out how she can best do that. It does not include going with a man who has another woman, however temporary that is. She is tuned into fairness and justice. She probably feels sorry for Barbara. She wants to help people, maybe even including you. She may think your crush on her is unhealthy and wants you to get over it. When she has figured out what she wants to do, she will be easier to get on with."

Tom amazes me with his ability to figure a person's inner nature. He is so right about Vicki. Inside she has burning mission to help troubled youths get their lives together.

"She's not perfect," says Tom. "She may not be able to see it from your point of view and is angry with you. It is rather unusual to want to have two girlfriends at the same time, in bed with one and with the other on ice as a replacement for when you want to get serious. I doubt that she accepts your criticism, either, of the way she used a lie detector on you. She would say you deserved it for being deceitful not just to her, but to Barbara."

"So you think I could still have a chance with her?"

"A chance. Not a certainty."

It is third year, and I know that it is time to resolve my love life and get stuck into the work. I will leave going to parties to the others this year. I love parties – I like the company and I like most of the people – but I want to make a break for it and see what I can do for my career. I will not be looking for any other girl. It has to be either Vicki or Barbara by the end of the week.

I want to talk with Vicki about my dilemma but I don't know what to say. I have difficulty understanding each other's views, and we both are strongly opinionated. I can sense a row coming on and maybe she can, too.

I resist the temptation to call Barbara for a date. If I do, Vicki will see that I have done the opposite to what I said I would do and will regard me as a cheat who would enter into a commitment with no intention of honouring it. When a cheat is discovered breaking an agreed rule, he may be excluded from further games. In some games, a cheat may be able to continue after suffering a forfeit, such as an apology or an exclusion from play for a period. I suppose Vicki will wipe me if I resume with Barbara but maybe I will have a chance with her later. I not only don't follow the conventional rules when it suits me, I make up new rules for others to follow.

I must have regular sex. I have enough experience to know its powerful effect on my ability to pursue an exacting study routine. There is a legend among the third years, that regular sex is essential to stay the demanding course and get a good quality degree. I believe it. Sexual intercourse sharpens performance. The effect of sex on performance has been tested in sport but not in academia. Some boxers and rugby players swear by having intercourse before they compete. Although even vigorous sex requires little energy, sports coaches try to prevent male athletes from having sex within a few hours before a game. Heart rates can be slightly lower. Although Muhammad Ali would not have sex within six weeks of a fight, few coaches discourage earlier sex. In my experience, regular sex does away with the distraction of unfulfilment and enables extreme concentration. The difficulty is in getting it, because females want you to spend time with them when your time is at a premium.

Whereas I refrain from sex the night before an exam, I find that weekly sex reduces dissatisfaction, conflicting with William Reich's theory that orgasm depletes dopamine in the brain and causes depression. My experience refutes his view, for if my partner and I don't reach orgasm, I am depressed, causing painful "blue rocks". His data are from rats that perhaps become more active when they are unfulfilled. In contrast, I work hardest after pumping rump, when I am happiest.

Another theory is that sex tricks a woman into "babysitting" the man she loves – nurturing him as she would her own infants, thanks to the oxytocin released when he plays with her breasts and his penis pokes her cervix. The chemical is one of several that exploit ancient neurobiological circuits. This theory focuses on the benefits a loving female can give, rather than those that a male contestant enjoys, whether from a loving female or an indifferent one.

On Friday we all go to the movies at the cinema on the Blackpool Road. Vicki is there but she does not show any interest in me. She does not even acknowledge me, walking past laughing and joking with Richard. She knew I was watching as she glanced over at me as she shared a bag of popcorn with him. I see no point in drawing out my agony any longer.

I have to decide between Barbara, who I am certain of but love less, and the lower probability of Vicki, who I love more. The expected value of the two's benefits, being the benefit times its probability, is about the same. Hence the dilemma.

How I long to lie with Vicki again, to remove her clothes and look at her naked, to feel her hold me and to make love to her, slowly because I know I will never leave her and she is relaxed knowing that. I will never be disloyal. It will be another world, where I am assured of freedom from the desertion I fear because we would marry and pledge to stay together come what may.

Another week has gone by and I have exceeded my compromise of 4weeks in quarantine and Vicki probably feels that by not actually finishing with Barbara I am trying to dominate her.

"Hi Vicki. I want to talk with you. How about a drink in pub this evening."

"What about Barbara?"

"I haven't spoken to her since before the holiday — 4 months ago."

"But you haven't finished with her?"

"I haven't said that, no.

"Why not?"

"I have been waiting for you."

"In Boston you promised you would."

"I haven't seen her or even talked."

"I don't want to talk with you until you finally finish with her."

Vicki turned and walked off.

If she wins on Barbara there may be no stopping her on other demands. She evidently has little interest in working hard at university and may make unwelcome demands on my time. My default option is the inertia of my erstwhile satisfactory relationship with Barbara. The inertia suggests I keep doing what I have been doing; in other words, Barbara.

I hate to turn my back on Vicki, but time is running out, and my relationship with Barbara could be irreparably damaged. The philosopher, Buradan, described a hungry donkey that finds itself between two equal piles of hay. Unable to choose, it starves to death.

I know that if I choose Vicki and our relationship comes to nothing, it would be devastating. She is too risky. Therefore, Barbara is my logical choice.

The decision is made. Nursing my grief, I telephone Barbara.

"Hello, Selwyn. What have you been doing?"

"Working, causing trouble and travelling around the USA."

"How long have you been back?"

"Four weeks."

"What have you been doing?"

"Recovering, moving in, getting organised and starting work."

"Did you miss me?"

"Yes. Did you miss me?"

"Yes."

"What have you been doing?"

"Waiting to hear from you. Getting drunk."

"Can I see you tomorrow? The same as usual?"

"Okay."

"Bye."

Barbara is friendly and does not seem to mind having been left in limbo, almost as if she has been expecting it. We take up where we left off, so much easier than going into a new relationship with Vicki, if that had been possible. With token cultural sociality, we go out to a pub, and then back to my flat and to bed.

One fine spring day, Barbara asks me to take us on a picnic in the country. It is soon clear it is her mother's idea, and I smell a trap. I hate being manipulated and immediately I want her mother's intervention to turn out to be counter-productive so it will not be repeated. The hamper they pack for a picnic is filled to bursting point with my favourite food. I drive to a local beauty spot and we eat on white linen with double damask dinner napkins, in the shade of a tree looking over the distant city. The stage is set for me to pop the question. Every animal, bird and insect seems to be pairing off around us in the warm sunlight.

"What is going to happen to us at the end of the year?" Barbara asks.

I am honest. "I don't know yet."

Barbara thought for some time. "You don't seem to have any emotions about us."

"I'm not going to worry about a situation before we get to it," I tell her. "Anything could happen."

We never discuss our relationship. It is a complaint I am familiar with, and there is some truth in it. I protest but I assiduously avoid talking about the future. I kiss her every time she tries to speak. I suspect that her waspish mother has advised her compliance so far and now is guiding her to negotiate a permanent relationship. It is the only response I can think of to avoid confrontation. I am sure it is not the response her mother wants. I get away with it this time, but I know that time is running out on my freedom in this relationship.

Barbara is my logical choice but I cannot face the future without a possibility of Vicki in it somewhere. I am on the lookout to amend my strategy with hope for a future relationship with Vicki, even though prospects at present are bleak. Too much is at stake with my work to risk finishing with Barbara. So I resume with her but only until the end of the year. How can I avoid her expecting a permanent relationship?

Rule 28: *In default of processes to negotiate mutually beneficial change, outcomes will be caused by inertia, which is the tendency to repeat past behaviours.*

CHAPTER 29   COMMODITY LOVE

Most people would expect me to give up on Vicki at this point. However, I have strong feelings for her and I churn ideas for keeping our relationship going.

I meet in hall an American student, Wilbur, doing a PhD in business economics. He tells me he has been speculating in commodities for three years and has made enough money to buy a sports car and go on skiing holidays. He is proposing that crude oil futures become tradeable in a commodity exchange market. It is a bold concept.

"Potentially, anything can be commoditised and futures traded," he says.

"Can love?" I ask.

"What kind of love?" he asks.

"Between two people."

"So one could be a seller and the other a buyer? What would they trade?"

I trot out the standard definition. "Love has three ingredients: intimacy, passion and commitment."

"Hmm," Wilbur ruminates. "Intimacy and passion are intangibles. But a person who wanted to acquire love could exchange their future commitment for the best love they can afford. This is what happens in arranged marriages. Intimacy and passion are subordinated. Perhaps that is why arranged marriages have gone out of favour."

"Negotiation of intimacy and passion could be decided beforehand, setting the price for exchange of love for commitment in a final transaction."

"Could negotiations be in terms of a 'price' of a particular love future between two people?" he asks.

"Hmm. I don't see why not," I reply, "although such a price would have several elements. For example, his and her obligations to provide resources, for wherever and whenever they are going to live together would have to be agreed."

"Love is not an ordinary commodity," Wilbur says. "Love is particular to two people, without a universal value. The marketplace cannot have anonymous buyers and sellers. It would merely be a meeting place where couples could circulate, get together and strike a bargain. Within the last 30,000 to 100,000 years, people have evolved a cognitive ability to detect cheating in exchange of one commodity for another. There would be a market, because both sellers and buyers could get several offers to choose between. 'Market pricing' would allow dealing with strangers and amounts of dowries to be paid for certain classes of bride or bridegroom."

I am fascinated that something as multi-faceted as a love relationship future could be subjected to market forces. I cannot afford the commitment for Vicki now but I may be able to at the end of the year. I decide to find out as much as I can about commodity futures trading from Wilbur. I take him out to dinner at a Chinese restaurant within walking distance.

After dinner, Wilbur explains to me how the commodity market works.

"Do you know what a 'spread' is with investments?" he asks me.

"Is it like putting your eggs in several different baskets?"

"Exactly. If things go badly, some of them may be okay. Suppose you want to have only two investments. Should they both be in the same thing?"

"No," I replied. "They should be diversified – in opposites."

"Correct. If one is in sunglasses, what could the other be in?"

"Umbrellas, or raincoats, or gumboots – not beach towels."

"Good," says Wilbur. "Those are diversifications for weather. Another example would be to bet on a future horse race, on two horses. One horse could be good in the dry and the other should be good in the wet. Then whatever the weather, you would be in with a good chance of winning. Are there other types of diversification?"

"Could you cover uncertainties that affect profit from both equally? For example, presence and absence of various types of disaster, disease, political leadership, fashion, competitor strategy or technological breakthrough."

"Very good," he says. "So far we have talked about investments that are complements. Now what do we call the relationship when investments are in items that have identical or very similar roles?"

"Substitutes?" I guess.

"Yes."

"For example, a sailor could have a girl in each port, so he can enjoy himself wherever his ship goes."

"Just like the sailor, an investor in commodity futures wants to spread the risk between commodities that are substitutes for each other," says Wilbur. "When the price of one goes down, the other goes down as well."

"This could apply to love commitments," I say. "It would be good to have a spread of girls who could substitute for each other, ideally with complementary qualities, to cover every situation. However, the value of such an arrangement could be affected by girls' predilection for married monogamy, and it would be difficult for a guy to openly hold simultaneous futures in two or more girls, not least because bigamy is illegal and adultery is grounds for divorce.

"Does this make sense? Love as a commodity future has obligations, on both seller and buyer, as part of a notional prenuptial agreement. Either the girl or the boy can be the buyer and the other is the seller. When a buyer takes a 'long position', he settles his or her obligations now and the seller has then to deliver hers, or his, by the closing date, which is when they start an exclusive relationship."

"It seems okay. Which girl are you talking about?"

"Vicki."

"That's the one who is playing hard to get?"

"Yes."

"You are in a relationship with Barbara already?

"Yes."

"Well she is the one you have in a long position."

"I agree. I acquired her on a no-strings basis and should be able to finish with her without loss of honour. My attention could have enhanced her attractiveness to, say, another lesser engineer."

"You really are up yourself, aren't you?"

"No more than I should be. Barbara and I could want to get from each other the best possible dowry at the lowest 'price' now, except that I want to make the minimum commitment in the Rake tradition."

"What is that tradition, exactly?"

"An attractive guy like me sometimes gives out his commitment to girls and takes it back when he has made a profit. I follow the 'Rake' tradition of the male whose participation in the market is to speculate in casual love. He does not ever intend to pay, but the girl cannot detect the difference between his offer and that of a genuine buyer. He sells out the girl at a profit when he has acquired kudos, connections, experience or materials from her and can present good reasons for leaving her. His honour may be intact and he makes a profit, but the girl may lose, although I have some social standing and would heroically try to avoid that."

"Barbara probably thinks she can reform you."

"There is no possibility of that with her," I say. "My price is more than she can afford."

"It won't be when the girls find out about you."

"They won't. I am medium on the guys' attractiveness ladder. I am provincial, rural and lower middle class and consequently I would not be so popular with an upwardly mobile girl even if I had good social skills, which I do not. I lack sexual experience, and I have learnt love-making skills through my observations of matings of domestic animals. Consequently, I am only of medium interest and unable to command a high price."

"Do not be too hard on yourself," says Wilbur. "You are socially obnoxious and your ideas about how to bond with a girl are crap, but you are very intelligent."

"Thank you, Wilbur. I haven't noticed you dripping with blondes. Now Vicki is at or near the top of the girls' ladder because she is popular with guys. She can command a very high price in commitments, obligations and conditions in a permanent relationship. For the guy she wants, she can relax obligations. For someone who is unacceptable, she can set a 'no way' condition."

"That could be your problem with her. She will not have you because you are weird."

"Even if that is true, everyone has their price. I could be unacceptable to a high-ranked female like Vicki, unless she lowered her price enough for me to reach by making maximum possible commitments, which I am not prepared to do at present. Guys and gals normally make love commitments slowly, a bit at a time, so they can pull out without major loss of face and position in their gender rankings.

"An ex-Selwyn girl would have a stigma."

"Your insults are amusing. Vicki's 'price' to me is the sum of the various commitments, obligations or conditions she would require to enter into an exclusive relationship with me. For me, entering into an exclusive love relationship would entail obligations and risks that I would not want to shoulder during Finals year.

"At the end of the year I hope to have a First Class degree and will better able to compete and get more obligations from her. Our 'price' would be most tractable at the end of my course when I expect to be best qualified. At present, I cannot afford the time for her. In other words, her price is too high and I may be better able to afford her later."

"So you have decided to take a short position with Vicki?"

"What do you think?"

"Well, it makes sense for you. But I doubt that Barbara or Vicki would tolerate it."

"They do not need to know. Does the jockey in a horse race need to know when a punter changes his bets to later races?"

I am excited that I can represent my relationships with Vicki and Barbara as trades in commodity futures. This model does not yet have the last word on how to conduct my affairs with integrity and honour, but it provides a coarse screening to distinguish a rip-off from a bargain. So far, it has been useful and I am improving it steadily. Some people may think my perspective of getting together is loveless, but it is love that ultimately sets the prices and will determine whether a trade can be done.

I am drawn to this model of mating, in which girls and guys choose exchanges of commitment not only in the present but in the future. They can "buy" or "sell" with payments for delivery now or in the future. It is even possible to "sell" now rights they do not hold. How could this change my relationships with Vicky and Barbara?

Rule 29: *All love matches are honoured in the same way, but each match dishonoured is dishonoured in a different way.*

CHAPTER 30 INVULNERABLE

When Vicki had me on the lie detector, the only time I had answered untruthfully was when I was asked:

"Have you wanted to have two girlfriends at the same time?"

"No," I lied.

Girls of my age are intolerably experimental with their emotions and the vagaries of monogamy can distract me from my work. There is less risk of disruption if I have two girls who live apart and who I consider are substitutes. If one is incapacitated, the other one can take over.

"The type of deal you want is called a straddle," Wilbur tells me. "You place a simultaneous buy and sell order on substitute commodities. Suppose one girl's love is like wheat and another's is like barley. My analysis of prices for the past 20 years shows that barley is normally about 20% of the price of wheat, but the gap now is closer, about 10%, with no good reason. It has to widen when the market corrects. That's how I make money. Do you know what short selling is?"

I am ready for this question because I looked it up the day before. "The sale of a borrowed commodity with the expectation that it will become more affordable?"

"Yes. It sounds an easy way to make a profit."

"No easier than going long. But it is not just a gamble. Some buyers are users who are prepared to pay a high price. So it's risky."

"It seems like you have to be in the know to make a steady profit," I say cautiously.

"That's right. You may be lucky once or twice but the speculators who make money study form and offset risks with other trades. I have an investment scheme that is a certainty. Are you interested?"

"How much?"

"Two hundred pounds should do it. Are you interested?"

"I can get the money on overdraft from my father's account, so long as it is returned when he pays the farm rent, at the end of September."

"That will be past the closing date and by then you will have, hopefully, a big profit."

"How confident are you of a profit?"

"It's a cinch."

"Why should the gap have a certain width?" I ask him.

"The gap is technological. The recent narrowing is a mistake by the market, an aberration. Barley is a less expensive substitute for wheat in livestock feeds. Normally, if the gap closes this much, wheat is preferred and barley rejected. New demand for wheat will drive the price of wheat up, while barley will fall, until the gap becomes wide enough for substitution to be attractive again and the gap returns to normal. The differences in milling, nutrition, storage and transport values create a negative feedback system that regulates a certain amount of substitution. In other words, the gap self-regulates itself constant. The only reason the gap could get narrower is if there is a change in the technology that favours substitution. For example, if someone discovers new nutrition benefits from barley compared with wheat, the gap would become narrower. I have searched industry literature and news articles but there is no reason for the gap to be so narrow. Today's market prices are out of kilter with those for the past twenty years."

"That's amazing."

"If you want, you can come in on my next trade. You will need at least 200 pounds. My broker operates on 2% 'margin', or deposit. So your investment will actually be 50 times 200, or 10,000 pounds. He will sell 5,000 pounds worth of barley short for you, expecting the price to go down. With the proceeds he will buy about 5,000 pounds worth of wheat, expecting the price to go up."

"Who is putting up the 98%?"

"No-one yet. Delivery is not until the end of September. That's why they are called 'futures'."

"If the gap under your straddle widens, that is, barley goes down and wheat goes up, you will make a killing."

When I look at the historical prices data he has graphed, it seems like a sure thing to me; they move up and down together with a gap that is almost constant.

"The best thing is that the straddle protects you against external risks, such as bad weather. If the wheat crop is destroyed, the money made on your wheat will cover your extra cost of buying back barley. If barley is destroyed, your extra cost will be offset by extra demand for your wheat."

In an epiphany, I realize the security of a straddle.

"So the long and short positions protect each other. Wow. It's brilliant. It seems like I can't lose. I'll do it."

Wilbur introduces me to his broker and I give him a cheque for the money. Two hundred pounds is a lot of money for me, compared with my rent of seven pounds a week.

That afternoon he leaves a message for me to call him.

"Margin call," he says. "Your 200 pounds is gone. The gap has narrowed even further. What are you going to do?"

I bite my lip. This is not what Wilbur said would happen. I hope he knows what he is doing.

"I'll go again," I say.

The following morning the broker leaves another message to call him. I have a sinking feeling.

"Margin call. The gap is still narrowing. You need to cover your losses," he tells me. "I need another 200 pounds from you. What are you going to do?"

It is a risky business, all right. I will have put in 600 and lost 400 in a day.

"I can't afford it," I say.

"Then you'll have to quit or break a leg. Which one?" the broker says.

"Are they both still narrowing?"

"Yes. Wheat is down a little. Barley is going up faster."

"Then close the barley."

"Will do."

When I tell Wilbur I am "out of" my barley position, he whistles. "I'm still hanging in there with the straddle. I really don't see why the gap has narrowed the way it has. That's why I'm putting my shirt on it. If I had to get out, I would not break a leg, as you have. I would quit both. I hate to be exposed like you are, owning 200 x 50 = 10,000 pounds worth of wheat with the price falling. They can make you take delivery, you know, even if it is worthless, and you still have to pay the price you bought it for, plus transport to your storage. I wouldn't be able to sleep at night. You had better pray for bad weather, crop disease, or a crop failure in China or Russia, to increase the wheat price. If there is an unexpected bumper wheat harvest, you could have to pay for a loss of all 10,000 pounds, or have to take delivery of several railway wagons of wheat on credit."

For the next three weeks, I anxiously study wheat price trends and weather reports. Slowly the September wheat price falls steadily, closing the gap as predicted, but I no longer have barley making a profit to cover my loss. I sell the wheat a week before the end of term for a total loss of 400 pounds. I have only a week to replace the money before my father checks his overdraft. I am distraught. It is more than I spend in a term and he cannot fail to notice that my expenditure has doubled. There are a couple of people who I can try for a loan before I sell my car.

Wilbur has made a good profit, and I ask him first.

"Sorry, I don't do loans," he says. "I'm already over-exposed to commodities without lending to other investors. You'll raise it somehow. The name of the game is resilience. Those who hang on get their profit from those who have to quit. To make money, it's best to have money."

I try to be philosophical about my loss. The straddle concept is brilliant but there are still risks and you have to be a long term player to win. I thank Wilbur for the experience and leave it at that. But I want to pursue the idea of a straddle in a notional commodity love market, as a way of protecting myself from hurt and distraction when love goes wrong. The love market seems to me to be inherently more predictable than grains and I can look forward to a win on every play.

Rule 30: *Players who are stayers take away the wagers of losers who quit.*

CHAPTER 31   LOVE STRADDLE

If I invest in a love straddle, I can enjoy Barbara now and put off a relationship with Vicki until after Finals. She doesn't want me now in any case. Her price is too high, more than I can afford. I would have to take a risk and give up Barbara, and then spend a lot of time with Vicki. Even then, it might not be enough. I could find myself alone and vulnerable when facing the most difficult competition of my life. I simply cannot afford Vicki at present.

After Finals, I hope that Vicki will accept me at a price I can afford. I will give up Barbara and have plenty of time for Vicki. I would be able to commit to her, sharing income from the good job I expect to get with a good degree.

My immediate problem is that unless I can borrow 400 pounds in the next day or two, my father could pull the rug out from under me, leaving me without any money to finish my degree. The bank will not be interested until I get a job, which will be too late. The only thing I can think of is to throw myself on the mercy of my friends, but it will be a big loss of face. I know of no-one else who has done this.

I start with Larry. "I need 400 pounds by the end of the week."

"Shit. How did that happen?"

I tell him about the grain straddle and how it turned out.

"Archer, you are a bloody fool!"

"It seemed quite safe."

"If it was without risk, as you thought, everyone would be in on it. Anyway, I'm sorry, but I can lend you only 50 quid because our wedding is coming up and I need every bean. Sorry."

I thought his wedding excuse was a joke.

"Thanks for that. I may have to take you up on it. I'm going to try some of the others."

"Try Richard. He's rolling in it."

I take Larry's advice and ask Richard.

"Richard, I need 400 pounds by the end of the week."

"Have you tried everyone else?"

"Not yet."

"Well, I may not be able to help. I would have to get it from a Trust and my parents are trustees and would have to approve it. What do you want if for?" I explain, as I did to Larry.

"Let me think about it," he says. "Ask me tomorrow."

The next day I feel hopeless about it and see him but don't mention it. Then, later when I am in my room forlornly trying to study, Richard comes in.

"Selwyn, I have the money ready, but it would be on conditions."

"What conditions?"

"I want you to stop chasing Vicki."

What a stroke of luck! Vicki doesn't want to know me and I want to sell her short. If I play my cards right I can get my hands on the two birds in the bush.

"Why do you want that?"

"I want Vick,." Richard says.

"But she may not want you."

"She might if she was sure you and Barbara are an item."

"But we're not. I'm just using Barbara because Vicki won't come across."

I hadn't told him I had decided to continue with Barbara.

"Do you think you will be able to get Vicki?"

"In July after Finals, maybe. At the moment, she needs more time than I have. How about I promise not to chase her until after June 30th. Is that worth something to you?"

"What would happen after June 30th?"

"I would go back to chasing her."

"You won't be here. You are thinking of getting a job overseas, aren't you?"

I had written to a mining company who wanted an engineer for their mine in South Africa. I didn't give the existence of the Apartheid system a second thought.

"I wouldn't leave until September. I can help you get a fair go with Vicki in three ways: by stopping chasing her myself; by making sure you can afford her after Finals; and by bequeathing her to you when I go overseas."

"What do you mean, 'afford her'?"

"Each girl has a unique value," I say. "The price varies between males and requires the girl's consent."

"Are you sure there is a market?", Richard asks.

"A girl's price has two components: the all-comers' market price; and an additional consent price set by the girl."

"What is the all-comers' market price?" he asks.

"This depends on the girl's position on the ladder of popularity with males. Have I talked about that with you?"

"Yeah, you did," Richard says. " Vicki is top rung. That's the problem."

"We can do a trade with her"

"How?"

"Vicki is an independent sort of girl and will want to represent herself," I say. "When the commitments are made and she has given him a consent price, if the guy can afford to close the deal in the bidding with allcomers, the deal will be done. He pays with either cash or commitment or with actions."

"The problem will be getting her consent," Richard says.

"Also, the allcomers' price for her could increase. What I can do is sell you a promise: you won't have to pay any more at the end of the year than Vicki's price to you is today."

"What is her price to me today?"

"It is more than my bid plus some."

"What is your bid?"

"Everything I have that I would commit to her: my health, my character, my possessions, my prospects and the activities I would do for her."

"Plus some."

"My guess is about another 20% to get a commitment out of her."

"That is your bid. Why not mine ?" Richard asks.

"Have you made a bid for her lately?"

"No ."

"That's why we should go by mine," I say. "We can work out the difference between us at the end of the year. The main thing that will change will be our prospects, depending on the levels of our degrees."

"What's your role in this going to be?" Richard asked.

"I am like a car broker," I tell him. "You know, you tell them what car you want, in what condition and they give you a price you will have to pay them. You give a deposit now, which is 400 pounds. They know the car market and where to get cars for sale from at the lowest prices. They bring cars for you to inspect. When you have chosen one, you pay them the amount agreed and they pocket the saving they have made. They may also charge you a fee, a percentage or a flat amount.

"So I know you want Vicki, but can't afford her now and expect to be able to. You won't have to pay any more than you would now. That's how a short works."

"What if her price goes up?"

"It's a risk I am prepared to take," I say.

"So you must think it is more likely her price will go down and you'll make a profit on that?"

"Who knows with Vicki? It's even-handed."

"So what's in it for you?" Richard asks.

"If you are unable to settle with me, I will not obtain her for you and keep your deposit."

"400 pounds! What are you going to be doing that's so difficult?"

"I am taking a risk that she will want more from you than from me," I answer. "I will have to pay the difference."

"If this gets out it is likely to cruel our wicket with Vicki," Richard says. "It has to be secret from her."

"Absolutely. The deal is both of us will drop her now and I promise you to buy her back in July, and with her consent, turn her over to you. Her price to you will be the same as to me today, plus 20% with a 400 pound non-refundable deposit."

"So why should she choose me?"

"She may prefer you."

"It seems unlikely. You seem to have cheated and lied yourself on to the top rung of the ladder."

"Fuck you too. I'll be going overseas and she has to stay here to finish her degree. So I will be setting you up with her. I will bequeath her to you."

"What if she sets her price higher than I can afford?"

"If her consent price is too high, the match with you is called off."

"But she might set it lower for you."

"As I said, I will be going away. Obviously, I can't deliver you a girl against her wishes but I can make sure you get a fair go with her. It could make all the difference. You'll get a lot of traction from this short."

"What if you don't come good? What if you are just setting this up to get Vicki?"

"I'll give you your money back, all 400, if Vicki and I start something before I go overseas."

"Fair enough. But this deal has to be strictly confidential."

"Of course."

"Shouldn't Vicki have validated it?"

"It doesn't concern her yet. It is an agreement between the two of us. Her consent to supply will be sought when I bid to cover my short with you, by June 30th."

"If you blab I will tell her you accepted 400 to stop seeing her. She won't be impressed."

I replied, "I would tell her that you have paid for me to get her for you at the end of the year and if she and I get together you would extort 400. That's pretty underhand, too."

"Do we need to put this in writing?" he says. "It would have no legal status."

"I'm not likely to forget," I say. "But you might, so I'll write it down while you write me a cheque."

Agreement

'I *Selwyn Archer (The Seller) agree at the Agreement Date to a short sale of the commodity love from Vicki Hillstone, (The Supplier, by consent) to Richard Armitage (The Buyer) for delivery by 30 June 1967.*

'*By June 30th, 1967 The Seller will endeavour to obtain the commodity love from The Supplier (by consent) for an exclusive relationship with The Buyer to commence on delivery and would continue after December 31st 1967. He will pay to The Buyer any difference in the amount of The Seller's equivalent obligations to The Supplier (by consent), between the date of this agreement and the date such relationship commences plus 20%.*

The Buyer will pay The Seller 400 pounds on the condition that The Seller avoids all social contact with The Supplier (by consent) before June 30, 1967. If The Seller commences an exclusive relationship with The Supplier (by consent) that continues after December 31st 1967, he will repay The Buyer 400 pounds by September 30th 1970. If no such

*relationship eventuates, The Seller agrees to leave the United Kingdom by
30 September 1967 and not to return except for visits longer than 2 weeks
until after September 30th 1970.*

This agreement is strictly confidential.

Signed Seller:

Selwyn Archer

Signed Buyer:

Richard Armitage

Agreement Date: November 16th 1966

We sign. I make a copy and give it to Richard. He gives me his
cheque, which I take straight to the bank.

I feel pleased about the arrangement, as I had planned to avoid
Vicki anyway. I intend to try and get together with her at the end
of the year and if I succeed, the penalty is steep but not impossible.
I intend to go overseas anyway; so again the arrangement suits me.

In brief, I sell Vicki short to Richard with the promise to deliver
to him, adjusting for differences in our commitments, and for the
price of her consent. If he cannot afford her price to him but I can
afford mine, the transfer to him is abandoned, the short is closed
and I may keep her.

"I am selling you a promise to deliver to you Vicki's love, with
her consent, by the end of June," I tell Richard. "In the meantime,
my relationship with her will be wound up, although there isn't
much between us at present."

"What will Vicki do?"

"Although we will cease social relations, it would be good if she
keeps an exclusive interest in me."

"You don't want much."

"No," I say, but I wonder if he is being sarcastic.

I do not tell Richard that this will be a very difficult time for
me. I am hungry to possess and control Vicki, believing she is the
only one who I can be happy with. Her rejection has distorted my
reality as if it is toxic, causing me suffering without end. When I
stop daydreaming and worrying about her, it will boost my on-task
study time significantly.

When I quit, my conscience nags me that Vicki won't understand
me. The Beatles' song, "You're Going to Lose That Girl", keeps
going through my head. But it is too late. In my mind, I have taken

a "short" position on Vicki, expecting to be better able to afford her high price at the end of my course. I put all my trust in the straddle, as my solution to coping with life without Vicki.

I can use my commitments recovered from Vicki to maintain my relationship with Barbara until after Finals. I am trying to minimize my commitments to Barbara. Her persistent demands for security are difficult to countenance without making some concessions.

"What's going to happen after Finals, Selwyn?" Barbara asks.

"I'm not sure. I may go overseas to a job."

"Do you want me to come with you?"

"No. At least, not at first. Maybe when I get established you could join me," I mumble vaguely.

There is a lot at stake, and I turn to Tom for advice while keeping my deal with Richard confidential. I explain to him the straddle concept with the example of the wheat and barley. I tell Tom I have a short position on Vicki where she buys her independence now and I get a better price after Finals.

"My straddle is worth more than the two positions separately," I explain. "Because Vicki is unaffordable, I can make do with Barbara. I will finish with Barbara when Vicki lowers her price or she values my commitment more highly."

Tom chews his food slowly, thinking.

"When you buy back Vicki, won't it be from the person you sold her future out to?"

"I am supposing she buys her own independence now and then sells it back to me later for less."

"A lot of men could be interested. What makes you think she won't be snapped up by then?"

"Her price could be too much for them. She knows I will bid high at the end of the year."

"Will you be able to handle it if she gets a taker now?" Tom asks.

"Do you mean will I be jealous? I have nothing to fear. If you take the fear out of jealousy, what's left? I can imagine losing her."

"Wouldn't you try to keep her?"

"No, I know she wants too much from me now. I would stick to my plan to get her back later, after Finals. My love life is now protected from whatever the World may throw in my direction.

A straddle protects my love relationship, by offsetting risks with opposite effects on my investment. I am protected from any external circumstances that could affect my corner of the love market, such as epidemic disease, financial crises, a third wave of Women's Liberation."

"Vicki the wheat and Barbara the barley. If the girls are substitutes, you would expect their prices to follow each other up and down, with the gap staying constant.

"I am short on Vicki and long on Barbara, expecting that if Vicki goes down, I will make money, and Barbara-the-substitute will also go down and I will lose money. So overall, I will break even."

Tom links his fingers behind his head and leans back confidently.

"I think I get it," he says, shaking his head. "I am appalled that you are trying to resolve issues of love, loyalty and morality by an economic strategy. Archer, it is clear that you are a cold-hearted, selfish and cynical bastard. You will deserve it if both women tell you to piss off!" He ends this tirade at yell volume and thumps his fist on the table, making the cutlery and china jump. I can tell he is impressed.

"It's strictly confidential, of course," I gloat. "I am going to have one or the other of them, whatever happens. I will be able to get on with my study undistracted by girls."

Tom isn't the same as me. He isn't hungry to get a First Class degree. So he doesn't understand my urgency to secure my sex life. He will take his time and can afford to be more gallant.

I am studying engineering for long hours to re-establish my lead in our class for Finals year. I am eating little and irregularly and become gaunt. Bruce my flat mate is practical and suspicious of theories, whereas I see the World through a screen of theoretical understanding.. When I tell him about my commodity theory of love, his response is to laugh, wag his finger at me and say in his Australian accent, "Selwyn, you are playing with bloody fire!" I do not tell him of my deal with Richard. No-one knows except Richard and I.

Later that day, Bruce puts his head around my door and quotes Shakespeare's Julius Caesar:

'Yond Cassius has a lean and hungry look; He thinks too much; such men are dangerous.'

I recognise that Bruce is concerned about me but I do not know how to be different. I am being true to what I believe in.

To implement my straddle I need to withdraw from Vicki while setting up to get together after my Finals. It is a tricky message and I dread delivering it. If I don't say anything, she could assume I no longer want her whereas the opposite is true.

When I go to her flat to tell her, she is out and I leave a note with Marion asking Vicki to come and see me or let me know when she will be in. When I don't hear from her, I recall all the other occasions when she has avoided communicating with me and I decide she can infer that she is on the back burner rather than me telling her. Maybe if she simmers for a while she won't be so tough.

Rule 31:*A straddle in the commodity of love has to be kept secret or the behaviours wanted will be opposed.*

PART 5: INSIDER TRADING (1967)

In which a short sale is made to a buyer who has a conflict of interest with the seller.

CHAPTER 32   SHORT FLING

In the following week I put my plan for a straddle into action. I stay away from the Union coffee lounge and avoid seeing our group and Vicki. I go on a date with Barbara for the first time in four months. Her ministrations help me to study better. At the same time my study is undistracted by thinking how to get together with Vicki. Then an event occurs that I had allowed for but had not realised how profoundly it would affect me.

One Saturday evening, I am asked to a party at Vicki's. I get the message from Roger. Why couldn't Vicki ask me directly? I do not reply. Instead, I keep my date with Barbara. Next morning I am up early and having breakfast when Roger drops in.

"Hey, Selwyn, Richard screwed Vicki last night," he says.

"Whaaat?" Richard is my flat mate, my best friend. I can hardly believe it.

Roger says what I am thinking: "What a bastard! I thought she was your girl."

"Not anymore," I fake, recalling how little I had seen of her lately. "She was my girl. But this is the end."

The news knocks me off my feet and I have to sit down. Room and furniture rock as my heart pumps adrenalin for a fight with Richard. I feel like vomiting. I try to hold up a heavy curtain of grief that is descending. I try to think what this means. I gaze into the heart of my relationship with Vicki and I feel disappointment that she has chosen to do this to me. She has hurt me badly where it hurts most, in my evaluation of myself. I want to hit back.

My first thought is, "She must want him more than me. This is the end of my hopes to get her." I had not expected Vicki to sell out to Richard. I had thought she would keep her price out of reach of any suitor. I didn't imagine her waiting for me until after Finals but that was the outcome on which my hopes are pinned.

I keep asking myself, "Why did you do this, Vicki?"

I find out from Roger that Richard was at the party at Vicki's and had gone to bed with her there.

I will find out from Richard. I ask him when he comes in later.

"Did you fuck Vicki last night?" He sighs and nods slowly, looking away. "Yeh."

He is competitive enough to cheat. Always having to be on top is his undoing.

I notice that he does not apologize or offer any mitigation. On the other hand, he is anything but gloating. I can't read his expression but I believe him. It makes sense he does not lie because his answer is yes, when he could be punched for it. As Oscar Wilde said, "A good friend will always stab you in the front."

"What was it like?" I ask him. Roger once said I was primitive, placid and existential.

"Aw, Vicki is, Vicki," Richard replies and shrugs, as if she is less than satisfactory. He seems miserable. It has not been much of a night for him, anyway.

"Was she a virgin?"

He shakes his head. "No. There was a guy in Spain when she was with her family on holiday."

My intuition is that he is telling the truth. I wonder if I should fight him. Whereas domestic dogs compete openly for females when they came on heat, primates have a dominance hierarchy that reduces serious injury. Usually the best fighter, who is the heaviest with the fastest reflexes, will be dominant and mate with many or all of the females.

Richard is a heavily built endomorph, whereas I am a mesomorph, of medium build but taller. He is very strong. We arm-wrestled once and he won. We have had frequent contests in arguments about issues of public affairs. Richard has been an unpleasant opponent, persisting with orthodox ideas to the point of rudeness. Maybe he figures he is an alpha male, but he does not dominate me.

In some animals, lower ranking males bring females to the dominant male who mates with them. Wild turkey males in Texas lure females away from other groups to mate with their dominant brother. There is nothing of this arrangement in my dealings with females and I have never passed a girl on to Richard. Nevertheless, I do not see that a punch-up will achieve anything at present.

I play The Beatles' album, "'Revolver'', as I study. The song, "She Said, She Said", ends with "cause you're making me feel like I've never been born". For a week I beat myself up. Then it appears that Vicki and Richard merely had a fling. There is not going to be a relationship.

I am angry about Richard's emotional intimacy with Vicki, although some sexual jealousy does come into it, too. A woman will be more angry if her sister seduces her husband than a stranger, contradicting genetic inheritances. Similarly, Richard is an emotional intimate of mine, a good friend, like a brother, and his betrayal of trust is hurtful.

But Vicki's betrayal is an immovable object beyond my comprehension, trying to stop me having anything further to do with her.

I turn in on myself, except for dates with Barbara. I work hard. I don't let this disaster deter or distract me from my goal. I am grieving inside but I keep on going. I know I will not get over this for a very long time. I hold it against Vicki. I hold it against Richard. But most of all I hold it against myself. I continue to puzzle over Vicki's motives.

"Why do you think she did it?" I ask Tom.

"You cannot complain," he says. "You told me you had cut her adrift or, what was your term, 'sold her short'. What did you expect? She was free to find another guy. She gave Richard a try."

"I had to accept that she could try other guys, but not Richard. That was a blow below the belt!"

"How come?"

"She knew it would cause trouble between Richard and me. She knew I wanted her and it would hurt me if she went with a guy who lived with me. She has driven a wedge between us, deliberately destroying our friendship as flat mates."

"Maybe you had hurt her."

"Two wrongs don't make a right. It was nasty and unnecessary."

"I think if you have a gripe about mateship, it is with him, not her."

"You may be right. A guy doesn't go with a friend's girl as long as the friend is still interested."

"Who says?"

"It's the custom where men are in teams together, such as in the military. If a woman causes trouble between two men, it can distract them and endanger lives. A man who tries to take another's woman is out of line."

"Did Richard know you still wanted Vicki?"

"I had a special relationship with her."

"Did that allow him to go with her?"

"Only at the end of the year."

"Did she know why you were keeping away from her?"

"No. No-one knows about my straddle except you and Richard."

"Well, you seem to have botched it," Tom says. "I warned you."

"Yes, you did."

"What will you do?"

"Work; carry on as if it didn't happen. What else can I do?"

Secretly, I launch a phalanx of imaginary emotional missiles of revenge and retribution at Richard and Vicki.

I am fortunate to have the straddle still intact, with Barbara to assuage my misery. I do not need to have any contact with Vicki about this. But I am not going to take it lying down.

Rule 32: *The glory lies not in the winning but in the not losing face.*

CHAPTER 33　RETALIATION

It may seem that Richard and Vicki have walked all over me, and I have not lifted a finger in protest; but slowly and inexorably, I am pursuing my revenge.

When the urge to punch Richard subsides, I focus on how to exact my revenge on him less dramatically and more punitively. It is final year now and the work steps up to a new level of output and difficulty. Richard is extremely competitive and is, I believe, going for a First Class degree like me. The strategy I choose is to out-compete him academically, so effectively that he will lose his self-respect.

"What did you get for the assignment," Richard asks me.

"A," I tell him.

"How did you get that? I thought you showed me your final paper and mine was the same. But I only got a B. Did you do more work?"

"I cannot remember."

"Can I have a look?"

Richard has compared our grades from every exercise, and when his are lower, which is usual, he has been obsessively conscientious in finding out where he has gone wrong and making corrections. I suspect that he, too, is going for a First. For him it is an even bigger deal, and he is always worrying that others may be getting ahead.

Whereas our gang has always shared the load and copied from each other, we now break ranks and compete individually. I have always been one of the leaders whose work is passed around and copied, but now I keep it to myself and hand it in directly without sharing. I have as little to do with Richard as possible, while still living in the same flat. Richard has relied on sharing with me to get finished in time and now finds himself on his own. I set a blistering pace, and he is soon struggling to keep up. I have increased the stress on him.

Vicki has shot herself in the foot with me, as if she is sure I am bad for her, but needs to quit dramatically. She has disqualified herself and burnt her bridges. I am repelled by her, because she thinks so badly of me, because of her abuse of Richard, and because of her rejection of my honest self as exposed to her on the lie detector. Being rejected in such a humiliating way by someone you are very fond of is hurtful. I have never experienced such a slight and wonder what I have done to deserve it. Foreign feelings fluster me. I would like her to apologize and be friends because, despite this slap in the face, I still love her.

Vicki is a she-cat. In my mind, she has been transformed from a gazelle into a cheetah, from a dainty herbivore into a shy, secretive, sleek and dangerous feline that has mauled me badly. It is a paradox that her feistiness in this and in her cavalier use of the lie detector is attractive; I am still fascinated by her but I am wary of getting near her. I love her at a distance. She may have burnt her bridges but our roads still lead towards each other, and a way of crossing the gulf between us may eventuate.

Sex with Barbara always seems illicit because she makes me take her home in the middle of the night and she sneaks into her parents' home like a teenager. Before sex, we go to nice pubs in commuter territory, she drinks a pear wine, Babycham, and we eat wholesome English fare. When we go walking, it is a brief stroll along a lane in the local hills. Drugs have never crossed our path. In short, like a middle-aged couple, we have kept to the straight and narrow. My plans are incompatible with her expectations and one of us is going to be disappointed.

I spend one afternoon and evening each week with Barbara and it always ends up in bed at my flat. Sex on Saturday night is so enjoyable that I can't get enough. On the other days, I masturbate, making up for years of unfulfilled lust. At first, I am wading through swamps of Puritan guilt. It is getting better, bringing relief without hours wasted on socialization.

Barbara is a steady support in my bold plan. When I pick her up for our weekly date, I am in quite a state, my head spinning with formulae, unable to relax or small talk. Gradually, she brings me back to earth and refuels my emotions for the week ahead.

Although Barbara helps me relax, she is too conservative for me. She eschews the Free Love mentality that is tearing down the old conventions of monogamous relationships. Whereas I thrill to the surrealism of The Beatles' 'Sergeant Pepper's Lonely Heart Club Band' album and numbers like 'With A Little Help from My Friends,' she is rather old-fashioned and likes the music of Peter, Paul and Mary and The Seekers. She wears skirts to just below her knee, wears flat heels and has her hair permed like Princess Anne.

I have an uneasy feeling that my relationship with Barbara is in deeper water than I intend. It has suited me go to bed with her for a few hours each week but now it could be leading me straight up the aisle at a time when I yearn for adventure as a single man. I play The Beatles' album, "Revolver", and although I usually can't understand the meaning of the lyrics, I like the line in "Love You Too" that goes, "There's people standing 'round who'll throw you in the ground". Although I am grieving for Vicki, I lose no more sleep over her fling with Richard. The straddle provides me with emotional security and the stability I need to devote myself to my studies. I am distant with Vicki waiting for a sign of remorse but with no intention of pursuing a relationship until after Finals when my straddle has to be settled.

Rule 33:*Any change in status quo prompts an opposing reaction in the responding system (Lenz's Law).*

CHAPTER 34   BOGGED DOWN

The Final Year juggernaut rolls into the straight leading to Final exams. There are sixty survivors in direct competition. It is a stressful situation. We are loaded down with revision tasks and rumours about what will be on the exam papers. I am guided by the fifth and last principle of the marathon: save enough energy for a burst to the line with an energetic performance in the exam.

I am still jealous and angry with Richard that he slept with Vicki. The rights he bought were for delivery from me at the end of the year. I have as little to do with him as possible, while still living in the same flat. We are on the same course schedule but I have stopped travelling and eating with him. Now when he uses the kitchen at the same time as me, I remain silent. We used to chat about almost everything, arguing just for the fun of it, even though he always had to win. He tries to talk to me, but I ignore him.

He is always worrying about his position and anxious that others may be getting ahead. Those who have failed earlier in the course have disappeared. Richard has become subdued and his huge explosive laughter has gone.

Final grading for the course depends on an assigned group project. When we receive our topics for our group projects, Richard's is tough and he asks me for help. I relent and discuss it with him.

"I know fuck-all about aspirin reactors," Richard admits miserably.

"All you have to do is find out what process a chemical company chose for a recent project," I say.

It is fully a month later that Richard shows me a photocopy of a journal article on a new method of aspirin synthesis.

"This could be the best technology," he says. "Or it could be a lemon. How would I know?"

Richard has the central design task with five students in his team using his results. This is our one and only test of ability to work in a team. He is deeply cynical about the task, and I wonder if he has chosen the right course. Again my advice is cautious. I suggest he talk with his supervisor but he seems to lack confidence to do that. I could have checked it myself. Two weeks later he is still stuck on the same issue. He is way behind, with the due date approaching.

Bruce tries to help him, too, but without success. He routinely quotes books, even when it is irrelevant. His favourite book is "Guys and Dolls". He keeps a toothpick between his teeth and affects a Bronx accent. One day as Richard goes into his room and closes the door, Bruce says to me:

Of all the players this country ever sees, there is no doubt but that the guy they call The Sky is the highest. He will bet all he has and no-one can bet any more than this.

I assume Bruce is trying to comment sagely on Richard's precarious position, for leaving his assignment until the last minute. He runs the risk of running out of time, and in Finals year failure to submit the Assignment is to fail the course.

Richard is aware of his position and very anxious. He comes into my room later the same day pondering a technical article, scratching his head.

"Shit," he says, several times. "This is taking too much time."

He has stopped taking care of his appearance. He has several days' stubble, with lank greasy hair, and wears the same clothes day after day. He smells of stale sweat.

"The others want to know my inputs and outputs. I don't have a clue where to start," he says, indicating the same paper, now well-thumbed, as if he has reread it many times.

He picks invisible fluff off his sweater.

I suggest how he can generate the information quickly to catch up, but he is not able to cope.

A few days later, Richard's tutor, who knows I live with him, stops me in the corridor of the department.

"Ah, Selwyn," he says. "I am looking for Richard. Do you know where he is?"

"No. He was at home when I left this morning."

"Is he coming in?"

"I don't know. Maybe not."

"How does he seem to you?"

"Tired. He isn't able to sleep. I think he's worried about his father's health."

"Would you get him to call me?"

When I tell Richard, he phones his tutor. The tutor tells him that the other students are complaining they need his input. The tutor wants Richard to bring in what he has done so far the next day.

"Can you show me how to do the calculations?" Richard asks me, desperately.

"How far along are you?" I ask.

He has barely started. He has written part of a chemical equation in a small very sloping hand, much smaller than his usual writing. It is almost illegible. I want to discuss it with him but he has difficulty concentrating. He does not understand a key concept that we learned in second year. He has somehow missed it, probably because he was partying.

I have an urge to tell him to go to hell but I put aside my resentment and write chemical equations for his reactions.

"Thanks. What about the outputs?"

I quickly scribble out calculations for the main reactant while he picks fluff and flicks it away.

"There. You just have to do the other outputs in the same way."

He stands studying my notes for hours. I suspect I am affecting him badly but I do not know how to reach out and help him. I am unable to imagine what he is going through. He seems like a horse refusing a jump, as if he is spooked. He eventually leaves to meet with his tutor.

About this time Bruce, my other flat mate, takes to quoting to me another line from Shakespeare's Julius Caesar:

"And Brutus was an honourable man."

Flatmates normally help each other with uni assignments. I think that Bruce is hinting that I am stabbing Richard unfairly in the back, as Brutus had done to Caesar, by stopping sharing. It seems that Bruce has discovered my revenge on Richard and I feel guilty as hell, because Richard, like Caesar, is a good guy. He thought I was finished with Vicki, with some reason, and therefore reckoned I wouldn't mind.

I have checked with my tutor and he is pleased with my design.

"Your solution method is radical, but I can't fault it," he told me. "You can get a publication out of this."

All I have left to do is type up my 100-page final report. Whereas I am flying high, Richard is in the depths. During the following week, he stays in his room. He lies on the bed with his eyes open and his arms by his side, as if he wants to die. On the few occasions when we pass each other in the passageway, he mumbles "Hi," with a blast of halitosis breath and the urine smell of his clothes. There is a sore at the corner of his mouth amongst the stubble.

"How are you?" I ask

His haggard, bloodshot eyes roll up and away.

"Okay."

"You don't seem okay to me. Let me take you to the doctor." I have never seen anyone in this condition before, but I think the doctor might know what is wrong with him.

"I'll be okay, thanks."

He turns away and goes back into his room.

Later on that day, he comes into my room.

"I have an interview tomorrow for a job in Canada, with Canoil," he speaks woodenly, as if he has been rehearsing what to say. "I don't have their phone number. Would you go along and tell them I cannot make it? It's at 10am in room S102."

"Okay," I agree.

I am there on time. A suited man sits behind the desk.

"Richard apologises that he can't make it," I tell him. "He's not well."

"Oh, I'm sorry," the Canadian drawls. "Are you interested?"

"What is the job?" I ask.

My career plan so far has been to wait until I get my degree before selling myself to the highest bidder. However, Canada seems very attractive as a destination from which to end my relationship with Barbara.

He explains what Canoil does and the several types of engineer they want to recruit. The more I find out, the more interested I become. They will have me if I can get a 2.1 degree or better, which is one rung below First Class. He tells me of a graduate from the previous year that I know who works there that I can contact.

"I am very interested," I tell him.

When I get back to the flat, Richard greets the news of my possible employment as if he has again been outcompeted. His lips are chapped and frayed.

"Okay. So you'll be going to Canada?" he says hopefully.

I think then that whatever hell he is in, I do not want him to be suffering like this. If I have brought this on, then will he ever forgive me? Or, for that matter, will I ever be able to forgive myself?

The next day, Bruce takes him to hospital. I hear he is in the mental illness ward being treated with strong drugs and asleep most of the time. Whether it is pressure of work, or the pressure of living with an autodidact, his nervous system has taken him into deep depression.

I do not dare to visit him in the mental hospital as he may think I have come to gloat and I will only make him worse. It sounds like a wacky place. I cannot think of what I would say to him. So I stay away, although the others, including Vicki, visit him. I wonder if she feels at all responsible. I hear that his electric shock treatment erases memories. I hope it will wipe his memory of the Vicki saga. Perhaps I should get some, too.

Now when it is too late I realize that I have been unfair to Richard. My hostility to him has derived from my indecision and jealousy. I did not realize that it would put him in hospital and I cannot face him. As I hunker down to revise for Finals, I am filled with regret.

Rule 34: *Competitors cannot count on collaboration but may agree to share some resources and restrict the demands of real competition.*

CHAPTER 35 FINAL EXAMS

My straddle works, and I am able to work steadily throughout third year. I have enough energy left after two and a half years in our course to take final exams on the burst, with huge cramming time carefully spent.

The work is like a drug, for the more revision I do, the more I want to do. I study exam papers from previous years, looking for patterns of topics, to predict what we will get, and prepare answers. When I stick to my notes, the work is tedious. I learn best using engineering theories to come up with new solutions to real-world problems.

As the exams near, I step up my effort level. The other guys often take time off to go out in the evening to a party. They ask me if I want to come. At first, I think they are being friendly but I soon realize they want to stop me getting ahead. Roger and Tom drive past my room on their way home as dawn is breaking and find me hitting the books, the same as when they left.

At last, Finals are upon us. The atmosphere is electric as sixty of us assemble outside the oak door of Main Hall. Bearing down on us from the architrave is a colourful heraldic shield with the university motto, "Credo Ad Astra". It means roughly "I think big". It seems especially apropos our situation. A few of us are finishing memorising from notes the remainder of three years of learning. Five minutes before the doors are due to open, someone starts singing "The Engineers' Wheel", and we all join in the mechanical chant, quietly at first and then with gusto.

The foul song is our revolt against a cruel system. We have suffered the competition of exams ever since the 11-plus, nine years ago, had our friends weeded out, with those of us who have survived reduced to eying each other as opponents. The great doors swing open to admit us, and the atmosphere is intense competition. We sit at single desks in precise rows. The exam papers are hidden from view inside folders. We are told to open them and peruse the paper for ten minutes. My perusal shows me that I can work out answers to most of the questions. As I start writing, in my mind I can hear The Supremes singing "The Happening" and this "earwig" continues, buoying me up throughout the exam.

I have come with three full fountain pens. Twice during each exam paper I refill all of them from a bottle of Quink. I have two slide rules for calculations. When one becomes warm from the friction of continual use and thermal expansion threatens to reduce accuracy, I change to the other.

For four hours I write like a whirling dervish, right up to when we are told to stop. The answer books have ten pages each. Most students get done in one, but I fill three. I finish mid-sentence when I am stuck, so the marker will be sympathetic and will mark the answer higher, because I was limited by time rather than by ability.

There are four exams, on four consecutive days. After each exam, I leave the hall exhausted and join the others in the Union bar, sitting stupefied, forgetting. There is little talk about the exam and by the time I go home to do final preparation for the next one, little of the subject matter remains in my memory. After the final exam I drink myself stupid, vomit and sleep for about twenty-four hours. The memory of the exam remains in nightmares to this day.

The level of our engineering degrees will be determined largely by performance in Finals. A good professional engineer is supposed to be able to solve problems from memory under pressure from competitors. This may have been the situation during World War II but it does not seem relevant today.

Immediately exams are over, Larry hands me a fancy wedding invitation. I sit down from shock. It is from a Mr & Mrs Weinstein to attend the marriage of their daughter Lisa to Larry Anapolis at Hepworth Synagogue in a month's time. It is a fate as far removed from my own planning as going to the North Pole.

"I'm gobsmacked! Larry, you a married man!"

"Why not?"

"I can't imagine myself getting married for years." I have a list of goals to accomplish, including years of travel and adventure, fast cars, fast women, a yacht and a pilot's licence.

"Have you told that to Barbara?" asks Larry.

"Yes."

"What does she say?"

"She accepts it. Larry, getting hitched is a serious thing. You should be careful what you get into. Are you sure you know what you're doing?"

"Yes, I'm sure."

"What's the point in getting married so young?"

"We want to be married."

I cannot get any sense out of him. It is true that I have told Barbara I am going away but I am not sure she accepts it. Larry is my first friend to marry. It should not come as a surprise to me, because their engagement was a year ago. I had thought it was simply a strategy of Larry's to bed a prim and proper girl. Now I understand why.

Larry's marrying Lisa puts my relationship with Barbara under a microscope. I should finish with her. We have been together for over a year and people will draw parallels, not least because Barbara and Lisa are friends from school. Whereas Larry has never looked at another girl, my attention has never been exclusively on Barbara. People know that I have the hots for Vicki.

This wedding is a spanner in my works. It brings home to me that already the hottest chicks are being snapped up. I do not plan to settle down until I want kids, not until about ten years' time. There is a price to pay, not only in getting the leftover girls, unless I go younger with fewer experiences in common, but also in being credited by employers with being more reliable and responsible. Larry, who is also joining Canoil, will be well ahead of me in getting promotions to positions requiring solidity, if I am still womanizing the way I plan to. Unless I can get Vicki to come across. Then we would plan together for our missions: mine is to help the poor and hers is to help troubled youths.

With exams over, I can concentrate on my neglected social relationships. Will I now be able to afford Vicki? Among the commitments she will want is to be exclusive, but will I have qualms about finishing with Barbara?

Rule 35: *Exams that require skills of remembering also develop skills of forgetting.*

CHAPTER 36 MAKING THE GRADE

Time crawls towards announcement of my results from the three year course. Our immediate futures rest on the grading of our degrees: as First; Second, level one or two; Third; or Ordinary Class. They will be our tickets to the future. Many of us have been offered jobs conditional upon achieving a particular class of degree. After three years of hard work we don't know where we stand. We are all anxious that by a combination of insufficient intelligence, inadequate preparation, too much cheating on exercises, bad nerves on exam day and bad luck in remembering the wrong formulae, we have blown it and failed. We could possibly get a degree at so low a level, that it will be a hindrance, rather than an asset, in getting a job. I have my fingers crossed: I want second level one or better for Canoil.

Although I am no longer seeing Vicki, it now seems myopic of me to have turned my back on her. I had earlier toyed with the idea of bringing Barbara out to Canada when I was settled, but now I am sure I want to be with Vicki, even if this means turning down Canoil and staying in the UK where she has family obligations besides uni. I will have to finish with Barbara in the next couple of days. With my degree up in the air, it is too difficult. If she thinks I have deliberately exploited her, I will have to face the music. I know I will need a very good result to attract Vicki, presuming she is interested. I will shortly be free to start a relationship with her to close my straddle. She is staying on for two more years in Liverpool to finish her course. I doubt if she will want me if I am going to Canada. I will wait until after I have my results to decide what to do.

I go into the Department daily as I wait for results. I wait with the others, relaxed but apprehensive. Now that the work is finished, my classmates open up. These visits usually turn into socials and we hang out in the Union Coffee Lounge and listen to The Beatles' new single, "All You Need Is Love". It is the lull before the storm of results, and we batten down the psychological hatches and for a couple of weeks we get to understand the meaning of "existentialism". We have an intense preoccupation with the present.

At last we are notified that results will be announced the next day at 10.00am.

At 9.45 there is a crowd packed around the Course Coordinator's office. We hush when he comes out and begins to read.

"Abingdon, James, Honours Second, Level One."

"Aldridge, Arthur, Ordinary, Pass."

"Shit," says Arthur.

No-one laughs, fearing he will be next.

The news is usually received in silence with only an exhalation of breath in the crowded silence. A few people swear and there are a few "wows" of pleasure. Slowly the names reach mine.

"Archer, Selwyn. First Class Honours."

"Yeeeeee hah!" I whoop, rodeo style, my yell shattering the silence and echoing around the dark and brooding corridors of the Engineering Department. It is a full-on cowboy whoop, learned at the Calgary Stampede the previous summer. Those who already know their fate are amused.

"You're a fucking cheat, Archer."

"How much did that cost you?"

Before you judge me as a conceited ass, consider for a moment that all of those assembled there had benefited from many hours I had put into community service, first as Secretary and then as Treasurer of the Engineering Society. This was not a glamorous post and I had been elected unopposed. My duties had included badgering individuals for their subscriptions, sometimes meeting rudeness.

"I'm busy, Archer! Come back later."

My precious time was regarded by some as cheap. I helped instigate a coffee service, with my friends rostered to help clean up the mess left by classmates who were too inconsiderate to bin their empty mugs. I had organised excursions, visits, functions and speakers, duties that reduced my study time. I was taken for granted. Consequently, when my degree success was announced, I wanted those present to realize that serving the community had not hindered me from achieving to my full potential. I had networked and tapped into the community's engineering experience.

Anyway, at the announcement of results, my yell racks up the tension, especially for those lower down the alphabet. Larry gets an Ordinary, as he had hoped. A rumour is that his pass rewards him for his excellent work as President of Engineering Society.

Tom gets a Second Level Two and he is pissed off. He left studying until too late and must have blown the exams.

Roger gets a Second Level One, which he says is okay, but I know he is disappointed, as he was hoping for a First.

When it is all over, we stay around mulling over the surprises in the results. I go to my tutor's office to say goodbye.

"First Class, eh, Archer! Well-deserved, too. Your assignment is a corker. I'm going to publish your method and you'll have your name on it. Not bad for an undergraduate! It's a brilliant piece of work: accurate and easy to use. You have a bright future in maths modelling. Why don't you stay on here and do a PhD? It will take only one year. There's a full scholarship available."

It is attractive but I have had enough of university for the moment.

"Thanks, but no. I want to get some experience in industry."

"You're joining the right outfit. Canoil's parent is United Oil and they are in the lead with their reservoir models. They have some whopping reservoirs to get your teeth into."

It will do for a start, I think.

We shake hands. He is a great teacher, one of several who are generous in passing on the skills of the profession. I am sad to be leaving but there is no reason to stay any longer.

I go over to the Students' Union. On the way I pass Vicki and tell her my result. She is very pleased for me, holding her hand over her mouth.

"A First," she gasped. "Oh, Selwyn! Well done. You worked so hard."

I am embarrassed that she has two more years of counselling studies ahead of her.

"I think you'll do well in counselling," is all I can think of to say.

"I'm doing my best."

I think she is, for the first time after three years. When she applies herself, as she is now, I suspect that she will get an excellent result. She understands people in a way that makes me feel inadequate. I have had a diet of maths, physics, chemistry and engineering for the past seven years. When I go to the theatre and see a Shakespeare play, I glimpse a world where people's characters are complex, with hidden motives. I realise my motives with girls have no more subtlety than our farm's rams when turned out with the ewes. Because of inexperience I do not understand Vicki's motives at the Cambridge Ball, in using the lie detector on me and in her fling with Richard. My infatuation with Vicki has primitive emotions, and during the time when my relationship with her has been postponed, there has not developed enough trust between us for the relationship to become exclusive and lasting. I am still love-addicted to Vicki, but it is bringing me only hunger pangs from an appetite that has little possibility of ever being fulfilled.

I must finish with Barbara. With Finals over, I have needed her less and sometimes I have forgotten to call her. I don't know exactly when or how to say goodbye to Barbara but I am not worried that she will be hurt, because it has always been likely. She is not dependent on me and seems to find plenty to do on the other six nights of the week. She has a good job and meets a lot of people.

When I phone her at work to finish with her, she congratulates me, saying she knows how much it means to me. Our relationship has lived in the shadow cast by my ambition. Now it is exposed to the cold light of day. Finishing with her seems ungrateful and mean, after sharing a bed with her every Saturday night for the past year.

"What will you do now?" she asks plaintively.

She knows that I no longer need her. I will do the dirty deed that evening.

"I'm going to take you out this evening. I'll pick you up at 6pm."

When I arrive her mother asks me in. Her father is in the lounge and shakes my hand.

"Congratulations."

He tells me it is in the newspaper that I had been awarded the Faculty prize for the best all-round student.

Then there is silence and they look at me as if I am supposed to do or say something. I feign disinterest and we go to my flat and to bed as usual. However, I forget to finish with her. My relationship with Barbara has reached a cross-roads. My plans to go to Canada are set. I have not asked her to go with me. In my mind there is a possibility, a small one, that I will want her to join me there later when I am settled, perhaps after a year. She is not my type but I like her and am grateful to her. I know that if I say anything about commitment, her mother will embark on a Plan. That would be most unwelcome, as I am rejoicing in my freedom from imperatives after fifteen years of discipline within the education system. Again, I put off finishing with her.

I feel foolish about my lie in Boston that I do not want to have two girlfriends at the same time. I realize that I have to finish with Barbara and fix the day. I am thwarted, for Barbara surprises me by going for a month's holiday in Majorca with Margot.

I spend the six weeks until I leave Liverpool socializing. We sit around, drinking coffee with our gang and generally having fun. For three years we have been on a high, feeling privileged. It has separated us from the local people and has kept us largely within the exclusive enclave of the Redbrick campus and our castle, the Students' Union Building. Although we have had a good time at uni, most of us are happy to be leaving.

Vicki socializes with us although she is not finishing. She is friendly with me but won't go out on a date.

"Will you eat out with me?" I ask.

"What about Barbara?" she says.

"She has gone to Majorca."

"Ask me again later, Selwyn," Vicki says, turning away.

My academic results are everything I hoped for and more, but I am unable to close my straddle with Richard for Vicki. Although Richard is getting better, he is not well enough for Vicki. So she is mine if she will have me. Until Barbara returns I cannot finish with her, and consequently my relationship with Vicki continues in limbo.

Rule 36: *When a person gains a professional qualification, they have more to commit in a love relationship and become more attractive to potential lovers.*

CHAPTER 37   BEST MAN

With Barbara away, Larry and Lisa's wedding is an opportunity to renew my relationship with Vicki. I hope to be able to plan a future together with her. I will finish with Barbara on her return.

I am pleased when Larry asks me to be Best Man. It will be a Jewish wedding. Larry tells me my overall job, as best goy, is to ride shotgun, so that he will be in good shape and relaxed for the wedding ceremony.

On the day before the wedding, I stay with Larry all day. I make him scrambled eggs and coffee. He writes a letter to Lisa, who he hasn't seen for a week and she replies. Her letter is a masterpiece of ambiguity and tasteful sexual innuendo.Larry gives me the wedding contract he will sign tomorrow to read, and I slip into my familiar analytical role.

Lisa is required to provide "conjugal rights", and he will give her "xxx". A word had been omitted.

"What word goes there. Is it 'sex'?" I ask.

"Usually 'children'," he laughs. "Any other ideas?"

"Why is it omitted?" I ask him, puzzled.

"I think it is left out for me to fill in. She wants me to add it, to show I want children with her. What do you think?"

"Could be."

I go on reading. In addition to esteeming, feeding and supporting each other, Lisa is bringing 100,000 pounds worth of valuables, while he will add assets of 100,000 pounds, which he promises he will pay down to the last cent even by mortgaging his property.

"That's a lot," I say. "Where do you have assets like that?"

"In my head," he says. "That's what my education is worth. It's like money in the bank."

"You are starting on 4000 pounds a year," I say. He is starting at Canoil on the same rate as me. "It will take you a very long time – twenty-five years. When do you have to have it by?"

"As long as it takes, unless we divorce. Then I would have to borrow it. What do you think?"

"You may not be able to afford a divorce for a while," I say.

"No," he says. "I'm taking a chance. She wants that much security."

"It seems pretty even-handed. Lisa puts in valuables, and you put in promises."

"It is traditional," he says. "Sometimes the man does not have any assets."

"He wouldn't be likely to get a girl who is loaded."

"She could keep her valuables for herself."

"It seems very mercenary."

"Love has a business side, like everything else."

"Yes." I give him back the contract. After that, we don't talk about money any more.

The other guys come with us to see Peter Sellers in "Doctor Strangelove". It is about Cold War brinkmanship that goes wrong. Larry has seen it six times.

Afterwards we go back to his flat, drink a couple of bottles of wine. There is sadness lurking, as this is the last time we will all be together. But Larry is his usual ebullient self. We are all happy for him and wish him the best.

The next morning, we all get dressed up at Larry's flat. We have white ties, pleated shirts, cummerbunds, tails, waistcoats, top hats and shiny black Oxfords hired by Lisa's father.Larry and I are met at the synagogue by the Rabbi and two men in suits. They witness his signing of the contract.

Larry has to identify Lisa, So, accompanied by a playing a fiddle, mandolin and guitar, we go into the bride's room. She is radiant, ensconced on a throne, surrounded by her family and friends, wearing a low-cut gown with a bodice sequinned with pink pearls and cascades of white satin folds. After a week apart, they only have eyes for each other. He covers her face with a veil. The Rabbi walks out first in the procession, followed by Larry and me, his parents, the grandparents, the groomsmen, the bridesmaids, the flower girl, the ring bearer, the bride, and finally her parents. I have never been in a synagogue before. We go outside on to the lawn where a canopy is festooned with flowers.

"This tent represents our married home," Larry tells me.

The two mothers break plates underfoot.

"This shows that a marriage is easily broken and can never be repaired," he says. He goes inside the canopy, and Lisa circles around the outside.

Bruce, who is Jewish, explains to me as we watch. "This represents the seven days of creation.".

Barbara is away in Majorca, and I am enjoying the wedding as a free agent. I look across at Vicki who is wearing a mini-dress that clings to her superb curves. When she looks at me I make goggle-eyes, showing my amazement at the proceedings, and she smiles.

A cantor sings the Hebrew words of a traditional song, achieving amazing nasal resonance. After swapping rings and receiving everyone's blessings, the Rabbi reads the contract aloud.

"The contract is now legally binding under Jewish law," Bruce whispers.

Larry wraps a glass in a piece of cloth and crushes it under his heel as guests yell, "Mazaltov".

"They are saying 'Good Luck'," Bruce says. "The broken glass shows that what has been done can never be undone. They say it is the last time he can put his foot down."

"Is that a joke?" I ask Bruce.

He nods, with a smile. He knows I never get jokes.

We all go into a hall and sit down to a feast. I am Master of Ceremonies, with five long tables of guests receding away from me. I feel very honoured but nervous that I will blow my speech.

When people have finished the first course, Lisa's father welcomes everyone. Then Larry thanks Lisa's parents and compliments the bridal party. After that I speak.

"My name is Selwyn Archer and I am the best man Larry could find for this job, because beside me he seems reasonably normal. It is hard to get a balanced view of Larry because he is essentially unbalanced or eccentric, as are all truly creative people. Getting married is one of the few conventions he has ever followed.

"Before I am howled down or thrown out on the street, I want to thank Larry, on behalf of the bridal party, for his thanking them, in his words, 'for the extraordinary efforts they have made to look good'. Larry is a spin artist but this was a wide. They asked me to say that what he meant to say is that they 'have set aside their individual and diverse excellences, to make

a uniformly beautiful group, as a frame for the infinitely greater beauty of the bride, for the splendour of this occasion.

"For almost three years, Larry has stuck out from our group like a sore thumb. There are twelve of us here today – stand up, please – enough for a cricket team. Larry, you can stay sitting down because you are the captain. Larry makes things happen. He is Chairman of the Engineering Society and has led us in organising dances, dinners and socials very profitably, speaking with my treasurer's hat on. Larry's leadership in our biggest project, the Channel Car crossing, was brilliant. He thought outside the box, floated a vision of something different, pumped us up to get it started, held us in a group when we would have fallen out, maintained our enthusiasm when we lost our way and kept us from going under when we were tired.

"Larry is a man who habitually controls situations. For example, he led us in putting on a dance called Public Hanging. The Liverpool Post received this letter:

Dear Editor,

Are your readers aware that students at the university are holding a dance at which a Public Hanging is advertised to take place? Even if no-one is hurt it will be a degrading spectacle. It is disgraceful that such a barbaric event should be celebrated by presenting it to young people as entertainment. Would you please persuade your readers to embargo this cruel event?

Yours sincerely

Iva Longdrop

"The writer was, of course, Larry. Every student for kilometres around was attracted by Larry's publicity stunts. Under his leadership, the Engineering Society enjoyed steady large revenue with corresponding benefits for members. I have heard he is working on a takeover bid for Apple Records.

"Captain Larry had foresight. On the paddle car stunt, he borrowed two powerful outboard motors to supplement the paddle wheels. The half-tide was running so strongly across Calais harbour entrance that we needed all the power we could muster to reach our destination. It is true to say that he has led England into Europe.

"If you were to ask, who is boss, Lisa or Larry, their friends would say 'We don't know, maybe neither.'

" These two seem to work it out naturally. When I went to the zoo the other day, the keeper, who was a woman, told me "The lioness is boss. At feeding time, she eats first and he has what's left. She is dominant."

"Okay," I said. "If I were to go in their cage, what would happen?"

"He would attack you," she replies.

"Then, who is dominant depends on the situation," I say.

"No," she replies, "he won't attack unless she says so."

"It is a true story .Everyone has a boss, even our captain. When Lisa tells Larry what to do, he does it. Besides being very beautiful, she has helped keep our group together. Working behind the scenes through Larry, she gets independent-minded engineers like us to collaborate as a united force. Their experience of working together and the friendships these two have forged have set the stage for their future success together as leaders.

"The three of us are going to Edmonton in Canada. Both Larry and I are joining Canoil. Larry is going into Sales, while I will start in Exploration. I will not explore for the North Pole, but for oil by drilling holes. Mark Twain described a mine as a hole in the ground with a liar on top. When I am in a hole it will be good to know I have Dave up top because he never tells lies and nor do I. Vicki, take note of that.

"Would you now rise and raise your classes to the Bride and Groom."

Afterwards, the band plays Hava Nagila and we dance the hora, with everyone's arms linked in a wheeling circle, changing direction, moving all as one. I hold Vicki on one side and Lisa's sister, the chief bridesmaid, on the other.

Vicki is stunning. Her hair is bobbed with a jewelled clasp, and she is wearing a light-blue pastel mini-dress stopping a hand-span above her knees. She has platform-soled knee-length white vinyl boots with blue polka dots and a matching shoulder bag with her camera and flash unit. When she takes a shot, she contorts her body, showing off her perfect legs and curvaceous physique.

We lift Lisa and Larry up on chairs over our heads. They hold a handkerchief between them, symbolising that they are now joined together. Then there is dancing for the rest of the evening. I dance with several girls. Vicki is in demand, and I have difficulty getting a dance with her.

"Great speech," she says as I take her in my arms. The band is playing the Beatles' "She's Leaving Home", a moving song about a girl leaving the parents who have nurtured her. As we pass Lisa and Larry, I see that Lisa is weeping. Larry has told me that leaving all her family in Liverpool and going to live in Canada is a big step for her. It will be the first time she has lived away from home.

I dance with Vicki. She is distant, and although she smiles beatifically, it is her public face. Inside, I can see sadness.

"You will have different friends next year," I say, enjoying being with her.

"Yes," she agrees. "Although Richard will probably still be here."

I keep down the jealousy that wells up in me.

"You'll have counselling friends, too."

"Yes," she says unenthusiastically.

"Are they different from us engineers?"

"Yes. They know about relationships."

It is true with me; I do not understand relationships. I want to ask her about her fling with Richard and what she thinks of my crush on her, shown in the lie detector test. But I don't have the courage. I can't face the possibility of even more rejection.

"Help me to take Larry and Lisa to their hotel, will you?" I ask her.

"Okay," Vicki says, with a smile. She seems pleased to be asked.

We go with the couple in their rented limousine to the hotel and make sure everything is all right. They will be staying at Lisa's parents' place after the honeymoon until they leave for Canada in two months' time.

"What did you think of the wedding?" Vicki asks.

"It seems very, er, final," I reply. "A couple would want to be sure of each other—that they trust each other."

I still don't trust Vicki completely, but I'm getting there. Now is the time to resume the relationship with her that I put off early in the year in order to concentrate on my studies. When Barbara comes back shortly, I will finish with her and try to revive my relationship with Vicki. I have given up on waiting for Vicki to un-clam or apologise about her fling with Richard. It isn't her style to meet me halfway. I am ready to capitulate.

Rule 37: *A wedding is a market where guests futures as love commodities are revalued.*

CHAPTER 38   COMING OF AGE

Vicki, and I, with Tom, Bruce and Roger, turn twenty-one around Finals time. We organise a birthday bash soon after Larry and Lisa's wedding. Most of us will be splitting from Liverpool after the degree ceremony in a couple of weeks' time and we don't know when we'll see each other again. We book the clubhouse at the uni's Naval Squadron through Bruce, who belongs. It is a grand mansion on the waterfront, but too small for family and friends from home to come. We book The Mods, a local group who do The Beatles, Beach Boys and Simon and Garfunkel songs. Our guest list has forty students and their partners. Most of the partners are friends with more than one of us, as we hang out in the same crowd.

"Will you go with me?" I ask Vicki.

"Won't you be going with Barbara?"

"No. She's still away. I am going to finish with her when she gets back."

Vicki hesitates. I had told her this before.

"This time I really will do it," I add.

"Hmm. I think I will go alone."

I decide to go alone, too. I will try to get together with Vicki at the party.

When I arrive, it is twilight and the car park is almost full. The mansion has Tudor black timbering infilled with white plastered walls and gabled window bays. Smokey oil lamps lead to a porch with a thick wooden door, slightly ajar. I go into a hallway. On the left is a large room where a four-piece rock group is playing vigorously beside a large unlit fireplace. The room is lit flashily by a chandelier and jammed full with people in their early twenties, the males in black ties and dinner suits and the girls in ball gowns. They are dancing, drinking, or both. Several people wave to me. In the room opposite, our volunteer barman pours me champagne.

The five of us each do a turn on the small stage. Vicki, Angela and Marion mime The Supremes' "Stop! In The Name Of Love". A steel band, friends of Tom, plays reggae music, and Roger and Tom compete in the limbo. Bruce plays Rolf's "Tie Me Kangaroo Down Sport" on his ukulele. Roger performs a series of card tricks he had purchased in a kit. My piece is "Toreador" from Bizet's "Carmen", which I play by trumpeting with my mouth like an elephant. My encore number is "La Paloma", and an ensemble of mouth-trumpeters joins in and ends the concert on a high note.

The band comes back on and starts into The Beatles' "With a Little Help from My Friends". I dance with Vicki. It is a close one, followed by Elvis Presley's, "Love Me Tender". It feels good to have my arms around her after so long. This may be my last chance of renewing the relationship with Vicki. Perhaps I can close out the short on her first and then dispose of my long position with Barbara after. I am apprehensive about finishing with Barbara as I fear a scene. It would be cowardly to do it by telephone when she returns from holiday. I will have to meet up and tell her.

I put my mouth close to Vicki's ear, to be heard above the music.

"What are you aiming for now you're twenty-one?" I shout. I genuinely want to know because what is inside her head has always been such a mystery to me.

"I want to find inner peace," she yells into my ear.

"How?" is all I can think of to say, because inner peace is not a topic I have heard engineering students mention.

"Meditation."

I imagine her sitting cross-legged on her bed.

"By yourself?" I ask hopefully, always ready to have a new experience with her.

"Yes. No! I'd like to meet someone who wants what I do," she tells me at the end of the song.

"Who?" I ask jealously.

Vicki laughs. "You are hopeless, Selwyn."

"Oh, I see. You were hypothesising such a person exists. Well, I want inner peace, too! I exist."

"You? You're too ambitious," she says. "You want to be a big shot. There's not much peace in that."

Suddenly the house plunges into darkness and the amplifiers stop working. The band is tinny and too quiet. The singer yells out the song with sixty pairs of feet shuffling on the creaky wooden floor. There is heavy breathing in the darkness and people collide often, with grunts, squeaks, giggles and apologies.

"Is there an engineer present?" an officious voice calls out.

There is laughter.

There is a loud slap, and a female voice says indignantly, "Keep your hands to yourself."

There is laughter.

"Deacon, cut out the foreplay!" someone calls out.

More laughter.

Then the band stops playing, and a pin-drop silence reigns. There is only the creaking of the floorboards, heavy breathing and an occasional muffled cough.

Just then I hear a voice call from the front door, "Hello? Anyone home?"

"No!" sixty voices yell.

I lead Vicki gingerly outside into the hall. My First Class degree has kudos, and I figure I may be able to attract Vicki by showing a large commitment to her. We sit on a settee beside each other in the dark.

"What if someone commits themselves totally to making you peaceful and happy?" I ask.

"It couldn't be a man. A man would want me for selfish reasons, for sex, for children, for his career, for his own peace and happiness – not for my happiness."

"He would be besotted with you," I say.

"Yes."

"He would have trust."

"He would be vulnerable, taking a risk," she says.

That is the problem; I do not fully trust Vicki. She has failed to meet my expectations several times – after my brother and sister visited in second year, in going to the Cambridge Ball, after the lie detector test – and I remember how angry she made me when she betrayed me with Richard.

"He won't be taking a risk if he fully trusts you," I say.

"I may want him to take a risk, to show how much he wants me. He would have to make sacrifices."

"What kind of sacrifices?" I ask.

"Abandon other plans; give up his goal."

"Gradually."

"Immediately."

"Wouldn't sacrifices be part of his commitment?"

"He would be vulnerable and have to trust me."

"Perhaps he couldn't commit totally at the outset."

"If not, I wouldn't want to start with him."

We are back to where we began.

I want to say, "Your argument is not reasonable. It is circular and unsound."

Instead I say, "Let's go back and dance."

I put my arms around Vicki and kiss her. Her mouth is soft and her tongue plays with mine. She presses against me and my body feels her generous breasts, rippling belly, firm mound and supple thighs. Her fingers weave through my hair.

Then the lights come on and the band starts up. I keep holding her as I feel the music resonating in her body. Then she pulls away and we sit down in the hall again.

"Vicki, what you are saying is unreasonable."

"Oh, you think so?" she says coolly. "Why do you think that?"

"Your premises are that true love requires total commitment and total commitment is trust; therefore, you conclude that true love requires trust. All right so far. Then you say that trust is total vulnerability and risk-taking. You say that sacrifice is risk-taking, such as giving up alternative plans and goals, which shows total commitment and true love."

I adopt my most reasonable tone. "Your conclusion is the same as your initial premise. Your argument is therefore circular. It cannot be falsified and is therefore unsound. Do you see that I cannot pull out of going to Canada before we renew our relationship? I need to be sure we will get along."

She turns away and listens to the others for a couple of minutes.

"So you are denying that I can require total commitment at the outset."

"Maybe you'll find someone; maybe not. Do you really want a man to give up everything for you on spec? Such a man would not have much going for him."

"Well, he should stop doing anything I don't like."

"Such as?"

"I'll leave you to figure that one out."

The music has stopped and we stand up.

"Another dance?" I ask gallantly.

"Thanks, but no thanks. Perhaps later." She walks away to join her friends. Once again Barbara has come between us.

Moments later there is a flash and the lights and amplifiers go off again. I sniff the air like a Labrador. I have learnt to identify plastics by their smells when burning. There is the floral smell of perfumes, but stronger underneath is the urine smell of sweat. On top is the acrid smell of burning plastic, which I know is from electrical insulation. I can smell several plastics. There is the soft candle wax smell of polyethylene from electrical wiring on fire. Burning polyvinyl chloride electrical insulation irritates my throat. Then there is the mousey smell of a styrenic thermoset, probably an electrical fitting.

I shout, "Fire! Fire!" and start searching in the darkness for a telephone, or for a kitchen with a tap and a saucepan. But the heat reaches me with the smell of wood smoke and pungent burning paint. I decide to get out and am caught up in the crowd of dancers jammed in the front door. People are shoving and climbing on top of each other to get out. My face is compressed against the head of a girl in front of me. Her smell is Vicki, a beautiful sweet smell like roses. With my hand I feel her face to be sure.

"It's me, Selwyn," I tell her in her ear.

She is too squashed to reply but she nods an acknowledgement.

There is the heady ammoniac odour of urine and the sharp smell of faeces as people are pulled down and trodden on. I hold Vicki up and we stumble through the heavy smoke, climb over the bodies and reach the outside, where we sink down weeping on the lawn.

"Thank you," she says to me, coughing. Her friends come and help her away.

We drag bodies away from the doorway to be carried into ambulances. I see the fire captain pause and taste the air, drawing it in all around his tongue where his sensors lie, checking for a particular smell. He probably recognises wood ash, cotton ash from curtains, wallpaper ash and wool ash from carpets. Wood particles taste resinous; cotton aromatic from the bituminous dyes; wallpaper gritty from the titanium oxide rutile filler; and wool fatty, from sheep. The taste he is searching for is not there – the taste on the side and bottom of the tongue of burning human hair and flesh, protein-heavy, fatty and sweet like the Sunday roast. When he is satisfied, he nods to his men. They turn on the water cannon and stand back as it knocks down the smouldering walls and the house collapses inwards away from adjoining houses.

Rule 38: *Love that is up in the air must eventually return to a safe roost.*

PART 6: LEG-BREAK (1967–1968)

In which I unexpectedly have to sell-out my long position, leaving me fully exposed to the possibility of a large loss on my short position.

CHAPTER 39   TRIAL BY CONSCIENCE

In the days after the fire, there are funerals for a classmate and two guests. Several others are in hospital with injuries. Recriminations worsen the trauma until victims and their families are able to grieve, some receiving counselling.

When Barbara and Margot return a few days after the accident, I am recovered. I overhear them talking about being drunk with some men they met on holiday. We take up where we left off. We always get together on Saturday night and we go straight to my flat and to bed. Barbara's behaviour in bed seems different, less inhibited, with experience of some variations. My instincts tell me that she has had sex with someone while she was away. I say nothing. Soon I will be free of her.

My family are coming up for the degree ceremony. I have been allocated three tickets that I assign to my parents and sister, telling myself that Barbara has work that day. I do not want my family to meet her. She is disappointed I do not have a ticket for her.

In the Great Hall on Degree Day, the feeling of being "special" that we have enjoyed for the past three years disappears. There are over a thousand new graduates assembled, indistinguishable in their rented gowns and mortarboards. We sit at the front, with our families behind us. The Vice Chancellor reminds us that we have been takers and now we should become givers of our skills to society, in worthwhile work. The lasting impression is conveyed that we have joined a powerful social class.

After the ceremony, we pose for group photos with our families and friends, throwing our hats in the air and leaping gleefully around. My father, who left school at fourteen to labour in the fields, is happy for me. Whereas his lack of education has enslaved him in a life of unremitting toil and although he is financially independent through hard work, my education has liberated me. I am enormously grateful that my parents have funded my escape from an inferior local position, to a world of opportunity. Moreover, quietly and in all humility, my father has shown me his model of human decency. I am only sorry I have not lived up to his example better in my treatment of Barbara.

With our way cleared to leave Liverpool, I go for a last outing with the guys to a movie. During the movie, I remember that I should have called Barbara earlier in the week to finish with her. She can't call me because I don't have a phone. She will be pissed off because I normally call her mid-week. It has been two weeks since she returned from Spain, and I cannot put it off any longer. Maybe by telephone will be easiest. I steel myself to finish with her at last. When we come out of the movie, I go into a telephone box and call her.

"Hello," she answers in her flat voice.

"Hi, Barbara. Sorry not to call before."

I lie; I am not sorry.

"I'm pregnant."

"What?"

"I'm pregnant."

"How do I know it's mine?"

"What do you mean?"

"It's not mine?"

I expected her to reassert that it is, to refute my null hypothesis with evidence, any evidence. She has to assert with conviction that it is mine.

"I never want to speak to you again!" She hangs up. It isn't how I had planned to finish with her. Her timid behaviour on the phone fuels my suspicion that she has been impregnated while on holiday. She is counting on my trusting her. Why should I?

This is the worst thing that has ever happened to me, and I fight down my panic. I leave the phone booth, stunned.

"I'll catch you up later," I tell the others. "Something has come up."

I do not regret questioning her. The burden of proof lies in her court. Now she can plainly see what common sense should have told her all along: I am never going to marry her. I have simply been playing with her, enjoying her, amusing myself. I am the archetypal philanderer and she should have recognised that. Is she really so stupid?

Perhaps she had thought her pregnancy would trap me, that I would take it for granted that I was the father and do the honourable thing, and that I could not bear the dishonour and the guilt of taking her virginity and using her. I can't forget that she had seemed available for sex on our first date. It is very likely that she has had sex with a man she met on holiday.

Whereas I can see the forest clearly, at ground level the view is obscured by individual trees. My courage waivers and my heart thumps with the adrenalin of fear. There is no-one to fight and nowhere to take flight. I walk several kilometres back to the flat, going over it in my mind. I have always been careful to use a condom. Why has she never gone on The Pill? She has never given me a reason. Why should I trust her? She could have wanted to use pregnancy to trap me. Our recent picnic indicated that she has been trying to get me to pop the question.

Could she have conceived while she was in Spain? Yes, there has been time. My accusation will irretrievably damage a relationship that is already too flimsy to parent a child adequately. As I walk, I ponder whether there is anything I can do. Does she need me to arrange for an abortion? No, my presence would cause confusion.

On the High Street, I run into Tom. I tell him everything. He listens, concerned, and understands. The weight becomes bearable.

"Think it through carefully before deciding anything," he advises me on parting.

"It's a bit late for that," I say. "I think it is decided. I have shown I do not trust her. That has damaged our relationship forever."

Tom suggests I get some distance away to think. I have told no-one else and I ask her to tell no-one. Sadly, we part.

I decide to go home in a day or two. I pack up all my things and wait to hear from Margot or Lisa in support of their friend. When they do not contact me, my heart hardens. I feel sorry for Barbara but I feel almost certain that I cannot be the father. If I am the father, then I am committing a grave injustice. If I am not the father, then it is evident that I have led Barbara to a desperate deception and I am blameworthy. Either way, it is too late to assume responsibility and I am destined for dishonour.

My thinking about Barbara has crystallized: there is no way Barbara and I could ever be a couple after this. I can see no reason to stay any longer. I load my things into my car. Barbara does not have my address or the phone number but she can get them from Richard or Tom via Margot.

Vicki drives past and waves. I am glad she doesn't stop. I am too ashamed to face her. After all my planning, it has all ended in my disgrace. I leave without saying goodbye.

Rule39: *Attribution of paternity is a matter of trust.*

CHAPTER 40   CLIFFHANGER

There are rules for assigning responsibility for a pregnancy that I do not know, and no-one explains. Consequently, I feel free to follow my conscience. The culpability seems to be like Schrodinger's Cat, whose state of life or death exists ambivalently. I both deny responsibility and suffer remorse at the same time.

When I get home, I say nothing about it. I have never mentioned Barbara to my parents. They would be less than helpful in deciding what to do, as it lies outside their experience. My mother's attitude to sex is Victorian. My father has never mentioned sexual relationships to me. Fortunately Howard is away, in Australia.

A few days later, when I come into the farmhouse from work, my mother attacks me.

"You ought to be ashamed of yourself!" She is her usual self-righteous self.

Barbara's mother has telephoned my mother. She is angry and threatens to have a maintenance order served on me that will prevent me from emigrating. Neither Barbara nor her mother has spoken with me, as I would ask how the pregnancy had occurred and why Barbara was not on The Pill.

I tell my parents my version of events, with Barbara getting pregnant on holiday. My mother does not believe me even though she has often warned me of girls who use pregnancy to trap boys.

By avoiding contact with Barbara, I believe I am doing what is best for her in the long term. She deserves more love than I have for her, or for the baby. I doubt that I could love it as much as most fathers, because I doubt I could make as happy a home with Barbara as a child has a right to have. Barbara and I have too little in common, and that is the tragedy. I can't love a woman whom I suspect of manipulation and duplicity. She will never love me now I have denied being the father.

I grit my teeth. A marriage could never succeed after this start. It is better that I distance myself from her rather than raise her hopes that I will accept responsibility if she keeps the baby.

Barbara's claim that I am the father is weak. She has left it to be inferred from our association rather than denying she has had another lover. Although she has been my sex partner for almost a year, there is the possibility of other males.

We have had intercourse once each week, amounting to about 50 occasions. Her ovulation on at most 6 out of 30 days could only have occurred on 10 of these days at random. I always used a condom, and although there is the possibility that semen overflowed the condom, the quantity would have been small and unlikely to reach the fallopian tubes causing fertilization. Pregnancy from our intercourse on these few occasions, protected as I always was by condoms, had been unlikely. In the month before she went on holiday, there was no reduction in or failure of my precautions. She would have been fertile on only one occasion and the chances of that day having a significant semen leakage are very small.

"I took precautions," I tell my mother. "I am almost certain that it wasn't me who made her pregnant."

My mother knows nothing of condom use and little of the conception process.

"It must have been you," she says. "She never had anyone else."

"The evidence says otherwise. I never told her I would marry her or that we would stay together after my course finished. When she tried to get me to agree to it, I would not, but I didn't dismiss it outright. If she assumed that would happen, she was foolish."

My mother nevertheless tells my sisters to beware of men like me who lead girls up the garden path. It is very hurtful. Barbara led herself up the garden path.

"She wanted to get pregnant. I only went to bed with her one evening a week. She never took The Pill. She told me she is pregnant on the phone; she couldn't tell me to my face. She has never said I am the father. Her friends have never backed her up to me. I've never met her social group and she may have had other boyfriends. At the time she conceived, she was in Spain on holiday, at a place where people jump into bed with each other all the time."

"Hmmph." I am used to my mother's disapproval of me. When it is unable to be articulated I realize her apparent dislike is real.

My father is less critical. "A solicitor's daughter! Tsk, tsk!" he says, as if the worst of the situation is that I have ruined an opportunity to get free legal advice.

213

I am in a quandary, facing either dishonour or the shackles of unwanted marriage. It is a terrible choice. If I continue to run, I will be a coward in my own eyes, an irresponsible boy leaving an innocent girl in the lurch. It clashes with the self-image I have of being a decent man who treats women kindly. I would become the type of man who I would protect my sisters from, a selfish cad. How will I be able to explain myself to decent girls in the future? I have vindicated Vicki's caution.

On the other hand, I can't imagine living with Barbara. I know next to nothing about her. What would we do together, besides having sex and caring for the baby? What interests does she have? Does she have home-making skills? We have never spent a whole night together, let alone a day; nor have we gone more than an hour away from Liverpool. She has never been with me when I get up in the morning, or seen me shave. How would she cope with living in Western Canada, in a harsh climate? What does she want? What does she care about? Would she be a good mother?

Could I be a good father when the child's paternity is in doubt? The child might not look like either of us, being dark with Mediterranean skin. It would be a constant reminder of her infidelity and dishonesty. I am not a hypocrite but it is one thing to cheat, another to use pregnancy to trap a person into an unwelcome partnership or even bondage. The possibility could have consequences far worse than leaving her alone with her pregnancy.

My mind keeps churning these options every waking hour, and the more I think about it, the less attractive the future seems. I begin to consider another option.

I ask my father for some farm work. He sets me driving a tractor that pulls a haymaking machine. I go around and around fields on our river flats, winding inwards, raking together a long row of hay for our baler to engorge.

I put in long lonely hours of tractor driving by the river, from dawn to dusk, raking hay. Our river land is a rectangular field bounded on three sides by hedges made of thorns and bent saplings. The fourth side drops away down a 30-metre-high vertical cliff onto boulders that fill the bed of the river.

I drive close to the cliff, not caring about the chance of the cliff collapsing. I am wearing radio earphones and listening to pop music. The Beatles' "A Day in the Life" reminds of the Tara Browne incident, wrongly regarded by some as an LSD-induced suicide. "He blew his mind out in a car." I feel bitter about how wrongly I am being judged and blamed.

I am driving across the headland, aware that if I don't turn the steering wheel, I will launch into space. The fall on to the solid limestone rocks would kill me even if the machine doesn't roll on top of me.

Will people think I have fallen asleep? I will not have to decide anything about Barbara and I will escape culpability and parental obligations.

I know that my suicide will be cruel to my family. I have been indoctrinated by my mother with the sad tale of a close neighbour's suicide, a married man with young children. His wife has moved away, presumably to escape the stigma. It is not a deterrent to me, but I have no desire to wound my parents or my siblings. I know that my father, at least, would miss me badly. My parents' lack of education is not an excuse for their being blind to my suffering.

I can't find any peace as I drive around that field, any reason to turn away from the cliff. Even the seagulls that ride the wind looking for worms seem doomed. I have considered everything I can think of and have become aware that I have no hope left. I am sinking down fast. I have unanswered questions. "Did she really expect that her pregnancy would be a better approach to marrying me?" The question blew away in the buffeting wind. There was no way of knowing, with the seagulls' screaming, "Die!"

I realise that although I am trapped and my prospects of relief dismal, suicide is not a way out. It will hurt my father. It would have no wide societal significance and merely recycle my substance early, with no lasting meaning. I will have to brave it out, choosing the least problematic of the options.

Barbara has got herself pregnant by not taking The Pill and she should take responsibility. I had done all that was reasonable for me to do to avoid her pregnancy and therefore I have behaved honourably.

The tractor gears grind forwards noisily, steadily, inexorably towards the cliff. I am about halfway towards the void now.

It is unbearable that I cannot show any support whatsoever for Barbara, without accepting fully responsible paternity. I want her to know that she was loved, in a way, but I cannot tell her now. To lose her friendship is a terrible pain. My ambivalence would only aggravate her wound and prevent healing. I want her to have kids under happy circumstances. I don't have enough mature affection to sustain a marriage, and the child would soon be fatherless. I have to either reject or accept responsibility. There is no halfway position. There is too much doubt in my mind. She has not looked me in the eye and said, "It is yours." Margot, her holiday companion, has not contacted me to vouch for her fidelity in Spain at around the time I infer conception to have taken place. She has not produced any evidence that counters my charge of infidelity, or vouches for her fidelity. I would trust her, except she has been trying to manipulate me into making a commitment.

There are about one hundred metres to go to the cliff. My awareness leaps to the stink of hot oil, the bouncing of the hard metal seat, the steering wheel wrenching against my hands with every hole and rock we drive over.

The clatter assails my ears of valves banging shut in the engine, of fuel exploding, of cams hitting rods, of rods lifting valves, of pistons hitting the crankshaft. I am just a cog with a job to do to keep the whole thing working smoothly.

I am within forty metres of going over the cliff.

By what right could I kill another of my kind? It is a right exercised by a victorious lion when he kills his predecessor's cubs. It is a right exercised by a kangaroo when in a drought it reaches into its pouch, pulls a suckling off its nipple and discards it. It is a right exercised by birds when in a famine they cease to regurgitate food into the gaping mouth of the weakest chick. It is the right that humans exercise when they abandon unwanted babies to community care or adoption or terminate unwanted pregnancies. They act for their own futurity by creating responsibility and acting accordingly.

As my thoughts re-iterate along these paths, I am aware that my behaviour has been dishonourable and I am filled with remorse. Barbara has trusted me to support her if things go wrong, and I have let her down. There is no-one I can talk to dispel my unease.

Twenty-five metres from the cliff, and my hands are gripping the steering wheel, ready to go straight over the cliff. We will plunge down, bounce, roll, and I will be killed. My pain will cease. They will think I went to sleep at the wheel, a tragic accident.

I used to sit beside my father in the Landrover and in between opening gates, spout my innermost secrets and hopes. He would say nothing and I would feel better. Often I was angry about being an adolescent and subject to arbitrary authority. He promised it would get better, if I was patient. There are only a few seconds left.

My father would understand the truth about the tractor and regret not having been there for me. My death would take the Sun from his life and he would live in the shadow of my gravestone.

Killing myself would be unjust and cruel to him. However badly I hurt, I cannot end my life. I love my father.

The front wheels reach the abyss. I pull the steering wheel hard around in a tight quarter circle on the uncut grass and I continue along the cliff top. Far below, the river tumbles between boulders. I will face the shame when it is brought to me. I will stay here on the farm and wait to hear from Barbara.

After several weeks Barbara's father writes that she will have a termination and requests I pay half. He is civil, without any recrimination. It is not a lot of money, and I guess he wants me to accept half the responsibility. I send it to him to make the arrangement and tell him, poor man, I am sorry. By making room for another, the chances are the next baby will have a better father who will love it more than I would.

The initial wrong is that I used her for so long and she allowed herself to be used. I first went out with her in default of a date with Vicki. I had my mind set on getting together with Vicki, and there is nowhere for Barbara to go in my emotions. I hope she will go on to have a happy life.

I wait with impatience for the sailing of my ship to Canada. The day finally arrives when tugs push us away from Southampton quay, breaking the streamers, out into The Solent, where Vicki learned to sail with her father. I feel a great weight lifting off me. I have left Priory Farm without looking back. I have said goodbye to my mother and promised to write. I have waved to my sister, shaken hands with my father and with Roger, who have brought me to Southampton. My father has tears in his eyes. Had I not been sure my father would miss me, I would be gone already, permanently. I wonder when I will see my family and friends again. I have not said goodbye to Vicki, but she has been with me in my heart during my ordeal.

My mother's parting words are "I'm pleased you are going. It's the best place for you, far away."

Then I depart from the country where I have experienced so much pleasure and pain, to make another start far away.

Rule 40: *Suicide has too much to lose and nothing lasting to offer, for those left behind.*

CHAPTER 41   CELIBATE REACTION

The great ship steams steadily down the Solent. As we slide past Portsmouth and into the westbound channel, I feel my worries of the past few months slipping away. There has been the uncertainty of Finals, the disastrous fire at the Naval Squadron clubhouse and the tragedy of Barbara's pregnancy.

I want to make a fresh start. I am off to join the exploration department of Canada's biggest oil company, Canoil. I hope that it will be the start of a glittering career. I stand on the foredeck, braced against the wind, as we smash through Atlantic rollers, thrilled to begin my next great adventure.

The other passengers are either married couples, many with kids, or elderly. I am lonely on a voyage to a new life and unable to share my feelings. However, I love the shipboard life, and by the time we reach the mouth of the St Lawrence River and are threading gingerly between the thousands of islands, I feel free of the archaic customs, mouldy rotting buildings and backward-looking society that are strangling the Old World.

We arrive at Montreal, the city where I worked during the vacation a year previously. I am itching to begin permanent employment in Calgary. Soon I am aboard a Canadian Pacific train as it rattles through a lace of metal roadways, weaves through the orange maple forests that skirt Lake Ontario, and then streaks westwards across an ocean of wheat.

The timeless train journey has intervals in which I am able to contemplate my goal, which is to engineer my way towards wealth and power in Canoil. After years as a student with little money, my ambitions are to own a sports car, learn to ski well, pilot an aircraft and ocean sail in a yacht. None of these requires female company; nor do I imagine myself in a relationship. I have had enough of girls for the time being.

When I arrive in Calgary, the Irelands make me welcome. I know James from when he was in the year ahead of me at uni.

James had recommended Canoil to me. He joined them a year ago. He has a full social life, with a new sports car and skiing at weekends. His girlfriend, Hayley, is a social worker from Sweden – a slender redheaded beauty. She tries to fix me up with girls but I am still grieving over Barbara's termination. They take me to parties and I meet several girls but stop short of having sex with them. I am fortunate to be able to start a new life where my previous relationships with females are not known. I am hurt by what has happened and avoid having sexual relationships with the females I meet.

Larry and Lisa are already in Calgary when I get there. He has started work at Canoil. I haven't seen them since their wedding reception in Liverpool. They welcome me to stay in their flat. It is their first married home and, far from feeling like an intruder, I have a great time with them exploring our new territory together.

At first, I am apprehensive that Lisa will blame me for her friend Barbara's pregnancy but the topic is never raised, and I wonder if she knows about it. She never mentions Barbara to me, and I don't enlighten her about our tragic parting. I assume Barbara has kept quiet and I see this as further evidence that I am not the father. Barbara's father writes saying she has had an abortion and is well. I feel like dirt.

I am reticent about a relationship with another girl. I live with Larry and Lisa as a determined bachelor, denying any emotional needs. I had played some guitar as a teenager, so I buy a guitar and teach myself the alternating thumb style and some Gordon Lightfoot songs. I start giving guitar lessons after work. Soon I give that up for a better business venture.

Larry and I moonlight, helping Lisa start a boutique, "Carnaby", selling the latest fashion in mini-dresses and hotpants to prairie farmers' daughters at a large profit. I am a partner and put in a thousand dollars I borrow from the bank. Besides capital, I research sites and do the interior and decor. Lisa sets the tone of the boutique, which is in a new downtown shopping mall. She wears mini-skirts, wide belts and skinny striped sweaters. Her footwear includes platform-soled leg-laced cork Roman sandals. They look great with her glossy black hair in bangs. Her green and silver eye make-up, with white lipstick, gives her a fashionable Cleopatra look. From the moment it opens, the store is a money-spinner.

When the boutique has been open a few months, Canoil transfers me to the Tundra Tar Sands Project at a remote location in northern Alberta. It is a world-class project with a team of engineers brought together to meet new technological challenges. They have an office building and an oil processing plant surrounded by acres of nodding donkey pumps amid a frozen tundra swamp. Having a First Class honours degree, I am something of a sensation when I arrive. The technology is innovative and has problems, and so expectations of me are high. I have few distractions in this all-male environment and I set to work with a will to succeed. I soon start contributing original ideas. This includes correcting the other engineers, and as a result I am disliked and left alone. My ideas are heard in silence and ignored until I assert them, when events normally vindicate me.

"Selwyn, what can possibly be gained by running cold water into the casing?" Mike says. "Won't it go into the pump and be brought up again?"

"At the moment it is so hot down there, the water in the pump flashes off steam and vapour locks. So no oil is produced," I reply. "The cold water will cool everything down so that it stays liquid in the pump and oil is produced."

"Well, I reckon the cold water will be produced, nothing more," Mike persists. "It's a waste of time and money."

"That would be correct if there is no mixing," I reply, "but I think the cold water will mix with the hot liquids."

"I'll have to think about it," says Mike. "A bore is not much good at mixing."

Everyone laughs. I don't get it.

"It all depends on whether the perforations are above or—"

"It was a joke, Selwyn," says Alan, "about a boring person not being a good social mixer."

"Ha ha. It sounds like Mike was making fun of me. Feel free, Mike. I'm used to it."

"Selwyn, don't take any notice of Mike. He's a stupid prick."

"We'll find out when we test it," I reply.

There were frequent clashes like this. My grudging acceptance by the others infuriates me. I am not able to participate in office banter and I have to have jokes explained. The Canadian idiom is often beyond me. My life is narrow but I enjoy it. I have several innovative design features tested successfully, and my salary is boosted accordingly.

Larry and Lisa are transferred east to Ottawa. They sell the boutique and return my capital plus several thousand dollars return on the fifteen dollars interest I have paid to the bank. I wouldn't have believed business could be so profitable. We consider starting a chain of boutiques across Canada, but we are not confident of being able to recruit honest store managers.

Back in Edmonton for a stint, my flatmate, Chris, asks me to a spring break-up party at his family's home near Mt Robson in Jasper National Park.

"What sort of a party is it?" I ask.

"You'll see," he says. "It is a get-together of local people who have been stranded in their cabins on the mountain all winter."

We get to a lay-by off a snow-ploughed road heading north into the Rocky Mountains from the Jasper Highway. We climb into the cab of a tracked vehicle that looks like a military tank fitted with a snowplough. With his father steering using brake levers, we force our way ahead slowly, with snow above window height. Gradually, we climb up to a plateau where his family looks after fifty horses used in the summer for tourist rides. The horses are corralled and being fed from a stack of hay, imported in the summer from lowland farms.

Chris's parents and sister have been cut off from the outside world since snow closed the road the previous fall. When we arrive, their welcome is joyful but muted by shyness, for they have not talked with anyone from the outside world for six months.

After introductions, it is difficult to get a word in edgeways. Chris's 19-year-old sister Annie, who looks like Dolly Parton, talks with a drawl and blushes prettily when I look at her. She has been educated at a girls' boarding school in Ottawa. Chris tells me she came home to get over a love affair that didn't work out. She is a kindred spirit.

Temperatures are rising daily, the ice and snow are melting and the roads are becoming passable. Everyone on the mountain is invited to their party the next evening.

"How do you let them know when to come?" I ask.

"Community radio station," says Chris. "Annie runs it."

We spend most of the day getting the place ready and preparing drinks and food. Annie has been learning the banjo all winter. She shows me her playing, at a dizzying lick that gets my feet tapping. She can also warble country and western blues, with a catch in her voice that makes the older folk cry.

I have brought my guitar, and that evening Annie and I play together for the mountain people. They are warm hairy characters who are glad to see each other after six months spent alone. We are soon doing pop songs together like "With a Little Help from My Friends" and "When I'm Sixty Four". Annie picks out the melody with arpeggios, at the same time singing the verses, while I strum and yell out the choruses, vamping up a storm. We get a few fast numbers going that get everyone on their feet, jumping around like the four Sioux Indians present. It is their land we are on.

When we take a break and I go outside, it is so cold I am warned to pee walking backwards, to avoid the icicle. When I go back in, someone has cut my guitar strings. It is a well-deserved musical criticism, as I can hardly carry a tune.

"Roly did it," Annie explains. "He was my boyfriend last year and he has probably been thinking about me all winter. I'm sorry."

I compare Roly and Annie with myself and Vicki. I can understand why he has done what he has done and feel sorry for him. When I go in, he tries to push into me, looking for a fight, but I step aside. Annie is a lovely girl, and I think it would take more than a fight to win her if I want her, which I do not. Apart from Roly, everyone has a great time. For me, it is a revelation of frontier life.

A month later, when Annie returns to live in Calgary, I see her several times. She has missed a lot of schooling, and the only job she can get is as a waitress. She is good at it and loves it. Annie may have modest qualifications but she is a first-rate person. She is naïve and innocent, too good for me. On one date she gives me her mandolin.

"No, it's too lovely." I say. "You keep it for someone more deserving."

It could be a symbol of her virginity, I am thinking.

"Take it," she says. "I don't play it. I won't have time to learn it now. I'm going to do a uni course in the evenings."

I do not have the heart to refuse. It is a very good instrument but I never learn to play it. Later, when I leave Canada, I give it away. I always feel like I obtained it under false pretences. However I stopmyself having sex with her. It takes all of my self-control to end my relationship with her before I hurt her. I am proud of that and set it against all the times when I used women badly.

After six months of celibacy, Hayley introduces me to a colleague social worker, Sally. She is a lovely girl, prim and proper at first, but after a month she becomes very amorous. I steel myself to resist her because I do not want to be tied down under any circumstances. Up to this time, I had only ever had sex with Barbara. I am still besotted with Vicki, who is seven thousand kilometres away in Liverpool. I write to her regularly, and she sometimes writes back. Although we have not been together for a long time she is the person who I most like to be with, and I miss her terribly. I don't how or when I will see her again, but she has a hold on me that nothing can distract. Even so, I meet some lovely girls, and my resolve weakens. Hayley introduces me to another social worker friend. She has a wild streak, and on a skiing weekend I quit my celibacy when we make love in a snowdrift.

I get a terse postcard from my brother, Howard, in Mexico, telling me he is on his way to see me and asking me if I have any contacts in the USA. I have not heard from him for two years as he only ever contacts people when he wants something. I do not put him in touch with any female friends because he treats women badly. By coincidence, I hear that week from Tom in San Francisco, where he works. I phone him and ask if he can put up Howard. Tom stayed at Priory Farm several times and knows Howard. Tom agrees but Howard can stay for two nights only, because it is his woman's place.

At Calgary on weekend visits, I meet attractive females who distract me from enforced celibacy at the all-male Tundra township but with restraint that precludes sexual relations. My preoccupation with Vicki continues at my remote location. If I can entice her to visit me, finally she will have an exclusive with me and we can renew our relationship.

Rule 41: *Females find celibacy in a man attractive.*

PART 7 MARGIN CALL (1968)

In which I attempt to negotiate a love future with Vicki.

CHAPTER 42   RUTTED RENEWAL

In the "summer of love", we follow our hearts' bidding, hoping with sincerity and optimism to begin a perfect relationship. I am partying, skiing, learning to fly and going on camping trips in the Rockies in my sports car. I write to Vicki and Richard, who are in Liverpool studying. Vicki is slow to reply but I exchange letters with Richard every few weeks. He tells me what she is doing.

#4 South Court,
Park Estate.
Mersey Avenue,
Liverpool.

14/03/68
Dear Selwyn,
Chuffed to get your letter. Bruce and I are working all hours. Jozef is in second year and enjoying a series of fresher girls. I am envious of your skiing as I didn't go this year and worked through the Christmas and Easter holidays. Doc Bishop is wearing the same suit. We have the first girl engineer in our year.
I see Vicki quite often. She is in second year and working hard. She has had several boyfriends but they don't last long. Angela has switched to counselling, too. They are still living together.
Dave Klein is Union President and Tony Benwood is Chairman of Deb Soc. Jozef ran for president but the socialists gave him a hard time in hustings. Tits Patricia is still around and both of them are doing well.
Yours studiously,
Richard

Strangely, after all we have been through, I trust Richard. It took him the whole of final term to recover from his nervous breakdown and he did not sit Finals. Now he is repeating final year. With me gone, he is acquitting himself with aplomb and is on track to secure a First Class degree. It is unlikely that his change in my absence is mere coincidence: his competitiveness was his undoing, and I had deliberately fuelled it. In my absence, he can do his best without worrying about beating me.

I hope Vicki will be envious of me, because I am still hurt from her betrayal with Richard and I am ashamed to admit my motivation for writing to her is partly to gloat. It is mean-spirited of me, but I want retribution.

c/o Canoil Ltd
Tundra Oil Project
Bear River Township
Alberta
Canada
25/03/68
Dear Vicki,

I hope you are enjoying Counselling and are managing okay without me.

I heard from Richard the other day that you are working hard, which I wish I was there to see. Also, that Angela is with you. So you will have old friends as well as new.

Here I am living in a caravan in the township and driving a carload of us to and from the pilot plant every day. Spring break-up is underway and the road varies from mush to ridged ice. The other two guys in the trailer are technicians and like to take me down as impractical. The other day it was so cold the LPG froze in its bottle and we had no heating. I was all for going to bed together but they used a petrol flamethrower to heat the frozen bottle, while I cowered under the table. Next season I will be ready to run a trap line with a sled and a team of huskies.

I would sure like to warm my hands on you, which is what the Choctaw Indians say when they mean, 'I am missing you'. I want to find out all about the new Vicki while still having some unfinished business with the previous Vicki. In particular, I want to explain my rapid and unfriendly departure from Liverpool, under difficult circumstances that you may not be aware of.

How about making me a visit after Easter? We could go on a skiing trip in the Rockies. I have been several times with James and Hayley, who I was telling you about. You need have no fear of the local population of Moose, Elk, Grizzlies, Mountain Lions, Wolverines, Racoons, Skunks and other varmints. They respect the skills I have learnt with a lariat. I would lasso

*them and tie them up, all except skunks, which I would keep well away
from.*

*We can trap our own food. There are tourist eateries in Banff where
the traditional food of the Choctaws is a short stack with clotted cream and
maple syrup.*

*I had better get on and do some work. While I have been writing, some
oil has run away. I will lead a posse to slip past it and, damn it, sometimes
work interrupts my leisure.*

With love,
Unrequitedly yours,
Selwyn

I am surprised and delighted when Vicki writes that she is
coming to ski in the Rocky Mountains with me. I reply that I will
pick her up in Calgary, to go on to Banff for a week of skiing. She
agrees.

I am alone at James' and Hayley's place, where I have been
staying, getting ready to pick up Vicki from the airport to go skiing,
when there is a knock at the door. On the doorstep with an inch of
stubble, a dark tan and a rucksack, is my older brother, Howard. I
haven't seen him for two years and have not missed him at all.

He punches me hard in the biceps, disabling my arm, and pushes
past me into the house.

"I'll sleep on the settee," he announces.

I haven't told James and Hayley he is coming and I need their
permission for Howard to stay.

"Leave your rucksack by the door," I tell him. "You may not be
able stay here."

"Oh, nice," he says, as if he is a victim of my inhospitality.

I question him about Tom. He says he stayed with him for a
week. I am annoyed because I had told him Tom could put him up
for no more than two days. Howard says there was no problem but
I don't believe him. I try to call Tom but there is no answer.

I am never in contact with Tom again, despite searching for him.
He doesn't answer my phone calls or letters. I am very concerned
as he is my best mate. I suspect that my brother has caused him a
big problem by overstaying his welcome, or damaged something,
or sponged too much, or got nasty when Tom asked him to leave.
Tom is short in stature, a ready target for Howard's bullying.

I am caught in a dilemma: should I leave my brother alone in Calgary, staying at the YMCA? Or take him with Vicki and me, with the possibility he will get in the way of a rapprochement? He knows Vicki from his visit to Liverpool two years earlier, when she was my girlfriend. Giving Howard the benefit of the doubt because I haven't seen him for a while, I tell him I will ask Vicki whether he can come with us.

"Vicki likes me," he says.

"Huh. She likes gorillas, too."

"Who do you know will lend me their skiing gear?"

I want to warn him of the fragile nature of my relationship with Vicki but I don't think he will understand this message and he would assume that she is available to him. Instead, I decide to say nothing, hoping that he has a remnant of common courtesy that will keep him out of our way.

James and Hayley kindly let Howard stay for the night.

"Do you have any skiing stuff I can borrow?" Howard asks.

"We are thinking of going skiing, too," James replies. I had warned James about Howard.

Next day, I wait in the arrivals lounge at Calgary airport for Vicki to arrive. When I get her alone, I will ask what happened between her and Richard. She may even counter by asking me about Barbara, and I will update her on all that has happened and the sad ending to that relationship. I will hug her and tell her I am sorry that I have been a hypocrite and ask her forgiveness. I am a little frightened by the power of her spell over me. I decide I will be wary of her until we have established meaningful communication about what happened between us. I have high hopes that our relationship will take off and we will finally get together.

I can hardly believe she is coming. I am so excited! At last, I have some evidence that she wants me. I doubt she is coming all this way to be with me unless she is interested in having a relationship.

When she comes through, she is even more beautiful than I remembered.

"It is great to see you," I tell her.

"You, too," she replies.

Her magic happens all over again. I begin to float around with a sense of unbounded joy that I have not felt since we first met.

When we set off to go skiing, Vicki asks to sit in the back of my car, where she reads a book. She seems rather withdrawn but it may be shyness with Howard there. I drive along the rutted ice tracks of the highway west to Banff. Howard is sitting beside me.

"We would be safer if you went faster," he says.

"We could slip off the crown of the road," I reply.

"You couldn't drive off this road if you tried," Howard says. "The ruts in the ice would hold you on."

Vicki's taciturn reading concerns me. I wonder if it is something to do with what has happened between us, or rather, what has not. I don't know what she knows about Barbara. I need to explain to Vicki why I had left her in Birmingham without saying goodbye. I am not going to raise the topic of Barbara's pregnancy with Vicki while Howard is there. It will have to wait until I can get her alone.

After about two hours, when we are in the desolate foothills, I have to move off the crown of the slippery road for an oncoming truck to come through. We skid off the road at speed and plough into an embankment of snow that has been heaped up to head height by a mechanical snow thrower. The snow forces up the hood as our safety belts hold us back. Steam from a ruptured cooling system envelopes us.

"Holy shit!" Howard exclaims.

"Are you okay?" I ask Vicki

"I'm okay," she says.

"Did you lose your place?" I ask about her book.

She does not reply.

The car is undriveable. It soon cools down and we are shivering. A vehicle going the other way stops and we ask them to take a message back to the local garage to send a recovery truck. I flag down a car going on towards our destination.

"Would you be able to take my two friends and their things on to Banff, please? Our car is undriveable."

The driver agrees.

"I'll see you at the Excelsior," naming the hotel I had booked. "Tell them my name and ask if you can move into your rooms. I should be there fairly soon."

Vicki and Howard take our bags and go.

I stay by the car. After half an hour, my face begins to freeze but I am careful not to scratch at the throbbing extremities. It is not uncommon for people to have bits of their ears, noses and chins lost, where they have rubbed and frozen tissue has come off. By the time a tow truck arrives from the garage with its warm cab, I am shaking uncontrollably and in fear of freezing to death. He winches my car back on to the road and loads it up. I go back with him to the garage and arrange for their mechanic to work on it, ready to collect when we return in a week's time.

There is a bus coming through shortly and I wait for it in the cafeteria. I hope Howard is not bothering Vicki.

As I ride in the bus to Banff, I am glad I am not driving because I can enjoy sundown retreating from the valleys, overhung by pink peaks. It is stunningly beautiful.

When I reach Banff, I find Vicki and Howard sitting in the hotel bar. Howard is surrounded by empty beer glasses, and Vicki is reading her book. Because Howard is there listening, I am reluctant to talk to her, expecting to have an opportunity later. We have a lot to talk about, and the sooner we do that the better.

I have mixed feelings about Vicki because of the hurt from her indifference on too many occasions, and now she is engrossed in a book and reluctant to talk. When we first met, our relationship floated very prettily until it ran aground on mistrust. Now I mistrust the book she is reading and I mistrust her, for no other reason than I cannot see what else to blame.

Rule 42: *A person's physical presence speaks volumes to those who are listening.*

CHAPTER 43 CHASED DESCENT

The next day we are having hot chocolate at the ski shop cafe at the foot of the piste. Vicki is eye-catching, wearing flared fluoro green ski pants and jacket, with a green knitted toque. We have made a couple of easy runs. We are all moderate skiers.

"You are a better skier than we are," I tell Howard. "We will slow you down. Why don't you go on ahead and make the most of it? We can meet later for lunch."

"I'd rather stay with you two," he says. "I will be able to give you a tip or two."

Howard sticks to Vicki like glue. Later, at the cafe, when he goes to get his lunch, I try to engage her in conversation.

"Did you see that bear back there?" I ask.

"Yes," she says looking up from her book.

"How do you feel about skiing with a bear around?"

"I don't know," she turns back to the book.

"What are you reading?"

"Kierkegaard."

"What's that about?"

"Existentialism and psychology." She answers my questions politely but I can see she doesn't want to talk.

"Is it good?"

"It makes you think – about how belief depends on doubt."

"And what do you believe in?"

"I'm not sure. Probably not Christianity."

"Nor I. My beliefs come from science, as you know."

"Science is too impersonal. Kierkegaard says that subjectivity is truth."

That seems like a contradiction to me.

"Can your truth be different from mine, then?" I badger Vicki.

"Yes, that's right."

"Give me an example."

"It's too difficult to talk about," she replies and carries on reading her book,

"That doesn't leave much to agree about then, does it?"

"No."

I am hurt by her reluctance to share her concerns with me. It is as if she is denying her feelings and has withdrawn, her ability to communicate paralysed. She seems weighed down by sadness or loss.

I want to ask her about her fling with Richard, but Howard is always there.

"Why don't you try one of the black runs?" I ask him. "I want to talk to Vicki alone."

"No, I'd rather ski together. Why don't we all try a black run?"

"You go first and try one for us."

"Let's all try one."

Howard couldn't be persuaded to leave Vicki and me together. When I fall behind with Vicki, who skis more cautiously, he climbs back up to us. If we go for coffee, he comes with us. The music playing in the ski lodge catches my mood, Jimi Hendrix's "If Six Was Nine". If existentialism is preoccupation with the present, Vicki is stuck in a hole and dragging me down.

I do not understand why she has come all the way here to cut herself off from me. It does not seem possible her withdrawal could possibly be shyness. I try to think about what she is feeling but I have seldom been successful in predicting females' behaviour in relationships with me correctly. I want to tell her that I love her, that I always will, and that I will help her overcome whatever difficulties she has.

There are obstacles between us. I want to tell her about Barbara and how that episode had ended in tragedy. I want to find out what happened between her and Richard. I need to talk with her but I cannot get started. I am waiting for an apology, explanation or discussion regarding her fling with Richard, for her to express a modicum of remorse. But she doesn't seem to be able to, or she wants to move on; I wish I knew which. In my mind, I run through possible conversation openings:

"I forgive you."

"I have finished with Barbara."

"I love you."

"Can we make a fresh start?"

I can never say these things because Howard is always there.

He styles himself after Ernest Hemingway, the gallivanting writer, and on Peter Ustinov, the raconteur, telling self-promoting stories about his adventures during his travels. Howard does not leave Vicki and me alone together and dances with her whenever she comes off the floor.

I wish I hadn't brought Howard. His bragging and cynicism are irritating.

We ski together and hard. In the evenings, after eating, we drink and dance ourselves to a standstill in the noisy bar and go to bed early. Vicki has one bedroom, and Howard and I the other.

I sometimes have black moods and I think that Vicki is in a mood, too, and that it will pass. It does not. In those days the words, stress and depression, are not in my vocabulary, and I only have a concept of a temporary malaise. I fall asleep thinking of her and wake up hoping that today we will start talking.

On our last day, Howard and Vicki share a chair on the ski lift in front of me, and he puts his arm around her. I am furious that my holiday, that was to have been a rapprochement with Vicki, has been spoiled by Howard. I realise I will have to assert myself with Howard or he will walk all over me.

When I get off the chair, I ski across his skis and put my shoulder into him, knocking him over.

"Bastard," he says. "What was that for?"

"Disrespect," I say, "For getting between me and Vicki."

Vicki hears this without comment.

"Fuck you," he says as he struggles to his feet. "She's not interested in you. I'll fucking trash you, crazy boy!"

I can hear his brain wheels grinding with malice.

"You'll have to catch me first," I say and take off along a trail leading to the top of the downhill.

"No problems," I hear him say. Over my shoulder, I see him lunge after me. This is going exactly as I planned.

I am in a crouch, head down, poles under my arms and bum up.

Howard is fifty metres behind me. When I reach the downhill, I turn and stand up high on my skis, using my body to brake against the wind, flowing like water and taking the fastest route through the moguls. My knees absorb the unevenness. I am only an average skier, a bit uncoordinated. Quite soon I begin to feel the pain of over-exertion in my thigh muscles, longing to rest, about to lose control. When I look behind, Howard is gaining and is now thirty metres behind me. I traverse off the piste into a forest trail.

He gets closer, intent on knocking me over, when he will stomp on me with his skis. I go fast around a sharp turn and over a 10-metre-high cliff with him close behind me.

The cliff is no surprise to me, as I found it yesterday and jumped down it several times, landing safely. But to Howard it comes as a surprise. He tries to stop, but is going too fast and falls over the edge. I land on my feet, turning to watch him as he falls steeply. Unimpeded by the soft powder snow he bounces off the hard ground. He rolls end over end down the scree slope, in a tangle of skis, until he comes to a stop. He doesn't move. I climb back to him. He is unconscious. I put him in a recovery position.

Vicki arrives. "You planned this, didn't you?" she says. I nod.

She says nothing. I suppose sibling rivalry doesn't need much comment.

I send Vicki down to a rescue station to phone for a stretcher. It takes the rest of the day to get him into hospital. He has broken both legs and six ribs. He is very quiet. Vicki hardly speaks to me. We leave him in the Banff hospital, and she requests I take her to the airport in Calgary.

"Pity Howard turned up when he did," I say as we drive back, the only time we are alone together. "We never even caught up with each other about Richard."

"I think your mind is already made up," she replied.

"I wanted to hear your side."

"There is nothing to tell. Nothing happened."

I can hardly believe what I am hearing. Can she be saying nothing happened between her and Richard? How can I have been so misled?

"I wish I had known," I said.

"So do I," she replied.

I couldn't think what to say next. The issue wasn't whether they went all the way, or trust, but the disdain she had shown me. True, I had postponed my interest in her, but two wrongs do not make a right. If I told her this it would seem like another criticism and would make matters worse. So I say nothing.

When I change the subject, I cannot get her to talk any more. She seems to be angry with me, as if the skiing accident was all my doing. I wonder if she meant to encourage Howard and make me jealous, causing our fighting and provoking Howard's accident.

Before she goes, at the departure gate, I try to kiss her on the mouth but she turns her head away and I have to be satisfied with a hug.

"I'll write," I say as I let her out.

"Yes, keep in touch," she says without much enthusiasm and walks through without so much as a backward glance.

I look back on Vicki's visit with profound regret. I had been waiting for her to express remorse for her fling with Richard, when throughout her visit she may actually have been displaying contrition. Or was it depression? Some apologies go deeper than words and maybe she had given them.

Three weeks later an ambulance brings Howard to my flat in Calgary. He is on crutches. A month later he is back to full health and works at a series of casual jobs, labouring on high-rise constructions. The accident does not subdue his tendency to get into trouble. Several times he gets into fights with other workers and is laid off.

At the flat, he terrorises my flatmate, Chris, who moves out. Howard contributes nothing to the running cost. Eventually, I demand half of the costs retrospectively for food and rent. He goes back to England, without as much as a thank you. I heave a sigh of relief and resume the social relations I broke off when he arrived.

With time, I become ashamed of my role in Howard's accident. The tragic consequence of Howard's visit is that I do not see Vicki again for several years. I keep in touch with her doings through Richard. We exchange letters every few weeks. He says he tells Vicki what I am up to and occasionally he tells me something about her. If Vicki is to be believed, Richard lied to me about their fling. Strangely, after all we have been through, I trust Richard's information even though I know he wants Vicki.

I like to think Richard has realised that we are made for each other and he is playing Cupid. But it is possible the opposite is true: that he is jealous and that he is discouraging us from getting together. For example, he may pass on to Vicki that I am womanizing. Anyway, when I fly over for a holiday to visit my family, Vicki is too busy to see me at Salisbury. I have to be content with a short telephone call with the woman I love.

I don't need much contact with Vicki to relieve my anxieties, because I imagine us getting together one day. Her other boyfriends must be temporary.

Rule 43: *Relationships have deep memories and unspoken uncertainties.*

CHAPTER 44   COLOUR CLASH

Later that year, in the summer, Richard writes that Vicki has a new boyfriend, William. He is an engineering student from a West African country, Bigeria. Unusual at LUT at that time, he is black-skinned. Like Vicki, he is involved in campus politics.

In jealousy, I imagine Vicki introducing him to her middle class family who would be puzzled by her choice. I wonder how Vicki's mother, a conservative English businesswoman, would regard the match. Up to this time, Vicki has seemed to be socially conforming. She is not a demonstrative person and with this partner she will be constantly in the public eye. Is her unconventional choice indicative of a new rebelliousness?

My scepticism reflects the racism normal in country England and redbrick engineering faculties at that time. I conclude that she must be very fond of him. However, I hope they won't last together and I will be able to revive our relationship once the debacle of our skiing holiday in the Rockies has receded in her memory. I write to Vicki, without mentioning William, the soliloquy that follows.

"Like moles, our lives are solitary, our souls always out of sight of others, our workings usually invisible except when, in the dead of night, we emerge to seek a mate. Urgently, we search our old tunnels looking for intersections with another, a soul mate. Sometimes we hear another's soft footfalls in the distance but when we get there, we find nothing – it is only an echo from the past. Blind from birth, we can find a mate by sharing, sound, touch, smell and taste, to discover empathy and build trust. After mating briefly, we return to solitude. Our imaginings remain within us, communicated only to our children, the history and traditions of our kind."

I write it to try to draw attention to the difficulties of cross-cultural matches and my continuing availability as a soul mate to share perceptions. I don't expect to get a reply and none comes. I doubt she would read it closely if she is, as Richard says, besotted with William. More than anything, she should realize how lonely I am without her, my soul mate.

It is unfortunate for our relationship that feminism ignites at this time. Its criticism of males is initially harsh and unfocussed. Men who like me are on the periphery of the Free Love and hippy movements inadvertently find themselves in the same reject bin with Chauvinists, bullies, misogynists and dishonest womanizers, when in fact their treatment of women is, by earlier standards, respectful, honourable and equal.

I hear from Richard that Vicki and William are a devoted couple. Their model of race relations is influential. Martin Luther King and Robert Kennedy have been assassinated, and in the aftermath there is racial tension between blacks and whites, spreading from the USA around the World, emancipation that is a reverse playback from the abolition of slavery in the USA in 1865, back to abolition in England in 1833. Jimi Hendrix's guitar screams defiance at American white society in the colour-blindness of his vision in his album, "Electric Ladyland".

A hundred years ago, Liverpool surpassed London and Bristol as the number one slave port in Europe. By 1792, 40,000 African slaves had been transported by Liverpool vessels alone to the plantations of America and the West Indies. From then, for the next sixty years, between forty and a hundred and ten ships sailed each year from Liverpool laden with slaves like cattle, and many died cruel deaths during their journey to America. A Liverpool actor lamented, "Every brick in this infernal town is cemented with an African's blood."

William's country, Bigeria, provided many of the slavers' victims, and I doubt that he could ever forget. Only a little older than living memory, the horror is controversial in Liverpool, as many people would prefer to forget. I wonder that Vicki, with her environs steeped in such an awful past, can trust someone with ancestors who had probably been enslaved. Would he not reflexively seek retribution for the awful injustices his people had suffered at the hands of the British, by letting her down when she is most vulnerable? In my jaundiced view, she is taking a risk in coupling with William.

Rule 44: *Unless there is reconciliation among different races, racial prejudice can endlessly update past discrimination.*

239

PART 8: SPREADING (1969–1972)

In which I invest in various prospects with a view to accumulating experience and resources to attract Vicki.

CHAPTER 45   WILD SOWING

When Howard at last leaves, I decide to get myself some fame to attract Vicki's attention by going back to the UK to do a PhD in management. It will take at least three years. I can get a grant that will pay for fees and a modest student lifestyle.

In the meantime, I have a good job in Calgary and a voracious sexual appetite starved by a year of celibacy. I decide to quit my job in a year's time to travel and seek romantic adventure before going back to the UK. I have to sow my wild oats before settling down. This has the negative connotation of irresponsible breeding, whereas I have been burnt already and I want to avoid that happening again. My ideal is to travel to South America for a year, with opportunities for relationships in romantic settings that are easy to end, by travelling on. I hope that when I get back to the UK, Vicki will be finished with William and more amenable than during our disastrous skiing holiday.

In the meantime, I prepare for a life of adventure by screwing my way through one after another of Hayley's single girlfriends. She and James throw me out, and I have to find another place to live.

"You have been treating my friends very badly," says Hayley, "like a man possessed. What's wrong with you?"

"I wish I knew," I admitted. "I can't seem to find what I'm looking for."

"What are you looking for?"

"I think a lot about Vicki. I have this anxiety right through me; an emptiness that hungers for her. It seems like romantic sex will appease it but it never does. So I move on to another girl, to try and find it there."

"I think you should discuss this with your doctor," says Hayley. "You can't stay here any longer, or I won't have any friends left."

I don't chase skirt in the office but I am always keyed up.

"Why do you look so worried?" colleagues ask me. "You are doing fine."

"I'm not worried," I reply.

I realise I have deep-seated anxiety from my childhood.

"How goes the battle?' one colleague always asks when we pass in the corridor. I want to punch him. I want to look like I'm on top of things, like a tycoon. His reminders that I do not are irritating. His observations are accurate, for I do see work as a battle, to be won by hard work. I feel I have a responsibility to apply my exceptional skills in solving technological problems for the benefit of my employer and society. I have a mission to better the lives of the poor, the helpless and those living under bigotry. Accomplishment of my mission depends on my work getting done, and I keep at it when workmates go off to enjoy themselves.

I move into a house where eight bachelors reside in style. At 6.00pm every weekday, cupboards and drawers slam shut, feet pound up stairs and six of us slide into seats around the dining room table. Mary, a fierce Scottish woman, wearing a white hospital gown, brings out the roast and vegetables. One of us carves as the others pass the plates around. We share in the cost of the house, with Annie cooking for us, cleaning up, making the beds and doing the washing. After dinner, we withdraw to the lounge and sit around quaffing port and discussing the events of the day or planning a weekend of rugby, skiing or girls.

The Round Table, as we call it, is a suburban male residence, a comfortable place to live, where men can get respite from female demands and enjoy each other's company. To get in, applicants must have unanimous approval. It is not practical to bring girls back there because the house is too quiet for privacy.

Canoil sends me to other cities for several months at a time. It has a cruel effect on my love life. Guys from out of town don't rate and suffer from the coming and going. Madly, I try to meet single women. I have time on my hands and I start giving guitar lessons at people's homes. My customers are all young virgin chicks and I am too professional to take advantage of them. I try nightclubs where there are cliques of girls who hang around asexual youths. They avoid me, an out-of-town lone wolf.

Back in Calgary, I try to scratch my itch for female company at rugby club parties. I stomp the night away to "Ob-la-di Ob-la-da" and music that releases energetic dancing. When my plans to leave

Canada next year are known, girls become even harder to attract. Everywhere I look I seem to see soft female faces, long female legs reaching up to alluring buttocks, firm breasts. It is tantalising. There are females where I work but they are off-limits. I have to masturbate, morning and night.

When I think of Vicki, I imagine her living in loving harmony with William in Liverpool. Then Richard writes that William has finished his course and gone home to Bigeria without her. He told her that he aims to be a politician, and white skin is unacceptable for a black politician's wife in Bigeria.

"He says black people back home won't accept her," Richard writes. "So he dumps her."

The situation is ironic. It is not Vicki's racial prejudice or her family's that splits them apart, as may have been expected, but William's. Probably he has known he will dump her all along and has used her badly. I am no better than he is, as he treated Vicki like I did Barbara.

It is strange how Vicki has let his lack of commitment get past her, when she has been so overzealous in stopping mine. If she had put him on a lie detector, she might have been saved from grief. Richard tells me she is very hurt. I fear she will become even more shy and reserved. I wonder if others see her in this way, or perhaps I am the odd one out in encountering this side of Vicki. My heart goes out to her but there is nothing I can do until I return to England and contact her. In any case, she may not want to have another relationship for some time.

When I am preparing to leave Canada, a friend at The Round Table arranges a blind date with Ruth, a school health advisor who lives with other teachers and nurses at the House of the Rising Sun. Her family live in Calgary. The girls do not like our salacious name for their communal home. Ruth has a healthy appetite for sex, and I am soon closely involved with her.

However, my plan is to throw in my job with Canoil and set out to travel for a year in Latin America, before going back to the UK to do a PhD. I long to join in the youth revolution that is passing me by. I feel unfulfilled in my business suit and tie, an imposter. Ruth wants to come with me to South America. Although it is only a few months since I met Ruth, she doesn't hesitate to try to push her way into my plans. I am determined to go alone, with more opportunities to meet people. I promise to write to her every week.

"You be sure to have a good time," she says bitterly. "Don't worry about me. I'll be okay."

"It's something I have to do. It was planned before I met you."

"I suppose you won't change your plans for me?"

"Could you take off with a girlfriend?"

"Who? Everyone I know is happy in their jobs."

"Well, I'm sorry but I am going alone."

If Ruth comes, I know it will severely cramp my modus operandum. My preferred travelling is in the lackadaisical denim style of Jack Kerouac's novel "On the Road," whereas Ruth's is the "ten capitals in ten weeks" coach tour style. If I go with her, my wild oats will be rolled.

For adventure, I want to be solo. Women are often envious of a man's ability to pursue promiscuous sex openly. Far from wanting to live on a pedestal of purity, most women are at least as carnal as men, but are less free to express it. Women watch male sport unashamed of their interest in male bodies. However, social mores make it more difficult for a woman to pursue a man than vice versa. A woman may have to live with her sexual hunger unmet.

When I tell my rugby club, Cloggers RFC, the day of my departure, they arrange a farewell piss-up in someone's basement. When I arrive, I find the group much in anticipation of a stripper they have hired. She is in a bikini and already performing, with an audience of about fifteen club stalwarts who are sitting around admiring her assets, as she bumps and grinds, wrapping her long legs around the structural timbers.

As I feared, I am nominated, as the man of the night, to participate in her act. I have been to one of these occasions before and I know that my role would be earthy,

I find it very embarrassing. She asks me to untie her top. Dramatically, she takes it off, revealing large well-formed breasts. I find my face in her cleavage.

"Windscreen wiper," someone yells, tilting his head from side to side as he hums, "Mmmmmm (Kiss) Mmmmmm (Kiss) Mmmmmm."

Laughter.

She wiggles her bottom in my face. Then I pull the cords on her bikini bottom. She holds it as she pole dances with a house stump. Then she removes it to applause and shouts.

"Woohoo!"

She is naked and gyrates to the music.

"Come on, Selwyn. Let's see you fuck her!"

I am expecting this request.

"No. Sorry, guys. I am shy, really. I couldn't possibly get it up."

"Faggot!" someone yells.

Everyone laughs.

It is traditional for the member leaving the club to comply. They try very hard to get me to perform but I stubbornly refuse. I guess the idea is that when you are leaving you are uninhibited and want to be remembered. Usually when club players leave Calgary, they will not be coming back and can go out in a blaze of glory with no repercussions. Their aim is to entertain club members with an athletic performance.

"Show us how you do it, Selwyn."

"No, sorry. I can't do it with anyone watching."

The nude girl comes over and sits on my thighs facing me, legs apart.

"Feeling a bit shy, are we?" she cajoles, unzipping my fly and holding me.

"Stop!" I tell her. "I just can't do it. Okay?"

"We can go in a bedroom," she says. "It will be nice; I promise."

I have no interest in this woman, or any woman, in this situation. I imagine that Vicki would be disgusted and horrified if I participate.

"I don't want to," I tell her. In case she is insulted I add, "It's not you."

She seems disappointed, gets up and walks away.

When a colleague invites himself to substitute for me, the assembly forgives me. Everyone looks on unperturbed as he indulges himself with spectacular flexibility and vigour. We are treated to the sight of his white buttocks pumping her on the floor in front of us as the team claps in time with the music. I close my eyes.

He gives a shout of triumph as he comes.

I wonder what she is thinking. She searches for her clothes, gets dressed quickly, takes her money without a word and leaves with her head hanging. I feel sorry for her.

The rugby players have a strange attitude to sex, wanting to debase an experience that is wonderful in private into a gross public spectacle. Can it be that good sex is unattainable to them? For a male club member to be seeking notoriety in this way he must be insecure, an exhibitionist and possibly a psychopath. However, I feel uneasy that my modus operandum may not be competitive. In bonobos, privacy is not an issue. Human privacy during intercourse is attributed to territory and monogamy. Since neither of these conditions is present, it is not surprising I am averse to participating in this act.

Distancing myself from the male chauvinism of engineers and rugby and my former friends is a big step for me. I cannot resist the clarion call of the youth revolution. If I wasn't leaving Canoil, they would probably throw me out. I am between two worlds in conflict. Now my anxiety is whether I will be acceptable to the other side. Once again, I begin redefining myself.

Rule 45: *A solo traveller will meet more people than those travelling in a couple or a group.*

CHAPTER 46 HIPPY LOVE

I metamorphose from a short-back-and-sides engineer in business suit, into a bearded longhaired hippy adorned in love beads, feathers, flowers and bells. I drive east across Canada in my station wagon, picking up draft dodgers from the USA. The Vietnam War loses popular support daily. I share joints with my passengers and listen to the music of the youth revolution: Bob Dylan, The Beatles, Hendrix and Joplin.

Hippies dress, talk and behave to shock mainline society. I visit Larry and Lisa in Ottawa. Larry is "straight", wears quality suits, ironed shirts and ties. They are in professional jobs and immersed in middle class culture. They conform to material consumption values. Hippies oppose their lifestyles and allegiances. I embarrass them. Employers and co-workers would be suspicious of their loyalties if they knew of their association with me.

I drive south-west to Kent State University with echoes still loud from the rioting and shooting of protestors there. I am a novice in the world of protest. I ask hippies how to protest. Opinions vary, but the anti-war movement seems to have broadened out into an anti-establishment movement. Passive resistance against the military, police and businesses is widely agreed. I have to buy petrol from the oil majors along the way to Texas and into Mexico. My lifts give me grass, and I soon adopt the affectations, attitudes and behaviour of a peace-loving drop-out, with a reflex for passive resistance.

Being a hippy means you have friends wherever you go. This is amazing for me, as I do not normally make friends easily.

Looking the part is important, and I go to some trouble to have long unkempt hair, old blue jeans, sunglasses, a bandanna and leather boots with medium heels. I learn to greet companions by touching knuckles and to give the peace sign at frequent intervals, especially to authority figures such as police. When something is good I say, "Ace, man", "Groovy", 'Far out", "Too much" or "Let it all hang out, Babe." If it is bad then, "Crap, man." If it is both good and bad, like an addictive drug, then it is "Shit, man." If it is difficult to understand, it is "Heavy, man." If it is difficult to understand because I am intoxicated, it is "Fucked, man." If I don't behave like a hippy because I am too intoxicated, or if I forget to exhibit my hipness, I am a "Shithead." This pantomime gets very tedious, and I long to have an objective discussion.

Hippies have values derived from universal peace and love. Working to get money is a betrayal of hipness, and I live free off people who can afford to give, especially the USA's Peace Corps volunteers who I seek out in every city. Free sharing of accommodation, food, marijuana, LSD and sex is expected in the communal utopia that is springing up in national and provincial capitals.

We are hostile to traditional authorities, armchair intellectuals and everybody who is not a hippy. Stealing from the rich and supermarkets is okay. The police are "pigs". The CIA controls Latin America by assassination. Global corporations such as the United Fruit Company control Latin American economies by crooked transfer pricing. Che Guevara is a hero because he mobilised resistance to tyranny. "Making love not war," "doing your own thing" and "letting it all hang out" are good. Bad are being straight, being earnest, being politically involved and being pro-establishment.

When I can, I leave the others and study books about Latin America to validate hippy claims of US tyranny. There is plenty of evidence in books that are obviously biased either for or against the US. It is impossible to be objective, and I do not feel comfortable with hippy beliefs.

We are against the war in Vietnam, and for legalisation of marijuana and free love. We condemn the USA for exploiting the countries of Central and South America and interfering with their political processes. We want free immigration into the USA and oppose racial discrimination. We oppose the prejudice against women, who must cease being regarded as sex objects and child raisers, by earning the same pay as men for the same work. We oppose the police who are corrupt pigs and we oppose the military that run the industrial economy for their own benefit. We oppose corporations that are motivated by pure greed. They must return profits to the people who they robbed. We want all countries to have peace and putting an end to poverty as their goals.

The best thing for me about the hippy movement is our lofty ideals and sassy girls.

Our revolutionary dreams are, funnily enough, traditional romantic love with hip girls. When I arrive in Mexico City, Hemingway's Mexico is singing in my veins as I lie on the grass near the city centre reading about the place. It reeks of adventure, fatalism and mob violence. I notice an attractive blonde, lying on the grass near me, reading too. I hello her. She is from California and waiting for her Mexican boyfriend. He has gone jaguar hunting in Yucatan. I am taken aback, as these lovely animals are nearing extinction. I decide it must be a metaphor for something in her imagination. I chat with her, and she seems on the level. When we stand up, she stretches luxuriously, limb by limb. She has pale green penetrating eyes. I ask her if I can take her out that evening.

"Come to my hotel room at exactly 8pm and I'll be waiting for you," she tells me. She gives me the address. I wonder what can go wrong. Maybe her boyfriend will be there and he will beat me up. I do not fight, except to protect women or my car. Or maybe she enjoys setting up a hoax and it will be someone else's room. I decide it is worth the chance of an adventure.

When I arrive at 8.00pm, it is an old mansion, with interior verandas around an inner court. I climb the staircase to the upper veranda. The door is ajar and the room is in darkness.

I think, "It's a vacant room." I knock on the door just in case.

"Come in," her voice calls. "Don't put on the light. I'm over here."

I feel my way over to a double bed where she is naked beneath the sheets.

"Get your clothes off and get in."

I strip off and get in beside her.

"I'm going to call you Miguel. That's my boyfriend's name."

Her body is wonderful and very friendly. At key moments, she calls me Miguel. She is fantasising the triumphant return of her boyfriend, and I see no reason to disappoint her.

"I killed two savage jaguars," I tell her. "Do you want hear about it?"

"Oh, yes!"

We spend several enjoyable hours as I regale her with hunting stories adapted from Hemingway's "Green Hills of Africa", alternating with making love. I had pursued the first jaguar until it was cornered, turned on the attack, leapt for my throat and landed on top of me, when I shot it. After a passionate intermission I tell her how, Tarzan-like, I tracked down and stalked the second one, from where it had killed and eaten an innocent village child. After following it across moonlit jungle glades like a shadow, I swung on a liana and dropped on it, strangling it with my bare hands.

Dawn is breaking as I end with the traditional reward of the jaguar hunter, vigorous sex in a succession of dominant positions. The spell is broken when she tells me her boyfriend will return at any moment. I leave in a hurry. I never see her during that night, nor learn her name, nor ever again set eyes on her, as far as I know.

As a sexual experience, I rated it at 8 out of 10.

The next day, I meet on the street an Australian hippy couple who are actors. They ride around with me for several weeks, as we visit the sights. Their world is affectionately peopled with Sheilas, bludgers, drongos, ratbags, drop-kicks, dingbats, dickheads and fuckwits. After they explained the meanings, I ask them if they are bludgers.

"Fuck you, nerdhead!" the guy says.

"Asshole!" the girl says.

This could have been affectionate banter, because they came with me in the car and I drove them around for three weeks.

One day we are walking along Avenida Insurgentes when we come to a university tower block where student protesters are hanging out the windows waving placards, protesting about Vietnam. Dressed in our colourful hand-loomed ponchos, with our beards, beads and long hair, our fingers ever ready with the peace sign, we receive a roar of welcome. It feels like we are part of a revolution that has so much support it is bound to succeed in reshaping the whole world for youth to enjoy.

The hippy actors like to be the centre of attention wherever we go, but I am an introvert and try to blend in. I am seldom successful because of my superior intelligence.

"Just say 'number 24'," I advised them in one restaurant.

They spent about half an hour getting the waitress to translate and pronounce the item they wanted. I regard the Spanish language as having beautiful sounds and sentiments but unfortunately obsolescent. The sooner everyone speaks English the better. Other languages are a nuisance.

I love Mexico; and one reason is that my dollars go a long way. I have money and I get respect, the same as I do in most places in the USA. In the UK you can only count on respect from your own class.

We smoke joints whenever we want, without being hassled by the police. There is cheap good quality pot available. I stay stoned for several weeks and do crazy things such as trying to keep up with the sunset by driving very fast. The circumference of the Earth is 25,000 miles and turns once in 24 hours; so the Sun sets at about 1000 miles per hour. Of course, I could not get my station wagon up to that speed, although I tried and nearly came off the road in the mountains. I realised that too much pot had affected my judgement. It is difficult to quit pot, because it releases me from the worrying that follows me whatever I do. I have a hunger for it deep within me, getting in the way of almost everything else. After a few days it recedes, and from then on I use pot on special occasions only, when I am with people who are unable to talk meaningfully and I do not have an excuse to leave.

While I have been travelling, Vicki has been working as a professional counsellor at a hospital in the UK. I send her a postcard.

Acapulco
June 1970
Dear Counsellor Vicki,
I hope your job is going okay.
I hope they know how smart you are.
Mexico is amazing. I am on the grass at the beach.
The waves are high.
Wish you were here.
Love
Selwyn.
PS Would you like to live in a commune?
PPS Please write to Poste Restante, San Salvador, ASAP as I will be there in about a month.

I doubt that Vicki will be impressed that I have become a dope fiend. She is quite conservative. I know it is just a phase I am going through, as they say. Although I enjoy it, it is addictive and may impair my mind skills.

In Mexico I meet some travellers who are spending two years riding horse-back from Peru to Canada. Hearing their adventures inspires me to go on a horseback expedition. My preference is to ride south through Argentina, with a companion, preferably a girl. I ask the girls I meet if they can ride.

I leave fabulous Mexico to get away from the actors, whose posturing irritates me. I drive out to the Yucatan, then to Belize and down to Panama, sightseeing along the way. In the capital cities there is much poverty.

I send Vicki another postcard.

San Salvador
July 22, 1970
Hi Vicki,
I have just watched on TV a recording of the Lunar Landing.
A local told me: "The Americans are Gods.
They can do anything.
We can't even get food for our next meal."
Love Selwyn
PS San Salvador exports bananas to the US.
Please write to Poste Restante, Panama City. I will be there in October.

Whereas the San Salvadorean's response was admiration of the US tinged with fear, this event was for me a triumph of science and engineering methods that are available to San Salvadoreans as soon as they can establish an economy that can pay for them. The problem is that their leaders are under the influence of religions. So they are stopped from controlling births, population growth absorbs public money, and most of the economy is dominated by poverty. The main hope is that science will oust religion from family planning.

Lambeth Hospital,
Sept 24, 1970
Hi Selwyn,

Got your card. The job is great. The patients are lovely, so hurting and needing.

I am very busy. It's work, work, work, but I love it.

Marion got married last weekend.

I went to the wedding with Richard, as friends.

He says he will write when he knows to where.

Yes, I would like to live in a commune with people I like. Are you sure you would like commune living? You are the least communal person I have ever met!

Love

Vicki

Vicki doesn't know me as a hippy. I have learnt to put up with other people for the benefit of their ideas and serious talk, although in my experience of hippies these do not occur often or with regularity. My interest in communes is in living with like-minded people, either in an existing commune or by starting one. I am excited that Vicki has the same idea and I will investigate possibilities.

I sell the station wagon in Panama and with a back pack and guitar I fly to Bogota. From there I take overnight buses south, so that I don't have to pay for accommodation. After some adventures I arrive in Lima where I meet Jill, an American teacher of English.

After we kiss a little I ask her, "How are you at riding a horse?"

"I love horses," she says with a New York accent. "They are so sweet."

Horses are not sweet: it is a ridiculous statement. Neither are they sour. Gustation acknowledges five basic tastes: sweet, sour, bitter; salt and protein. The taste of a horse is the bitter ammoniac or urine-like taste of sweat, depending on temperature, work and washing.

"Have you done some riding?" I ask.

"Oh, yes, I've been on a horse many times."

This answer does not answer my question fully, but her eyes are smiling with so much promise of a good time that I give her the benefit of the doubt.

"How would you like to come with me to Asuncion in Paraguay and ride south through the Argentinian grasslands?"

"How long would that take, Selwyn?" she asks.

"The distance is one thousand miles. If we take it easy and do twelve miles every day, then three months."

"Hmm," she replies. "Three months in the saddle. When we finish we will be able to get work as gauchos!"

Although I suspect she has little experience on a horse, her spirit is excellent and she will be able to learn en route. She throws in her job and we set off to Argentina to find horses we can buy. A week later we arrive and seek horses for sale from gauchos. Like cowboys, they do their work on horseback. They do not want to sell, or they will be out of work. We ask station owners, estancieros, but the stations are huge and the owners are not interested in selling horses to gringos, because if they have an accident, they could hold them responsible.

Eventually, our search for horses by bus reaches a lake at Santa Rosa near Cordoba in the Argentine pampas. For a week, we try living rough, as we will on the trail. We use a tarpaulin as a makeshift tent. We cook Quaker oats, beef steaks and capsicums over an open fire. Collecting enough wood for a fire takes most time. When it rains, it is challenging but it does not dampen the romance. Jill passes the camping test with flying colours. Now all we need is horses.

We travel on by bus, asking at way stations without much encouragement. We take a break at Buenos Aires and cross the River Plate to Montevideo. At the Rowing Club we meet the son of an Uruguayan estanciero.

"I think my father will have two horses you can have," he tells us.

"Will they be expensive?" Jill asks him. She is a shrewd shopper.

"No, very cheap. We have many. I go home this weekend. If you want you can ride them."

"Thank you. We would like that very much."

"How you say, I am honoured if you be my guests."

"We are delighted to accept."

He drives us there and we find his family well-off, owning a large and wonderful ranch. They make us very welcome. We go for a ride on the Pampas. Our horses are well-behaved. My saddle is a sheep skin, with the wool uppermost, held in place by a broad strap around the horse's girth. Although there are stirrups, compared with a fully mounted English saddle it is uncomfortable. However, the horses are willing, and I know I will get used to this type of riding. My horse is responsive and I enjoy myself.

Jill is in difficulty. She is unable to rise in the trot and bounces around painfully. She stays at a walk to avoid being shaken We are unable to teach her to trot. She is clearly out of her element and unable to keep up. I am disappointed that she does not keep on trying, for the basic gait of our epic journey must be a trot, or it will take forever.

It is a fabulous ride, as our host takes us to see peccaries, coypu, capybara, javelina and tapirs in their natural habitats.

On our return, I look quizzically at Jill.

"No," she shakes her head. "I can't do it."

I consider leaving her and looking for another girl companion rider but I have grown attached to her. My interest in living like gypsies in a horse trekking commune has abated. A nomadic commune may be possible in an eastern country but roadside travelling and living in South America would be difficult and dangerous . It is the end of the dream that brought us together and from Peru to Uruguay.

With horse trekking abandoned, I decide to pursue living in a static commune, where I might persuade Vicki to join me. Jill is not much interested but we continue travelling together for the time being. I hope she will change her mind.

Rule 46: *Even when the proponents are enthusiastic, plans that require entirely new behaviours are likely to fail.*

CHAPTER 47   COMMUNES

We thank our Uruguayan hosts at the horse ranch and go on by bus to Asuncion in Paraguay, where we will visit a former commune. Jill is sceptical but I welcome her challenges to my ideas. Even if I cannot convince her, I want to be prepared when I get back to the UK and try to persuade Vicki to join me.

On the way I read a history of the New Australia commune in Paraguay, founded in 1892 by William Lane, a prophet of anarchical communism. The Paraguayan government wanted to repopulate after the Great War of 1864-1870 in which Paraguay was utterly defeated and nine out of ten males died. The population was recovering from the bloody war with its neighbours. Lane was given 75,000 hectares of land. He brought a shipload of 220 mainly male socialists who were disenchanted with life in Australia after the shearers' strike was broken in 1891.

"There were so few men that women took over the restoration of agriculture, industry and commerce," I tell Jill.

"In between taking care of kids," she added.

"A woman with a job would leave care of her children to other women, as we do today," I say.

"Were the New Australia men welcomed by the women?" asked Jill.

"They were short of men and must have been disappointed when the dictatorial and idealistic Lane set racist rules that prevented the predominantly single males from consorting with the local women. Alcohol was forbidden and he insisted on monogamy. He lived with his wife and three sons. The commune was unsuccessful and Lane left to go to New Zealand in 1899."

We meet Gabriela at Cosme, where the commune had been set up on land given by the government. She is a descendant of one of the original New Australia socialists. She lives in the US, where she is a psychology lecturer, and is visiting relatives.

Gabriela tells us, "The biggest problem in any commune where there is much work to do is achieving egalitarianism. Some people cheat, leaving others to do their work."

"That's easy," I replied. "You can bring it out in the open and embarrass the hell out of them."

"Selwyn," says Jill, "that may be okay for someone with a hangover. What about someone who claims to have injured his back?"

At least Jill is seriously considering commune living.

"Yeah," chimed in Gabriela, "are you going to wait until a cheat tells you about it?" I am not sure if this is meant to be sarcastic but I am polite and let it go.

"No, you could fix it before that. You make sure it's the people closest to them who will suffer."

"How?"

"Put them in work teams with their friends and base the egalitarianism on the work done by the team."

"But how are you going to know who is a shirker?" asks Jill patiently. "Shirkers won't be accepted by any of the teams, except for a team of shirkers. Then what do you do?"

"Make the shirkers team captains."

"If you know who they are." Jill sounds impatient. I ignore this.

"They will try to get the best workers in their own team. After choosing, there could be election of captains."

"Selwyn, that seems okay, but there must be something wrong with it because I have never been anywhere that does it that way."

"Maybe no-one has figured it out before," I say. I like it very much when I suggest solutions, because people usually try very hard to show I'm wrong.

"We still don't know who the shirkers are," says Jill, looking up from a magazine she is reading.

"That was a problem here. They didn't know who they were until it was too late," says Gabriela.

Jill puts down her magazine and rolls her eyes rudely. "Told you so."

"Perhaps new commune members could present references," I suggest.

"They did that. But shirking comes and goes. There are a few dyed-in-the-wool shirkers and many who want to punish their former friends for something."

"It is a major problem," I admit, but I am not beaten and will work on it. I think Jill is stuck on the difficulty of labelling someone a shirker, whereas the real difficulty is in getting shirkers to lift their game. I will be interested to discuss this with Vicki when I get home.

"What is it about cults that enables them to survive?" Jill asks. "Is it a supernatural leader?"

"No. Socialist cults are successful, too, with a leader who is merely respected," says Gabriela.

"Then what is it that the leader has to do?" asks Jill.

"Give out rewards and punishments," I say.

"What rewards and punishments?"

"Going to heaven and hell."

"In a socialist commune?"

"A technological heaven and hell."

"What would a technological heaven be like?"

"High quality living and health care, no work, holiday house, rich food, good booze, good sex. Stylish living."

"Okay, so that is the carrot. What about the stick? What would a technological hell have?"

"No energy, polluted water and bad air. Insanitary conditions, disease, smell and noise," I reply.

"That is ordinary everyday living for most people on the planet. That's not a technological hell."

"What is?"

"Drug addiction, murder, abduction, rape, torture, imprisonment."

"I agree. Okay for a mass market run by a tyrant, but not for a commune. Can you see why religious communes are more successful? Their hells are conjured up and they don't have to worry about the media or prison riots."

"The negative reinforcer, God, is offsite and cheap to deploy. Generating fear from being cast down supernaturally into everlasting fires, with gnashing of teeth, requires less skilled labour than torture."

"Are rewards and punishments necessary?"

"Yes, for conditioning people to obey rules they may not like."

"What sort of rules?" asks Jill.

"Paying their taxes. Giving their assets. Bringing in an income. Working. Praying. Making obeisances or sacrificing to the leader. There can be hundreds of rules."

"How is a commune defined, then?" Jill asks.

Gabriela answered. "I looked this up. A commune is an intentional community of people living together, sharing common interests."

"What kinds are there?" Jill asks.

"I—" begins Gabriella.

"My analysis," I interrupt, pleased to be able to reveal the results of several hours of research, "is that everything about a commune depends on its know-how or technology and who provides the material and resources it needs."

"Okay, how does that explain a religious commune or cult?"

"Such communes have a purpose or mission and they need god's approval to pursue it. Getting the support of established religions can be difficult."

"What about a permaculture commune?" she asks.

"Their know-how is in converting wastes and natural materials into food for humans. They rely on access to land, water and other resources."

"I get the idea of the technology having needs provided from outside. What other types of commune are there?"

I am enjoying recalling my analysis. "Project communes, like for the Ascent of Mount Everest; primary industry communes, like a Masai village with its herd; product communes, like pottery collectives; and consumption communes, like a camp-out of drug users."

When I finish, Jill asks, "How do your technology types help me appreciate communes?" It is a hostile question, originating possibly from the way I had pushed Gabriela's response to Jill's question aside.

This is the kind of challenge I like. "The needs for materials may be of great interest to law enforcement officers in communes where drug taking, or growing particular crops are proscribed. It would be of interest to sponsors wanting to promote commune living. A similar analysis of the other types would reveal communes where different types of key technology are most valued."

I turn to Gabriela, "What is your idea, Gabriella?"

She shakes her head. "Communes are first about emotions, not technology. The most visible feature of a commune is the emotional bonding to the whole group rather than to any sub-group. Members are experienced with emotions beyond social collectivity."

"What do you mean 'emotions beyond social collectivity'?" Jill asks. She likes other people and collaborates naturally. She is warming to commune living.

Emotions are a black box to me. I try to hide mine and do not have many feelings.

"How do the emotions affect communal life?" I ask.

Gabriela explains: "A commune could be a group with a love of music, not musical technology, but as a communal emotional experience."

I cannot think of ever having a communal emotional experience.

Jill asks: "Do you think the New Australia people enjoyed a communal emotional experience beyond collectivity?"

"Sexual hunger, I should think," I say, sotto voce.

Neither of the women laugh.

"Possibly they thrilled in realizing they were involved in an experiment in socialism, testing the ideas of Marx and Engels," says Gabriela. "They may have had group emotions separate from the collective ethos, Lane's leadership and shortages of women."

She smiles at me tolerantly.

"It may not have been a strong emotional bonding," I say. "Lane lived here for only 7 years before quitting. The dissatisfaction of the single men due to lack of women is usually seen as the cause of the failure. Mosquitoes and humidity made the work hard. Most males will work hard in the presence of women and slack off in their absence. They deserted Lane's leadership and turned for comfort to the Guarani women and rum."

"What should Lane have done?"

"He was right to put a barrier between the commune and the community," I say. "Communes that assimilate often disintegrate. He needed an alternative supply of women for the single men. He could possibly have attracted more lefty women from Australia. If not, when there are more fewer women than men, the solution is for the men to share the women. A woman is inclined to be generous towards any man who, when he might be the father, will take responsibility for her child. The more men she can get in that position, the better off she is likely to be."

"No way," says Jill. "One man is enough."

"One is too many," says Gabriela rudely. "I think I'll turn in."

I think Gabriela means one man at a time. Although Jill is very loyal, she is quite demanding and protective, smothering me. If we had another man travelling with us, I would want to share Jill on alternate weeks. It is not likely to be attractive to her until another guy is available.

It is very hot in Paraguay. The next morning we farewell Gabriela and are relieved to fly out to Quito in the Andes, which is at higher altitude and much cooler.

When we arrive in Quito, we hear of a commune in the Ecuadorian jungle near the border with Brazil. We travel there by bus and truck and, for the final leg, down a headwater of the Amazon River by canoe. It puts us ashore into solid jungle, with only an overhung path to follow. After ten minutes climb, we reach a beautiful open plan house, thatched with reeds, on high ground above the flood-line, looking down the river. There is no-one there. There are no doors and we wait inside in the heat for about an hour. Then a man wearing a Stetson materializes out of the jungle, with a machete in one hand and a large bunch of bananas on his shoulder. He is bare to the waist, with long hair down his back, his face shaven but pock-marked. He tells us how the commune started.

"We were a dozen couples. The government in Quito granted us a long-term lease on one hundred hectares of rain forest. We helped each other to build our houses and plant crops. Then it all began to go wrong. It is difficult to stay healthy here because of tropical diseases such as malaria. The nearest doctor is two days' travel away. It is difficult to grow enough to sell to pay for essentials such as medications. First, the women left. Then, one by one, the men did, too. I'm the only one left," he says sadly.

He pauses, fidgeting with embarrassment.

"I would appreciate $10 from each of you. You can sleep here tonight. I'll provide a meal of beans and rice, with plantain."

Jim is the only one remaining on the commune's land. We have come all this way for nothing. We follow him on a walking tour through the thickly jungled land. He shows us the plantains and sweet potatoes he is growing.

We gladly give him the money and spend a pleasant evening talking about his experiences. He is a tough survivor and says he has the respect of the Indians with his self-taught knowledge of tropical medicine that he uses to treat them. I briefly consider staying there, but I can see it will be a hard life, unrelieved by female company, not like the communal life I am seeking. We learned little about married life in a commune, except that here they had tried monogamy. That problem was the unsupportable lifestyle expectations of the women. Malaria is cruel and the treatment is expensive. He has learnt Indian medicine and is surviving.

Jim is quite intelligent and we have some good conversation.

"People who live in communes are 'communists', aren't they?" Jill asked me. "I mean, the Red-under-the-bed type of communist." She had lowered her voice and looked around before she asked this question.

"Your furtive behaviour amazes me," I say as I mimic her, laughing. "It is very unlikely that Robert McNamara has the CIA monitoring the allegiance of the Quito government by posting listening devices here in the jungle."

"It could be an involuntary association," I say. "The same as when you look around to see who is listening before you fart."

Jim laughs. Jill blushes.

"I do not," she says emphatically. "The great frequency with which you divert my questions on to trivial side-issues indicates an overused obfuscation strategy designed to protect your know-it-all image when you know fuck-all about it."

"I am sorry, Jill," I say. "It must be against the rules to suggest that a woman farts, even with consideration for others. Now, what is your question?"

Jill laughs. "Are all people who live in communes communists?"

"Hmm. How long do you have?" I ask her.

"Why?"

"I can answer 'Almost all,' or I can explain how Robert McNamara used to pick out so-called 'communists' to bully."

"Explain, Selwyn, please."

"I'll try to. Jim, would you correct me, if I get it wrong? It is unlikely, as I will keep to the basic logic, which I think Jill is most comfortable with."

Jill turns to Jim. "He's always like this."

"Indeed I am, which is fortunate. Now, the main proposition is that the communists that the US government opposes are egalitarians."

"Shouldn't such fairness be applauded?" asks Jill.

Even though we are as bad in the UK, I try to distance myself. "Not in America, because to be egalitarian you tax the rich and give to the poor."

"Which one is worse?"

"They are equally bad."

"Why?"

I am without authority and do not feel any remorse in admitting this failing on behalf of all Americans. "They are un-American. Communism is un-American. Therefore Americans are anti-Communist. It is a tautology. Such fallacy is not unusual. A tautology lies at the heart of every belief system, including Science and Christianity. Science observes; what is observed is Science. How do we know Christ is the son of God? Because it says so in the Bible. What is the Bible? The word of God. How do we know that? It says so in the Bible. It is a matter of belief. I digress. Americans believe in selfishness, or its euphemism, Freedom."

"Why not egalitarianism?"

"You could go on a ramble through US constitutional history, but just accept that Americans have no interest in it at all."

"Americans believe in being selfish? What about the common good and community?"

"They are not allowed to interfere with the processes of selfishness called market capitalism."

"Then communes are nowhere," Jill says sadly.

"What is more, Americans are required to allow each other to be selfish," I tell her, "whereas a commune or collective needs some unselfishness to stay together, because there are people wanting to rip it apart. McNamara was most opposed to egalitarians who had much unselfishness or even opposed selfishness."

Jill reinforces my point, "The US government doesn't like people who oppose selfishness. Such a commune is impossible."

"The government must have very selfish people," says Gabriela.

"They are. People like us elect them," I reply.

Jim interrupts, "It is changing, slowly."

I brush this comment aside. "In the meantime, egalitarian communes like this one have to hide out. Out of sight, out of mind."

Jill asks, "Jim, perhaps it is also because of change that the other members have been able to go home?"

"Maybe."

"How long will you stay here, alone?" she asks him.

"As long as I can, Jill," says Jim. "I love it here. Maybe I'll move in with the Indians."

Soon afterwards, we say goodnight. It is glorious sleeping in a hammock, fading out on the shouts of monkeys and with parrots shrieking all around, and fading in again at daybreak. I wonder if Vicki would like it here.

After a breakfast of fruit, we thank Jim and leave to catch the mail canoe downstream.

Jill and I have found that with living in communes, selfishness prevents cohesion. Its complement, egalitarianism, won't work. A compromise may be better than either alone. If we can find a commune with enough selfishness to motivate people and enough egalitarianism to hold them together, then Vicki and I may be able to design a lifestyle for living together.

RULE 47: *A commune needs a religion, an ideology or a charismatic leader, as well as isolation from the outside world.*

CHAPTER 48   INTENTIONS

Further down the Amazon, the mail canoe puts in at a jungle path. We get out, taking our packs. The canoe continues downriver.

"I hope the natives are friendly," Jill remarks as we push through the vegetation overhanging a path.

"There's only one way to find out," I reply.

We come to a large clearing with a church and buildings of an agricultural mission. We meet an American woman of about thirty, with a good figure, wearing khaki cotton twill jacket and shorts with army boots.

"Anne Sawyer," she says, shaking hands. "I have been flying in and out doing my post-doctoral research for several years. I am an anthropologist and am investigating the Indian tribes around here."

"Jill and I are into evolutionary psychology," I add to make our interest respectable. "We are going around visiting communes to find out how they tick. Are you interested in mating?"

She looks at me, then at Jill and smiles. She is not sure if I am kidding. "What did you have in mind?"

I smile back. "We want to find out whether promiscuity provides social cohesion in human communes the way it does with bonobos."

"This is the place to come to find out about mating in communes," she says. "The people who live around here have many different ways of doing it."

"What are some differences between communes?" Jill asks.

"The ratio of males to females," she replies. "The Indians here have famines and are into infanticide, the same as indigenous people in other places. Over a long period, they let up to half their infants die. Other places are on record where it is higher. It changes the gender balance."

"Do they let girls or boys die?"

"It seems to vary with the food outlook and the population saturation level. When they want to boost their numbers, they let boys die. When there are too many of them and they are going to fight for more territory, they let girls die. It is necessary for dealing with problems of over- or under-population. The death of 70% of infants at certain times has been found in some indigenous communities."

"They must plan fifteen years ahead," I comment.

"I'm not sure the elders sit down and say, 'Now, we're going to plan.' Things just happen naturally. When there are more women than men, they tend to have polygyny, with the better-off males having more than one wife. When there are more men than women, the most attractive women have several men.

"However, the bigger picture is of multi-mating. For example, some tribes believe that babies are made from semen – the more the better. Therefore, a woman on her wedding day may have intercourse with every male guest, maybe twenty men. The men then believe her child is partly theirs and will provide food and help to her look after it. So, promiscuity is cohesive."

"It's the women I feel sorry for," says Jill.

"The women say they enjoy it," replies Anne.

I wonder what Vicki would think.

"Let's have a glass of wine," says Anne.

She goes into the kitchen and comes back with a bottle of red and a corkscrew. "Have you been to an Indian village?"

"Only briefly, in the mail canoe."

Anne offers to take us to a nearby village but we decline, wanting to allow the native people their privacy. She has been there long enough that she is almost invisible to them. We drink the wine and thank her for her information. The next day we fly out in a DC3 from the commune's airstrip to Quito.

Jill receives a message that her father has been seriously injured in a car crash. She has to go home to the USA immediately. I go with her out to the airport and see her off. When she goes through to boarding, I am sad. She has been very close. Despite my affection for Jill, after living with her for three months, she never tips me over into wanting to settle down with her, the way Vicki does. The obstacle with Jill is that she is reluctant to compromise her disinterest in my goals. We will write to each other.

After Jill goes, I write to Vicki. I believe she is more compromising than before.

Quito

November 18th 1970

Dear Vicki,

It was an honour to receive a rare letter from you, written on Sept 2, in Panama. I am relieved that you are happy counselling. I suppose there is no end to the work, as I cannot imagine you ever signing off a patient unless they no longer want your treatment, which is unlikely. So I imagine you are keeping busy, as usual.

I intend to test your theory that I would not like living in a commune. I am quite concerned, as you are usually right. It is true that I do not like having to follow rules. The solution I have in mind is to start a commune that has rules I want.

I am delighted that you, too, would like to live in a commune with people you like. I have been following my nose in tracking down various communes, taking me over to Uruguay in the east and back again.

Some types of commune I am investigating are:

1. urban craft commune: Lima pottery
2. child education commune: Lima
3. horseback trekking commune
4. performing commune: theatre; circus
5. criminal commune: piracy; Ned Kelly; Argentina
6. island commune: book, "Island", Aldous Huxley.
7. horse-drawn wagon travelling commune: gypsies
8. river or barge trading commune
9. ship mission commune: racing Brazil; circumnavigation
10. travelling camping commune, moving by trekking or public transport
11. agricultural commune
12. horticulture commune; permaculture
13. jungle or tropical subsistence farming commune: Amazon
14. jungle cultural research commune: Amazon
15. social mission commune: nuns, monks
16. religious mission commune: Amazon missionaries
17. religious sect: Hutterites; Mennenites
18. religious cult community: Waco
19. I am comparing these for the following attributes:
20. achievement of own intent
21. happiness of various types of participant
22. stability and survival

23. *personal cost*
24. *duration of stay of participants*
25. *ease of recruiting new members*
26. *leadership needs*
27. *gender constraints*
28. *behavioural constraints e.g. monogamy*
29. *suitability for participants to bear and raise children.*

My major conclusion so far is that the only communes I can find that are functioning properly are run by religions or cults. Not being religious, I/we are unlikely to find an existing commune we can join. Therefore, I/we would need to start our own commune. I believe we can achieve the commitment needed from participants with a group social mission interpreted scientifically (by me) and promoted by a popular leader (you).

I have not yet analysed how to find the most suitable location for such a farout commune.

Would you send me your ideas about this?

With love,

Selwyn

PS Please write to me in Lima where I will be in early December.

I post my letter on the way to buy a railway ticket to Guayaquil on the Pacific coast.

It has been an interesting time visiting communes. My finding is that an egalitarian commune can be promoted by communication, religion and promiscuity. What gender roles should I consider for communal living?

RULE 48: *Stability in sexual relations is essential for the enculturation of a commune.*

CHAPTER 49   POLYGNY

"Could multi-mating, or polygyny, be acceptable in a predominantly male or female commune, or should a commune require monogamy?" I muse. "In Paraguay the female to male ratio varied between 4:1 and 10:1 after the war. The solution adopted was to legalize polygamy, in which a man could have more than one wife. It was not uncommon for one man to father children with three or four women."

After seeing Jill off in Quito, I travelled on alone, for the first time in months, by train to the port of Guayaquil. There I embarked on a voyage across the Equator to the fabled Galapagos Islands, several days out in the Pacific. My ship is an Ecuadorian navy patrol boat.

I am not alone for long. When I go aboard, I meet a group of four female hippies from the US. Georgia is tall and confident, in her high-heeled boots. She is their leader. Vanessa, who I set my sights on, is medium height with blond plaits and a dreamy, self-absorbed face. Estelle is short and dark with thick glasses, with an independent outlook and a great sense of humour. Her best friend is Stacey, tall, with a happy-go-lucky grin and a mop of shiny curly brown hair. She is good-natured and practical.

The girls are in Ecuador to participate in an aid programme. It has fallen through, leaving them in the lurch, without much money. They are using the last of their money sightseeing and will then persuade their families to buy them air tickets home.

Our ship reaches the islands in a couple of days and then visits each in turn. Her crew row us ashore in longboats each day. Temperatures at midday are in the 40s, and the dark volcanic rock absorbs the heat, becomes too hot to touch and radiates it, making the rocky beach unbearably hot.

We ogle and photograph strange animals that are so tame we can reach out and touch them. Predation was unknown until humans arrived. Only here could Charles Darwin get close enough to birds' beaks to realize that they are adaptations from a common ancestor. We spent our time together getting stoned on the beach, dipping in the cold water where playful seals join us. We visit reptile and bird inhabitants at their homes.

Vanessa is tantalising in her bikini, but unfortunately the men's and women's hammocks are separate on the ship. After two celibate weeks at sea I arrive at a cheap hotel in Lima with the four girls. I am ready to consummate my friendship with Vanessa and with the other three, too, if possible. I suggest we get one large room for all of us. The other girls seem interested, but Vanessa objects.

"I would like Selwyn and I to have some privacy," she says.

"It isn't as if you have anything to hide from them, is there?" I comment.

"I know where you are coming from and I don't like it," she says. "I am not doing group sex."

"It could be fun," says Georgia. "If Selwyn is up to it."

Estelle and Stacey giggle.

Vanessa thinks for a moment. "Not tonight; I want Selwyn all to myself. How about group sex tomorrow night, okay?"

We all agree. Vanessa and I get our own room, leaving the other three to share a room, with Georgia in a single bed and Estelle with Stacey in a double. It seems quite likely that the two share more than the bed, because the way they are together suggests bisexuality.

Georgia is absent making a phone call at the post office when I first meet the group and take up with Vanessa. When she arrives she leaves me with Vanessa, I suppose by some rule such as precedence. Now I want to be alpha male to all four of them. Georgia is the alpha female and she knows she is most attractive, setting me a challenge.

"I am looking forward to tonight," I tell her.

"Of course you are," she says, "even though you haven't earned such treatment."

"How do you mean?" I ask.

"Normally a girl only takes up with a man who has other women if he is generous and kind. We haven't seen much evidence of either from you."

Ungrateful bitch, I think. Women have large appetites for rich living, and a polygynous man needs to be wealthy. But I am not going to take this put-down.

"Oh, is that how it works? I think that women normally bring a dowry, and when you lot didn't, I couldn't just leave you penniless. As a result, in case you didn't notice, I have been paying the hotel and food bills. By the way, I don't expect any thanks, although sex with you would do nicely."

"Typical male sexist objectification of women. Sex, with me, is not a commodity. It is linked to my emotions and feelings. I don't think you know what they are. I only have sex with people I like. Group sex for you is something you do by yourself with other people present."

I am not sure what she means, but other girls earlier have complained to me that I don't have emotions and don't show my feelings. That is correct. I try to do without emotions because they are difficult to control.

"But you said yesterday it could be fun."

"For the others. They haven't yet transcended to self-fulfilment the way I have. They will enjoy your selfish endeavours."

It is a blow to my plans when the next morning, Georgia changes her ticket to go back to the USA immediately. I suspect her parents have sent her a ticket. Georgia had seemed bitter, and I wondered whether her ideas had come from feminism. On reflection, her leaving is a blessing in disguise.

The rest of us set off for Cuzco in Peru by bus, on the way to the Incan ruins at Machu Picchu. That evening, Estelle meets Jarl, a Dane, and they get a room together. Vanessa, Stacey and I take a room with one very large bed. Stacey is in the middle, and I caress her while she does the same to Vanessa. I bring Stacey to orgasm, at the same time as she induces a climax in the narcissistic Vanessa that is even noisier than she was with me the previous night.

I fall asleep and awake in the night to find the two girls talking. I get out, go around, and get in the other side so Vanessa is in the middle. By now I know just what she likes. With our legs interlocked at the groin, like two pairs of scissors, Vanessa and I enjoy each other while she stimulates her friend, Stacey.

Sex with these two women together is a dream come true. In a threesome, even with a lot of talk, someone would surprise the other two with their urgency and this would stimulate the other two. Each female is different, and the attraction of multi-mating is novelty. When I cannot have Vicki, having more than one girl is less of an indulgence and more of a compulsion. It is a recurring dream of mine to be in bed with several girls at once.

I love women, and every one of them has something unique. As I try with Stacey and Vanessa to scratch the itch of love I feel for Vicki deep inside me, I imagine I am with Vicki who is a composite of her own special qualities, plus Bridget's idealism, Linda's body, Barbara's selflessness, Jill's passion and so on. My worrying over Vicki drives me to seek satisfaction with as many women as possible.

After three nights together, in the morning Vanessa asks me, "How do you feel about me now? How would you be if there are just the two of us?"

My early warning defence system detects emotional missiles heading in my direction and springs into action. "Why? Has Stacey said something?"

"No. I want to know your feelings for me."

"I feel very attracted to you."

"That's not what I mean," says Vanessa "Do you like me and want to be with me alone?"

This is getting difficult.

"I like you very much,," I reply." We could be alone; but what about Stacey?"

'You don't get it, do you? Do you feel that any bonds have grown between us?"

"Oh, I see. Yes, certainly."

"Emotional bonds?" she asks.

"Yes."

"Like love?"

I know that when females attack with love-seeking missiles, the only defence is to pretend love and counter attack. Hippy men like me have a dream of free love.

"Yes," I reply, "I'm almost sure."

"I'm not sure either."

"Is that because you are not sure of your feelings or because you don't know if the feelings you have are love?" I ask.

"Sometimes I think all you care about is sex – or multi-mating," she says. "Mating is not what it is all about for me, as if I am one of a herd," she sniffs.

I know it would be appropriate to put my arms around her at this point but I cannot bear displays of affection. Another response that sometimes works is to feign insult.

"That is so untrue," I say. " I don't want to continue this conversation."

I go and find Stacey. Another advantage of multi-mating for the male is that his vulnerability to being womanless is reduced, and his women need to compete by behaving well towards him. My love straddle with Vicki and Barbara was an example. Advantages for females are access to and security from a high-quality male, with assistance in child-raising from his other women.

RULE 49: *Monogamy's exclusivity increases covert competition.*

CHAPTER 50   LOVE IN RUINS

In Cuzco, as in Quito, the Quechuan indigenous women dominate activity in livestock farming, commerce, social activities, child-raising and home activities. Male activity is low and features chewing of coca leaves. In a polyandrous community, it is possible that a woman would have more than one man. If there is a shortage of women, men near the bottom of the hierarchy, who could not expect a wife, would benefit from the additional demand for males.

After two more polyamorous nights in Cuzco, the five of us take a bus to Machu Picchu.

The Macchu Picchu ruins of the temple and horticultural terraces are at a remote and easily defended location where an Incan sex cult could have existed until the 15th century . The community is believed to have been a cult led by high priests. There is speculation on the demise of the Machu Picchu Incas. About eighty female skeletons for every male have been excavated there. Parthogenesis, or virgin birth, without males, is unlikely. It has been discovered in up to one hundred species of reptiles, fish and birds but is extremely rare in humans. It seems most likely to have been a polygynous society.

Our guide tells us that the site was probably populated by a handful of high priests and many beautiful maidens brought there from all over the empire to be their servants. Such a polygynous society could easily have been ravaged by a few Conquistadors. Perhaps polygyny works when the few males are not required to fight.

On a hunch, I lead our group away from the tourist site along a little-used path going away from Machu Picchu.

"Where are you taking us?" asks Vanessa.

"We may be able to find a quiet place to camp out. It would be nice to stay here, rather than go back out to a hotel."

We passed a sign saying "Entrado Prohibido" (Entry Forbidden).

"Hmm," I say, looking at the sign. "That says something that Spanish speakers need to know, not us." We carry on walking along a narrow ancient track along the precipitous mountainside.

After a two-hour walk, delayed by the overgrown path in disrepair, we come to extensive unrestored stonework on a hilltop that commands a view of the valley. The absence of tourists, tourist signs and tourist pathways dramatizes the disappearance of the occupants. They say on arrival of the Spanish Conquistadors, the Inca king leapt to his death from a high place, and thereafter the civilisation rapidly declined.

The unrestored ruins have many of the same features we observed at Machu Picchu, such as immaculate walling with stones having dished surfaces in contact, to fit together and resist displacement during the many earthquakes that frequent this tectonic zone. On a grassy hilltop amid the ruins, we take off our packs and clothes and lie stark naked on our ponchos. Presently, Vanessa, Stacey and I make love. The thin air seems to pulsate with the husky panpipe tones and cantata rhythms of the Quechuan Indians that are with us, from a performance in Quito. These are the most sublime moments of my life. Estelle and Jarl are making love nearby; then Estelle comes over and joins in with us. The girls enjoy each other. Lesbian activity can prepare a female for a male.

For three days we read, talk and make love in our condor's eyrie with its 360-degree view at the junction of three cleft Andean valleys. The empty reflective sky seems to bear down on sharp ridges that rise like gothic arches from thick piers, stretching away along the nave-like valley of an immense imaginary cathedral, with us perched in the gallery halfway up. In the evening, my mind soars on gusts from a vast pipe organ playing Mozart's "Requiem", with sublime throbs and refrains that dignify the fading of the light from the windows high above. Night steals in along the valley floors, a procession of the innocent to safety from the devils that populate the night, until finally, with one crashing chord that echoes and re-echoes into silence, we fold our wings as darkness settles upon us.

We obtain drinking water from a channel cut through the rock six hundred years ago. Our hunger makes us high but short-tempered. I try to keep my females together at my spot and away from Jarl. I spend a lot of time posturing to try to attract Estelle away from him. I play on my guitar Simon and Garfunkel's haunting melody, "The Sounds of Silence".

I find myself flirting with Estelle, even though I don't mean to. I could run myself ragged keeping these females rounded up and in my harem. Polygamy is hard work, and allowing Jarl in for multi-mating comes naturally. We have returned to the sexual promiscuity of a peaceful species, bonobo monkeys, regarded by scientists as humans' closest ancestor. Humans have inherited genitals with a capability for multi-mating in a peaceable stable society.

We have brought no food, and on the third day, Jarl and I put on our clothes to go down to the village for provisions. We descend a steep path. As we enter the village we pass a swimming pool. Through the wire we can see a bevy of bare-breasted women talking together in the shallow end. Trippy with hunger, we pay to go in and strip off in a cubicle. We run out naked, laughing and as high as kites and jump into the deep end. Immediately, a middle-aged man calls a pool attendant who hurries away.

We are treading water, ogling the females, when two policemen arrive and beckon us over to the side. They tell us that we under arrest for nakedness. The man in the water wearing shorts, they tell us, is the police chief. It turns out the "naked" women are his family, and the females with their breasts bared are wearing bikini bottoms. The police hand us towels to cover ourselves as we get out. We put on our clothes and, feeling foolish and scared, we are escorted to the village jail, a rat-infested brick cell.

They keep us locked up all day, refusing us access to a telephone and refusing to inform our consulates. Eventually, with the aid of a dictionary, I apologize formally and profusely, explaining our mistake of deducing the women were naked. They walk us down the railway tracks out of town and tell us to keep going, but we circle back to the others.

"We are starving," complained Vanessa, "and all you think about is naked women and what you call mating. Women are just sex objects to you. It is sickening."

Vanessa flushes as if she could be angry. "Some of us like to think we have personalities, skills, conversation and experiences that are equally attractive. But men always focus on the physical first. Why? Because most men think with their dicks."

"The behaviour you are complaining about is instinctive. Men can't voluntarily change that. Women need to cover up, Vanessa."

Soon after, Jarl leaves us to go back to France. Our itinerant polygamous commune, three women and me, sets out for Chile, where we hear there is a very favourable exchange rate and low cost of living as capital flees Allende's democratic socialism. My conscience in profiting from the flight from democratic socialism is appeased by the knowledge that my purchase will strengthen the Chilean peso and improve the regime's standing in a small but possibly decisive way.

On my way there, I collect the Christmas card below and one from my mother, from the post office in Lima.

December 10th 1970
To: Selwyn
Merry Christmas
From: Vicki
I hope you find a commune with a turkey!
I am going to my parents' with my brother.
Love
Vicki

From Lima, we hitchhike to the beach at Arica in the north, where the desert reaches the sea. We live on the beach for several weeks in a tent. The three girls fall under the spell of a group of unemployed young men. Their prospects are dismal. The three girls have little money. I treat them to food and occasional entertainments, without expectation that it will be returned. I am pleased to help them but I begin to wonder where it will end as I want to keep as much of my funds as possible to support my studies in London when my travelling finishes.

They desert me and sleep elsewhere. Vanessa comes to me two days later begging for $50 for Jorge to obtain a passport. He wants to go to Peru to get work. I am suspicious that the money is to be shared amongst the girls. Vanessa knows I have money, saved up from my job in Canada. I have only a small amount with me, in cash and as travellers' cheques, which I keep in a pouch I hang around my neck, inside my shirt. I think that if I am going to finance them, the least they could do is to maintain the cosy sleeping arrangements I enjoyed at Machu Picchu.

"Why should I support him?"

"You could change his life for the better."

"He should come and see me personally. I don't know where or with whom you are sleeping. If you want me to give you money, then you have to sleep here."

"I am an independent woman," Vanessa tells me."You have been trying to exploit me because you have been fortunate in being able to earn enough to save money. Like most women, I cannot earn enough to save and have to depend on a man. It is oppression, and I have no hesitation in taking your money. You cannot force me to have sex with you."

They come back that night and I enjoy another glorious night. In the morning I go out early to gather pipis. When I get back they have gone, and so has $100 from my money pouch, which I had hidden in my backpack. I am angered by Vanessa's treachery and saddened that my friendship means so little to her. The worst feature of multi-mating is that women are less independent than when they have a "captive" monogamous male. Children, too, probably prefer to have an identifiable father.

Anne had told me that multi-mating is common in native communities. After a woman has intercourse with many of the men, the men accept possible paternity and ensure that she and the child have safety, shelter, food and other assistance. Thus, multi-mating binds communities together.

My finding is that there could be a case for starting a commune based on multi-mating and polygamy. I want it to attract Vicki. I doubt she will be attracted by polygamy with me, or polyamory or multi-mating, and the commune must have flexibility for a plurality of relationships.I am not planning to share Vicki with any other males. I would be content in monogamy with her, within a multi-mating commune. I am not keen on sharing Vicki, even though Richard tells me it is happening.

Arica,
Chile.
January 1971

Dear Vicki,
Thanks for your Christmas card. My Christmas was spent camping on the beach here, with a feast of the abundant shellfish called pipis. I made a soup from them, in an empty can.

I have been travelling in several countries investigating examples of commune living. The successful ones have been religious. I have learnt something.

These must be avoided:
1. *religion or zealous idealism that changes the commune into a cult*
2. *autocratic leadership*
3. *absence of medical facilities*
4. *all males or all females*
5. *pooling of personal assets*
6. *difficult physical environments*
7. *difficult social environments*
8. *ageism*
9. *sexism*

Some advantages of a commune could be:
1. *companionship with like-minded people*
2. *fulfilment by donation and sharing of skills with others*
3. *better child-raising and education for all ages*
4. *economy by sharing of resources*
5. *affording of better services and facilities*
6. *more free time to follow own pursuits*
7. *sharing of caring for young, sick, disabled and aged*
8. *freedom with option of individual living*
9. *sexual freedom.*

As you can see, commune living has many advantages, provided certain pitfalls are avoided.

My investigation is not yet concluded, as I want to visit communes in other places, e.g. Israel. A particular arrangement I am investigating is polygyny. This practice is widespread in human societies today and was normal in humans before agriculture was adopted. I also have yet to decide on the requirements for commune leadership.

As you know, I love you and want to live with you, either in an existing commune or in one we start somewhere.

I trust this information will be of interest to you and look forward to having the opportunity to discuss it with you when I get back, with a view to achieving a wonderful lifestyle.

I expect to be back in the UK in April.

With love,

Selwyn

PS: Please write to Poste Restante, Rio De Janeiro, Brazil.

Rule 50: *A polygamous man needs wealth to support his second and later women better than other men would.*

CHAPTER 51   SAILING CREWS

I cross the continent from Santiago to Rio for Carnival. When I arrive, I go first to the Yacht Club. Competitors in the inaugural Cape Town to Rio yacht race are arriving. The winner, *Ocean Spirit*, skippered by Robin Knox Johnstone, has already arrived, taking 23 days and 42 minutes and arriving in darkness without ceremony. The fanfare is about to be turned on for the next arrival.

As I stand in the crowd on the jetty, someone points and everyone cranes their necks. Visible across Guanabara Bay is the white blob of a spinnaker.

"Who is it?" someone asks.

"*Ermelo*," replies a South African looking through binoculars. "I'd know that spinnaker anywhere! It is Bryce Cullan's boat."

A motor boat putt-putts out to the finishing line with three officials standing in a row, in navy blazers and panamas. As the yacht crosses, a puff of smoke and the boom of a small cannon bring cheering and clapping for second place.

As the yacht comes nosing into the jetty at our feet there are eight crew lined up along the foredeck wearing white T-shirts that brag "Ermelo". Eight beards, with glimpses of brown faces. We clap them in and stand to attention as the scratchy PA system plays "God Save The Queen" and then the Brazilian national anthem. The crew pose on the foredeck for news cameras, with the skipper sitting on a winch in front, flanked by the smaller men on one knee and the tall beefy winch men, with their muscular arms folded, behind.

The crowd disperses to the rowdy bar inside, where The Beach Boys are harmonising the arpeggios of the "Sloop John B". I go in with them. I push through and buy a couple of tankards of beer, offering one to Bryce as he comes in. He takes it and drinks deeply.

"Ah. That's great."

"Did you run out of beer?"

"Yes, about two weeks ago. And rum, too. Nothing but water since."

"Did you have enough water?"

"Of course. We are very careful."

"How was the race?"

"Bloody awful. No wind for days at a time. We never saw another boat after the first day."

"I'm Selwyn Archer," I say, offering my hand.

"Bryce Cullan," he says, shaking.

The owner and skipper of *Ermelo* is a tall, blond-haired, raw-boned policeman in his thirties, with a South African accent.

"Congratulations," I tell him. "I wonder if you have any places in your crew. I need to get back to the UK for uni."

"I'm going to Jamaica," he warns.

"Close enough! I'd love to sail with you."

"Have you any experience?"

I tell him about the uni sailing club and about crossing the English Channel in a car. He is interested in the car project.

"What do you do when you're not sailing?"

I tell him I am an engineer and that I have been travelling. I don't let him see I am a hippy. I have shaved and put on a business shirt and trousers. Yachties and hippies are worlds apart. "Come aboard at six bells," he tells me, "and meet the crew." He turns away to talk to someone he knows.

It is a new race event, and some skippers had not realised the conditions. The South Atlantic, at these latitudes, is one of the least windy stretches of ocean in the World. Three weeks in a small space with nothing to do has tested relationships beyond endurance. That afternoon I watch as dispirited crews arrive, disembark and go straight to the airport, without speaking to each other.

There are plenty of crewing positions available. I post my letter to Vicki as I take my pack from the hotel to the yacht club.

Rio de Janeiro,
February 14th 1971
Dear Vicki,
Will you be my Valentine?XXXX

I am in town for the Carnival, which is on the four days before Lent, starting on Ash Wednesday. The indulgence is followed by abstinence: very Christian.

I have been here over a week and I noticed that the streets are being cleaned up and decorations put up. When I asked where all the beggars and tramps had gone, a local told me they had been rounded up, put on a ship and dumped out at sea. It is shocking! Although the citizens appear relaxed and friendly, I think the story could be true.

Here music is the social medium. One day I hear a complex rhythm coming from under a tree. There are about twenty youths gathered. Each is contributing to the sound, one with an empty bottle hit with a stick, another with a tin can hit by hand and others pounding blocks of wood together. The result is an intricate rhythm with many layered parts, vibrant and pleasant. Solo pieces feature in turn, as in an orchestral concert. I sat down and listened as they proudly displayed their musical culture.

The place starts throbbing at dusk, and everyone goes into the barriadas, or shanty towns, and packs into the samba schools to dance and drink, or rather crush together and drink, as there is not enough space for dancing. The Carnival is a competition between neighbourhood Samba schools, ending in a freaked out procession with elaborate floats and much noise, music, sexy dancing and bare skin.

To Samba you do a normal walk, either with a partner or by yourself. Relax your hips and legs to have fluid, loose steps, shuffling from foot to foot. Then add in the energetic frevo step with some small jumps that land in lunges. Other popular Brazilian dances are the Bossa Nova and Forro. "The Girl From Ipanema" is Bossa Nova, and I have learnt to play it on my guitar. I am looking forward to learning these with you.

I hope you have given some consideration to the commune variables I have written about in my last two letters: types of commune; their attributes; their advantages; things to be avoided.

After Carnival I hope to get a sailing boat home, hopefully in a crew where I can study commune dynamics at sea, as I am particularly keen on starting a sailing commune with you. I hope to join a crew of eight South Africans on a yacht going to the West Indies, from where I will fly home. We sail in about a week.

Love
Selwyn

I step aboard *Ermelo* with my pack promptly at 6.00pm. Her crew are gathering for sundowners in the cockpit. There are five young South African men. Three others have already flown back to Cape Town. A young Brazilian woman, Maria, is there, Like me she is joining the crew. Bryce shows the two of us over *Ermelo*. He is taking her to Jamaica where he plans to run charters and hopes to earn enough to buy out his partners.

I meet the rest of the crew. Alan is the same age as me. He is a solicitor from Kensington in London and flew down to Cape Town for the race. He is an experienced heavy weather sailor from racing in around-Britain races. He went to a famous boys' school and he is very social and pleasant.

Greg is a little older and an accountant from Durban. He is quiet, tall, beefy and punctilious. An experienced navigator, he has been with *Ermelo* ever since she was launched. The other two males are younger.

Maria flew over for Carnival from Johannesburg, where she is a casino croupier. She has ideas of yacht-hopping to exotic places. She met Bryce at the yacht club yesterday but hasn't moved her gear aboard yet. She is young and lithe with a gamin physique, skin the colour of white tea, a mop of curly black hair, very white teeth, a broad smile and an attractive face. She is wearing tight-fitting jeans and a figure hugging T-shirt. Her face has Caucasian and Negroid elements. She is vivacious and fun.

After the introductions I sit with the others in the cockpit, watching the Sun go down behind the hills. They tell in-jokes that refer back to the race, and I feel like an outsider. Bryce is sitting next to Maria.

"Where are you going to sleep, Greg?" someone asks.

Greg looks at Bryce for an answer.

"He'll have to take Bruce's bunk," Bryce says. Bruce had flown home to look after some business.

I never know what is happening in a nuanced conversation like this one until it is explained to me. I learn later from Greg that he has been sharing the master's cabin with Bryce, but he is now being ejected for Maria to sleep in there, so that Bryce can have sex with her.

"Is that okay, Greg?" Bryce asks politely.

"I suppose. But I wouldn't like to be Maria!"

There is a pindrop silence.

"What do you mean, Greg?" asks Bryce, taken aback.

"Your snoring!" says Greg.

Everyone laughs and looks at Maria.

"If she can't take it, I might have to put her ashore," Bryce threatens. It doesn't seem as if he is talking about snoring, but Maria gamely tries to ignore his threat.

"Well, It can't be too bad or you would have moved out already, Greg," she says. "Can anyone tell me if you can hear it in the crew quarters?" Maria laughs nervously and looks around.

The master's cabin is behind the cockpit. I figure out she is sounding us out as to whether we will be able to hear her if she screams. It is another matter whether any crew will come to her aid.

I catch her eye and give her a small nod. Perhaps because I am a newcomer, too, I feel an obligation to look after her.

"No, not so far," says Alan laughing. "But if we do hear anything we'll be pretty pissed off. The Skipper may have privileges but they don't include robbing us of our beauty sleep." He seems to have only a minimal interest in Maria's predicament.

"It will take more than sleep to make you beautiful, Alan," quips Bryce, changing the subject.

Maybe Alan, too, would help her. I can see the other two wouldn't go against Bryce. He looks and talks tough like a skipper, and his stories about policing show he is a physical man. He is a Boer and fiercely proud of the white ascendency and Apartheid system. His views are very different from mine, but I respect his right to air them on his own boat. I will notconfronting him, unless he is directly affecting me or those I care for.

I play on my guitar Dylan's "The Times They Are A-changing". They listen unmoved, not being sympathetic to the youth revolution. So next I bash out "Michael Row the Boat Ashore" and they join in lustily. When I get to "Sister help to trim the sail", Bryce interrupts me.

"Do you know 'Sloop John B'?"

I arpeggio the chords, singing falsetto, and they all join in on the chorus.

We sing for another hour and then I turn in. Maria goes ashore for the night. My hammock is on the top in the damp and smelly forward cabin.

In the morning Maria brings her stuff on board.

"We will sail after lunch," Bryce announces.

The morning is spent in a flurry of activity as all the crew help prepare the yacht. We take out all the sails, dry them in the Sun, fold them carefully and stow them in the sail locker with the eyes of the sails uppermost ready to be cleated and lofted. We fill the water tanks, and clean the head and galley. We fill our tanks with water and stow the food and booze brought by Bryce. Then we wash the decks and take our last showers in the clubhouse.

When everything is shipshape we bring in the mooring lines and motor out, putting up the sails as we go. Bryce turns off the motor. The only sounds are the slosh from our bow wave, with gurgles from the keel and the creak of taut sheets as we reach northwards with the wind abeam. We sit together along the starboard gunwale, watching Corcovado Peak with the white statue of Christ, arms outstretched, slowly sink from view. This is an adventure I wouldn't miss for quids.

As the Sun dives down, Rio is a glow on the horizon. We have sundowners of a tot of rum apiece in the cockpit. Bryce's singing is terrible, but no-one tells him to stop. Greg in the galley passes up to us in the cockpit a dinner of pies and beans. We drink more rum. Gradually, the guys disappear below to their bunks, leaving just Alan and I with Bryce and Maria. Bryce tries to put his arm around her but she moves away. I keep the chat going, to give time for Bryce to sober up, but eventually he tells her that she has to turn in now so as not to come in later and disturb him. They say goodnight to me and go to their cabin like Goldilocks and the big bad wolf.

In the morning Maria is hollow-eyed and Bryce is more crabby than usual. The day passes uneventfully until Bryce, who is drunk again at sundown, regales us with stories of how he implements the Apartheid laws in his job, brutalizing black men and black women. Maria is pale, clearly terrified. She goes below. I presume her classification is the same as an Indian and not black. Nevertheless, she is part negro and is afraid of the monstrous Bryce. The other guys seem to think he is okay. They are inured to the racism of the police in South Africa. Bryce tells story after story of his bigotry until I can stand it no more and turn in.

Next day, Bryce has breakfast as usual, but it is mid-morning before Maria appears, with a black eye. When Bryce goes below for a minute, she crosses the cockpit and sits beside me. She whispers, "He hit me. Unless I have sex with him he's going to put me ashore in Recife. I don't have any money."

Before I can say anything, Bryce comes back and sees her talking to me.

"How are you getting along?" he asks me, as if being aware of my presence for the first time.

"Maria has told me you have hit her. When I get off this boat I will seek an International Citizens Arrest Warrant from the International Common Law Court of Justice."

Bryce is taken aback. "It was an accident," he answers. "You need to keep focussed on your sailing or you might never get to where you want to go. It can get pretty rough out here. Accidents happen. We're in international waters. There's no law out here and people can do what they like."

It is an ugly threat. She is in danger, and so am I, if I try to help her.

"She has human rights and International Court Law applies," I tell him. "She is not going to sleep in your cabin anymore. You keep your hands off her. She'll sleep in the crews' bunks when they're on shift."

"So what will happen when they come off shift?"

"She'll change to another bunk."

"You're kidding! Would you kick her out? No way. You'll climb in beside her. You want her, don't you? Why should she be with you when it's my boat? She'll have to sleep in the bow locker, with the door closed so the guys can get some privacy changing their gear."

The locker is a cupboard.

"It's full of gear. There's no ventilation."

"The door is slatted and she can sleep on top of the kit bags. I'm not having her take the crew's minds off their jobs. She'll soon come back to my cabin. You'll see."

Maria shakes her head.

I say to her, "Is that okay?"

She nods, relieved.

"You can have the black bitch," Bryce says, getting up, "until we get to Recife."

Our watch, Alan and me, take on Maria. We are on from midnight to 8.00am, and the watch ends when we get breakfast for everyone. She stays with us at all times, learning how to steer a compass course, trim the sails and help in a sail change.

I love sailing, travelling as free as the wind. A sailing boat has to be rigged carefully and continually adjusted for maximum efficiency. Alan and Maria resist the tiny changes I order when it is my turn at the helm.

"Let out the jib," I tell Maria.

"I just did," she says.

"Well, please let it out a little further. It isn't doing any work."

She makes the adjustment.

"Thank you. Get the Genoa ready, please. Get Alan to help you."

Alan is down below, getting our 4.00am lunch.

"But we just took it down."

"Well, the wind has slackened off again. This jib isn't doing much."

"Okay. But let's wait until Alan comes up."

"Let's hope he's not too long. There's wind going to waste."

"Selwyn, it isn't a race. It isn't as if the wind is paid for. Who cares about efficiency – other than you?"

"Don't you want to get there soonest?"

"No, I am enjoying this. Let it last forever."

Rule 51:*A captain who is a tyrant will be opposed.*

CHAPTER 52   SLAM DUNK

Three days out from Rio, a terrible storm blows up. Waves break over us, and the helmsman has to be lashed to the binnacle to stop being swept overboard. We run east before 30-metre-high waves with only a tiny storm jib set. After four days it blows itself out. We don't know where we are, but figure we are halfway to West Africa. We turn around and head west.

Our spirits are high from surviving the storm, but we are exhausted. Conditions become calm, and we begin to enjoy ourselves again. The three of us chat together in the early hours, getting to know each other under the vaulted Milky Way.

"I wish this night will go on and on forever," says Maria.

"Me, too," says Alan. "I feel like stardust, blowing through space, my destiny unknown, and there is nothing I can do to change it. So I am happy going with the flow."

"Before this trip, I had never noticed the Milky Way," I say. "I didn't think it matters, like wallpaper. There is no point to looking at it. I like to be in control of my immediate surroundings."

"Can I ask what is the purpose of your life, Selwyn?" asked Maria.

"I want to have a normal life, marry, have children and raise them to respect and dedicate their lives to the things that are important to me: peace, independence, science, logic."

"You seem to have a spiritual approach to non-spiritual matters, Selwyn," she says. "What about you, Alan?"

"I tend to go day by day. I want to make a difference to family, friends and strangers, too. The more people and the better the difference, the more successful I will be."

"He sounds like a politician," I say to Maria. "What about you?"

"I do not have so much ability to change the world outside me. I will be content when I die if I have acted wisely for myself and the people near me and have done the best I can with what I have, without hurting others."

"Yours is the most humble, Maria. I think you are the kindest of us," I say.

Maria is lovely, but I yearn for Vicki. My commune plan is to sail with Vicki, if possible in these waters.

When the look-out sings out "Land ahoy" we are off the easternmost bulge of South America. We go into Recife for supplies, dropping anchor about two kilometres out, as the port is shallow.

All seven of us squeeze into the ship's dinghy. Alan, our best oarsman, rows us into the Recife Yacht Club. Maria brings her pack to take with her but Bryce tells her there isn't enough room in the dinghy for it and he will put her ashore tomorrow. She has been keeping out of his way, and he seems to be backing down on wanting her to leave. She is well-liked by the crew and has made herself useful. If he makes her go now, he will be unpopular.

We have lunch at the club. Then we help Bryce carry supplies down to the dinghy from the supermarket over the road. Most of it is cans of beer. I can't believe we will all fit in but we sit on the supplies with about 2 cm of freeboard.

"Steady! You'll have us in the water!" warns Alan.

We are quite drunk and we sing at the top of our voices. I organise us to sing in three parts: "Row, row, row your boat." We are making a lot of noise and laughing. When we are about halfway, we see a wave breaking continuously, pouring water down as if in slow motion, like a bore. It cannot be that, as the bay is wide and open to the sea. No-one has seen this phenomenon before, and we are mesmerised.

"Let's get a closer look," I say.

Alan is rowing us towards it when suddenly, from under a flat sea, a wave rears up and dumps us. The dinghy turns over, and before we can grab it, it is carried away on a breaking wave, leaving us in the water surrounded by groceries and bobbing cans of beer. The shore is about a kilometre away. It will be a demanding swim.

Without a word, the guys set off swimming for the shore. I start to follow when I hear Maria call faintly.

"Help! I can't swim!"

She is clinging to an oar, trying to keep her head above water. I swim over to her and get her in a lifesaving position, floating on her back with her head on my chest. I tell myself not to have sexual designs on this girl. I feel privileged to be able to help her.

"Thank you," she says.

I begin backstroking with one arm and kicking steadily, with only the experience of one lesson in my school's pool. It is a long way but I will be able to take rests.

I wonder for a moment why it has fallen to me to take her in alone. I suppose the other guys' swimming may not be good, or maybe they are too drunk to care for anyone except themselves.

I change my backstroke to the other arm for a while, and then back again.

I am getting tired. I get her to hold on to my shoulders in front, with her body under me as I swim breaststroke. It is slower but easier. I ask her to kick to help me. Feeling her lithe body moving under me is exciting, and I want her. I think she feels me against her. She smiles at me. I look away to hide my embarrassment.

There is a shout from ahead, and I tread water to see. It is nearly dark. One of the guys is waving to me, pointing along the shore to the right.

"Oil," he shouts. "Go around."

Just our luck. I turn and follow him parallel to the shore. But I am tired and I am having difficulty, trying to cough up water from my lungs. He shows no sign of turning in towards the shore. I am desperate, thinking I might not make it. I turn and head for shore closest us and swim into the slick. My arms are coated with black goo, and there is an oily taste in my mouth. The oil becomes thick and heavy, with globs sticking to Maria's hair. I curse whoever spilled this. It gets into my eyes and they become bleary. I take my direction from the Sun. My limbs are so heavy I can hardly move them. Just when I am thinking I have had it, a wave lifts us, then another and another. Maria is torn out of my grip and we are dumped by a breaker. She disappears and I swim in a circle frantically. My foot touches her and I pull her up to the surface, both of us coughing weakly. Then my foot touches the beach and I first walk, then crawl, hauling her up onto the sand, where I collapse, exhausted.

The others come and look at us. We are covered with black filth. They find it funny.

"They won't let you into the sailing club like that," says Bryce.

Because I know he is a racist bastard, I think it is a racist comment.

"Or you into the life-saving club," I say.

"Aren't we the big hero?" he sneers. "One guess who gets into your hammock tonight."

Maria looks at him but says nothing.

We all walk along to the sailing club and the guys all go in. They have no oil on them. Maria stays outside with me. Alan comes out with a couple of buckets, some rags, a bar of soap and a bottle of diesel.

"Diesel? Hell! Don't they have any liquid detergent or turps?" I ask.

"Sorry, this is all they have."

I had used diesel on the farm to clean my hands and arms after working on engines. It isn't much good as a skin cleaner – too oily – but better than nothing. My skin hurts. It is sunburnt through my T-shirt from sailing under the noonday sun at the Equator. There is no shade near the tap. Now I have to suffer the stinging diesel as we fry in full sun while trying to clean up. By the time I am reasonably clean, I am feeling pinpricks all over my skin. I am feeling nauseous and have a throbbing headache. Maria seems to be okay. Her dark skin isn't sunburnt like mine.

Bryce buys more groceries, and a local yachtie takes us all out to *Ermelo* in his runabout. Maria collects her things and goes ashore with him. She is going to Sao Paolo for a visit with her family. I lend her $30 for the bus fare; she will send it to me in England.

"Thank you for saving me," she says simply. With a hug, she is gone, all her belongings in a kitbag over her shoulder. She leaves a piece of paper in my hand. It is her addresses, in Brazil and South Africa. I feel like I did with Vicki after the lie detector, as if there is nothing more I can do at present. If something is meant to happen between us, it will.

By the time we clear the headland, I am alternately vomiting and lying in my bunk in a pool of sweat. My head is thumping, and I take some aspirin. I want to shit but I have been constipated ever since boarding *Ermelo* a week previously. Alan tells me boats affect some people that way.

Next morning, everything is fuzzy and distant. I become delirious and do not know where I am. Alan takes my temperature and it is dangerously high. Bryce shows no concern.

I remember he comes up to my bunk and looks at me.

"Well, we can't get a doctor out here," he says. "We're beyond radio contact."

"Can we go back in?" asks Alan.

"Not for that useless hippy," Bryce says. He must have looked in my pack and seen my bandanas and love beads. "If he dies, we'll slip him over the side when the others are asleep and no-one will be any the wiser."

"You can't do that!" exclaims Alan. Of all the crew, he has been the friendliest. I always have difficulty making friends. I don't know why.

"Just watch me," Bryce says.

Bryce's hammock-side visit does nothing to lift my spirits. Fortunately, Alan recognises I am dehydrated and makes me drink mug after mug of water and bathes me with a cool wet sponge.

After about four days I begin to feel better. I lurch up to the cockpit for sundowners. They give me a big hand.

"That's the best imitation of dying I've ever seen," says Bryce callously. His compliments always have a sting.

"With all that diesel in you, watch out your farts don't ignite," someone jokes.

"Ha ha."

"Have you had a shit yet?" asks Alan.

"Yes."

"Alleluia!"

It is glorious to feel well and sit in the cockpit as we rollick along to the West Indies on a broad beam reach. I decide then and there to start a sailing commune. I wonder what type of crew would be most fun for Vicki and me to sail with. We have seen that with Maria the conventional wisdom, "A woman on board causes trouble", is correct. Ships' crews are traditionally all-male, but women are gaining acceptance, in all-women crews. I have heard that mixed crews have problems on long voyages. An all-women crew could be most desirable, depending on the intention of the commune and who is the leader.

A week later we arrive at Trinidad's yacht club at Port of Spain. I say my goodbyes and take a plane home to the UK. After a week of my mother's cooking, I am right as rain. I go back to Liverpool to start a PhD.

I soon as I reach the UK I telephone Vicki, but she is too busy counselling adolescents for me to visit. I had last seen her during our abortive holiday in the Rockies three years previously, but I have written and telephoned regularly, even though she seldom replies. Every time I talk with her, a knife twists in my guts because of how she betrayed me with Richard. I think if we can get together and talk, I will get over it. According to Richard, she is in a relationship with a guy. So I do not persist.

When I left Canada I promised to write regularly to Ruth. I have written to her every week or two during my travels and she wrote back, when she could, because sometimes I was unable to supply an itinerary. When I begin my PhD in Liverpool, I can see it will be at least four years before I can settle down, and longer if I start a sailing commune. I know that Ruth wants to have a baby and it will be too long to keep her waiting. I write to her ending our correspondence.

From my experience on *Ermelo*, I predict that a shipboard commune would have to be single-gender and carefully recruited to ensure stability. A leader living separately can be of the other gender, if relationships are transparent. My preference is to captain an all-female crew, in partnership with Vicki.

Soon after returning to the UK, I receive in the post the contract for my short sale to Richard, with a note from him.

Welcome back, Selwyn. I guess I won't be able to collect on this now. So you can have her, if you can get her. Good luck, Richard.

Three years since graduation have passed, and my contract, to leave Vicki to Richard in the UK, has now expired. I tear up the bill. It has repaid my father, which is the main aim. My short on Vicki, taken after the lie detector test, is still open. I want to close with her as soon as possible, if I can afford her price now.

Rule 52: *Mixed gender groups are unstable in close quarters.*

CHAPTER 53   AGAPEMONE LEADERSHIP

I begin my postgraduate studies at my undergraduate campus. To progress my plan for a sailing commune, I need to investigate the leadership needs of an all-female crew and recruit Vicki to share leadership with me. The success of my polygamous sailing commune will depend upon my success at recruiting women and my leadership thereafter. I want to lead both women and men in my own organisation to go to foreign places and help poor people.

I hear about a flamboyant polygamous commune called the Agapemone, or Abode of Love, that operated for over 80 years, with a large group of females under sole male leadership. The first leader of the cult was Henry Prince, who left the Church of England in 1843, when he was thirty-two, claiming that the Holy Ghost had taken up residence in his body. I find enough information in publications to fill out a picture of the commune.

Prince was a charismatic, fiery preacher who recruited wealthy women by preaching in resort towns on the south coast and in London. He acquired 200 acres of land near Spaxton in Somerset, and on these spacious grounds, behind a 15-foot high wall, built a church, residences and garden cottages, with recreation gazebos, outhouses, conservatories and stables.

I imagine an impassioned organ playing the hymn, "O Perfect Love", being sung shrilly in the chapel by the women, balanced by the fruity descant of Henry Prince as he struts in maroon velvet and brocaded finery, eying off the members of the congregation as he selected his next bed partner.

The sect proclaimed the imminent second coming of Jesus. Henry Prince travelled in a gilt carriage with a team of four and outriders, from London to his cult's headquarters, attracting female followers along the way. He took up luxurious residence in 1846. Ten years later there were more than 200 people attending to his various needs, most of them female.

He was the only male living in the 20-room residence, pursuing a sacred sex life with his favourite women. Some had his children. The cult was sustained by lonely young spinsters and middle-aged women from the rich upper class, looking for excitement, who gained entry to the cult by liquefying their assets and paying the money into his bank account.

He and his rector, styled as the Prophet Elijah, were the Two Witnesses of Revelation. He said he was immortal, did what he wanted and justified it by divine revelation. His authority was absolute. He purified girl virgins, notoriously by raping one on the chapel altar before his congregation. She became pregnant, and he declared the baby a "devil's child" and not his own. He had children with several women, and these grew up at the Agapemone. Some later lived in the local village. People who knew them said they seemed quite normal, although defensive about their lives spent in the cult.

When he died in 1899, his followers were shocked. A new Beloved Leader appeared and the cult continued. However, when the new leader died in 1927, the cult declined and the property was sold in 1958.

The Agapemone experience is relevant to leadership, not least because, like Henry Prince, I was introduced to the Church of England at St Mark's College, Brecon, in Wales, to study to become a clergyman. I went there as a teenager, to attend summer courses for senior school students who might be interested in studying full time to become a clergyman. I was about ten years younger than Henry Prince when he attended Brecon College. I was excited as I hung up my clothes in the oaken wardrobe in an ancient student room. Past the crumbling window mullions was a verdant quadrangle, boxed in by buttressed and gargoyled walls of buildings, crouching ready with their traditions.

Like Prince I was very interested in females. Perhaps because they were barred from ministry, the females who went to Brecon College with me seemed less devoted than the males. Three times daily I knelt painfully, spending a half of each day in prayer or chanting dogma. I was more interested in the girls than in the praying. I passed some of this time flirting and holding hands with some very attractive girls, who were there for orientation on how to become a clergyman's wife. Unfortunately, we were closely supervised, but I developed a crush on one girl while kissing another. Unfortunately, they both lived too far away from my home. It was the first time I had access to females for kissing, and I tried out several. Each was different. I was fascinated.

I did not confront the college's academic staff, as he did, nor foment student rebellion on religious issues. I did that later, at Liverpool University of Technology when I became a leader of postgraduate student protests against the administration. I negotiated with the department's Professor, whose specialty was game theory, power and negotiation. He was a tough nut but cared about student welfare and achievement. Particular cases of injustice to students were my best ammunition. I suspect Henry Prince would have been in a similar situation, with ecclesiastical arguments, at Brecon College, where he spoke for a wide circle of male friends.

I was elected student chairman of the management postgraduates after an impassioned speech about the virtues of free time and how the course assessment load could be reduced. Like Henry Prince, I wanted to be a leader, and like him, I had a lust for women and polygamy.

Although I had been elected with a fraction of the class's votes, gradually I gain the support of most students. I had a close group, who I called my disciples. I imagined them to be like Henry Prince's Brecon College brethren, the first Agapemonites.

My interest turns to forming a missionary sailing commune. I had learned from school and university that males are incapable of forming a group without infighting unless held together by a common cause: a competition such as in rugby, or warfare, or commerce, or by a religion. I believe that a group of forty women whose mission is to better the lives of children who are poor, helpless and living under bigotry can achieve greatness. Henry Prince had the same understanding and allowed very few males into the Abode of Love and kept them away from the women. I would inspire them with beliefs tantamount to a religion derived from science. They would unite and achieve fulfillment in our mission.

The other intent of my commune is to attract Vicki. I am circumspect about approaching her and will wait until my plan is nearing fruition before mentioning it to her.

Vicki is working as a counsellor at a school near her hometown, Salisbury. When I visit her, we sometimes go to Salisbury Cathedral, arguably the most beautiful building in England. How can it be, I ask myself, that such a building has been constructed with such care? We enter the building through the ornate Gothic doors and walk along the nave towards the distant altar. My eyes are drawn from the arches repeating on either side, to the higher level of the triforium, with the clerestorey arches high above that and the apex of the magnificent vaulted ceiling.

When there is a service or choir practice, we sit and listen to the soaring voices of the choir of girls and boys from the Cathedral School, complemented by the voices of professional tenors, counter-tenors and basses. I lead Vicki up the stairs to the back bench where the adult choristers sing. Their stations are surrounded by ornate carving. In the gloom, in the recesses of the choir, I kneel and show her decorative work that has the same level of detail and finish as those in more prominent view beside the presbytery.

Who would want these obscure corners of the cathedral to be decorated so elaborately? I tell Vicki that I believe the intricate carving, beyond ordinary purview, is evidence that the carvers believed they were being divinely supervised and judged. It is ironical that I am on my knees when I find the answer as to who supervised the carvings beside me.

The stonemasons, wood workers and other skilled workers laboured neither for money nor earthly favour, but to secure their place in Heaven. It is likely that they received little pay, and then only intermittently, under the overall direction of clergy inspired by God. Their work was a sincere prayer, continuing for decades amid hunger, religious controversy, tyranny and insurrection. The work was larger than their lives, and they continued it without thought of earthly self-aggrandisement.

The artisans' dedication reminds me of the faith of the mechanic in "Zen and the Art of Motorcycle Maintenance", by Robert Pirsig. Such is the devotion of the craftsmen, the Cathedral is a masterpiece. I come away with my belief revitalized that when humans are joined in a common cause, they can accomplish great works beyond our wildest imagination. Ken Follet, in his book, "Pillars of the Earth", has captured the spirit of the artisans.

"People can do anything they want," says Vicki, "if they want it enough."

"Doesn't that make you think big?" I ask her.

"Yes. I, too, am ambitious for my ideas."

We stand looking at a stained glass window.

"Wouldn't it be good if my mission could be the same as yours?"

"It would," Vicki says. "Let me know what you want me to do."

"I will."

I start planning a sailing commune in detail. I think that Vicki will be most attracted to join it if we have a commune that will achieve her mission of helping troubled youths get their lives together. I devise a sailing commune with a mission to aid children at disaster locations worldwide. I decide to recruit a crew of forty women.

I call the project Mission Figurehead. A figurehead, often a woman naked to the waist, is an icon on a sailing ship that embodies the spirit of the ship, to placate the gods of the sea and ensure a safe voyage.

Until Vicky comes in, I will reluctantly act as leader. Whereas I am not comfortable in the limelight, I know I will be a competent leader until Vicki takes over. I need to get her agreement as soon as possible.

If I can inspire our crew with a spiritual mission, as Henry Prince did at Agapemone, we can achieve great things. I think we can best attract Vicki if we headquarter on a sailing ship. She has sailed and enjoys it. Many women do not take to the rugged conditions encountered offshore on yachts, but comfortable conditions are possible on a catamaran.

As a base for helping the poor, a ship has the advantage of being mobile and able to bring help close to where it is needed. We can travel the World, contributing our skills where they are most needed. A group of about forty women will be ideal. The teams will be big enough to make a visible impact at a disaster and few enough to be flexible.

A catamaran to accommodate forty women in luxury would be about 40 metres long and cost about 3 million pounds. With funds for operating for two years, we will need about 100,000 pounds from each crew member, a sum affordable by professional women of 25 to 50 years who can realise funds by taking mortgages on their shares of property.

To be happy, most women need eligible men, and they would encounter these ashore, in the tradition of sailors. When a woman married an Agapemonite man, an acquaintance of Henry Prince, she had to leave and forfeit her entry fee of 6,000 pounds. I propose a similar arrangement, that if a woman wants to leave she can sell her share to an approved woman. It is essential that the project attracts suitable women and continues to attract replacements.

Although I am planning to emulate Henry Prince's Agapemone with a scientific mission rather than a cult, I decide to keep this link to myself. I know that Vicki would regard the Abode of Love as a perversion and my interest in it as perverted.

I am working with urgency, planning Mission Figurehead and neglecting my uni studies. I figure that my investigations of communes and leadership are relevant to my research into alternative systems of government. I want to be able to do a field study of the crew of the ship.

Rule 53: *The greater the leader's appeal to religious belief, the less his or her authority will be questioned.*

CHAPTER 54   ATTRACTING FOLLOWERS

A sociology research student I know in hall gives me a list of upper and middle class households in Liverpool City with single or separated women in the age range I want. I book a private room in an exclusive restaurant on two nights, a week apart. I send invitations by mail, with RSVP and a choice of dates.

On the first Tuesday evening, I count fifty-seven women in evening wear around the sumptuous, candlelit tables. My assistant, moustachioed Manfred Brash, has helped me create a festive ambiance in the hall with lights, music and flowers. He is a colleague research student who is good at the things I am not: socialising and getting people's support. He is dressed in the black velvet suit and bow tie I bought for him. I am wearing a claret velvet suit and a garland of flowers. I have hired and parked my rented white Ferrari conspicuously outside. The best way to loosen purse strings is to appear well-heeled, with a higher purpose than relieving them of their money. As the women arrive, they receive a brochure with an artist's impression of a schooner under full sail under the banner heading, "Mission Figurehead: Will This Be Your New Home?" Our background music is the Cat Stevens album, "Catch Bull at Four".

When the uniformed waiters finish serving dessert and refill the champagne and wine glasses, I stand up and survey the dining room. It feels good to be in such company, even though I will have to borrow to pay the bill. I straighten my bow tie and undo the jacket of my suit to show my tartan waistcoat. Manfred is seated at a small table on one side, where he can overlook the proceedings and help with any problems in how I am coming across. He taps on a glass. They all look at me. Manfred busies himself writing.

The women seem curious and are giving me their full attention. I speak with quiet self-confidence.

"Good evening ladies. Welcome to the inaugural meeting of Mission Figurehead. I am Selwyn Archer," I say, and my voice becomes expansive. *"I am a spiritual adventurer, and my project is Mission*

Figurehead. Our ship will sail the seven seas to natural disasters and drop anchor for up to several months. We will rescue people and help them restore their lives, using the skills you bring to us and new ones we will teach you. Our ship will be an orphanage that, in cooperation with the local communities, will take care of infants and young children who would otherwise perish. We will return them later, when they can be cared for properly or, with their communities' permission, arrange adoption.

"My experience is as a ship's captain and mission leader in exploration of the South and North Poles. I began as an altar boy in my local Church of England church and then attended Brecon College to enter the ministry. I loved the sense of mission but despised the dogma, pomp and ceremony. I am now a professional engineer. I have retained my interest in spirituality. When people share a mission they can accomplish more than they can individually and through teamwork and science. They can even perform miracles."

No-one smiles. Good, I had worried about that line. Manfred Brash looks around and continues his writing.

"Mission Figurehead will be run as a team of women under my captaincy. It is the best way to organise to achieve our mission. With men in any number, there would be competition and conflict that would detract from our mission. Women work together better without men. The ship and accommodation will be built to the highest standards of safety and luxury.

"I need women who are 25 to 50, are looking for a change, can raise 100,000 pounds and want to work at disaster relief. Women who have established careers with skills we can use are wanted, as well as women who can learn skills to help those in need.

"I want life aboard to be filled with pleasure and fun. Sex is less important, but women who need it will be able to arrange to spend time with a man through their democratically elected leaders."

I pause for this to sink in. There are a few smiles, as if it may be a joke.

"The arrangements for a woman to be with a man do not include a married life aboard. If a woman wants an exclusive relationship with a male, the couple will have to leave the ship. I am firmly convinced that polygamy offers women more choices of better quality males. However, in this country polygamy is illegal, and so the relationships with men will be informal. The men aboard will be recruited by the women. About 4 or 5 males will probably be sufficient.

"The process is that if you are interested, write your name and contacts on the form inside the brochure. I will interview you and take you for a trial voyage to find out how you would like living under sail. If your application is successful, financial details are explained on the back of your menu.

"In a few minutes, I will answer your questions. First, would you introduce yourselves and tell us of any experience you have that could help our mission, such as skills you have, or interests you would like to develop."

I turn to the woman seated on my left. "Would you begin, Emma, please?"

Manfred Brash hands me his notes, and I read them as I listen to the women taking it in turns to tell their backgrounds and interests.

"Great start – awestruck by your gear, car and spread. Asking each other about you, no-one knows anything. Mystery man. Talking with each other about what Mission Figurehead can possibly be. Wild guesses, cynicism, some suspicion because not in media. Realize all single, footloose, moneyed. No-one said they couldn't afford it. Excitement. Destinations in Earthquake zones okay. Bob up over tsunamis. Some want to run it past their solicitors.

Angie, at right, red dress, hostile feminist, anti-male leadership. Why do they need you?

Wendy, left back in green, has sailed in Around Britain races and suspicious of your skippering. Some support for blue dress. Can we pull out after a year? 100, 000 pounds for a year is expensive. How can I sell my share?

All but Angie interested in sex with you. Lesbian? How would committee decide who next?

Overall, a bit too dictatorial and inflexible. Show listening and flexibility with questions.

The introductions have reached Angie. I concentrate on her because feminist influence is gaining ground every day and could sabotage my project.

"My name is Angie," she begins. "I work as a barrister for Women's Liberation. Unlike you, I was not targeted to attend this evening, but a member sent me her invitation. If anyone would like me to leave, then would you raise your hand and I will go."

She pauses and looks around. I would love to throw her out but I do not dare.

She looks straight at me.

"Selwyn Archer, I suspect you are a fraud and a philanderer. Do you honestly think that any of these women believe it when you say that for you sex is less important than your mission? If so, why are you not recruiting an all-male crew?"

"Angie, I welcome you here. An all-male crew would lack credibility for running the orphanage. Also, women would be more effective in organising and running compassionate care operations. If there were also men, their rivalry could cause conflict between them."

Angie looks down at her notes.

"Who the hell do you think you are to be sole supplier of sex to 40 women?"

"That is not the idea. There do not have to be any men available for our 40 women. I plan to have a monogamous relationship with a woman who will join us later. Workers on ships and in orphanages run by nuns have traditionally foregone heterosexual activities. Sailors have made the most of shore leave. Centuries of experience show that sexual activity in both ships and nunneries disrupts order and reduces mission effectiveness. Mission Figurehead will be run by women in full partnership with me."

If they buy that, I think, they will buy the rest of it. I haven't told them about my plan to attract Vicki as my partner, possibly as First Mate, or even taking over from me as captain if she wants to.

"Can the women sail without you?"

"Only if I agree, because I will have a majority of shares under my control."

"Can a woman become captain?"

She is determined to show that Mission Figurehead would be male-dominated despite its all-female crew. I want to get Angie off this tack.

"Yes, if I agree," I replied. "However, I do not think this will be an issue. My captaincy will be to achieve our mission of aiding disaster victims. I have a scientific outlook and am open to change."

"Will we be able to quit at any time?"

"Yes, provided there is another suitably qualified woman to take your place. There will be women who are waiting for an opportunity to join in, and you will be able to sell your share to one of them, probably at a profit."

That seems to satisfy Angie.

"Captain Archer, what experience of sailing a ship of this size do you have?" asks Wendy.

"I have been too busy training as an engineer to have time for much ocean cruising. I have done a month on a 30-metre ketch, taking turns to skipper her. We were caught in a storm, with waves going right over us. So I have a respect for the sea. As an engineer, I understand the forces involved in sailing and how to keep safe. I would like to have more experience, and before you join us aboard I will have a done a shakedown voyage and know how to sail her safely and efficiently."

I reassure them about issues such as discipline, medical expertise, running of the orphanage and long-term plans. When there are no more questions, the women talk together informally, and I take the names and contact details of those who want to try a day sail with me.

When they have all gone, Manfred Brash asks, "How many did we get?"

"Twelve," I say, counting application forms. "Six may sign up. Not bad, eh? The next step is to ask them for a twenty percent deposit."

"One hundred and twenty thousand pounds would be a good start. Are you going to be up to the interviewing?"

Manfred has a steady girlfriend and is unable to help. I phone each of the twelve women. Some are merely curious but others are genuinely inspired by my offer. Those interested come to each of my rallies, creating a snowball effect. Morale is high. The excitement of these social gatherings entices others to join. I hold them at exotic venues, and they bring their friends. I am the main attraction, and I try to develop a rapport with each of them. My social skills are poor, and I keep notes on a file card for each of them, listing their concerns and interests. I study these before each meeting where they will be present, using their name badges to access my information.

Steadily, the number of recruits needed to fund the laying of the keel is increasing. Several pay a deposit immediately to secure a place, and I am able to use the money to guarantee my borrowing to pay my bills. I begin preliminary work with a Merseyside shipwright on a design for our ship. Also, I am looking for a small sailing cruiser to take other applicants day sailing.

I am aware that it will take persuasion to tear Vicki away from her work with troubled adolescents, which she finds very rewarding. Joining Mission Figurehead is a lifestyle change, and I think I can best attract her by taking her sailing. Buying a small yacht becomes a priority.

Rule 54: *Single women are attracted by a resourceful man who recognises their individuality in an ambitious plan esteemed by their community.*

CHAPTER 55   MATE TEST

With the last of my savings, I buy a small yacht, *Minetta*. I spend several months getting familiar with her, sailing in the Mersey shipping channels out from Liverpool.

I ask Vicki if she will come up and go sailing with me for a week, cruising to the Isle of Man in the middle of the Irish Sea, 78 miles out from Liverpool. Rather than telephoning her, I write because it is difficult to get her attention on the telephone. Richard tells me she has been seeing a guy.

I am delighted when she writes agreeing to come, and I telephone. We set a date for the following month in the school summer holiday.

I prepare *Minetta* with the required safety equipment. I get the short-wave radio working; it could be important in an emergency. I buy a radar reflector to run up the mast so that ships can see us and avoid collisions when we are sailing at night. I check all the lights are working. If we are caught by bad weather at sea, we will run back to port or behind the island. I buy large-scale charts for Isle of Man waters.

We need food for about two days each way. I cook up lasagna, chilli con carne, beef stroganoff and korma curry and freeze them in meal-size quantities in plastic bags. They will thaw after about four days in the icebox, but will last long enough unless we are delayed by bad weather.

Vicki arrives at my room in Hall as arranged, and we spend a pleasant evening together, going over the charts and listening to Janis Joplin. She tells me she is seeing someone. I take this to mean she doesn't want to start anything with me – at least, not immediately. I have arranged a guest room in Hall overnight. We turn in early, separately.

We are up at dawn, and the radio forecasts light winds with a change coming through at midday. I drive down to the marina, and we put the food and supplies aboard. I go through the 53-point checking routine I have developed. Vicki, realising how important my routine is to me, is careful to follow my instructions to the T. When everything is shipshape, she casts off and we motor out into the shipping channel and put up the sails. Vicki is a great deckhand and sets the sails without instruction from me. When we clear the harbour leads, we settle into a tack with the wind abeam from the port side and follow a compass course for the Isle which is over the horizon. We sit side by side in the cockpit and chat about this and that.

I can hardly believe my good fortune to be sailing with Vicki after dreaming about her for so long. She wears a nautical striped T-shirt, deck shoes and the briefest of shorts that barely contain her perfect buttocks. At first, she scarcely seems real. My desire for her is so strong, my voice seems thick to me, and whenever I brush against her the hairs on my arms and legs become erect, as if every cell in my body has become enamoured with her. I am as tongue-tied with her as I have always been.. We only talk about our voyage, whereas I want to talk about our relationship. I fear finding out that she is keen on the person she is seeing.

Later in the morning, the wind drops and the sails flap and jerk on their ropes. It seems to go on interminably. Without warning, *Minetta* is knocked flat by a strong gust. The mast goes under and the sails fill with water, stopping us from self-righting. Water pours in over the gunwale as we climb over the lifelines and walk backward out on the keel, using our weight to try and right her. But the sails are buried deep, and we have to get down on our knees and crawl backwards out to the end of the keel. Our knees bleed from the small limpets on the keel. Slowly, the sails empty and she begins to come up. When the sails break free from the sea, she springs upright, dunking us in. We swim around to the other side and into the cockpit over the coaming. She is almost full and there are only a few inches of freeboard. Waves are still filling her.

"We have to bail," I pant. "She could go down."

"Doesn't she float?" says Vicki, her voice shrill with alarm.

"No," I say. "But almost, she's made of wood."

"What about the lead in the keel?" Vicki asks as she starts bucketing water out of the cockpit

"I few more bucketfuls and we'll be okay," I say.

I swim through into the cabin. I notice that the radio is underwater. The flares are floating. I hope their bag is waterproof. A raft of food and clothes floats in the cabin. I find another plastic bucket.

"Put this on," I say, handing her a lifejacket.

I put one on, too, and join her in scooping bucketfuls over the side.

Minetta holds more water than I realised. By the time we are down to the cockpit seats, we are gasping and exhausted. We sit dispiritedly and take stock of our situation. With a misty horizon of under a kilometre, our piece of ocean is empty. Using the compass, I bring *Minetta* sluggishly back onto course. The wind is blowing steadily from over the stern a little to starboard, and she wallows along with the sails wet, misshapen and limp.

"How much further is it?" Vicki asks, between breaths.

"We're about one-third of the way – about 10 hours of sailing to go."

"Can we go back?"

"The motor is stuffed. It could take even longer."

Vicki looks around her grimly. The mist seems to be closing in.

"Are you sure you can find the island?"

I hesitate. It is a small island with some high ground. On a clear day, it is visible from 10 miles. By the time we get there, it will be dark. There is a lighthouse and light buoys that lead into the harbour. I look Vicki directly in the eyes.

"Yes, I know where we are now within a few miles, and this course will take us there."

I can see she is not convinced. Unless she accepts my captaincy, there is little hope of our getting together on Mission Figurehead. Because she has so much experience, I need to communicate with her.

"What do you think?" I ask her.

She stares ahead. "Can we go aground?"

The island's shores are steep and rocky. The depth finder is not working. We can use a lead weight on a rope, but the warning would come too late.

"No," I say. "We can get a fix from the lighthouse. We will be able to see lights on the island before we reach it."

Vicki is silent and reflective. I know that she is putting on a brave face. She doesn't dwell on the other difficulties that her experience would have revealed to her. We have no electricity and no running lights to warn away other craft. Will we be able to find the navigation chart, will it be intact and is there a torch to read it? There isn't time to search now.

Her face is composed. Answers will come in the fullness of time.

She gives me a smile. It does not daunt her that we will have to spend the night on *Minetta* with our bedding soaked. This is not important. She is a sailor and knows that such inconveniences do happen from time to time.

"Okay," she says. "Shall we go on with the bailing?"

It goes better after that. Her voice is so reasonable and her actions so helpful she seems like an invaluable extension of myself. We are a team. We get out as much of the water as we can. Vicki takes the helm while I remove the head from the motor, dry it out and reassemble it. It takes about an hour.

I hesitate before pulling the starting rope.

"Wish me luck," I say to her.

"Fingers crossed and hope to die," she replies.

After the third pull, the motor starts.

I shout above the racket, "Do you want to go back to Liverpool?"

"No way! This is fun."

I love her then with every fibre of my being. Because we can deal with this and enjoy it, life together will be a glorious adventure. She must see this, too.

Visibility improves; we see the lighthouse and use a soggy chart to find our way into the harbour. We tie up as night falls.

"Thanks. You were great," I say, giving her a hug.

"You were pretty good, too."

We hang out our bedding to dry. The friendly skipper of a neighbouring yacht lends us sleeping bags. We eat cold chilli con carne and turn in.

We stay on the island for three days, seeing the sights and enjoying being with each other. The Sun comes out, and we sunbathe on the golden teak deck, with only the sound of waves lapping against the hull, loose halyards flapping against the mast and the crackle of the masthead flag. I try to kiss her but she turns her head away.

"No, sorry, Selwyn. It would be good, but I'm not free at the moment. It would be a commitment I couldn't keep."

We spend our evenings at the pub in conversation with local people and then eat at the restaurant, before climbing aboard and into our sleeping bags.

I ask if she thinks her man is the one.

"Possibly," she says doubtfully.

That seemed to kill the conversation, but in a moment of inspiration, I had prepared conversation topics for the voyage. I asked her if she thought children had rights. She had told me she had taken part in a debate on this topic while I was away.

"Children should be able to grow up healthy and free," she says. "They have ownership
of their bodies."

"They should be able to do what they like," I joke.

"You are not far off," she laughed. "They have freedoms of —"

"Speech and —". I am stuck.

'Thought,' she prompts. "Also, freedom of choice and the right to make decisions. The last one is different – freedom from fear."

We talk for a while about how to free children from fear, and I outline Mission Figurehead. I do not try to recruit her as she knows I want her to come. She seems interested, and I say I will put her on the distribution list.

We buy a small radio, and on the return voyage we sing along to The Beatles' "Oh Darling"; "I would never do her harm but she didn't need me anymore and I nearly broke down and cried."

Back in Liverpool, we part with a hug before she sets off to drive back to Salisbury. I want her more than ever and hope to resume the relationship with her that has been thwarted so many times in the past. I will not pressure her to join Mission Figurehead until we have a full crew of committed women. She will take some convincing to commit, but I am counting on her adventurous nature to bring her aboard.

Now that I have more details of how Mission Figurehead will work, I have a prospectus printed and ask the recruits who have not yet paid to pay their deposits. I want to check out each applicant's sailing aptitude and offer to take applicants for a day-sail in *Minetta* to help them make up their minds.

Rule 55: *A couple who can sail together can live together.*

CHAPTER 56 RECRUITER'S ITCH

Since returning from South America, getting enough sex to relieve my anxiety takes much of my time. I return to living in Sidmouth Hall where everything is laid on, including undergraduate girls in Falmouth Hall next door.

I have a list of Mission Figurehead women to interview. One of the first is Clare, a Liverpudlian nurse. A practising Catholic, she wants to travel and help people in poor countries. She has money left by her grandmother. When I take her sailing on Minetta, she is wearing a skimpy bikini.

Clare connects with the real world, as I do, by hunches and weird intuition. I am at the helm and Clare is working a winch on the jib when she says, "I expect you are comparing me with your girlfriend?"

That is exactly what I am doing. "She has had more experience," I reply, "but you have potential."

"What about sexual experience?"

"We're not that close, yet."

"Is that why you want me?"

I laugh. "Who says I want you?"

"Well, do you?"

"Maybe," I say. "You are very attractive."

"Sorry, but I'm saving it until I get married."

"Okay, then." We continue chatting about other things.

I don't do virgins. They deserve better. Their first time should be for love. With me, it is something I do because I don't know how to stop.

Later on, we sail back to *Minetta's* mooring and pack up.

"Clare, I think we're going to get along just fine. I hope you'll sign up for Mission Figurehead. We especially need nurses; your sailing aptitude is a bonus."

Sandra is an American girl who is open and demanding about sex. She is a hopeless sailor and becomes seasick on a flat sea. She has money from a shrewd real estate investment in Liverpool. She wears her extroverted personality on her collar, unlike demure Vicki who is so quiet and introverted that her personality is all but invisible. Sandra is unable to enjoy herself without talking, which she does incessantly. At her insistence we have sex under water in Albert Dock in broad daylight, overlooked by art galleries and museums.

"In Albert Dock?" I query.

"Yes, absolutely," she enthused.

"We could be arrested," I say.

"That's the whole point. It will be art revealing a new use for a public resource."

"Where else have you done it?" I asked her.

"Hyde Park, in London. The British Museum. Lots of places. Come on, be a sport."

"Okay, but on the condition that we are quick about it," I warn her.

"Oh, all right. How about tomorrow morning?" she says.

"Why not? Shall we meet there, as if by coincidence, or arrive together?"

"Coincidence would be fun," she says.

"Especially if there is someone else there in the water."

"To be safe, we should shake hands first," she proposes.

"This is England, after all," I conclude.

We meet in Albert Dock the next morning as planned. Although Sandra is an extrovert and the dockside walkways are thronged with tourists, I am an introvert and our sexual encounter is brief.

At Sidmouth Hall, I run into Hugh Stevenson, another doctoral student in engineering. He is a tall, spare figure with long black hair, a bushy black beard, wearing immaculate white suits he makes himself. He is given to religious monologues and rants. His eyes are wide and stare sightlessly over your head when he speaks. Despite the proximity of our rooms in hall, we don't often stop to talk. I have told him about Mission Figurehead. One day he asks me how my recruitment is going.

"It's going very well," I tell him. "I have six applicants tested and ready to go. I have another seven lined up."

"How are you testing them?"

"I take them sailing. I find out what skills they have that they can use on the ship."

"The real test will come when you ask them for the money," he says. "Do you think they will trust you enough?"

"Their payments go into a trust account of the National Bank. Several have paid the deposit already."

He seems impressed. I explain to him how the members' payments will be secured by shares in the physical ship and how they can get their money back.

"Are you taking couples?"

"No. Just single women."

"I've got to hand it to you: you have a way with women," he comments as we part.

I am involved in interviewing women almost every day.

Lynn is physically strong, extroverted and idealistic. She is a freelance news reporter from London's East End. She is fiercely independent and regards males as largely superfluous. She owns a half-share in a house with her ex-husband. She is an experienced sailor. When I deliberately capsize *Minetta* to test her seawomanship, she reacts fearlessly and effectively. She wants to be First Mate.

"Why did you go for twin hulls?" she asks.

"The kids and hospital staff will be more comfortable than in a monohull."

"It makes sense. Cats are faster, too. I've done the Round Britain in a cat."

"Your experience would be useful."

"I'd like to do some skippering," she says.

"No, sorry. I'm skipper."

"What if I have more experience?" Lynn sounds annoyed.

"As I said before, your experience would be useful."

This is not going well, I think. Then I remember that people find me rigid, and I wonder if there can be a compromise.

"You could have command for a watch, when I'm below. What title would you prefer?"

"'First Mate' is usual. "That would be okay."

"Great. Will you have a drop of grog with me?"

We get on well over a couple of rums. Lynn is most interested in having new experiences. Within the space afforded by *Minetta*'s small cabin, she reveals a penchant for unusual sex positions. She seems likely to be a stalwart of our crew, and I welcome her in some style.

Deborah is my most exotic recruit. She is a former Olympic gold medallist ice skating soloist from Montreal. She is in Liverpool to run international workshops for ice skating coaches. When I walk down the street with her, she has the magnetic self-assurance and poise that royalty inherits and athletes attain with fame. People on the street see her coming, stop, back up in doorways and push past each other to get a better view.

Over a few years, she has lost flexibility and strength-to-weight ratio and disappeared from the World rankings. She has gone from Olympic Champion to being unplaced in competitions over a very short time. She is in shock and depressed. She hates her work and wants to quit the rink but she has very little education to fall back on. She will be able to borrow the money for Mission Figurehead from her parents.

"Do you think you will find helping orphaned children rewarding?" I asked her.

"Yes, that's why I am applying."

"Could you teach children ice skating?"

"Yes, but it is not kind or caring. I had a terrible childhood. I want to give some children the love that I never had."

"Could you marry and have children?"

"That is want I want. But I want to do some real living first, have an adventure."

"Perhaps you will meet a man!"

Although Deborah has wonderful control of her body, she has difficulty grasping sailing principles. Even analysis of forces in skating is foreign to her. Sex with her is rote and clinical, lacking in passion. Our sex could achieve extreme positions but she is too controlling and rules out some reasonable activities. She is judgemental and precipitate, rather than keeping matters open and relying on her perceptions, as Vicki does. I hope that she will learn to be more amenable and provide sex that maintains excitement. She is a caring person, and I welcome her to join our crew.

Keeping some of my recruits interested in Mission Figurehead, while recruiting others, is demanding. I have to keep having sex with them to get them committed to pay the hefty deposit required. As the number of payers climbs slowly towards the magic number of twenty, half a full crew, I find attending to the women so demanding that I don't often get around to any academic work. My life is frenetic. I am high on a sex wave with The Stones' "Let's Spend the Night Together" echoing in my head. I have interviewed all the people recruited at my dinners. By November, I have stopped taking applicants for a sail in *Minetta*, due to bad weather. Instead, I take them up to my room. I play them the B side of Blind Faith's LP, "Sea Of Joy", the most erotic music I know.

I meet Sally while waiting to see my uni department's professor. Sally is his secretary, a prim and proper woman with some sailing experience and money from her divorce settlement. She likes children and is excited at the prospect of working with orphans. She refuses to come to my room in hall in case someone sees her. When I take her out in *Minetta*, she amazes me by caressing the G spot on my prostate. I experience an orgasm on a new plane of pleasure.

She is very cerebral and maintains a distance between us during sex that keeps me coming back for more. She will be an asset to Mission Figurehead's crew. I see Sally regularly, as her boss, the professor, is concerned about my lack of progress and has me come weekly to see him at his office. She acknowledges me with a wry smile, distracting me from the perilous state of my doctoral studies.

"Good morning," I greet her.

"Good morning," she replies demurely.

"Are you looking forward to setting sail?"

"Oh yes. Are you?"

"Of course, but I have to get my research up to the field study stage."

I had told her previously about my plan to study our crew.

"Do you think you will be sufficiently detached?"

"You mean too involved? If it is anything like recruiting, then I will be exhausted."

"Perhaps you need to be more selective?"

"What criterion do you suggest?"

"Pleasure?" she suggests.

"It's difficult to put one's finger on it," I replied with a smile, "but certainly pleasure comes into it."

She laughed. "Then perhaps you will need a research assistant."

"I would not look further than you for that position."

Her phone rings. She stands up to show me in to the professor. If he knew what was taking my attention, I have little doubt he would have me thrown out. Sally is very discreet, and our sexual adventures remain hidden from him.

My recruitment continues whenever I have the opportunity. I need a constant supply of partners to assuage the fearful itch that keeps me hungering for sex. It surprises me that, even after they had paid their deposit, few of the women show interest in the details of Mission Figurehead. I conclude that most of these females are existential and conduct their relationships from a need-to-know perspective. I begin to regard them as a happy-go-lucky crew.

A worrying aspect of my sexual appetite is a growing desire for novelty and a corresponding inhibition in seeking it. As I drive home in the rush-hour traffic, I see in my rear-view mirror an attractive woman in an open sports car. From her alluring face and sexy car, I can imagine an attractive body. She seems to be smiling at me; it is tantalising. I like a girl who flirts. But although Vicki is a flirt, she is too introverted to respond to a stranger. When we are brought to a halt by congestion, I put on the handbrake, get out of my car and walk back to her, with a hundred pairs of eyes boring into me.

"Hello," I say in my most sing-song friendly voice. "I was right. You are beautiful. My apologies for being so forward, but you seem to be just what I am looking for: a truly beautiful and hopefully intelligent person."

I am thinking, "Randy, too."

"I would like to chat. How about giving me your name and phone number and I'll call you this evening?"

I hold out a notepad and pen. She shakes her head.

"I'll tell you about myself. I'm a doctoral student at the LUT. We don't have any women in our department. So I'm desperate to meet a beautiful woman like you, so desperate I am driven to this—"

A horn blows. The cars in front of mine move forward.

She looks in her rear view as if about to seek help.

I proffer the pad and pen again.

She grabs it and jots down a number.

A horn blows. I thank her, get into my car and catch up to the car in front.

I do not know her name. My biggest turn-on is if the woman I am having sex with is anonymous. My emotions are engaged with Vicki. I call the number that evening. She answers and we chat. Belinda is an accountant. She admits it is a boring job, but she says she doesn't mind that. It would have concerned Vicki, who fears getting into a rut. She lacks Vicki's spontaneity. I invite her to go to London for the weekend but she wants more notice. Instead, I take her up to my room. She turns out to be a nymphomaniac, as compelled as myself. We have a lot of quality sex. She is not interested in Mission Figurehead, does not want a relationship and is only interested in having sex with me. I have no reason to see her except to appease my need for sex. When I am with her, I forget the fear gnawing in my guts. I see her briefly almost every day.

I need more and more sex. Sowing my wild oats has left me with a sex habit, an addiction; no matter how often I satisfy my lust, it never goes way. Sexual activity is as much a pleasure for me as compulsive scratching of an itch, when you know you are worsening it. Each orgasm is merely a tickle and a sneeze, whereas the sex itch is deep in my bones, an irritating and painful lesion for which sex is a salve, but which nothing can cure. Getting sex compels my attention, almost all the time.

I ogle neatly turned ankles, firm breasts and long legs reaching up to curved buttocks. I am preoccupied with finding my next sex fix, although it brings me very little pleasure. I am like a bonobo monkey for whom sex is a handshake. It is how I keep my females sweet. Bonobos use sex to solve power problems, whereas other men use power to solve sexual problems.

It takes increasingly bizarre sex, abuse and submission to scratch my itch. My partners are beginning to feel humiliated, and I wonder how long before I am into perversion and even criminality.

"You are a cold-hearted unfeeling pig," said one girl as she declined further involvement with the project.

"Can't you tell I'm feeling down tonight?" another asked. "I don't supply sex on tap whenever you want it."

"I wouldn't trust you as captain," another said. "If we were sinking, I think you would save yourself first."

It is true. My philosophy of self-altruism is to self-sustain before helping others. The women's needs for sex are very demanding, and if I do not put myself first I know they will quickly reduce me to a state of emotional exhaustion.

When I take a holiday to get away from the women, I meet Mathy, from Sri Lanka. I am with Manfred on an excursion to a ski resort in Austria. Mathy is doing a PhD, too, at Leeds uni. I tell her about Mission Figurehead, and she and her girlfriend are immediately interested. She says her parents may sponsor her share in the venture.

In a double bed in the ski chalet, Manfred and I have four-way coition with them. It is my first homosexual experience. His hard hairy body is quite different from the soft smooth girls, and I find it very unattractive. Nevertheless, I make him happy, and the girls are wonderful together. Afterwards, I am beset by guilt. I know Vicki would not approve. I seem to be on a sexual ride with a train of events that are becoming more and more distasteful. With no end in sight, satisfying my needs for sexual adventure coincides with the wants of the women I am recruiting. I know I cannot keep on going like this, but I don't know how to stop.

Rule 56: *Women are more attracted by adventurers than by adventures.*

CHAPTER 57   DIRE STRAITS

I have to prevent my females from straying away, and recruit more by seducing them. There is a steady stream of women to and from my room in Sidmouth Hall. I am close to establishing a harem of forty women. We all meet together monthly to discuss the ship's design and orient ourselves to our humanitarian tasks. The women have organised themselves into task forces to offer assistance, of well-organised expertise and facilities, for the various disaster situations we expect to encounter.

There are probably social rules for a polygamous man, but I am not aware of them. I have my own code, which is to be available to everyone regularly and equally. Even more important, I am discreet and never pass on information from one lover to another, to discourage gossip. I live in some trepidation that the women will organise themselves against me, but until we are at sea and my monopoly takes effect, the women are not limited in any way from relationships with men.

Our ship will be built in six months, and we will embark for Haiti, where we will assist in recovery from the recent earthquake. If there is a worse disaster somewhere else in the meantime, we will go there instead. The ship will have powerful engines, and we will be able to reach most locations in time to take a leading role in rescuing, treating and rehabilitating victims.

The construction phase of the Mission is now underway. The whole crew meet with the boat builder for a tour of the boatyard and design office. Afterwards we dine in a private room at the local pub. I speak about our mission and what to expect.

After a group photo, I introduce five of our crew with special expertise. They have volunteered to take charge of specifying the various systems that the boat builder will now design to our specification.

Bernadette, a general practitioner, will design the paediatric hospital, and Clare, a nurse, the orphanage. Accommodation and food will be specified by Sally, who is a stickler for efficient organisation and has headed hospitality services for a prestigious hotel chain. Lynn, our First Mate, is to select the sailing equipment, using her extensive experience in skippering in offshore sailing races. Olga, a mechanical engineer who designs systems for ocean liners, will design the electrical, instrument, fuel, water and refuse systems. My job is to coordinate them all and see that they work with the boat builder to solve problems and arrive at efficient designs.

When forty women have paid their deposits, we celebrate with a party for the whole group. The women are in high spirits, and a wild party ensues.

I do not want publicity, but a reporter interviews me. An item appears in the local paper:

WOMEN'S MISSION OF MERCY TO SAIL TO DISASTERS

Forty women will give up their homes and jobs to join Selwyn Archer, 25, on a yacht that will sail to rescue children from disasters. The women, who are mostly professionals between twenty and forty, will use their skills to help local people recover from earthquakes, cyclones, tsunamis, bushfires and floods. The proposed Mission Figurehead ship will have a paediatric hospital and an orphanage. It will anchor near disaster areas and help children to locate relatives. It will help communities to get back on their feet. Selwyn Archer, the project founder and ship's skipper, said, "We want to work as a group to rescue children in most need, cooperating with local authorities. Our group is made up of women who have the skills to contribute to recovery working in teams.

I borrow a four-person tent from the Sea Cadets and set it up in a grassy area of the boatyard for the girls to stay in when they come down, which is almost every day. I stay most nights, and we become lovers and good friends. Four women is an exciting experience for me. Women have a much greater capacity for sexual arousal than men, and our fivesome is able to generate and satisfy passion beyond the capability of any pairing I have ever experienced.

Sometimes I am the indulged one, with every body part being stimulated until I melt. At others, I am one of a team coaxing orgasm after orgasm from one or more of the girls. At first, I am self-conscious in these roles, but gradually I grow to trust the girls and am able to express my wants and affection freely. Of course, I have my favourites on some days, but I reach a balance, with equal regard for each.

The girls each settle into a role they enjoy. For example, one is the initiator, another does the hard work, another's skill is in exquisite tortures, and another provides counterpoint of different attractions. Based on our experience in the tent, we adopt a four-person cabin with a double and two single bunks as our basic crew accommodation unit. I had specified for Vicki and myself a cabin with a double bunk. Without her, my sleeping arrangements could be like a Kenyan chieftain, who shares his time between the huts of his wives, arranged in a pecking order of proximity to his own.

When the major design features have been decided, an artist prepares images of the yacht's elegant exterior and luxurious interior for a glossy brochure. We compose a time schedule, showing the launch in six months, and include it in the brochure. We send it to every participant with an invoice for the final instalment.

Cheques arrive in the mail, but only in dribs and drabs. A few days before the due date only a fraction has come in. I am on the verge of despair, imagining that the women have changed their minds.

Then, over a period of a few days, to my great relief, all the outstanding money comes flooding in. We are euphoric.

My impetus to develop Mission Figurehead has come from wanting to go adventuring with Vicki under sail. Ever since Vicki and I sailed to the Isle of Man in *Minetta*, I had wanted to entice her into more sailing. She is still working as a counsellor in the same school near Salisbury. I am hoping that she will welcome the opportunity for professional development and adventure in Mission Figurehead, and that at last we will be able to have a relationship. For Vicki, communal life holds fewer attractions than for me, because she prefers to commune not with people but with the sea, in privacy, or in a couple. She would have ample opportunity for that with me.

When I am ready to present my scheme to her, I visit Vicki at her home. I hug her and with our bodies pressed together, I blurt out my pitch I have prepared.

"I love you so much, Vicki. I want to be with you always."

She hugs me again.

"Thank you, Selwyn. This is very sudden. Are you sure we would be good for each other?"

"Absolutely. Our Isle of Man sail showed that, didn't it?"

"It was fun. But I think living together all the time would be different."

She remains silent.

"How would you like to live together on a ship with forty others for a year or two?"

I outline the Mission Figurehead plan, only omitting my polygamy idea.

Vicki is interested and asks several questions.

"So you want me to put in 100,000 pounds as soon as possible?"

"We are all doing that. If you don't have enough savings, you will be able to borrow it. I can give you paperwork to take to the bank that guarantees your share."

Then she asks me about the others.

"Did you say all forty will be women?"

"Yes. As I wrote to you, it has to be all men or all women, and men would have difficulty in being accepted with children."

"I see."

"Here is our newsletter with a photo of everyone and their resumes. You will be able to meet them at our next get-together. They are excellent people, and there is a terrific atmosphere of togetherness. I know you'll love us."

"Talking about love, where do you and I fit in exactly? You are skipper and I—"

"You would be my partner."

"What would the forty women think of that?"

"No problems."

"I think they would be jealous. What if I don't come?"

"I will be very disappointed."

"Will you still go? Oh, I get it. You will be the stud skipper with sex coming out of your ears. Knowing you, you have already made a start on this. You weren't going to tell me." Vicki is angry.

"Everything I have done has been to get you together with me," I tell her.

"How did you recruit these women?"

"I invited suitable people to a series of dinners and sought their participation. If they signed up I interviewed them."

I didn't mention Henry Prince or taking them sailing on *Minetta*.

"Did you have sex with any of them?"

"A few," I lied.

"How many?" Vicki asked.

"Maybe twenty."

Vicki turned away and was silent for a full minute. Then she exploded. Her voice is raised and cutting.

"Even if your morals were acceptable, which they are not, how would you think I would feel on a boat with twenty women you have had sex with?"

I couldn't relate to that situation at all. "How?" I say.

Vicki throws up her hands in exasperation and speaks to me intently.

"Selwyn, imagine I invited you to a party with twenty men present who you knew I have had sex with. How would you feel?"

That was easier.

"It depends on how you finished with them," I say. " If they all dumped you, I would be wary of you. But if you dumped all of them, I would feel superior. Don't you feel superior with forty women and I have chosen you?"

"Ah—", she gave a shriek and held her head."

"Selwyn, you are fucking impossible," she yells." Now get out."

I cannot see what Vicki's problem was. Despite this setback, I continue living in the tent with the girls and designing the ship's systems. As we add the finishing touches to our specification, the story below appears on the front page of the local paper.

SHIP LOVE CULT DENIED

A Mission Figurehead sailing ship, proposed to be crewed by forty women and led by a single man, is accused of being a "sex cult", a source has reported. The women are to be available for sex with Selwyn Archer, a 25-year-old engineering student, either individually or in groups. Mr Archer has denied this. "Our ship will be a children's hospital and orphanage," he said. "Traditionally, such organisations have been staffed by females, such as nuns, with a strong sense of mission. Our mission is to rescue children from disasters. Sailing ships have also been single-gender. There are several sailing boats crewed by women, and they have been successful in competition with men. In port, the women will be free to have relationships that do not reduce their effectiveness in achieving our mission."

He said that the group had no particular religion and therefore could not be a cult. He expects to be joined shortly by a woman friend with whom he would have an exclusive relationship.

Despite my denial, the "cult" label sticks, and local people start coming around to stare at us. There is hostility.

"Perverts!" a woman calls out. "We don't want your type here."

At night, local thugs often climb the boatyard fence, curious to see what the five of us are doing in our tent, but the lights are off and there is nothing to see. They soon leave.

As I climb wearily up the staircase to my room at Sidmouth Hall, after farewelling a recruit, I am accosted by Hugh. He has something on his mind.

"Hello, Selwyn," he says, stopping on the landing. "Do you have a minute?"

"Sure." I walk back down to his level. "What can I do for you?"

"I am concerned about your promiscuous behaviour. You are a greedy, selfish monster. You are only interested in having sex with as many women as possible."

"It's got nothing to do with you."

"It does affect me. I live here. I'm on to you. I want you to know that I disapprove, very strongly, of your promiscuous sexual activities."

"Love doesn't have to be monogamous," I say. "Every woman is unique."

"Well, I'm a Christian, and you are a cheat. Your Love Boat story is a fraud. You're not going anywhere except to prison."

"Where did you get all this from?"

"Let's just say a disgruntled female."

It could be any one of half a dozen I had rejected as unsuitable.

"Anyway, so what if I get my end away now and then?"

"It's a sin against God."

"Fuck off, Hugh. Mind your own business. I love and respect women."

"Respect? You don't know the meaning of the word. You are a sex cheat, a monster."

He pushes past me and is gone.

I hear the words of the song, "Your Cheatin' Heart" in my mind. It will tell on me; I had been told on, and it hurt

I feel as though Hugh has tarred and feathered me, as was done to Henry Prince by locals angered by the goings on at the Abode of Love. Women find me courteous and attractive, and I have no trouble getting girls into bed. On the other hand, men have little time for my blunt and dramatic assertions and like to challenge my philosophies.

Hugh's criticism hurts, and the next day I go down to Manfred's research laboratory to get his advice. We have been too busy to see much of each other since our foursome in Austria. I find him hard at work testing a new reservoir model. His model is a bottle-sized cylinder of rock cut from an oil-bearing layer underground. He is pressuring one end with water to drive out oil with the water flowing through it. I take him for coffee, tell him about Hugh's outburst and ask him whether what I am doing is as bad as he is making out.

"Do you think Hugh's right? Am I a sex fiend?" I know I sound pathetic.

"You certainly seem compelled to chase skirt. It depends on how much satisfaction you are getting."

"Not much. These days I have to have kinky sex."

"I think you have a problem with relationships. You are getting heaps of sex but missing out on love."

"Aren't they the same thing?"

"You are so primitive. Sex is the part of love known as passion. Love includes other things, like intimacy and commitment. You are missing out on them. You are behaving like your bull at Priory Farm."

"If you think he doesn't enjoy himself, forget it. He's always keen."

"Yes, but it is very brief and then what does he do?"

"He looks over the gate."

"He wants out. Without intimacy and commitment, sex soon becomes unsatisfactory, a reflex, instead of an experience that becomes better and better."

"What I really want is a steady bird to be in love with. If only I could get my hands on Vicki."

"You have been saying that for the past six years. Why don't you tell her?"

"I did, when we went sailing, but she had someone and was not interested in a relationship."

"Are you sure? She would hardly have gone sailing with you if she wasn't!"

"She says she couldn't make a commitment at present. I don't know why not."

"If you want her to think well of you, you had better keep quiet about your harem of forty sailor women. A Lothario image isn't politically correct these days."

"When Vicki joins the crew, I will be monogamous if she wants."

"Do you think she will join?"

"There's a chance."

"Do you think she wants you?"

Manfred has told me previously that my fellow students regard me as egotistical, selfish, insensitive, uncaring and disloyal. It is jealousy. However, Vicki's affection for me is a question I have been asking myself for too long, without coming to an answer.

"No," I admit. "Not like this. I don't think she does."

"Then forget her and get on with your life."

"I need a regular woman for support."

"Have you come across a female you could settle down with?"

"Maybe." I can think of several among the recruits who I could love. Also, several girls I know from previously.

"Well, go to it. You don't have to decide anything overnight. Make up your mind a bit at a time. Recognising you have a serious problem, as you have done, will put you on the road to recovery."

I thank Manfred for his advice and go back to the struggle of writing up my MPhil thesis, the final step before a PhD. But I find it difficult to concentrate. I must resolve the Vicki question as soon as possible.

Rule 57: *Free love has a moral cost to an ethical relationship.*

CHAPTER 58   UNHITCHED

I phone Vicki to try one more time.

"Hi, Vicki. I was wondering if I could persuade you to change your mind about coming with us on the ship."

"Hi, Selwyn. You don't give up easily. I'm perfectly happy doing what I am doing."

"You can come back to it."

"I see from the article you sent that you expect us to have an exclusive relationship. Isn't that rather presumptuous of you?"

"I—"

"It is also totally out of character for you to have an exclusive relationship with anyone, especially me!"

"Ouch!"

"You seem to be using sex to escape from the challenge of your doctoral work," she tells me. "You are unconsciously avoiding the unpleasant truth that you have bitten off more than you can chew."

I could see she was right.

"I just need to do more work," I say.

"Some endeavors require a maturity we do not possess. For example, until a baby's brain is ready to coordinate all the skills needed, it cannot walk, no matter how much it tries and practises. It is the same with algebra; the brain has to be capable of abstract visualization. In your case you are tackling issues of management requiring an understanding of motivation and behaviour in organizations that you may not have yet. You can only acquire that by going out and immersing yourself in those situations. Does that make sense?"

"So you think I am using sex as an anesthetic, to reduce my awareness of my academic inability."

"Yes. Or you may be trying to repeat a pleasure sensation you had before your senses became dulled by indulgence. You may yearn for the buzz from that first intercourse and you do not have the will power to stop trying to regain it. Your sexual exploits seem to have a lot of hubris."

"What do you mean by 'hubris'?"

"You are too full of yourself, sexually."

"Meaning I'm really pretty ordinary."

"Yes. You have become addicted to sex and you have imaginings that show poor judgment. They say that sex addicts try to relive the rush of their first experience. Is that you?"

"Maybe. I'm not getting that first rush or even the highs I used to. Maybe I am a sex addict then. Crikey!"

"You seem to have a predisposition for addiction and even if you can control your sexual urges you would become dependent on something else."

"Like what?"

"It could be another dysfunctional behaviour, such as compulsive golf, gambling, shopping, bargain hunting, shop theft, excessive tidiness, cleaning germs, dieting, exercising, love, sex, anorexia, muscular spasms, or a religious practice."

"What about booze?"

"Yes, excessive sex is a consumption addiction, and you might switch to over-consuming something else. You might sublime your craving into overeating, chocolate, tea, coffee, coca cola, wine, beer, spirits, marijuana, cocaine, heroin or petrol sniffing. To feed your habit, your mind will drive you to find something else other than sex."

"Isn't there any way out? Is this inevitable?"

"If you join Alcoholics Anonymous, you are encouraged to believe in a Higher Power and follow a set of behaviours in twelve steps that would enable you to control your addiction."

"But I'm not an alcoholic."

"It's the same process for controlling sexaholism."

"I cannot believe in a Higher Power. I am an atheist. Is there any other way?"

"You may be able to stop your sex addiction by yourself. Individuals can bring all sorts of compulsive behaviour under control by their own methods."

"I want to put all that behind me. I want to be in a monogamous relationship with you. I have all along. If you come on Mission Figurehead with me, I swear I won't cheat on you."

"There's no way I'll come with you. You have had sex with so many of those women that I would be unable to establish normal relations with them."

"Oh, hell! I didn't think of that."

"Do you feel you have been conning these women?" she asks me. "In your mind, is it a sex junket?"

"'No. It was to be a commune you would want to join, with me as your partner. Won't you reconsider?'"

"Selwyn, no. Keep in touch."

It is what she always says as she goes.

I leave the foyer telephone booth, stung by the realization of my sex addiction and by Vicki's rejection. She has probably been put off by my sexual hyperactivity. She just isn't interested.

It is the end of a dream for me, because I will have to find another way to revive our relationship. Whereas in Mission Figurehead she would have my undivided attention, I realise now she may have foreseen my being lured away by our resident sirens. She had reason to think that I would be unfaithful, as testified to by my polygamous design and the way I am ensconced at the boatyard with my four designers. Vicki may have found out about them from friends among the crew.

I decide to keep Mission Figurehead going without Vicki. The project has enough women, and although I will miss Vicki, I will have as much female company as I want. With 4-person cabins, I can sleep with a different group on ten consecutive nights. It is an established fact that humans, both male and female, enjoy novel sexual partners.

The boat builder is to commence in a month and is ordering materials.

WOMEN TO BE LED BY MAN

Mission Figurehead is a scheme for a sailing ship crewed by 40 women, devised by Selwyn Archer, a 25-year-old hippy engineer. The ship will sail to rescuechildren from disasters. "It is not unusual for a predominantly female group to be led by a male," he said. "Schools and hospitals often have a mainly female staff with a male principal or CEO. The women do their jobs with female leaders, such as matrons or deputies who are in charge of day-to-day operations. Mission Figurehead will have females in charge of sailing, care of rescued children and crew welfare. My job is to coordinate and deal with external threats and opportunities. We are definitely not a cult, as we do not have a religion."

Construction of the specialised ship has commenced.

We are beset by reporters who look for scandal in our crew's unusual gender make-up. After the media publish defamatory articles about my sexual propensities, I commence legal action, but several letters arrive from crew members informing us they are pulling out, requesting return of their money.

I have to postpone construction while I endeavour to attract more women. I have the brochure and the other girls to persuade them. As usual, I take them out for a sail in Minetta. I also entertain them in my room at Sidmouth Hall.

Despite my best efforts, attrition exceeds my recruitment rate. I try to keep positive but doubt begins to creep into the project.

On every weekend after our return from skiing, Mathy takes a bus to Liverpool and we spend a night together in bed. Like Vicki, she is reserved and sincere, but she is rather too docile and not my type. I am about to finish with her when she tells me she is pregnant.

Shocked, I go and see Manfred, hoping for some sympathy.

"One of you has made a mistake," he says.

"She seemed reliable," I reply lamely.

"Well, she wasn't," he says. "We're getting older and have older birds. Some of them are desperate to settle down and figure that if they get pregnant we'll marry them. From now on we will have to take precautions ourselves, like using condoms."

Although she would keep the baby if I wanted, we quickly establish that she should have an abortion. We find a doctor who puts us in contact with an abortion clinic. On the day, I drive her there, give her my half of the money as agreed, and wait outside, wishing I am dead. She comes out after about an hour, weeping quietly. I feel deeply ashamed. The situation reminds me of the Barbara termination.

I cannot think of anything to say or do that will make it better. So I take her to the bus station.

"I'm sorry," is all I can find to say as she climbs on to the bus.

"Goodbye," she says politely.

The bus takes her away.

When I return to Sidmouth Hall, my mind is numb with grief from the tragedy. Added to this is Hugh's criticism. I am unable to study because of worrying about what is happening to me. I feel doomed to failure, in my course, in my relationships, as a person, in my life. For the first time, I feel disabled but I don't understand by what. I decide that my sex binge is over.

I call a meeting of all the participants, presenting the facts. We are down to only twenty-five women to pay for the boat. My recommendation that we cancel the project is accepted. I still have about 90% of the money, and will return it to the women. It is sad because many have sold their homes and tendered resignations at work. Looking foolish for believing in our mission, they have to re-establish their lives. I tell the bad news to the boat-builder. A few months later, he goes bankrupt.

My attention reverts to my university course just in time to prepare the MPhil submission prerequisite for PhD entry. The concepts give me difficulty that is magnified by time stress. I sink into a black depression, worse by far than any I have experienced before. This impasse seems to be an augury of things to come with my research topic, and I am in despair about ever finishing. I feel absolutely alone and vulnerable.

There and then, I decide I must get a partner to help me through the difficulties. I want someone who will be there for me, come what may. The cost is that I will have to make a long-term commitment to her. By the time I am thirty I will have finished my PhD thesis and be ready to settle down. I need a girlfriend who is prepared to wait. I have to be sure now that she is the one I will want to marry.

I lie on my bed and think about the women I most like. Vicki is my ideal partner but she continues not to want to see me.

My feeling of inability to cope continues. I want a woman who will love me and who I will love. She should be attractive, intelligent and kind, a lifelong learner. I figure I probably already know such a woman. Several women I can think of fit the bill and may want to move into a flat with me. Which one should I settle down with? I run through a mental list of the possibilities, evaluating their suitability as marriage partners. They are all far from ideal. It becomes a question of which one I dislike least.

I show Manfred my shortlist.

"Which one is best?" he asks.

"I don't know. It is difficult to combine their good points and their bad points."

"Okay. Which one has the most good points?"

"This one; but she has some very bad points."

"Which one has the fewest bad points?"

"This one. But she hasn't much going for her."

"But she won't make you unhappy. She's the one. If you can't have the best, you can at least avoid the worst."

I think back to three years previously when I was on a plane, landing in Calgary. I headed for the cab rank to take me back to my dreary cold room and my empty lonely life.

"Hello, Selwyn," a voice said behind me.

It was Ruth, come all the way through the snow to the airport to fetch me home. I hardly knew her, having had only a handful of dates with her before going on holiday. We embraced and kissed. Her coat is real fur, deliciously illicit, presumably acquired before the new morality. Her new car seemed solid and confident. My life took on a happier complexion. No girl had ever come to an airport to fetch me before. Ruth had wanted me, whereas Vicki had been indifferent or disinterested when I tried to talk with her at home from Heathrow airport.

Now, two years later, I telephone Ruth from Liverpool.

"Ruth, it's Selwyn."

"Selwyn! Where are you?"

"Liverpool."

"It's great to hear from you! How are you?"

"Missing you. How are you?"

"I'm going to New Zealand soon. I have a good job there."

"Could you come this way? I'd like to spend some time with you."

"It may be possible to change my flights. I'll let you know. Have you changed?"

"Yes, this time I'm sure."

I give her my telephone number and wait to hear from her. She calls back and says she can come and will arrive in three weeks' time.

While I wait for Ruth to arrive, I grapple with my hunger for women. I realise time is almost up and I try to crack on to every good-looking woman I come across. When I try to study, I get a hard-on and think about women. Masturbation brings only temporary relief, and I do it so often I become sore. I hope that soon I will be able get my mind off sex and on to finishing my PhD. I alleviate my perpetual anxiety with smoking and drinking scotch, neither of which I can afford.

Rule 58: *Addiction can occur when a person attempts to quell anxiety with fondly remembered sensations of a dispelling experience.*

PART 9 TAKING DELIVERY (1973-1975)

In which I reduce exposure to my short position by a long position commitment with a remote closing date. This has unforeseen costs.

CHAPTER 59   REBOUND DECEPTION

Ruth arrives in Liverpool on a visit, and we start living together. She is a very compliant flat-mate. We share the lounge of a two-up in a genteel old house off Ashgrove Road. I have my research grant money, which isn't much. She gets work as a school health advisor. Whereas I avoid doing inessential domestic chores, she cooks and cleans and even makes the bed. I am a kept man. The tide of feminism has yet to flood in, and I feel no guilt. I like being cared for; it is a good arrangement while it lasts.

Ruth goes to Women's Liberation meetings. She dresses in yellow or green overalls, grows her hair long, wearing it big and frizzy or tied back. She volunteers at the local family planning centre. She goes on protest marches and at the local Sainsbury's supermarket she sticks labels on South African canned goods: "Don't support Apartheid. Don't buy SA goods".

The rest of my life continues much as before except for the tourniquet on the flow of girls. Her sexuality is compliant, and sex with her is like brushing my teeth. My work becomes more ordered and effective. At home, my wishes are respected and my things are left scattered as I leave them lying around. Even when a flagon of fruit and sugar I am fermenting to make wine explodes in the linen cupboard, soaking her clothes, she does not complain.

Although life is good, in some aspects it is lacking. Our intimacy and passion seem quite stilted, and I feel that she does not forgive me for ending our correspondence a year previously. Ruth's hostessing is superficial, and she does not reciprocate the warmth and humour I value in my friends.

"What does a school health advisor do?" Richard asks when he and a girlfriend are at our place for dinner.

"I teach about diet and care of teeth, hair and skin."

"Contraception?"

"No. I am only allowed to cover reproduction."

"How do you feel about that?"

"It stinks."

"Have you complained?"

"No. There's no point. It's the school governors. They are hopeless."

That ends the discussion. Ruth has a closed mind on many issues and she is not interested in my friends' views. She does not think much of them, and they stop coming around.

Consequently, at first Ruth does not tip the balance in favour of settling down. In my mind, I compare her with Vicki, whose astute listening and intelligence are always attractive to others. We like the same type of people and our talk is a rollercoaster that sometimes lasts until dawn.

Vicki seems rather ineffectual and a dreamer. Although she gives little away, I prefer her more considerate posture to life. She is more respectful and honest with me. If I could go to Vicki, I would. We are similar and would grow together, with real affection.

Since Ruth arrived, Vicki is unfriendly on the phone. I get my information about Vicki from Richard.

"How's Vicki?" I ask him.

"Okay," he says. "I saw her at a party a couple of weeks ago. She has a guy, er, Jon. I think that was his name."

It doesn't seem to come to anything, although my information is secondhand.

Sometimes I think that my admiration for Vicki is an illusion, that she is simply the one that got away, that her attraction is simply unrequited love. Was her mystery simply that of the unattainable? Like Mount Everest, do I have to climb into her affections simply because she is there? I tell myself, "You have to face it: you are never going to have Vicki."

At other times, I feel thwarted, and my passion for Vicki is intense. My wanting for her burns through time and space and circumstance. My fondest hope is that our relationship will come home to roost like an albatross alighting after an Atlantic crossing.

For some time, Ruth has been talking about wanting to get married. I tell her that it could take another two years before I finish my PhD, and I will not be ready to settle down or have a baby until then.

After about a year Ruth surprises me by packing her suitcase to leave, even though things have been going pretty well for the past few weeks.

"Either we get married, or I'm leaving now," she says.

"What about the other alternatives?" I ask.

"What are they?"

"You can give me moral support with my PhD and if that doesn't become marriage, leave then, when I'm finished."

"I have to know now."

"Why?"

She doesn't answer, and I assume she feels insecure, which is quite usual in a relationship. Ruth is breaking the verbal agreement we had when she moved in, that we won't settle down until I have finished my PhD.

In my mind, I run though the advantages and disadvantages of settling down. I am twenty-seven, and although I am short of my target of thirty, I have had a pretty good innings. My amygdala is beginning to caution me to slow down. Ruth says she can wait a few more years until I finish before having a baby. Our age is similar. Perhaps being married won't make as much difference to my work as I had feared.

Ruth's proposal seems to put me at a tipping point, and I may go either way. If there was a prospect of getting together with Vicki, I would let Ruth go. I am inclined to let her go, anyway. What finally tips the balance are Ruth's diligent efforts to take care of me as I struggle with my PhD. Slowly and reluctantly, I agree to get married.

The wedding is in mid-summer at a small chapel near Priory Farm. I am an unenthusiastic bridegroom and I take no part in making the arrangements. I am so out of it I can't be bothered to choose a best man. They do not tell me the wedding programme, as if it is a shotgun wedding. My mother and Howard do want to get shot of me, it is true. My happiness is not a consideration. A crowd of friends drives up from Liverpool for the occasion. I am in a state of shock. We have a barbeque on the river bank afterwards, but there are no speeches.

I invite Vicki to the wedding, because I want her to share in my life the way I want to share in hers. She comes by herself. I wonder how she feels behind her inscrutable smile that seems to indicate she is happy for us. She can see to what she has driven me, on the rebound. For me it is tragic that I am marrying the wrong woman. I think of her throughout the service, and I am in a cold sweat. I stutter my way through the responses. When we get to my vows, I am surprised when my voice comes out loudly, the way it does to deter any lurking infidels or demons when I am scared in an empty car park or in darkness at night. Vicki gives us a lemon extractor as a wedding present, and I wonder if it is to be a reminder that our relationship went sour.

When I sign the register, there is an audible sigh of relief from the congregation. My bachelor antics have unsettled people. My friends wondered where my sexual odyssey was taking me, and they are reassured that convention is being observed in the motherly woman I am marrying.

As I take the pen from Ruth to sign, I notice her date of birth. She is five years older than me. Her biological clock is approaching midnight. My heart sinks as I realise I have been duped. There will be no hiatus for me to complete my PhD. Even worse, if she has misled me in this, can I trust her at all?

Rule 59:*Marriage changes a relationship, with unpleasant as well as pleasant surprises.*

CHAPTER 60   LIBERATION LOSER

Within hours of the wedding, Ruth's true qualities are revealed. They are the opposite of Vicki's. She is slippery, and I never can discover her true feelings about anything. She is seldom direct and almost never reasonable.

I realize I have been misled by Ruth's obliging countenance. Her caring face is the shop window of her profession. Her interest in me is selfish and loveless. I realize when it is too late.

Ruth begins nagging me about smoking. I enjoy my daily packet of Peter Stuyvesant's and I am affronted. She complains about passive smoking long before the concept has been named, or found unhealthy. She has never complained even once about my smoking before we are married. I resent her assumption that she can assert rights once she is married that she had not mentioned when she was single.

"The terms of our marriage are," I tell her, "that our relationship will continue more or less as before!"

"I do not remember that," she says."Anyway, you should be more flexible."

"I am prepared to discuss things and, if necessary, compromise. But you expect me to capitulate on your every whim!"

"Fuck you," she says and walks away.

She disparages my friends and is intolerant of their beliefs. They stay away and stop inviting us around. I become socially isolated and demoralized. Our marriage is founded on the dishonesty that lured me to the altar, and I feel devastated. Ruth's misandry possibly results from a decade of failed relationships with men. She is bitter that I left her in Canada and that after corresponding for more than a year, I abruptly dismissed her.

When I telephone out of the blue from Liverpool, Ruth is desperate to have a baby. She does not reveal her dislike for me immediately, but waits until after we are married. Then she wreaks her vengeance on me, guided by Germaine Greer's feminist diatribe, *The Female Eunuch*. Greer scorns contemporary notions of love, romance and the nuclear family and urges women to think beyond their social conditioning to *"discover that they have a will"*.

Within a few weeks of our wedding, Ruth has asserted her feminism, with such radical vehemence, that I feel my life has marched into a brick wall. She imagines herself as a champion of women creating a peaceful world in which men's aggressiveness will be subordinated to female peacemakers. Her manner is inflammatory, and she sets out to antagonise me. She switches abruptly from a deferent to a bullying personality. She reveals that she is a misandrist, a male hater, criticizing my persona and reneging on our agreement that I will finish my doctorate before starting a baby.

"If I don't have a baby soon, it may be too late."

"Not until I have finished my research."

"Oh, phooey! What does that matter?"

"A baby is a huge distraction. I might never finish."

"I will be over thirty, when there is an increased risk the baby is disabled."

"You agreed that you would wait."

"If you loved me, you wouldn't be so cruel."

In bed she becomes frigid, whinging and demanding. Sex for her is when I pay ritual homage.

The radical feminism that Ruth reveals is unpleasant. My new wife goes out to meetings with Women's Liberation activists on several nights each week. She comes home spouting about how women are bonding to undermine the capitalist system. Because I am studying this system, her mindless invective grates on me. Women, they say, will use power for peace instead of war, caused by men being in control in the past. Overnight, her attitude changes from dutiful fiancée to implacable foe. Men, she says, cause war, harmful technologies and all social problems. I am a barely tolerated specimen of a species destined for extinction. Women don't need men any more, thanks to the new reproduction technologies. Anything a man can do, a woman can do better. When we go sailing, she uses a plastic spout to piss over the stern, standing up.

According to Ruth, men are no longer necessary, as women can control their own fertility without marriage. Women are no longer sexual objects and tools of men. They should give up "fripperies"

– shoes, pretty clothes and make-up – and stop indulging in shopping. The crusade for equal pay for women makes huge gains when a female Secretary of State for Employment is appointed and the Dagenham women strike for and get equal pay and conditions. Contraceptive pills become available at Family Planning Clinics, abortion is legalised, women's refuges are set up, the Miss World pageant is disrupted as a "cattle market" and gender discrimination is outlawed.

"I am not interested in re-wallpapering the bedroom," I tell her."It isn't as if we own the place." We live in a rented two room flat and sublet one room.

"Why not?"

"I would prefer to spend my time doing something cultural. It doesn't need re-doing. I am not interested in material appearances."

"So I suppose you want me to do the wallpapering by myself?"

"I'll help you with the difficult bits."

"As if I don't do enough around here already."

"I didn't say that."

She had already flounced off. As it turned out, I helped her with all the wallpapering of the bedroom. After that, she embarks on a programme of redecorating. She cajoles me into repainting every wall and ceiling in the place. To me, this is a waste of time and money, but I try hard to make her happy.

When this is done, she says the duvet cover no longer matches the decor and she is going to buy a new one. It is not a large expense but by this time, my grant has run out and I am living on my slender savings. Our few purchases are carefully considered. When she says she is going to Selfridges to buy one, I invite myself along.

"Why do you want to come?" she asks me.

"It will be a joint purchase, will it not?"

"Yes, but it's fine. I can get it by myself."

"How will you know I will like it? Do you know my taste in duvets?"

"It's probably weird. I am not going to get one that's weird. Our bed is in our living room, and I will not have something weird there."

"We'll have to compromise. When are you leaving?"

The reason I go with her, which I don't dare state, is that I don't like her taste in such things. I like colourful abstract patterns, whereas she invariably chooses subdued pastel floral patterns.

We go up to the bedding section and come to a display with about thirty different duvets. I look over Ruth's shoulder as she starts to browse through them. When she concentrates on pastel flower themes that I dislike, I think I should speak now, or be forever ignored.

"Ruth, our tastes are different. We need to use a process that will arrive at the best possible compromise without causing us to argue or fall out. Do you agree?" I am studying management science and optimistic about a scientific compromise.

"Actually, I don't," says Ruth. "This should be for me to decide, as a woman. Women know about decor. Men don't. They know about cars."

We had talked about changing our car. This is a bribe. But I won't be corrupted.

"A quid pro quo isn't the same as equality!" I tell her.

"Then how do we decide?" she says.

"We each select our three favourites. Then we will each rank all six, from first down to sixth. Then we add up our scores. The best possible score is 2, 1 from each of us, and the worst 12. We will select the duvet that has the lowest score."

"Okay, I'll try it," Ruth says suspiciously.

We each choose our three, I make up a list and each of us rank all 6, between 1 and 6. Then I add the two lists together.

"There are several sevens, eights and a nine. Not much compromise there. But here's one with 6. I rated it 2nd and you put it 4th. That's the best compromise."

"Which one is it?"

"This one."

We both look at it, unimpressed.

"Are you sure?" Ruth asks.

I check the numbers.

"Yes, this is it," I say, picking it up and heading for the checkout. "Let's go."

When we get home, Ruth puts it on the bed. Neither of us says anything.

A week later, Ruth says, "You know that duvet? It's horrible. I hate it. I hope you are satisfied."

"No," I say. "I don't like it, either. It's our lowest common denominator. We could be worse off, though. We should be thankful we don't have one we dislike even more. At least we're still talking to each other."

"In future," she raises her voice, "I'm going to choose the decor!"

It is the first time I recognise that my marriage is irredeemably a mistake.

Rule 60: *When a person is a professional counsellor, it is difficult for a lover to distinguish professional care from love.*

CHAPTER 61 DILEMMA

When Ruth announces she is pregnant, at first I cannot believe it.

"Pregnant?" I say. "How can that be? We agreed you would not get pregnant until my PhD is finished!"

"I am tired of waiting."

It is the second time I recognise that my marriage is irredeemably a mistake. Next, she opposes my continuing the PhD, an act of sheer treachery. Whereas I had assumed that married couples followed the rules they had established when they were single, I suddenly find myself at the mercy of a woman who will stop at nothing to get her own way. Ruth is fundamentally dishonest. She has cheated me about her age, about her affection for me and about her motives for marriage. It is a condition of our marriage that we will wait until my PhD is in the bag before starting a baby. Ruth has ignored it.

The only female I stay in touch with is Vicki but she talks only briefly, on the telephone. I have no-one I can discuss my marriage with. Anxiety is my constant companion. My consumption of cigarettes and alcohol slowly increases. I am having trouble with my research project and with my supervisor. I have to apply for an extension of my grant. I sense a crisis is approaching, and that I am absolutely alone.

I find I have married a hijacker whose agenda excludes the PhD that she had agreed I could complete. Will I be able to oppose her and complete it?

I am tortured by apprehension as, after three years of strenuous research, I wait to hear if the PhD research grant for my thesis to end the Cold War will be extended. When there is a change of government in England, interest in my topic of planning objectives disappears. The new government will not support my work to the finish.

346

I recall that my motivation to do a PhD is to attract Vicki's attention. It seems less relevant now I am married to Ruth.

Next, the Social Science Department takes over the Governance and Industrial Research Unit, grabbing our research money. Extension of my grant is unlikely. My only source of research funds dries up. I am disappointed but not deterred. Once I have started down a particular track, it takes a lot to divert me on to another. I have no income and no alternative other than to live off Ruth, a situation which she resents.

Without asking me, autocratic Ruth makes matters worse by purchasing a house under mortgage when we will shortly be without any income. This move puts me under extreme pressure to leave uni and get a job as soon as possible.

"I need another year," I tell Ruth. "I can't quit now or it will be four years' work with nothing to show for it."

"Do you mean you will not get a piece of paper saying 'PhD'? " she asks. "Or is it that you have not ended the Cold War?"

I detect a note of sarcasm in her voice. She has always thought what I am doing is a waste of time.

"Both," I say, "because I am very close to finishing."

"So you have been saying for the past year."

How can I abandon four years of hard work? I am unable to raise a bank loan without an income; nor do I know of any opportunities for part-time work because such income reduces a student's grant by an equal amount.

I have no-one to support me. My family think what I am doing is a waste of time and money, as is all university research. My only recourse is to work harder and apply myself to writing-up, in the hope of finding a sponsor. My thesis now occupies my thoughts 24 hours per day, through sleepless nights.

I am excited about my theory: I have a mechanism for stopping the Cold War! The religions can grease the wheels of devolved planning and bring the East and West together. The two sides will coordinate and unite through religions both sides practise in common, spanning the Berlin Wall and East-West border. I am exuberant and lie in bed quivering with excitement, unable to sleep, going over my success and elaborating my theory time after time to be absolutely sure.

"How are you going to pay the mortgage when I stop work?" Ruth bullies me.

"The Head of Department may have some money for me. He mentioned it the other day."

"How long ago was that, exactly?"

"Two weeks."

"Then it doesn't seem likely. Time has run out. You must get a job. We need money. It is time to quit."

When our marriage folds, as it surely will if I do not comply with her, she will get custody. Ruth will have the unassailable advantage of being the birth mother and suckling our child. She will be able to raise our child by her feminist precepts. Women are united to overcome the overpopulation, war, famine and poverty that men have caused. She is not the least interested that my research topic is aimed to do precisely that. Because I am a male she regards me as an encumbrance.

As I toss and turn, I imagine there is polarised conflict, with frozen ideas at two geographic poles. There is planned collectivism in the north and east, with market-oriented individualism in the south and west. I mount an expedition to bring representatives from these two poles together at a mutually acceptable place, such as Berlin. There they will plan a shared civilisation that will last a thousand years. All I have to do is describe how, through religions that span the frontier, the two disparate planning methods will work in unison and the Wall will fall.

An urgent need for this solution is verified in almost every news broadcast. The situation of the Cold War is grim as the nuclear arsenals increase in kilotonnes equivalent of TNT. I throw myself into my work, unable to relax, and go without sleep. "Stress" is not a concept that I have come across or understand. I am not aware what is happening to me, as the stressors multiply and load me to breaking point.

Rule 61: *To solve an ideological conflict, old ideas need to be replaced by an idea that unites adversaries.*

CHAPTER 62   BIPOLAR EXPEDITION NORTH

Nearing exhaustion, with my thoughts churning, I go to the library, find a quiet corner and sink into a reverie.

Subsistence farmers in tropical forests join in teams to build each other houses in clearings. Each family joins with neighbours in working their land to supply themselves, as well as less fortunate people, with food. This is the archetypal small collective. I imagine migration of the original collectivists north from Africa, and review anthropologies of the peoples who settled along the way. I rouse myself and begin writing a record of my mental exploration of this heretofore uncharted territory.

My course to the collective pole takes me through an arid wasteland of academic detritus, a landscape of useless theories. I follow the philosopher, Karl Popper's, dictum to clear a track through the underbrush of minor academic papers, to reveal the tall trees of iconic understanding. As an iconoclast, I use my data to fell a few giants, to expose my own theory to the light of recognition, thus enabling it to grow in stature.

As the climate becomes cooler and drier, the forest gives way to open woodland. Lichens of controversy grow on the wetter side of the tree trunks that face the prevailing westerly wind. I navigate ever northwards by leaving these on my right as I climb steadily up through the foothills.

When I reach the savannah, tropical subsistence communes give way to larger collectives. On the plains of the Russo-Chinese border, the cooperative farms are very large in area, operating as instruments of the state with national vision. Here the famines are worst. The grain produced is exported to the capital under armed guard to prevent theft by the hungry local people who helped grow it. The soils are being run down, the desert is advancing and the people in the collectives are demoralized.

Beyond that, the empty desert shrinks away to tundra. Academics seldom venture this far north, and I come upon species of hypotheses that no-one is interested in, standing at the margins of the various disciplines. There is not much succour here, and for the first time I realise my isolation and vulnerability. Lately, the forces against me have intensified. As the days approach the northern summer solstice, the Sun circles around me, low on the horizon. I lose my bearings and begin to wander aimlessly, unable to get any closer to the collective North Pole.

What a relief it is when I am found by a party of journalists. They are following a herd of indigenous people migrating across the tundra between research centres where they receive food. I am suffering from hypothermia, and they undress me and put me in a sleeping bag with a naked post-doctoral student, a female, who warms me up by skin contact. It seems like a dream. They give me food and alcohol in exchange for some hypotheses.

I give them an hypothesis that in a collective, people allow their leaders to be corrupt. This enables them to act as surrogates for the illegal selfishness they inherit. They allow local leaders to corrupt, and thus usurp, control over the system of altruism imposed by the central leaders. In this way, altruism gives way to self-altruism.

Self-altruism, the philosophy of my cancelled Mission Figurehead, makes sense here. It is obvious that here on the tundra you must sustain yourself first, so that you are able to look after others. It contradicts Christian concepts of charity that are not self-sustaining. Oxygen masks on aeroplanes are for adults to put on themselves before helping children.

It is too difficult to test collectivism against self-altruism. It was nomads such as these, living in harsh environments, who first formed collectives. When survival of the individual is threatened, subscription to kin groups and subspecies groups is worthwhile. The basic unit of survival becomes a group, not an individual. However, the fitness of collectives for survival cannot be tested for, according to Popper, it is a tautology. Fitness and survival are the same thing when we measure them.

It is the last contact I have with reality, for when I leave them my mood is elated. I ignore their advice and set off in a direction they predict will lead away from collectivism towards the opposite pole and selfishness. I give up on finding a pole in the north and east with advantages for collectives, except as a figment of imagination, when selfish needs have been met.

On my trek south, I lose track of time.

"Selwyn, I'd like you to come home now," Ruth telephones me at the university.

"I am not here," I answer. "I am on an expedition."

"What are you doing?" she demands.

"I am on my way to the South Pole from the west."

It is not strictly correct but difficult to explain precisely.

"I can't hear you properly. There seems to be interference."

"It must be the Aurora Borealis," I say.

I suspect the CIA are listening. Paranoia has set in and I am seldom alone.

"Selwyn! Stop it at once," she orders. "I do not want you getting off on some atmospheric effect. Find out where you are and get back to a straight and narrow thesis."

"I'm nearly there."

"Exactly where are you?"

I pause, wondering whether it is best to humour her.

"I am in the Arctic. The Map coordinates are 121151121. Wow! It's a palindrome. Maybe I should head in the opposite direction."

"You are talking nonsense, Selwyn. The sooner you work out where you are, the sooner you'll get your damned thesis finished."

The wind blows quietly past, and fine snow gathers in drifts as I think how to answer her.

"I'm trying but there aren't any road signs. I can't seem to move backwards or forwards." I laugh hysterically. "I'm stuck, bogged down in the soft snow of communist propaganda!"

It is then that I fall into a crevasse-like dilemma that tests my messianic powers.

I know that at the North Pole, some people work hard but not directly for themselves. I can't decide from watching movies of collectivists at work which one of two motivations explains their diligent labour under arduous conditions. On one side is the belief that people work best for a common purpose that captures their imagination. On the other is working hard to provide loyal support to kinfolk.

The closest I can get to a North Pole is a vision supported by a religion that oversees artisan and slave collectives. The USA's moon landing was inspired by the nationalism of John F Kennedy: "Ask not what your country can do for you; ask what you can do for your country!" Visions such as these can be refuted, whereas a religion cannot. Maybe slaves built Stonehenge and the Pyramids. The vision required by artisans to build a great cathedral had been revealed to me in an epiphany at Salisbury Cathedral, when Vicki and I visited. The best evocation I can find is in the book, "Pillars of the Earth", by Ken Follett, about the building of a great cathedral.

Artisan and slave collectives are apples and oranges. I vacillate for three days without sleep, thinking about whether they really can work together under religious supervision. I become incoherent. I have lost objectivity and retrace my steps. When I cannot write a chain of causality for collective organisation in words, I try for two more days without sleep to relate planning algorithms in diagrams and then in symbols and formulae, filling page after page with equations. But when I go back over them, their meaning is not clear to me. I rewrite them over and over again, never managing to capture collectivist planning in either prose or maths that is common to both the USA and USSR. I am going around in circles.

My colleagues from uni visit me at home at Ruth's behest. They try to rescue me, but I laugh and pull several into rhetorical crevasses, showing off how one can get out. My exuberance worries them, and they want me to take a holiday. I stay home for a few days. I want to spend my time drinking whisky, dancing and having sex, but Ruth wants to sleep. My sleeplessness is causing me to hallucinate. When I explain to Ruth that I am a messiah, she wants me to go with her to the doctor, but I refuse because he is under the control of the Cold War conspiracy.

When I try to explain to her my theory, Ruth tells me, "You are talking gibberish."

I have to talk about it with someone. I seek help from Professor Shapner, our department head. I tell him where my research is up to.

"You are making good progress," Professor Shapner tells me. "I'll try to get your grant extended. I am concerned about your health. You need to take a holiday."

"I have never felt better," I say.

In fact, I have a bad headache. I have been without sleep for five days.

Against all advice, I prepare for a final assault on the North Pole. I am going there to find an everyday collective. The problem is that I don't know in what direction to go.

Ruth persuades me to lie down and rest. I plan to redecorate the hallway walls with tiles like those on the floor. The pattern intrigues me. It shows how international diplomacy depends on everyday volunteering, such as offering to do the washing up. I wake Ruth up to tell her my ideas but she is unimpressed.

"I don't understand what you are on about any more," she says.

"It's a new paradigm that tears up the previous theories and has a new viewpoint on almost everything," I tell her."I cannot explain it in one thesis. It's too big."

I want to keep talking but she pretends to sleep. I toss and turn until the early hours. Then I get up and go out to the study to work.

Ruth's night is sleepless, too. In the morning, before going to work, she confronts me.

"I want to you to come with me to the doctor."

"There's nothing wrong with me," I tell her.

Ruth makes an appointment to see my doctor the next morning, which is Saturday.

When I leave home, for the first time in a week, I think we are going to base camp. When we arrive at the doctor's, I refuse to go in with Ruth and return home instead. In the afternoon, my sister, Heather, comes with us. I do not want to go to the doctor's as there is nothing wrong with me, but the two of them browbeat me into walking there and going in.

"How do you feel?" the doctor asks me.

"I never felt better," I tell him. "How about you?"

He eyes me balefully.

"Who am I?" he asks.

I do not answer.

"Who are you?" he asks me.

"I have a mission," I tell him, "to save the World."

"How are you going to do that?"

"Why should I tell you?"

"I will try to help you."

"I do not need your help. I want to go."

"Why do you think I want to help you."

I don't answer. I am sure he is KGB, knows about my theory and wants to kill me.

"You are ill," he tells me. "I want you to take this pill now. It will help you get some sleep."

"What evidence is there that I am ill?" I demand. "If my breath stank like yours I'd have halitosis. I ought to be paid a fee for putting up with it."

He looks angry.

"Take the pill now, Selwyn."

"You are a shaman, a glorified medicine man, naked and painted beneath your suit."

"Selwyn, this pill will help you."

"That is not a testable hypothesis. I don't believe you. You are trying to poison me."

Ruth and Heather tell me I can trust him. Their combined persistence persuades me, and I swallow the pill.

The doctor has the last laugh. When I get home, my tongue sticks out involuntarily. I am embarrassed and badly frightened. I have heard that people can swallow their tongues. My eyes bulge out as I struggle for breath. I fear I am about to asphyxiate. I am convulsed by the desire to vomit and double up, gagging. Ruth calls for medical help. Jesus never had it half as bad as me.

God sends his heavenly chariot disguised as an ambulance. Two burly angels, who say they are psychiatric nurses, give me a white garment to put on.

"The other way round," they tell me, as I shuck on the straitjacket. "It is standard procedure with mania." They tie me in so I can't move my arms.

Being tied up is totally humiliating. With the klaxon blaring, we speed to hospital. It is a hive of activity. Hundreds of political prisoners shuffle in lines to be processed by white-coated officials. When it is my turn, I denounce my doctor for poisoning me. I am put in a room with chairs around the walls where about a dozen sad-looking patients sit. Because they seem without hope, I relieve their sadness by reminding them in a loud voice, "You are all mad." None of them disputes it, which confirms in my mind that I am the only person who is totally sane and I don't need to die just yet.

"Listen to your feelings," an inner voice seems to be telling me.

I don't want to be with such hopeless people. At the first opportunity, I escape out the back door and head for home through the streets of suburbia on foot. My heart pounds in my ears. My sense of direction, which is unreliable at the best of times, gives me only weak clues about which direction to head in. I seek the help of a lady with a shopping trolley.

"Can you tell me the way, please?"

"Where to?"

I pause. I hadn't thought of this complication.

"I don't know," I admit.

"Where do you live, luv?"

"I'm not sure. Maybe at Ayston."

"That's a long way. You can get a bus over there, number 162."

"Thank you."

While I wait at the bus stop, I see on the ground a small piece of cast aluminium shaped like a letter A and pick it up. I know immediately that it has something to do with my friend Tom. He works for an aluminium company in the USA. I have not heard from him for years, since Howard stayed there. A higher power obviously wants me to contact him. I don't have Tom's address or telephone number. If I think about him, maybe he will call. Then a bus comes and I put the piece in my pocket.

I have not been on a bus for some time and I have forgotten how to pay. So I give the driver a handful of change from my pocket.

"Where you going, mate?"

"Ayston."

"High Street?"

"Maybe. Where else do you go?"

"Lochlan Road, Park Road, Town Hall, Swimming Pool, Library, Grosvenor Close. Just moved here, have you?"

"About three years ago."

"Blimey. Well, I'll let you off at Town Hall. You can ask there. That's one pound sixty pence."

"Thank you."

"Here's your change. You may need it."

When I get off, I am completely lost. My heart thumps in my chest as I fight panic. Two men along the street are looking at me. They could be CIA. I walk in the opposite direction. I can't remember my street address. With mounting fearfulness, I walk the length of the High Street trying to see somewhere I might remember. What if I cannot find my way? Would it be best to sleep in a park? Then I walk further, past the Town Hall, and eventually I see a vaguely familiar street name and follow it. It is a great relief when I reach my street, Worthing Street.

I have now been awake for eight days and I am aware that I am hallucinating. My vision is distorted, with some objects looming up too close and others seeming to be falling away, like looking through the wrong end of a telescope. But it is the fear that I am being hunted by the white-coated goons from St Peter's Gate that is worst. I let myself into our home, tired and footsore. I lie on my bed and search for sleep in a head exhausted and dulled. I have been chosen for the Second Coming or as The Messiah, I am not sure which, to denounce the Cold War conspiracy. I cannot picture God, but I feel my life has been taken over by a higher power and I am immortal. It is exciting to realize that of all the 4,100,000,000 people on the planet, I am the only one chosen, and I wonder what I have to do to keep my job. I am exhausted. So I take the pills they promise will help me sleep.

Rule 62: *Leaders of collectives are allowed to replace altruism with self-altruism.*

CHAPTER 63   TIME OUT

I wake up with my thoughts fuddled. It is a resurrection. The pills work brilliantly. My thoughts are woolly; so I don't bother to think. I sit out in the Sun in our back garden and watch the cabbages grow. They seemed accepting, as if I can be like them.

I attend the hospital day-care centre for two months. I talk with the inmates and play the guitar. Gradually, the mania that has gripped my sleepless mind is replaced by the certainty that as a messiah, my role is to detect the Cold War conspiracy. I have to conceal my special identity from Ruth and from the doctors. I know they would explain away the strange events that impress on me continually as coincidences. In my view, there is ample evidence that I am specially chosen for a mission that a higher power will one day reveal to me.

I believe I am in control, not only of the British Government, but of every organisation and every person and their activities, including the play of children outside in the street. I feel a huge responsibility to watch and wait, my thoughts churning with realisation of the connectedness of everything to everything else.

My disciples, Richard, Steve and Vicki, drop in after work to visit me at home. Their visits are dissolved by my fertile imagination into a pageant of biblical scenes. Richard is the apostle John and Vicki is playing Mary Magdalene to my Jesus. I do not recall exact roles in the Bible, but I am allowed to create a new ministry as I go.

Vicki sits beside me in the back garden. We look at the cabbages. Conversation is difficult for me and very slow because of my medication. I am embarrassed. She will never want me after seeing me like this. She tells me about a book, "The Plague", by Albert Camus. Irrationality of life is inevitable and human reaction towards the plague is "absurd".

Poor Vicki. She tries to bring me back to reality with questions about what I am experiencing but I resist her intrusion and hide in my shell. If I come out, the reality of my marriage, my thesis and finances is more frightening than the world I have escaped to.

"Do you hear voices?" Vicki tries.

I shake my head. The messiah communicates by thought transference.

"Do you have delusions of being specially chosen?" she asks.

Again, I shake my head. It is not a delusion; it is real. This conversation is a delusion.

"Can you remember a time when you first stopped liking yourself?"

I can remember, all right; they brought my baby sister home from the hospital and I became a nuisance, to be minimised and got rid of. But I say nothing.

"Can you tell me your thoughts at this moment?"

It is too painful. I say nothing. I want her to go away.

"Do you want me to stay?"

I shake my head.

"Well, goodbye. I hope you get better soon, Selwyn. You are ill and you need to talk about what you are experiencing. The sooner you do that, the sooner you will recover. You will be able to make a full recovery. Remember that I am your friend. I will always be here for you to talk with."

"Thank you, Vicki. I'm sorry."

I am sorry that I cannot tell her. She will never want me if she sees how broken I am.

"Goodbye, Selwyn."

She goes and sadness comes.

Did Jesus make out with Mary, I wonder.

I wonder if I will ever see her again.

Richard is a regular visitor, and I am always glad to see him. Since his breakdown, I have forgiven him for his fling with Vicki. Maybe he is secretly glad that I, too, have succumbed. As Gore Vidal said, "Whenever a friend succeeds, a little something in me dies". Richard wants to know what I am thinking about and I tell him. I explain to him patiently that the collective pole I am seeking is eluding me.

"So why have you been searching for collectives in the north?" he says.

I tell him my theory of sailing upwind or downwind and the different types of people.

"Communes develop in harsh environments where unity is essential," he tells me.

"But there aren't any collectives at the North Pole," I reply. "At least, I can't find any."

"No collectives? What about Eskimos? An Eskimo village is a collective, if ever I saw one. Not much selfishness going on there!"

"But they're kin," I object. "That doesn't count. A collective has people who you are not related to. Eskimos hang out in families, not collectives."

"What about Eskimo villages with several different families?" he suggests. "They share everything. They are a collective."

"What do you mean they share everything?"

"Space. The living place."

"That's not true altruism," I reply. "They get close together to keep warm, to trade, to keep away bears. These are selfish reasons. A collective must have unselfish sharing, or altruism."

"They share time unselfishly," Richard proposes.

"Time?"

"Whenever they take it in turns. To check for a seal on the ice they can hunt. Or when taking away pieces of blubber from a kill. It's not a selfish feeding frenzy like Tasmanian Devils or hyenas. It's orderly. They share time."

I shake my head. "But it's not true altruism, either, because they know that their turn will be reciprocated very soon. True altruism is giving to strangers without expectation of an immediate payback. "

"Then maybe you are right: there is no collective altruism in the north."

"Well, of course there bloody is," I say impatiently. "I just can't find it. What about when they protect their neighbours' children from the fucking wolves, even when they don't have any children of their own?"

"Hmm. Yes, that's altruism, all right," he admits grudgingly. "They could have a child-protection collective."

I sense victory. "Yes, they do. And what about all the other altruism that goes on, such as partner-swapping? I dare say Eskimos are monogamous some of the time, but how do you think they fill those long winter nights, hey?"

"Hokey pokey, heh?"

I am triumphant. "Ha ha. The idea is not a 'getting a fair share of something' type of selfish; it's a reciprocation, a collective based on altruism."

"Ha ha, reciprocation; a good concept. But why Eskimos? Why not with other indigenous people?"

"It is an evolutionary response to a restrictive environment," I say. "It is the best way of spending darkness when you are surrounded by snow."

"Having sex isn't altruism."

"It's just a surmise," I shrug. "It could be true."

"I do not think so. Anyway, if collectives worked," says Richard in the loud voice that he uses to present a cynical viewpoint as an insight, "we would already be living in one."

"Doing hokey pokey—"

I try to laugh but I can't.

After he has gone, I feel completely hopeless and recognise the feeling as depression. My few downers before this were picnics. It is as if I have been paralysed and am unable to anything, even simple tasks like making a cup of coffee. All I can do is hunker down and reflect on my own weaknesses, over and over again.

After several weeks of this, I become able to think about the outside world. I go back over my thesis, time after time. I become convinced that I have to rescue the Russians and Chinese from the clutches of the frozen north by exploring in the south and then finding a compromise position. Therefore, I pretend to be normal and stop going to the day-care centre.

Rule 63: *A compromise between two alternative systems is unlikely to be better than either, but will at least reduce conflict between them.*

CHAPTER 64   BIPOLAR EXPEDITION SOUTH

I resume my work at the university, supposedly writing up my thesis. Secretly, I go back to untying the Cold War knot in my thoughts, filling notebook after notebook with ideas, diagrams and equations. I am on the second part of my expedition, to investigate the nature of true selfishness at the South Pole of the Cold War nexus.

To tease out the aetiology of selfishness, I follow the trail of the more selfish humans from Africa who crossed the North Atlantic and spread along the eastern seaboard of the Americas. There is much evidence of anti-collective selfishness, such as desertion, slavery, mutiny, punishment, sabotage, piracy, insurrection, genocide and religious extremism. The routes branch off to places where alternative societies with individual freedom exist now or once flourished. They eschewed mutualism and displaced indigenous people from the land, sometimes as thinly disguised genocide, all with religious approval.

When my journey reaches Patagonia and the frozen south, I climb up from the iceberged sea until the sled becomes a hindrance in the soft snow and boulder fields. I know I have to keep going, from effect to logical cause, to reach the ultimate cause of selfishness. I had set off well enough, going against the ocean currents, against the drift of icebergs and then up the glaciers of Antarctica, seeking to find the frozen source of individualism. Scott of the Antarctic showed how individualism and self-sacrifice are noble companions. When my supplies dwindle and fit into a backpack, I have no further use for the dogs and I slaughter them. The only dog I spare is a black Labrador who follows me around. I cook the others' meat by burning the sled and cache a half of it for the return journey.

The going is dismally slow. I am mired in bogs of circular argument. I choose the most direct route, discarding sophistry and applying Ockham's Razor. The black dog follows at a distance, fearing the fate of his companions. The way is marked by the remains of camps where individuals have dropped their expedition's equipment and returned the way they came. Utilitarians who had reached this far turned their attention to benefiting the state and had split away towards the other pole via the Pacific. They wanted a government that would limit selfishness and in so doing killed the bird that laid the golden egg.

It is bitterly cold, and the only life is a colony of seals, grouped in a defensive collective, and a handful of polar bears whose collective behaviours are predicted but have not been observed.

Capitalist freedom is grounded on the bedrock of Darwin's theory of survival of the fittest. My modification is that after individuals have promoted their genes selfishly, as explained by E O Wilson, in their kin groups, they sometimes show altruism and undertake collective action, such as combining to fight an intruder. I believe lions and elephants do this, although these could be kin groups. We seem to be the only animal that practices true altruism.

As I trudge across the ice, I consider how my behaviour would be different if I had companions, and whether they would improve my survival prospects. I conclude that because I am above average, I would be better off alone.

In the Cold War, is there a morality that maintains a balance between the two sides? If so, is it less a war than an incompatibility between two moral crusades? Capitalists and collectivists deal with each other through centralised international diplomacy. A secret underground source shows me evidence of an agreement between the Americans and the communists to stage the Cuban missile crisis in 1962. Following this lead, I go back and investigate the correspondence between Roosevelt and Stalin in 1945, first at Yalta and then at Potsdam. I find ample evidence that the two sides had conspired to effect a mock confrontation based on the atomic bomb, and all the posturing had been empty. Roosevelt and Stalin had agreed that this weapon should never be used, but merely brandished to maintain cohesion within their own ravening side. The Cold War that blighted the lives of billions was a ritual confrontation, with empty posturing.

Mao Tse Tung, who is a party to a three-way agreement, has sought to inculcate altruism by Cultural Revolution and his little-read book. He has steadily escalated the military conflict with the

US in Vietnam. The war is now so unpopular in the US that the Americans want to withdraw.

I feel stupid that I have overlooked the true dynamics of the Cold War until now. The impasse is not between two separate natural philosophies, as I had thought, but between two incompatible peaks of one giant iceberg that is drifting, out of control. Submerged between them is a conspiracy of technological development that is keeping the populace of our planet enthralled with materialism and employed, even if not gainfully. When I seek the source of material images, the trail leads underground.

I find a line scratched on a rock by Richard Dawkins: "Let us try to teach generosity and altruism, because we are born selfish." I am puzzled, because the logic is not self-evident. Selfishness that self-sustains is good, and altruism that creates dependence on others is bad. People need self-altruism, which is self-sustaining altruism. That it is not happening is because of a conspiracy between the Cold War opponents. The US promotes selfishness and opposes altruism, while on the other side the USSR has adopted the converse, promoting altruism and opposing selfishness.

I follow the black dog down into the darkness, risking discovery by security personnel employed to keep the conspiracy hidden. The evidence I find is a survival shelter, deep enough to escape damage from the inferno above. Lights are on, and through an open door I can see it has food, equipment and hydropower needed for about 100 people to stay here indefinitely. Labels inform the occupants of facility functions and hazards. Every label is written in Russian, Chinese and English. I am able to peel off a label from the door, "Exit Code 27", and put it in my backpack.

Fearful of a patrol, I walk back the way I have come, but I get lost. My supplies are finished, and I am sustained by metabolic absorption of fat and muscles from my body. The eye of the bipolar hurricane crossing my psyche is now blowing from a direction opposite the manic phase earlier, into depression. I indulge in orgies of recrimination and self-loathing. I have wanted to be a hero to attract Vicki, but my expedition is an example of the very selfishness it is investigating

I conserve body energy by lying in my sleeping bag in a foetal position. I have no desire to return to a world where, in the name of freedom, individuals spend their days slaving to supply meaningless excesses of conspicuous and addictive consumption. It is a world where the authorities deny community, so that people will be motivated by status anxiety to consume and to work, to pay their debts, and to produce missiles.

After a month, I am skin and bone and have no energy to continue. It is safest to stay underground. There isn't any leader I can trust enough to tell my findings to. If there is a way to persuade the public to exclude national politicians from public policy-making altogether, the conspiracy of the Cold War can be ended. Overcoming the cheesy smell of the black dog, I kill and eat it. I regain strength.

I should maintain the life given me by my parents and set a positive example. I want to see Vicki again. She may not be impressed by how I have become lost, but there is a chance that she will understand and forgive me. Although I regret Ruth's baby, it will have as full support from me as if it had arrived by an unflawed process, by a fertilisation I wanted. Spurred on by claustrophobia, I stand up weakly with aching limbs. I stumble back the way I came, scrambling down the watercourse.

I find my way back, consuming the caches of food I left on the way in.

When I get home, I take a few weeks off work and recover my health. When I return to uni, I continue drafting my thesis, preparing to be interviewed on television and calling for religious communities to make simultaneous demands for disarmament in both the USA and USSR, especially in West and East Germany. When I distribute drafts to other researchers for comment, the silence is deafening. Most people are accustomed to saying nothing about others' new ideas unless their own territory is threatened.

I get an appointment with Professor Shapner to discuss my findings. I sit in his office as he goes through my report.

"You have done a lot of work," he says. "As for what I think about your theory, I am reluctant to give it to you straight because you are not well. Your judgement seems to have been affected."

"What do you mean?" I ask.

"You think there is a conspiracy, a secret understanding between the Russians and the Americans? What is your evidence for that?" Professor Shapner smiles paternally.

I tell him about the underground shelter and show him the door label I brought back.

"Hmm. I suppose it could indicate international cooperation," he says."It could come from several places: Shanghai, Vladivostok, Vancouver. Where was this underground shelter?"

"Antarctica," I say.

"How did you get there?"

I can only dimly remember. "I travelled overland through Patagonia to Tierra Del Fuego, and then across the ice with a dog team."

"But the sea doesn't freeze over to provide a land bridge, even in the winter. You must have gone by sea?"

"I have forgotten."

"How long ago was this?"

"Several months."

"When did you get back?"

"Last weekend."

"But I saw you two months ago. Then I heard you were away with a mental illness."

"That's right."

"What other evidence of a conspiracy do you have?"

I tell him about Potsdam and the Cuban Missile Crisis.

"It's not direct evidence," says Professor Shapner defensively. "You have inferred from Stalin's and Roosevelt's behaviour that they were up to no good. Other explanations are more likely. For example, they were building trust to negotiate."

"It's a fine line."

"Do you really think the missile transporters in Red Square, the fleets of nuclear subs, the loaded missile silos and the ICBM early warning system exist merely to keep the leaders in Moscow and Washington in power?" he asks incredulously.

"Yes, I do."

"Do you believe that the leadership on both sides is committed to the nuclear confrontation as a stabilising force? Do you believe they are so enamoured of each other's intelligence that they believe that a secret mutualism is the only way forward? Isn't it possible that the military people are more committed to a zero sum future?" Shapner sounds irritated.

"They are certainly gung-ho, but not that gung-ho. It is logical that a nuclear war would be such a disaster, the presidents would agree to have a charade of antipathy," I answer.

"Is it not cynical to believe that arms escalation has no other purpose than to consolidate the two presidencies?" snaps Professor Shapner.

"Yes, I believe it is."

"Are they facing a prisoners' dilemma where they secretly cooperate in keeping quiet about their treacherous deceptions to avoid the consequences that would rebound on to them if they both confessed?" He sounds sceptical.

"Yes, I believe they are. They would be out of office."

Exasperated, he says, "Were Stalin's purges and McCarthy's witch-hunts contrived?"

"Yes, I believe they were."

Professor Shapner shook his head. "When there are two possible explanations, should we not adopt Ockham's Razor and choose the simpler one? The simpler one is the official line, that we fear USSR aggression. Isn't your evidence from Potsdam and from the Cuban Missile Crisis more likely to indicate incompetency rather than conspiracy?"

"I suppose it is possible," I accept reluctantly.

"It is very possible," he says, thumping his fist on the desk. "I don't believe your conspiracy exists anywhere other than in your head, the same as your imaginary trip to the Antarctic. It is an international conflict, not a corrupted two-player zero sum game as you suggest. A conspiracy is just not credible. You will not submit it as a doctoral thesis in this department!"

He calms down.

"I'm sorry to be so negative when you are unwell. Think about what I have told you. Write up your theory, comparing it with the conventional theory as I have told it. Your comparison must show the conventional theory fits the data better. Then you will be able to submit it for the Master of Philosophy degree. Any questions?"

"So I can't write up my conspiracy thesis for a PhD?"

He rolls his eyes. "No! Thank you, Archer. Close the door as you leave."

"Thank you, Professor," I say.

I think about what he says. Very reluctantly, over several weeks as I write up my comparison of the conflicting theories, I abandon my conspiracy theory. According to social psychology, if someone changes their behaviour, they will internalize new attitudes required. It comes as a relief, and my depression lifts. Feeling foolish, I revert to my theory of using religion and science to control the confrontation at a devolved level. In my MPhil introduction, I present the philosophical divide between the two sides.

In the west and south, there is an unwritten acceptance of any new technology, with the onus on opponents to show reasons why it should be restricted. The philosophy follows from Popper's science, in which any idea is allowed, provided there is the capability to falsify it. It allows for a society to have rapid growth, with all the trappings of selfish dreams, modern theisms implanted by corporations for profit.

It is unlike growth in the ancient theistic forests of the east and north. Those have tremendous waste. People lead empty, vacuous lives. They want collectives, but corporations assiduously differentiate their customers to isolate them and increase their consumption.

I meet with Professor Shapner in his office to review my progress.

"How is the MPhil write-up coming along?"

"My data fit the conventional theory better than a conspiracy, as you instructed."

"What a pity," he says. "Your conspiracy theory is correct but is more complicated than needed. The difference cannot be attributed to the presidents' whims. There are two incompatible systems, capitalism and communism."

"Is incompatibility the problem?" I interrupt.

"No, not at all. They can co-exist happily – in different places. The Cold War is simply a competition to show strength and recruit countries that are undecided to their side."

"Why do they need the recruits?"

"For strength," the professor laughed. "It's a circular argument and unsound. The premise that the two are in zero sum competition is false. They could have a symbiotic relationship, each stabilising the other." He throws up his arms. "But people are uncomfortable with ambiguity. We live in a crazy one-eyed world. They believe monotheism should prevail when obviously there needs to be duality, or we will have tyranny."

"So, in your view the Cold War is necessary?"

"Not necessary. But inevitable."

"Well, I believe it can be stopped."

"How?"

"When enough people on both sides work through the same churches for a unity that builds bridges between the USA and USSR, limiting the centralisation of power, the Cold War will be stopped."

"Then people will want competition in another arena. You can't deny human nature."

"You mean Vietnam? I mean in an arena beyond the Cold War."

"There will be other wars."

"We should face that when we come to it. In the meantime, I want to submit a doctoral thesis that proposes a religious solution to the present Cold War."

"I am not convinced it will work. Religion is not something we get involved with in this department. You will have to change your enrolment to the School of Social Science, if you can. They may have some funds for you to pursue this type of thing. I wish you luck."

I have already crossed swords with the School of Social Science. My solution lies in their academic territory, and they insist that I have to do field work in Russia and America. I do not have time or funds. I leave feeling defeated by an academic system organised by tradition and unable to address problems where other disciplines are prominent. Neither do I have time to align my thesis with the academic culture of the School. I have to quit and look for a job.

My bipolar expedition is ended, and I have succeeded, in a limited way. Later, I realize that due to the success of my bipolar expedition, I have contributed spiritually, or even prefigured, processes that eventually ended the Cold War.

Rule 64: *There is a public conspiracy that creates an illusion of moral competition between ideologies of individual and collective consumption.*

CHAPTER 65   DECLINING BLAME

In contravention of our pre-marriage agreement, Ruth is pregnant. With a baby on the way, she compounds the stress on me by buying a house with a mortgage requiring an income she will soon lose. I will have to get a job. Moreover, she loads me to breaking point with inactionable worries about having a disabled baby. By nature, I am unable to provide much practical and emotional support. I blame her for creating stresses that carry me down into the depths of mental illness.

Instead of leaving her because of the pregnancy, I shoulder my load and try to keep going, even though there are luminous signs of overload. If there is a faulty circuit breaker and no-one has ever before overloaded it, is there a predisposition to break down? I think not. I worry unproductively all day, and my mind churns uselessly all night. My overload is unsupported, my circuit-breaker fails, and after a sleepless week I become deranged. A paranoid delusion takes over my mind: that my suffering, like that of Jesus, is evidence that I, too, have been selected as a messiah. I infer that God, who moves in mysterious ways, must have big plans for me.

Vicki visits me at home a couple of times. She slips into her professional role as a counsellor and is concerned that I am receiving medication rather than counselling. Medication does not deal with underlying causes. I realize that what led me into trouble was wanting to be a hero. It is a selfish motive. I do not tell her that I did it to attract her. But I am a hero to myself, as my bipolar expedition succeeded in finding a solution to the Cold War.

Vicki eyes me curiously, keeping a professional distance, as I tell her a skeletal account of my expedition.

"Selwyn, how do the hospital people explain your breakdown?"

"Schizo-affective disorder."

"What does that mean?"

"Symptoms part-way between the delusions of schizophrenia and the mania and depression of bipolar."

"Do you still have any symptoms?"

"No," I lie, for I have a big secret.

Being The Messiah is real to me, not a delusion. It is my escape route from the anxiety that has dogged my heels from childhood, exacerbated by anxiety from being married to bossy Ruth. For other people who deal with me, the illness has few repercussions other than a susceptibility to stress, paranoid suspicions and a silent preoccupation with coincidences that renders me unresponsive and sometimes unreliable. Gradually, these behaviours ameliorate.

I veg out in hospital day-care. Mental illness is little understood, and the effectiveness of medications is discovered by trial and error. Fortunately, there are more trials than errors, and within a few months I am ready to resume work.

By reflection, I have realized the errors of my expedition and how to avoid repeating them. I am learning to remain detached from my work and retain emotional balance. In future, I must avoid isolation and maintain relationships. I need to articulate my work better to family and friends and build up support.

With the help of medication, the depression has gone. I finish writing up my description of the Cold War as a symbiosis between two incompatible systems and am awarded a MPhil. It is a devastating blow to have to settle for this when I had done sufficient work for a PhD.

James, my friend and colleague from Calgary, has started an energy engineering consultancy in London. He generously offers me a good job and I gladly fall back on the skills I learned when I was with Canoil.

Ruth gives birth to a lovely baby girl, Nicola. I am delighted. My life is suddenly restricted to care for a tiny person who is very rewarding. I love being a father.

I do well in my job with James' company, and my pay increases. While I am ill, Ruth takes over running our household and dealing with banks, utilities and services. When I recover, she is reluctant to give me back control of my pay. She denies me an equal say in joint matters, even if she does not understand them and I do. In particular, she shuts me out from moulding the behaviour of Nicola, claiming her expertise has precedence on every issue. She has no interest in my career and personal growth. She bullies me by claiming the higher moral ground in every argument because she is female and therefore understands. I infer that she regards me as fatally flawed and from a sub-species of mental defectives who cannot expect equal rights.

"This is about my rights as a mother on behalf of our child," she says. "You wouldn't understand."

Ruth never seems to value my skills. She makes rash property purchases, ignoring my analyses and caution to get advice. When I want to evaluate alternatives rationally using technical advisers, she bullies me into submission.

"I am going ahead with this now, whether you like it or not," she says. "If you won't sign, I'm leaving you and taking Nicola."

So I sign. I will not leave my baby with Ruth.

Then she bullies me into returning home.

"I'm going back to Canada," she informs me. "Are you coming?"

"But I've just landed a great job here in London. Let's go later."

"I'm going now, whether you come or not. And I'm taking Nicola."

I know she would have, too. It isn't hard to see that she would get custody. So, I have to go with her, or abdicate responsibility for Nicola.

When I manage to get Vicki alone and tell her of my misery with Ruth, she is unsympathetic.

"Why don't you stand up to her? Do you think she would really go back to Canada without you?"

"Yes, I do. She has no further use for me."

"Why don't you let her go?"

"I couldn't live without Nicola. A kid deserves to have two parents." Vicki is surprised by my loyalty to baby Nicola.

"You could be sacrificing your own happiness."

I try to work out what she means. Vicki's eyes are unfathomable as she holds my gaze. I thought then she meant being unhappy with Ruth. Later, I realise Vicki could be offering happiness with her. But it is Nicola's happiness that I care most about.

If only I had persisted and been patient, I might have married Vicki, as I have been in love with her all along. Ruth and I are incompatible, and stitch by stitch the bonds holding us together are coming undone. I wonder how I can renew my relationship with Vicki without deserting Nicola, but it seems hopeless.

Rule 65: *Strong characters are greedy and steal the rights of the meek, rather than compromising to achieve a healthy balance.*

PART 10: NARROWING GAINS
(1976–2002)

In this part, the ethical cost of selling out my long commitment is too high, and closing my short too expensive, but I am able to stay in a straddle by renewing my short at a reducing price.

CHAPTER 66   PUSHES AND PULLS

After five years away, we go back to Canada with our baby and settle in Calgary, Ruth's hometown. Ruth gets pregnant again. She worries that the baby could be affected after she is in contact with German Measles. I have more responsibility at work than I can cope with, and I am sleepless. Not wanting another psychosis, I seek refuge in a mental hospital for three weeks. Ruth's family look after her.

When the baby arrives, we bring it home from hospital to our new house. I am thrilled to be a father again, with a son, Michael. The house is unfinished, and I use every spare moment and weekends plastering, painting and concreting. During this time, Ruth complains continually.

"When are you going to carpet the bedroom?" she asks.

"When I've painted it," I reply.

"When will that be?"

"I'm not sure. I'm going as fast as I can."

Ruth is dictatorial, as usual. The stress at home affects my work. I become sleepless with worry and begin to crack up. I feel really bad leaving her with a tiny baby, but her family again look after her while I go back into hospital for two weeks. Away from her, I quickly recover. When I come out, I am able to finish the house, and our lives revolve around our two children and each other. I have to overlook Ruth's pushy nature, which is so much like my mother's. Anxiety stalks me, and I often visit the paranoid world in which I am The Messiah. In my regular appointments with a psychiatrist, I never tell about these delusions because I need these bolt holes for survival with Ruth.

I come back to the UK every few years to visit my family in Yorkshire and several old friends. At first, Ruth, Nicola and Michael come with me and we go to see Vicki at Salisbury, not far from Heathrow. It is a one-hour drive along the M6 and down the A303. After leaving the motorway, we come upon the town of Salisbury on the flat river floodplain, spread around its cathedral, like a dinner plate turning upwards around the outside, with splashes of grey, orange and green. It is a beautiful place.

At the outskirts, I switch on to a side road. Vicki's house is down a narrow overgrown lane in a quiet hamlet. Her quaint cottage is half-timbered in the Tudor style, infilled with brick herringbones. A weathercock swings lazily above a thatched roof. The air is rich with mossy green smells. Inside are low narrow doorways, beamed ceilings and steep spiral stairways in stone, with smells of candles and wood smoke from the open fire. Behind the house are stables converted into a garage, a modern studio with vinyl smells, a walled vegetable garden, an orchard with fruit trees and a full apple barn with the nutty smell of Cox's Orange Pippins.

It is a rather awkward visit. We all sit on the settee and try not to stare at her. I have not told Ruth how much Vicki means to me, but she probably guesses and doesn't care. When we arrive, Vicki and I hug warmly.

The house is Vicki's childhood home. After her father died, her mother moved into in a modern flat near the town centre, with a full-time carer. Vicki visits her every day. She has taken over the family home and put in central heating. She has added works of art to the walls and some exotic furniture pieces. It is an exquisite residence.

Vicki makes us welcome. I had written to her several times, hearing back only once. I assume that is the way it is when so much is at stake.

"How do you like it over there?" Vicki asks.

"It's great," I say.

"What do you like about it?"

"Equality – no class system."

"Everyone's working class, then?"

"More or less, yes."

"What do you miss most in the UK?"

It is her, and she knows it, but I answer in a plummy voice.

"Culture – you are so much more civilised here."

"Do you mean middle class culture?" Vicki says.

"Why should we import foreign elitism?" says Ruth defensively.

"Why is Canadian culture set at the least common denominator of beer, football and xenophobia?"

"They have them here, too, Selwyn," says Vicki, changing the subject.

"Great." I am loyal to my adopted home. "Our engineering tends to be hijacked by cowboy politicians, but we are not hampered by regulations and traditions as you are here."

"Well, maybe there is an upside. I'm glad you like it."

Vicki is an eternal optimist. She is sympathetic, too, and I love her more and more. It bothers me that she is single. I want her to have children. She smiles at the baby, radiating quiet self-confidence like the Mona Lisa. But she also shows puzzlement as though wondering why we have all descended on her.

I want to show her what she is missing. I want these visits to convey to her how much joy my children bring me. It is the way they trust me and show affection, with an arm around my leg, or a little hand reaching up for mine.

Perhaps it is mean of me to show off our baby when Vicki is feeling the social pressure from her biological clock. I want her to have children before it is too late. I long to be free to have children with her.

"I hope you find a guy who wants children," I say, "so he will give you a push in the right direction."

It is as close as I think I should come to a delicate topic. My love is in my eyes, but I try not to let Ruth see that.

Vicki laughs. "I am trying – assuming you are using push as a euphemism."

I am embarrassed. "No, I mean—"

"She knows what you mean, Selwyn," interrupted Ruth."We should be going."

Vicki glances at my two beautiful blond-haired children and then at me. Her eyes disdain me as an irresolute romantic, fully committed elsewhere.

As we leave I notice that her things are put away, which is unusual for her. It seems like she is living somewhere else, probably with a man. I feel jealous and wonder who he is.

When I am alone with Vicki, I feel that I belong there, as if we should always be together. It is by bad luck that so far we have been out of phase with each other. With good luck, we can be together soon.

"Do you ever get homesick?" she asks.

"Sometimes."

"How are you getting on at home?"

Our house rings with children's laughter – but rarely Ruth's or mine. I realize how I have been putting others' needs before my own.

My instincts are that my growing unhappiness originates from my dealings with Ruth. I do not reveal to Vicki the sad state of my marriage. I am haunted by my wedding vow, "Until death do us part". My attitude to marriage at this time reeks of hubris: I am openly contemptuous of colleagues who quit their marriages, insinuating that they are not putting enough effort into making them work, as I am doing. Proust wrote, "Happy families are all alike; every unhappy family is unhappy in its own way."

I never consider leaving Ruth. My kids need two parents who are in harmony. I am in denial that our marriage is failing. I simply have to put up with the stress and anxiety.

I find out very little from Vicki in our encounters. Getting any information from her is like getting blood from a stone. She is habitually secretive.

"Have you found a man yet?" I ask.

"Several," she answers, "but none steady. I'm still looking."

I want to say, "'Don't look any further. You can have me.'"

To leave Ruth with the kids is not an option. No-one in my family has ever divorced. It would have a bad effect on the children, and I can't contemplate it. My only hope is in the distant future, when the kids leave home.

Instead, I say, "He'll be a lucky guy."

Rule 66: *Whereas in nature's garden a marriage is ideally a "companion planting", some couples compete or conflict, or shade each other and need to be separated.*

CHAPTER 67   FERTILITY LIMITED

On one of my visits, Vicki and I drive to Stonehenge near her home. We stroll past the massive blocks of limestone, stopping to read the guidebook. Skylarks twitter high overhead as we sit on the grass and speculate about the people who built this monument. Both Vicki and I are interested in organisation and motivation problems.

"What sort of people would cut these and bring them 200 kilometres from Wales, across land and water?" I ask.

"Slaves?"

"The construction work went on for 1300 years," I say. "Do slaves become assimilated? The skeletons there are of local people, from the Stonehenge district. What kept them going?"

"They must have been highly motivated?" suggests Vicki.

"By the carrot or the stick, do you think?"

"Fear of earthly punishment wouldn't work for long because they would run away. Religion would be better. They couldn't escape a vengeful god or the devil; they would be found wherever they ran to."

"Perhaps they had carrots: wouldn't promises of wealth, fertility, health, life everlasting and reincarnation be more effective?" I ask her. "It's hard to know" she says. "Monument building seems to have gone out of fashion."

"Do you think so?" I reply. "What about skyscrapers, bridges, tunnels, roads, hospitals, power stations and shopping centres?"

"They're not monuments. They have utility," she answers.

"Perhaps Stonehenge had utility, too," I suggest.

"Oh?"

"It is impossible that anything so difficult to build did not have utility for someone"

"Perhaps it is a model, of a social cell in their society," she muses.

"Hmm. Concentric rings of individuals linked horizontally higher up."

"But supported by individuals of lower stature in the outer circle," she continues.

"Who or what could they represent?"

"Perhaps the smaller stones are children?" Vicki asks.

"They could be," I say. "There are fewer children – less than replacement."

"Could these people have planned to dwindle away? Or transcend?" Vicki suggests.

"Perhaps the opposite," I reply. "It could be a place for their spirits to dwell."

"Have they perpetuated themselves—with a memorial?"

"It could be."

I figure it would be impolite, given her childlessness, to remind Vicki that nowadays many people regard their children as their memorial. It seems a crime against natural law for a person of Vicki's large calibre not to have children. She should disseminate her genes and teach her behaviour, to leave descendants like herself who would enrich the gene pool and civil society.

Vicki's solo status brings out the herd bull in me. I have an urge to round her up into my harem. I picture a wildebeeste herd, as it drifts from horizon to horizon across the savannah in a tide of migration. Frenetic bulls gallop through, jousting with each other briefly, separating out heifers and unmated cows and ushering them to join their harems.

I have no right to expect her to have children.

Women's Liberation is in full flood, a revolution in which women cease to attune their lives to males. They take responsibility for their own sexuality and demand equality with men in economic, social, psychological, political and moral spheres. The extent of Vicki's subscription to feminism is unknown to me, although I suspect that she has adopted them lock, stock and barrel. She is very career-oriented and seems happy and engrossed in her work. She often reveals the joy she finds in her career.

I contrast stone-age women's preoccupations and how they may be symbolised.

"Fertility has an element of chance; perhaps the gods need to be appeased. Could Stonehenge be a simulation of the uterus and birth canal?" I ask Vicki.

"Hmmm."

"Our visit could appease the gods. Today may be a turning point for you, Vicki. But you need a man as well!"

"I have a man!" she protests. "Haven't I told you about Gossie?"

This is a long-awaited development.

"No, I'm all ears!"

We have arrived back at her place, I fetch a bottle of red wine I have brought, pull the cork out and pour each of us a glass.

"Cheers!" we toast each other.

"Now tell me about Gossie."

Jealousy wells up in me. I think it possible she has decided years ago to remain unmarried and childless. She has not valued highly enough the opportunities she has had to pass on her genes and behaviours to her own exclusive offspring. She could regard other ways of perpetuating herself as just as good. She has not been short of suitors, but Vicki has not been able to settle for less than zeniths in intimacy, passion and commitment. Perhaps she wants too much, or she values her independence too much to accept less. I suppose that Vicki likes children but not enough to have one.

Perhaps she feels like someone who is encouraged to get a dog: it is a lifelong responsibility that she has not wanted. Unlike a dog, having a baby risks enslavement, either by disability or by a demanding partner. For quite a few years, having a child inevitably subtracts from career success. If she has children, she would have to give up work for the time being, which she would be loathe to do.

She seems too cerebral, too detached, to be a mother. She values very highly the serenity she has achieved. It seems likely that she does not want to engage with the worries of parenthood. For her, fulfilment does not require children, and its attainment would be obstructed by them. It is difficult to imagine her changing nappies; she seems made for a life of contemplation.

Her position in bucking convention is becoming harder for her to sustain, as the choice is being taken away from her by the ticking of her biological clock. Now the situation is urgent. Vicki seems unable to find a suitable man and her predicament tugs at my heart strings. I want her to have children, anyone's children, before it is too late. She is on my conscience. I am arrogant enough to think maybe I stole away some of her child-bearing time by prevarication.

Vicki seems reluctant to tell me about him.

I repeat, "What does Gossie do?"

"Gossie is a condom salesman."

I don't reply immediately. "Where?" I asked evenly, with steely control of my face.

"Africa, mainly. He sells to governments. They distribute them."

"I expect he has opposition?"

"Roman Catholics and Moslems, mainly. He stays away from places where they rule."

"How fantastically wanted he must feel, to be solving hunger, disease, poverty – the really big problems."

"Yes, he is very wanted."

"By you, too?"

"Yes, mainly. Sometimes. Of course. You know how it is."

"No. I don't. How is it?"

"Oh, Selwyn, you know. Our amity is, less than complete. We overlap quite a bit, but we're independent. He stays at his own place – when he's here."

"Does he want children?"

"He lives for his work. He's a, a sort of, missionary."

"Converting people to contraception. It is as important as disease prevention – but more difficult to sell?"

"No, they go together. Where there is disease, people have many children. So some will survive. When disease is prevented, fewer children are wanted."

"With every doctor, a condom salesman."

"With every vaccination, a bonus condom."

"With every mosquito net, a bonus condom."

"They are co-products; they go together."

"We do, too, Vicki."

I go to hold her, but she moves away.

"What about Ruth? And Nicola and Michael?"

I am not sure what she means, whether she is reminding me to think of their welfare, that I cannot desert them to be with her, or that I should do just that. I have a responsibility, but I am so attracted to her that if I thought she would respect me for it, I would desert my little ones; but I imagine she would not. It is a classic Catch 22. If I want her enough, I must desert my children. But if I do so, I feel sure she wouldn't want me. It does not occur to me to check my assumption with her.

I don't know what commitment she has to Gossie, and she is not forthcoming about that. There is something ironic about Vicki's relationship with a contraceptive salesman at a time when she should be having children. On the other hand, he could be reluctant to become a parent.

It seems that he is a smokescreen, to silence her well-meaning friends with children who, like me, urge her to get a man. Vicki is an idealist and has a mission to help people. I can picture both of them childless, riding in the cab of a truck, delivering a container full of condoms to Africa.

I imagine she tells people that she and Gossie want kids, as childlessness is not fashionable, and childless couples are assumed infertile and expected to seek to adopt a child. Voluntary childlessness menaces the family ethic, the populate or perish mentality. So Vicki and Gossie tell people, year after year, that they are trying for a baby, when they are not. Now, when Vicki is losing her ability to choose, she may be having second thoughts.

On my next visit, I learn she has finished with Gossie and is searching in earnest for another man. She is seen with a man who was written up as having the highest taxable income of anyone in the United Kingdom. Nothing comes of it.

On these visits, I leave Vicki and the UK regretfully. Although I have a good job and a comfortable home in beautiful surroundings, living with Ruth is lonely and stressful. She takes no interest in my career and guards from me her own understanding of and thinking about our children. We are closest together when I sit on the veranda and drink a bottle of red with her. She has one glass and I drink the rest, in silence.

Rule 67: *Contraception is an effective aid to development of populous countries.*

CHAPTER 68 RELOCATION REFUSAL

On another of my visits to Salisbury Cathedral with Vicki I remark, "Living would be easier within a strong religion, don't you think?"

"Perhaps. There are faiths other than religions, you know."

"I agree," I say. "I suppose my career is built on a sort of faith."

"Mine, too. If only our workplaces had as much faith as there was here when this was being built."

We pause at the ornate entrance to the cathedral.

"It drips with love and care," says Vicki. "No shoddiness or planned obsolescence about this building. They knew they were building forever."

"Which comes first, the vision of the building, or the reverence?"

"Perhaps both together," Vicki says. "The architect and stonemasons had a vision, and reverence achieved it."

"The people lived like slaves in fear of the Normans after the conquest," I replied. "Their takeover was brutal. Perhaps the cathedral was to be a place of sanctity that even the Normans would respect."

Vicki stood back admiring the fluting on the columns. "The stonemasons were evidently supervised by an all-seeing God," Vicki told me. "This is perfection."

We admired the wooden altar screen. "No human supervisor could have caused this carving," I say.

"By serving God with diligence that glorified him, the sculptor ensured a place for his family and himself in heaven," Vicki explained.

"The cathedral was to be an ultimate icon, a synthesis of stylised forms, each having a track record of durability and reverence, repeated many times," I say in awe.

Vicki draws my attention to a wooden figure at the end of a pew.

"Look how the sculptor has adapted the folds in that garment to a knot in the wood. He didn't chisel through it blindly. He was aware, not in a state of religious transport."

"He could do that because the carving is one of a kind, and he could regard the figure as pre-existing in the material, as is usual in modern work. But it is an exception. Repetition, corresponding to ideal forms, is the ethic that drove Salisbury cathedral to perfection."

"It is the same in workplaces," says Vicki. "Faith in ourselves, like the cathedral builders' faith, is not enough. We need a vision or community mission, like Stonehenge. Like the pyramid at Giza. Like Machu Picchu. Like putting a man on the Moon. Our school isn't driven like that, yet, but we are trying. We need somewhere with ideal forms we can copy."

"Professional standards?" I suggest

"More than that. Does Canoil have a mission?"

"Probably, but it is interpreted higher up. Something to do with exploring boldly and safely, I think. Since I was promoted to Engineering Manager, all I have been able to do is grapple with my own faith, looking inwards."

"Your work is technical?"

"Yes, but I want to get into line management."

"Could you relate the work of your people to your corporate mission?"

I nod. It is that obvious. Vicki helps me as a mentor to develop empathy with subordinates. I need to do this. She knows more about how to do my job than I do. I am in awe of her understanding of what makes individuals tick. If only I could be with her every day.

Ruth sees to it that I do not regain enough self-confidence after my mental illness to challenge her control. She monopolizes the family decision-making that she grabbed when I was ill, keeping me isolated by discouraging friendships, retaining control over disposal of my income and, when I confront her, threatening to leave me, taking Nicola and Michael. I always back down. The children are very important to me.

Can Vicki understand the pull on me of my children? It is they who are keeping me in Canada. Vicki won't come to Canada because she believes her mother and family need her in England. I am being pulled from opposite directions, and it is tearing me apart. No-one who is not a parent with a distant lover can realize my pain. It is there when I wake up, it is there whenever I relax from the imperatives of the day, it is there in the long evenings, there when I go to bed, there when I imagine her touching me, needing me, there until sleep releases me.

Ruth's dominance over our sexual relations means that my needs are not being met. She assumes she can enforce a regimen on our love-making. For me, sex needs to be as much mental as physical. For Ruth, it is merely physical.

I am usually able to forget my family worries at work. I express interest in moving out of a technical career into management. The Personnel Manager informs me of an upcoming management aptitude test for young engineers at my level. I will answer a written questionnaire at my desk. It sounds threatening. So I ask an older engineer what the company means by "management aptitude". He laughs. "It's whether you conform with the group," he says. "Try to answer like everyone else." He explains that managers are under enormous normative pressure to be politically correct and not appear discriminatory. My real self has to remain hidden.

When I start on the questionnaire, I am glad of his advice because the questions often test hypothetical situations where values are personal and controversial. For example, one of the questions is, "Have you ever felt sexually attracted to someone of the same gender?" As a teenager, I had, but I had never done anything about it. Fortunately, I infer from my informant's advice that a manager in our company will answer "No" like the group. So that is my answer.

Another question is, "Did you ever want to make love to your mother?" I can recall, as a very small child, that I was under my mother's spell, until her beating broke it. I answer "No" because it is an incestuous and perverted desire, despite being frequent, according to Freud, and respectable in Sophocles' tragedy, "Oedipus the King". There are many more such questions. It is demanding to anticipate the group morality in obscure and bizarre situations, but I manage to suppress my individuality.

My answers are sufficiently close to median, for I am promoted to oilfield manager at Moose Hills. It is a good opportunity for our family to get out of the rut we are stuck in.

"How would you like to live in Moose Hills for a couple of years?" I ask Ruth over breakfast. "We need a change. We have been here for years. This is my big chance to make it into management. It will be good experience for you, too."

A Moose Hills engineer's woman competes by promoting her man's career. That is the opposite of how a feminist like Ruth perceives her man's career. It is her career versus his. My career threatens her freedom.

"I won't go," she snaps, setting a stack of hot pancakes in front of me.

Ruth has seen Elizabeth Taylor's brand of feminism in "Who's Afraid of Virginia Woolf?" "Would I be able to work as a school health advisor in Moose Hills?" she says. "I think not. Will I to live my life in order to advance your career? No way. What about me? Am I not a person, too?"

"They have schools around there that need sex education counsellors. Could you adapt your school health advisor skills to sex education?" I murmur, breathing in the steamy aroma, like butterscotch. I reach for the maple syrup.

"No. We're not moving." She hands me a bowl of whipped cream, hesitating as she considers pushing it into my face.

Her glib defiance infuriates me.

"You married an engineer," I say through my teeth. "Moving to places is a part of the job."

She spits back at me, "And you married a school health advisor, and she doesn't go where she can't get a job." She slams a bowl of fried bacon on the table. I serve several strips on to my plate, their smell heightening the resinous odour of the maple syrup.

"You can look after the kids for a couple of years. What's wrong with you? If your pay was double, then I would take turns with you." I bite into a pancake wrapped around crispy bacon, with syrup and cream. It is delicious. "You'll like it at Moose Hills."

"No," she shakes her head.

Ruth weeps silently, leaning over the kitchen sink.

"Aren't you being a teeny bit precious, my precious?"

I don't often do sarcasm, and it comes out as a sneer.

"You don't seem to like me anymore."

"I do like you," I lie.

I have lost my appetite, scrape the rest of my breakfast into the bin and stalk out.

"I have to stay with my kids," I explain to my boss. He is not sympathetic.

"Don't take no for an answer! Women nearly always oppose transfers to the sticks because of their kids' schooling, or because they need 24-hour access to specialists. My experience is that when the man insists and they live there for a while, the woman comes to like it. Women are naturally more cautious and need encouragement to do something different. It is not part of their self-image to be without family and friends. They think they have to have access to good shops, good hairdressers and sophisticated recreation. They can't picture themselves happily dressed in thermals, jeans, lumber jackets and muddy boots. They will meet great people and learn to love it out there. So, I urge you, don't take no for an answer!"

I try again with Ruth, but the answer is still no.

I analyse the situation, using physics concepts to calculate a position of balance between each of our inertias, which are our tendencies to continue doing what we are already doing. A couple have balance when each applies his or her own inertia at their partner's distance from the point of compromise, along a dimension of difference between them in terms of where, how soon and how much cost for the alternative each prefers. It sounds more complex than it is.

"What's the longest you would go for?" I ask Ruth.

"I told you: I'm not going."

"I want to go for as long as it takes, maybe three years," I tell her.

"Well, go, then."

"Here's the compromise: let's assume each of us has the same amount of inertia to keep doing what we have been doing. Then we go for midway between us, half of my three plus your zero is one and a half years."

"No. I have much more keeping me here than you do, much more inertia. You can change jobs, but I could lose contact with my friends forever."

"Okay. Let's say you have twice as much inertia as I have. You sacrifice two times one year and I sacrifice one times two years, which is equal. Then your compromise that balances is that we go for one year more than the zero you want. It is two years less than I want. Get it?"

"So, what are you suggesting? We go to Moose Hills for one year?"

"Yes. Then if you don't like it we will move back and I will get another job."

But Ruth is, as usual, uncompromising. "No. I'm not moving."

My boss reassigns me to less interesting work and seems to forget I exist. I am humiliated.

I see little of my children in their early years, and this is becoming a problem for me as they become older. Through the week, I leave for work while they are still in bed and arrive home after they are in bed. At weekends, Ruth encourages them to stay indoors rather than helping me with my outside chores.

"I would like Michael to help me water the trees," I tell Ruth.

"He's tidying up his room," she says.

"How soon will he be finished?"

"Then he has to do his homework."

If parenting is largely role modelling, then Ruth is trying to stop me. It is at this time that I become aware that Ruth has a reflex that always stops her being on my side. She is blocking the Sun from my life and stopping me from growing. She has started to criticize my ejaculation control now that I have accepted she is incapable of orgasms with me. She seems determined to make mine unpleasant.

I have caught myself disliking her. She wants my career halted. She seems jealous of my much higher pay, even though I pool it with hers. She retrains and transfers to pursue a career in management where she will be able to catch up with my earnings. I am happy that she should be able to do this but not that it has become a zero sum competition between us where she tries to pull me down.

By refusing to transfer, I am sidelined. For two years, my career is on halt. Before, as a very bright young engineer on the make, I was included in social groups and slowly developing informal acquaintance with several geeky guys like myself. After, no-one could be bothered with me and I am labelled an oddball.

When I am offered a job at Trapper Lake that I can commute to weekly, as Engineering Department Manager, I accept it gladly. It saves my bacon in the career stakes, because I could be forgotten forever where I am now. The worst part is that I would only get to see the kids at weekends. That is a terrible privation because I am not there for their triumphs, disasters and everyday growing up. My influence on them is displaced by Ruth who takes over deciding their issues and disciplining them.

"Butt out, Selwyn," she says. "We have moved on from there. You don't understand."

Her pushy takeover is difficult to accept, but there is nothing I can do. Ruth doesn't join me for a drink on the veranda any more. It suits me. These days I take a cask of red wine. It's better company.

Rule 68: *Compromise is not possible in a zero sum game.*

CHAPTER 69 EXPERIENCING OFFSPRING

Tension goes out of my relationship with Vicki when we reach forty. She is still single and childless. She is soft and vulnerable, and her life seems dedicated to counselling her clutch of school students, the way that other women are devoted to their children. I admire her ability to put herself in others' shoes and understand their motives and fears.

When I visit her, she tells me how she sometimes takes care of her brother's children. She is like Julie Andrews in "The Sound of Music" who, instead of singing, counsels the delighted youngsters. Their Aunt has each one in turn lie on a couch, and there they squirm out their most secret thoughts. Their mother is jealous of their rapport with her.

"I had no idea," she tells Vicki on one of the few occasions Vicki deems it wise to break the child's confidence and reveal a problem to its mother. "How do you do it?"

I have long known Vicki is a gifted counsellor. It is a luxury for children to have the uncritical attention of an adult, especially one who understands their innermost thoughts.

Vicki asks, "When you look at yourself in a mirror, Carla, what do you think?"

"My hair is okay but my nose is ugly."

"Why do you think that?"

"It is too big."

"How do you know that?"

"The girls at school tease me."

"What do you do then?"

"I cry."

"Why."

"Because my nose is ugly."

"Why aren't you crying now, then?"

"I don't know."

"It could be because your nose is okay."

Aunt Vicki doesn't tell them what they should be thinking, the way their parents do.

If she catches children being unkind to each other, she gently reveals to them their motives, which they are incapable of realizing unaided, with the gentle sarcasm affected by schoolteachers.

"Now, Simon. Do you have something in your fist to give to Charles?"

Simon, about to deliver a punch, nods. "Yes, Aunt."

"Oh, good. Show me, what you have, please."

There is nothing in his fist.

"Well, I can't see anything. It must have got away. You need to be more careful, don't you, Simon?"

"Yes, Aunt."

Through her they discover that they can choose how they behave, so as to have rich and mysterious private lives, as befits the unique individuals that they are. It is fun learning this from Vicki, who is their favourite adult. They behave maturely for her – until the next time they want her special attention.

One day I am at her place when she comes back from a country ramble with them, her hair in bangs, dressed in a mini-dress, black tights, an army greatcoat and gum boots. The children arrive keeping pace with her, stride for stride, singing the song "I Love to Go a-wandering".

They have picked blackberries from bramble hedges, staining their fingers and mouths. They have discovered a thrush's nest with perfectly proportioned, teardrop-shaped eggs, paste-blue flecked with brown. They have learnt the names of the birds they have disturbed and the names of the different types of tree they have climbed.

When they are old enough, her nieces and nephew come up on the train to her town-house in London and stay overnight. She takes them out into the West End, dressed up for their first visit to the theatre, opera or ballet. These are highlights in her life. As friends who live in her area move away, her social life reduces. Dinner parties are few and far between. She is too attractive and single for women to befriend because their men may be looking for some sport or a change. Her life is increasingly absorbed in her work and growing her gardens, which are a profusion of colour, with the help of a gardener.

Although I don't see Vicki often, it is with growing intimacy. I imagine myself through Vicki's eyes as a mid-forties man still rising in a management career, with two adolescent children and a wife he doesn't love. Her own career is successful, too, not so much in money, but rich in rewards from helping young people to lead healthy lives. I understand the importance of what she does from the needs of my own children. Vicki's and my love of young people bonds us, as we strive to apply our experience to their happiness. I wish Vicki could live with me and help me with Nicola and Michael. As they enter adolescence they are troubled by the rift between Ruth and me. They are helped by their school counsellor. I wish it could be Vicki.

When I next visit Vicki, I see her going to waste. She is a warm and interactive person, and it seems wrong that she lives by herself. The ground under her two large apple trees is strewn with fallen Granny Smiths. I help her gather them into her apple barn. After filling several buckets each, I remain hunched over, with my knuckles hanging to the ground, whooping like a chimpanzee in "Planet of the Apes".

"Hoo! Hoo! Hoohoohoo!"

Vicki, laughing, replies in the same style. "Hoo! Hoo! Hoohoo!"

We leap up and down and dance around each other crazily, laughing hysterically. I try to grab her and we collapse in a heap, with Vicki on top of me. We haven't been together doing rough and tumble since we were undergraduates many years ago. Suddenly, the game is over, and we clamber to our feet, embarrassed. I have remembered my loyalty to my children.

We go back to filling buckets.

"These are bruised," I say. "They won't store for long. They have to be picked before they're ripe and handled gently."

"Says the engineer to the school counsellor," quips Vicki, unsmiling. "You had better be on your way to visit your family now."

I know that she wants commitment, but I can neither give it nor refuse it. All I am sure of is that I feel too uncomfortable to be decisive, and I simply want to put it off until later. I hope that time will show me my feelings better. I have known Vicki and wanted her for a long time now, but still my feelings for her are strangers, and I cannot compare them with the sureness of my loyalty to my children.

Long before I met Ruth, I had held Vicki, kissed her and lain beside her. My clumsy hands have never persuaded her to the unity I so much want. She is showing me more affection on my visits now, but I am not free to go to her until Nicola and Michael leave home – unless something happens before then and I can honourably leave them. I believe they need both parents for their success as students and in life afterwards.

I am still recovering from my failure to achieve a PhD. Vicki knows that I have a thesis in me that has never been finally submitted. As every day passes, events render it obsolete.

"What do you think of Gorbachev's developments in Russia? Glasnost and Perestroika?"

"You mean, how do they affect my thesis?"

"Yes, on how to stop the Cold War."

"Glasnost is openness and an end to censorship, whereas Perestroika means political restructuring. There has also been Uskorenie, or economic reform. They have allowed state enterprises to supply customer demand. It's only a small step from there to our market capitalism."

"Was that what you were trying to achieve, one system in the West and East?"

"Yes. The sides are drawing closer. The Cold War will soon be over, I think."

"Has your work been used?"

"They say a problem can't be solved until it has been described. I did describe it."

"Then you did succeed."

I hold her then, our bodies pressed together. She knows how I still grieve for leaving Liverpool without a PhD. She feels so good. I ache to hold her the way I had when we first met. I want to say to Vicki, "It won't be long now until we're together", but I remain silent rather than mislead her.

"What about Nicola and Michael?" she says again.

"They are doing fine," I say eventually.

When I say goodbye I caress her face and kiss her on the cheeks and forehead.

Vicki pulls away and I leave to go home.

On my way home, I am thinking about a Canoil problem on the desk I am going back to, when I recall some fun I am having with my kids.

"What do you do at work all week, Dad?" Nicola asks, as I leave to go to Trapper Lake for the week.

"I am building a spanking machine," I tell them. "I will bring it home soon. Today I have to make it bigger, because you have grown."

This stops that question for another year.

Ruth is convinced that I am harming our children, but I persist in providing ideas for imagination.

"Dad, what do you really do at work?" asks Michael one day at dinner.

"We have pools of oil underground," I explain.

"How did the oil get there?" asked Michael.

"It is made by micro-organisms."

"What's a micro-orgasm, Dad?"

Nicola is watching me closely and I choose my words carefully.

"A micro-organism is a tiny animal. It eats vegetation and its poo has oil in it, which collects in pools"

"Yuck.".

"My job is to put the foot-valve where it can pump out oil to go into people's cars."

They know what a foot-valve is, because we pump from our house dam to irrigate our lawn. Each weekend in warm weather I carry one of the children down to the dam on my shoulders. I leave them on the bank by the motor and wade out to hammer a stake into the bottom and tie the foot-valve to it. With a bucket, I pour water into the pump and prime it by filling the pipe to the foot-valve. The foot-valve stops water flowing back out into the dam. Then I start the motor, which pumps water up to our lawn. They know that unless the foot-valve is submerged, the pump's rotor will spin in the air without sucking up any water.

"It sounds like a stupid job to me," says Nicola. "My friend's Dad is on TV. Why don't you get a job on TV, Dad?"

"I like my job. Looking after foot-valves is an important job because if I didn't do it, you would have to walk to school. Do you know why?"

They think in silence.

"Because there wouldn't be any gas?"says Nicola.

"Correct. We use oil to make gasoline."

"Do you put on bathers at work, Dad?" Michael says.

Michael has assumed that the oil pool is like our dam.

"Yes. I put a clothes peg on my nose, too."

"Oil is stinky! Your job is yucky, Dad." They had watched me change the oil in our cars.

"It is. But I have to do it to get money for the supermarket!"

One weekend at tea, I told them that at work we have had an exciting week.

"We discovered a new pool of oil this week, kids! Think of that. What do you think the first thing I have to do is?"

The children try to imagine the implications.

"Hammer in a stake for a foot-balve?" asks Michael.

"Aw, Michael, that's not first, stupid!" interrupts Nicola, who is several years older. "He has to poke with a stick to find the deepest place. Then hammer in a stake and tie the foot-valve to it, right in the middle."

It is stunning inductive logic, from the known into the unknown. We do indeed find the top and bottom of the oil layer to know at what level to pump from to get out the most oil. It is a good feeling that the children understand something of the technology I work with. I hope they will continue to connect with my job and me, so that my life's work amounts to something for the future, other than money.

"Excellent, Nicola! Well done, Michael!"

My two children are quite different in the way they understand events. Nicola relates behaviour to the past. She hesitates before speaking, always considers her words first and likes to make references to historical examples of a situation as much as possible. When she speaks she does so with charm and charisma, pulling out all the stops to persuade.

Michael obtains his authority by observing and analyzing to discover the logic of the present. He responds quickly, with breathtaking inferences. People who do not know him sometimes do not recognize his ability.

Neither Nicola nor Michael is slow to take the risk of imagining solutions to problems, but in my workplace there are too many employees who wait for others to think of solutions. My job as a manager is increasingly to stimulate and harness people's imaginations, persuading them to strive to achieve corporate objectives. It challenges me more than reservoir engineering ever did. But reservoir engineering is our basic technology, and I have set my sights on rising to become CEO, through expertise, loyalty and hard work. I am successful as a manager, but my position is obscure, and advance will be slow unless I can get some push from below or pull from above.

Rule 69: *Reality and imagination occur in a cycle with no ultimate cause, like chickens and eggs. Big changes in reality go with big imaginings.*

CHAPTER 70   REFLECTING SUCCESS

I am promoted to Manager of the Trapper Lake Oil Field but the work is dull routine, and time drags. I drink a lot alone after work and when I go home at weekends. I feel myself growing older, impaled on an obscure branch of the hierarchy. My boss, the division manager, hardly knows I exist. I am not friendly with anyone in our Toronto head office. Then I have an idea.

At uni I had learnt that in 18th Century London, Michael Faraday was a young man of humble origin and an apprentice bookbinder. He was fascinated by science, but he had no opportunities to do any research. Science was a rich man's hobby, and experiments were conducted in private laboratories.

Faraday's hero was Sir Humphrey Davy, and he attended his lectures at the Royal Society where Davy presented the work done by employees in his laboratory on an exciting new form of energy, electricity. He wrote down every word of his lectures and copied his illustrations. He collated these and bound them into a book, which he presented to Sir Humphrey. At the same time he asked him for a job in his research laboratory.

Flattered, Davey had replied, "This is most appreciated, young man. You can work for me, starting immediately."

Davy was so impressed, he allowed Faraday to experiment and test his own ideas. Soon Faraday invented the electric motor, the electric generator, electroplating of metals, electro-refining and many more.

Following Faraday's example, I looked for a leader at Canoil who might be persuaded to foster my endeavours. In Canoil's annual report I read Chairman Ralph Gooder's profile.

Chairman of the board is Ralph Gooder. He graduated from Ottawa University in environmental science and was recruited by Canoil's Toronto oil refinery. He conducted successful experiments, reduced impacts on the environment and became refinery manager. He served as Chairman of the

Canadian Petroleum Association and is on the government's National Environment Council, most recently as its Chairman. As General Manager of Canoil's Marketing Division, he renewed the company's 1250 service stations. On the retirement of WO Sanderson, he was appointed CEO. He oversaw a period of unprecedented growth, now continuing under Robert Walker. Gooder has served for 4 years as a director and has been elected Chairman of The Board.

I figure that although Gooder had worked his way up, he may be susceptible to sycophancy and be able to open doors for me.

I take a week of my annual holiday and go to Toronto. There I gather together all of Gooder's public statements from company files, from the files of the Canadian Petroleum Committee, the National Energy Committee, newspapers and magazines. I obtain copies of the minutes of provincial and local authority meetings where he had spoken about large projects, such as the Toronto oil refinery, and from special occasions where he had been an invited speaker, such as graduations and environmental association dinners. He is a popular and prolific speaker and it is a large task. He is a trendsetter who is often controversial. Fortunately, the company has most of the important speeches on record in well-organised paper files, and I am able to get photocopies. I tell CEO Robert Walker what I am doing, in secrecy from Gooder. He likes the project and kindly lends me library staff who help enthusiastically; otherwise, I would not have enough time.

Back at Trapper Lake, I key in every one of Gooder's speeches and press releases on my computer and save them on floppy disks. It takes me every weekday evening for six months. Then I compile the material serially with a common font and add a comprehensive index of events and speech topics. When I finish, I have a 300-page document. I have five copies printed on parchment and bound with embossed gold-lettering on leather covers. At the next opportunity, when he has come over for a Board meeting in Calgary, I make an excuse to go to Calgary and catch Gooder coming out of the boardroom afterwards.

I have only seen him in photos before. He is an imposing figure, tall with silver hair and a millionaire's suntan.

"Excuse me, Mr Gooder, Sir; I would like to give you this."

I hand him one of the books.

He reads aloud, "Ralph Gooder, Chairman of Canoil Limited, Public Statements."

He looks inside, turns to the contents page that doubles as a timeline of his public appearances and is silent.

Eventually he says, "This is impressive. And who are you?" He eyes me suspiciously.

"Selwyn Archer, Sir. I am Manager at Canoil's Trapper Lake Field. I have put this together in my spare time."

"I don't get it. Why did you do this?"

"I admire your career, Sir. I want to have a career like yours myself, Sir, if I am good enough. I want to ask you, how can I advance when I am stuck at Trapper Lake?"

"Hmm. You should ask Bob Walker that question. He's CEO. I'll talk to him."

"Thank you, Sir. Here are three other copies you can have, Sir. I have told Bob about this. Would you give him a copy?"

"Yes, I will. Thank you very much, young man."

"My pleasure, Sir. I have learnt a lot about Canoil and the work of a senior manager."

"Have you, now? Good, I'm glad you have. Bye."

A few days later, when I am back at Trapper Lake, I receive a phone call from Bob Walker, CEO. It is unusual for him to phone staff because he normally communicates through the hierarchy, and I am four levels below him.

"Archer, how would you like to come over here to Toronto for a couple of years?"

"I would like that very much, Sir. What would I be doing?"

"Special projects. You won't have a set territory, but you will go in and deal with problems we identify – a sort of executive analyst. I think it's a role you would be good at."

"How would I get people to co-operate?" I sometimes have difficulty getting subordinates to do what I want.

"You will be working for me, and people will cooperate. Leadership is something you need to work on. I have talked with your manager. Don't let what I have to say ruffle your feathers. You are not a warm person, and people don't follow you willingly. If you don't give people a feeling of security, they won't willingly go with you, even on an excursion to paradise. On the other hand, you have a talent for recognising and coming up with solutions for problems, and that's what I want you for. When you need people to co-operate, I'll come in and back you up."

Walker's evaluation of my people skills and leadership threatens my ambition to be CEO. I regard most people as self-seeking and unable to see beyond their experiences. So I usually don't bother with the slow process of consultation, and my changes are opposed. But with Walker's backing, people should be more flexible. I will practise being warm with people, and my leadership should improve.

"It is a wonderful opportunity."

"It's also very challenging. If it's too much for you, you will be able to go back to Trapper Lake."

"What if I succeed?"

"You could get a division GM position."

"Wow! I will do my best not to disappoint you, Sir."

"Good morning, Selwyn." He ends the call.

I say a small prayer of thanks to Faraday for his idea.

That evening, I tell Ruth, Nicola and Michael about his offer. When Ruth finds out we will have a lot more money, live in cosmopolitan Toronto and socialize with general managers, she agrees to the move. Her competition with my career is put on hold.

Gradually, Ruth and I have begun to lead separate lives. I visit England by myself again, on a company errand, flying business class. I want to see Vicki alone. I make full use of the free drinks. I am glad when Ruth stops coming with me, as she always insists on a rigid pre-planned itinerary, whereas I prefer flexibility and spontaneity. This difference is exacerbated by the ongoing struggle for control between us. It is unpleasant.

Every time I am in England, I feel compelled to contact Vicki, even though she sometimes does not have time to see me. We spend our brief time together talking. We sometimes talk in the dining room, dominated by a long carved wooden table. The surface is covered with heaps of professional correspondence and papers, except for one end, where I can sit in a chair and spill my guts, as she walks along tending the piles and listening to me. The kitchen has a round table in an upholstered nook, where I can talk with her as she prepares our food.

She loves to counsel me, slipping into her work role. There is the formal sitting room, with a deep armchair where I recline as she draws me out, sitting over me. I lie back and pour out my truths, as if to an oracle. Vicki has a gift for bringing my worries to the surface. Her prompting and questions keep our conversation going while she simultaneously attends to an untidy mountain of correspondence. By not seeming to have all her attention focussed on me and listening with only one ear, she encourages me to air confidences that have never before seen the light of day. She is an astute listener and says just enough to keep me talking.

Vicki's questioning sympathetically explores and observes my innermost self. My reflection and insight improve under her benign observation. She is the only person who has ever taken such an interest in me. In default of the affection I crave, it is flattering. I talk to no-one else the way I talk with Vicki. When I talk to her, it helps me understand myself. Her attention is like a drug and induces in me an indulgent self-absorption.

"I don't know why I married Ruth," I say to Vicki. "I must have been stupid."

"You were in love."

"She didn't show her true colours until we were married."

"Perhaps you encourage women to push you around."

"Hmm. Maybe."

Her questions make me realize how my marriage is suffocating me. The only place I can get air to breathe is when I am with Vicki.

Sometimes when I have visited, Vicki is less well-organised and muddles through her piles of papers frantically. Although she does not yet confide in me, her life must have its ups and downs, too. I think how good I would be for her, bringing into her life order and efficiency

I assume that she doesn't want to encourage me to leave Ruth and come to her, because of the bad effect on the children and on me from being away from them. In other words, she doesn't want the role of home-wrecker on her conscience, and this is why she steadfastly keeps her correspondence with me to a minimum.

After I am promoted, work takes up most of my time, but I am able to see Vicki more often. I do not think she wants me to leave my marriage, and our relationship remains platonic.

Rule 70: *An employee is most valued when he or she goes beyond the call of duty in showing his or her alignment with the goals of the top manager.*

CHAPTER 71   DEEP END

While our family is in Toronto, the four of us take a week's holiday and we all fly down to an apartment we own in Mexico, at a fishing village on the Pacific. We have been going there as a family most Christmas and Easter holidays every year since the kids were babies. It makes the long Canadian winter more bearable. These days, the kids usually bring school friends with them.

Zapulco has perfect waves rolling into a concave bay, where they hang poised and crash over on to foam that surges up to a white sandy beach. Board and body surfing are excellent. The beach is fringed with coconut palms, their fronds stirring in the breeze. Hammocks are strung under them in dappled shade or under palm-thatched shelters.   Behind are cafés and apartments, where time stands still.

We hire a sailing sloop and sail out into the Pacific and along the coast. It requires teamwork. I am an authoritarian sea captain, in a Basil Fawlty-like way. My posture is unacceptable to Ruth.

"Get the map out," I order her. "Will we go aground if we stay on this tack?"

"Are you talking to me, or is there a dog on board?"

We anchor overnight at some inlet and play sevens or Scrabble on the galley table with the kids. We talk about this and that; Nicola and Michael try out their new opinions and skills of persuasion. I coach them to use logic and persuasive argument, rather than personal attacks and deceit.

One holiday when we are anchored along the coast, I decide to have the kids experience the magnificence of night sailing that I had so enjoyed on the midnight watch on *Ermelo* a decade earlier.

"I do not want to sail at night," Ruth objects. "It is dangerous enough in daylight."

"There is no additional danger. Navigation is easier. There are a couple of light buoys along the coast and then a lighthouse at Zapulco."

"Come on, Mum. It will be fun," says Michael.

Ruth gives in.

"Okay, but be careful."

When we sail out into deep water, I am surprised by the size of the waves. We lift and lift, suspend in space before dropping down and landing with a crash. There is no moon yet, and I can just see Ruth's pale face as she grips handholds in the cockpit.

When we turn south, we pick up speed, alternating gently between crests and troughs. It is exhilarating, and I point out features of the night sky to Ruth and the children.

"The great blaze of light we are following is the Milky Way. It is the great saucer of stars that is our galaxy and as we look up we are seeing it from inside the disc, edge on, one-third of the radius from the centre."

"Watch out, Selwyn," Ruth exclaims, as we plunge down a wave.

The onshore wind is picking up, and we are scudding along at very high hull speeds, requiring constant attention to the tiller. When the wave we are on drops below the rudder, it turns uselessly in the air with the danger of broaching, turning sideways abruptly.

"There's the lighthouse, straight ahead," I say with relief.

When I relax my attention for a moment to light a cigarette, suddenly we broach, swinging into the wind. A giant wave smashes into the bows, bringing us to a standstill with the sails flapping wildly. The usually commanding Ruth and our children are silent and fearful in the blackness. Water breaks over the bows, and a deluge runs back over the cabin roof on to us in the cockpit. Another wave or two could capsize us.

"Take down the Genoa and put up the number three foresail," I order.

"Do not fall overboard, kids," Ruth warns, at last able to control something.

It would be difficult to find a swimmer in the dark.

Ruth lets out the halyard as Michael drags down the Genoa, unclips it and stows it in the cabin. Nicola is already on the foredeck, clipping the next jib sail on to the forestay. She changes the snap shackle, and Ruth pulls the jib up, finally tightening the halyard and cleating it off.

When they have finished with the jib, I order, "Reef the main."

They ratchet the boom, winding on the giant sail. All the while, I am keeping our nose into the wind as we bob over the rollers.

Finally, these reduced sails are sheeted taut in the strengthened wind, and we resume our course at lower speed. We reach Zapulco harbour safely.

"Well done, crew," I say.

Ruth sighs with relief. "I thought we were goners that time. This is my last time night sailing."

"That was fun, Dad," says Michael.

"I'll stick to day sailing, like Mum," says Nicola.

As they become older, our children are less interested in sailing and prefer to spend their days hanging out in groups, mostly with Canadians staying in nearby apartments. When they are undergraduates, they go off with friends and we seldom see them, except when they come back for food or sleep or both. The idyllic holiday setting creates a party mood, and they rotate their noise and wild behaviour around various parents' holiday homes.

While the kids are out, Ruth and I can find little of common interest. Ruth initiates and controls all of our sex, which has become less frequent. We can find little to say to each other, and I spend more and more time alone. My work occupies my thoughts. To escape from worries, I drink, or puff "Acapulco gold".

Increasing quantities of grog and pot are unable to mask my unhappiness, and they affect my self-esteem, health and judgement. I become incapable of responding appropriately to problems that arise. When I am awake I am usually inebriated and an embarrassment to the others. I try to join in their small talk, but I lack the social skills and remain silent except for an occasional bizarre or angry outburst. They start leaving me behind when they go out, and it is hurtful.

"Where have you been all afternoon?" I ask them.

"We went shopping in town," Michael answers.

"Why didn't you tell me you were going? I have been worried."

"You were fast asleep and snoring. We didn't think you would want to come."

"It would have been nice to be asked."

One afternoon we all go to the beach. My thinking is blurred, and I have trouble keeping my balance. I am very unfit, have put on weight, and don't have much stamina. In a haze of alcohol,

I wobble across the road with them to the beach opposite our apartment. The afternoon sea breeze is lifting sizable waves, and body surfers are out in force.

"Dad, you are too stoned," says Nicola. "You'll drown yourself."

"Do you mind?" I say. "I go better when I have had a drink."

The water is cold, and I collect my senses as I wade out and begin swimming. I turn down a series of dumpers, diving through the base of the waves at the last moment before they crash down on me. Ruth and Nicola are talking in knee-deep water near the beach.

Michael and I thresh down the face of a wave and get picked up. I can see him out of the corner of my eye as we are swept in towards the beach in the fast-moving surf.

With barely a ripple on the surface to warn me, I am caught in a rip too strong to swim against. It carries me, swimming uselessly until I am exhausted, out to sea beyond the breakers. I am floundering and panicking, with water in my lungs, when Michael arrives and holds my head up.

"Okay, Dad, take it easy. Get your breath. That's it."

I am able to kick a little to help as he pulls me in further along the beach. It is hard work for him, and he is shattered. He is only an adolescent and he has shown terrific courage.

"Thanks, son, you were wonderful," I gasp.

Ruth has no sympathy. "Michael could have drowned. You had better stay out of the water when you are drunk."

It is quite clear whom she values most.

I realize my use of alcohol is pretty irresponsible. Other people I know use it socially and in moderation. My use is solitary and out of control. I have tried to limit myself without success. It is taking more and more to get me drunk. When I am drunk I feel sorry for myself and keep going until I am paralytic. It can't go on like this or it will kill me. Because I can't drink in moderation, I will have to give up completely. When I do, I will need another way of alleviating the anxiety that is like a parasitic growth in my subconscious.

I never think for more than a moment that I should leave Ruth. Both Nicola and Michael know something is wrong, but it does not seem to impact upon them much. They have a reasonably happy home. Friends come for parties and sleepovers. They are asked to parties, as if their home is normal enough. Nicola cuts loose sometimes, galloping her horse and jumping fences. Michael roars off on his trail bike. They seem happy enough. Ruth and I are growing further apart, but it seems tolerable.

A few weeks later when in London for a meeting, I am able to drop in on Vicki. When I give her perfume I have bought on the plane, she seems puzzled. Now that I have come on my own to see her, I want to talk about us, but I cannot think what to say. All we have together are these brief visits and years of near-emptiness in between. I have nothing substantial to tell her. We exchange Christmas cards, and hers are always from the same children's charity, seeming to me to advertise her affinity for new life that she, for reasons best known to herself, has declined to contribute to.

Vicki seldom drinks alcohol and never becomes intoxicated.

"My psyche is difficult enough to manage when I'm sober," she says.

Outside her work, Vicki seems to lack self-confidence. She is a good listener and helps men find ideal partners. She is dutiful to her father and brother. She is intensely private, with inviolable inertia, and I speculate that she may be unable to compromise sufficiently to connect with a man.

I hide my drinking from her and stay sober on my visits, although it makes me irritable. This worries me, for I don't want to clash with her. I suffer oceans of guilt for my drinking but know that Vicki would be unsympathetic as she strongly disapproves of drunkenness. I know that as long as I plan to go to her, I must quit my drinking.

As we part, I hug her close and run my hands over her back and waist, and she pulls in against me. I run my fingers through her hair and feel the shape of her delicate ears. It is difficult to stop when I have to leave. I try to kiss her but she pushes me away.

"What about Ruth?" she asks.

"She's okay," I reply.

Later, on reflection, I am not sure if she is reminding me I should honour the wedding vows that she had heard me recite at our wedding. Or is she prompting me to focus on how to end my relationship with her competitor who she wants me to oust? The former seems more like the courteous Vicki that I know.

Rule 71: *Drug dependencies create dependencies on others.*

CHAPTER 72   MODEL DISMISSAL

When I walk into the packed conference I have arranged for researchers at our Calgary and Edmonton laboratories, for them to present their work to me, the buzz of conversation becomes an awkward silence. I am a Toronto boofhead doing a purge. My petroleum engineering expertise is legendary. I have trained with Canoil's USA parent company as a reservoir specialist. I am familiar with the pantheon of recovery technologies being developed or tested here. The CEO, Ralph Gooder, expects me to check that we are getting value for money from these boffins.

They fear me as a turncoat, someone nurtured here who has gone east and come back as a potential traitor. I know their weaknesses and I may rip into their projects using "inside" knowledge. They know me personally, or by reputation, as someone they cannot count on for loyalty. So far in my auspicious career, I have displayed loyalty only to the company and one person – me.

On my first day, four projects are presented. I know most of this work from a meeting I attended three years ago. So far, I have suggested minor changes to two projects and a major change to another. The other one is to be wound up. No shedding of staff will be necessary because they are to be transferred to a new project.

On the second day, my treat is to take everyone to a local hotel for lunch. I surreptitiously drink half a dozen Bacardis and coke. When we return to the conference room, the presenter of the project is Graham Antcliff, who I have known for fifteen years. I am summarising his presentation of miscible flooding because mine and Vicki's relationship is involved with this technology during much of the remainder of my story.

"My team's work is to come up with a design for miscible flooding," Graham begins. "I know Selwyn did not like our model last time but I hope to convince him that we have been successful in using it to test alternative designs." He shows a slide of the laboratory model that he explained to me three years ago. It looks like a large fish tank with very thick glass , full to the top with sand, covered with wires to an instrument panel.

"Miscible flooding is the last stage of oil production. The first is exploration and locates depths to domes, and other types of trap, using mini-earthquakes made with explosives, that bounce sound waves off underground layers. We drill into the traps to find if oil has collected over hundreds of millions of years. If there is oil in the trap, it is inside the pores of a rock and flows out under its own pressure, or by lowering pumps down the well."

I begin thirsting for some alcohol.

"Next, if there is gas above the oil, the expanding gas can push the oil into the wells. Eventually the pressure falls and the layer of groundwater below the oil moves slowly upwards. Water clings to rock better than oil does, gets under the oil, lifts it off and carries it to the well. This is called primary production and recovers about 15% of the original oil until only water is produced.."

"Why does the oil stop flowing out, anybody?"

"Groundwater has lifted off all it can from the rock," answered an engineer.

"Good answer. I'm glad no-one answered 'because it has all gone' because most of it, about 85%, is still down there."

"Next we convert some of the holes to water injection and flush out more oil. This is called secondary production. By drilling additional holes we can get recovery up to 30%.

"The rest of the oil is trapped in 'dead-end' pore spaces, like cars parked in cul-de-sacs. The water traffic can't get in to wash the oil globules out. Unless there is a way of bringing them out, they are lost, wasted. What type of substance do we need?"

"A detergent."

"Surfactants form emulsions that are difficult to process. Another way?"

"A solvent."

"We can inject a solvent and dry-clean the rock. Miscible flooding is a breakthrough concept. It has been tested and it works. A good solvent can increase recovery to about 90% of the original oil. This is called tertiary recovery."

There is a murmur of interest..

"It is amazing. Look, I'll show you. I want you to understand how miscible flooding works because it is something we are going to hear a lot more about in the future, as oil gets scarcer."

He picked up one of two identical metal trays, with rectangular sponges on them, like those used for car washing. The trays have drain spouts with plastic tubing going to beakers on the floor.

"This sponge represents an oil reservoir. It has holes connected together through it, like pores in the limestone of a coral reef. I soaked it in oil earlier today. Some of the oil has drained into the tray and out into the beaker. For a real reservoir, the beaker is a tank on the surface, up near the ceiling, with the oil being pumped up to it. The oil has stopped flowing now, representing several years of field time. A lot of oil is still in the sponge, in pores with closed ends and clinging to the walls of pores."

"What does the tray represent?" asks one of the engineers.

"Beneath the reservoir rock is rock without any holes in it. The gas above the oil in the sponge is air. But underground the top is sealed by another impervious layer, or tray, and at the top of the sponge is natural gas at high pressure. Including the effect of groundwater coming in from below it pushes out about 15%.

"What if the gas channels down into the well?" another engineer asks.

Antcliff makes a show of putting on his glasses and looks. "There is less oil at the sides of the sponge. Is that what you mean?"

"Gas pressure release," someone says.

"Ah! Wind?" hr says..

There is laughter.

"A reservoir is rather like a full rectum," Antcliff says. "Gas channels down and there is a blow-out."

More laughter.

"A blow out is to be avoided. We want to keep the gas in to push out oil, the first 15% or so by unassisted primary production methods. At the same time, water is flowing in slowly lower down in the rock, creeping through capillaries behind the advancing oil."

"It is like Indian bikini bottoms then," says an engineer. He pauses and people look at him. "Creeping up behind."

There is laughter.

"Very amusing, gentlemen, " says Antcliff.

He pours a beaker of water into the tray.

"This is secondary recovery. The sponge sops it up, because water likes rock and clings to it, going under the oil and lifting it off. It flows into the closed pores, and beads of oil come back out. Water can get out about another 15% of the original oil, giving at most 30% recovery."

He picks up a beaker containing a pale greenish liquid.

"This is kerosene. It is part of the crude oil produced, separated by a distillation plant on the surface. We pump it back down into the reservoir rock, where it 'dry-cleans' the rock. It gets out most of the oil left behind by the water. Because it mixes into the crude oil, we call the process 'miscible flooding'".

Antcliff pours the kerosene into the tray. They watch as the flow of black crude oil increases.

"This is tertiary recovery. Where is the best place to put in the solvent, at the top. in the middle or at the bottom?"

"In the laboratory model, it is better at the top, or at the bottom, where it can mix vertically. Theoretically, the bottom should be best, because the kerosene floats up in water and oil, giving better mixing It is too slow for us to see this gravity effect in our models. If there are shale barriers, liking icing between layers of a sponge cake, it is better to inject directly into the middle of each layer."

"How do you inject the solvent?"

"Because we need to dissolve the whole of the crude oil and the solvent is a quarter of the volume, we need to extend it with something, or it can't reach it all. We are already injecting water. Mixing the solvent with water and injecting an emulsion is convenient".

To reach more of the oil, we fracture the rock, opening up natural cracks."

"Injection into a natural crack is called an enema," someone comments. There is laughter.

"The solvent flushes out the oil – like a laxative." He paused as the audience chuckles.

"Anal retention is the main problem stopping this process being adopted,," Antcliff jests."Piles of oil are being wasted even though miscible flooding was discovered in the 1960s."

More laughter. Graham Antcliff shows a couple of slides with the results from the group's laboratory model.

"To summarise, our simulation of miscible flooding shows it is most suitable for reservoirs that have high porosity, like this sponge. Our best potential is overseas at Bigeria's Panypo oilfield. It is a shallow reef, and we believe we can get out over 90% of the oil."

Alarm bells sound in my head.

I interrupt him. "Graham, have you communicated with the Bigerians about this?"

"Yes. We have written to the Bigerian Energy Minister, suggesting a joint study. We haven't heard back yet."

"I see."

Although the idea is a favourite of mine, I am sure Antcliff's group have achieved nothing of practical value in the last three years, and it makes me angry. I wait for a few more questions and then I stand up.

"The presentations this morning were informative, whereas since lunch we have been entertained with the idea of miscible flooding, rather than presented how miscible flooding is to be developed as a field technology. Graham, with your laboratory model, you have persisted in gathering more and more useless data. If you can tell me one consequence for our field operations of your work in the last three years, I will reconsider."

Antcliff's face turns the colour of a beetroot. I wait.

"We, er, have found out the effect of, viscosity."

I interrupt, "That is a fine-tuning variable. The place to investigate it is in the field, with a pilot plant, at the Tundra Tar Sands. Do you have a proposal for doing that?"

Antcliff sheepishly shakes his head.

"Your sponge model has amusing ideas about diarrhoea and constipation, but the rock model you have been using is shit, as I told you three years ago. Your testing should be in the field, but there is no proposal for a pilot plant. Am I correct? I thought so. The processes are, you will remember: pumping the solvent down the bore; flowing it to where the oil is; dispersing the oil in it; dissolving it; extracting it from closed spaces; flowing it away to the producing well and then to surface; and separating it for recycling. None would occur in the field in the same way as in the laboratory. Your model, the rock one, speeds up the processes and therefore cannot show optimal field conditions. It is not surprising you have nothing to say about these processes, as you have learnt nothing at all to tell us about what we want to know: how to do a miscible flood."

I liked to show off my experience and learning, especially my grasp of theoretical aspects.

"You have persisted with these worthless experiments, despite my telling you here, three years ago, to stop. It would have been better if you had spent your time sweeping the laboratory floors."

There is absolute silence. Antcliff stares at me, his face pale.

"What is more, you have contacted the Bigerian Government without being authorised to do so. Canoil has delicate relations with Bigeria. The country is in the throes of a famine, and we don't want any possibility of upsetting them. It is well-known that all correspondence outside the company has to be cleared with senior management, but you seem to have ignored that.

"I want a pilot plant to be constructed at Tundra Tar Sands as soon as possible. The others in the miscible flooding team will prepare a proposal for such a plant as their top priority."

I turn to the lab manager. "Trevor, I want to talk with you privately. Good afternoon, gentlemen. We will have the remaining presentations tomorrow."

As I stalk out, you could cut the air with a knife. It is a dictatorial display. Bob has told me I need to be more relaxed. My social interaction is too rigid, I am too blunt and I bully people. I am irritable because I am craving alcohol. I suppose I have been too hard on Antcliff in front of the others. I regret that it had to end up like this for I have known Antcliff for years as a friend and I don't have many friends left.

I go straight to Trevor's office. He puts the blame fully on Graham Antcliff. However, it is obvious that neither of them has shown sufficient loyalty to the company or to me in persisting with this nonsense. I inform him that I will be recommending that both he and Antcliff are fired. It would be better for them if they resign within the week. I ask him to inform Antcliff.

"Can we appeal?"

"Yes, to the CEO, Bob Walker."

Their appeal will be a waste of time because I know Bob will back me up. I will be widely hated, but if I return to Alberta as Division General Manager, my requirements will be met.

I go back to my hotel and open a bottle of beer in my room. I long to discuss the situation and my feelings with Vicki, but the UK is seven hours ahead of Calgary and she will be in bed. If I had her with me and could call on her common sense and people skills, I would be so much better at my job. It almost seems as though events are conspiring to make my life difficult. I cannot see anything I can do about it except watch out for storm clouds and hope for a silver lining.

As my work increasingly involves human and ethical issues, I need Vicki to unburden myself to. My responsibilities weigh heavily upon me.

Rule 72: *Simulation is like masturbation: some people like it better than the real thing.*

CHAPTER 73   HUNGER TREK

When I arrive back at my office in Toronto, Chairman Ralph Gooder's secretary brings me a copy of an article from *The Independent*, a non-establishment but authoritative Ottawa newspaper.

FAMINE RELIEF AND THE GOODER OIL IN BIGERIA

In northern Bigeria, Syrad Abdul Razak and her husband Abdi Shamarcke Razak stand together and dejectedly survey their land and home. The house is one of five in a cluster of mud wall and thatch dwellings above the Panypo oil reservoir. Inside is one room, with a mud fireplace at one side and the sleeping area at the other. Each house has a hectare of land. It is bare earth and they have no seed. They have eaten their corn, their poultry and their cow over a month ago. There is no food left. Their only food for the past three days has been flowers and berries they have picked from bushes beside the dry creek bed.

"My husband, we can stay here no longer," says Syrad.

"Yes, it is time to go to the south," replies Abdi. "I have prayed and I believe we are meant to go. Allah is great."

Twenty years previously, the government granted a foreign company, Canoil, an oil exploration and production licence over this area. They discovered oil below the Razak's home. A donkey pump is nodding in a fenced-off area at the boundary of their property. Below their home, one of hundreds of barrels of oil is in the holes in the rock, where it has reposed since the Jurassic era, when dinosaurs walked the Earth. The pump has caused a pressure reduction, and some of the oil begins to move slowly through the rock towards the well.

Two kilometres above, Syrad gathers her four small children together. She and her husband each carry a baby, with a blanket over the other shoulder, containing cooking utensils and other things they have been unable to sell for food. They begin walking to Panypo, the local village. They hope there may be a handout of food aid, as there was several weeks ago.

The government has called in several international aid organizations for assistance and they have set up a camp at Panypo. People flock to the station, but a militia hijacks a large truck bringing food and takes it to their chiefs across the border. There it is sold for guns and ammunition. The aid is fuelling the fighting in the country, instead of helping its struggling citizens. As the Razak family nears the village, their path runs together with other paths and evacuating families. People are fleeing from Panypo. They tell them the militia is burning houses and killing people. They detour around the village and begin to walk alongside the main road going south to the oil port near Akar, the capital.

As it nears the well, the oil begins to speed up as it runs through cracks in the rock. Oil is coming in all around the well to join the flow. Water is also coming up from below the oil. Soon the oil and water mixture is hurrying through the passages and finally squirts through a hole in a vertical iron pipe. It gathers in a pool, with its surface rising up the pipe until it is sucked into the chamber of a pump and lifted by a piston vertically to the surface. There it passes through pipes under the ground surface. It gathers together with the oil from other wells into a large pipe that flows away past the Razak's house to the centre of the oilfield. There slugs of liquid are blown by the gas into a large horizontal cylindrical tank. Water and gas are separated from the oil. Water is piped back and injected back into the reservoir below the oil level. The gas and oil flow away in two pipelines beside the main road,

The Razak family is in trouble. The youngest child is no longer able to keep up, being weak with diarrhea. The family stops for shelter in a dry water culvert. The child dies in the night. They leave the body to the jackals and exchange half their possessions for a few handfuls of rice.

They reach pumping station number 2. It is under permanent guard by three soldiers who have a Landrover and sleep in a tent. Syrad begs for food and water, and they give her a little of each. They walk on, towards the south where Syrad and Abdi hope to be able to get work and food.

At the pumping station the oil pressure is raised to go over the low hills ahead. In the past, rebels have diverted oil into barrels for their own use. Over the border is a distillation still that can take out gasoline for vehicle use and kero for heating.

The Razaks are a few kilometres further on when a militia of eight men roar up on motorbikes. They round up a group of walkers and start yelling at them in a language they do not understand, the language of the ruling Fetani tribe. They want valuables, but the Razaks have long ago used their few pieces of silver to buy food. When the walkers do not comply, *the Fetanis become angry. They start shooting the men. They make Abdi kneel down and machine gun him in the back, despite Syrad's pleading and screams. The child clings to her, sobbing silently. The babies sense their mother's distress but are too weak to cry. When the group produces no more valuables, the bandits shoot the rest of the men. Then they roar off.*

The gas pipeline stops in the capital city, Akar. It is distributed to industries by the government. Much is stolen through illegal connections.

The oil passes through another half a dozen pumping stations, each guarded by the Army, and flows away placidly through its pipe under the surface. Before Syrad and the children have reached a quarter of the distance, the oil reaches the coast at the oil port, Kosoto. It runs into one of several enormous holding tanks on the shore beside the tanker loading jetty, guarded by the army.

Syrad, her brain numb and physically exhausted, abandons one of the babies and continues walking, forlornly. She carries one baby, and the child tries to keep up. The last of the fat on her body has been consumed, and her body is obtaining energy by running down her muscles, which become weaker and weaker. They pass families that have given up and are sitting under bushes waiting to die.

Mixed with other crude oil in a huge tank, the oil that left Panypo a week earlier at the same time as the Razak family is pumped into an oil tanker's hold. When the tanker is filled, it noses slowly away from the loading jetty and tugs push it out into the seaway to start for Canada on the other side of the World.

The second baby dies of starvation when Syrad's milk dries up. She places the baby's body under a tree where the circling vultures cannot see it. Then she resumes walking, holding the hand of the last of her four children, going slowly now. The child is too tired and weak to brush away the swarms of flies that cluster on her face. She knows instinctively not to complain, that keeping going is her only hope

After crossing the Atlantic Ocean, the oil tanker slows down in the St Lawrence Seaway and slides through locks up to Montreal, where it discharges the oil into tankage. A pump sends it to the Sarnia oil refinery near Toronto, 500 kms away, where I work at Canoil's head office. Within a few days, gasoline made from it is being pumped into my wife's car at a gas station.

When a truck stops for them, Syrad and the child stare, hollow-eyed. An aid worker helps them to get in. When the truck is filled with famine victims, it takes them to an aid station where they are given a soup made from maize. Then they get back in the truck and are taken to a camp a day's journey to the south, where they are led to a tent.

My wife pays at the gas station with her credit card. She uses the petrol commuting to work on the expressway, most of it burned while waiting in lines of traffic. None of her money will reach the remainder of the Razak family, whose deserted home remains above where the oil came from.

Canoil's Chairman Ralph Gooder says, "We pay for the oil to the elected Bigerian Government, according to our contract. It would be illegal under Bigerian law to give any of the money to the starving Hotu people. We employ local people and support local communities."

The remaining two of the six Razaks have plenty of time. They wait in their refugee camp for conditions at home in Panypo to improve. A national election is scheduled in a year's time. If it is held and enough Hotus have survived to win the election, Syrad is hopeful that some of the oil money will flow back to the north of the country, and they will be able to go home.

It will be the Hotus' turn to eat.

Greg Castles for *The Independent* in Akar
The article has a note written on the top:

Selwyn, contact "Shaver" Ronson in Ottawa and check for a better way of paying. R

Later that morning, Gooder calls me into his office.
"Selwyn, nice job in Calgary."
I sent him my report of the conference. He gives me a big smile.
"You didn't ask Graham Antcliff."
"He's past his use-by date. Get rid of him. Now, I would like you to transfer to Edmonton as Division General Manager. Think you can handle that?"
I am thrilled. I have hit the big time.
"Yes, no worries. Thank you, Sir."
"Call me Bob. Any questions?"
Another big smile.
"No, er, Bob."
"Good morning, Selwyn."
I phone Ruth and tell her the news.
"Why not Calgary?" she complains. "I am losing touch with my family and friends there."

By now, I realize that nothing I do can please Ruth.

"It may not be for long. If I make the grade, the next step up to CEO would probably be in Calgary."

She says nothing. I hang up.

I phone Manfred Brash, who was with me at Liverpool uni and helped with my recruitment drive for Mission Figurehead. He is working in London for a consultant. On my recent visit, he complains that he is finding the work dull.

"Manfred, how would you like some excitement? How would you like to join Canoil in Edmonton as assistant to the Division GM – me?"

Manfred congratulates me and says he will let me know.

Next, I have to get up to speed on the Bigerian situation.

"What's happening?" I ask our manager, on the telephone at the Bigerian oil port, Kosoto.

"The government has banned reporting of famines," he tells me. "I am getting news from our people at the oilfields. There is a rebel army of Hotus, calling themselves the People's Party, led by Abdul Misoto. He trained with al Qaida and is being supplied with food and munitions from over the border with Zanabwe. If they shut down our oil production, the Okonjo Government will be in trouble. The supply chain is fragile. It has military protection from saboteurs along its full length. The army has a platoon stationed at every oilfield, guards at pumping stations and regular patrols all along the trunk pipeline to our marine loading facility. The navy has turned the port into a fortress. Tanker ships are escorted in and out by gunboats. Pro-government militias are terrorising Hotus who may support the rebels. Despite the army guard, it would be easy for the rebels to blow up the pipeline."

Ralph sends me a copy of the telex Bob received from the rebel leader.

"To Robert Walker, CEO of Canoil,

I am the leader of the starving Hotu people. We demand that Prime Minister Okonjo provide food relief to us. Unless food is provided, we will stop the production of oil from our people's land. We also demand that Canoil pay to our Bigerian People's Party, for distribution to the Hotu people, 50% of payments for oil produced from Hotu lands. Payment for oil shipped in July must be paid into the Party's Trust Account, in my name, at the Commonwealth Bank in Zanabwe, by 31st August.

Abdul Misoto

President,

Bigerian People's Party.

I call Bob to find out his reaction.

"My feeling is we should do what Abdul Misoto wants," Walker tells me. "That way we can have a bob each way on a coup and the election."

I agree with Bob. It is good to know that Canoil has a man of principle at the helm.

I phoned Vicki to get her take on this situation. She said she would take it to her group.

"Who are your group?"

"We call ourselves Friends of Overseas Development, or FOOD."

"What do you do?"

"One thing is we are interested in what Canoil is doing in Bigeria."

It is ominous. However, they may be able to offer ideas.

"Vicki, whatever we do has to be approved by Ottawa. Why? Because they licence us to import Bigerian oil. Yes, we can and will suggest it to them but their main interest is the Canadian voter, who is a motorist. Yes, I know it is wrong, but that's the way our democracy works. Most Canadians neither know nor want to know about the famine in Bigeria."

Although it is not my responsibility, I fear that the situation may have dreadful consequences. I hope that I will consider everything that I need to in dealing with Ottawa.

Rule 73: *The owners of a resource expect to receive a fair share in benefits, as well as efficient extraction, to sustain their future.*

CHAPTER 74   EQUAL PAY

Next morning, while I am packing up my office, Ralph's secretary brings me a short news item on the second page of the Toronto Star.

BIGERIANREBELSTHREATENCANOILPRODUCTION

Rebel leader Abdul Misoto is demanding a 50% share of oil payments being made by Canoil to the Okonjo Government. He has threatened to stop Canoil from producing oil, using force against the Bigerian Army who are defending oil facilities. Last year, 473 million barrels, 26% of Canoil's production, worth USD33 billion, was sourced from Bigeria. Energy Minister Tinibu commented, "Petroleum exports from Bigeria are made under a contract between Canoil and the elected Government. The contract includes a failure to make correct payment clause which can result in immediate stoppage of supply."

Canoil CEO, Robert Walker, was not available for comment.

I decide we should wait for a few days before responding to Misoto.

I have moved into my Edmonton office when Manfred walks in. I walk around to shake hands.

"Great to have you aboard, Manfred."

"It's good to be here," he says.

I give him the Bigerian file to read. We have lunch and I fill him in on the situation.

"Do you think Bob Walker is leaking the story?" I ask Manfred.

"I don't know who else, unless it was another Board member," he replies."You said Bob disapproves of Okonjo's corrupt government."

"I wonder if Walker might have put Misoto up to it in the first place."

"That's a very off-the-wall thing to say," says Manfred. "You are suggesting that Canoil has been interfering in Bigerian politics. Ottawa wouldn't like that."

"How can you be sure Ottawa don't know already?" I replied.

"I am sure. I know how Ottawa works. I did a job over here a few months back. It's best that we don't mention it again."

I feel rather stupid. I am fortunate to have Manfred point it out when I make mistakes in interpreting situations, as I am not as good at it as my job demands.

Later that week, Bob telephones me.

"I have just been in a Board meeting. I told them my view of the situation in Bigeria. They don't see it my way."

"How do they see it?"

"They insist our first allegiance is to Canadians to keep the oil flowing," the CEO says. "They will back Okonjo's elected government, continuing to pay all the money to that genocidal bastard, even if he cancels the next election and becomes a dictator."

"What do you think should happen?"

"I wanted the Board to agree to a compromise, that Canoil pays 25% of the money to Misoto, but the vote went against me," Bob says.

"How did they leave it?"

"Gooder told me afterwards, 'If you won't keep supporting Okonjo 100%, we will get someone who will.' I think he means you, Selwyn."

Bob is clearly uptight. Ignoring Misoto's plea comes at a price. He must face the media and take the blame for the agony of the thousands of starving and dying Bigerians. It is an unenviable task.

I am dreading having to fire Antcliff. I have known him since I joined Canoil and have chatted with him a number of times, at company conferences and meetings. He is older than I am but far enough from retirement to still have a mortgage. He is a specialist and will find it difficult getting another job .

I dial his number at the laboratory.

"Is that Graham Antcliff?"

"Yes."

"Good morning, Graham. Selwyn Archer here. I expect Trevor has told you?"

I begin to fiddle with a wart on the palm of my left hand.

"Yes, he says I have to resign – by Friday? You can't do that to me!"

The wart has been there for years, slowly getting larger. I try to dig under it with the nail on the forefinger of my other hand.

"Graham, you leave me no choice."

"Just because you want to do field tests, instead of doing lab tests, is not a reason—"

"It's not that. You have set yourself up against company policies – defiantly."

I hold the phone with my shoulder and get the wart in a pincer grip. With a jerk, I try to yank it out. A piece comes off the top on one side. The roots don't budge.

"Trevor knew what I was doing. He didn't try to stop me."

"He says he warned you."

"It's not true."

"He says he told you several times to stop the miscible work. And you didn't. You were supposed to switch to other tar sands work."

"We had to finish the trials we had started, or we would be throwing our results away."

I pinch the wart as hard as I can between my nails and yank again. My forefinger nail tears down to the quick. Blood begins to ooze around the bottom of the wart.

"It wasn't for you to decide when you would stop," I say sharply. "I clearly told you to stop, more than three years ago."

I take a tissue and dab at the blood.

"We have found out a lot."

"Not in my opinion. That is not the issue. I told you to stop. You have shown flagrant disregard of policy. Now you have spilled the beans to the Bigerian Government – without authority."

I consider yanking again, but my nail is broken. I could use another, nail, my second finger. There could be blood everywhere.

"I was teeing up a field trial. That's what you want, isn't it? They are very interested in having a trial."

"I'll bet they are, but not for Canoil's benefit. You don't have the big picture – and you have opened a can of worms. You knew you needed clearance, but you flagrantly did your own thing."

I look at the wart carefully. I notice for the first time that deep inside, the centre is black. Could it be a malignant cancer?

"Canoil should help the Bigerians. They are starving!"

"I agree, but it is not your job to decide that."

You hypocrite, I say to myself. It is not my job either. I cannot forget the story about the Razak family in *The Independent*. I believe that helping those starving people should transcend corporate and job boundaries. Yet here I am punishing a man for acting on his conscience.

I can see the blackness in the wart growing. Is my hypocrisy and selfishness causing my inner self to get out of control?

"There are thousands dying. Doing a field trial would help a little, ," says Antcliff.

"Robert Walker and the Board decide who and how Canoil will help. Not you; not me."

"They don't give a shit about people who are starving. They only care about feeding greedy fat cat shareholders and collecting their obscene pay."

He was right. However, he, too, is paid by Canoil. I know just what to say because I have said it before to other disgruntled staff.

"You do not have authority to spend shareholders' money on that. You can send the rebels as much of your severance money as you want."

"You nasty bastard. It will be a pleasure to stop working for you."

"I'm sorry you feel like that, Graham. We used to see things the same way. Is there anything else to talk about?"

"You have changed. You used to have a heart. All you care about now is your career and keeping in with straights. In the end, it will destroy you."

I realise at that moment the evil that Canoil is doing and that he is right. I am without empathy for people in trouble. I have become an evil person.

I will make an appointment with my doctor to have the wart removed.

"Goodbye, Graham."

"Go to hell."

Antcliff hangs up. I feel quite bad about myself, although I never doubt that I am right in firing him. His philanthropy is incoherent, the incomplete thinking of a man unsuited to his position with Canoil. But I know instinctively that Canoil is not being a good world citizen. If I can, I will change Canoil so that it is. I want Vicki to be proud of what I do.

I follow up on Gooder's suggestion to visit "Shaver" Ronson at the Foreign Office. We need to know the Government's attitude to the Bigerian rebels. The issue of the oil payments is still around, and I need to be up to speed in case it erupts. Manfred drives me to Edmonton public airport for a flight to Ottawa scheduled at 9.30am.

Manfred keeps the big car astride the rounded icy road, so we won't slide off into the walls of snow built up by snow-throwing machines. I am eating a hamburger. I eat to soothe my nerves. These days I get anxious about almost everything. My life is in my head, and it is a crock of worries. Hardly anything is the way I want it to be. As we near the airport, there is more traffic and the road is salted, producing brownish slush.

The flight is delayed by ice on the runway, and we arrive in Ottawa late. Fortunately, the Minister is able to reschedule.

"Our eyes are open wide on this, Selwyn," Ronson says, "but there is nothing we can do. It is their problem, not ours. Bob can't see that As he will have told you, Canoil is giving Okonjo a fortune, equal to about 40% of GDP. But only a half of your payments appear on the books and most of it goes to the army. None of your money is going to help the starving people. Okonjo and his cronies are stashing the rest away in their Swiss bank accounts.

Overseas aid is being channelled to Okonjo's people, who are mostly in the south. With drought in the north and little aid getting through, he is practising genocide on the Hotus. Misoto is trying to pre-empt an election with a coup, presumably because he is likely to lose."

"Can we change who we pay for the oil to?" I ask.

"I don't need to know who you are paying," he says, "as long as we are getting receipts for it from the Bigerian government, as required under the contract."

"We pay them enough to feed the entire nation," I tell him.

" We are also sending food aid, despite not much getting through to the starving," Ronson says. "They have a system. If you destabilize it, you do so at the peril of your shareholders, your people in Bigeria and your customers. Okonjo will get his come-uppance in the election. We have to assume at this stage he will hold one."

When I get back to the office, I make my report to the Board. Ronson wants Canoil on the Okonjo bench as his tribe slug it out with Misoto. I can see that Bob is on a collision course with Ronson.

I sympathize with Bob's point of view, but Canoil should not go against Ronson. Perhaps Gooder can take it up with the Foreign Minister.

I report to Gooder accordingly. This problem is on my conscience, and the spectre of the Razak family tragedy and thousands dying from starvation haunts me. I am losing sight of my ideals to help people. I try to forget the awfulness by burying myself in my work. My high salary seems poor compensation for the way my personal ethics are being violated in this job. I wonder if I will be brought to resign, like Robert Walker, for moral reasons.

Worrying about it makes me feel hungry. These days I always feel hungry. When my work is stressful, I eat. I send out for some doughnuts. They are the English type, greasy balls of flour with jam inside and coated with sugar, the way I like them.

On my next visit, Vicki uncovers my alcoholism and blames my anxiety as the cause. She warns me that stopping drinking does not end alcoholism. I must beware of the possibility of the need emerging somewhere else.

"Provided I have someone who understands how I am feeling, anxiety isn't a problem. You are magic. When I talk with you, my worries disappear. Being with you makes me forget my worries, better even than drinking alcohol."

"Selwyn, do you think our relationship is healthy?"

"It seems almost an addiction," I reply.

I need her so badly.

"I have heard of love addiction," says Vicki."You have a dependency problem. You have to get on top of it, as it is affecting others. I wouldn't want to have a relationship with you unless you are having effective treatment. You need the help of a psychotherapist."

It's been a bad week. That evening, I drink a bottle of red wine followed by a four-litre cask of wine and get a splitting headache. I have a sleepless night, waking only to vomit on my feet as I try to make it to the sink.

Rule 74: *Corporations may not respect ethical responses of employees.*

CHAPTER 75   DRINKER DECIDES

I wake up to the Edmonton dawn chorus and lie there, in a hell where I have to choose between alcohol products. How will I recapture the euphoria of that first taste of the blackberry wine I made, long ago at home on the farm?

The choices are either Tunley Red Claret or casks of Vinolli Cabernet Shiraz from the State liquor store. The Vinolli has delicious flavours of blackberry and plum and hints of pepper, but it is expensive. The Tunley Red Claret is cheap but has a mixed-up sour taste, with a hint of preservative, sulphur dioxide.

The other option is my home-made banana and apple wine, which is still fermenting in the garage. It isn't ready yet, and the taste will be yeasty, with only about 6% alcohol, whereas the Vinolli could be up to 12% and the Red Claret 10%. Drinking my home-made wine would save me driving 1.7 km to the liquor store and there are fewer chemicals.

I still have a headache from last night's Vinolli cask. I threw up at 2.15 am. I remember dozing off afterwards sitting on the toilet, in a cold sweat with my head spinning. Every time I tried lying down in bed, I became nauseous, jumped up and retched into the en suite sink. Ruth woke up and put in earplugs.

We still share a bedroom but that is all.

I am worried about the state of our marriage. The despotic Ruth and I can barely tolerate each other. I want to be with Vicki, in England 6,800 kilometres away. I am also worried about my kids. I haven't succeeded in having a conversation with them lately, and it feels like living with strangers. I want to have a happy home. In Yorkshire, 7000 kilometres away, my father is losing his mind to Parkinson's Disease, and from over here there is nothing I can do to help him.

After I get up and have breakfast, I drive Nicola to school on my way to work downtown. It is 28.6 kilometres along the St Arthur Trail on to Fair Road. We come off at Nicola's school, Archibald

High School at Aberdeen North. I drive at the optimal speed for fuel efficiency, indicated by the instrument I have installed on the panel. Her answers to my attempts at conversation are monosyllabic. After dropping her off, I join the traffic crawling along Jasper Avenue into the city centre. I reach 102 Ave and 104 Street, park and take the lift up to my office, arriving 3.4 minutes late for work. No-one is concerned. I am the manager of that floor, and people know I put in extra time outside the office. I work steadily through my in-tray, my brain on automatic, while I think about a past sailing trip, as I cruise towards the challenge of refuelling with a few drinks at lunchtime.

At mid-morning, I try to arrange some drinking to look forward to. I inquire if there are any farewell dos that day for people who are retiring, being transferred or quitting. Today there isn't one. I am getting desperate, until an oilfield contracting company's representative calls and asks me out to a restaurant. I leave the office at 1.00pm. We share a bottle of wine; he has two small glasses and I drink the rest. I get back to the office exactly at 2.00pm for a meeting.

Most managers at lunchtime restaurant meetings drink. There is an office joke. "If you say something stupid and stink of booze, they will think you are drunk and forgive you. If you don't stink of booze, they won't forgive you for being stupid."

After the meeting, I doze with micro-sleeps on and off at my desk. I have a newspaper, open at the business pages, in front of me and pretend to be reading but fall asleep sitting up. Gradually, my head lowers until my chin rests on my chest, and then I bend at the waist until my forehead rests on the paper. A tremendous start throws me upright. I look out of the corner of my eye to see if anyone has seen me through the glass wall of my office. Then I go back to reading the paper, and the dismal cycle is repeated.

I wake up whenever the telephone rings, or when one of my team knocks and comes in. I jerk awake instantly, concealing my startle with motion such as looking in my desk drawer. At about 4.00pm, the prospect of buying wine, going home and getting a drink wakes me up. I imagine myself skolling glasses of red, in satisfying gulps.

At about 5.05pm, an hour before I normally leave, I get a call from Reception that Nicola is waiting for me in the foyer. She must have stayed downtown late for a school function or something. I am pleased to have the excuse to leave on time. Most of the managers leave at 6.00pm, but I will make up the time as soon as possible. I grab my things and collect her, and we walk down to the car.

"What have you been up to, sweetie?" I ask her.

"School play rehearsal."

"How did it go?"

She shrugs her shoulders. "All right."

I am half-hearted about my job, too. It is a long time since I felt joyful about my work, or about anything. I turn on the radio news channel. The traffic builds up steadily, and halfway home it is a bumper to bumper, with darkness closing in. The back of my head gets fizzy, and I know I am about to micro-sleep. I roll down the window, turn the radio up loud and slap my face. The traffic slows and becomes a stop-start crawl.

When I hear a horn blow behind me, I wake up with a jerk. There is a gap of twenty metres to the next car ahead.

"Jeez, Dad. Don't go to sleep!"

Surprised and wide-awake now, I drive up to the next car and stop, my heart pounding.

"Talk to me!" I say to Nicola. "I hardly slept last night!"

"Did you drop off? What were you thinking about?"

"It is more efficient to move forward in a few large steps rather than many small ones," I say, admitting nothing. "It saves wear and tear on the brakes and uses less petrol."

"You did go to sleep, didn't you?"

"Tell me about your favourite subject at school."

Dutifully, she starts telling me about her history class. History is my least favourite subject. I strive to concentrate.

When a horn blows, my momentary blackout ends.

"Dad!"

Frightened into alertness, I drive on again. What if I drop off at the wheel when I'm moving? My commuting is getting more dangerous every day. I know Nicola will tell Ruth about this. Ruth will put on a performance. My position is indefensible. When I don't get enough sleep I should stay at home. I have to go to work. If I stay away, they will learn to get by without me, and senior management will soon make that a permanent arrangement. I have a mortgage and two children at uni, together with a holiday home financed by the company.

If only there is something Nicola and I can talk about. Then I have an idea.

"What do you think about Camp David? George Bush and Boris Yeltsin have declared the Cold War over!"

"It's awesome, Dad! You must be pleased. That's what you were doing your PhD on, isn't it?"

"Yes. It hasn't happened in exactly the way I predicted. The Soviets' move to state enterprise is a convergence between the two sides' ideology. I believe cooperation between the religions on both sides played a role, with a move towards my philosophy of self-altruism. This is what I suggested should happen."

"Does it bother you that the solution doesn't have your name on it, like Kissinger's?"

"No. University research usually stays in the background."

"Do you like the job you have now more?"

"Sometimes. I have more responsibility – but less authority. I sometimes have to do what I'm told."

I start thinking about Vicki's spat and what to do about paying the Bigerian oil money to the Hotus.

When we are almost home, I drive off into a liquor store. Leaving Nicola in the car, I go in and buy a 4-litre cask of Vinolli and another 4-litre cask of Tunley. I ask for them to be put in shopping bags for me to carry out, as I am ashamed to be seen carrying casks of wine. Drunken Native Indians buy wine casks, whereas general managers of divisions should have cases of champagne delivered. The cask wine I buy is low quality. I figure it will reduce the quantity I imbibe.

The cost is no more than many other households spend on good liquor. So the oppressive Ruth is unable to complain about my habit being too expensive. I try to conceal from her how much I drink by paying cash for it. I will not discuss my drinking with her.

When I get into the car with the two carrier bags, Nicola says, "Do you want me to tell you about the American Civil War?"

The shame I am feeling is multiplied by her innocence.

"Yes, I would like to know about that," I tell her.

But I am unable to concentrate and follow her explanation. For the remainder of the journey home, while she tells me about the

War, I am calculating whether to begin with the good wine or the cheap wine, in case I don't finish both. I mentally calculate the unit cost of pure alcohol from each of the two casks.

When we get home, I put my briefcase on my desk in the study as if I have important work to do and take the casks into the walk-in pantry. From the glasses cupboard, I select one of my four favourite lead crystal wine goblets. I polish it with a tea towel and fill it from the Vinolli cask. I take a swig of wine and rinse it around my mouth, compressing my cheeks to squeeze it through the gaps between my teeth. I tip my head back and gargle as if it is a mouthwash, feeling it splashing up over my soft palate. The first of the alcohol to be absorbed into my blood starts coming through, with a slight numbness at the nape of my neck. I throw back another four full goblets in quick succession, enough to empty a regular bottle. I feel the alcohol surging into my blood and starting to anaesthetise my anxiety. Over the years, it has taken more and more wine to relax me. Recently it takes a whole cask, or about 20 goblets with 200mL each.

As I go to my study and begin looking at some papers from work, I notice several home repair and maintenance jobs that need attention. I worry that I will never get them done. I make a list on the back of an envelope and this reduces the worry, although I know I will lose the list. As I am passing through the kitchen to refill my glass for the umpteenth time, Michael arrives after catching a local bus home from a football practice at his school. He reads the signs correctly.

"Hi, Dad. Getting drunk, I see," he says, as if commenting on the weather.

"Let those without blame be the first to get stoned," I reply, my voice slurred.

I feel inadequate to be a parent to two such wonderful children. As it is Friday, I am simply anaesthetising myself to forget a stressful week.

"Dad, are we still going down to Zapulco tomorrow?" Michael asks hopefully.

I had forgotten that this is the third weekend in the month, when we normally go to Mexico. Although Ruth and I avoid each other, for our children we try to keep up the facade of a united family.

"Do you want to go?"

"Well, I asked Connie and Jamie."

"Did they ask their parents?"

"Yup. They can come."

"Then, if your mother still wants to go, we'll all go."

I feel hungry. I find my dinner in the oven and Ruth watching television.

"Hello. Thanks for dinner, Ruth. Are you okay to go to Zapulco tomorrow?"

She thinks for a full minute before replying, as if she is playing a chess move against me.

"Is Michael coming?"

"Yes, with two friends."

"What time?"

"The usual; leave here at 7.00am."

"Is Nicola coming?"

"I'm not sure. She was going horse trekking in the foothills. I was taking the horse float."

"We can't leave her here by herself. She has some wild friends."

"I'll tell her that she has to come then."

"No way! You will put her back up. Leave it to me."

"What would I do without you?" I mutter. Nicola's wildness could be her escape from our unhappy home. I wish I could escape from it, too.

Every Friday I drink myself stupid and start thinking about Vicki on the other side of the World. I am hamstrung in a loveless marriage, and Vicki is all alone. At least, she was by herself last time I was over there; she has probably had more blokes than I have girls over the years. A couple of times I have heard from Richard she has a man living with her. But her boyfriends have become less frequent and they don't seem to stay for long now.

I finish dinner and go back to the Vinolli. Then I finish writing the report that Nicola interrupted. I write carefully, enjoying myself with a familiar feeling of numbness low down under the back of my head, in the cerebellum which controls my balance. When I get up to refill my glass, I stagger and have to hold on to the furniture. As I finish the Vinolli and start on the Tunley, the numbness spreads up into the occipital lobe at the back of my head. I have difficulty focussing on my writing. I started in a stylish longhand, with flourishes, for my secretary to type up. But now my parietal lobe and sensorimotor lobes on top of my head have lost sensation, and my writing is an ugly squiggle. When the Tunley takes over my frontal lobe, my problem-solving dithers and my writing slows to an indeterminate halt.

When I go into the lounge for the TV news, the screen is so blurred and the sound so distant that I know my De Broca's area is shutting down.

"I am sick of politics," Ruth says. "Who cares that the Prime Minister met with the President of France?"

It seems more like diplomacy than politics. She looks at me as if I should say something, but I cannot remember what she has just said or what my thought was. Nothing matters.

"I totally agree with you," I say, trying not to slur my words, hoping they fit the occasion.

She looks at me and shakes her head, as if I am failing dismally. Then she turns back to the news.

I have a splitting headache and I go to the en suite. When I vomit, it is a relief, and my headache eases. I go to bed and sprawl fully clothed on my back. I wake up with a snort and I know I am snoring resoundingly. I am getting insufficient random-eye-movement sleep, and tomorrow I will be catching up by micro-sleeping. When the irascible Ruth comes to bed, she prods me awake, pushing me over on to my side to reduce my snoring.

Later that night, as I sit on the toilet retching, I decide I have reached the end of this particular road. If I keep going, I will kill myself and maybe innocent people, too. Vicki will not want to be with me. It is rock bottom, and I resolve there and then to give up drinking. Whenever I want a drink, I will have a cup of coffee instead and bury myself in my work. I intend to get to the top of Canoil, and alcohol is not going to stop me.

Instead of becoming drunk, my desire for Vicki's approval is my strength to stop drinking.

The next morning at 10.00am, I check the time in England: 5.00pm, a good time to call on a Saturday. I dial Vicki's number.

"Hello?"

"Vicki, it's Selwyn!"

"Sorry, Selwyn. I can't talk now. I have to meet someone. Are you okay?"

"Yes. Are you?"

"Yes. Oh, there was something. You are with Canoil, aren't you?"

"Yes." I wondered what was coming.

"The BBC had a story last night about Bigeria. They say Canoil is paying the oil money to the government, who are the Fetani tribe, while the people where the oil comes from are the Hotus and starving. Do you know about that?"

"A little."

"Well, I am totally pissed off with Canoil. For God's sake, behave responsibly and give some of your oil money to the Hotus." Vicki is very idealistic and is always on the side of the underdog.

"I agree, Vicki, but there is not much I can do. The Board are against it."

"Those fuckers should be bombed. Find a way of getting the money to the Hotus, or I will be very disappointed in you!"

"I have no authority to access that account."

"What's your position?"

"GM Exploration and Production."

"Really? Well, there can't be many prats above you. Bend some ears and kick some asses."

"It won't work."

"You won't know until you have tried, Selwyn. Goodbye."

"Bye."

Phew! I hang up sadly. I know Vicki can be a fiery idealist , but I have never before heard her so wound up about anything. Besides wanting to make a difference, I wonder what can have rattled the bars of her cage.

A few months later, I have to go to London and I drop in on Vicki.

"I have quit drinking," I tell her.

"Oh, Selwyn! That's fantastic. You must be so happy about that."

Vicki explains to me that I am fearful of Ruth when she threatens to leave and take the children away from me. Because I choose not to fight this, I used to flee, using alcohol as an anaesthetic to take away the anxiety. How will I flee now?

I tell Vicki that now I stay working, when I would previously have been drinking.

"That's not the way to deal with Ruth. You have merely shifted the need, and it will emerge somewhere else. What should you do?"

"I don't know."

"Stand up to her," said Vicki. "Then you won't have the anxiety from her bullying."

"Easier said than done."

"You need help. Here is the address of someone who can help you."

She gives me the card of a psychotherapist. I have no idea what that might entail and I am too suspicious to find out. I have read some of Freud's writing, and it is unscientific rubbish. Having Vicki's understanding helps me to resist alcohol, to have the strength to stay away from the horrid stuff. Now I can concentrate on overcoming my unhappiness from my marriage to Ruth by working harder and drinking cups of coffee.

Rule 75: *Alcoholism may anaesthetize awareness of a dysfunctional marriage.*

CHAPTER 76   IMPASSIONATE REFUSAL

When I want a drink, I bury myself in work. I work to excess. I become intoxicated with work. At the same time, I know I have to deal with the underlying problem: the uncompromising Ruth.

She tries to bolster our flagging relationship with spending. That summer, Ruth and I look into investing in a residential unit overlooking Lake Louise in the Rocky Mountains. We have inspected several with an agent and are having lunch in a café.

"We should put a deposit on that last one," says Ruth, "before someone else does."

"What do you like about it?"

"I just like it. I have a good feeling about it."

"I like it, too, but I don't think it is as good as the one with the sundial."

"Who wants a sundial?"

"No, I mean the one with a sundial that had an extra room, and the lawn is big enough for a tennis court."

"I liked the other one more. It has a better view up the valley."

"I don't think so. Its view is about the same! I've told you my reasons. What else do you prefer about it?"

"I told you. Everything."

"Well, that can't be right. It is more expensive, for one thing."

"That's because it's better!"

"Yes, but in what way is it better? It has one less room."

"Well, I liked it more! It seemed better to me. I want to put a deposit on it."

"Hold on! What's the rush? If we miss out, there are others. Let's go back and have a second look."

"No. I am going now to give them a cheque, and if you don't like it you can lump it."

"You'll be buying it for yourself. I won't sign the contract."

"If you don't, I'm leaving you and taking the kids, you selfish bastard."

"Selfish? I'm prepared to compromise but you won't."

"No, you aren't. You always oppose whatever I want."

"I'm not opposing you."

"Good. Well, that's settled. I'll see you at the car." Ruth pays a deposit from our joint account and I sign the contract. We only stay there a few times. We sell the place several years later at a loss.

As soon as I put out a fire in one place it springs up again in another. Ruth has a very high inertia in real estate evaluation. Once she gets an idea in her head, nothing will stop her. Her gut-feeling approach is part of her personality and clashes with my analysis and caution. She imagines that she has a shrewd ability to pick winners, whereas her record is well below average. To have any say at all, I have to make huge compromises and capitulate.

I am like a plant trying to grow in her shade, unable to photosynthesize or gain enough nourishment. I am withering, parts of my brain are dying and I am depressed. Ruth considers herself an expert in knowing her sexual needs, for which I am an inert object. Because I have to abase myself to her, as if I am a machine for her sexual use, my dislike for her has grown into repulsion.

With Ruth, sex is homage, a service or duty that I must provide when I am able. Sex with Ruth is an ugly and humiliating act that she dominates without passion. Her sex is unfriendly, as if she is inured to passion. It is humiliating to me to be treated like a vibrator. One day, after a particularly mechanical performance, I decide I will stop having sex with her, for my own self-respect. Stopping sex with her is the only way I can redress the humiliation I am suffering.

I have made up my mind and I never turn back. No more do I have sex with her.

Although she is distant, having Vicki's support means a great deal to me. Endlessly, I long for her. I know I would have an ideal relationship with her. I cannot use alcohol to flee from Ruth, for my mental health, but I can take a stand against her. I start to contest Ruth's domination in every area of our relationship.

When she next touches me, as she does when she wants me to start, I turn away from her. I am going to retain what is left of my self-respect.

"What's the matter with you?" she demands.

"I don't want to do it," I reply.

For her, as a member of the Silent Generation, doing one's duty is most important. It is outside her understanding that I am declining further participation. For some time she considers that it reflects a personal failing of mine.

"Are you ill?" Ruth asks.

"No."

"Is there someone else? Are you writing to that Vicki in England?"

"No." I do write but she doesn't respond to my letters. So it doesn't count.

"Are you impotent?"

"No."

I had masturbated in bed that morning. I thought she would have noticed. Over the past week, Nicola and Michael have heard the vituperative Ruth address me with suspicion, ridicule, humiliation, insults and threats. They are worried that Dad has something wrong with him, something bad for Mummy they will have to put up with.

"Are you homosexual?" Ruth asks.

"No."

She makes this accusation in front of Nicola and Michael, as we are having breakfast. Nicola has left school, and is waiting to start uni. Michael will be going into the senior school next.

Nicola thinks for a moment, and then turns to me.

"Do you have sex with men, Daddy?" Her eyes and mouth are wide, aghast.

Michael stops eating and looks at me.

"No, I do not," I say. "Your mother is making things up."

"Why?" persists Nicola.

"Because he won't tell me!" Ruth bursts into tears and throws down a plate onto the tiled floor. It smashes loudly. "Your father is being nasty to me, and I am trying to find out why."

"Dad, why are you being nasty to Mum?" Nicola asks.

"I am not. I won't do something she wants me to."

"What thing?"

"Use your imagination, Nicola," I say.

"You won't have sex with her, will you? Why not?"

"I don't want to; that's all."

"Why does he have to do it?" Nicola asks Ruth. "Who says?"

Ruth shakes her head.

"You should respect him," says Nicola."You can't force someone to have sex."

Eventually, Ruth infers why I am refusing to have sex with her. My freedom from her attempts to dominate me is more important. I will not succumb to her. Like Nicola's horse, that panics and breaks its halter when it is tied up, I am too strong to be re-trained to obedience. It is a heavy blow to her self-esteem.

Giving up sex with the wooden Ruth is easier than giving up alcohol. Not having sex with another woman is harder. I ogle attractive females avidly. Sex has become a scarce-remembered pleasure of a past life. As long as I live with Ruth, I will be loyal. I become very interested in and aroused by other females. The best of them is Vicki, a focal point for my imagination during masturbation, which becomes a regular part of my life.

Ruth is distraught in our loveless marriage, but I am happier now that my disaffection is out in the open. Our eventual parting is assumed, when the children leave home. I look forward to the prospect of going to Vicki.

Too late, Ruth tries to turn the clock back. She is in the kitchen when I come in to make myself a cup of instant coffee. Neither of us speaks, and the atmosphere is strained. I look at her but say nothing.

"What do you think the problem is between us?" Ruth asks.

"We have different affinities," I answer, obfuscating the domination issue. If I raise it, there is no chance that she will change her behaviour to respect me. "You are a Silent and I am a Boomer."

"Those are American marketing classifications. Why should that affect us?"

"It is not just marketing, but lifestyle differences. Silents are older, staid, quiet types who look for authority to do their duty. That's you to a tee. Boomers are younger, self-centred, hedonistic, disrespectful of authority but hard workers."

"Self-centred is right," she says nastily.

"It's your own fault. You lied about your age. If you had been truthful I would never have got together with you."

"I did not lie."

"You misled me!"

"Well, you misled me. You kept me waiting for a year while you had a grand old time in South America. Then you came back and dumped me!"

"When I changed my mind, you didn't have to take up with me."

"Maybe I was desperate."

"You told me you loved me."

"So?"

I want out. Absence of truthfulness in a person damns them in my eyes. Lying in an application is acceptable when it does not reduce performance, but blatant lying to secure a position and then defaulting on performance is another.

When Ruth eventually realizes that the reason I won't have sex with her is because I don't want to, it is as if a bubble has burst. She is devastated. It is a massive insult to her femininity. We both know, without saying it, that what love there was has died and is beyond resuscitation. I know that I will never have sex with her again. We carry on, subdued, respecting the corpse of our marriage.

In the last few years I had given up alcohol, smoking, and now sex with Ruth. The opiates for my anxiety are now my work and also eating. I begin to put on weight. As I become more and more engrossed in running Canoil, my time spent at work is increasing, but anxiety about the business has become a frequent visitor. There is little in my life except my work, and overworking is becoming a habit.

The snag about dedicating myself to my job is that I am too emotionally involved with it.

"You need to relax more," my boss, CEO Robert Walker, tells me. "Go fishing or hunting. Get your mind onto something else."

But I don't have anyone to do such things with. Being an immigrant is not easy. Since I hung up my rugby boots, the only activity I have found in Edmonton where I can fully take part, is my work with Canoil. I used to socialize with Ruth's family, but when I was drinking heavily I got pretty obnoxious, and she stopped inviting me to her family gatherings.

I am surprised one evening when Ruth tells me she is going to telephone my brother, Howard, in England.

"Why?" I ask.

"I am telling him I am on his side."

Howard and I are on opposite sides in a family feud. I have stopped corresponding with Howard for his cruel treatment of our father, for locking him away in a home for demented people. Although he has dementia, his mental faculties are often normal. It is another instance of his bullying. For me, it is the final straw. I have not had any contact with Howard for several years. Nor has Ruth.

"Why are you on his side?" I ask Ruth.

"You're in the wrong," she accuses. "You should leave it to Howard."

"He is bullying my father. I want you to have nothing to do with him, until he moves Dad into a better place. If you are not with me on this, you are against me."

"I'm against you." She moves towards me, pushing out her jaw in a caricature of rude defiance. She is normally physically timid, and I wonder what she is up to. "You're a pig," she says. She steps even closer, right up to me. Suddenly, I realise what her game is.

"Stop that, Mum," says Michael.

"Go ahead: call him," I say and walk off.

But she doesn't.

I have heard of this ploy. I suspect a solicitor is advising her to provoke me into hitting her, with a witness present. Then she will have the moral high ground in deserting me. She knows how to push my buttons. However, all she achieves is to discover I abhor domestic violence.

After that, any pretence of intimacy disappears. We deal with each other with minimal civility at arm's length, as if our only joint interest, other than Michael and Nicola, is economic. I move into the spare bedroom.

I begin to feel better. I cease to feel even a tiny bit depressed. It seems most likely to follow from the change in my relationship with Ruth.

My life continues to be stressful, both at home and at work, but I have my special messianic powers to deal with situations intuitively. Out with stressful thinking.

"What do you think we should do about Misoto?" I ask Manfred.

I hand him the folder.

Next morning he brings it back with his analysis.

"Insist on transparency. Ronson will back us – I checked. Tell Misoto who we are giving the money to and how much. Perhaps the Bigerian government can be shamed into more humane use of the money."

"Hmm. Okay, where do we start?"

"Get the account numbers and names we pay the money to now."

"I've tried that," I say, "through Bob, but Gooder refused."

"That was when you were working for Bob," Manfred says. "Gooder had a down on Bob. Persuade Gooder yourself."

He doesn't take much persuading.

"Here they are." He gives me a page with half a dozen names, each with a Swiss bank account number. "These are Okonjo's cronies – senior Ministers, probably. They take 50% between them, Okonjo gets 20% and the other five get 6% each. This one at the bottom is the Government account, where the other 50% goes. You realize this information is dynamite. It could start a civil war and cut off our oil supply. So use it carefully."

Here is the evidence that Canoil has been cooperating in diverting a huge amount of Bigerian public money into corrupt private accounts. I have an idea and talk to Bob.

I phone Vicki. "I have discovered we are paying half the oil money into private Swiss bank accounts. Do not quote me or Canoil on that."

"I suspected as much," she replies. "The thing is, how are you going to stop it, without causing a civil war?"

"Our goal is to get relief to the famine victims in Bigeria," I say. "I am talking with Bob about making Okonjo an offer he can't refuse."

"About bloody time, too," she says.

It is safer for Vicki if she doesn't know the details. She showed me how she locks the front door at night, on my last visit to her place, buried in the dark Wiltshire lanes. There are two separate strong mechanical locks with keys, and an electronic alarm system. They are evidence of the lonely frightened nights she passes there, but she does not complain to me. I want to stay with her, to keep her safe. My hope is growing of being with Vicki soon.

"How are Nicola and Michael?" she asks.

"Michael has a girl friend."

"How do you feel about that?"

"They seem to have become intimate very quickly."

"Well, we know who he gets that from."

I change the subject. "Nicola wants a gap year overseas."

"She could stay here and get a job in Salisbury."

"That would be terrific. Thank you, Vicki. I'll let you know."

It would be good for Nicola, as she needs a lifestyle role model for an accomplished single female. Nicola is keen but Ruth is opposed.

I tell Vicki of my withdrawal from sex with Ruth.

"Is there anything left holding you together," Vicki asks, "apart from your kids?"

"No, but we still live together and do things together because of the kids."

When I talk about it, I feel better, less stressed, immediately. I realise my marriage has to end. I want to tell Vicki when this will be, but I am not yet able to focus on what the end will be like.

Rule 76: *Good sex is a necessary but not sufficient condition for a loving marriage.*

CHAPTER 77   JEALOUSY PROVOKED

As arranged with Vicki, I find the key in its hiding place, disarm the alarm and let myself in. Vicki is politically active and fears reprisal. I bring in my suitcase from my rented car and leave it in the hall. Then I put the chain on the door again.

The sitting room is as I remember it from my last visit, several years before. It is comfortable, with antique furnishings. The ceiling is crisscrossed by blackened hand-hewn wooden beams, and the outer walls are thick and irregular, with small windows, so that the room is rather dark. The kitchen is modern with many appliances. I make myself a cup of tea and sit down to relax after my journey from Edmonton. I hear a tractor in the field next to the house. From the clatter, I deduce it is trimming the hedge.

Twenty minutes later there is a knock on the front door. I undo the chain and open it. There stands a stocky rustic figure, bewhiskered, in a green boiler suit, with canvas leggings over hobnail boots, and wearing a battered trilby hat . His complexion has the ruddy hue of one who works outdoors, and he looks muscular from physical work. I cannot tell his age; it might be anywhere between thirty and fifty. The sound of the tractor outside has ceased. He stands up close to me, as if I am on his territory. Omitting any salutations or niceties, he speaks plainly.

"Ooer you, then?" he asks me. His accent is West Country, with burrs and questions signalled by raising of pitch on the final syllable. His narrowed eyes bore into me.

"I'm a friend of Vicki," I tell him defensively, feeling like an intruder. "From Canada."

"Canada! I didn't know she had any friends coming from Canada," he grumbles, as if she should have told him. "And where might you know 'er from?" he persists, as if he is running a security check.

"We were at university together."

"Which university would that be?"

"Liverpool."

"I see," he sounds disappointed, as though he won't be able to throw me out. "Ow long might you be 'ere fer, den?"

"Just a couple of days. I'm on my way to visiting my family in Yorkshire and have dropped in here, from Heathrow."

His face is inexpressive as if he doesn't entirely believe me. He seems excessively zealous. Either he is a current lover or an over-possessive friend or neighbour. It is doubtful that an employee could be so bold, unless his duties include security. I feel jealous, and I can see that he is feeling the same way. I think he may want a fight, but I am careful to talk about the brevity of my visit and my distant home, and that seems to defuse the situation.

"You're a friend of Vicki's, are you?" I venture.

"You could say that," he says.

His eyes pierce into me, as if his relationship with her is a private matter.

"Oi looks after 'er garden. I'll be around if there's any problems."

He turns abruptly and stomps away. The tractor revs up and resumes its working.

When Vicki comes home, a couple of hours later, it is almost dark. I glimpse him hanging around outside. He could see us hug and go inside hand in hand. I hug her in front of a window, so he can see, if he is watching, how things stand between us.

"There was a man earlier, asking me questions about what I was doing here – a man with a beard."

"Oh, that's Colin," she says, as if that would explain everything. "He's been trimming the hedges."

It reminds me of Mellors the gamekeeper in "Lady Chatterley's Lover", a man who once enjoyed a high social standing but of necessity has become a gardener. I wonder if Vicki has taken her loneliness to him by instinct rather than by design. She has no impotent husband encouraging her impregnation by someone within her class, but an affair with her gardener would breach class etiquette and she would keep it a secret. Probably, like me, he has fallen for her and is jealous. I keep a question mark over the incident.

With my marriage reduced to a holding operation, I imagine getting together with Vicki soon. I will leave Ruth to rule as she wants, as soon as Nicola and Michael will be advantaged by my living in England, with Vicki as their stepmother. Vicki would make an excellent stepmother, placing the children's needs before her own. Vicki seemed to encourage me to stay with Ruth when our children were small, because they would be badly affected by a separation. Vicki could now be a great help to Michael and Nicola.

Michael is rather a wild young man and could go off the rails. Ruth has allowed him to have an unsavoury girlfriend. She is into dope, has other much older boyfriends and is unemployed.

"He has been skipping school and hanging out with Carla and her layabout friends," I tell Ruth, who seems oblivious to what is going on.

"The school will deal with it."

"I don't think so. They're into dope."

"I find Carla quite charming, in a punkish way."

"You mean the razor blade earrings?"

"It's just a fad. They copy the Heavy Metal groups."

"That's what I thought. Dope and head banging. Michael should be working hard. I want to hold a meeting with the school. Will you come?"

"I suppose. But that won't get him away from Carla."

"What will?"

"Experience," she says. "He will find out that Carla is going nowhere and trying to hold him back with her."

"By the time he realizes that, it may be too late for him. I want him at that meeting, even if I have to drag him."

"Why?"

"I want him to realize he has a problem."

"What problem?"

"Carla is his problem. This has gone on for too long."

I know Ruth's angle. Michael may be reacting to our marriage breakdown.

The meeting with the school is brief. Our marriage problems are not raised. Michael is required to sign in and out at the office every day. The deputy is to supervise that.

"Putting a band-aid on it won't heal it," Ruth says afterwards.

"At least we will know if the infection is worsening," I reply.

It does get worse.

Michael is so distracted by Carla that his final year at school is about to become a disaster. One night, on the way to bed, I catch him studying.

"This is a pleasant change," I say. "Has anything happened that I need to know about?"

He puts down his pen and looks at me. "I am finished with that thieving bitch, Carla. You are right, she is no good: too lazy to work and expects me to support her."

"How is she taking it?"

"I haven't heard from her."

"How long has it been since you finished?"

"Four days."

"Well done, son. Keep up the good work and you might just scrape into engineering, if that's what you want still."

"I'm just working as hard as I can to catch up."

"That's the way. Good night."

Vicki is an activist in the UK against Canoil's role in Bigeria. Already she has been involved in picketing outside our British affiliate's board meeting in London. When I am visiting next, she holds a meeting while I am there.

"Selwyn, when you told me you were coming, I arranged for our FOOD group to come around and talk with you about Canoil and Bigeria."

"I could eat some food. What have you got, Vicki?"

"Selwyn, you don't need food. You should eat only at mealtimes."

"Okay, I'll try. Now, how many are you expecting?"

"Only about four of them. It's a subcommittee."

"What do you talk about?"

"Okonjo is carrying on the same as always," Vicki asserts, as if it is my fault. "I am losing a lot of credibility with the girls. They think I should stop talking with you until you do something."

"I have been working on Bob, and he is fully onside with paying Misoto. But Gooder and the Board won't hear of it."

Vicki slams her fist down on the stainless steel draining board, making the china and cutlery bounce. "For fuck's sake, what's wrong with them? Can't they see people are dying like flies over there?"

"They will not accept it as their responsibility. Bob is sticking his neck out in reminding them at every Board meeting—"

Vicki hurls her wune glass at me and I duck just in time. "It is their responsibility. They are a fucking disgrace. We are going to picket your next Board meeting."

"It would be counter-productive," I tell her. "The Board will never be influenced by illegal action. They would show that they are responsible to shareholders, not the public, and especially not a group acting illegally. Be patient. Bob is providing them with photos and statistics of deaths, and we think they will soon come around."

"Tell Bob," she spits the word, "that we are totally pissed off with Canoil. We have stopped buying Canoil products. Our membership is growing fast."

"Now calm down," I say. "Tell me how you see the problem and how Canoil should respond."

When I draw Vicki out, she calms down, and we have a lot to talk about.

Her group arrives at the time arranged, and after introductions, we get straight down to business. Vicki starts the ball rolling.

"We had a meeting last night to discuss it. We decided that the Bigerian people need outside help to get organised for development."

"You and I talked about that, Vicki. Did you tell them we are going to pay all the oil money into the Government's account, not half into private Swiss bank accounts?"

"Yes. We thought that was a good start."

"Uh-oh. You want us to do something more? I told you I am doubtful about getting Board approval for that. Anyway, go on. What else?"

A middle-aged Australian man who says he had worked in Bigeria asks me, "Can Canoil take some responsibility for developing fair government in Bigeria? Everyone except Okonjo and his cronies wants stronger regional governments."

A woman who worked in publishing interrupted him. "Canoil has a vital role in nurturing Bigeria's internal stability and helping the tribal groups behave responsibly."

"What can Canoil do?" I ask.

"You can prevent the national government usurping all the power."

"You mean insist on dealing with regions?" asked a youngish man who is studying international relations.

"Exactly."

"But projects like your Panypo pilot plant are of national and international consequence," he says.

"I agree."

"You cannot pay all the Bigerian oil money to tin-pot regional outfits," the first man says. "What makes you think you should?"

"Canoil normally pays whoever administers oil production. So if it is a regional

authority—"

"That's right. Pay them. They are closer to the oil action. But if the benefits are to be spread nationally, why does not Canoil pay equal amounts per capita to each of the regional governments?"

"Hold on," I say. "We do not want to govern them. How that is done is their business. We prefer to give it to a national government to distribute."

"We know. That's easiest in the short term. You have seen the dog's breakfast that Okonjo has made of that. Enough is enough. Canoil will be doing everyone except Okonjo and his cronies a big favour by distributing the funds fairly."

"Could Canoil set the ball rolling by sending the oil money to the regional government offices?" Vicki asked."It would be a major change to the power system in Bigeria, but it seems worth a try."

"Fortunately, our contract does not give the official, address or bank account where the money has to be paid. It merely says 'to be paid to the Government of Bigeria.' So we would be legal," I say.

"You had better tell them it's coming first," warned the middle-aged man."You can ask for account details from the regional offices."

"They'll have a lovely surprise when you transfer hundreds of millions of dollar," says Vicki.

"No less than they deserve. Thanks, Vicki. Thanks, you guys. That's terrific. I think it may work."

After they had gone, I tell Vicki, "That went well."

It is the first time Vicki and I have worked together on something. Her idealism and intuitive grasp of the problem have left me amazed. There is no limit to what we could achieve together. .

"I can't do much at present, until I'm CEO," I say. "It may not be long. Bob has made himself unpopular by advocating we support the rebels. If he keeps going, he could get the chop. If I keep my head down, they may pass the ball to me. Then I'll be able to do some of the things we have been talking about. Coffee?"

"No, thanks."

I get myself a cup.

"It is so good that you have quit drinking. How long has it been?"

"A year."

"Do you feel any better for it?"

"Much better. I was poisoning myself."

"You seem tense."

"Drinking used to relax me."

"What is making you tense?"

"I am not sure. I get wound up, most of the time."

"Is it Ruth still? We talked about how to insulate myself from her demands, her moods, her nagging and her tantrums. Are you doing that?"

"Yes, that is much better now."

"Are you still fretting and worrying from your childhood fear of desertion that we talked about?"

"Maybe."

"What do you do about it?"

"I work. It helps me relax."

"Eating soothes it, too, doesn't it?"

I pull in my bulging tummy. Since stopping drinking, I have had an insatiable hunger.

As usual, she recommends counselling. As usual, I do nothing about it. I am too busy in my job to have much time for thought about myself or anyone else. I am so intent on managing without alcohol that my other dependencies change for the worse.

Rule 77: *Beware that consumption which, prevents the scratch but not the itch.*

CHAPTER 78   CHIEF OILMAN

One morning, as I am working my way through the in-tray in my Edmonton office, I get a call from Bob in Toronto.

"I have put in my resignation to Ralph," he says. "I can no longer support Okonjo while he steals the food from millions of starving Bigerians. I want you to know this is what really happened, before the spin doctors get hold of it."

"Will Ralph accept it?"

"Oh yes. He is expecting it."

It saddens me that Bob is going. He is a man of great integrity and the type of engineer who operates from long experience and gut feelings, rather than by economic reasoning and rational thought, as I try to do. In one story about him, he showed great bravery in going back into a wellhead fire at great risk to himself and dragging out an injured roustabout. I hope I will be considered for his job, although my credentials may be less impressive.

I feel a little guilty for encouraging Bob to get nasty with Gooder about the famine victims, resulting in his resignation and my getting his job. Bob should have persisted; his resignation won't change any minds.

When I reach my office, there is a message to call Ralph Gooder in Toronto. His secretary is expecting my call and puts me straight through.

"Selwyn, I have news for you," the Chairman says without any preliminaries. "Bob has a medical problem and wants to retire. I want you to take over as CEO. Bob says that he supported you when you needed to lead people. I will be available to help you with that.

"The other day I sat beside Manfred on a plane. He is sensitive to politics and people. He has been helping you with communications, I hear. You should continue having him check what you send out.

"There is one thing I forgot to mention. The Board recognises that you are a highly creative problem-solver, and that is what we want you to spend your time on. I want you as the Board's heat-seeking missile who identifies, analyses and stops problems before they hit us. It is a difficult job. The Board is pleased with how you have been handling the Bigeria situation and they have full confidence in you. Sometimes you have, er, advanced thoughts, and these can be misunderstood. We want you to run those types of communications past me. Manfred can screen them out for me. Is that going to be a problem?"

I am a little concerned that Ralph sees limits to my leadership ability. Everyone has an Achilles heel, and this is mine. I know I have put people off by being too directive, and it has been good having Bob's support. I hope this will continue under Ralph. I will be running my own show, with Ralph's and Manfred's approval. Ralph knows the bare details of my mental illness, and this is a precaution. It is unusual but I can live with it. As Messiah, I must expect to suffer to save the World.

"No, that will be okay."

"Good. We're expecting great things from you, Selwyn. These days, most of the increase in gasoline cost at the pump goes back to the wellhead. The action is going to be in production. There is no-one in the country who knows more about the producing game than you do. We are putting our trust in your instincts."

"That's kind of you," I say, "but as you know, I go by the logic of the technology and rational economics, rather than instincts."

"That's what I mean. I want you to take the heat out of the enhanced recovery issue, here in Canada and in Bigeria. As you know, Walker had a bee in his bonnet about helping the starving Bigerians. The Board has made a donation of $2 millions to aid agencies to provide help in Bigeria. Bob was out of line with shareholders. I think it would be good for us if you had a meeting with Charles. Rumour has it that Ottawa is going to take over oil exploration and production licencing from the provinces. We need to state our opposition early. Ottawa already has too much control through taxes."

Charles Picard, the mercurial Prime Minister, is pitting his government against foreign-owned oil companies. It is an aspect of Picardmania, the excitement of teenagers for Canadian nationalism. Picard's government is bringing Quebec back into a

Canada separated from Britain. Canoil, being largely US-owned, is vulnerable.

Gooder continues, "I took the liberty of sending Ian across to you with the Kingair this morning, in case you want it. You will always need to check with me on political implications. I know what you are capable of, Selwyn, and I am counting on you to be a moderate and reliable leader."

My heart sinks. Moderate: he had used the word carefully, as if he had planned to drop it in to tell me that my immoderate workaholism is a problem. If he knows, then it must be right around the office. I don't know how he has found out, as I put in my long hours when most people have gone home. My managers put in extra time, following my example. They could have complained that I am too demanding to work for. I will have to behave in a more exemplary manner. I need to kick my workaholism. The thought makes me hungry.

"The job is yours if you want it. You can do it from over there, in Calgary. Our centre of gravity has moved over there now that Calgary has direct flights to everywhere. I will be here in Toronto, and the Board will meet here. I would like you to move to Calgary as soon as possible. I will keep in touch with you constantly, but you will be running your own show, using me and the Board as a rubber stamp."

I get most satisfaction in life from my job. I have let my marriage and Vicki take second and third place. This promotion could ruin my private life. The job could come between Vicki and me even further. It will be demanding, and my secretary will fill my time with Canoil business meetings. I might not be able to get to the UK with time to see her as often. Perhaps my kids will leave home soon, and the impossible Ruth and I will separate. She will get half of everything. Perhaps I can persuade Vicki to join me in Calgary. Otherwise, I will need to have enough to be with Vicki in England and eventually retire there.

"What rewards are you offering?" I ask.

I know that after today it will be difficult to get an increase.

"You'll get more than Bob," Ralph told me. "The job is bigger now. We've had McNabs compare it with others, and you would get $15 million, plus up to $5 million in shares at issue price, depending on performance, plus the usual perks. What do you say?"

"Thank you, Ralph. I accept."

We talk briefly about his priorities. It is easy for me to understand him, from my familiarity with his speeches and press releases in the book I made for him.

"Congratulations, Selwyn. I look forward to working with you."

"I will do my best for Canoil, Sir."

"Ralph to you. Bye."

I have an extraordinary floating feeling. At last, it has happened: I am CEO. I have been working towards this all of my career. I have been doing the Division Manager's job satisfactorily for the past five years, and there is little challenge remaining. This change is just what the doctor ordered.

When I hear a car horn from the driveway, I find Nicola in her car. It is chock full of her belongings. Ruth is there looking glum.

"Where are you going?" I ask..

"Toronto," she said. "I've been accepted to do a PhD."

"Congratulations. What is your area of research?"

"Social psychology."

"That will be fun. Don't you want to have a farewell party?"

"Nah, I hate long goodbyes. I'm leaving now."

"Where are you going to stay?" I ask Nicola.

"I know someone in Regina. If I get tired, I'll get a motel."

"Here's some cash, all I have on me. It's not much."

"Gee. Thanks, Dad."

"Have you said goodbye to Michael?"

"Yeah. I hope you'll all look after each other."

"I'll miss you, Nicola.."

"Me too, Dad," she says, her eyes moist.

She drives away.

"It had to happen one day," I say to Ruth.

She says nothing and walks inside, her head down.

When I tell Vicki of my promotion, for once she is impressed.

"Chief Executive?" says Vicki. "Holy cow! I suppose you are stuck in Canada now."

"That's true, but the job makes high demands, and I won't be able to do it for long. Ten years maximum."

"Ten years? That's forever. How old are your kids now?"

"Nicola is 23 and Michael is 21."

I tell her about Nicola's leaving. I begin to mist up and go croaky. Vicki waits for me to continue.

"Vicki, I had a lump in my throat. She had lived with us all her life, and now she has gone far away, all by herself."

Vicki is silent as I recall how Nicola gets out of her car and puts her arms around me.

"Vicki, I watched her leave through my tears."

"Were they tears of happiness?" Vicki asks.

"Of loss. She left so abruptly. I am grieving for her."

"Maybe you and Ruth's differences —"

"Drove her away. Yes."

"Have you heard from her?"

"Yes. She has found a place to live in Toronto and has started a PhD."

"You should be happy that she's doing what she wants. You still have Michael with you. What is he doing?"

"He's staying here to finish honours, then doing a PhD in Calgary."

"So he will be living with you. How long will all that take?" she says.

"A minimum of four years."

"If Nicola stays in Toronto, then it's just Michael who needs you in Calgary."

I may not want to quit Canoil after four years. Vicki does not say anything.

"Why don't you come over here to live?" I ask.

"I've told you a hundred times."

She has too. Vicki will not consider coming to live in Canada. It is as if the very walls of her home are imploring her not to leave. I must wait for Michael to finish at uni before I can come back to the UK. It is easy to imagine living with her. It would be good to get back to a decent climate where I can jog and hike in the winter instead of being cooped up indoors. My university friends are in the UK, and we could visit them at weekends. It should be possible to get a good job. But Vicki is the major attraction.

"Maybe I'll get fired soon. It's a tough job."

"I won't hold my breath."

My plans are not encouraging for her, and we both know it.

Caroline, my secretary, will move down to Calgary at the weekend. She calls the Prime Minister's secretary, arranges a brief meeting for tomorrow and tells Ian to get the Kingair ready to fly to Ottawa.

I send Manfred home to get some clothes for me. I stay on at the office reading through the CEO's emails forwarded from Bob's old office. Caroline brings coffee and biscuits. She tells me that the CEO's car and driver are waiting for me in the underground car park, to take me to the airport.

"Can you get me Prime Minister Okonjo's email address? You may have to telephone."

"Okay," she replies.

I write this email.

Dear Prime Minister,

"Our company is concerned about the welfare of your nation's famine victims, especially those who live near the oil resources that produce the oil we purchase from the Bigerian Government and who should be sharing in your people's prosperity that our payments can provide.

We have received a request from General Misoto for us to send to his organisation 50% of our payments for Bigerian oil. Payments to General Misoto would not accord with our contract with the Bigerian Government. However, we will confirm our responsibility to all the Bigerian people by paying 100% into the one government account that was previously used for 50%. Payment of 50% into Swiss bank accounts will cease. This change is expected to provide more relief for famine victims throughout Bigeria, according to need.

Would you cooperate with a UN team appointed to inspect the implementation of an enlarged relief programme?

We will review the situation in three months to determine whether there has been an increase in relief to famine victims throughout Bigeria, according to need. If it has not, a more devolved and transparent payment protocol will be adopted, within the terms of the contract, such that starving Bigerians obtain more food.

Yours truly,
Selwyn Archer
CEO, Canoil Ltd

I asked my secretary to check it.

"That's telling the bastard," she says.

"Watermark it strictly confidential," I say."I have sent a blind copy to Vicki."

Then I wrote another to Frank McGann, our General Manager in Akar.

Dear Frank,

Would you contact regional offices of the Bigerian Government that administer health, welfare and education to all parts of Bigeria without overlap. Request the following:

a) bank account number to receive equal per capita regional share of Canoil payments for oil purchase from Bigeria;

b) names of 3 officials representing health, welfare and education required to countersign all withdrawals from that account;

c) electoral roll population number and names.

Above to be received in this office by COB Friday.

Thank you

Selwyn Archer

CEO, Canoil Ltd

When I have finished sending these and looking though the paperwork, I take the lift down to the basement.

"May I drive you somewhere, Sir?"

The voice comes from the open driver's window of the CEO's Lincoln Continental with bulletproof windows. The door opens, and a wide man of about thirty, wearing an army camouflage suit, gets out. I have seen him there before, but we have never met. We shake hands. His grip crushes my hand painfully.

"My name is Thug, Sir," he says. "I do security and driving. I'll look after you, Sir. Is that okay, Sir?"

He is tall, solid and looks fit, with a ruddy complexion, as if he spends a lot of time in the open.

"Call me Selwyn," I say. "Did you say your name is Thug?"

"That's what they call me."

"How did you come by that name?"

"It's really Tug," he pronounces it carefully, "from working on tugboats in Vancouver. But my front teeth got knocked out playing rugby, in the army. Now they call me Thug."

He smiles, showing a wide gap in his front teeth. With his broken nose and cauliflower ears, it seems like an appropriate name. The front of Thug's car is set up as an arsenal, with a machine gun clipped under the roof, a machine pistol below the dashboard and a handgun in the driver side pocket. He pulls out a tear gas grenade, from under the drivers' seat.

"The best defence is attack," he says. "I have four of these babies under here."

I have difficulty doing up the safety belt. My body is a disgrace. I wish I could lose weight. Maybe I should get one of those stomach bag rings that stop you eating. Then I would have to do something else when I'm anxious, like pacing to and fro, changing feet, chomping or swallowing all the time.

"Would you take me to the Kingair?" I tell him. We set off for the airport. Thug asks if I am interested in what today's newspapers are saying. He gives me an insightful summary, laced with entertaining gossip he had heard from other drivers.

"The rebels in Bigeria have got the media on their side," he says. "There was a story on the radio how corrupt the Bigerian government is and that oil company CEOs are psychopaths with no feelings for the starving millions."

"Thanks for the tip. We think the Bigerian government is better than most," I tell Thug. "As for being a psychopath, it is difficult to help the people who are starving without starting a civil war. Then they would call us butchers or something."

Thug drove me around the airport to the private terminal where Ian is waiting with the Kingair. We have to wait for ten minutes until Manfred joins me with suitcases.

"See you in few days, Sir!" Thug says. "Have a good trip."

Rule 78: *Corporate hierarchies separate decision-making from real effects on real people.*

CHAPTER 79 INEFFICIENT RECOVERY

I am having breakfast in my hotel room in Ottawa when Manfred shows me a front-page story in the Toronto Star. There is a photo of cars queuing at a petrol station below the headline:

CANOIL RECOVERIES IMPROVE?

Prime Minister Picard told the Toronto Star in an exclusive interview today: "We are investigating why there has been no increase in recovery of oil underground, even though oil prices have increased. We want to know the oil companies' plans to adopt technologies capable of higher recoveries."

"We recover as much of an oil resource as is economical" said Selwyn Archer, newly appointed CEO of Canoil a week ago, at an emergency meeting of the Western Producers Forum. The Forum discussed the Government's concern that oil recovery is low.

"There is insufficient incentive to invest in expensive processes such as miscible flooding. The laboratory testing phase has been completed and we are engaged in field pilot testing. The process requires special conditions present at only one of our oilfields, Tundra Tar Sands," Archer said.

In an earlier test at their Silver Atoll oilfield, Canoil obtained 90% oil recovery, compared with the average recovery calculated by Alberta Resources Council of 30%.

"Oil producers are reluctant to invest in technology for higher recovery as they fear competition would increase oil supply and lower oil prices," said Angela Gillow, President of the Petroleum Conservation Action Group. "The companies restrict competition to exploration and use identical antiquated production technologies.

"If companies paid a rental based on oil remaining, instead of acreage, they would get more oil out of the ground instead of wasting it," she said.

"The resource rental idea was tried in the UK. It didn't work," Archer said. "Enhanced recovery costs an arm and a leg. We are waiting on the results of the miscible flood pilot test before committing to a demonstration plant."

Canoil commenced pilot plant testing at the Tundra Tar Sands five years ago. The company has shut down research into miscible flooding at its Calgary Production Research Laboratories.

A meeting of Prime Minister Charles Picard and CEO Selwyn Archer is planned for later today.

Walter Raschig, Staff Reporter, Technology, *Toronto Star*

I am pleased to see my name on the front page of the nation's most popular newspaper, and I ask Manfred to send a copy of the article to Vicki. I have not been in contact with her much lately. I want her to know that important matters are keeping me busy.

When I telephone, I think that she can't talk because there is someone with her who she doesn't want to hear us. It is abundantly clear that she doesn't want to talk to me now, and I wonder what has happened. I am jealous, but I forgive her for what I believe are casual relationships with men.

With an effort, I switch my attention to responding to the article.

"I wasn't expecting this to be dropped on us," I tell Manfred. "You would think the media are running the country. But Picard may have asked Raschig to write it."

"Hmm. It's quite likely," Manfred agrees.

"Are we going to have an answer for him?" I ask. "The meeting's at 4 pm."

"We could call off the meeting."

"We're here now. We can't call it off and slink away. Maybe we can use the meeting to find out what the government wants. We can start the negotiation ball rolling."

"I think you should get any negotiation checked by Ralph," says Manfred.

I scowled at him.

"Sorry. Just doing my job," he says.

"Dead right, you're sorry," I replied angrily."How can I be chief executive if I can't execute anything?"

Manfred helps himself to coffee and a bagel. He doesn't answer for a while.

"It sounds as though Antcliff has spilled the beans on Silver Attoll," Manfred says. "Canoil is leaking like a sieve."

"I know Raschig," I tell him."He was at the Forum. He has put the words in Picard's mouth. He has taken my comment, added to it the Silver Attoll information from someone in Canoil, perhaps Bob Walker or Graham Antcliff, and come up with two plus two equals five, an insult to oil companies' integrity. Oil company bashing is a popular sport. By the way, is this room safe?" Security is an issue as corporations compete for government favour.

"Yes, I checked with the hotel. They swept it yesterday just before we arrived," Manfred replies.

"Our strategy is to produce the best of the oil from a lease first," I say. "We pay as little in royalties and taxes as we can. Then we make a token investment in secondary recovery and obtain a little more oil. "

"Like the other companies," Manfred added.

"We never invest much in oil recovery—" I begin again.

"Because it is on leased land, not our own," Manfred interrupts.

"And profits would be readily visible and attract hefty taxes."

"Or even nationalisation," he says.

I lean back in my chair. "We always resist government intervention in our oil recovery operations."

"We prefer to explore for new oilfields," Manfred says to keep it going.

"Absolutely. Everyone does. We can keep to ourselves what we've found."

"We can shift profits to where we are making losses," he says.

"The situation is changing, Manfred," I say, munching on a bagel. "The World is running out of new oilfields, and oil companies have to work with governments. They have caught on that what we are doing is not in the national or public interest. They want us to invest in more efficient recovery methods."

"Like miscible flooding."

I nod. "Exactly. But miscible flooding is like opening a can of worms, eh, Manfred?"

"Why are they picking on us?" he asks, through a mouthful of bagel. "Why not pick on a car manufacturer? They get 20% energy efficiency at best. They waste more oil than we do! Our 30% is not bad."

"No, we waste more," I tell him. "We leave 70 out of 100 barrels underground, and of the 30 we do get out, there are only 20 left after refining and transporting to the pump. Cars waste 80% of that, that is, 16% of the initial oil. The 70% we leave underground is more than four times as much."

"I see," Manfred says. "The ball is in our court."

"Only 4% of the initial oil is useful. The car manufacturers will be in trouble, too, before long."

"Appalling, isn't it? The government is going to be difficult to deal with on this. The conservationists have a lot of traction with them."

I pour myself some coffee.

It is a shock to realize the size of this recovery problem that has sneaked up on us. "I suppose Canoil has to respond," I comment. "If this takes hold, it could turn the company upside down. My job could be on the line. I had Production Division before. And I sat on Silver Atoll."

He looks at me. "You had reason to. Silver Atoll is a special situation. The question is whether we will have to use miscible flooding in other places to stay in business."

I pause. "In a small way at first, only where we have to; don't you think?"

I am eating a croissant.

He reflects. "You mean, we should race to be second?"

I shake my head. "They'll see through that. We are biggest, and they expect us to lead the way. Our argument would be full of holes. It will be better to get the public to pay for miscible flooding, by tax concessions on existing production."

"Okay, now let's get to work. What do I tell the PM? It is going to be difficult to bullshit him on this one."

It is my job to get him off our back. He will expect assured results from an oil technology that is a game of chance. If it works, he will be the winner. If it does not work, how can I not be the loser?

Rule 79: *Leaseholders of a resource have less interest in sustaining it than the owners.*

CHAPTER 80   YES PRIME MINISTER

At 4.00pm I am shown into the Prime Minister's office. Charles Picard comes to greet me. We have met previously on several formal occasions, but never one on one.

"Good afternoon, Selwyn," he begins briskly.

"Good afternoon, Prime Minister."

"Congratulations on your new position. I look forward to working closely with you. Robert was a friend of mine, but I'm afraid he got rather carried away by the plight of those poor starving people. Anyway, we won't talk about that today. You asked for a meeting?"

"I want to find out the government's concern about oil recovery that you mentioned last week."

"Have you seen today's *Toronto Star*?"

"Yes. I am very concerned that our production technology is being perceived as less than optimum. We keep to standards that are world's best practice."

Picard remains standing, facing me, referring to a paper he holds.

"The behaviour of the oil industry is not acceptable to my government," he says doggedly. "You are operating a cartel with a 'slash and burn' mentality, worthy of subsistence farmers in developing countries, where more of the natural resource is available for the taking. That is not the situation with Canada's oil resources. Oil companies are not making enough investment in recovering all the oil before moving on. The technologies you use are basic and inefficient. When your returns dwindle, you cry poor, obtain tax concessions to move to a new plot and begin again. You leave behind you a trail of ruined oil reservoirs and mineral deposits. They are too far gone to be salvaged later. Your high profits have gone to your shareholders in the United States."

"Prime Minister," I say quietly, "Canoil operates lawfully. May I summarise Canoil's position in current legislation?"

I refer to notes Manfred has prepared.

"First, we are paying for leases that entitle us to extract unspecified amounts of minerals.

Second, we are required to install and maintain extraction facilities, of our own choosing.

Third, the amount we extract should be sustained according to the sustainability criteria.

Fourth, the percentage recovery of the extraction is one of several sustainability criteria.

Fifth, the government may not renew the lease if the lessee does not extract sufficient oil.

Sixth, and finally, leases do not preserve access to extract the remainder. Prime Minister, do you accept this as a fair summary of our position?"

Picard replies with disdain, "Do not imagine that by doing nothing illegal you and the other oil companies are behaving like good corporate citizens. You show a minimum of loyalty by investing as little in Canada as possible." His voice has increased steadily in volume and now he is yelling. "It is treason!"

He goes behind his desk and sits down, leaving me standing. I am filled with indignation that anyone, especially the Prime Minister, should criticize my company's lawful operations. I try not to let my resentment show in my voice.

"Prime Minister, our production operations have to be commercial, and where we can make a profit from secondary recovery, we invest accordingly."

Picard gets up, and we both sit at a small round table.

"Archer, do not give me that bullshit. I know you have been using transfer pricing to make your profits elsewhere. You are not going to fuck this nation on my watch, whatever the legislation is. We will change it. The picture that is emerging is that the oil companies are pulling the wool over our eyes. Primary production has been presented as tapping oil resources, getting something for nothing and therefore doing a good job. In reality, you are wasting oil willy-nilly, and I am going to stop you. Is that clear?"

"It is not something for noth—"

"Archer," he interrupts me, "you may be acting legally, but the Canadian people can see that your industry has dug itself into very deep hole, or shall I say bore? It won't do. My government is going to bring down legislation to make you act responsibly. Before you are granted a production lease, you are going to have to declare what technology you are going to use, and it will have to be one that recovers most of the oil. From now on, primary production methods alone will not be accepted. Does that make sense?"

My collar and tie are so tight they hurt, and I loosen them.

"Prime Minister, Canoil will only invest in technologies that appear to be profitable."

"Yes, of course. We will suspend royalties and taxes, until the investment is paid back."

My heart leaps. This is more than I thought we could get.

I reply steadily. "Prime Minister, I will have to consult with my colleagues and get back to you about it. The rocks in some oil reservoirs are too tight to recover much oil, and nothing worthwhile can be done about it. We would want a case-by-case evaluation of every secondary recovery proposal."

"Point taken, Archer. In a nutshell, you are saying that we should not force mineral companies to lose money, because they are willing to do what is reasonable. Is that your position?"

"Yes, Prime Minister."

"I don't believe it. I look forward to getting a detailed proposal from you on what is reasonable. Then we will see who is going to pay for it. Now, I have to leave you as I have a prior commitment in the House."

He shakes hands and is gone.

We return to Calgary. Manfred has driven down from Edmonton and collects us from the airport. We stay at a hotel. Next morning, everything goes pear-shaped. I awake to a yell from the forecourt. I come out on the balcony eating a croissant.

There is a shout, "No. Leave him. The police are coming!"

I hear car doors slamming and voices. When I look outside, I see Thug feeding an electrical cable over our balcony hand over hand. When I go across the balcony and look over, I see the bottom of a pair of boots. They are on the feet of a person being lowered down the side of the building held by the cable around his ankles. When he reaches the ground, Thug throws the rest of the cable down to him. The man unties himself and stands up.

"Where's my camera?" he shouts shakily up to Thug.

There is a movie camera and tripod on the balcony. Thug points to it and crooks his little finger at the cameraman menacingly. I presume the cameraman has climbed up to the balcony to get some candid shots of me. Thug has done his duty as my bodyguard.

The cameraman shakes his head, "No, I'm not going up there again."

"What's going on?" I ask Thug.

"Bastard was trying to film you through the window."

I take Thug inside, and grab a croissant and cup of coffee.

"Don't antagonise the press any more than you have to," I tell him quietly but firmly.

"Yes, I know. This was necessary," Thug says. "They won't try any stunts like that again."

"Thank you, Thug."

"My pleasure," he says.

I go outside on the balcony. There are groups of reporters standing around, crammed in the early morning cold. They beckon to me to face their cameras. I remember to be cooperative.

"Good morning, Selwyn," one calls. "Will you comment on the news?"

"What news?"

The reporter holds up a newspaper with the headline, "CEO PROMISES OIL CHANGE".

I ask to see the paper and they throw it up. The story speculates on how the change I had discussed with the Prime Minister would be received by the oil industry.

Charles Picard has notified the oil industry of regulation of oilfield technologies to reduce wastage of oil resources underground. Oil companies will have to operate secondary recovery technologies from the start of production, or licences will be refused

Canoil CEO, Selwyn Archer, on behalf of oil producers, is attempting to negotiate suspension of royalties and taxes on existing production to pay the investment cost of the additional technology.

"Production of sub-economic resources requires Government support," he said. *"Oil companies have the expertise to choose the best technologies to develop and apply. Government assistance to develop and test new technologies is welcomed."*

The industry opposes government interference in what they see as their proprietary expertise.

An oil industry observer said today, "There is no way the oil majors are going to have some tin-pot provincial government telling them what technology to use, even if they will get a tax holiday for an approved technology. They could lose heavily if it doesn't work. Governments govern; they don't engineer."

Trent Camberwell, *Ottawa Post*

I clench my teeth and swear, annoyed. I had not realised that my friendly chat with Trent at the airport would be quoted as an outcome of the meeting. The words I am quoted as saying have been magnified and dramatised. I will demand the *Ottawa Post* withdraw them, although this will merely amplify the discord with the Government.

I haven't yet taken the PM's proposal to our board or to our parent company, United Oil. Ralph Gooder will be cross.

"Rubbish! I deny ever saying that," I tell the clamouring journalists.

"What did you say?"

"Sorry, no comment."

I go in from the balcony. Manfred is eating breakfast. I pass him the newspaper, and he reads the article.

"Ralph is not going to like this," he comments.

"Would you work out how to extricate ourselves from this shit? We'll go into the office and calm him down shortly."

Gooder's likely anger is making me anxious. I scoop jam into another croissant and try to loosen my belt because it is cutting into me, but it is not long enough. I am a fat man, and I wonder if Vicki will be repelled.

I have not heard from Vicki for a while. The following week, I make an excuse to go over to the UK by myself. When I talk with her, I always end up in a couch posture, revealing my innermost secrets to her. Mostly, I tell her about my addiction issues and what Nicola and Michael have been doing, because our correspondence has been a few letters from me and a card or two from her.

As usual, Vicki does not say much about herself. On my visits, I talk and talk. Vicki throws in an "Uh-huh" or "What did you do?" now and then, as I suppose she does when she is counselling students.

"Okonjo is still starving the Hotus?" she says, as if she regrets her loss of temper on my last visit. "There are families living in refugee camps outside Akar who have been there five years now."

"That long? Really? Well, I feel bad because I got Bob all fired up, and he lost his job over it. Now I am CEO and we have done what I call the 'Swiss Roll'. It is too early to expect much change. Any day now, relief should start arriving at the starving."

"Do you think he'll do what you tell him?"

"Probably. You can never be sure with a drop-kick like him. Now let's talk about living together."

She has to rush away to a meeting at her school. We hug and kiss perfunctorily.

"Keep in touch," she says.

"Will do," I say as we part.

I leave without finding out her thinking about us. I feel like a block of ice, cool and hard. I believe that love will overcome all obstacles between us. I return to a loveless marriage that has my full commitment, at present. My job is precarious, but losing it and returning to the UK and Vicki is becoming attractive.

Rule 80: *Sustainable use of the people's resources is difficult to legislate.*

CHAPTER 81   SNOWMAN COMETH

Thug drives me to an apartment he has rented for us in Calgary, overlooking the Bow River. When I get out at the front door, he shoulders his pack from the car trunk and puts it down in the lobby. There are a pair of skis and a pair of snowshoes attached.

"Can I put up my tent on the back lawn?" he asks.

I am surprised. "What for?" I ask.

"For me to live in."

It is a cold day, about minus 20 degrees Celsius. I am wrapped up in an overcoat, scarf, gloves and hat with ear muffs. Thug has nothing on under a thin cotton camouflage suit.

"Won't you be cold?"

"No. It's cosy."

"Okay," I say. I am thinking that perhaps he suffers from some sort of claustrophobia. It is a temperature I have skied at. If there is wind they shut down the chair lifts in case of mechanical failure, when people suspended would freeze.

"Do you have food?"

"I'll use that barbecue over there, if it's okay." He points to a recreation area, draped in snow.

"Is there fuel?" I ask.

"Firewood," he says pointing to a mound of snow.

He takes me up to the apartment, lets me in and gives me the keys. Most of our belongings are in boxes in the lounge. Ruth and Michael will be arriving later in the week. Thug helps me unpack linen and make up a bed. He has brought groceries and cooks me a steak dinner.

"Thank you, Thug," I say when I have finished eating. I feel like going to bed. Thug is a godsend.

I say, "That will be all, Thug."

I feel like a phony.

"Good night, Sir."

He goes outside.

469

A few days later, our move from Edmonton to the apartment in Calgary is complete. I awake early, around 3.00am. I only need four hours of sleep. I get up and begin work.

At 7.00am, our Philippine maid serves me a breakfast of eggs sunnyside, tomato, bacon and hash browns. Then I wake up Michael, who is flying in the Kingair to the Tundra Tar Sands project. I go out the front to help Thug get Michael's car ready. He is parked in the outside parking lot. It has snowed. I find Thug lying back in a recliner on the new snow, wearing just a skivvy and jeans. It is bitterly cold, with a hazy sun and a light wind. I shiver in my overcoat.

"Morning, Thug! Can you have Michael's car ready in half an hour?"

"Sure can, boss!" he answers, springing up.

"Aren't you cold?" I ask.

"No," he says, "I disdain the winter. It's a mental thing. With practice, your body adjusts."

"Rather you than me. Why do you do it?"

"It's my hobby. Can I take Saturday and Sunday off? I want to go hiking in the foothills. There has been a heavy snowfall and there will be some fantastic cross-country skiing."

"Who are you going with?" I ask.

"By myself," Thug replies. "I like to go at my own speed. I get a lift into the mountains from downhill skiers. I meet them at a petrol station on the highway and they drop me off. I never know where or when I am going to come out."

"Well, take care. There are avalanches, crevasses and grizzly bears, besides the cold."

"I know how to deal with them. I plan my route carefully and take a rifle."

"I'll need you first thing on Monday!"

"Okay, boss."

Winter in Calgary can be grim. Thug and I dig out Michael's car, heaping the snow up to shoulder height. Using scrapers, we remove ice from the windshield and rear window. When Michael comes out, we unplug the heating elements for the engine coolant, the sump heaters for the engine oil, an under-battery heater and an interior warming fan.

"Thanks, Thug, Dad."

"Have a good trip, son."

Michael is going to the Tundra Oil Sands to gather data for his honours research project. He pulls carefully on the door handle to prevent snapping castings brittle with cold. He drives away slowly, until the bumping of the frozen tyres stops. When he gets to the airport, he will park his car and plug in the electrical devices so he will be able to drive it when he returns. I wonder how much longer I will have to stay in such an inhospitable climate. The likelihood of getting Vicki to come and live with me here is zero.

On my next visit to England, I wonder if Vicki notices how I have put on weight. If she has, she doesn't say anything.

I tell her that famine relief is starting to come through to Panypo.

"Okonjo is a bastard," she says, "but he is essentially a nationalist and a democrat, and it is good you are supporting his government."

It doesn't surprise me that she knows so much about Bigerian politics as she was going with a student from Bigeria. Vicki is such a humanitarian.

"What if they are genociding again, like we suspected seven years ago?" I ask.

"Take it to the United Nations," Vicki says. "It is up to the oppressed people to retaliate, obtain the support of neighbours, hide or flee the country."

I don't agree, but hers is the orthodox view. I ask her something that has intrigued me for some time.

"Do you think that if Okonjo really is a tyrant, one of his victims will eventually take him out?" I asked her. "Someone usually catches up with a bully. Will he be taken out by a suicidal bomber?"

"What do you think?"

"That seems possible, but it cannot be an assumption in international diplomacy."

"Perhaps not," Vicki says. "But neither should we assume we can deal with it. When foreigners dismantle a nation's system of governance, what they replace it with is usually worse than the tyranny itself."

"What if genocide is endemic in Bigeria?" I ask her. "Should we just accept that?"

"Have you heard of resources diplomacy? It worked against Apartheid in South Africa."

"Okay, I'll start canvassing an embargo option."

Vicki has a very strong humanitarian view of developments in Bigeria. I wish I had Vicki with me in Canada. Michael's perspective is sometimes incisive, but I am operating under a handicap without the support of independent adults. It would be good to have friends. Work colleagues have a company-biased viewpoint. In my job, one error of judgement can bring me down.

Rule 81: *Democratic voting brings representation of majority allegiances. It does not bring fair representation of people's rights, wants or needs.*

CHAPTER 82   WORK HABIT

One Saturday there is a happy diversion when Nicola and Scot, a boyfriend, are due to arrive from Toronto. Ruth and I take the Lincoln to the airport as Thug is away winter hiking. Ruth drives with me in the passenger seat.

We meet Scot for the first time in the arrival lounge. He is tall and dark, with a slight stoop, reminding me of the parson at home in the Dales. We walk out to the car park together.

"Been hitting the bottle, Dad?" Nicola asks when Ruth takes the wheel.

"No. I don't touch it anymore, as you know."

"Dad! Congratulations!"

"Now he's hooked on work," Ruth says bitterly. "I have to drive or he may fall asleep."

"Why do you have to work such long hours?" Nicola asks.

"By your ad hoc fallacy, I will take it you mean, 'Do I have to work long hours?' No, I don't have to. I enjoy it," I reply. "Now, perhaps Scot will tell us about his research?"

Scot is doing a PhD in mechanical engineering, designing artificial limbs for accident victims.

"I hope you haven't come all this way because Nicola has told you I am an android?"

"What do you mean?"

"It's a joke. My nickname when I was your age was Spock. He was an android, wasn't he?"

"Yes."

No-one seems to like my joke, but I am used to that.

When we get home, I pour out a selection of soft drinks. I don't mind them drinking alcohol, but since I quit, I reduce temptation by not keeping any at the bar. Guests are warned to bring their own.

I am looking forward to unburdening myself about work. Scot is chatting with the manipulative Ruth in the kitchen. I am sure that she will be trying to change his behaviour in some way. Nicola's PhD is in leadership, and she always quizzes me about what is happening at Canoil. I tell her about our dilemma in paying for the oil from Bigeria, including Okonjo's taking of the money.

Nicola interrupts me. "So your response is to simply ignore the rebels?"

"Of course not. I went to Ottawa yesterday to talk about the alternatives."

I couldn't tell her about the Swiss Roll yet. I told her about half the money going to Swiss bank accounts.

"Did you consider letting Misoto have some of the oil money?"

"No. Misoto would be just as selfish."

"But more money would get through to the starving."

"The feds think that by paying their elected government, we are preventing civil war."

"How can there be a fair distribution of the money while we support corruption?"

"Canada needs a stable supply of oil. If there is civil war, the supply could stop and Canada's economy would be disrupted. Then you might not get your research grant renewed!"

"If you believe that you should be paying the people of Bigeria for the oil, what you're doing is immoral. It's wrong to give the money to corrupt officials. If you can't see that, you aren't thinking it through. You are working too hard and it could be affecting your judgement."

"I enjoy my work," I tell her. "My judgement is okay. We have intervened in Bigeria, through Okonjo, and I have received reports that famine relief is increasing right across Bigeria."

"Really! That's fantastic, Dad!"

Nicola calls out the news to Scot and Ruth. Then Nicola takes a different tack.

"Dad, how many hours per week are you working?"

"I only need six hours of sleep."

"You could be a workaholic. They say a workaholic works long and hard for three reasons: because he has to do the job properly; because he can't leave it to anyone else; and because he has lots of energy to spare. You can call these perfectionism, inability to delegate and high energy."

"Hmm. I suppose I am guilty of all three, but that's not uncommon."

"I have a checklist here to test if you are a workaholic. Now tell me, do you always worry that people expect you to get more done?"

"Nearly always."

"Do you want to be busy all the time, even with unnecessary tasks?"

"Umm, yes."

"Will the extra time you spend at work be worth it, by keeping your job, improving your skills, improving your pay or bettering your prospects?" Nicola asks.

"Hmm. That's a tough one. It is difficult to say when 'extra' starts. It's hard to know what is expected in my job, other than total dedication."

"It seems to be a case of Parkinson's Law: I mean the work expands to fill the time you have available."

"I have to put in extra time to make up for not being good at some aspects of the job. I neglect to communicate with those around me, and I am often misunderstood. I lack the ability to empathize with others, and we expend a lot of energy at cross-purposes."

"Are these long hours hurting the people you love?" is the next question.

When I don't answer, Nicola says, "Yes. Mum is very unhappy. I wonder how much I am hurting Vicki too? Nicola is unaware of the perilous state of our marriage. She knows I quit sex with her mother years ago. She is too young to understand the significance of that in a middle-aged couple's marriage. Youngsters assume sex becomes less important.

"Dad, your answers show acute workaholism. You can see how dysfunctional your behaviour has become. You're sick. If it wasn't so common you'ld be in a clinic, chilling out."

"I have to be on the job twenty-four seven. I drop back to less when I can. It's been seven years since I quit alcohol. I quit smoking five years ago. So don't hassle me about workaholism. I am still in control. I am okay."

"In your dreams! You're going to kill yourself and possibly a lot of innocent Bigerians too! You need some other thing to get off on."

"I have started having timeouts drinking coffee."

"Great. It'll be okay unless you drink huge amounts. It would be better if you reduce your working hours."

"I'll cut back when I can."

"I'll phone to see how you're going."

"Thanks, Nicola."

We hug, and I feel Nicola rest her head on my chest as if she's listening to my heartbeat. I realise then how much she loves me and is worried about me.

I telephone Vicki.

"Selwyn, how are you? When are you coming over?"

"Sorry, I haven't had a chance. I have had one problem after another over here, mostly to do with drilling in the Arctic. I miss you, too. Why don't you come over for a holiday for a few days?"

"I'm going to Spain with Anne next week."

I have never heard of Anne before. She doesn't suggest another time, and I wonder what sort of relationship we now have.

"Nicola called," I tell Vicki. "She has submitted her thesis and – get this – she and Scot are going to live together."

"Tell her congratulations on submitting," Vicki says. "Who is Scot?"

I tell her about him.

"He sounds perfect for Nicola. How is Michael getting on?"

"He is finishing his honours year. He is following in my footsteps in studying reservoir engineering. However, he seems to be doing very little work at all."

"Do you know why?" Vicki asks.

"Thug told me he brought a girl home yesterday afternoon. 'Is she a regular girlfriend, or what?' I asked Michael. 'Maybe. What's it to you?' he replied. 'Was the girl you brought back the day before a regular girlfriend, too?' I asked him. 'Isn't it okay to have more than one girlfriend?' he asked."

Vicki laughs.

"Who does that remind you of? What did you say?"

"No, not if you want a relationship."

"I hope you didn't tell him about your sex addiction when you were doing a PhD."

"No fear!"

I tell Vicki the good news that famine relief is getting through to Panypo and other Hotu areas.

"Far out! Is that in response to the change in banking arrangements that you haven't told me about?" she asked.

"It could be. Otherwise, it's an amazing coincidence."

"Congratulations, Selwyn!"

"Thank you. I'm going to Bigeria shortly."

"That will be interesting."

"Have you been there?" I asked her.

"No. Almost, though. I found out about it. It's different."

"Is that why you didn't go?"

"No. Something came up." Like she was dumped, I thought.

"Okay, you have a good trip," I tell her.

"You, too. Bye."

Rule 82: *Excessive working is an accepted way of abdicating family and community responsibilities.*

CHAPTER 83   TECHNOLOGY COMPLAINT

On Saturday, I am at home having breakfast with Michael, when Manfred faxes me this story from *Inside Out*, a counter-culture newspaper.

CAN CANOIL FOLLIES IN BIGERIA CONTINUE?

President Okonjo is demanding more efficient oil production. He has ordered Canoil, Canada's largest oil company, to install a more efficient type of technology at the Panypo oil field. If it does not, its production lease will not be renewed.

Bigerian oil production has been recovering after the lifting of the embargo during the Misoto-led insurrection. The Misoto government lasted only one year.

Energy Minister Tinibu, in a press release earlier today, said, "Primary oil production at the Panypo field will recover only 20%, leaving 80% of the oil in the ground. Traditional secondary recovery by water-flooding will increase recovery to only about 30% but miscible flooding can recover up to 90%. In miscible flooding, solvent is distilled off the oil produced and recycled to extract more oil from the rock."

Frank McGann, Canoil's General Manager in Akar, said, "We expect that primary production at the Panypo oilfield in Bigeria will not be completed for at least three years. Investment now in secondary recovery technology, by tried and true methods, would be uneconomic. We will consider other options for secondary recovery on their merits. Miscible flooding has performed very well at two oil fields but may not be suitable for conditions at Panypo. We will choose a method giving a high recovery, but other factors, such as investment cost, have to be considered."

Canoil has been testing miscible flooding technology at its Tundra Tar Sands pilot plant for the past nine years.

Is Canoil ripping off nations and ruining their oilfields because they can produce enough oil without much investment? Why are they not investing in miscible flooding at Bigerian oilfields?

The ill-fated rebel coup is now history. Misoto took over the wellheads and pipeline and demanded 50% of oil revenue before they would allow production to be resumed. When Okonjo refused, Misoto drove south, gathering the support of hundreds of fighters on the way, arming them with guns seized from pipeline guards who had deserted their posts. The procession of rebel vehicles, surrounded by an armed mob of Hotus, attacked Okonjo's command centre in Akar. Okonjo came out, followed by his staff. The rebels imprisoned them. Misoto declared himself Prime Minister and formed a government.

The oil companies embargoed Bigerian oil, demanding holding of an election. When an election was held, Okonjo regained power.

How valid is the Bigerian Government's complaint? Inside Out is waiting to find out Canoil's response.

My first thought is that this is payback to Canoil for the Swiss Roll. Okonjo, using Tinibu as his mouthpiece, is letting Canoil know that trying to outmuscle him does not pay. I reread it slowly as I eat toast and marmalade. This allegation of inefficiency has come out of the blue. Ungrateful bastards, after our loyalty in embargoing Misoto's government. We put Okonjo back in power; now this. I suppose he is trying to look like he's in charge. The recovery issue has Canoil's name plastered across it and is a fire visible to the Canadian government. I have to put it out. I mumble and mutter to myself as I peruse the situation and work out what to do.

Energy Minister Tinibu's comments are unusually proficient. On a hunch, I send a telex to Richard in London.

Hello Richard. Would you please supply full name and academic results of Vicki's erstwhile boyfriend from Bigeria while at LUT. William Something? Thanks, Selwyn.

The next day, I receive Richard's reply:

William Tinibu, B.Sc.Hons, Eng 1966, M.Phil,, Pet Eng, 1968. Seeking tips? Cheers, Richard.

My hunch is correct. Vicki's heartthrob, William, is William Tinibu, and he is now Energy Minister of Bigeria. I can vaguely remember him at Liverpool uni. I can imagine that when she knew him, he was full of ideals and plans for the good of his people. Now he is a leader in a corrupt regime. No wonder Vicki has been up in arms about his government's virtual genocide.

I think it strange that an educated man like William is serving under such an oppressive leader as Okonjo. He had entered the undergraduate course in engineering at Liverpool the year before me and stayed on to do petroleum engineering research when I left to join Canoil. He and Vicki began a relationship after our ill-fated skiing holiday with Howard.

I feel envious of William that Vicki had loved him. To have become a minister he must be quite a guy. However, Canoil's annual budget is larger than Bigeria's, so I'm not doing too badly myself. He must be a ruthless career man to have ditched Vicki. I will look for an opportunity to revenge Vicki, but I will check if she wants that. It is strange the antipathy I feel towards Tinibu. I want to protect Vicki.

Vicki does know I love her, from the lie detector and our subsequent meetings. Whenever I try to kiss her, she always turns her head aside and asks me about Ruth, Nicola and Michael. Does her question prompt me to make alternative arrangements for them? Or is it simply to remind me where my loyalties should lie?

I tell her that Nicola has a post-doc job, has Scot to look after her and is independent. I only have to stay in Calgary for Michael, who is about to start his PhD.

"How long will Michael take?" Vicki asks.

"If all goes well, three years," I reply.

On Monday in the office, Manfred comes in.

"I told you at the time the Silver Atoll results would get out," said Manfred. He has been looking into the leak to the Bigerians about our miscible flooding project.

"Do you know who leaked it?"

"No. Unless it was one of the engineers on the Tundra Tar Sands Project, who are looking at it. Let's face it, quite a few people inside the company are interested in miscible flooding, since Silver Atoll. It could be any of them. Or it could be someone who knew about the project and held a grudge against you."

"Graham Antcliff is that man. I fired him for incompetent research on the project ten years ago. He must be in his seventies now. He wouldn't care if no-one employs him. So he tells his story to *Inside Out*."

"Why?"

"Not for money; *Inside Out* can't afford to pay anything. He is a whistle-blower. He always had high ideals of what Canoil should be doing. Also, he wanted revenge on me for sacking him. If it is Antcliff, he will regret it. That information belongs to us, and he stole it. We will charge him with theft."

A secretary brings in a bag of bagels and cups of coffee.

"Why have Bigeria picked up on this?"

"Tinibu may be a sincere reservoir engineer, but it is likely that Okonjo is telling him to use it as a red herring. He wants to take Bigerian voters' attention off their misery. Instead of hating Okonjo for his theft and sloth, they will hate Canoil for our theft and sloth."

"We are doing a miscible flooding test at the Tundra Tar Sands, aren't we?" Manfred interjected.

"Yes."

"And our calculations show none of the other oil reservoirs we own outright is attractive yet for miscible flooding."

"Yes, that's true."

"Well, then, we are not doing 'nothing', as *Inside Out* are claiming."

"Okay, I'll run with that. Let's hope the spin will shut them up. Thanks, Manfred."

I can't run anymore. My tummy is too big. I can remember it is only a year or two ago when my belly didn't hang down over my belt.

I will arrange to meet Tinibu and spin him a line that we are doing everything that is reasonable. I want to discover surreptitiously what attracted Vicki to him.

My work as a cool-headed CEO has deteriorated into an all-comers' slugging match. I am hemmed in by enemies who I am decking one by one. I am tired, and when I do not have time to visit Vicki, I relieve my anxiety by working even harder, to the point of exhaustion.

Rule 83: *A new technology can become a football in a ritual political game.*

CHAPTER 84 YACHT HOPPER

I take another helping of the steak and kidney pie our housekeeper has cooked.

"It's okay to have girlfriends, as long as it doesn't distract you from your work. I want you to get your PhD finished."

"Why?"

I couldn't tell him the real reason was so that I could leave his mother and go to Vicki.

"I want you to be finished and get a job and be independent, so I don't have to worry about you."

"You don't have to worry about me now, Dad."

"You wish. Tell me: how far have you got?"

"I don't want to talk about it."

He gets up from the table, goes to his room and then leaves the apartment, slamming the door behind him.

I worry that he won't apply himself. His honours thesis must have been satisfactory because he was invited to go on to a PhD. I am keen that he does a PhD because I failed to complete mine. If I had had more support, I would have overcome the difficulties and finished, instead of having a nervous breakdown. I can support Michael and scaffold him with a well-funded practical research environment where he can make a worthwhile contribution and finish as quickly as possible. He has a great opportunity due to my position at Canoil.

As the weeks go by, running into him either coming in or going out with a different female each time, I become very concerned about his progress.

"Michael, how are you getting on finding a problem to investigate for your PhD?"

"Still looking, Dad," he replies

"You don't need to find an alternative to Darcy's Law," I say. Darcy's law is to a reservoir engineer what Ohm's Law is to an electrical engineer.

"Don't worry, Dad. It's under control."

The young can affect a casualness of which I am envious.

"Yes, but is it your self-control or social control?"

I put some gum in my mouth and turn away. It is all I can do to stop from shouting at him.

One day about a month after starting as a research student, when we are weekending at Zapulco, Michael comes to me.

"I've decided to defer uni, Dad. My heart isn't in it."

"What have you been trying to do?"

"A literature survey. It's so boring. I need adventure. I'm going for a job advertised on a yacht as a deckhand and barman, cruising to Hawaii and then on to the Pacific Islands for a year. When I get back, I'll be able to get into my research."

My heart sinks. It will delay my plans to go to Vicki. I am not at all concerned about his safety. He is experienced at looking out for himself on yachts. He might not be going if his home life hadn't been so affected by the fighting between the pugnacious Ruth and me, which must be distracting him from his studies.

"Will the uni let you defer?"

"They don't like it, but if I quit altogether, they'll lose their sponsor's money. So, they have agreed."

"It seems your mind is made up then."

I recall my own travels in Latin America. I am pleased with Michael and hope he will have as much fun as I did.

The conventional Ruth opposes his going. The romance of yachts and solo travel off the beaten track have never caught her imagination. But she is over-ruled.

He wins the job against hundreds of applicants. We go down to the Zapulco yacht club to meet the crew and to see him off. The yacht is a huge catamaran with every luxury. It is kitted out for heavy weather. Her owner, a French businessman, has sailed the Pacific Islands before.

"Pirates can be a problem," he says. "You have to negotiate with them in a language they understand."

He reaches into a locker beside him and brings out a machine gun and hand grenade.

"They understand these," he says, "and leave us alone."

The other two men in the crew seem like decent types, and we leave Michael with them to prepare for the voyage, with an early morning start the next day. I lie awake that night worrying about all that can go wrong for Michael. In case he is held for ransom, I keep a stash of cash hidden ready. This is one of the most difficult times as his parent. I set it against all the times that he has brought me joy.

I briefly consider quitting Canoil and going to England to be with Vicki. If I am not there when he comes back, I doubt that Michael will finish his PhD. He needs my support. Instead of three more years of waiting to go to Vicki, it will now be four.

Michael calls home regularly, and gradually my fears for his safety leave me. He changes to a different yacht in Hawaii. He travels through the islands, changing yachts several times more, and lives on a small idyllic island near Fiji for several months. I wait anxiously for his return. Michael's letters tell he is leading the life of Riley.

Vicki accepts my delay due to Michael's defection with a typically English stiff upper lip. She can no more tell me her hopes and fears than I can tell her why I always come to visit her and why I don't leave the imperious Ruth. She was at our wedding. She heard me recite, "To have and to hold, until death us do part". Already I've reneged on the holding bit. I am beginning to think I should renege on the whole thing.

It seems unlikely that Vicki can be waiting for me, uncomplaining, after nearly twenty years. To wait for so long, without dismissing or berating me, means she must be disinterested or have extraordinary faith. She is much closer to enlightenment than I am. She has the placidity of Da Vinci's Madonna. Her dependants are her students. They are always with her in spirit, and she with them.

Vicki is extraordinarily successful in her difficult work of counselling senior school students. They trust her and she is able to work wonders. She is so valued by her colleagues that they come to her for advice with their own difficulties. It is a rare day when she comes home without a box of chocolates or a bottle of wine from a thankful workmate.

When I visit Vicki, I usually take her something – perfume, bracelet, necklace or a wristwatch. On my next visit, I give her a gift of a ring, slipping it on to the middle finger of a hand that has never worn an engagement ring – at least, not to my knowledge.

It is at about this time that a feeling of impending disaster comes upon me. I have never experienced anything like it before. I am startled by the least movement, ready for fight or flight. My job exposes me to danger from disgruntled people, Canadians as well as foreigners from the countries where Canoil is active. It could possibly concern a natural disaster or a man-made one. Calgary is blessed in being well away from the east Pacific subduction zone, and earthquakes and volcanic eruptions are unlikely. I conclude that my dread is for something else – an attack, or a man-made disaster such as a terrorist bombing, a gas explosion or a road accident. I purchase first aid kits for our home and each car, make an evacuation plan and lay in a stock of canned food that I keep in the garage.

My preparations for an unknown disaster relieve the fear that sometimes almost paralyses me. I am pessimistic and watchful, which are quite out of character. I can't say what my premonition concerns, only that something dreadful is about to happen.

Rule 84: *Portents of disaster may be subconsciously sensed and interpreted.*

CHAPTER 85   ULTIMATE TRUST

A few months later, *The Western Free Press* carries the headline:

BIGERIAN OIL THREAT

Bigerian Energy Minister Tinibu has informed international oil companies that he will not renew oil production leases unless satisfactory facilities for secondary recovery are installed. At present, none of the companies who have applied for renewal has installed them.

Since production commenced ten years ago, oil has been produced using primary facilities. Secondary technologies are normally installed when primary production declines. They extend the life of the field by increasing oil recovery.

CEO of Canoil, Selwyn Archer, said, 'Our proposals for secondary recovery by water injection are on the table. We are waiting for a detailed response from the Government.'

Water injection is the predominant technology used for secondary recovery from Canadian oilfields. It is not yet clear whether Canoil's water injection proposal will be acceptable to the Bigerian government.

Ralph Gooder phones about the article.

"What's wrong with our water injection proposal for Panypo?"

"The Bigerians say it will leave too much oil. Tinibu wants a miscible flood. He is reiterating it with teeth."

"But the technology is unproven."

"We have told them that, but Tinibu is adamant."

"Who is he to know? He must not understand the difficulties. That bastard Antcliff must be leading him up the garden path. Have you got the evidence we need to nail him for theft of the Silver Atoll data yet?"

"No, but if the Bigerians show it to us, we can use that. We have photos of him talking to Tinibu at the conference in Dallas."

"We need to persuade Tinibu that water injection is best practice."

We talk about how to respond to Tinibu's threat.

"I'm thinking of going to see him in Bigeria." I say.

"Good idea."

Later that week I fly via New York and London to Bigeria. On the way, Ruth the shopper is flying to Toronto with me. I buy comprehensive travel insurance. We travel first class because I would need two seats in economy and I would be uncomfortable in business class. In first I get as much food as I want. I can keep a hostess busy.

Manfred suggests I take Concorde, the Anglo-French super jet, across the Atlantic.

"It's expensive," he says, "about the same as first class, but it's quick, and you will gain two working days. You can leave JFK at the end of a day in New York, sleep for six hours on board and arrive in London in time for breakfast and a full day's work. You can have a night out there, and the next morning you can be in Bigeria in time for a working lunch. On the way back, leaving Heathrow at 7 pm on Concorde, you can arrive in New York in the afternoon and be back in Calgary in time for a night at home."

"You have convinced me," I say. "How come Boeing haven't gone supersonic?"

"It's a niche market; too small."

"I hope there aren't any niches in the flying gear!"

"They're safe as houses. A perfect record."

I think about visiting Vicki in England. I haven't heard from her since the last time I was over, when she was so inviting. Perhaps I could spend the night there on the way to Bigeria. Her place is about an hour from Heathrow. I call, but there is no answer, either on her house phone or mobile. I decide to call again when I get there.

It is early morning as I climb the mobile boarding stairs. Fear grips me as I stoop to enter the tubular cylinder of Concorde. It is tiny, with a narrow central aisle and two seats on either side. I cannot stand upright. I have a moment of claustrophobia. My bulk barely fits into a seat, and I am unable to move. I am next to a porthole that overlooks the gaping rectangular arsehole of a monster jet engine. There is another further out, hanging from a huge expanse of aluminium wing. I look for cracks in the worn metal, but it looks sound and I relax a little.

They close and bolt the hatch. I feel like an astronaut. They tow us away from the other aircraft, and the four Rollers take turns to leap into life. It sounds like four electric lawnmowers, a high-pitched whine, underscored by the howl of air being shredded. Awkwardly, like a pelican unused to walking, we sashay down to the extreme end of the JFK take-off runway, where a limp windsock hangs dispiritedly. The portside navigation light bounces red off the runway marker posts as we wait for clearance. A Lufthansa swoops past and sticks to the runway. We bounce a little from its gusts.

We start out to the centre of the runway, turn ninety degrees and come to a pendulous halt. Every metre of runway is needed and we power up until we are dancing behind the brakes. With a lunge forward, I shake to the thunder of torrents of fuel being torched a few metres away from me, the glow of the flames reflecting out the exhaust. Faster and faster we go, until it seems certain we must crash over the end of the runway. I grip the armrests. Just in time, the nose elevates impossibly high and we lift off into a steep climb.

In front of me, inlaid in the partition separating the cockpit, is a plate-sized dial with a needle showing we are at 0.5 mach and accelerating. One mach is the speed of sound, about 1200 kilometres per hour. Our speed climbs, with a jolt as we go through one mach and up to one point eight, 2200 kilometres per hour. There we stay for about three hours, half the Boeing time, until we slow down over England and bustle to a standstill at Heathrow.

I eventually contact Vicki and drive down to her place. Her normally pale cheeks are tanned from a holiday in the Sun, from which she returned the previous day. She is relaxed, and after dinner we kiss passionately for the first time since university. It is a betrayal of my marriage, but there is no chance of any reconciliation with the forceful Ruth. Since Michael dropped out, Ruth and I have not spoken to each other. That night I agonise over whether to try going to Vicki's bedroom, but in the end I decide not to. Next morning, as we have breakfast together, we seem to belong together.

It is sweltering hot when I arrive in Bigeria. A Tinibu assistant meets me at the airport in a black stretch limo. I get a stabbing pain in my balls when I sit down, because I have put on so much weight my pants are too tight.

"I am looking forward to meeting Minister Tinibu," I tell him. "He went to Liverpool university in England, where I studied."

"Together?"

"In different classes, but around the same time. I don't think we met."

I tell him I had done my research in reservoir engineering.

"Then you should have good understanding of the Minister's concern about low oil recovery."

"Yes. Tell me, is Minister Tinibu married now?"

"Yes, for many years."

"Does he have any children?"

"Eighteen, I think."

"It is many."

"It is typical for a big man. He has four wives."

I understood now why he would not take Vicki home with him.

"Really?" I say. "Then he must be a very busy man."

The aide laughed and cracked a weak joke. People expect fat people to laugh at anything.

We arrived at an imposing building, the Oil Ministry, and I was led up to Tinibu's office. The big man is sitting behind a massive mahogany desk, with the national flag draped down the wall behind him. He is pleasant, warm and friendly. We chat about Liverpool uni over coffee. He can remember me vaguely from Engineering Society and our cross-channel car project. He remembers some of the lecturers, but does not share in my enthusiasm for Dr Bishop, the logic king, who he found to be a bore.

I would like to have asked him about Vicki and hear him explain how he had conned her, but I didn't know how to go about it. I might upset him and Canoil could suffer. So I left it alone.

He oversees Bigeria's oil production, and his idea is to increase oil recovery by having the companies submit secondary recovery proposals for approval or lose their licences.

"Your government's intervention is unnecessary, " I say. "It is in our interest to increase oil recovery."

"But you are not doing it!" he throws up his hands in frustration.

I want to deny this without making him angry.

My head shake is brief. I say quietly, "We have been producing in Bigeria for only ten years, and primary recovery is not finished yet."

Tinibu's forefinger stabs at me. "That," he speaks slowly and loudly, "is the crux of the matter. You must start secondary recovery right from the start! It is not good enough to rely on the gas and water already there to drive the oil out of the rock. Too much oil is getting bypassed and left behind!"

This is going to be difficult. He is a powerful man who knows enough reservoir engineering to buck the global oil companies' conventional use of technology. I decide to fog his aggressiveness, by agreeing with whatever he says.

"William," I sit forward, "you are absolutely right. Too much oil is getting left behind. The technologies for getting it out are experimental and have to be developed on site. For example, we are testing detergent flooding in a pilot project at the Foothills oilfield in western Alberta. It will be several years before we know whether it is economically attractive."

"Yes, yes, I know about that," he drums his fingers on his desk. "But detergents emulsify the oil, making it difficult to treat. What I want to know is what Canoil is doing about applying alternative secondary recovery methods."

"We have given you our proposal for the Panypo field."

"But it is for water injection. Did you consider using miscible flooding?"

"Minister," I say, bending low and looking up to him, so as not to seem threatening, "may I ask you, how do you know about miscible flooding?"

William hesitated. We both know it is Canoil's proprietary technology.

"I have seen the Silver Atoll data," he admits slowly, sitting uncomfortably.

"Oh? With respect, Minister, would you be able to tell me, from where did you obtain that data?"

Receiving stolen data is an offence in Canada.

"We believe the data are so encouraging that the method needs to be applied to every Bigerian oil reservoir." He punches his fist into his palm decisively, ignoring my question.

"Sir, if Graham Antcliff showed you that data, Canoil will have him charged with theft," I respond, holding his gaze. "With respect, Sir, I am very concerned that he has told you that the technology can be applied in every Bigerian oil field. That advice would be incorrect.

Canoil has been testing the technology for three years at our Tundra Tar Sands pilot plant, and the technology has complications that we are working out. When the technology is ready, we will approach you to start a pilot at, say, the Panypo field."

"It is too late. We do not have tar sands; we need miscible flooding now, not in five years time."

An aide brings in tea and sandwiches. We stop and chat as we eat, comparing the weather in Akar with the weather in Liverpool. There is no air conditioning, and sweat is running down my forehead and into my eyes. The fatter you get, the more heat you have to lose. Moving takes more energy, but unfortunately the fatter you get, the harder it is to lose heat because you have less surface area per kilogram. Tinibu is also plump, his face glistening.

Tinibu mentions the coming election, and I realise he needs a result to demonstrate his government's control over foreign oil companies, of which Canoil is the largest. His threat to cancel production licences may be able to be met by installing a pilot facility to investigate secondary recovery. It could be presented to the people as tangible evidence of the government's control over Canoil.

"William," I continued, "you will understand that pressures are higher at the primary stage. We need to develop methods for injecting the solvent at high pressure. If we construct a pilot plant at Panypo next year, would the government share in the cost?"

He looks up at the ceiling for a moment with his tongue in his cheek. "We would support it but we will not share in the cost." He shakes his head. "You will produce enough additional oil to pay for it. Anyway, your contract terms are already very much in your favour."

"Such a plant would be expensive, maybe 30 million Canadian dollars initially, and 10 million a year to run it. Our licence would have to be renewed under the same terms, with the same tax and royalty concessions as we are getting in Canada for secondary recovery investment, to be fair to us."

"Okay," Tinibu says slowly. "You are driving a hard bargain."

I close my folder, with finality. "Our Board may not accept my proposal. What then?"

Tinibu shakes his head. "They must accept it. Or Canoil will be shut out from Bigerian oil." He turns away and looks out the window.

I stand up and move towards the door. "If you will excuse me, Minister, there seems little left to say, only that our Board will not be threatened. If your government stops the oil, the global oil industry will unite against you and you will not be able to sell it."

"Mister Archer, our party may improve its election chances if our government does take on the global oil companies in that way. The country would unite behind us!" He stands up, leaning forward with his hands on the desk, nodding smugly as if certain of this outcome. "Like Thatcher and the Falklands, Okonjo will be popular if he stops our oil being destroyed by foreigners."

I pause and turn to face him. "William, our game goes beyond the next election. Remember how ten years ago we supported your government against Misoto, and our embargo lost him the election? That embargo cost us dearly. We trusted Okonjo, and he owes us. You should trust us now to do the right thing with Bigeria's oil."

Tinibu waves me to sit down again. He sits down himself. "Selwyn, you are right. Tell me, can the Bigerian people trust Canoil to make the most of our oil resources?" Before I can answer, he holds up a hand. "No, I don't think so. If you set up a pilot plant, it would be evidence of Canoil's commitment to increasing oil recovery. What do you say?"

We discuss this. No-one would support another embargo so soon. I tell him I will do my best to get our Board to agree to a pilot plant at Panypo.

"Thank you for coming, Selwyn," William says, as we shake hands on parting. "You are right. A long-term relationship like ours is based on trust. When you make a commitment to efficiency, we will renew our commitment to your company."

I nearly replied, "You snaky bastard! You are tearing up the existing trust, in Canoil's ongoing relationship with Bigeria, merely to force us into a token surrender, to get yourself and your party re-elected. Vicki is fortunate to have escaped your ugly corrupted grasp."

Walking down the stairs I use the handrail, as I cannot see where I am putting my feet because of my belly. The meeting has made me hungry. I have found that William is a political heavyweight. I have no confidence in him, and the feeling of imminent catastrophe is unnerving.

Vicki always goes by her gut feelings rather than reasoning things out. Perhaps William had seemed to her like a reliable guy who was going places. It did not occur to her that he would go without her. It is despicable behaviour, and if he had perpetrated it in commerce rather than romance, Vicki could have sued him under civil law as a confidence trickster. Now I have to be careful he won't pull a similar heist with me.

Rule 85: Trust is the ongoing aspect of commitments made and kept; to last, it must have a framework of mutual interest.

CHAPTER 86   LOYAL REFLEX

On my way back, I catch Vicki about to leave for work. I drive to the local village and shop for ingredients for a banquet. When Vicki eventually comes home, I get a good look at her for the first time in several years. She is the same as when I first met her, slim and shapely. I hug her. She feels even better than ever. My body has always responded eagerly to hers, and I tremble as I kiss her on the lips again. Our bodies press together, and the years apart melt away.

That evening we step around each other in the small kitchen as we cook together a dinner of roast duck à l'orange and vegetables. When we brush against each other, her touch is electric. We eat by candlelight slowly, savouring the rich food. Vicki relaxes, and we delight in conversation for hours. As usual, she asks me all about Nicola and Michael. I feel sure that she would care for them, welcome them into her life and, if necessary, help me support them, if we were together. Vicki is my ideal woman, honest and gentle.

We sit on a sofa side by side with our coffee, quietly talking and laughing together. I kick off my shoes, put my arm around her and slump back, pulling her down beside me and putting my feet up. Then I pulled her along so we are lying full length beside each other. I feel my erection against her mound.

"Sidmouth Hall," I say.

"No visitors after 10 pm," she replies.

That was the previous time. I knew she would remember.

Vicki is a little greyer, with a few lines around her eyes. Her essence has matured for thirty-six years with steady improvement. She is more spicy, with stronger flavours and mellow edges.

We alternately kiss and talk. She is delightful and funny. We get on so well together. Afterwards, we wash up. She asks me searching questions, and I do most of the talking.

"I met with William Tinibu in Bigeria the other day. Did you know he's Energy Minister?"

His name brings indifference to her face.

"Oh, really? I didn't know you knew him," was all she says, as if she already knew he is minister there.

"I do not think I had ever spoken to him before. But we spent a half a day talking."

I told her he had four wives and eighteen children. She laughed, a belly laugh of unalloyed joy. I suppose she had realised for the first time the true nature of her competition. She had never stood a chance.

I tell her that Canoil is going to enter into an agreement with him.

"Well, don't believe a thing he says," she tells me. "He is only interested in promoting himself."

"That's politics for you. He must have been like that when you knew him."

"No. He was an engineer but he changed during the time I knew him."

"Perhaps you changed, too?"

"Yes, I did. I found my vocation, counselling kids."

"Would like some payback for his cheating?"

"He didn't exactly cheat," she replies. "He refused to have me as his wife. By the sound of it, it's just as well. I wouldn't want to be his wife even if I was number one, sharing with three others. Thanks for the offer, but I don't want you to do anything to him."

"What about his corruption? He was having oil money put in his Swiss bank account."

"I know. I will deal with him about that myself."

William had figured Vicki would not be accepted in Bigeria. Looking as she does, with her ideals, she could never have fitted in.

We spend the evening talking about the past. I don't have an opportunity to air my plan. As usual, I am not sure where I stand with her. Mustering my loyalty to my family, I say goodnight and go to bed, in the guest bedroom on the other side of a staircase from her own bedroom. I lie in bed hearing the sounds of her moving about and wishing I was in her bed. There is a light knock on my door.

"Yes," I call.

The door opens a crack. "It's me. Is there anything you want?" she asks in a small voice. It takes me completely by surprise. If I had been prepared, I would have acted differently. When I am surprised by events, I always try to respond along familiar pathways, to return to a semblance of order.

Who would know if I accepted this implicit offer of what I have badly wanted for so long? Could this be a private bonding experience that would at last bring my commitment to Vicki that I had been putting off? Afterwards, I could leave Ruth, make arrangements to support Michael, quit my job and move back here to live with Vicki. This could be an opportunity to test the waters before I take the plunge.

I want to be an honourable man. For years I hurt and disappointed women, but when I married I vowed to keep myself for Ruth, for better or for worse. Now it is worse, what right do I have to forsake her for another? But fifteen years of abstinence has atrophied my self-confidence. I have been sustained by hope of this, but now the opportunity has arrived, I do not have the courage to flout loyalties I wear like shackles. I am a prisoner of habit, for whom being loyal to Ruth and our children has become a reflex.

"No, thanks," I say.

If there is one thing I would change, those words would have been, "Yes, please."

"Good night," she says.

As she closes the door, I can hardly believe that what she has just said could be an invitation to passion. Maybe it is polite hostessing. Her words are clichéd and perhaps they were meant as a joke. If I went to her, it would be embarrassing and hurtful to be rejected again. I try to imagine what Vicki is thinking. If it was an invitation, it would have taken courage and humility to say those words. Her feelings are hard to imagine. I should investigate. It is safer not to know. My aim in life with women has sunk to avoiding disappointment. I lie in bed, going over and over whether to take the risk of finding out, until eventually I fall asleep.

In the morning, Vicki is distant. I feel confused, scarcely in control of my emotions. I ask Vicki if she will come with me to Salisbury Cathedral, a monument that has harboured my belief in humanity's goodness for so long. I kneel in a pew with Vicki beside me and try to pray. I cannot remember how to pray. Instead, I think about Vicki and the difficult life she has led, caring first for her sick father and then for her old mother. I want her to be happy. Then I think about the two of us and how I want to be together with her permanently. Then I remember my children and Ruth, how they had done their best for me and that I can't let them down.

We walk out along the cavernous aisle. I am feeling wrung out and labile. I squeeze Vicki's hand, and she returns the gesture as if she understands my torment. With our fingers entwined, we stroll through the town as I tell her of my plan to leave Ruth when Michael leaves home and how I will then come over to be with her.

"How soon?" she asks.

"Three years," I reply. "He should be back from his travels in a few months' time. A PhD normally takes three years but he will have a running start."

"It's a long time," she says without commitment.

"I have to be there for him. Without moral support, he won't be able to keep going. The myopic Ruth wants him gone, finished or not, the same as she did with my PhD. Three years will soon pass."

"Maybe," she shrugs.

I sense she is reaching the limit of her patience with me. When I leave, I hug Vicki close, with a brief kiss. I drive away to visit my family and friends.

On the return trip, taking off in a Concorde from Heathrow, I pass near Vicki's place. The day before, when a Concorde passed over Vicki's place, the noise was so loud our conversation had been drowned out. She told me about the noise regulations. Vicki had flown the Concorde to New York before and told me what to expect.

"They try to accelerate quickly through the sound barrier, because vibrations aren't lost as sound but resonate. The vibrations shake the aircraft and can damage it. They build up like a wave that suddenly spreads out and down, causing a bang on the ground. This is reduced if they fly fast through the barrier.

"When they started flying, they used to go supersonic over land, but farmers complained that the bang frightened their animals. Cows stampeded and went off their milk. Sheep rushed together and trod on their lambs. A few glass windows smashed and things rattled off shelves. So Concorde was banned from going supersonic over land. As a result, they take off in two stages."

"Thank you for that, Vicki. You are more scientifically competent than I thought."

Vicki glares at me for some reason. Perhaps women do not like to be thought of as technically competent.

When I hug Vicki farewell, our lips touch briefly.

Today the Concorde levels off at about 0.95 mach as we leave Heathrow. When we pass Bristol and are well down the Severn estuary, we have a "second take-off". We are pulled back in our seats as we are hurled up to 1.8 mach.

The second take-off reminds me of my undergraduate study strategy, with a blistering first year, cruising through second and taking off again at maximum power in third year.

I arrive back at JFK early enough to be able to follow the Sun on to Toronto where I meet with the Board the same day. I stay overnight with Nicola and Scot. They are wonderful young people and I wish I could see them more often.

The dread feeling is still with me. Danger is threatening, but I have no idea what it can be. Small movements in the corner of my eye startle me.

Rule 86: *There are only a few opportunities in a lifetime which, when taken on a flooding tide, can lift and carry a person to commanding new heights.*

PART 11 FORCE MAJEURE
(2003-2004)

In which an accident is caused by unforeseen forces with disastrous consequences.

CHAPTER 87 RISKY INVESTMENT

"Gentlemen," Chairman Ralph Gooder says, "we are now certain the Silver Atoll data were leaked by a former Canoil employee, Graham Antcliff. He will be charged with theft. Moreover, he has passed this information on to the Bigerian Government. This has opened a can of worms, not only in Bigeria, but also here. Bigeria's oil minister has threatened not to renew companies' production licences. Selwyn has just come back from Bigeria with a proposal."

I tell them of my discussions with Tinibu and how he wants a pilot plant.

"How much would the pilot plant cost?" asks a director risen from our ranks of accountants.

"Thirty million to get started and ten million a year," I tell him.

"Peanuts," someone says.

"There could be additional costs," I begin. "We have little experience of this technology and none at all at the high pressures in the oil reservoir at Panypo. There is a possibility that the plant will be unsuccessful. My risk assessment has considered— "

"Yes, yes, Selwyn," says Gooder. "What is the risk of an accident?"

My instincts continue to warn me of danger, and I am countering by being ultra-cautious.

"A very significant one," I warn. "The operating conditions we have to use are, frankly, dangerous. The greatest risk—"

"Thank you, Selwyn," says Gooder. "Gentlemen, if there is an accident and we kill Bigerian people, we could find ourselves nationalised."

The Board Members scan the pages of my proposal in the Board papers in silence.

Presently, Gooder says, "Do we have to put in a pilot plant? We are walking away from an important principle: 'Threatening Canoil will not get you what you want'."

"If we don't, they will not renew our licence."

Silence as they carry on reading.

"Can we get a tax holiday?" Gooder asks.

"They have agreed to it in principle," I respond.

"We can get it from Picard here; so we should be able to get it from Okonjo there," the bean counter says.

Gooder puts down the proposal and leans back. "As an investment, it looks barely attractive on paper."

"Meaning?"

"We need more to cover the extra risks: the possibility of an accident, taxes and nationalisation," replies Gooder.

"We may have to absorb them," I comment. "Otherwise, Bigeria will call the King's New Clothes on us when we propose our standard water injection technology and they ridicule it in the media. There could be a backlash here."

"Good point, Selwyn. This could keep the feds off our back."

Another member added, "This pilot plant could take years to get going and in the end be inconclusive."

"That would be ideal. There's safety, too, to consider," says Gooder, "as Selwyn is warning us. It has to be a safe pilot plant or we could lose the lot."

In the end, the Board agree to invest in the pilot plant, which must be as safe as possible. They send me to New York and then to London to reassure investors that the local press has merely been engaging in a new variation on the old theme of "oil company bashing" that occurs from time to time. Also, I explain the investment in a pilot plant. Manfred is with me and helps with the technical questions. Manfred and I are successful in getting support for the pilot plant in both the UK and New York. When we get back, we will put together a team who will start working up a design.

When I visit Vicki, she seems rather off-hand, and I wonder if by holding back last time I have failed her test of serious interest. I want to explain my position and that I want her more than ever, but I don't have the words. I feel any reference to what happened last time would break the magic of that moment. Our relationship seems like a lifeboat that we trust to save us, although we have never tried it out afloat.

Although I have always played it straight with Vicki and she trusts me, after thirty-seven years I am still unable to make a firm commitment to her. I am living with Ruth, joined only by our interest in our children. Michael wrote three months ago that he is living in a thatched hut with an earthen floor on a small Pacific Island. He is catching fish to eat and harvesting coconuts to sell. He does not mention returning but does mention he is with a girl.

A chip off the old block, I think.

"How long do you think it will be until Michael returns?" asks Vicki.

"About six months. Then he will have been away a year, which is what he planned."

"How long will his studies take?"

"At least two and a half years."

"Anything could happen in two and a half years," Vicki says disconsolately.

I take this to mean that if the right man comes along she would grab him. I am worried that Michael will drop out but I tell Vicki that he will be back soon and that the day when I will be able to quit my job, leave Canada and return to the UK is getting closer.

Rule 87: *Technologies often benefit a few at the expense of many, but there is no agreed method for just compensation of losers.*

CHAPTER 88 PRODIGAL RETURNS

It is a Friday evening when the telephone rings at home. I get to it first.

"Hello?"

"Dad! It's me, Michael!"

Neither Ruth nor I have heard from him for four months. He has been away a year. I had not set a contact rule with him but I was about to start looking for him, without knowing where to start.

"Michael! Are you okay? Where are you?"

"I'm in Hawaii. I'm okay. Tired, though. How are you? I'll be in Calgary tomorrow afternoon at 3.10pm."

"Fantastic. I've so missed you."

I did not say "we." I had long since stopped speaking for his mother. Anyway, he and comptroller Ruth are usually at odds about something.

"How's Mum?" he asks.

"The same."

"The same good, or the same bad?"

"Hmm. Baddish."

The rift between Ruth and me may have driven him away. He went in search of adventure. In the year he had been gone, we had heard from him only a few times, calling from one or other of the Pacific Islands.

We both go to the airport. Ruth drives because I have been working long hours and I am tired. We always pull together for Michael. We wait outside Arrivals, anxious to see what condition he will be in.

Then he is there with his pack and big hugs. He is six foot and strongly, not heavily, built. He is the picture of a seafarer, in calf-length faded blue shorts with a rope belt, blue and white deck shoes, stripy blue T-shirt and kitbag. He has biceps from pulling on ropes, a wiry body and thighs from standing on heaving decks; he is a picture of health. His hair is short in a crew-cut, light-brown gone yellow, and his fair skin is tanned light-brown.

Michael has been away a year, crewing from Fiji to Tonga, to New Zealand, to New Caledonia and flying back from Vanuatu. It is great to have him home.

"How are you?" I ask.

"Not too bad, but I don't feel good. I have tropical infections and parasites in my blood and intestines. I'm going to the doctor first thing on Monday."

As soon as we get him home, he has a bath. I resist the urge to go into my study. I don't want him to know I am addicted to work. We sit together, slouched back in armchairs in the lounge. I get him a beer and Ruth a brandy, while I have ginger beer. I wonder if the alcohol-fuelled yachtie social life has affected him. It seems strange preparation for the resilience he will need to complete a PhD. I hope he will have matured and will be able to concentrate on his research. It is difficult to know how much support at home he will need.

He has been in touch with Nicola while he has been away.

"When am I going to meet Scot?" he asks, on the phone. "No, I don't want to do any more travelling for a while. Why don't you two come over here? That would be great."

I am delighted that he and Nicola get on so well. Ruth starts planning for their visit.

His usual ebullience is still with him, and he wants to know about everyone and everything, guffawing at his own jokes. I keep him talking. Ruth cannot imagine herself in the situations he has been in and seems to have lost touch with him. She is uncharacteristically quiet.

"So did you find yourself, during your travels?" I ask.

"I found what I didn't want. I had wanted to live a simple life, living off nature. In Fiji, I lived in a grass hut with an earth floor for three months and fished for my food. That was enough for me. It was a good life but difficult for someone used to our civilisation."

He is tired then and goes to bed for almost 24 hours.

He resumes his PhD work in good spirits. He stays away at the uni research centre until the early hours, sleeps until noon and goes back to work again. I live for his weekends at our home, when his laughter rings out through our sombre apartment. He is a Generation Y and cut his teeth on a keyboard. He is a prodigious multi-tasker and takes over our lounge, flicking TV Channels as he analyses data on his laptop, while using Facebook to keep in touch with his mammoth list of friends worldwide, at the same time as chatting on Skype with several respondents, while a girlfriend on our landline gets just enough attention to realise that she has yet to make much of an impression.

"Hello, Yolanda. Sorry. I was already on Skype with someone. What were you saying? Ha ha. Yes. No, sorry. I will be at work then. Yes, I do work weekends. Maybe next month I'll have more time. Yes. Thanks. Bye."

Michael picks up where he left off, building a math model of miscible flooding.

Now I have to wait for Michael to finish his PhD. I want to be there for him, to protect and support his endeavours in the abstract and lonely work of PhD research. Ruth doesn't understand the internal battles Michael has to fight to keep going, the times when he detests what he has to do.

Late at night, unable to sleep, I sometimes find him working quietly in his room. He puts his work aside and gives me all his attention. We usually talk about technical issues but sometimes we talk about his girlfriends. He isn't looking to settle down, as some of them want, and he is leaving a trail of broken hearts. When he brings girls home, he always introduces me. I am impressed by the attractiveness, intelligence and idealism of these young women.

In the past year while he has been gone, my marriage with the obdurate Ruth has deteriorated. His return restores the mutuality between us. He is more than an arbitrator and tries to bring us together.

"Dad, would you clean up your study? It's bothering Mum."

"Everything bothers her."

"Well, your study needs cleaning, it's bothering me, too. Would you please clean it?"

"Oh, all right. Would you ask your mother not to move my stuff from where I leave it?"

"Oh, Dad! You shouldn't leave it around."

"I live here, too, remember. I put stuff where I need it. It is efficient!"

"I don't agree. It is not efficient for her. You'll have to ask her yourself."

Threes have a bad reputation for stability, because two may take sides against the third. But Michael is assiduously neutral and finds common ground between us. When he supports one of us against the other, it is for his own interest or for objective reasons. We come to depend on him for our stability.

I write to Vicki I explain that Michael is at a critical stage of doing a PhD and needs my support. But I know she is tired of coming second to my family. She has slowly but surely drawn me away from Ruth and probably thinks I am cheating by staying with her. I long to be able to tell her that Ruth and I are finished; yet I cannot do that as long as Ruth and I are living together, which looks like being until Michael finally leaves. My concern for Michael is magnified by the sense of impending doom that is intruding on me night and day.

Vicki and I have inertia keeping us going on with what we have been doing. Vicki, having lived alone for so long, could have concerns about sharing her home and life with me. We will both have adjustment challenges. We have never discussed this, and I wonder if this is the main reason she will not live with me in Canada.

Although Michael is back, he might not take up his postponed PhD. This time I won't hesitate. I will quit Canoil, leave Ruth and go to the UK.

Rule 88: *A person does not understand an idea until they are able to express it in language.*

CHAPTER 89   RISK EXPORTED

"So have you told the university you are back, Michael?" I ask at breakfast, as I contemplate having another bowl of muesli.

"Yeah. I went in the other day. David has managed to have the Gatz money transferred here." He has a Gatz Foundation scholarship.

"For petroleum reservoir work?"

"Yes."

"For another three years?"

"Four."

I have a sinking feeling. Universities keep their PhD students' noses to the grindstone as long as possible. A PhD student has to have strong support. I know from bitter experience. Michael could need my support for up to another four years. I cannot leave him here doing a PhD and go to join Vicki in England. I have doubts whether Vicki will wait for me that long. All I can do to hurry him is to provide work where I can ensure a timely outcome. I pour both of us some fresh coffee.

"Michael, you said you want a field project. How would you like to be part of a design team for a miscible flooding pilot?"

"What type of reservoir?"

"Reef."

"How depleted is it?"

"Maybe ten percent recovery. No secondary yet."

"Where?"

"Bigeria, the Panypo field."

I start clearing the dishes.

"Wow! I heard that we had something happening there."

"You would work with our design team."

"Is there a deadline?"

"As soon as possible. They need someone to focus on safety issues. After the design is finished you would go over to supervise construction for a start-up next year."

"That would be perfect! I'd love that." He gets up and gives me a hug. "Thanks, Dad!"

Later that week, Michael attends a meeting with me and the design team for the pilot plant. There are six assorted engineers, including Michael, plus four drafting technicians. My molar teeth are clenched and hurting. My reputation is on the line with this project.

"I've called you all together to consider our design brief."

I read from my overhead projection:

'To extract as much of the oil remaining in the Panypo reservoir rock as is profitable, by penetrating the pore spaces to reach it, mobilising it, dissolving it in a solvent distilled from the oil, and maintaining reservoir pressure while we optimise the process. The solvent is to be injected below the oil layer into fractures made in the aquifer, by injecting at very high pressures. Safety is the highest priority.

"What accident scenario is most likely?" asked one of the draftsmen.

"Quite frankly, I don't know," I say. "This project will be pushing several boundaries. Previous testing, at Silver Atoll and Tundra Tar Sands, has been at much lower pressures."

"What safety standards do we use, Canadian or Bigerian?"

"Bigerian."

"Bigerian safety standards are lower," an engineer says. "Is it ethical to do tests that endanger people overseas for the benefit of Canadians who decline such danger?"

It is a curly question. Everyone has heard of global corporations testing out new drugs on uncomplaining Africans, in order to check their safety. But I know it would be a faux pas to say that African lives are cheaper. I know the correct answer from an earlier project.

"Developing countries, by accepting more risk, can get access to many cutting edge technologies that will benefit their people and help them develop. New pharmaceuticals, GM crops and deep offshore drilling are examples. Developing countries choose to have these tests. William Tinibu, the Bigerian Minister for Energy is initiating this project.

"I have prepared a schedule of design deadlines that will enable it to be approved by the Bigerians, so that we can start construction at Panypo at the beginning of next year. We will manufacture and preassemble most of the hardware here in Calgary and fly it out there. Construction should then be finished by mid-year next. Are there any other questions?"

I tear open a can of Coke and drink a mouthful.

"About safety, could there be spontaneous combustion?" someone asks.

"Yeah, I studied it for honours," says Michael. "If there is an air leak inwards, at high pressure you can get conditions like a diesel engine cylinder where, without a spark, the mixture explodes."

"Thanks, Michael," I say.

"Would air leak into a pressurised solvent system?" someone else asks.

"Easily," I reply. "I'll send you our consultant's report. If oxygen reaches only a few percent, at the temperatures and pressures we have, spontaneous combustion could cause an explosion that rips the plant apart. If oxygen rises above one percent the plant must be shut down."

There are other technical questions, and then the group disperses to continue their design work. I am satisfied that we are doing everything that is humanly possible for the safety of this project.

I write to Vicki that Michael has returned from sailing and is back in harness for a PhD. Vicki is showing signs of impatience with me over Michael. I suppose most parents would seize their own chance of happiness, leaving Michael to sink or swim. Vicki had seen me sink, when I disintegrated into a cabbage, and she would understand why I had to be there to scaffold Michael, within this one window of three or four years.

At the back of my mind, there still lurks a presentiment of approaching disaster. I feel helpless to do anything except maintain a vigilant watch.

Rule 89: *Rich countries avoid risk by using poor countries with lower safety standards to test technologies.*

CHAPTER 90   LOYALTY SPLIT

After clearing the final hurdle for the pilot plant in New York, with approval from our parent, the United Oil Company, I fly into Heathrow. I am stopping off in London to meet with Robertson UK, who will be constructing the plant. I hope to have time to drive down to Salisbury to see Vicki. After that, I go to Bigeria to finalize our commitment with Minister for Energy, William Tinibu. As usual, I have not told Vicki I am coming.

"Selwyn!" she answers the phone. "Where are you?"

"Heathrow."

"Are you coming down? You can stay if you want."

"It would only be for the night."

"Well, come anyway!"

I arrive just as it is getting dark, and I sip ginger beer as she cooks a roast dinner. We talk, catching up from almost a year apart. I feel comfortable with her, as if I am at home there.

"Are you hungry?" she asks.

"Travelling makes me hungry. Come to think of it, just about everything makes me hungry."

"You seem larger somehow?"

"Yes, and it bothers me. If I had some self-respect, I would have the will to lose weight. But to get any self-respect, I have to lose weight."

"It seems to be a chicken and egg problem. You'll have to break the cycle. Don't you get some self-respect from your important job?"

"No, I'm a workaholic. Does an alcoholic respect booze? No, he hates it. I despise my job. It makes me hungry all the time."

Suddenly, in an epiphany, I realise that I really am addicted to work. I am amazed and disappointed that my hard work, instead of being a heroic sacrifice, is nothing but a further manifestation of my predisposition for addiction. I am out of the alcoholic frypan and into the workaholic fire! Addiction transfer, they call it.

"Perhaps if you deal with the workaholism first, you will be able to tackle foodaholism after. Why don't you quit and get an easier job?"

"I wouldn't have any self-respect then, either."

"Well, why don't you lose some weight, then?"

"When I exercise, I just eat more."

"Do you diet?"

"When I diet, I eat more when I stop."

"Hmm." Vicki seems nonplussed. "What you need is a change of attitude. That's easiest after a heart attack, if you are still alive."

She continues cutting up vegetables for dinner.

I ask her then what I can do about the premonition of imminent disaster that keeps dogging me.

"You worry a lot, don't you?"

"Yes, but I deal with worries, and they go away. This is different. I cannot pin it down to anything."

"Addictions are regarded by some people as driven by anxiety."

"I know. I have always had anxiety, as you know, but it has become worse quite recently."

"It's probably nothing. There is nothing you can do. So put it out of your mind."

Later that evening I squeeze my way up the narrow ancient staircase. Tired, I fall into a wonderfully comfortable guest bed, with crisp white linen and a duvet that keeps me toasty warm, but is so light I can barely feel it on me. I am tired but happy to be close to Vicki. I agonise over whether to go to her bedroom, but still I am stopped by my marriage.

Vicki and I have never talked about our relationship. So imagine my surprise when she says, "Selwyn, can we talk about how you see our relationship? How loyal are you to Canoil? Is it a case of a 'Man Who His Mates Cannot Replace'?"

"Not at all. They can get by without me."

Vicki puts her head on one side, in her endearing way, and asks me, "How powerful is your pull to stay in Canada, compared with the pull for you to come to the UK?"

"It is like a tug-o-war with teams pulling on me from both sides of the Atlantic. Michael, Nicola and Canoil are pulling one way, opposed by you, my family, friends and other attractions in the

UK pulling the other. Your side would win, except there is a risk our relationship would fizzle."

"Why should we fizzle?"

"You tell me. It has happened before."

"When?"

"At least four times: at the May Ball; after the lie detector; when you went with Richard; and when we went skiing in the Rockies."

"God!" Vicki exclaimed. "Those were risks under your control. You went wandering off, you horny sod! But you are right; we may be incompatible. You seem to have calculated that I am not worth taking a risk for," she says dispiritedly.

Our communication continues to be stilted and incomplete. She has stopped asking when Michael will be finished, and the wait until I can return to the UK seems too long to hold her interest. In the morning, I kiss Vicki goodbye and leave for my appointment in London. I hope to be back in the UK soon, for my visit has renewed my love for her. I want very much to be free to live with her. I will, sooner rather than later, bugger the consequences.

Rule 90:*A person's altruistic loyalties are divided among those in receipt of his or her commitments.*

CHAPTER 91 SPAGHETTI LAUNCH

Six months later, I am sitting in a makeshift grandstand under the shade of a creaking galvanised iron roof, as puffs of cumulus try to block the baking tropical sun. God, I am unfit, I tell myself, mopping my brow with a handkerchief. I could hardly climb up into this seat reserved for me. Behind me, most of our field crew are here, talking quietly together.

Michael has been stationed here at the Panypo Oilfield for several months, setting up the monitoring systems for the pilot plant. Yesterday he picked me up from the airport and took me to a hotel in Akar where I caught up on my sleep before setting off for Panypo.

The grandstand overlooks the one hectare of oil processing plant. There is a distillation column, trickling steam like a Saturn launch vehicle, horizontal pressure vessels the size of buses, pumps, and multi-lane highways of pipes radiating out to the oil wells with their Christmas trees at intervals all around.

Michael comes out of the control room and walks over to where I am sitting in the stand. We may once have been taken for brothers. They used to tell me I had a boyish look, but since the fat took over, no-one has made that mistake.

"Is everything ready, Michael?"

"Yes," he says confidently.

"How did they get on yesterday without you?"

"They brought in several tankers of kerosene and pumped it into the reservoir with water. The pressure was high enough to cause fracturing."

"Have all the safety systems been tested?" I asked.

"Yup. This baby is so well-monitored that any dangerous condition will shut her down in seconds."

"Good. When's Tinibu getting here?"

"Any time now."

Half an hour later, a white Land Rover with the Bigerian national flag fluttering, bumps across the site towards us, flanked by two motorcycle outriders and leading a procession of government vehicles. It stops and Tinibu gets out. He is wearing an army general's uniform with gold braid.

"Good morning, Minister," I greet him. "Thank you for coming. When you are ready we will sit in the stand while they get ready for you to start the process."

Tinibu shakes hands and sits beside me in the stand.

"I knew you wouldn't miss it," I say. "Once an engineer, always an engineer."

"I have been looking forward to today," he says."It is important to my country's future."

I think, "Probably more important than the famine."

The rest of the small stand fills with his aides and our people. I introduce him to Michael.

"Minister Tinibu was at Liverpool uni."

"We have at least one experience there in common," William says, smiling. He means Vicki.

I wonder if he is a compulsive smartass because he is insecure.

"How will we know it's working?" he asks, changing the subject.

"See that vessel?" Michael points. "On the pipe leaving at this end there is a circular sight glass. Inside is a yellow and black striped spinner that will show when we are producing oil."

"Are we ready?" I ask Michael. He nods.

"Minister, would you please go with Michael and press the button?"

Tinibu climbs down and goes with Michael into the control room. A klaxon sounds, warning people to clear the site.

Then we hear the strangled howl of liquid being impelled out of pumps, the grainy cavitation of shock waves from bubbles collapsing, as the pressure on the solvent increases in the pipes.

Tinibu comes back from the control room and takes his seat.

There is the squishing of liquid being torn apart through valves and past obstacles as it flows out along the pipeways that criss-cross each other. The noise level increases as the pressure builds up until we have to yell to hear each other. It quietens down, and we can hear the steel pipes clicking and vibrating as the pressure mounts. We can see them stretching and bending. I had not realised the extreme pressures required and the demands this would make on the hardware. In my wide experience of the petroleum industry, this is undoubtedly the highest pressure and the most dangerous plant I have ever encountered. I experience a moment of foolishness and regret for having championed this project. It crosses my mind to order a shutdown, but my reputation and Canoil's is at stake. To concede an error of such magnitude could herald our exclusion from the Bigerian oil industry.

I look at Tinibu and see he is mesmerised by the tortured screaming of the compressors. The yellow and black spinner starts rotating rapidly. I am thinking that everything seems to be working okay when, without any warning, the safety valve on top of the tall distillation column suddenly jets out a colourless light-bending gas in a roar. A second later, there is a loud sputter as slugs of liquid from the venting pipe shoot into the waste pit a hundred metres away to our left. They are coming from a pipe, laid along the undulating surface of the ground, from the injection well-head in front of us. With a whoosh, the pit bursts into flames. The pipe kicks, and then, shooting out a torch-like flame, it flails wildly, like a lashing garden hose, half a foot in diameter and made of steel.

"Get down," I yell at the people in the stand.

It whirls around picking up speed until it is just a blur and slashes whip-like through one wall of the control room and out of the other, cutting the upper part off as cleanly as a knife slices through butter. The top of the control room drops down and rests on the bottom half. Michael is in there and must be cut apart and dead.

Filled with the certainty of horror, I get up and run towards the control room. I have a good head in emergencies. Everyone else is running in the opposite direction. As I climb down from the grandstand, I yell, "Michael!" into the mêlée, but no-one can hear me.

There is an explosive release of gas as the blind rams on the blow-out preventer drive in, severing the production tubing and shutting in the well. The pipe stops flailing. Silence resounds, but the thunder of the discharge echoes as I run across. It is several seconds before I can hear pounding from inside the wrecked door of the control room.

"Michael!" I yell again.

"Here," comes the reply.

Thank you, God, or whoever. How else could he have survived? Suddenly, the well-head hisses with a gas leak building up to a roar. I flatten myself flat on the ground as the heavy well-head Christmas tree flips back and steel pipe accelerates up vertically from underground, like a skinny Saturn launch vehicle a kilometre long, clothed in a jacket of flame, clustering high overhead like a clump of black spaghetti, falling down safely away from us. Fumes from liquid erupting from the wellhead wash over me, my eyes weep and I lose consciousness.

Rule 91: *A technology required to adhere to an inaccessible natural system is inherently uncertain.*

CHAPTER 92   THRONE DISCOVERY

The ceiling spins down to a stop like a vinyl on a turntable. I am flat on my back on a bed. My eyes can move and I see the top of a wardrobe, a glass-fronted cabinet and a doorway. I can move my head a little. I am in a hospital. I cannot feel pain anywhere, but I am nauseous. What has happened? Oh, I remember! The start-up! Where is Michael? I must find out if he is all right.

"Nurse," I call out. "Nurse. Is anyone there? Hello!"

"Here, Sir. Do not move. How are you feeling?"

A smiling black face.

"Well, thank you. Where am I?"

"In the Botibo Hospital."

"What happened?"

"You were brought in unconscious from breathing in fumes, Sir. You are lucky to be alive!"

"How long ago?"

"Yesterday. It takes time for petrol fumes to go out of your body. Doctor will come soon and see you are okay, Sir."

"Is Michael, my son, here?"

"Is he coming to visit you?"

"No, he was in the accident."

"There are some more patients here from the Panypo accident." She gestured to the next bed. "Here is Energy Minister Tinibu. Is your son a white?"

"Yes."

She went out and came back a minute later.

"There are some others from Panypo but they are not your son."

"Is there anywhere he could be?"

"I'll check if he's been admitted."

"Okay, Sir."

While she is gone, I roll on to my side. I can see William Tinibu in the next bed. He is either unconscious or sleeping.

518

Then a Caucasian woman walks in. For a moment, I think I am dreaming. It is Vicki.

"Selwyn! How are you?"

She gives me a peck on the cheek. I recover my voice.

"What are you doing here, Vicki?"

"I came when I heard of the accident."

"That was lovely of you. I don't know where Michael is."

Just then the nurse comes back. She shakes her head. "He's not been admitted here, Sir."

"I'll check with the ambulances," Vicki says, going out. She comes back a few minutes later. "No-one knows anything. Perhaps he's okay and staying somewhere else."

It doesn't seem likely.

"Hello, Vicki."

It is William, turned onto his side in the next bed. Vicki, turns partly towards him and speaks to him formally, as if to discourage further interaction.

"Hello, William. How are you?"

"I am okay. I have a headache; that is all. How have you been?"

She speaks to him warily, without trust. "I am well, William. Thank you."

"I never realised Selwyn was your friend before me at Liverpool until now."

"Selwyn and I have been friends for nearly forty years, William," Vicki says stiffly. "He has been telling me you had oil money going into your Swiss bank account, while your countrymen were starving. I could hardly believe it. Is it true?"

"No. I did not do that," Tinibu shook his head vigorously.

"William, you are a liar. Now, I am going to talk with Selwyn about finding Michael," she says, turning away from him and addressing me. "Selwyn, I'll go and check with the other victims who are conscious. They may have seen what happened to him." She leaves.

"That is one sharp-tongued lady," says William, shamefacedly.

"You had it coming."

"Hmm. I remember Michael going into the control room," says William, changing the subject, "and how you went down there and shouted for him after the gas pipe smashed through."

"I heard him," I say. "He was alive. Then I blacked out."

"I saw you fall down," says Tinibu. "It is the last thing I remember."

With a heavy heart, I run through the possibilities. I have to act quickly. I get out of bed and almost fall over, as my balance is affected. I hate going to the toilet; I'm so fat I can hardly reach my bum. Normally I try to ignore pressure on my anal sphincter and am constantly constipated, with haemorrhoids. Afterwards, I look for my clothes but they are not in the wardrobe.

In my hospital gown, with bare buttocks, I go confidently out of the room and down the corridor past the nurses' station. They do not look up. I continue and go down the stairs one floor. In the crowded reception area, I run into Vicki, going the other way.

"Any news?"

She shakes her head. "Selwyn! What are you doing?"

I grab her arm, turn her around towards the exit door and walk her alongside me.

"We're going to find Michael."

"But—"

"Sh—"

I walk her out of the main entrance and put her into a taxi, with all the dignity that my bare bottom can afford. I climb in the other side.

"Good afternoon, driver," I say boldly to the driver.

"Yes, Sir," he says, looking at me doubtfully, as if I may be mentally ill.

"We would like to go to Panypo Oilfield."

"Panypo Oilfield?" he looks at me, incredulous.

"Yes, Panypo Oilfield. Is there a problem?"

"The accident place?"

"That's right."

"I no go there," he shakes his head.

"Why not?"

"Too far."

"How far?"

"Maybe two hours."

"I will pay there and back."

"Five t'ousan zlotis?"

"Okay."

"Where you have money? Show, please."

I turn to Vicki. "Do you have any money?"

"Only a little. Six hundred."

I manage to get eye contact with the driver. "Sorry, I do not have cash here. My money is at our company office at Panypo. My company is Canoil. I am the chief man of Canoil. You will get your money." I nodded encouragingly. "It is an emergency, to find my son."

Vicki nodded and smiled grimly. "It is true."

Faced with the two of us nodding and smiling, his caution is overcome.

"Okay, Chief." He starts the car.

"Quickly, man," I say, as I spot a nurse and two orderlies running down the hospital steps towards us. We drive away just as they reach the car.

It is just as well my backside is well-padded, because I can feel the diff through the car seat. I bounce and jar like on a steel tractor seat on the farm. It is a bumpy, dusty ride to Panypo, and I go to sleep.

"Are you well enough for this?" Vicki asks me.

"I am tired. Wake me up when we get there," I yawn.

The next thing I am aware of is Vicki poking me in the ribs.

"Mr President, we have reached your Panypo field office!"

The Canoil office is not much more than a hut. I struggle to get out of the taxi; it would be okay for a midget. The receptionist does not have any money. She says the manager is at the plant but the telephone system is not working because it was damaged in the accident.

I persuade the taxi driver to take us to the plant. We ask directions from villagers along the way. We can see the plant from afar by the plume of black smoke. When we arrive, we can see a well-head gushing oil that is burning as it runs through a surface channel into a creek. There is a sad-looking group of local people sitting under a tree. Vicki and I run hand in hand up to the damaged control room and pound on the jammed door.

"Michael," I yell.

There is no reply. We run back to the group.

"Can someone help us open the door?"

They are amused by my bare bottom in the hospital gown. In Bigeria, I get respect for my size, because fat is a sign of a fat wallet. But they are not going to help me until Vicki speaks up.

"He is the Canoil chief man," Vicki says. "We have come from the hospital to find his son. We need to get into the control room. We need a strong man."

They all look around at a big man with very big muscles, who gets slowly to his feet and stomps beside us towards the jammed door. The sweat pours off me. The inside of my thighs are sore where they rub together.

"Me Aziz," he says.

"Me Selwyn," I reply. "This Vicki."

"You find Michael?" he asks.

"Yes. Was inside," I point at the control room.

We are nearly there now. Aziz stops.

"No, him not," he points, shakes his head and wags his finger. "Him at village Chief house."

"Him okay?" I ask.

He shakes his head. "Maybe deaded." He grimaces, rolling his eyes back.

This is terrible news.

"Can we go there now?" I say to Aziz.

"Okay."

The taxi driver refuses to go any further, but Aziz picks him up and puts him in the taxi behind the wheel and shuts the door. When Aziz squeezes in the other side, the taxi is down on its axles. We drive slowly to a nearby village. The village, like others we have driven past, consists of a circle of dung and thatch dwellings, around an enclosure with a mound of dung where a herd is protected from predators at night. There is a central community house and a water well. The Chief's hut stands out from the others in being made of galvanised iron, presumably obtained during the construction. A portaloo stands prominently to one side.

We find Michael, lying in a hut, still too woozy from his gassing to walk.

"Michael!" I kneel down and hug him. "How did you get here? How come the swinging pipe didn't get you?"

"I heard an explosion and dived under the table...something smashed through the roof... the door was jammed... I crawled

through a hole at the back... there was gas...I fell into the portaloo...
shut the door.. don't remember...must have passed out."

"How come the rescue party missed you?"

"...couldn't open the door."

"Then what happened?"

"Later, they came back...chief tried to steal the portaloo....for a
status symbol."

"A loo is a status symbol?"

"A confessional and throne...realised someone inside... got me
out. ....brought me back here."

"What luck!" says Vicki.

"Michael, this is Vicki," I say. "The last time she saw you was
when you were about six years old."

"Hi, Vicki," Michael says. "I don't think I can remember you.
Do you work with Dad?"

"No. We are old friends. We were at uni together."

"Oh, I see," he says, realising ours is no ordinary friendship.
He didn't get his astute social awareness from me. "I need to sleep
now."

My shirt is stuck to my back. The problem with getting obese is
that your clothes are always too tight.

After a tour of the village and meeting some of the people, the
Chief's wife asks us in for drinks. After tea and chocolate biscuits,
Michael revives and joins us. We make small talk, and then I say,
"When you feel up to it, we need to talk about what went wrong."

"I don't know," he says. "There seemed to be a large increase in
pressure in the well or reservoir."

"A movement in the rocks could have let a pocket of gas at very
high pressure somewhere else into the reservoir. We sometimes
hit high pressure pockets when we are drilling, and they wreak
havoc."

"It would have to be huge to pressure up the whole reservoir."

"It seems unlikely."

We try to think of another explanation.

"What I noticed was that the well pressure increased very
quickly."

"As if there had been an explosion in the well itself."

"Was the oxygen content of the kero high enough for 'dieseling'?"

"No," says Michael. "It was under one percent. Spontaneous combustion needs five percent."

"What other reaction could it be?" I ask. Michael has more chemistry than me.

"Not cracking or polymerisation."

"Could more oxygen suddenly get in there?" I am exploring the possibilities.

"The pump seals were okay."

"Could oxygen be stored anywhere underground?" I have never heard of it happening before, but I ask anyway.

"It would have to be put there recently. It's too reactive to be stored for long," Michael says.

Suddenly I have an idea."What about combustion of the oil with something other than oxygen?"

"Sulphur! That's it!" Michael exclaims. "Gas wells can get deposits of sulphur in them, can't they?"

"That's right, compounds called mercaptans," I tell him. "But this is an oil well, right?"

"Originally, but it was gassed out when we started. We drilled it deeper for injection but it was flowing gas right up until we started injecting kero. There was no liquid to carry away the sulphur. It could have been coating the whole of the inside of the production tubing."

"And when it contacted hot kero at very high pressure—"

"Ker BAM!" Michael says. "It spontaneously combusted."

"What rotten luck!" I say.

By afternoon, Michael is mobile again and the cabby drives a very full car back to the hospital. He departs with a fare large enough to buy a new taxi. We find Tinibu and the others are all recovered and discharged, apart from two who have died.

Tinibu is at the town's best hotel. He has a broken wrist in plaster. I explain the likely cause of the accident.

Tinibu snorts with derision. "I see. I want the oilfield operating normally as soon as possible," he orders his offsider. "This project will be dismantled and forgotten. I will have to be satisfied with water injection."

"Bigerians forget when it is convenient to do so," I say pointedly to Vicki within Tinibu's hearing.

She nods and glares at Tinibu. He is pretending to be reading something and glances up at me, and then Vicki, guiltily.

"When Michael was in the convenience, they even forgot him," Vicki guffawed.

Vicki's response to others' seriousness is to try and lighten the mood with a quip here or a playful question there, aimed to show that naivety and dilettantism like hers is not to be overlooked.

Tinibu scowls at me but says nothing. If Vicki had not been there, I think he would have had us shot.

"If we leave now we can get to Akar in daylight," Michael tells me.

I offer Tinibu a lift but he has his own vehicle waiting. So we part company.

When we get to Akar, Vicki, Michael and I have separate rooms in the Sofitel. Our plane leaves the next day. We have dinner together, and then Michael goes off for a drink with a friend. Vicki and I are alone at last and I can give her all my attention.

RULE 92: *There is risk in transferring technologies as new applications in complex natural environments.*

CHAPTER 93   IMPORTUNATE OCCASION

In Akar, Vicki and I go for a stroll into the city centre. On the way back, we pass through a park. Scarlet petals, from an overarching flame tree, carpet the pathway. They seem to portend a special occasion. We walk slowly over them, holding hands.

I look at her and she smiles. The wind blows her hair across her face, and she pushes it back. I put my arm around her. As she brushes against me, the erector muscles in the hairs on my arm and leg on that side prickle with excitement.

A few tables are taken in the Veranda Bar and we sit away from them, with our chairs side by side overlooking the colourful garden. The wind has dropped, and the flowers glitter in the sunlight.

"Would you like a cocktail?" I say, looking at the drinks menu. "You can have a Martini, Singapore Sling, Daiquiri, Orgasm, Black Russian, Chapman —"

"An Orgasm sounds interesting, " she interrupts with a twitch of a smile. "What is it?"

"I haven't tried it for ages. It says here it's a mixture of Cointreau, Baileys and Irish Cream."

"Mmm, sounds nice. Perhaps we could have one later? Let's start with champagne. How about getting a bottle? Oh, now I remember. You don't drink alcohol."

"No. But you go ahead. Have an Orgasm. I'll have a coffee."

I order and they bring the drinks. She links our drinking arms through each other, with our elbows on the table.

"A penny for them," she says, grinning.

"I was remembering all the times I have wanted to have sex with you but couldn't."

"What makes you think this time is any different?" she asks coyly. "I am having an Orgasm by myself."

"It takes two to Tango," I smile. "Ladies first but simultaneous is better."

"I think you are all talk," Vicki laughs. "Well, drink up then."

By the time we finish our drinks, we are pushing our tongues into each other's mouths. Although it is enticing, we have not brushed our teeth, and it seems we are taking unnecessary risks with germs.

"I have been wanting to have sex with you for a very long time."

"Why?"

"I love you."

She kisses my cheek. We stand up and head for the elevators, hand in hand. Vicki comes to my room with me. When we are inside, I wrap my arms around her. She feels warm and real.

"Let's take our clothes off," she says.

By the time I hang up my suit and brush my teeth, she is under the sheet.

"Come one, what are you hanging about for?"

As I get in I put the light out.

I find her and we hold each other close. As I run my hands up her back, I marvel at the firmness of her body and the smoothness of her skin. I have imagined this for forty years but my body fails to rise to the occasion.

"Tonight is your first night out of hospital. Could that be the problem?" she asks.

"It could be PTCS. Post-traumatic cock syndrome." She laughs.

"I haven't had sex for thirteen years," I say. "The mechanism is rusted up and jammed."

"I'll bet you lubricate it and work it regularly!"

"I mean the psychological gizmo. It's stuck."

"How do you feel about me?" she asks.

As I normally deny having feelings, it takes me some time to work out what I should say. I am glad it is dark and I don't have to put on a face.

"I love you and I want to have sex with you. I want it so much I am all wound up. You have rejected me so many times, my subconscious is refusing to be made vulnerable. The issue for me is trust, as it has been all along."

Vicki moves away from me. "Are you saying you don't trust me? After I have flown halfway around the World to look after you?" She is indignant.

"I trust you in that, but I worry about your commitment to me. Did you know that in animal matings, when they are capable of injuring each other, they have elaborate and protracted courting rituals? Horses are an example. A mare can kick a stallion and make him infertile, and he is as good as dead. So he is circumspect, spending a lot of time making sure she's ready before he steps into the firing line. Because I love you so much, I fear what you can do to me. It is a big risk. I need time with you, getting used to you. Then trust will happen."

"I see. But we never do have much time together." She is forlorn.

"We will, before long; I promise you. I will leave Ruth, quit Canoil and come back to the UK. I will bring Michael with me, if I have to." I have said it to her before.

"I am tired of waiting, but you're a lovely man, and I understand you have other people to think about. I trust you when you say it won't be long. Can we trust each other enough to sleep together?"

"Yes. Goodnight, Vicki."

"Goodnight."

We fit together well and sleep in each other's arms.

I am up at 4.00am as usual. I make myself coffee and sit and work quietly until Vicki gets up. We go down to breakfast together. She is distant.

"Are we okay?" I ask her.

"Yes, I think so," she says. "You are not exactly the warm cuddly type, are you? Is your work that important?"

"No, but I can't lie in bed awake, even with you. Unless I get up and write my thoughts down, my mind churns around in circles. Did you miss me in bed?"

"I did. It might be a long time until next time. I wanted to be able to remember what you are like. I thought you were going to reduce your working time to sensible hours?"

"I'm sorry. Maybe I can change my ways." She had heard that before, too.

After breakfast, we pack and go out to the airport with Michael. We lie back in recliners in business class. She seems pensive.

"Do you want to talk about living together when I come over?"

I had long imagined this conversation, with her being welcoming.

"What about it?" she replies and yawns.

"I want our lives to overlap as much as possible," I say. "I want to be with you in every way I can."

"Sex is one thing we can do," she says, "or at least, try. What else? Remember, I'll be working." "I want to get a job, too. It might take a while until I'm acclimatised to UK business. What about weekends? What do you do then?"

"Routine stuff, visiting people – like my family."

"Will I be able to join in?" "You may not want to. You know you're not social."

"We could go up to London, see a show."

"That would be nice, once in a while."

Discouraged, I fall silent. She goes to sleep.

When we reach Heathrow, we go through Immigration together, leaving Michael in the transit lounge. We collect her bag and take it to her car. There doesn't seem to be any point in prolonging my stay..As we hug beside her car, we are both lost in our thoughts. I had seen a lot of Vicki in the past few days and needed time to reflect.

"I have to get back to Calgary," I say. "Thank you for coming to look after us. It was very kind of you."

"You can trust me," she says.

A quick kiss; she gets into her car, gives me a brave smile and starts the engine. She backs out, and I watch as she drives away into the distance.

I turn and walk. My life has lurched forward. The foreboding returns. I call Nicola to see if she is okay. She is fine. I feel bruised but I have to keep going. Michael is expecting me in the terminal.

On the flight back, Michael asks me about Vicki.

"Dad, what's your relationship with Vicki?"

"We are just good friends, Michael. I visit her when I am in England."

There was a long pause.

"Are you going to leave Mum?"

"No. Nor will I leave you."

"Thanks, Dad."

Michael goes to sleep.

I find out when I am back in Canada a few days later that they are commencing water injection at Panypo. The accident, however, is not forgotten.

We had been home in Canada a week when news comes through that the Okonjo Government has been ousted in a rebel coup by the

Hotus, the same tribe that had seized power twelve years earlier. I telephone our office in Akar, and they give me a report from a newsman travelling with the rebel command cavalcade. He has told them that army guards at the Panypo oilfield were disheartened by the government's abandonment of the burnt-out pilot project and fled from the rebels' attack.

There is no news of Tinibu. Okonjo had sacked him from his position as Energy Minister when he arrived back from the disaster. I had inadvertently heaped trouble on him.

Eventually I am back in my office, working quietly on my Board papers, trying to relax.

"Oh, no!" I groan aloud. The same feeling that something disastrous is about to happen has come back to me, as if the Panypo disaster has been a sideshow.

When I am notified that the rebels have seized the Panypo oilfield and forced the Canoil personnel to shut in the wells, I tell the office manager to evacuate Canoil personnel from Bigeria as soon as possible. I arrange with Ottawa for an Air Canada 707 to divert on its way from Cape Town to London. It will land at Akar airport about midday.

Cessation of oil exports from Bigerian is causing gasoline prices to rise sharply in Canada. The government's response is to appoint a Commission of Inquiry.

Press release
COMMISSION OF INQUIRY INTO OIL RECOVERY

The cause of the recent explosion at Panypo in Bigeria in which two Canoil workers were killed, is to be investigated by a Commission to be led by consultant petroleum engineer Dr Arnold Southwell.

The Commission of Inquiry will investigate results from new technology being tested by Canoil, both in Canada and overseas, to determine the need for government control over oil recovery technologies and for concessional royalties and taxes. Safety, oil recovery and economic performance will be evaluated.

"Both the Canadian and Bigerian governments are about to reap the rewards of their interference," I tell Manfred.

"You mean the votes lost over the Tundra Tar Sands project and the accident in Bigeria?"

"Exactly. Already the Opposition are using them as examples of inept government. They let us use the Tundra pilot to get concessions when we should have shut it down, and they made us build a pilot plant that exploded in Bigeria."

"The government has not improved oil recovery anywhere," Manfred says.

"Southwell will have to recommend the government pulls out and leaves it up to us."

"I hope he will see it that way."

"The commission will be looking for a scapegoat for our government to save face, Manfred."

"Will they pick on you?" he asked.

I shrugged. "Who else?"

Rule 93: *In any system, the greater the number of independent variables that are uncontrolled, the lower the confidence in any one outcome.*

PART 12 FINAL JIBE (2005)

In which events conspire to put asunder that which I could not.

CHAPTER 94 COMPANY RETREAT

The stress of the past months catches up with me, and Michael, Ruth and I decide to go to the company's house at Montego Bay, Jamaica, for two week's holiday. If necessary, I can deal with important matters from there.

At the last minute, Michael pulls out, due to a better offer of a skiing holiday with friends. Michael's selfishness reminds me of myself at the same age.

"Well, you have a good time."

"I'm sorry to let you down, Dad, but you can take Mum and have a great holiday without me."

Perhaps he thinks a rapprochement is possible. He is an optimist. I consider cancelling, but Ruth and I may just as well be at each other's throats in an exotic outdoor setting as in mundane indoors in wintry Calgary.

Canoil's King Air twin turboprop takes us down. The plane is based in Calgary, and I decide who can use it. Ian is waiting on the runway for us at Calgary airport in white shirt, tie, epaulets and peaked hat with gold braid. I climb into the co-pilot's seat with difficulty, due to my size, and start going through the checklist. Ruth has the passenger cabin to herself. It can seat thirteen, but Ian has set it up with a couple of bunks, a bar for Ruth, snack foods for me and a coffee maker. He pulls up the stairs, bolts the door and gets into the pilot's seat.

We cruise down across the mid-western states, landing at St Louis, halfway, to refuel. It has taken eight hours, and I am tired and hungry. We park the plane for refuelling and call for pizzas and fruit salad to be brought out from the terminal building. As I sign the account for the fuel, the food arrives. We put it on the wing and eat as we stretch our legs.

"I am looking forward to a good night's sleep," says euphemistic Ruth. "I hope you are not going to snore, Selwyn."

"Come on! What's wrong with a bit of snoring?"

"Yours is particularly penetrating," she says, "since you put on so much weight."

"Yes," Ian agrees. "It even reaches me in the cockpit."

"If you sleep on your side it may be okay," Ruth suggests.

"Okay for you. But uncomfortable for me. All right, I'll try," I say reluctantly.

At midnight the alarm goes off, and I go forward and join Ian. We taxi out to the runway with our fuselage lights flashing and take off through some stratus. I am going for an instruments rating, and the flight in the small hours is a great experience. It is thrilling to be hurtled blindly through the night by complex machinery with so many systems helping us. It is an ego trip, a tonic of empowerment.

Dawn is coming up over the Gulf as we pass over the Bahamas and turn around Guantanamo into the Sun, for the final leg into Montego Bay. The King Air needs a kilometre of gravel runway, and although it is only a small airport, there is an ample safety margin for take-off.

For me, those freezing winters and cold wet summers in the Dales seem a long way away. I have been fortunate to rise to the top of a large corporation in a foreign country. I have provided my family with regular holidays at our residential unit at Zapulco, with sailing cruises up and down the Mexican coast. Our youngsters outgrew family holidays with us, and we sold it when I became CEO. Now we can use the Kingair and Canoil's house at Montego Bay. It is used mostly by senior management for conferences.

We touch down and slither to a halt in a cloud of dust in front of the make-shift terminal building. I have radioed Garfield, our housekeeper, and he is there to meet us. The local Customs man is not there, but will come out to the house for a meal and a drink with Ian later.

We drive through the village, with its dirt floor dwellings and barefooted children. I don't feel that my wealth is unfair or that I owe them anything. There are two views of our intrusion. On one hand, the local people copy us, aspiring to our wealth and lifestyles and developing their economy. On the other hand, I am envious of these people and their simple lives. Our empathy with them helps them appreciate the high quality of their lifestyle and enjoy the beauty around them.

Ian recounts how two peasants are labouring in a vineyard beside an autostrada in Italy, when a latest model Ferrari drives past.

"Hey, Alberto, look at that! How beautiful," says one.

"I don't like it," says the other. "The price of that car is more than I will earn in my whole lifetime. It makes me feel very small."

"Isn't it a wonderful life that a person can have such a thing!" exclaimed the other. "One day perhaps your son or my daughter will own one. Think of the pleasure they will have!"

My role is to enjoy my wealth and beautiful things. The local people will enjoy seeing how it is possible to live, to have hope and to be motivated to acquire wealth by working for it, as I have.

It is important to have hope. During my travels in South America I noticed that in urban communities with high unemployment, there are many places selling lottery tickets. The more poverty there is, the richer the interior of the local church. Where there is little opportunity to better one's life, hope can only be sustained by luck, or by faith in a rich after-life.

I am in beautiful surroundings, and work takes second place to enjoying myself. Canoil's beach house at Montego Bay opens on to a deserted lagoon with white sand shaded by coconut palms. Garfield and his family have their own small house nearby.

Here is a different social set – the rich. In the season, during the northern winter when we would be shivering in Calgary's unpleasantly variable climate, we can snorkel over the reef and go to parties held for moneyed Jamaicans and expatriates every evening. On the day we arrive, our neighbours take Ruth and me with them to a local club. The place is a hubbub of conversation. We have dinner in polite silence. Afterwards, we dance a tango and a waltz but sit down when the band plays reggae. The stately Ruth won't try to dance reggae. The silence between us is like a heavy chain.

That night, as I lie in my bedroom alone, I think of my last visit to Vicki. I continue to visit Vicki every year or two, when I am in the UK on business. Last time, we danced in her lounge to a Bob Marley tape. Vicki is a really good dancer, and her bare midriff and hips take on a separate life, balanced by her upper torso, swinging sexily as she steps backwards and forwards and around me. The hypnotic rhythm and her erotic dancing are tantalising. I try to kiss her but she pushes me away.

"What about Ruth?" she says.

It worries me that Ruth is so unhappy with me, and I consider how I can extricate myself from my marriage with honour. I doubt that local people would persist with marriages having as little interaction as ours. Garfield tiptoes around us as if we are a minefield. We are like opponents brought together for conspicuous consumption, with a truce. When there is kindness, it is hollow, the mere following of tradition.

Overbearing Ruth sleeps late. Her snoring has increased, and I move into a separate bedroom, something I have wanted to do for years, but Ruth has talked me out of it. Now she doesn't object, as she has given up hope of resuming a sexual relationship with me.

"Can I get you anything, Ruth?" I ask the next morning.

She shakes her head, without making eye contact. I seldom see her without a drink in her hand. Ruth's brooding silence is already spoiling my weekend. It is one of the most beautiful places in the World, but I feel life is passing me by.

How much more could I enjoy being here with Vicki. We would recreate in each other's company. While I paint, she would write. Perhaps we could work on an illustrated book or film together. Then the house would ring with laughter, there would be intelligent conversation, we could meditate together and be fulfilled.

I feel I am riding a wave of activity that is about to dump me with catastrophic consequences. My love affair with Vicki is being left behind through neglect, my career is peaking out and my family life hangs by a thread. Ruth and I are pulling each other down, but I cannot walk out yet, at least not until Michael finishes his PhD. I refuse to sink under a pile of addictive work and disappear without trace. At all costs, I am going to stay on this wave. I need to get away from it all and come back refreshed.

"I want to go on a cruise," I tell Ruth the landlubber. "You'll come, won't you?"

She thinks about it, without answering. It is obvious she does not relish the prospect. I presume she is working out the consequences of going and of not going.

"How long for?" she asks.

"Maybe a week. We could go to Grand Cayman."

"I'll tell you later," she says, as if she has to consult her social diary.

It irritates me that she isn't more keen to participate in my favourite pastime, sailing. I am aware, too, that I approve of little that she does. The gap between us is widening.

Rule 94: *People who are happy experience joy in the same way, but each person who is unhappy suffers in a different way.*

CHAPTER 95   PREMONITION

It is a family tradition that we go sailing together. I want to go cruising whenever we go down to Montego Bay. Usually I take Ruth to crew for me, which she has done with reluctance since our boat broached at Zapulco at night, for she has not wanted to sail with me since. When there is wind and the yacht heels over, as it is designed to do with perfect safety, Ruth is immobilised by fear. Nevertheless, to her credit she has always come. It is our only surviving joint activity, other than providing for our kids.

Canoilster is a luxurious 12 -metre cruising sloop, moored at the yacht club. Although we have come down several times, I have been too busy with work to get away. I haven't cruised for over a year and am determined to go – without Ruth, if necessary. I can make Garfield come.

"We can reach Grand Cayman in two days," I tell Ruth. "I'll call Hans and Lottie and see if we can stay at their place. You and Lottie can go off shopping, while Hans and I split the mainbrace."

Ruth the cautious is thoughtful before she replies. Now she shakes her head.

"No, I'm too scared of sailing with you."

I can take Garfield, our houseman, who has sailed with me sometimes, on day cruises. If he comes, Ruth will only have his wife, Marjory, to take care of her at the house. It is not safe to leave them.

"I need you to help with the sails."

"And you won't put up that big sail that pulled us over at Zapulco?"

I bite my lip. We had a capsize at Zapulco ages ago when we were too slow taking down the spinnaker. I thought she had forgotten. I hate her putting restrictions on how I sail the boat. I control my anger, for taking Garfield is a last resort. He, too, prefers dry land and would have to have his arm twisted.

"The spinnaker? No. I promise. It will be okay to go slowly."

"And we won't tip over on our side?"

"No, the wind is from the east and we'll be reaching, with the hull almost upright."

"Could we hit any reefs?

"Oh, come on. There's only deep water from here to Grand Cayman. With this wind, we'll be there in a couple of days. I'll give the Kings a call."

Ruth likes the Kings. While she studies the map, I telephone.

"They will have lunch for us when we arrive," I tell her. "C'mon, you will enjoy it."

"Will it be a rough?"

"No, like a millpond. The wind will be abeam both going and coming back; just a slow roll. No pounding into waves, I promise."

"Will we be sailing at night?"

"Yes, but it will be very safe, using the self-steering vane. It will be bliss under the stars."

"Why do you need me to come?"

"I think you'll enjoy it. Also, it will be safer for me, if something goes wrong." I could have said I liked her company, but it would have been dishonest.

"What could go wrong?"

"I could slip and fall overboard."

"Okay," she says reluctantly. "I'll come, so long as I don't have to take the helm. What time do we leave?"

"On Sunday, at first light, say 6 am. I'll ask cookie to get breakfast for 5.30. Thanks for coming. We'll have a great time."

The next morning at first light, Marjory, Garfield's wife, makes me fried bacon, baked beans and eggs, and Garfield drives us to the yacht club nearby. As usual, I am stressing about following all the routines, schedules and rituals I have accumulated over the years. Everything has to be prepared in a certain way. Everybody has to do things the way I want, when I want. As we prepare to leave home, I spit out my orders tersely and negatively through my teeth.

"Have you brought coffee?"

"Instant."

"Life jackets?"

"I left them aboard last time."

"Sunscreen?"

"Yes."

"Hats?"

"I couldn't find yours."

"Shit. It must be in Calgary." I am curt, but there is nothing I can do about it. I am wound up.

"You need one."

"I'll put a towel over my head, like a hajib."

When we get to the marina, I find our dinghy, collect the outboard from the locker and attach it to the stern. We put our gear in. We are taking plenty of food: frozen meats and pies, dairy foods, fresh fruit, fresh vegetables and canned foods. We motor out to the anchorage. It is just before low tide. Canoilster is swinging gently at anchor, in about three metres of water, in one of several parallel lines of moored yachts. There are yachts, a good way apart, all around her. We bring the tender alongside. Her hull is covered in a leafy algal stubble; our sailing will wash most of it off. She is swinging into a ten-knot northerly wind, with about ten metres of heavy anchor chain jerking on it now and then.

We clamber aboard. I am surprised at the effort it takes now that I am heavier. Garfield puts our things up on the transom and takes the dinghy back.

"Ruth, would you unlace the sail covers?"

A few minutes later, she reports back.

"Done that."

"Okay. Help me get the main up. Feed the leach into the track."

It gets stuck.

"What's the problem?"

"It won't feed."

"Pull it back, and I'll try again."

Eventually we get the sails up. They flap and flutter in the breeze as I tighten the halyards. The scene is bathed in a peculiar early morning light. I feel as if something awful is about to happen, as I have for the past six months, but now the feeling of impending doom is stronger. There is nothing I can do except be ultra-safe as we prepare Canoilster to sail out into the ocean.

Rule 95: *The mind may subconsciously command involuntary behaviour to resolve cognitive dissonance.*

CHAPTER 96 HEADING OUT

I switch on the electric winch to draw in the anchor. Suddenly, from the bows we hear the machine-gun chatter of the chain links bouncing over the pulley sprockets. The chain begins rattling out uncontrolled. The breeze is pushing us back into the line of yachts behind us. I know what to do because it has happened before.

"Put the chain back in the sprockets," I ask Ruth.

She hesitates. She has never done this before but she has seen me do it. Today I need to stay at the helm to steer away from a collision. I am less nimble than I used to be, before I put on weight.

"Quick!" I say. "I'll feed you some slack chain."

Ruth edges gingerly forward on the starboard side, holding on to the lifelines to keep her balance. She struggles with and eventually lifts the heavy anchor chain, twisting it to re-engage with the drive wheel sprockets. I start the winch again; it bites and starts taking in the slack chain. By this time we are well out in the channel with our nose into the wind, with the sails flapping. I spin the wheel to turn us to head along the channel. There is a jerk as we break out the anchor plough from the sea floor.

"Damn," I swear, as both sails jerk full on the wrong side. The sails are pushing us the wrong way, back towards the closed end of the channel. I pull in the mainsheet to get some headway with the boom to starboard, ready to go about. The mainsail fills and Ruth, who is edging her way aft on the starboard side, has her path blocked and has to go forward again, pushing the full jib aside and stepping around the forestay, to start aft along the port side.

We are headed back towards the line of moored boats. I need to be on the other tack but we don't yet have enough speed to go about.

I am struggling with too many things to do at once. I have to navigate, steer the boat, haul in the sheets, switch off the anchor winch as it arrives in its channel, and keep an eye on Ruth. I am not good at multi-tasking, and *Canoilster* is turning in fits and starts, rather than smoothly and predictably. Ruth the snail is coming aft on the port side now. We are within metres of the moored boats. I have to jibe to avoid collision, immediately.

"Hurry!" I yell, putting the helm across to bring us around, pulling in both sails to assist. Ruth is coming slowly aft, holding on to the lifelines, and reaches the shrouds and cabin roof. The jibe is imminent. She is edging past the cabin, when there is a gust, the mainsail fills from the other side and the boom swings across, picking up speed.

"Get down!" I shout, as it swings faster and faster. I pull the mainsheet in as fast as I can, to try and stop it, but I am too slow. Ruth stoops, but not low enough. It swings right across and hits her on the side of the head, sounding like a gong. She squeals and pitches sideways over the port lifeline into the water, going under. I run forward. She has not come up. I dive in where she disappeared.

The water is clear and I swim around in a circle under water trying to see her, but cannot find her. I have to come up for air. On my second dive, I see her and grab her. I kick upwards as fast as I can, hauling her up to the surface.

There is no time to lose. I get her nose and mouth above water but she isn't breathing. I hold her head up and yell for help. A few minutes later, a young man in an inflatable reaches us. She is a dead weight, and we can't get her inside. We hold her arms over the side and set off for the closest land, pushed by the tiny outboard motor. There is a sandbank about two hundred metres away, and we head for it.

Progress seems dreadfully slow, even with the outboard going flat-out. When we reach the sand bank, a couple of people wade out and we drag her ashore. She looks dead.

"Turn her down the beach," I order, dragging her around, face down.

I pump on her back. Immediately, water gushes out of her mouth, several litres. She vomits and goes into a fit of coughing. I keep her in the recovery position to stop her getting vomit into her lungs. Then she begins wailing, a long yell. She is delirious, and I try to quiet her, but when she sees me she yells even louder. A small crowd has gathered, and someone has a blanket that we put over her.

"The coastguard helicopter will be here in about ten minutes," someone says.

She quietens and remains conscious.

When the helicopter arrives they put her on a stretcher. I can go with her if I want, but there are two medics and there is nothing I can do. They take off in a flurry of sand and spray.

I get a lift out to *Canoilster*, which is caught against another boat. I take her back and anchor her. There is little damage. I get a lift back to shore, and call Garfield to fetch me. Taking some things for Ruth from the beach house, I set out in the Landrover for Kingston hospital, half a day away, where the helicopter is taking her.

I feel responsible for Ruth's accident. I am wracked by anxiety. I know in my bones that she will blame me and never forgive me. If she is badly injured, I will never forgive myself.

Rule 96:*A sin of omission is less blameworthy than a sin of commission.*

CHAPTER 97   RECUPERATION

I arrive at the hospital in the Jamaican capital three hours later. I find her on a trolley in a corridor.

"How are you?" I ask.

"Not good," she replies. "Not that anyone around here cares." She has been on this trolley all day and is feeling unloved and sorry for herself. "Where are my things? Didn't you bring them?"

"Shit! I forgot."

She wails piteously that I have not brought her nightie and slippers and other items for a stay in hospital. Her hospital gown leaves her bottom uncovered, and she is too embarrassed to go to the toilet.

"I can't walk along the corridor like this!"

She cries, as if my neglect is deliberate. It is the first time I am in this position; I have been unable to empathize with her and have not realized my responsibilities. I am distraught that Ruth has suffered an accident while under my care.

"I'm sorry," I tell her. "It was my fault. I should have gone forward myself."

She says nothing. She does not seem to be forgiving me. I go off and buy the things she wants in local shops.

When the hospital emergency doctor comes he informs me of her condition. Her breathing has recovered from immersion. She has been CAT-scanned and there doesn't appear to be any serious brain damage. There is a lump on the side of her head with a cut that has been stitched up.

Her head wound requires dressing only every couple of days, but they are going to keep her in under observation. The doctor is concerned about how traumatised she is. She is too frightened to go home. I get the impression from the doctor that Ruth believes I deliberately caused the accident.

"How did it happen?" the doctor asks me.

"The wind got behind the mainsail. It brought the boom across fast, and it hit her before she could duck down out of the way."

"A jibe?"

"Ah! You sail?"

"I've done a little. Did you expect it to happen?"

"Not so soon. She was slower coming aft than I expected, and it caught her."

"Did you warn her?"

"Yes. I called out, 'Get down!'"

"What did she do?"

"She bent over, but not enough."

"Has anything like this happened to her before?"

"No. Normally I leave the helm and go forward myself."

"What did you do last time it jammed."

"I went forward myself. I was younger and quicker."

"Ah, yes. So you had both slowed down, maybe?"

"Yes, I can see that now."

There was nothing to suggest it was deliberate. I had led the rescuers. There are no grounds for police involvement. Nevertheless, Ruth doesn't want to go home and she continues to be suspicious of me. They allow her to stay in the hospital. I apologise again profusely, but after that we have nothing to say to each other. So I go home. It seems pointless waiting at the hospital. I telephone twice each day to bring her home but she wants to stay there.

"I don't want to be at home with you. I want to be cared for," she complains.

Unable to neglect my job any longer, I return alone to Calgary. If necessary, I can be in Kingston within a day. After two weeks, the hospital insists on discharging her, and I take the King Air down with two nurses and bring her back. She is able to walk into our place, but her posture indicates trauma, and she takes herself to bed. I hire a nurse-housekeeper-cook to look after her, supervised by her doctor.

She is a demanding patient and at first will not turn over in bed or pick up a book without help. Her doctor reassures me that her injuries are psychological, and it will take time for her to recover her self-confidence.

Her employer grants her sick leave. She has worked regularly since we have been back in Calgary, but her job as school health advisor is difficult as parents have become more demanding and litigious. She says she will probably retire.

At the back of my mind there is guilt, for I had been careless in planning and in dealing with the developing situation on the yacht. I should have chosen the collision with the other yacht. The consequences would have been a few scratches and a dint in my bank account. I am in a hell of guilt, for a sin of omission, and I become a victim of my conscience. I am mortified when the premonition of disaster resumes, as if the oilfield and Ruth's accidents are merely preludes to something truly dreadful that has yet to happen. I try to follow Vicki's advice and put the worry aside, but I cannot. I almost sink back into working all hours but catch myself in time.

With Ruth laid up, life at home is more tolerable. I love having the run of the apartment. Ruth has always made me feel as if I am there on sufferance, allowed in only a few rooms. Now when I put things down, they are still there when I came back. It is empowering and a foretaste of what life would be like without her.

She discouraged me from cooking, being a very good cook and wanting to do it herself. On the few occasions I had wanted to cook something, she had stood over me and made me use her methods until I quit. Now I have a wonderful time preparing foods in my own way.

I do the shopping for the first time in thirty years and purchase foods that Ruth had refused to buy: bacon, mushrooms, kippers, pork pies, lamb chops, rhubarb and parsnips. I develop a love of cooking, starting with recipes from books. Increasingly, I improvise. I tend to nibble when I cook, and my bulk becomes unpleasant.

Ruth will not eat food I prepare. She complains about everything and picks at the food prepared by her housekeeper. I visit Ruth in her bedroom several times each day, sometimes with flowers or chocolates. I enquire about her health, and we make small talk until we run out of things to say and I end my visit. After a week of this, I leave her in the care of her housekeeper and stay in the CEO suite at the office through the week, checking on her progress by telephone.

When I come home at the weekends, my snoring in the next room spoils her sleep. It takes a month before she recovers sufficiently to get out of bed. She avoids me and goes out to visit friends. These jaunts are a tonic, and she comes back revitalised. We are finished in all but living in the same place. She needs to get away on holiday, and I book a flight for her to visit Nicola and Scot in Toronto for a couple of weeks.

She says she will never go to the Montego Bay house again.

When she goes to stay with Nicola and Scot, I realise for the first time not only that I can live without Ruth; I prefer it. I await her return with trepidation.

Rule 97: *Renewal of atrophied senses from a change in responsibilities is challenging and can bring unexpected pleasures.*

CHAPTER 98 SEPARATE INTERSECTION

When the intrepid Ruth comes back from Toronto, she asks Michael to collect her from the airport. She comes in the side door from the garage and goes directly to my study where I am reading a novel. While she has been away, I have been able to reduce my working hours. They are still long but I take frequent time out to relax.

"Hello," I say getting up. "Welcome back!"

We have long since dispensed with kissing each other.

"Sit down," she says. "This may be a shock."

I sit down again, wondering what is coming. She seems to have rehearsed her part and is enjoying it.

"You know how we're always bringing each other down?"

I don't know what she means. True, I have been deliberately thwarting her. I suppose she means my passive resistance. Yes, that must be it. Alternatively, she sees what she has been doing as taking me down. I have never intended that with her. In order to move on, I will agree.

"Yes."

"Well, I'm leaving you." She pauses for a reaction.

She once told me of a friend of hers, who she admired for telling her husband this out of the blue, like she is telling me now. She left and he was badly hurt, which pleased her.

I do not give Ruth that satisfaction. I look at my book and think, "Oh, yeah. I've heard that before." She has threatened it often enough, to get her own way.

"I'll take my stuff and go this weekend." I say nothing. "Okay? Understand?"

She seems disappointed that I don't react. In fact, I don't believe it. We have been together more than thirty years. People do not leave each other after so many years together, in my experience, unless they have a damn good reason. She has gone without sex from me for thirteen years, but that is not a sufficient reason to separate. That couldn't be it. My snoring upsets her, but I sleep in a separate room. I don't hit her. What other reason could she have to leave? Could she have someone else and want to live with them, like I do Vicki? It doesn't seem likely. She must be upset by something and will get over it. She has threatened to leave before.

I go back to my novel.

On Sunday, Ruth gets out suitcases and boxes and starts to put things in. I recall this is the day she said she would go. She really is going. My immediate reaction is a spike of elation. Free at last!

"Where are you going?" I ask.

"Janet's place."

Janet is Ruth's sister. She continues packing. I suppose she must be going to rotate living at the homes of her sisters and brother until she gets a place of her own.

She finishes packing and lines up the boxes and suitcases by the door. There are six. I am surprised that she is taking so little and leaving so many things that I know are rightfully hers or she is fond of.

"Aren't you going to take the food mixer I gave you?" I asked. "Or what about this bowl? It was a wedding present. Don't you want it?"

"I'm taking away only what I brought to our marriage and things I acquired in my own right. That is the custom when the wife leaves the married home."

Sadness wells up within me and I become numb. This must be the disaster I could feel in my bones months ago.

After that, it happens very quickly. Two nephews arrive and load her things into our new car. She gets in and they all drive off. I am left alone, thinking that her taking the new car without discussing it is the last time she will be able to bully me.

When she has gone, my anxiety is acute. My head feels like it is about to explode, and I am aware that my spine has locked in an uncomfortable position. I alternate between feeling nauseous and eating the contents of the fridge. Unprepared for solitude, I wander through the apartment, remembering some good times we shared. Michael comes back to the apartment from the research centre to look after me. He is taking the rest of the day off work.

"Where has she gone?" I asked him.

"She's on her way to Toronto."

"Toronto? Who is she going to stay with?"

"George Watt. He has come up to drive back with her."

"Who," I ask Michael, "is George Watt?"

Michael tells me that he was her boyfriend when they were at university together, forty years ago. His wife was killed in an accident two years ago.

"So when she was visiting Nicola and Scot, she was seeing her new man?"

"I guess so."

I am dumbfounded. Ruth's infidelity explains so much. Not knowing when this affair had started leaves Ruth's loyalty questionable for the duration of our marriage. Ruth's departure without warning had been carefully planned over a long period, possibly many years. I had no idea George Watt existed and didn't know when his influence first affected our marriage. It might have been all along. Her dealings with him were underhand. In contrast, whenever I had visited Vicki, she came with me and our children, or I reassured her after each visit that it was innocent.

When I was with Ruth, I had yearned for Vicki. Now, against all logic I grieve for Ruth. Loss of a spouse is rated for stress severity as the most traumatic of life's events, even above loss of a child. Although Ruth had not died and I had ceased to interact with her at the end, we had been together almost half a lifetime. The separation brings me despair and even panic. There is the terror of the unknown. Michael suffers it, too, but youth is more flexible and he is able to be stronger.

"It seems bad now, Dad," he says, " but it will soon seem like a change for the better."

"It has torn up yours and Nicola's past," my voice strangles. "I have no-one with whom to share my memories of your childhoods."

"There's us. We were there, too."

He gives me a hug and gets lunch. Over the next few weeks, he supports and counsels me until I begin to regain the independence and self-confidence that have been sidelined since I married Ruth.

Chunks of my cerebral cortex seem to have atrophied, and I can barely function on my own. I have to learn to use our mobile phone. It takes weeks before I can send a SMS. I buy a GPS for my car now my navigator has gone.

It surprises me how disabled I am without Ruth. Before, my life had run with a flat tyre and couldn't get up to speed. After, with the wheel taken off, I am unable to go anywhere until I am repaired. I am hurting from the loss of a part of myself.

I know I am not ready yet to make plans to go to Vicki even though time may be running desperately short.. I need time to grieve and understand, to adjust to being single.

Because Ruth is a native Calgarian, my social life has been mostly with Ruth's large family and friends. There were always birthday parties and family get-togethers. Suddenly, I am totally isolated. Loneliness stalks me like a shadow. I have to learn to do things that I used to do with other people, by myself, even going for a walk,.

Immediately Ruth leaves, my health improves. The medical conditions I acquired since we married disappear.

"I used to believe I was The Messiah," I confessed to Manfred. "I was that crazy."

It was strange to be telling this secret of my daily life for the past three decades.

"I thought you were a bit strange at times," says Manfred, "as though you were getting instructions from someplace else."

"It is behind me now. It was a bolthole in my subconscious to get away from Ruth."

"What was it you couldn't face?" he asks.

"Being treated like I am second rate. I had an alternative reality in which I was a hero. Being ordinary all the time is going to take some getting used to."

It does not take long. The psychiatrist who had treated me since shortly after I married is able to close my case, as symptoms cease. I no longer have delusions and paranoia.

While I was married to Ruth, I was unable to make new friends. She seemed to discourage me, especially with females. Now she is gone, I can resume where I left off when I was single. I can mix with who I like.

I want to be independent and healed when I go to Vicki. My recovery from Ruth seems to be slow but sure. To rush to her in the state that Ruth left me in could jeopardize the relationship I have waited so long to renew.

Rule 98: *The longer a relationship has lasted, the greater is the trauma of separation and following improvement in wellness.*

PART 13 LEG MEND (2006)

With Ruth gone, my selling short of Vicki, done years ago while at university, is now for the first time fully exposed and vulnerable to changes in her situation. There is no time to lose before I seek closure, or renewal of my straddle.

CHAPTER 99   DEVOLUTION

Since Ruth left, I have not been able to get over to the UK to see Vicki for over a year, due to pressure of work. I fear I am losing touch with her.

"Hello, Vicki. Selwyn here."

"Oh, Selwyn. Look I can't talk just now. Would you write, please?"

"Okay. Bye."

As usual, she is reluctant to use the telephone. I write with my news about separating from Ruth, but to my consternation she does not reply. I imagine she does not want to communicate with me until I can tell her a definite plan, which I am not yet able to do.

Canoil is the nation's largest oil company, and we are headquartered in our own building in downtown Calgary. After Ruth leaves, I usually go home in the evening to stay in touch with Michael. My day begins when the alarm goes off at 4.00am. Thug brings me into work from home, and I shave and shower in the CEO's suite. Breakfast arrives from the shop across the street: orange juice, pancakes, maple syrup and coffee. I sit at the breakfast bar, glancing through the morning papers. Next to the breakfast room there is a sitting room. Beyond that is the boardroom, with my office and my secretary's and Manfred's offices next to it.

After breakfast I go through into my office and start work at my desk. My job means a lot to me; enabling me to appease my anxiety demons by overwork rather than by drinking. I am anxious that my performance as CEO is under scrutiny, that they will find out I am a no-good impostor. I innovate and plan for others with some regard for their views but prefer to work in isolation from them. It is not a popular style, but I feel meetings are mostly a waste of time.

At 7.00am, Manfred arrives. Yesterday we listed tasks that need attention and today we review the list, discussing each item. My weekly Board meeting is at 10.00am. There are ongoing negotiations with indigenous people about a drilling site on the

Northwest Shelf in the Arctic. We need to decide whether to drill another well in the Timor Gulf, in an area claimed by the Timor Government. Most bizarre, we have to come up with a new brand name to put on our thousands of petrol pumps across Canada.

I tell Manfred what to put in the Board papers and he goes out. I stretch my legs. When I look in the mirror I think I look worried. I have far too much on my plate. The only way out of trouble with problems, that I know of, is to do more work. I can delegate or move items down my priority list but I am reluctant to do this. I know exactly how to deal best with each item. I spend several hours preparing for today's meeting, working out how to present each item to get approval to proceed.

I call the Lands Manager when he comes in at 9.00am, as the Board will want to see progress on the indigenous issue. I go over the whole situation with him. Unfortunately, he does not grasp the nettle and I have to tell him an amount to offer to get the ball rolling.

I take a few minutes to sit back. Just then, Manfred brings in the morning mail. As he goes through it with me, I nod off. I wake up when he shows me a class action filed by our roustabouts at Tundra Tar Sands. They claim that exposure to the tar has given them cancer. I am instantly alert, as this is potentially catastrophic for Canoil. I have not heard of this action before, and I get Manfred to take it to our legal people for advice.

Manfred comes back. "There is a bloke from the CBC outside, a journalist."

"Find out what he wants."

"Bigeria. Your response to the rebels' demands for oil money."

"Fuck, fuck, fuck. Not that again. I thought we had sorted it six years ago with our Swiss

Roll."

"Apparently not."

"Tell him, sorry; it's too early. Maybe this time tomorrow. Make an appointment."

I stand up and write on the whiteboard a diagram analysing the risks of our situation in Bigeria. My diagram compares "do nothing", with "pay the rebels" with the "devolution" alternative that Vicki's group had proposed at her place six years ago. My analysis supports "devolution".

"We didn't use the devolution option last time," I tell Manfred, "because Okonjo responded to our Swiss Roll. Since then the money has been leaking away faster and faster until now we have this crisis. I am fucking fed up with those corrupt bastards. This time we'll fix them for good."

The Board members arrive and come through into the Board Room. The Chairman begins with the usual apologies, minutes and auditor's report. The first motion is the mid-year financial report. There is an increase in dividend that we have worked hard to achieve. It is voted to be accepted unanimously.

Next I have a motion about the indigenous situation in the Arctic. I give a verbal update, and my proposal is accepted. Then we turn to the Timor Gulf drilling. I have a motion that we go ahead regardless of the opposition and explain why in detail. The vote is narrow and it only just gets over the line, with three members voting against. I am affronted by this unjustified rejection of my leadership. I had failed to win the support of almost half the Board, and it is an insult that stings.

Just then Manfred comes in.

"Bigerian protestors are outside."

"What do they want?

"They have a placard saying 'Bigerian Oil Money for All Bigerians'."

"Why are they here now?"

"This morning the CBC broadcast that our Board is considering it today."

"How do they know that?"

"I told them. Sorry," says Manfred, very sheepishly. "I didn't think it would matter."

Everyone looked at him curiously. Journalists are skilled at winkeling out information.

"Selwyn, would you tell us what we should do about them?" Gooder asks.

I give the Board a rundown on the situation in Bigeria while they eat sandwiches and drink fruit juice. They have been accustomed to drink a few lagers during meetings, but I have stopped that, arguing that the Board's decisions should not be made under the influence of alcohol. There has been some grumbling.

"As a major player, Canoil can organize concerted oil company action involving alternative supplies. We can even get an embargo that Ottawa would accept."

"What about Okonjo?" one of the directors asks.

"Okonjo is a fly in the ointment. We can sideline him," I reply.

"About time," someone said. "How?"

"We will re-direct our payments for oil we purchase to eight regional government bank accounts under the signatures of their health, welfare and education bosses."

"Can we do that?"

"Our contract doesn't exclude it; so, yes. Frank McGann, our GM in Akar, has almost finished updating the details and talking with the bosses who will operate the accounts."

"Any more questions?"

There is noise outside from the protestors.

I groan inwardly when Gooder postpones the meeting, to be held in secret, in two days time. They haven't approved my proposal. The Board members leave secretly through the car park in the basement.

For a few moments I am in despair, wondering if I should resign.

"Call me tonight after 10pm," Gooder tells me as he leaves.

I wonder why so late. He has never done this before, and I am apprehensive that he will ask me to resign. I worry that he has detected that I am affected by sleep deprivation and is concerned that my cognitive functions are impaired.

Gooder is an oil man through and through, and his acumen mirrors the technological opportunism of our business. He believes in doing our homework using the best analytical techniques to manage a portfolio of attractive projects with calculated risks, in the likelihood that a few will come to fruition and return a satisfactory profit overall. I spend the afternoon going over and refining my analysis of the Bigerian situation. I have never felt so stressed. I want to run away but I cannot.

As work is my favourite activity, I need to relax, but there is a procession of visitors with complaints, or people who have been overlooked for promotion, or people who have tenders and contracts they want to be okayed, or people who want to deliver confidential information. I work straight through. I delegate to Manfred when I can.

When I look in the bathroom mirror later, my face is haggard, with bags under my bloodshot eyes. I am very concerned about talking with the Chairman tonight. I could find myself out of a job. I have to show I can hack the tough going. I return to my desk and continue, rushing to complete several matters that need my final touch.

Then Michael arrives in my office unannounced.

"Are you okay, Dad?" he asks when he sees me. "You look like shit." It is his way of being sympathetic and supportive.

"I didn't get much sleep last night, and today is turning into a disaster. I'm sorry, but I can only give you a few minutes. Is there something you want?"

"Nothing in particular but I'm finding evidence that oil recovery at Canoil's oilfields overseas is low."

"Keep that to yourself for the moment," I say. "If the exporters get hold of that, they will use it as a stick to beat us with. Put it in your thesis. I am very concerned and doing all I can, but it is difficult to persuade governments in developing countries to invest in secondary and tertiary recovery facilities."

"Isn't that a Catch 22 situation?"

"How do you mean?"

"They would invest if they could see the improvement, but until they see the improvement they won't invest."

"Exactly. It's a conundrum. Perhaps your thesis can tell us how to break out of the vicious circle. Put it in the Discussion you are writing. When will you be completely finished, do you think?"

He doesn't know that I am eagerly waiting for him to finish before quitting my job and joining Vicki in England. Michael does not realize that my loyalty to him is causing me to sacrifice so much. It takes a parent to realize how my loyalty to my son is greater than my loyalty to my lover.

"I should be ready to submit by the end of the year."

"That long? You need to get finished as soon as possible!"

"I'm going as fast as I can, Dad! I am writing up the disaster, and new information is still coming in."

By the time we finish, it is 8.00pm. I pick up the folder on the brand name change. We need to replace the name, CANOIL, on the gasoline bowsers at our 2100 service stations across the nation. I consider the alternatives put up by Marketing but they are unsatisfactory. I call Manfred in, and we come up with CANGAS. I will try to get the Chairman's approval later this evening.

It is now 10.00pm and time I called the Chairman. I have been on the job 17 hours now. I go over my risk evaluation calculation on the whiteboard one last time. It makes good sense. It should have been prepared by our engineers, but the analysis they sent me is useless. I believe I have the best risk analysis skills in the company. That's why I'm in this job.

Nevertheless, I am fearful when I call the Chairman.

"This evening I have been talking with Ottawa, New York and London," I tell Gooder. "Some of them had to get out of bed."

"Tell me, why don't we just send the money to the human welfare departments in Akar?"

"If we do that, Okonjo will just send someone round to gather it back for himself. Most of it will end up in his cronies' private bank accounts, the same as before the Swiss Roll."

"That's what we thought. I have Ottawa's approval for what they call our devolution move. It's radical but they like it. Do it, Selwyn and good luck. The shit is going to hit the fan from Bigeria to Bombay to Bogota. It had better work."

"It will."

What a relief. Gooder offers to explain what we are doing to Okonjo, warning that if he obstructs the devolution, we will open negotiations with the rebels. I accept, thankfully.

Finally he gives me the okay on the CANGAS name. I am delighted.

Sometimes being CEO is sweet.

By the time Gooder finishes with me, it is midnight. I email our treasury with the approval; I have already primed them, and money will start flowing into provincial Bigerian government bank accounts tomorrow.

I decide to stay the night in the CEO suite. I heat up a frozen dinner and eat it watching the late News. Then I get ready for bed. As I brush my teeth, I tell myself: today I made a difference. Vicki would be proud of me.

RULE 99: *Devolution denies despots domination.*

CHAPTER 100 SELF-INDULGENCE

Despite my position as CEO of the nation's largest oil company, I feel unfulfilled and empty as I sit at my desk where I have given my very best for the past nine years. I have lived my life so far mostly without the pleasures of having friends, partly by choice. I have put everything into my career. Now I am lonely, my career goal is achieved and I want to move on, to be with Vicki. Since bringing my working hours under control, I am racked by anxieties and self-pity that churn my intestines, producing secretions that demand food to prevent self-digestion and ulcers in the emptiness. I soothe my anxiety by eating.

My conscience grapples with a voracious appetite for almost any food. I could probably eat snails, bêche de mer, tripe, brains and haggis. I prefer dishes such as roast lamb, steak Diane, beef stroganoff, spaghetti Bolognese, lasagne, moussaka, hamburger, schnitzel, chicken tandoori, korma curry, paella, cod and chips, Caesar salad, stir-fried beef in black bean sauce, goulash, tempura, sashimi, fondue, chicken satay, enchiladas, ratatouille and smoked salmon.

When I exercise regularly on the machines in the room next door, my weight reduces. Then something upsets me, and the emptiness and hunger are too much, my willpower gives way and I binge eat, putting back on all the weight I have taken off – plus more.

The dessert course is usually where I come unstuck. My will has least power in refusing chocolate, fudge, cheesecake, shortbread, mango, ice cream, creme brulée, tiramisu, cream caramel, sorbet, soufflé, apple torte, crêpe soufflé, apple strudel, Black Forest cake and chocolate fondue.

I am obese. When all is going well, I can fight my hunger. But when I am beset by failure and overwhelmed by self-pity, I give in and binge, undoing my weight reduction and getting fatter. I scoff and scoff, hating myself for it. The worst of it is that my fatness makes me less attractive and less popular and excludes the possibility of being admired rather than regarded as a curiosity. I am spiralling downwards towards gross obesity, with the shortfall in my achievements becoming hopeless. I know that unless I get help, my food addiction will kill me.

One morning I double up with pain in my chest. I buzz and Manfred comes in.

"What's up, boss?"

"My heart, I think."

He calls an ambulance and they take me out on a stretcher. I feel acutely embarrassed because I know this is self-inflicted.

At the hospital, the specialist shakes his head.

"You were lucky this time, but you'll be back soon unless you get some weight off and your arteries cleaned up. Is your job stressful?"

"Very," I nodded.

"You should think of doing something else."

When I get home I get a trainer and start exercising regularly. I am very overweight, and even a short flight of stairs brings me to a standstill. I have been trying to get into better shape before visiting Vicki again as she may be put off by my obesity. Lately I have not made enough time for her, and I feel neglectful.

I have achieved my ideal of becoming an oil tycoon, as CEO of Canoil. I have reached my level of maximum incompetence, as predicted by the Peter Principle. Now I am aimless and drifting, and my anxiety is manifesting now as workaholism and food addiction.

They say sexaholics die of syphilis, alcoholics die of liver failure, workaholics die of cancer or suicide, and foodaholics die of heart disease. My addictions are killing me, but I haven't quite hit rock bottom yet. I can extricate myself without outside help. I would quit my job, but I cannot walk out on Canoil just yet. The company has supported me through thick and thin. I will keep going until I can hand over a tidy ship to a new CEO.

I will try to bring my foodaholism under control by keeping a diary that reflects on my working day and family life. I find reflection helps me relax.

I will soon be with Vicki. Until I fall asleep, I imagine sailing with her. I feel too exposed to Vicki, and I will try and offset my short on her with a long on a new woman. I need to be in a straddle.

Rule 100: *Every action for employee health is countered by an equal adverse effect on organisational well-being.*

CHAPTER 101   WHISTLEBLOWER

While I am waiting to resign, the Commission into the Panypo disaster brings down its report, and the government publishes its findings.

Press release
COMMISSION OF INQUIRY INTO OIL RECOVERY

The Commission, today submitted its report to the government. The main conclusions are as follows.

1. Testing at the Tundra Tar Sands has been unsuccessful; Canoil has kept it going to obtain concessional revenues, and the Provincial Government should withdraw these;

2. Canoil acted legally but allowed political pressure to overcome sound judgement in agreeing to construct and operate the pilot plant at Panypo;

3. The explosion at Panypo was caused by application of a technology under severe conditions without adequate testing under milder conditions;

4. The technology has future promise to achieve higher oil recoveries with safety;

5. There has been no public benefit from government control;

6. Government control and concessions should be withdrawn as soon as possible.

Ian Southwell (Dr)
Chairman

"It is totally unfair to suggest my judgement is unsound," I tell Manfred. "I had to choose between the shutting down of oil exports from Bigeria or constructing a pilot plant."

"You crossed the PM, and this is payback."

"Oh? How did I cross him?"

"When he yelled about oil recovery, instead of promising to raise efficiency, you read him the rules. He would not have been amused. Pinning the accident on you is convenient."

"If I had refused the pilot plant, I would have been blamed for an oil import crisis. I am to blame either way – a scapegoat."

"This is it, old boy," says Manfred. "The Board is bound to haul you over the coals."

First, I have to face the media. I have not been able to clear my approach with Ralph Gooder. I decide to blame the accident in Bigeria on teething problems, rather than on the intrinsic nature of the technology in pressurising volatile hydrocarbons to spontaneous combustion pressures.

Later that morning I sit in a large room, full of reporters and observers, in front of the Commission's Committee, with a bank of media cameras trained on me.

Dr Southwell refers to the questions raised in the press article, "Canoil Leaves It in the Ground", by Walter Raschig, who is sitting in the audience. Then he outlines today's news of the collapse of the Okonjo government and Canoil's evacuation, which followed the Panypo accident.

"Before the accident last month, was the best way to increase Canadian oil recovery to test Canoil's technology in Bigeria?" he asks.

This is my opportunity to contest the Commission's finding that my judgement had been unsound. I fumble, as usual, as I raise the microphone. My answer is a stock reply, and I try not to drone, a tendency I have.

"Every oilfield is different, and extracting more oil is easier from some than from others. The technologies have to be tested under local conditions. The test in Bigeria was under extreme conditions and revealed a previously unknown problem. The test was small-scale and was successful in avoiding a major loss."

Next Southwell asked, "Do you agree with the Prime Minister's assertion that 'Oil and mineral companies leave behind them a trail of ruined oil reservoirs'?"

It appears my telephone conversation with the PM was recorded. The public wants blood, and I have been chosen to be sacrificed. I won't play the part, though. I remember my teenage vow, taken forty-five years earlier, to dedicate my life to bettering the lives of the poor and helpless. Now I have my last chance to redeem myself. I will call The King's New Clothes from a firm belief in objectivity. I will not accept the blame. I will lay it squarely where it belongs. It will mean the end of my career, but I have had enough. I have been careful when negotiating my contract that my payout will be the same whether I resign or am sacked. It is enough for me to live on for five years. After that, I have my superannuation. I have nothing to lose and my self-respect to gain from telling it the way it is.

"Yes," I say."I cannot speak for other oil companies, but I agree that Canoil ruins oil reservoirs."

The room suddenly becomes very quiet.

"Mister Archer, you are a reservoir engineer. What is your view of oil recovery in Canada?"

If I expose the failure of the government to create an environment for investment in oil recovery, it could bring immediate action. The poor and helpless will be served. I draw myself up to my full height, hold my suit lapels, pull my chin in, and in ringing tones denounce the connivance of our government at all levels with oil companies.

"Canoil obeys the resource extraction laws. The laws are weak and allow oil companies to waste oil resources by grabbing the easy to get, most profitable part, first. It is cheaper to find a new reservoir than to get more oil out of an old one. Our shareholders only want profit and don't give a hoot about waste. The government has only itself and its predecessors to blame for allowing low oil recovery. Governments court the oil industry and are in cahoots. In my opinion, the current legislature lacks the will to do anything thing about it."

The room erupts, as people start yelling, first at me and then at each other. The chairman postpones the session.

Feeling pleased with myself, I go back to my hotel room and email my resignation to Ralph. It crosses with one from him telling me I am fired for exceeding my authority in dealing with the government. Reporters keep calling, but I refuse to see them. They are as much a part of the shameful scam as the politicians, government bureaucrats and shareholders, for they do not understand the problem and merely parrot stakeholders' biased excuses without making an effort to understand and analyse. I am sick of the lot of them. It feels good to be free.

The Board accepts my resignation and glosses over my treason largely by ignoring it. Ralph issues a press release announcing my resignation.

Press release
OIL CEO REPLACED

Selwyn Archer is to step down as chief executive of Canoil from July 1st. He will be succeeded by Gary Ackman, formerly GM of Production Division.

Canoil Chairman Ralph Goodman said, "The Canoil board is saddened to lose Selwyn, who has worked tirelessly, increased the company's financial performance and contributed to development of civil society in Canada and in countries where it operates overseas.

"We are fortunate to have Gary Ackman as his successor. He has worked in petroleum production in various countries and made strong contributions to the efficiency of our operations."

Ackman said, "I am honoured to be given the job of maintaining and enhancing Canoil's reputation and performance in Canada, as well as overseas. I have great admiration for Selwyn and what he has achieved and I will endeavour to bring Canoil through the current controversies unscathed."

Commenting on his decision to step down, Archer said, "The drought in Bigeria is a tragedy. I have done everything within my power to keep the oil flowing and funds going into the country to be distributed fairly by their government to the starving people. I want to thank all the employees of Canoil involved in that effort for their loyal endeavours, also all of Canoil's employees who have served the company with dedication while I have been CEO.

"Company operations will be safe in Gary Ackman's hands. I have always found him to be a loyal and competent colleague. My decision to step down will enable Canoil to embark on new relationships within Canada, in Bigeria and elsewhere overseas, that will ensure continued prosperity, new opportunities and more efficient use of petroleum resources."

My criticism has rolled off the oil industry like water from a duck's back. The oil companies do their business in a certain way, and it will take more than my exposé to change anything.

Gary Ackman can take up with the Bigerian rebel leader where I left off with Tinibu. It will not include miscible flooding at Panypo. I expect much of our payments to Bigeria will soon revert to government members' Swiss bank accounts.

I forward to him an email from Tinibu's successor in the rebel government, requesting we pay restitution of CDN$19 billion for loss of national income due to the Panypo disaster and subsequent shutting down of oil exports. If the money is not paid, the rebels are threatening to nationalise Canoil's facilities. Gary can deal with that.

Michael now has enough data for a PhD thesis that defines some boundary conditions of miscible flooding. He should be able to submit his thesis in six months, and then I will go to Vicki in the UK. My letters to her lately have not been acknowledged, and I have not been able to speak with her on the telephone. Since the Panypo disaster I have been distracted from visiting her, and she may be piqued. I hope that she will understand how my job has been all-absorbing, but now I am free. At last we will be together properly. In the meantime, I make sure that Michael is supported at home with everything he needs at this crucial time.

I try to imagine Vicki's response to my whistleblowing. She would view it as the sour and negative denoument of an ineffective CEO. I am leaving Canoil without a way forward and blaming the government for trying to do their job. Had the Bigeria technology worked, my tenure would be celebrated as an epoch of seminal innovation in the World oil industry.

I reflected on the Panypo disaster. It had resulted from an uncontrolled condition, absence of the oxidant sulphur, rather than failure of the miscible flooding concept. If it would be possible to prevent sulphur deposition, the test should be repeated.

Michael had given me a copy of the discussion section of his thesis to peruse. I read it carefully. He had listed various methods to eliminate the sulphur hazard and was optimistic that the problem could be overcome. He is proposing an investigation of these and if a method can be confidently selected, another Panypo test should be undertaken. He ends that his study confirms the high investment return potential of the new technology, that teething problems can be expected and that a future with greatly increased oil recoveries both in Canada and overseas is assured.

When I finish reading I am convinced that is my duty to see Michael's conclusion is communicated to oil industry investors and Government technocrats across Canada. I begin by congratulating Michael and asking him would he come with me to discuss his study with Commission Chairman Southwell. I make an appointment with him for the next week.

At last I feel my trials as CEO at Canoil have not been in vain.

On a recliner on the lawn at home, enjoying the summer heat where Thug used to enjoy the winter, I feel like a new healthy person, without Ruth and the CEO job to worry about. I looked at myself in a mirror earlier and saw a dude that I can live with. It is the first time in my life that I have been able to look at myself with equanimity. Until now, my image has always brought me a feeling of dissatisfaction or downright displeasure.

Although I am fat, I am losing weight. When the hunger pangs hit, I drink coffee. Will I be attractive enough to be able to revive my relationship with Vicki?

Rule 101: *Over-eating is a response to deep-seated anxiety.*

CHAPTER 102   REGENERATIVE AFFAIR

There is no problem with my appetite for sex. Ruth's departure has re-awakened my hormones, and I eye every female I come across for sexual potential. The bare thighs and naked midriffs of Calgary girls who crowd the shopping malls induce in me lustful hankerings.

My grief at losing Ruth has diminished, but I am unfit and apprehensive of finally getting together with Vicki. In particular, I have never had sexual intercourse with her, and I have been celibate since I quit sex with Ruth thirteen years ago. Since my dismal performance in the hotel room in Akar, I have been unsure of my sexual ability with Vicki. Her receptiveness has not been repeated, and I don't know for sure if she will want a sexual relationship or just want to be good friends.

I have lost hair on the top and temples and turned grey, with reduced muscle and body tone, but I am still somewhat young-looking and alert for my age. Apart from a belly large enough to indicate overweight, I am still an attractive man. My GP tells me my talk reveals unusual lack of empathy and off-putting self-centricity, but these qualities are not unusual in retired executives.

Nevertheless, I decide to attempt to start a relationship with another female, to develop my libido ready for Vicki. I need to get fit for sex.

When I turn my attention to finding, meeting and starting a relationship, which I have not done for thirty-five years, the techniques I require are different. It takes me some time to realise that there are only a few modes of conduct that can access cultured females, and those I used in my twenties are unsuitable. At first, I explore the possibilities of meeting attractive females in public places. For example, when out for a walk, I match strides with a female walker and draw alongside, remarking on our surroundings. I find she invariably takes a byway, speeds up, slows down or doubles back. When I follow, she heads for the nearest crowd or shop and hides.

For the first time in my life I feel lonely. I miss something. I don't talk to anyone all weekend. I feel like a robot without a controller. I have circuits that are part of the real me and they are not being used. I am a nice guy, and people are missing out. With people it seems they are either all over you or they don't want to know you at all. There is no halfway point.

When I discover that a woman can be lured into talking with me in a restaurant or art gallery, I strike up a conversation about food or art or some other innocuous topic. However, soon the conversation dries up and she moves away or leaves if I suggest coffee or a walk, as if the social risk is too great.

In the meantime, I seem to be acceptable to some single women in my apartment building. In fact, several women seem to follow me around and pop up unexpectedly. I am quite unused to this and cannot take their advances seriously, as there are conflicts of interest with my role as neighbouring property owner. Unfortunately, I am unable to meet a woman who values me for what I am, rather than what I earn or what I own.

When I complain about my problem to Michael, he tells me about a dating service called Amour. Michael helps me enter data for my profile. I don't have long to wait. After one dud coffee meeting with a respondent who can't see the funny side of computer dating, I meet Helen and fall madly in lust.

Helen is a zany woman, bohemian and spiritual, with whom I recapture some of the existentialism of my hippy days. We complement each other, me with my analysing and she with her gut feelings. Together, we campaign to conserve public lands, fauna and flora, indigenous culture and heritage buildings. Our balmy days fill with writing to government ministers, historical researches, community meetings, protest marches, press releases and providing information to our legal representatives. The teamwork contrasts with my past, and I learn to value the perspectives brought by people whose careers are very different from mine.

Helen and I play tennis, swim, walk, cook, eat and go to the theatre together. We talk a lot and we attend cultural events, introducing me to a side of Calgary life I had not previously encountered. She is a psychologist and is not fazed by my behaviour, even at its most antisocial. Within a few months I have thoroughly tested my wedding tackle and found it to be in good working order.

I imagine meeting with Vicki and being together after so long. She is an intensely private woman, and our separate lives have barely overlapped. It will be an adventure getting to know each other sexually and taking up where we left off, in the Akar Hotel a year ago. Our encounter will not be without risk, for our communications have been brief, with long intervals between them.

After knowing Vicki for so long, I trust her completely. I hope that she feels the same about me, as she should do, ever since she analysed the polygraph from the lie detector. It is chance that has kept us apart. Very soon we will be together, as we should have been all along had there not been several chance occurrences, such as Howard spoiling our skiing holiday.

Michael finishes writing and submits his thesis. He is offered a post-doctoral position in the USA, accepts and leaves. I am alone in Calgary except for Helen. She meets Nicola, Scot and Michael when they come back on visits, and they get along well together. Helen and I have become close, and I know I am lucky to find her.

I book a return flight to England. If things work out with Vicki, I will still need to come back, to move out of the apartment in Calgary and sell it. My children will lose their home, but neither of them is now living in Calgary, and they will gain a home in England. I warn them that I could want them to come to England to meet with Vicki, who they haven't seen since they were small.

Helen knows nothing of Vicki or my plans in England. I tell her I am going on holiday to visit my family in the Dales. She helps me pack and drives me to the airport. I will miss her. I feel indifferent to my own and others' fates in this high-stakes game I am playing. It has taken so long and so much anguish to reach this point that I am numbed to having feelings about the outcome. I just want the final play to be over.

Rule 102: *A man may have a satisfactory relationship with a woman while secretly burning with the flame of a greater love.*

CHAPTER 103   MATING FLIGHT

I am comfortable in my imagined cocoon in business class where I have been recalling my long involvement with Vicki, to be ready to connect with her and move on together soon after we land.

On the whole, I have led a fortunate life. I have always wanted to be an oilman and, having succeeded, I am ready for change. I have quit an important job and I feel useless now because I have nothing to do. I have money from my payout and I can afford to have all the order, symmetry and beauty in my life that I want, except that I need company to enjoy them. I hope that will change when I get together with Vicki. There are so many things we can do.

I enjoy an excellent dinner without requesting more. I feel empty but I doze and think about Helen, feeling bad about how she took me to the airport and saw me off at an ungodly hour. I am being disloyal in going to see Vicki. She thinks I am going over to see my father, who has become too deaf for me to talk with on the phone. She knows nothing of my plans with Vicki. Anyway, the possibility of a permanent relationship with Vicki may be a figment of my imagination. After all, there is nothing concrete between us.

Supper is served. After coffee I watch a documentary with an enchanting sequence of the courtship dancing of a pair of elegant birds, brolgas, at Lake Eyre in Australia. I think of how the lie detector test has limited my attempts to attract Vicki. After declaring my love so ardently, without her reciprocating, further advances have seemed superfluous, and my visits with her have been brief and years apart. I summon my flight attendant and buy Vicki perfume, as I usually do.

I begin to feel nervous about how Vicki will receive me. I hope she won't be too repelled by my weight gain. I received a Christmas card from her as usual – with just a few words that she is very busy. Being busy is not so much an indicator of her lifestyle as the manifestation of a chronically preoccupied personality. I know parts of her well, while others remain a mystery. Our feelings for each other run deep, worn into a canyon of mutual interest during all the time we have been together while apart.

As usual, she will ask about Nicola and Michael. This time I will be able to tell her they are perfectly independent. They know of her but not of my obsession with her. I don't know how well they will take to her. How warmly will they welcome her as their stepmother? I never have been able to predict relationships.

Perhaps Vicki has little interest in being together with me, or any other man. She enjoys being single, and that is the reason she has never married or had children. There is nothing I can do about it. I switch off the light, recline my seat and doze off. Within a few hours, my future will be decided.

The "fasten seat belt" gong wakes me. I stretch, feeling refreshed. The flight to Heathrow has gone quickly. I have relaxed with my eyes closed, reviewing my visits with Vicki, from meeting her at Liverpool uni forty years ago until now when I can at last be with her.

I switch on the seatback monitor in front of me to get the pilot's view. The runway stretches ahead as we settle into our approach. There is only a small chance of an accident on landing. Beside me, I glimpse England's carefully uniform houses and streets, reposing wetly in the clouded half-light of the morning drizzle. It is a sombre prospect, but today it cannot dampen my ebullience at finally getting together with the love of my life.

Rule 103: A very old relationship, with sparse brief encounters, is as unpredictable as a new relationship.

PART 14 UNEQUALLED DEMAND (2007)

In which an unexpected event causes me to rationalise and renew my love investment portfolio.

CHAPTER 104   GAZUMPED

We thud onto the tarmac with a sickening bounce. The brake flaps pop up, and the reverse thrust roars. I am almost at the end of a very long journey. Things can still go wrong, but one way or another, my situation will soon be resolved. After years of speculation and attempting to bring this day forward, the final roulette is in spin, and I am resigned to the fall of the ball.

On the moving walkway there is a spring in my step as I speed eagerly towards my ultimate destiny. Helping me are thoughtful passenger direction signs, part of the brand new terminal make-over. There is satisfaction in joining the short line of British passport holders when I enter the arrival hall. Queued up like sheep are hundreds of sullen foreigners, crammed together in the other half of the building, probably because England is full and doesn't want them.

I am ebullient and chat with the official directing traffic at passport control. She is an ex-Afghani girl and is all smiles as she welcomes me to her adoptive country. It is a good sign that a war victim can have such a responsible position. There is justice.

I had planned to call Vicki from the baggage hall, but to my surprise my suitcase arrives there at the same time as I do. I ask myself, how can they be so quick? It is a good sign too, and I go on to Customs riding a wave of optimism. Things are going well.

I declare the bottle of perfume I have bought for Vicki, even though it is not necessary. I go to the red side because I have found, from long experience, that the red side is quicker than the green.

I wheel out through the sliding glass door to an audience of expectant faces. Vicki is not there. Of course not; she doesn't know I'm coming. She lives close to Heathrow, and I always just drop in, with a call from the airport. Since I left Canoil, it has not been very often. I find a quiet corner and switch on my mobile. My hand is shaking and my mouth is dry. I find her name, Vicki Hillstone, and place a call. My heart is thumping.

"Hello?" she answers.

"Vicki, this is Selwyn. I'm at Heathrow."

"Selwyn! How are you?"

"Terrific. Can I come and see you?"

There is a slight pause. Something is different.

"Selwyn, I am married now – about a year ago."

I am not prepared for this. I feel panic. I didn't even know there was another man in her life. My feelings for her are in turmoil. Why didn't she tell me? What did I do wrong? Maybe I can learn something that will help me go forward from here. I have to keep going and get out of the numbing blackness. As usual, I try not to show any emotion.

"Congratulations. Who is the lucky guy?"

Speaking these words into this plastic object, I feel foolish. What does it matter? Is there anything that still does matter? I want to smash it on the ground and stamp on it.

"Peter Huntley."

I have never heard of him.

"Are you happy?" I ask.

"Yes, very," she enthuses.

"What kind of man is he?"

"An engineer. He's been working in the oil industry."   Like me. So it wasn't my affiliation that came between us, at least.

"Where?"

"Canada."   Like me again. How extraordinary!

"Canadian?"

"English."

"What uni?"

"Manchester."

A redbrick like Liverpool.

"Grammar school?"

"Yes."   I can hardly believe the similarity. So, it isn't my social class that was the problem, as I thought. Then what was it?

"I would like to meet him." Curiosity. Study the enemy.

"I don't know."

"Just a quick visit. I can be over there in an hour."

"Let me check with Peter."

She is gone for several minutes. I spend the time imagining what he would be saying about her man friend coming over.

"Okay," she says slowly, as if I am leaning on her and she would prefer I didn't come. "You can come for tea."

"Thank you. That will be nice. Coffee would be better. See you around four o'clock, then?"

"Bye."

I hang up. Suddenly I am in a strange world. I am having difficulty focussing on anything. My steps are unsure as I make my way to the Europcar counter.

"My name is—," I pause while I try to remember who I used to be. My voice is shaky. "Archer. Selwyn Archer. I have a car booked."

The receptionist is used to senile people who are about to fall off the face of life's rock climb. Her job is to get them to go somewhere else to do it. She speaks kindly, in a patronising way, making a good effort not to swamp me with information while giving me necessary directions.

"This is your contract with us, in which you agree to pay for any damage to the vehicle. Would you sign here, Sir?"

I put on my glasses. Everything is too much effort to read. I sign in a white space.

"This is the insurance agreement, in which you will pay for the first 300 pounds of any damage. Would you read this and sign here, Sir?"

I sign.

I have entered a dream and no longer care about anything. I am merely an observer of the strange events that occur in the life I am being denied.

"Now, you can choose a vehicle from Pool B, 1800 automatic, or Pool C, 1600 manual. Which do you prefer?"

"B."

I choose quite randomly from the options she gives me.

"You can return the car with a full tank or be charged to fill it. You can decide that later." She takes an imprint of my credit card. "Our delivery person will take you to choose your car. Just wait over there, please. Happy motoring, Sir."

A genderless delivery person – I cannot tell which – takes me to the cars. I choose the one that looks fastest. It is a make I don't know. He or she shows me where to put the keys in, and I drive out onto the M4. There are five lanes, and they all seem to have cars speeding much faster than my mere 80 miles per hour. I am driving badly but I don't care. Vicki is taken. With the windscreen wipers on by mistake, I move into the centre lane and turn on the radio loudly so I cannot hear the horns behind me.

In my awakened dream, I fall down a bobsleigh chute at high velocity with no self-control and expect that if I hang on I will be ejected at the bottom into Vicki's front yard. I have driven the route before, but my memory is working in retrospect; after I have gone wrong, I remember how to do it right and go back. After back-tracking huge distances between exits, I eventually escape from the motorway correctly at her exit and am conveyed along narrower and narrower country lanes between high hedges growing from ivied embankments. I remember sadly these were once the homes of hedgehogs, badgers, foxes and rabbits, until they were run over. This reverie and others take me across a welter of intersections and past my turns. I have to travel a long way until I can find gateways with puddles without deep holes in them where I can turn around. On the verges of my dream, an abyss threatens, but the danger is too near and present for any action.

I recognise her place as I pass it, go back and skid into the front yard. Only fate has brought me here, for my skills seem to have deserted me. Feeling surprised to have arrived at all, I get out of my dream. I am embarrassed at having commanded my former lover's attention.

The house softly melts into its gardens. The Elizabethan timbering is infilled with red sandstone bricks around casement windows with small leaded panes. It is timeless and blends into the surroundings, with a weathercock on the chimney, commanding the direction of the wind.

Vicki comes out from the front door and we hug briefly.

Her man sticks out his hand as victors do when you lose at rugby.

"Peter Huntley." He doesn't sound as though he's gloating.

"How do you do, Peter. Selwyn Archer," I say. "Congratulations on your marriage."

I give Vicki a present of some porcelain figurines I bought in the village. I will give the perfume to one of my sisters. Vicki opens the parcel.

"Oh, lovely. I collect these."

I go inside. Nothing seems to have changed. Peter and I sit in the breakfast room as Vicki makes the tea. We compare careers in Canada. He has been in oil, too. We used to know some people in common. I am surprised to find he has known Vicki for six years. He married her when his divorce came through. The similarity between us is eerie, more than a coincidence, as if Vicki has a fetish for our type or has searched for a substitute for me. Peter is not unlike me physically, either, about the same height, medium build, brown hair and fair skin. The main difference is that I have a belly.

Vicki seems to have had her own love straddle. Maybe she learned it from me.

We are both on edge and relieved when Vicki joins us, pours us tea and hands around chocolate biscuits. Vicki looks at me and smiles.

"How have you been, Selwyn?" she says in her faltering, little-girl tongue-tied way.

"Okay. This is a surprise," I say.

They both look at me curiously.

"Now tell me, why did you snub me at the St John's Ball?"

Vicki flushes.

"I can't remember. Perhaps you were double-timing me. You usually were."

Touché. She has never spoken to me like this before.

"That's not fair. You knew from the lie detector test that I was crazy about you."

Peter looks from one to the other of us apprehensively.

"Oh, that," she says. "I had forgotten about it. Anyway, you were with another girl at the time."

"Barbara. She was just a fill-in."

"You were using her for sex," Vicki raised her voice a notch, accusing. "You had even sold out on me to Richard in some crazy commodity scheme."

It was because she was being a prude, but I couldn't say this now, in front of Peter. I didn't want to embarrass Vicki. I glance at Peter. His face is whitish.

"Because I couldn't wait around for you any longer," I say. I sounded as though she is a hopeless case. "Then you had a fling with Richard."

"Are you still carrying a grudge about that?" Vicki laughed. "Nothing happened. I was trying to jolt you back to reality, but it backfired."

"Well, it tore me apart."

"No, it did not. All you seemed to care about was your work. But you got a first and well-deserved."

"Then when you came to Canada and we went skiing, you started flirting with my brother."

"I did n—"

"Did you arrange for him to turn up like that?" I interrupted.

"No, of course not," she turned and walked into the kitchen, and then came back. "You always think there's a conspiracy. I've never known anyone with so many grudges, suspicions and conspiracy theories," she says. "You are your own worst enemy."

She stood up and busied herself in the kitchen.

"You know what was bothering me when we went skiing?" Vicki asked, coming over.

"No."

"I wanted an explanation of why you had left Liverpool without saying goodbye. And I still don't know."

"I thought you knew. Barbara got pregnant. I was not the father. She had an abortion."

Vicki is silent for a moment.

"I see. I'm sorry about that. I thought it was something I had done. You should have told me."

"I was too ashamed."

"But it wasn't yours."

"I can't be absolutely sure. Remember, there was no DNA testing then."

I tried to think of something else to say.

"How long ago did you start seeing each other?" I ask Peter.

"Six years." He says it defiantly, as if it is arguable.

She had never mentioned him. I suppose she had her own straddle and had sold me short. I could hardly blame her for that.

Vicki started talking. "Selwyn, I think you need counselling. You seem to me you are suffering from a condition that is making life difficult for you and for others."

"What others?" I ask.

"Well, me, for instance. You have never considered my feelings and you have treated me badly. Your family on the farm, too, from what you have told me. Then there's Barbara. And Ruth."

Her words are like whiplashes.

"What do you mean? I'm pretty normal," I say, knowing I am lying.

"I do not think so," she says. Peter is smiling nervously.

"I have always tried to treat you well, Vicki. I could never tell what you were thinking, whether you had any feelings."

"I do not label people," she says. "I'm not sure if you have Asperger's Syndrome or Obsessive Compulsive Personality Disorder or both. They could relate to your bipolar episode. It's not my expertise. You need to get psychological counselling."

My indignation collapses.

"What are the symptoms of this Asperger's Syndrome?"

"There are lots of checklists on the Internet. There are three areas where sufferers are in deficit: they do not reveal their emotions and feelings to others; they do not empathise with others; and they lack social skills. Oh, and they have poor communication."

"I thought I was okay at showing people what I am thinking."

"No. People never know where they stand with you. They are scared of you as if by repressing your feelings you might go off like a bomb."

"Really? Are you scared of me?"

"Not now. I realise that you do have feelings, but you have learnt not to show people you like them. You want to keep people away, so you can do your analysis thing obsessively."

"I empathize with you, don't I?"

"Sometimes. But you did not show the consideration I wanted. You have never seemed to realize how you can affect others."

"Shit. I knew my social skills were not crash-hot."

"We haven't done much socialising together, but I remember what you were like at uni. If you wanted something from a person, you just went up to them and asked for it. When you had finished with them, you walked off, leaving them feeling used. You never bothered to find out about them or build a rapport. You are a control freak."

"People hide from me. It takes too long to get to know them."

"Exactly. So you have never bothered."

"You can't have it both ways. If I had spent my time socializing, I would never have reached CEO of a large corporation."

"You make moves on people, like it is a game of chess."

"Isn't it?"

"No, at least, it wasn't for me. Or for others you pushed around. Now you have done that, you are on your own, Selwyn."

I feel sorry for myself.

"I would like to have friends but I don't have the knack."

"Maybe you can learn it."

"The worst thing is that I have lost you. What was the main problem about me for you?"

"You were too selfish and insensitive to my needs. You didn't follow the social rules. You didn't show me affection."

"I gave you presents all the time."

"Yes, but I wanted you to be intimate and share my worries and hopes."

"Me, too. I guess communication is not our long suit."

"I agree it was partly my fault. I tend to be too secretive."

"I never knew where I stood with you, Vicki."

"I have heard that from others. Perhaps I am a bit of a flirt. But we were talking about you."

"What are the symptoms of this 'Obsessive Compulsive Personality Disorder'?"

"You always seem to be obsessed with your work, with being efficient, planning things and keeping to schedules."

"Aren't those admirable qualities? People who are disorganized create problems for others."

"In moderation, I agree, but you caused me problems by being inflexible and closed to my ideas."

"What sort of ideas?"

"It took you a very long time to listen to me about helping starving people in Bigeria. Your values were to keep the oil flowing to Canada, and you wouldn't listen to me for over a year."

"I didn't realize that was such a problem for you."

"You are reluctant to take on new ideas. You are rigid and stubborn."

"I see it now."

"Another symptom has been your reluctance to delegate your work to others. You took on more and more, because you say others would not do things your way. You always want people to do things your way, don't you, as if they are stupid."

"Most of them are."

"That's a symptom, Selwyn, of perfectionism and inability to delegate. You are overconscientious. No-one wants you to do everything yourself, even if their standards might be lower. They don't want to be totally dependent on you."

"They are managing without me now, I suppose."

"That's right. Another thing: you have a different view of money. For you, money is viewed as something to be hoarded for future catastrophes. From what you told me, Canoil got itself offside with the Canadian Government by refusing to invest at the oil fields. I daresay your stingy outlook was well-received by your masters in New York, but for just about everyone else, Canoil during your reign was ruled by conservatism. You are to the right of Attila the Hun. Your tenure won't be remembered for its investment in the future, will it?"

I reflected for a moment and realised that I had achieved very little. I had been reactive. Oil recoveries are as low now as before Michael and I almost gave our lives to improve them.

"I wish you had told me this before."

"I did tell you, but you were not listening. Your miserliness is not ignorance; it is a symptom of deep-seated illness. You are compelled to be inflexible and obsessive to control the anxiety that is in every cell in your body, like a highly-strung horse that frets and champs without ceasing and develops bad habits of head-tossing and pacing. You have tension in you that you have soothed by bad behaviour and substance abuse. It is sad for me, too, when I have to tell you that your relationship with me has been an obsession."

"Are you saying my interest in you has been sick?"

My thoughts go back to the exhilaration and excitement of that first meeting with Vicki in the coffee lounge. Then I remember our first kiss and the feel of her body and lips. I want that again. She is more intoxicating than drink. With her, I am comfortable. With Vicki, I am not driven to be independent, well-organised and efficient, as I usually am. I can relax at her place without feeling compelled to do anything

"Selwyn, you have a dependency problem. If it's not me, or sex, or alcohol, or work, or food, or coffee, it's whatever comes next."

I hadn't thought of her like that before.

"What has caused it?" I ask.

"Anxiety. Tell me when it started?"

"I have always been anxious."

"Did it start when you were a child?" Vicki asks.

"I can remember confrontations with my mother, after which she would ignore me for days."

"What do you mean, ignore you?"

"When I came to her for attention she would tell me I was bad and to go away."

'How did that make you feel?"

"I feared desertion, that it was all over with her."

"And was it?"

"She would tell me I was the worst of all her five children and I worried her. The only joy she had with me was that I would be leaving home."

"What did you do?"

"I spent as much time as I could with my father. He accepted me and even seemed to like me."

"Did you like yourself?"

"No, I was no good. People did not like me. I did not know why. Sometimes I thought about suicide. I self-harmed by diving off walls on to my head and playing recklessly, for example, climbing trees that were dangerous."

"Did you play with anyone?"

"My brother Howard let me come with him birds-nesting, provided I did not complain to our parents about his bullying."

"Were you anxious about anything else?"

"I was under pressure from my mother to do well at school. It was very competitive."

"And at university?"

"That's when I started obsessing about you, after the lie detector test."

It was comforting that someone, Vicki, knew how very much I could love and wanted to be loved. That thought had helped soothe my anxiety about attention for the following forty years.

There was much I did not understand, especially about relationships. If I could be together with Vicki, I could learn these things, but my chances of getting with her now are zilch.

Peter is in good health and seems like he is neurotypical. His hobby is flying. He could have an accident.

"He could kill himself," Vicky tells me later, when he is going on about his aerobatic plane. I think she is telling me the only possible way I can get her now is over his dead body.

"Thanks for the advice, Vicki," I say, getting up to leave. "I will make an appointment to see a counsellor when I get back to Calgary." I am defeated.

"Where are you going now?" she asks, concerned. She can tell I am partly in shock, although I am trying not to show my feelings.

"I'm staying with Richard for a few days. Then I'll be going on to Larry's, Roger's and Jozef's."

"Give them my regards," she says.

A small hug and handshake with Peter. He seems like a nice guy. Vicki deserves to be happy.

"I will. Bye for now."

First, I must call Helen at home. With Vicki unobtainable, or at least in a very distant short, I need to rollover my straddle and acquire Helen in a long position. It's just as well I am not vulnerable, or right about now I would be desperate.

Rule 104: *At settlement time, love is traded like a commodity future and goes to the highest bidder.*

CHAPTER 105 RESOLUTION

"Why didn't you tell me she was married?" I ask Richard when I see him in London the next day.

"I didn't know," he says. "I haven't been in touch with her lately."

Richard has had marriage problems.

"Did you know she had Peter?" I ask.

"Yes. I met him several years ago, but I didn't know they were living together, let alone married."

If I had known they were together, I might not have taken any notice because Vicki often had guys hanging around.

"What do you think decided her to get married?" I ask.

He shrugged. "Maybe she was getting lonelier as she got older."

Perhaps Vicki had tied the knot with Peter to please her mother, before she died.

It was ironic that Vicki had married a man whose appearance and background could have been a substitute for me. Vicki had seemed to be dealing with men as a commodity, too, and may have been operating a straddle of her own with Peter, keeping me in the short position for later. She had probably taken a long position with him years before when it seemed that my commitment to Michael, workaholism and my career in Canada had made me unobtainable.

Mine was a sublime love. Of the three ingredients of love – commitment, intimacy and passion – all three were lacking. Of passion, there was only our undergraduate fondling until that fateful Akar hotel bedroom. Of intimacy, it was growing but slowly, as we only had our few meetings. Of commitment, I never could get further than a short position in a straddle, withdrawing from her but promising to recommit at some future settlement time that never eventuated. Yet this love, incomplete and unfulfilled, brought joy and hope to my life that relieved the stress of my unhappy marriage.

I respect Vicki's advice about counselling and visit specialists. They find that I have a susceptibility to three different chronic stress and anxiety disorders, possibly caused by insufficient positive attention in childhood and as a teenager. When I was two and a half, after my sister was born, my mother treated me as a liability. Fears of desertion caused an abscess of anxiety to flare up deep inside me. Without the attention and love that I craved, I developed a habit of anxiety that I have soothed by a series of addictions throughout my life, or suffered stress disorders. First, chronic Asperger's Syndrome manifested in a trail of broken relationships. Then, under the stress of my marriage with Ruth, I suffered a manic depressive psychosis and a series of dependency illnesses. I have been addicted, in turn, to my father, Vicki, sex, alcohol, work, food, chocolate, and now coffee.

I am flawed. My sex-addicted life now seems harmful to the innocent women I have preyed on. I have an overwhelming sense of guilt, but Helen relates it to illness.

"Why did I have a series of addictions?" I ask Helen.

"Possibly when you were a little child, fear of desertion by a parent could have caused your deep-seated anxiety. Did you have such a fear?"

"Yes. I feared my mother."

"Could you have eased those anxieties in compulsive love for your father? Or for another sibling? Or later for a girl? Was there such a person?"

"How do you mean, compulsive love?"

"Unconditional love; it didn't matter what the person did, you loved them the same," Helen says.

"Yes, my father. Also my sister, Heather."

"Your fear of your mother caused you to love them unconditionally?"

"I think so, until I went away. I left home to go to uni."

"How did you manage your anxiety at uni?"

"I studied obsessively. And there were girls."

"You loved the girls unconditionally?"

"No, I tried several before I fixed on Vicki."

"What happened?"

"She put me in a lie detector."

"Did you lie?"

"No. I declared my love for her."

"Did it encourage your narcissism?"

"It seemed logical that she would reciprocate."

"So you transferred your compulsive love to her. You became obsessed with her."

"What do you mean by obsessed?"

Helen quoted me the words of a French philosopher.

"Obsessional does not necessarily mean sexual obsession, not even obsession for this or for that in particular; to be an obsessional means to find oneself caught in a mechanism, in a trap increasingly demanding and endless."

(Lacan, 1957)

"Yes, I wanted more and more attention from her. I was obsessive. Do you think she eased my anxiety?"

"Yes, as a distraction that soothed the fear," Helen says. "When you were anxious about the threatening parent or about your career, you escaped the worry by concentrating your thoughts into compulsive love, first for your father, then for your sister, and then for this Vicki."

It makes sense. After the lie detector test, in which I laid bare my soul to Vicki, she knew me better than anyone, and I felt compelled to gain more approval by having a relationship with her. I became obsessed with her. I was aware it was unhealthy and I tried to make myself less vulnerable to her by having other women.

"You seem to have misread women's aversion to male duplicity."

"Polygamy is accepted in most societies."

"Yes, but the man makes his previous wives secure before chasing another. You seemed to be avoiding commitment and threatening her strong personal value of exclusivity."

Perhaps I should have explained to Vicki the commitment in my short sale to Richard and my commodity straddle.

"How long have you had a crush on Vicki?" Helen asks.

"Forever. Since final year uni."

"Do you mean you still have it?"

"Yes."

"Does she reciprocate?"

"Not since she married Peter. Before, her responses were mostly minimal, but enough to maintain my obsession." I tell Helen about my correspondence and visits with Vicki.

"Only an obsessed person and one with Asperger's would have persisted the way you did with so little encouragement," she tells me. "You don't have feelings that are easily hurt. It didn't matter to you whether Vicki reciprocated or not. You kept writing and visiting. What happened when you married Ruth?"

"Subconsciously, I knew our marriage was a mistake from the beginning. I became manic and then depressed. It was my way of escaping."

"Asperger's is a way of escaping," Helen says. "You withdrew to a limited area, and gained the attention you craved by becoming very good at a certain skill."

"Analysis."

"Is it a skill you can perform solo, with excellence, without being held back by others?"

"Yes. Independence is essential to me."

"You did not bother to learn about other people or how to engage in social behaviour?"

"No, because I found I couldn't analyse people," I tell Helen."People have feelings, and predicting them defies scientific methods. Even testing by a lie detector is not scientific. I cannot control people and feel uncomfortable dealing with them."

"You had a nervous breakdown. How did that affect your obsession with Vicki?"

"She wanted me to get counselling."

"And did you?"

"No. I needed my Messiah delusion to escape from Ruth's pushiness. I thought that to talk about it would confirm a label of schizophrenia, with all the stigma that would bring. So I kept the delusions secret."

"How long did that last?"

"About thirty years, until Ruth left. Then for the first time I could bring myself to tell people about my Messiah delusion. Then like a mist in sunlight, it faded and disappeared. It left me and has never returned."

The best memento of my marriage is my children, Nicola and Michael. I am in contact with them regularly. I live with Helen in Calgary and work as a board member for several oil companies.

Canoil was unsuccessful with miscible flooding at the Tundra Tar Sands due to channelling of the solvent. Other oil companies experimented, but none was able to reproduce the results at Silver Atoll. Oil recoveries stubbornly remained at around 30% although several experiments that injected other fluids gave promising results.

My lack of success with Vicki had more complex causes. My obsession with her probably began as a Stockholm Effect from the lie detector. She became my captor when she measured my infatuation for her. Infatuation is normally short-lived and has an addictive component. I kept it going, by addiction to Vicki and by a disorder of the autistic spectrum, having restricted, repetitive features, that includes Asperger's. They made it difficult for me to change my behaviour. Neither physical love nor even reciprocity were necessary.

My visits to her in England, years apart, had nothing if not constancy. That was what I wanted, predictable solace from the spiritual torture of my unhappy marriage. She was one bolt hole, of several I used. Mental illness, alcoholism, workaholism and foodaholism were others.

As my addiction to her diminished, I remained obsessed with Vicki, because I valued her loving, caring, loyalty and commonsense. Her healing and idealism nourished me through bad times. She liked me and I may have enjoyed some narcissism. She told me she admired my intelligence, ability to focus and persistence.

My obsession with her is unhealthy. Vicki and I have personalities that clash. I am an independent thinker, analyse everything and delight in arriving at outlandish opinions. Vicki often finds my opinions threatening. I try to dominate her intuition and feelings, bringing her emotional distress and self-blame. These escalate into conflict between us, when she dislikes me but I ignore her. To get rid of the conflict and get the support that she craves she tends to lash out at me irrationally or manipulate me. By concentrating on our tried and true routines, such clashes have been few.

Our personality differences may be no more problematic than for most couples. Normally, young love overlooks them and as the relationship matures there is adjustment. Because our relationship is still young, we have differences that are still there after a very long time. Perhaps Vicki would like to end it, but feels that I might fall off a psychological cliff, not knowing I have that covered.

My feelings for Vicki have changed. I have desired her for successively: sex, polygamy, children, a relationship, cohabitation, her as a person, her insight into my world, her wisdom and her intellectual correspondence. Taking half a lifetime, with autism repeating my behaviour, this shift seems un-dramatic at a distance, as if it could have resulted from environmental change.

I am still in touch with other friends from uni: Richard, divorced, remarried and separated with a daughter, Jozef divorced and in a second marriage with a son and daughter, Larry and Lisa, Roger and Linda, all in first marriages with grandchildren. Helen and I see them regularly on our travels together.

Changes in my physical, social and heterosexual environments can explain less of my change in feelings for Vicki than our interaction and my maturation. Scanning the past of my interactions with Vicki, a narrow view can magnify irregular change and pick out epiphanies and quantum changes. I am fortunate to have met Vicki Hillstone. I still contact her for a visit or a chat on the phone when I am in the UK. From her I have learnt I am an okay person, despite my shortcomings. She lets me love her and I can wait. An image of her smile warms the cold places in my heart.

I do not mention Helen to her, or that ours is an interim relationship. Vicki knows what I'm like. Her place in my straddle allows her full freedom. If it becomes possible, I still want to close out my short on her and exchange my love for hers, at my best price.

Until then, I also have a long position and am invulnerable.

Rule 105: *Whereas polygamy and bigamy are illegal, a commodity straddle on love futures is legal and less vulnerable than monogamy.*

BIBLIOGRAPHY

Austen, Jane. Pride and Prejudice.

Camus, Albert. The Plague.

Dawkins, Richard. The Selfish Gene.

Follett, Ken. Pillars of the Earth.

Greer , Germaine. The Female Eunuch.

Hobbs, Thomas. Leviathan, 1651.

Lacan, Jacques. Interview. Published in L'Express, May 1957.

Lawrence, DH. Lady Chatterley's Lover.

Persig, Robert. Zen and the Art of Motorcycle Maintenance.

Proust, M. Anna Karenina

Segrave, Kerry. Lie Detectors: A Social History. McFarland, 2004.

Shaw, George Bernard, Pygmalion.

Wilson, EO. Sociobiology

Huxley, A. Island.

Lacan, Jacques Interview Published in L'Express in May 1957

AUTHOR BIO

Martin Knox is a fiction writer living in Brisbane, Australia. He studied chemical engineering and management science at UK universities, receiving BSc Hons 1st Class and M.Sc. His research was into alternative models of government planning.

He worked in the UK, Canada, the USA and Australia in nuclear, tar sands, petroleum, coal and coal-to-oil industries.

He travelled in Central and South America and sailed by yacht from Rio to Trinidad.

He settled in Australia with his family and worked as an evaluation engineer for coal mining projects . At age 40 he became a high school Science and English teacher. He wrote curriculum materials for teaching multistrand science to senior students by distance education and taught students in classes online.

He is divorced from two marriages, with children and grandchildren.

He is active in public decision-making on development, population, growth, water and resources issues and he has written a series of futuristic political thrillers yet to be published. His speculative fiction novel The Grass Is Always Browner was published by Zeus Publications in 2011.

He is interested in psychology and relationships. He is currently writing a crime fiction novel. He is involved with writers' groups, book clubs, current affairs discussion groups and art.

For further information see
www.lovestraddleanovel.wordpress.com